Clash of Stone and Steel

By Karen C.P. McDermott

ISBN (paperback): 979-8-9898117-4-8
ISBN (eBook): 979-8-9898117-5-5

Book Cover by Mick Estabrook

1st edition 2025
10 9 8 7 6 5 4 3 2 1

For Joshua Hamel, the original Samhail (aka Sammhael). Thank you for letting me take the big guy for a ride.

And for all of Samhail's fans who thought I did him wrong in the first two books. I hope I've redeemed myself.

Pronunciation Guide

People

Samhail = SAM-heyl
Talyn = TA-luhn
Cyra = SEE-ruh
Bressen = BREH-sen
Surgeon = SUR-jun
Serise = SUR-ees
Aidan = ĀY-den
Jasper = JAS-per
Maziren = MAZ-ur-in
Axenus = AX-en-uhs
Jaylan = JĀY-lin
Brix = BRIKS
Raina = RAY-nuh
Glenora = Gle-NOR-ah
Phaedrus = FAY-druhs
Aramis = AIR-ah-mis
Sandrian = SAN-dree-an
Morland = MOHR-land
Clarice = Cla-REES
Magdalene = MAG-dah-leen
Praya = PRAY-uh
Ariel = EHR-ee-ul

Places

Thasia = THAY-zhuh
Callanus = KAL-an-uhs
Polaris = Puh-LAH-rus
Gendris = JEN-dris
Fernweh = FURN-way
Hiraeth = HĬ-rayth
Solandis = Sō-LAN-dus
Derridan = DAIR-ĭ-den
Seatherny = SEE-thur-nee
Rowe = RŌ, Rown = RŌN
Kern = KURN

Other

Angelus = AN-jell-us
Perimortal = PEHR-ĭ-mohr-tl
Demoni =Deh-MAH-nee

Triumvirate (Trī-UM-ver-et): A group of three people who share power.

In the book, the country of Thasia is ruled by a group of three lords and/or ladies, each of whom also oversees one of the country's three territories. Callanus is the main capital. Bressen rules Hiraeth, whose capital is Solandis. Aidan rules Derridan, whose capital is Seatherny. And Polaris is currently overseen by the High Council in its capital city of Gendris. Cyra is from Fernweh, a small town in the south of Polaris.

Content Advisory

This book includes mature (18+) subjects and potentially upsetting situations that include graphic violence, death, threats of SA, accounts of past SA and torture, dubious consent due to false identity, and multiple explicit depictions of sex, including some non-traditional sexual practices and proclivities.*

*For a list of kinks and tropes, see https://karencpmcdermott.com/clash-of-stone-and-steel

Recap of Previous Books in the Series

If you need a reminder of what happened previously, please visit the links below for a brief summary of the major action and plot points.

Recap of *The Last Triumvirate* (Book 1)

https://karencpmcdermott.com/tlt1-summary

Recap of *Of Wrath and Storms* (Book 2)

https://karencpmcdermott.com/tlt2-owas-summary

Map of Thasia and Surrounding Countries

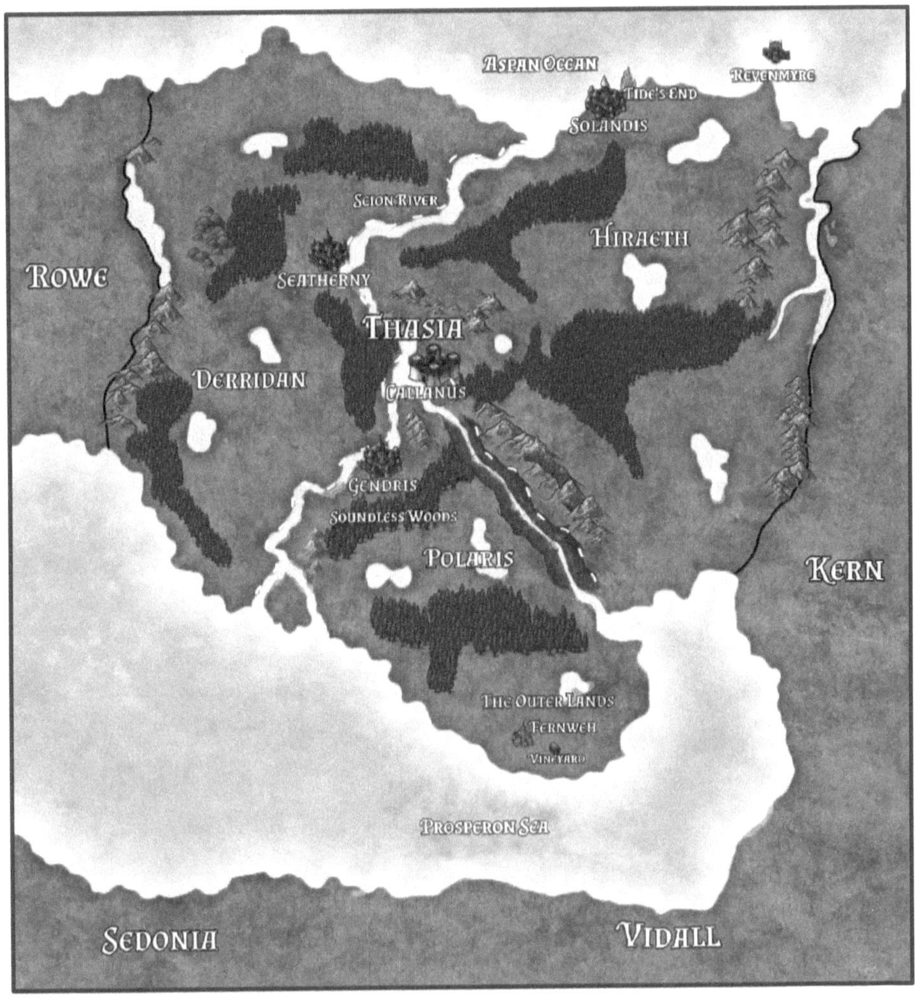

Tandem Reading Guide

The stories in this book (Book 3) and in *Nemesis Rising* (Book 4) overlap, so the two books can be read in tandem. That is, readers can switch back and forth between the two books as the story progresses, depending on what experience the reader wants. Doing the tandem read will let you be a little more 'in the know' if you so desire, but the author does not recommend reading one way over the other. Notations are also included at the ends of chapters of both books to tell readers when to switch.

NOTE: If you choose the tandem read, you will begin with the Prologue of Book 4, *Nemesis Rising*.

Recommended Tandem Reading Order:

Nemesis Rising (Bk 4), Prologue
Clash of Stone and Steel (Bk 3), Prologue-Chapter 14
Nemesis Rising (Bk 4), Chapter 1
Clash of Stone and Steel (Bk 3), Chapter 15
Nemesis Rising (Bk 4), Chapters 2-3
Clash of Stone and Steel (Bk 3), Chapter 16
Nemesis Rising (Bk 4), Chapters 4-7
Clash of Stone and Steel (Bk 3), Chapter 17
Nemesis Rising (Bk 4), Chapters 8-10
Clash of Stone and Steel (Bk 3), Chapters 18-21
Nemesis Rising (Bk 4), Chapters 11-12
Clash of Stone and Steel (Bk 3), Chapters 22-26
Nemesis Rising (Bk 4), Chapters 13-16
Clash of Stone and Steel (Bk 3), Chapters 27-30
Nemesis Rising (Bk 4), Chapter 17
Clash of Stone and Steel (Bk 3), Chapter 31
Nemesis Rising (Bk 4), Chapter 18
Clash of Stone and Steel (Bk 3), Chapters 32-33
Nemesis Rising (Bk 4), Chapters 19-20
Clash of Stone and Steel (Bk 3), Chapters 34-35
Nemesis Rising (Bk 4), Chapters 21-23
Clash of Stone and Steel (Bk 3), Chapter 36

Prologue

Talyn

Talyn of Avril – "The Raptor" to those who paid her to kill their enemies – stood over the sleeping couple and wondered if she should end them now and be done with it.

The man and woman slept soundly, so she could easily slit their throats. The only complication was the size of the bed. It was huge, and the couple slept in the middle, so she'd have to port to reach them, but she could strike quickly enough that both would be dead before they knew what happened.

That wasn't her assignment, though. Not yet.

Talyn studied the man. He was an exceptional-looking male, more beautiful than handsome. His night-black hair stood out starkly against the pillow, and she knew even from brief glimpses that his bright turquoise eyes were mesmerizing under lids heavy with long lashes. It would be a travesty to kill someone as stunning as him, but she'd do it.

Actually, she was looking forward to it. He oozed arrogance most of the time, and that alone made her want to stab him.

The woman sleeping beside him was another story.

She was beautiful as well, with haunting silver eyes so light they almost glowed, and rich brown hair that now spilled across her pillow as if being blown in the wind. Together the pair made a devastating couple.

While Talyn wanted to kill the man, her feelings about the woman were less clear. The lady was the main reason she was here in the first place, but nothing Talyn had seen of her said she deserved to die.

If anything, Talyn felt the urge to protect the woman. Just a week or so ago, she'd heard a scream come from this bedroom, and she'd rushed to see what the matter was. Never mind that she was supposed to be a servant and shouldn't be rushing toward danger quite so eagerly. She'd flung open the door without knocking and called to the woman.

She'd stopped short when she found Cyra, the Lady of Hiraeth, sprawled on the bed with her husband's head between her legs.

Talyn realized immediately she'd grossly misinterpreted Cyra's scream, and she'd been about to leave when she noticed Lord Bressen, Cyra's husband, had pinned the lady's wrists to the bed.

Talyn had stopped, suddenly not so sure everything was as innocent as it seemed. Some men believed they owned their wives and could have them anytime they wanted, regardless of the woman's wishes, and she wondered just how willing Cyra was.

"Are you sure you're alright, my lady?" Talyn had asked.

Lord Bressen had looked over his shoulder, amused she'd dared to question his intent, but she hadn't backed down. She'd kept her eyes locked on Cyra's, watching for any hint of duress. Talyn had a dagger at each hip hidden under her dress, and it would've taken seconds to draw them and port to the bed to plunge them into the lord's neck.

Whether seconds would have been fast enough was the question.

Lord Bressen was a mind wraith, probably the most powerful one to ever exist if the stories were true. Mind wraiths weren't common in general, but one of his ability was almost unheard of.

Lesser mind wraiths could read people's thoughts, while more powerful ones could compel a person to do things. Lord Bressen could do all that, plus glamour people into seeing things that weren't there. He could reportedly control the minds of hundreds of people at once, and it was rumored his ability to dominate a person's will was so strong he could compel them to drop dead with one thought.

As if that wasn't enough, he was also an angelus, a winged being that came with its own innate set of terrifying powers.

No, if Talyn had needed to strike at Lord Bressen to save Cyra, it was by no means certain she could've succeeded before he killed her. Fast as she was, she wasn't faster than someone's mind. She kept a mental shield up as a precaution, but the shield would only slow the lord down, not stop him entirely.

Talyn had been relieved when Cyra assured her she was fine, and the lord had released his wife's wrists. Still, there'd been a wild look in Cyra's eyes that had haunted Talyn ever since.

She looked down at the sleeping couple again. They looked perfectly happy and peaceful at that moment. Cyra's body was free of the bruises she supposedly got while training, and the two were curled around each other, their heads tipped together as if they'd fallen asleep whispering to each other. Cyra's hand rested lightly on the lord's chest while his arm lay across her waist under the covers.

Talyn had spent years sneaking into people's bedrooms to kill them, but she'd never seen anyone sleep this way before, pressed together as if love drew them close, even while unconscious. She rarely encountered couples sleeping in each other's arms. Most liked their space. In any case, if Cyra was afraid of her husband, her body language didn't show it.

Talyn took her hands off the hilts of the daggers sheathed beneath her dress and resigned herself to waiting. She wasn't sure why she'd ported into the bedchamber tonight to begin with. Maybe curiosity, or maybe the need to do something daring so she didn't go mad from the monotony. She'd been working as Cyra's lady's maid for several weeks now, trying to gather information for Sandrian, but spying wasn't her usual role.

She was an assassin, and she liked it because there was a certain rush that came with the job, one that – ironically – made her feel alive even as she took the life of another.

Spying was different. There was some danger involved, but it wasn't the same feeling.

This job was more dangerous than most, given that both the lord and lady could read minds, but Talyn's masquing power – her ability to shift her body into that of another – allowed her to mask her mind to a degree, even beyond a normal mind shield. It was an added perk of the power.

Still, she didn't want to be here any longer than she had to be. She'd sent Sandrian a message a day or two ago letting him know the lord and lady had returned from their ocean voyage and had retrieved the collar and rings he wanted. She'd been unable to get them for him, though, and he'd sent back a message telling her he'd take care of it.

Talyn was about to go back to bed when Cyra stirred, and she tensed. She may have been angling for some action, but she wasn't stupid. Being caught here at one in the morning would be a problem, and she'd been careless to come.

Cyra gasped and bolted upright in bed.

Talyn ported immediately, throwing herself across the room and around a corner across from the bathing chamber. She thought Cyra might've seen her for a brief second before she was able to port, but perhaps the lady had been too muddled with sleep to understand what she'd seen. Talyn's heart hammered in her chest as she waited for Cyra to scream or sound the alarm, but the woman did neither.

Bressen's voice met Talyn's ears. "Cyra? What is it? Are you alright?"

"I…I was in a nightmare, but not mine," Cyra said. "Somehow I dream walked into Axenus's nightmare."

Axenus…It took a moment for Talyn to summon the image of the merman, but his garnet-colored hair, cerulean eyes, and lightly iridescent skin finally swam to the surface of her mind. Axenus was the second of the three devastatingly handsome men that lived in the house.

And the third of those men…Gods above.

Talyn thought she was immune to fits of thigh-clenching arousal, but when she'd seen that third man for the first time, Protector save her. She wondered how the servants got anything done with these men around. She'd seen most of the women, and even a few men, blatantly staring at them on occasion. For that matter, she had no idea how Cyra herself managed to be around them.

Talyn was lost in her thoughts when the rest of Cyra's words hit her.

"Somehow I dream walked into Axenus's nightmare."

Fuck. Cyra could dream walk.

As if Talyn didn't have enough to worry about with the lord and lady's mind reading abilities, now she also had to make sure she didn't dream anything that might give her away.

Sandrian wasn't paying her nearly enough to do this job.

Talyn eyed the door across the room, but she was too far from it to port outside in one shot. Her range was about twenty feet, and the door was more than that. She'd have to port a few feet in front of it and then onto the other side, but she didn't dare do that with Bressen and Cyra awake. She tried to listen, to at least gather more information while she was here, but she was having trouble hearing what they were saying as they spoke in low voices. Only a few words drifted to her.

"Axenus said he owed you a debt," Cyra said, her voice barely reaching Talyn. "You freed him, didn't you."

Talyn raised a brow. There was a debt between the Lord of Hiraeth and the merman? She wasn't sure if or how this information might be useful, but she stowed it away for future reference. She knew Axenus was training Cyra to use her magic. Was that the debt Axenus was paying to Lord Bressen?

Talyn had never met a syphon until Cyra of Hiraeth, but no one else had either as far as she knew. Syphons were the most powerful perimortals in the world due to their ability to draw powers from other perimortals, but so far the Lady of Hiraeth didn't seem like much of a threat. She'd been raised among mortals for the first couple decades of her life, so she'd had no powers to draw on during that time other than the natural elemental ones around her. Or so Talyn had learned from other servants, whose knowledge seemed to rival a royal spy network.

Talyn heard movement on the bed and chanced a quick look around the corner. Cyra was lying with her back against the lord's chest, his arms around her shoulders. Talyn strained to hear what they were saying, but the lord's mouth was close to Cyra's ear, speaking low.

It was another minute or so before Bressen's voice rose enough for

Talyn to hear. "Nemesis damn me. That's all? How many partners?"

Talyn frowned and listened harder, but the couple had lowered their voices again.

"Your arrogance is truly astounding," Cyra said to her husband a little while later, and Talyn nearly snorted. At least they agreed on one thing.

A minute later, there was more shifting on the bed, and Talyn peeked around to find the lord now on top of his wife.

Nemesis take her. She should've seen that coming.

On the other hand, this might be the chance she needed to get away.

Talyn watched as Bressen entered his wife, making her gasp. The lady cried out as he thrust into her hard, and Talyn again wondered if Cyra enjoyed her sex rough or if she was a prisoner to her husband's desires.

She pulled back. She couldn't worry about it now. She needed to get out of here while she had the chance.

She glanced around the corner to be sure the couple was distracted, then she ported to within a few feet of the bedchamber door. She barely materialized when she ported again outside into the large sitting room. She put her ear to the door, but the sounds of fucking continued inside, and she breathed a sigh of relief.

She moved to the door of the sitting room and opened it very slowly, listening for any noise in the hall. Hearing none, she slipped out to hurry back toward the servants' wing.

She moved quickly on feet practiced in silence, looking back once to be sure the bedroom door was still closed. Just as she turned back around, though, she ran into something solid.

Talyn barely managed to hold in her squeak of surprise as large, rough hands closed around her upper arms to steady her, and she raked her eyes up the body of the absolutely huge man before her.

There he was. The third of the trio of exquisite men in the house, and her personal favorite. Even in the dark, the man's stature and long, stark-white hair told her exactly who it was.

Samhail.

She'd heard of him before coming to Solandis. Nearly everyone in her line of work had, but the bits and pieces of information that had reached her over the years hadn't done the man justice. Big, imposing, and gorgeous seemed wholly inadequate descriptors for him.

Talyn knew from Sandrian that Samhail was a gargoyle, although she didn't fully understand what that meant. She'd heard of gargoyles before, had seen their stone likenesses on the roofs of temples, often with water spouting from their mouths, but she wasn't sure how they were related to what Samhail was. Supposedly he could shift into a giant stone monster, but if this man could transform into something more intimidating than what he already was, she couldn't imagine it.

Talyn had done a double take the first time she'd seen him. Lord Bressen was tall, but Samhail had more than half a foot on him. One might've expected a man his size to lumber or trudge, but Samhail strode purposefully wherever he went, his long, thickly-muscled legs eating up the distance between him and his destination.

His white hair fell well past his shoulders, where he almost always wore it loose, and his eyes were so dark Talyn just assumed they were black. She also rarely saw him without the two long, razor-sharp blades that crisscrossed his back, and now was no exception.

Talyn balked. Why in the name of the Trinity was the man prowling the house at one o'clock in the morning fully armed?

"I didn't expect to encounter anyone but guards at this hour," Samhail said to her, "and you don't look like a guard."

His voice was deep but strangely smooth, and it did things to Talyn's insides and between her legs she couldn't think about right now. He hadn't released her yet, and being this close to him wasn't helping.

The assassin in her was a bit offended by his words, but in fairness, she was wearing her servant's dress right now. Thank the Protector she'd opted to wear the face of the lady's maid she was masquerading as and not her own face despite the late hour, or not looking like a guard would've been the least of her worries.

"No, sir. I'm Lady Cyra's maid," she said, the tremor in her voice mostly unfeigned.

Samhail occupied an exalted place in the household, and she'd been told at her orientation to use the honorific when addressing him.

He let go of her arms and paused a moment. "Leeda?" he said, seeming to pull the name she was using from the recesses of his mind. "Your name is Leeda."

She nodded, surprised he knew that.

"What are you doing out of your quarters so late, Leeda?" he asked.

Nemesis take her. She should've had an excuse ready. She was used to sneaking around and frequently had to come up with reasons why she was somewhere she wasn't supposed to be, but there was something overwhelming about Samhail's presence that left her mind blank.

Talyn's hand flew to the gold chain at her throat that held a large locket etched with a bird on it. "My necklace," she said quickly. "I lost it earlier. It's special to me, and I couldn't sleep until I found it."

She saw his frown, even in the dark.

"Where did you find it?" he asked.

"I was cleaning the lord and lady's sitting room this afternoon," Talyn said. "It fell off in there."

The only door in this hall led to Bressen and Cyra's chambers, so there was no other reason she could give for being down here. She might've been able to get away with saying she'd found the necklace in the hall, but there'd be questions as to why no one else had found it earlier.

Samhail's brows went up. "So you snuck into the lord and lady's chambers to look for your necklace?"

Talyn swallowed. It was like she'd never fucking done this before.

"I'm sorry," she said nervously. "The necklace was a gift from my sister. Please don't tell them."

She must've put the right amount of fear and humility in her voice because he nodded once after a pause.

"You should get back to your quarters now, Leeda," he said.

She bobbed a quick curtsey. "Yes, sir. Thank you."

Talyn brushed past him, resisting the urge to run her hand over his muscled forearm, and hurried toward the stairwell.

She glanced back quickly to see Samhail disappear around the corner into the hall she'd just come from, and she sent up another prayer of thanks he hadn't caught her porting. Trying to explain why she had such a rare power would've been challenging at best.

Minutes later, Talyn finally slipped back into her room and let her features morph into her own. Her body stretched up a few inches as her skin changed from olive to golden, and her brown hair spilled further down her back as it turned a shiny copper blonde.

In her own form, Talyn was beautiful, with striking features that demanded attention. She had a pert nose, high cheekbones, and full lips that one man had told her – just before she'd slit his throat – would look incredible wrapped around his cock.

She'd learned long ago her true features were entirely too conspicuous for the work she did, so when she was on a job, she made herself as forgettable as possible with common coloring, average height, and facial features that would easily be lost in a crowd.

The only time she wore her true shape and face nowadays was when she was alone. No one else had seen her real face in nearly a decade as far as she knew. Outside her rooms, out in the world, she was someone else. She was always playing a part, wearing a costume. She put on faces and bodies the way other women applied makeup or donned new clothes.

She'd left her room at an inn once wearing her own face by accident. She'd been in a hurry and stepped out into the hall without thinking, but the second she'd crossed the threshold, she'd suddenly felt naked, exposed. She'd shifted quickly before anyone saw her, darkening her hair and skin and flattening her hips and chest into those of a boy. She shrunk herself five inches and pushed her body farther away from who she really was than she'd ever done before until she finally heaved a sigh of relief and headed out to meet her newest client.

Only the people she killed ever saw the one other face she wore regularly, the one so much like her own, but not hers.

Talyn laid down on her bed. Tomorrow she needed to start making a more concerted effort to learn about Samhail. If she did have to kill the Lord and Lady of Hiraeth, he would be the biggest obstacle to her success.

She'd seen Samhail and Lord Bressen spar once before, and once was enough to know they were both warriors of an entirely different caliber than she was used to. As impressive as Samhail was, though, she could tell he was holding back when he sparred with the lord, and she longed to see what he could do when he wasn't governing himself. Part of her even wanted to match her own skills against him. She was good with a blade, and she suspected her ability to port might give her a fighting chance against him.

Maybe one of these days she'd get the chance to see.

Chapter 1

Four Days Later

Samhail

Every muscle in Samhail's body was strung taut as a bowstring while he fought to keep from jumping into the fight playing out before him.

He stood in the training yard with his arms crossed and his teeth clenched as he watched one of the house guards exchange sword blows with his student. He only managed to hold himself in check because crushing the guard's skull in with his bare hands would likely deter any others from agreeing to this assignment in the future.

Across from the guard, Cyra just managed to get her sword up in time to block the man's swing, and a bit of tension eased in Samhail's body. Cyra spun to the side and went on the offensive, swinging her sword low, then immediately striking high.

Samhail's muscles twitched with each move she made, as if his own body was trying to go through the motions with her, or as if he could somehow mentally impart to her what she should do next.

He could probably do the latter if he lowered his mind shield and allowed her to read his thoughts, but that wouldn't help her learn to make her own combat decisions. She'd been improving slowly before now, but the events a few days ago had lit something inside her, and Cyra had redoubled her efforts to master her fighting skills in their lessons.

Samhail knew he had things easier than Axenus did. The merman was tasked with helping Cyra train her magical powers, and that job had gotten infinitely harder in the last few days. Not only had Cyra's powers grown exponentially, thanks to the gods themselves, but the same tragic events that had spurred her to improve her fighting skills had also made both Cyra and her powers much more volatile.

Axenus had once told Cyra her powers were a wagon she'd been 'riding with the brake on' and that it was time to release the brake and push the wagon down a hill.

Well, the merman had gotten his wish, and Samhail wondered if he now regretted it.

Samhail ground his teeth as Cyra just barely dodged another blow.

Enlisting one of the household guards to help in Cyra's training had seemed like a good idea at the time, but he'd underestimated how difficult it would be for him to stand here and watch as the lady tried to defend herself, occasionally taking blows from the guard's blunted sword that would leave angry bruises. Cyra had already taken one nasty blow to her back that made Samhail flinch, and it had taken every ounce of his control not to blast the guard across the training yard with a forcefield.

Cyra could heal herself, of course, but it didn't make watching any easier. Aside from Samhail's concern for her as a friend, the divine imperative was sorely testing his resolve to stay out of the fight.

Samhail had enlisted the guard's help to begin with because it was getting harder for him to train with Cyra himself. When she'd just been learning to use a sword, it was easy enough to practice with her since he'd only had to use minimal effort. It took a little while for him to get used to swinging the smaller practice sword just slowly and lightly enough that he didn't hurt Cyra if he hit her during practice, but he'd eventually gotten a feel for it.

Now that Cyra had improved her swordsmanship, however, he needed to put more effort into both attacking and defending when he fought. Unfortunately, the extra effort made muscle memory and instinct kick in, and it was more difficult to restrain himself.

Yesterday when he and Cyra fought, she'd executed a clever move to almost land a blow to his exposed side, and Samhail had only just barely gotten his sword up to block it in time. More than a century's worth of fighting instincts had taken over, and his body had acted automatically to counter Cyra's attack with one of his own.

Before he could stop himself, he'd pivoted and swung his sword at her, landing a blow to her side that knocked her to the ground and nearly cracked one of her ribs. Cyra had cried out in pain, and he'd immediately dropped his sword, then dropped to his knees beside her to see if she was alright. At the same time, pain had shot through his head as the divine imperative reminded him he was supposed to protect her, not hurt her.

Samhail was close to seven feet tall, and his body was densely packed muscle, honed to lethal perfection by decades of training and combat. Cyra was half his size and had only started training to fight a few months ago. In short, it was entirely too dangerous for him to continue fighting with her, so he'd asked one of the smaller guards – relatively speaking – to stand in for him when it was time for Cyra to do some sparring.

The guard, Yarris, had been hesitant at first, afraid he might hurt the Lady of Hiraeth and draw the wrath of her husband, Lord Bressen.

Bressen was extremely dangerous when provoked, and he was also fiercely protective of Cyra, so Yarris's reluctance was understandable. Samhail had assured the man he'd take full responsibility for anything that happened during training, and he promised to keep a close eye on things to make sure nothing unfortunate occurred in the first place.

In the end, a hefty bonus to Yarris's pay had succeeded where promises and reassurances had not.

This was Cyra's first day training with Yarris, and so far, it had worked out relatively well. The only issue was the damned divine imperative that kept demanding Samhail step in and protect Cyra from Yarris.

In addition to being a powerful syphon, Cyra was also a Hand of the Gods, a perimortal chosen by the Trinity to carry out a particular god's will in the mortal realm. As a gargoyle, Samhail was part of a race of beings created thousands of years ago with an obligation to protect the Trinity and all those who served them. If Samhail himself hurt Cyra, he'd experience piercing pain in his head, or so he'd learned. If anyone else tried to hurt her, he felt a deep-seeded compulsion to help her.

Samhail's body tensed again as Yarris effected a series of attacks that put Cyra on the defensive.

Yarris had tried to go easy on the lady at first, assuming she wasn't terribly skilled with a sword, but Cyra had shown him soon enough just what she could do, and Samhail felt a swell of pride at her progress. Yarris learned quickly that going easy on her would only result in his own injury, and he'd stepped up his efforts. He had Cyra retreating now, and if she didn't find a way to turn the tables on him soon, she was headed for another ugly bruise.

Cyra tried to gain some ground and get back on the offensive, but Yarris hadn't left her any opening. In her attempt to get in a swing of her own, Cyra left her midriff unprotected, and Yarris saw the vulnerability. Samhail's hands clenched into fists as Yarris swung his blunted sword for Cyra, but just before it hit, an invisible force knocked Yarris to the side, and the guard went sprawling across the ground on his back.

Both Cyra and Yarris looked at Samhail, and Samhail looked down to see his hand extended toward Yarris.

"Fuck," he swore as he advanced toward the guard.

Yarris's eyes widened in fear, and he scrambled backward as Samhail strode toward him, but Samhail only held out a hand. Yarris flinched but realized the hand was an offer of help. He took it after a moment of hesitation, and Samhail pulled him effortlessly to his feet.

"My apologies, Yarris," Samhail said as the guard eyed him with surprise. "The forcefield was a reflex. I'll keep it under better control next time. You did nothing wrong."

He turned to Cyra. "You, on the other hand, let him put you on the run, then you tried to go on offense prematurely. What could you have done differently?"

"Kneed him in the groin when we locked swords that first time?" Cyra suggested, and Yarris flinched again.

Samhail felt her words between his own legs but inclined his head.

"You could've done that," he admitted reluctantly, "but we should get Yarris some protection for future sessions before you try it."

Cyra gave Yarris an apologetic look, and the man returned it with an unenthusiastic shrug of understanding.

"But there was something else you could've done as well," he told her.

"Yarris leaves his right shoulder vulnerable on his cross-swing," Cyra observed. "If I can get my blade around, I can take out his sword arm."

Yarris blinked in shock, as if this was news to him.

"Good," Samhail said. "That's what I would've done." He looked at Yarris. "You might want to fix that, or you'll have a very sore shoulder when she's done with you."

Yarris nodded slowly.

"That's enough for today," Samhail said.

"No!" Cyra cried. "Let's go again. I can do this."

"Tomorrow," Samhail said. "You've been at this almost two hours. You need to eat and rest."

"I need to train," Cyra insisted.

Samhail set his jaw again. He recognized the look of stubbornness and wild desperation in her face. It was a look he knew well, since he'd worn it himself decades ago after that battle in the war when Morland had captured his mind and almost used him to kill Bressen. He'd never felt more helpless in his life than when he'd been barreling toward Bressen with every intention of ripping the man he considered a brother in half.

He still wasn't sure how he'd broken Morland's hold on him, but he'd thrown himself into training after that, both physically and mentally. The physical training had helped him work off his frustrations, but he'd pushed his body farther and farther until he'd collapsed in the training yard one day and a healer had to be called. It had never occurred to him he had physical limits, but he'd found them that day.

Even worse had been the day he'd learned his mental limits. Morland had been able to take over his mind because he'd never worked all that much on strengthening his mind shield when he was younger. He'd been arrogant and always assumed his physical strength would get him out of trouble, but it had taken Morland mere seconds to get past his rudimentary mind shield on the battlefield that day, and then his mind had no longer been his own.

Morland had controlled him as easily as a puppeteer, and Samhail vowed later it would never happen again. He'd enlisted Bressen to help him strengthen his mind shield, but there too he'd pushed himself beyond his limits. He remembered making Bressen attack his shield harder and harder until his friend had refused to push any more. Samhail hadn't slept in days by that point, and he'd lashed out, crazed with desperation, and attacked Bressen himself.

He'd woken up three days later with no further memory of what had happened. He suspected Bressen had crashed through his mind shield and rendered him unconscious, forcing him to get the much-needed rest he'd been denying himself, but he'd never asked Bressen exactly what happened, and Bressen never offered.

So yes, Samhail recognized and understood that look in Cyra's eyes. She'd moved her training time with Axenus to an hour earlier to get more time to work on her magic, and she'd pushed Samhail to extend their lessons longer and longer each day. She was now training for more than four hours straight every morning. He'd have to ask Bressen if she was sleeping at all, because he suspected she wasn't. In any case, he wasn't going to let her burn out like he had.

"We're done for today," Samhail said using a tone that normally made seasoned warriors shiver. Cyra only glared at him.

He turned to Yarris and jerked his head toward the door. "Thanks for your help, Yarris. We'll see you here tomorrow."

Yarris spared only a quick glance at Cyra before mumbling a 'Yes, sir' to Samhail and turning again to bow to her. "My lady," the man said as he scurried past her out of the yard.

"We're done," Samhail said to her again. "It's time for lunch."

"I'm the lady here, and I'll say when we're done," she snapped back.

Samhail arched a brow. Cyra wasn't the type to pull rank, so the fact she'd just tried told him just how far out of herself she really was. It was time to rein her back in.

"I don't care if you're the Hand of the Nemesis or the Queen of Arystria or whatever other titles you're using nowadays. They mean nothing in this training yard," he told her. "In this yard, I'm in charge, and I say you're done for today."

Her eyes narrowed at him, and he knew even before her body tensed she'd taken it as a challenge.

"Cyra," he warned.

She ignored his tone and launched herself at him, blunted practice sword raised. Samhail sighed and dodged her first two swipes with the sword, which only enraged her. She pulled back the blade again and swung it across her body with all her might, clearly forgetting everything he'd taught her about leaving herself open. He pulled back again, just out of reach of the blade, and Cyra nearly spun herself around as the strike she expected to make didn't stop her momentum.

With her back to him now, Samhail lunged forward and grabbed her around the shoulders to pull her back against his chest. He knocked the sword out of her hand with a quick blow to her wrist and then lifted her off the ground so her feet dangled in the air. Cyra screamed her frustration as she found herself immobilized and weaponless. She struggled against him, trying to jerk and wiggle free, but he only tightened his hold on her until she grunted.

"Let go of me!" she screamed.

"Yield," he said calmly.

"Never!"

Samhail was about to chuckle at her stubbornness when he realized he was suddenly holding empty air. He whirled around, looking for Cyra in the training yard as panic rolled over him.

"Cyra! Where are you?" he called to her. He stopped as he spotted her near the weapons rack pulling another sword from it.

"What the fuck just happened?" he asked, more to himself than her.

Cyra didn't answer, but suddenly she was in front of him again, swinging the new sword. He blinked in surprise, but this time he simply put up a hand and caught the blade in mid-swing as Cyra tried to slash at him. The sting of the metal on his palm hurt only for a second before his hand closed around the blunted blade so she couldn't swing it again.

"Let go!" she yelled as she tugged at the sword.

"Since when can you port?" he asked her.

"I discovered it on the ship after we found *The Stalwart*," she answered, still pulling at the sword.

"Who did you syphon it from?" he asked more urgently.

"I don't know!"

She was still trying to jerk the sword from his hand, but he pulled it from her instead and chucked it across the yard.

"Cyra, stop right now, or this will be our last training session."

She stopped instantly, her eyes going wide. She shook her head. "Samhail, no, please…"

Samhail swore loudly as tears gathered in her eyes, but she stepped back from him and wiped furiously at them.

"I'm fine," she said, still wiping the moisture away.

"You're not fine," he said gently, "but no one expects you to be after what happened."

She looked away from him, but he saw the tears threaten in her eyes again and sighed. He stepped toward her and brushed a thumb across her cheek. It was perhaps too tender a gesture to make out in the open as they were, but he didn't care. He hated seeing her upset.

"Would…a hug help?" he asked.

Her gaze snapped to his in disbelief. "You're actually offering a hug?"

"Only for the next five seconds," he said, "so if you want one…"

She threw herself into his arms and laid her head on his chest. Mercifully, it didn't sound like she was crying, and Samhail wrapped his long arms around her. He put a hand on her head and held her for a moment before she finally pulled back from him.

"Thank you," she said. "I'm sorry for attacking you."

"I've been where you are before. I understand," he said. "If you need to work out your frustrations, that's fine. We can do that."

She looked at him as if seeking clarification of what he meant, so he added, "In the training yard. But I won't let you push yourself to exhaustion and burnout. Recovery time is as important as training time."

She crossed her arms. "I remember being told a few months ago we don't always get to fight under ideal conditions, that sometimes it's a good idea to see what your body is capable of when you're not at your best."

Samhail frowned. "These are very different circumstances. You aren't just tired, you're exhausted, mentally and physically. At some point you do need to take a break. In fact, those are your orders for the afternoon. Take a nap. Read a book. I don't care, just spend the rest of the afternoon resting, or I'm canceling our training session for tomorrow, and I'll have Axenus cancel his with you as well."

"Axenus doesn't answer to you," she said, her anger resurfacing.

"No, but he'll agree you need rest, and if we take it to Bressen-"

"Fine," she said, holding up a hand. "You win."

"Speaking of Axenus, does he know you can port?" Samhail asked.

"Yes, he was with me and Bressen when I discovered it," she said.

"And you have no idea who you syphoned it from?"

"No. It's possible I've had it for months and only just discovered it. I've been careful about not touching the perimortals I meet lately."

"That's a handy ability to have," he said. "Porting is fairly rare. Has Axenus worked with you on using it?"

"I completely forgot I had it until now," Cyra said, and suddenly she looked as bone-weary as she sounded.

"I'll make a deal with you," Samhail said. "If you take it easy the next few days, rest, and don't push yourself too hard, next week we'll start incorporating some of your magical abilities into your combat training."

Cyra's face brightened. "You promise?"

"I promise."

"Deal," she said. She bent to pick up the first practice sword he'd knocked out of her hand.

"Leave it," he said. "I'll clean up here. Go have lunch."

She looked surprised but nodded and headed toward the door into the house. When she was gone, Samhail went around the yard to collect the equipment they'd used and put it back on the rack. Then he sat down on the bench, rested his elbows on his knees, and let his head drop. His body sagged, and he pushed out a long, deep breath.

Normally he wouldn't show such vulnerability out in the open, but both his energy and his ability to care if someone was watching had left him. It killed him to see Cyra this upset, this unhinged…

And it was all his fault.

He'd been careless days ago when they'd faced Sandrian, Morland, and Magdalene at the abandoned temple. He'd been so focused on getting to Sandrian he hadn't seen that spear coming until it was lodged in his pelvis. Granted, he hadn't recognized Morland in his mortal body, but he should've been ready for the attack regardless. As a result of his negligence, he'd been powerless to help when things had truly gone sideways, and the result was that Cyra's father was now dead.

Aramis had been told to wait outside the temple until he was needed, but he'd snuck in to help and stabbed one of Sandrian's guards just when Samhail was sure everything had gone to all hells.

Chaos erupted when Aramis attacked the guard, and it had given them time to remove the spear from Samhail's hip and heal the wound. The only thing Samhail could think as Aramis had worked on him was that he had to join the fight as soon as possible. The second he was fully healed, he'd shifted into his gargoyle form and launched himself toward the horde of symbionts Sandrian had brought, creatures that could take over human bodies. It hadn't occurred to Samhail to order Aramis back outside or – better yet – get the healer out of harm's way before he'd begun tearing the creatures to pieces.

He should've gotten Aramis to safety. He should've gone after Magdalene instead of the symbionts. There were any number of things he could've or should've done to ensure the safety of Cyra's father, but he'd been so short-sighted. Now Aramis was dead, and Cyra was grieving the loss of the parent she'd only just found. She didn't seem to blame him for Aramis, but she didn't need to. He blamed himself.

Samhail had visited the temple in Solandis that same day when they'd returned. He wasn't sure what had compelled him to go, but he'd stayed outside and crouched on the parapet of the roof as he rethought every move he'd made – or hadn't made. A torrent of rain beat down on him, soaking his hair and clothes, and he'd looked over at one point to realize he was in almost the exact same pose as one of the ridiculous stone gargoyles that perched atop the roof. His 'replacement.'

He'd wanted to rip the grotesque thing off and send it crashing to the ground. He'd been just as useless that day as the lifeless piece of stone.

Samhail lifted his head as the feeling of being watched stole over him where he sat in the training yard now. His attention snapped to the side when he thought he saw movement near the house, but there was nothing there when he looked.

Except maybe a faint cloud of smoke? Had a guard been watching him while out on a break perhaps?

He shook his head. Cyra wasn't the only one wound too tight after their battle at the abandoned temple. He'd thought Morland was dead once before only to find the man was still alive, just in another body. Now the man was seemingly dead again, but Samhail couldn't shake the feeling Morland had once again managed to elude death.

Morland had shattered Samhail's peace of mind on that battlefield twenty-five years ago, and he wasn't sure he'd ever rest easy again until he knew without a doubt the man who'd held his mind hostage was gone.

Chapter 2

Samhail

Samhail wasn't surprised to find Axenus in Bressen's study when he entered. The merman met with Bressen regularly before lunch to update him on Cyra's progress in their magic lessons, and he was often still there when Samhail arrived to give his own updates.

"Axe," was all Samhail said by way of greeting as he sat down in the other chair across the desk from Bressen.

"Sam," Axenus answered, and Samhail growled. He didn't do nicknames, but Axenus knew that.

Bressen rolled his eyes and sighed. "The two of you have Cyra so confused. She can't tell if you're enemies or best friends."

Samhail and Axenus glanced at each other.

"Enemies," they said together.

Bressen snorted.

In truth, Samhail liked and respected Axenus. He'd just never tell him so in a million years. Doing so would be too…familiar.

He and Bressen had met Axenus when Bressen had been sent to Sedonia by his father during the war to secure Queen Clarice's alliance for Thasia. Unfortunately, Bressen had discovered Clarice was keeping Axenus as a slave, forcing him to serve her in bed when he wasn't being kept in a tank of water just barely big enough to hold him. Bressen had risked everything to save Axenus, and he'd paid dearly for doing so.

It was Samhail that Bressen had called to aid in Axenus's escape, and Samhail had been happy to help. He was horrified to learn what Axenus had endured for years, but that knowledge came with some awkwardness.

As Samhail had once told Cyra, gargoyles didn't do caring well, and his unease with showing concern had manifested into the antagonistic friendship he now had with Axenus. It was his way to hold the merman at arm's length, to not show pity for what had happened to him.

He was sure Axenus preferred the antagonism to pity anyway, so this was how they existed, as friends who seemed like enemies to anyone who didn't know them.

"Were either of you planning to tell me Cyra can port now?" Samhail asked, glancing between the two men.

"Gods damn me, I forgot about that," Axenus said, sitting forward in his chair. "I need to make a list of what she's syphoned. It's getting too hard to remember everything she can do now."

"Should we be worried about where she picked it up?" Samhail asked, swallowing down the urge to hassle Axenus about the oversight.

"Not yet," Bressen said. "She probably came into contact with a priest or priestess at the Priory who had the power. I'll ask Phaedrus if anyone there can port when I see him later today. He's bringing someone over who's willing to let Cyra syphon their power to create wards. That's a power she should have."

"Why not ask Phaedrus for a list of the powers of all the priests and priestesses?" Samhail suggested. "Let Cyra syphon everything she can."

"I'd be hesitant to do that until we know more about how her powers work," Axenus said. "It's possible she can only hold so many abilities at a time before the other ones she has either go away or weaken. We don't know what limitations, if any, she may have, so it's best to just let her syphon what she needs for now."

Samhail frowned. "Do we have any reason to think she might lose some of the powers she already has?"

"Maziren let Cyra syphon her strength at the temple," Bressen said. "It's how Cyra broke Sandrian's wrist and my caronium cuff, but she no longer seems to have that strength now."

Samhail blinked in surprise. "When the fuck did that happen? And, again, why am I only hearing about this now?"

"I'm the magic instructor," Axenus said coolly. "When there's something you need to know about practice swords and straw pads, we'll let you know."

Samhail knew Axenus was just trying to rankle him, as was their way, but the comment still stoked his ire, and his answer was sharper than he intended.

"I was going to start incorporating magic into Cyra's combat training in a few days," he snapped at the merman. "It might help to know what she does and doesn't have at her disposal." He fixed his gaze on Axenus. "And anytime you want to train with me, I'd be happy to show you just what I can do with a practice sword and a straw pad."

To his credit, Axenus didn't flinch at the threat in Samhail's voice. In fact, he just sighed and admitted, "I probably should get back into the training yard at some point now that we're heading for war."

"How was your session with Cyra?" Bressen asked Samhail.

"She's pushing herself too hard," he said. "She attacked me today when I told her it was time to stop."

Bressen's brows shot up. "And how did that work out for her?"

"Not well. Until she remembered she could port," Samhail said. He looked pointedly at Axenus, who shrugged one shoulder.

"Axenus said much the same thing," Bressen said with a sigh. "Cyra didn't attack him, but she's pushing herself too hard."

"How is she sleeping?" Samhail asked. "When you let her sleep, that is," he added, giving his friend a knowing half-grin. It was well-known, even among the staff at Tide's End, just how much time Bressen and Cyra spent fucking each other.

Bressen started to speak, then stopped to reconsider his words.

"To be honest," he said finally, "she's the one keeping *me* up, which only supports what both of you have been saying. She's not handling what happened well. She blames herself for Aramis."

Samhail tensed. "I told her to take the rest of the day off and relax or I'd stop training her," he said, then looked at Axenus. "I need you to back me on this if she refuses to rest."

Axenus nodded. "I'm sure that decree went over well."

Samhail pushed a deep breath out through his nose. "You don't want to know what I had to do to smooth it over."

His tone was ominous, but he opened his mind a sliver to show Bressen the image of him hugging Cyra, and the lord pressed his lips together to hide his smile.

"So what do we do?" Axenus asked.

Samhail willed his cock not to harden as he thought about what Bressen's solution had been the last time Cyra was struggling with something. Samhail didn't think he'd be receiving an invitation to Bressen and Cyra's bed again anytime soon, though. They'd agreed that the last time had been *the* last time.

"The deal to buy the vineyard in Solandis went through this morning," Bressen said. "I just let Cyra know before Axe arrived, and she looked happier than I've seen her in days. I hope getting back to something she loves will channel her energy into something productive. If she decides to take a break from training for a while, I'd ask you both to let her."

Samhail and Axenus nodded.

"The timing is good anyway," Samhail said. "I'll need to start making regular trips to the training camps to see how the soldiers are doing."

"We're still getting things set up, but yes," Bressen answered. "You'll need to start overseeing things soon."

"You both remember we won't be able to fight this like a normal war, right?" Axenus ventured. "Having our men face off across a battlefield with these symbionts seems rather futile."

Samhail caught Bressen's eye, but the lord didn't seem to understand what Axenus was talking about either.

"What do you mean, Axe?" Bressen asked.

Axenus looked between Samhail and Bressen as if he thought they might be joking with him, and Samhail had the urge to shake the merman.

"You said those things can replicate themselves, didn't you?" Axenus asked. "If they wound you, whatever that blue substance is can seep inside you and take over your mind? If we send men into battle and they're wounded, the creatures will start taking over their bodies, and we'll end up being outnumbered very quickly."

Samhail met Bressen's gaze again, and he saw the same shock he knew must be on his own face. "Fuck me," he swore. "I forgot about that."

"Me too," Bressen admitted. "Three hells. That means every casualty on our side is a potential new enemy."

They'd only learned recently about the existence of the creatures they now referred to as symbionts. Bressen and Cyra had found evidence of them at one of the villages that had been attacked in Derridan a few weeks ago, but they hadn't seen what they looked like until the night before Bressen and Cyra's wedding. Cyra and Raina had gone to a gambling den to celebrate when the establishment was attacked by the creatures.

The things were human in shape with dark blue bodies, clawed hands, and glowing yellow eyes. Their bodies were hard, as if the blue symbiotic shell was an exoskeleton, and normal blades mostly glanced off them. Only Samhail's own exceptionally sharp blades had done any real damage, and even then he'd had to put some strength behind driving his sword through them.

The most horrifying thing about the symbionts, though, was that when they wounded someone, the dark blue substance that covered their human hosts could separate off so that part of it seeped into the wound and turned the other person into a new host. As far as they knew, there was no way to separate the creatures from their hosts without killing both.

The idea of facing an army of hard-to-kill creatures with claws and nearly impenetrable skin was daunting enough. That any of their soldiers who were wounded could be turned into symbionts to swell the enemy's numbers was unthinkable, and Samhail's stomach twisted at the thought.

"Gods above," Bressen breathed. "What the fuck are we going to do? He's right. We can't just send soldiers into battle like normal."

The three of them sat in silence for a long moment.

"I'll...I'll figure something out," Samhail said.

He had no idea what, but he felt like he should say something. He was Bressen's general after all. It was his job to figure this out.

"Would the gargoyles fight?" Bressen asked him. "The symbionts weren't able to so much as scratch you back at the temple when you changed into your stone form. If we could recruit them…"

Bressen let the thought hang in the air, and Samhail grimaced.

"Ajax would certainly fight for us," Samhail said, mentioning the gargoyle they'd recently met when Cyra had freed him from four hundred years of imprisonment in a magical necklace. "He feels he owes Cyra, so she could call in that favor."

"And your family?" Bressen pressed.

Samhail sat for a moment, willing the cold dread in his bones to ease.

"They might fight, but I'm not sure how much I'd trust them," he said finally. "The twins aren't completely right in the head, Sadira enjoys cruelty a little too much, and Soldier…well, he's a vicious bastard on a good day. He might decide to fight for Sandrian just to spite me."

"This is your family?" Axenus asked incredulously.

Samhail shrugged. "My siblings, yes."

"You have four siblings?" Axenus pressed. "That's a huge number of children for a perimortal family."

Samhail shrugged again. "My parents did a lot of fucking, and they were apparently the exception to the rule in terms of fertility."

Axenus's eyes widened in shock.

"Speaking of your parents, would they fight?" Bressen asked.

"They might," Samhail said. "My father is getting old and hasn't been in a battle for centuries, but he could be talked into it if I can impress on him the severity of the situation. My mother will be far easier to recruit."

Bressen nodded. "Would we have better odds of convincing them to help if I reached out or if you did?" he asked.

Samhail thought for a moment. "Your chances are even either way."

"I'll reach out then," Bressen said. "The request should come from me if it doesn't matter."

"Remember the symbionts were once human, and many, if not most, will have been turned against their will," Axenus cut in. "We need to look for a way to separate the creatures from them safely or we'll just be killing a lot of innocent people."

Samhail and Bressen looked at each other again.

"You're just full of fun reminders today, Axe," Samhail grumbled.

How in the name of the Trinity was he supposed to plan for a war where they couldn't hurt the other side?

Bressen sighed. "We'll see what we can do," he said, "but in the meantime, we need to find people who can fight the symbionts without being injured, or we need to protect our soldiers from head to toe so they don't leave the creatures an opening to take over their bodies."

"Do you want me to do some research?" Axenus asked. "I can see if there's any record of these things and any information on how to separate them from their human hosts."

"I'll put Phaedrus on it," Bressen said. "I may need you to take a trip soon. We need to start recruiting allies."

"Where do you need me to go?" Axenus asked.

"Kern," Bressen said. "They stayed out of the war with Sandrian the first time, but I'm hoping they'll be more willing to help, given the higher stakes, especially since they share a border with us. The Primus who rules there is getting old, but I'm told his eldest son has started preparing for the transition of power. Perhaps the son will be more open to joining our cause and can convince his father."

Axenus nodded. "When do I need to leave?"

"Not yet. I'm still negotiating a visit for you. Until then, we'll have to come up with the best way for you to approach the situation."

Bressen paused, and Samhail could tell something was eating at him.

"What is it?" Samhail asked.

Bressen exhaled deeply. "I have a proposal for Kern that may sway them to our side, but it won't go over well with everyone."

Both Samhail and Axenus waited for the lord to go on, but Bressen only said, "I'm not at liberty to say more just yet."

"Whatever you need me to do," Axenus said with an acquiescent nod.

Samhail almost rolled his eyes. Even after a quarter century of friendship, Axenus hadn't let go of the deference he had for Bressen.

Samhail showed Bressen the respect befitting his title in public, but when it was just the two of them and Cyra, that all fell away, and they were like normal friends. There was no yes-my-lording or anything that suggested Bressen was in any way above him in station, and that only made Samhail respect Bressen all the more. They'd seen each other in too many ridiculous situations — most of them drunken — for either of them to stand on protocol when they were alone or just among friends. Axenus had never quite reached that level of comfort with Bressen, so the merman still balanced the few liberties he took with a lingering formality.

Bressen suddenly arched back against his chair and gripped the armrests until his knuckles went white. He sucked in a hard breath through his teeth, and Samhail shot forward in his chair, searching for a sign of what was wrong.

"Bressen? Are you alright?" he asked.

Bressen closed his eyes as his breathing became labored.

"Bressen!" Samhail said. He launched himself out of his chair, looking for an enemy to fight.

"Bressen?" Axenus pressed as he stood as well.

Bressen swallowed. "I'm fine," he said, his voice carefully restrained. "I just need to speak with my wife about appropriate times to practice her mind powers."

Samhail and Axenus just looked at him before understanding dawned on Samhail and he grinned.

"She's got your cock hard right now, doesn't she," he said with a chuckle. His body relaxed as his gaze dipped to Bressen's groin to confirm his suspicion. The lord was definitely aroused.

Bressen only groaned.

"I'm not sure whether to be impressed or terrified," Axenus said as he studied the mask of erotic torment on Bressen's face.

"It's like she's under the desk with her lips wrapped around my cock," Bressen ground out.

Axenus's expression shifted toward terrified, but Samhail chuckled.

"You can't push her out?" Samhail asked.

"Fuck!" Bressen swore loudly as his head kicked back. "Not without hurting her. You both should leave. You don't want to see how this ends."

Axenus headed immediately for the door, but Samhail only crossed his arms in amusement. "On the contrary, I definitely want to see how this ends," he said.

"Out!" Bressen yelled before his eyes rolled back in his head.

Samhail sighed but turned to follow Axenus out. Bressen was already tearing at the fastenings of his pants to free his cock, and the thought of what Cyra was doing to his friend made him a little hard himself.

Cyra was a beautiful, effortlessly sensuous creature, and remembering the couple times he'd fucked her always aroused him. He rarely fucked women more than once, but if Bressen ever allowed it again, he'd be happy to take Cyra whenever he could. She was the only woman he'd met so far that had kept his interest, and he loved the feel of her writhing in pleasure beneath him. She belonged to Bressen, though, and as disappointing as that was, he accepted it.

The strange thing was that seeing Bressen and Cyra together almost – *almost* – made him want something similar. Or at least it made him want to find a woman he found alluring enough to fuck regularly. He generally enjoyed the hunt, as Bressen once had, but it was becoming tiring. There was a process to choosing a companion for the night, of getting to know her just enough that he didn't feel like a cad taking her to bed, and then of hoping she was able to even take his large cock.

The appendage between Samhail's legs wasn't monstrous, but it was big enough that once in a while the woman he had for the night couldn't take him without pain. In those cases, he pleasured her with his tongue and hoped she'd return the favor. Generally she did, but there were a few times he'd had to get himself off.

He had a secret when it came to his tongue that he'd never told anyone else, not even Bressen. The women he pleasured were often spent when he was done with them, so in those cases, he took care of himself.

Samhail closed the door to the study behind him as he left and smiled as he heard Bressen roar with pleasure on the other side. His own groin ached now, but it was too early in the day to head into the city. He'd find his own release now to take the edge off, then go into Solandis tonight to find a woman – or maybe two – to finish him properly.

It was the one thing he still had that Bressen didn't.

Options.

Chapter 3

Several Minutes Earlier

Talyn

Talyn strode down the hall toward her quarters in the servants' wing as quickly as she could with the message leaf clutched tightly in her hand. Thank the Protector she had quick reflexes and was able to snatch the message out of the air to port away with it before anyone saw her.

Well, she suspected Samhail might've seen movement out of the corner of his eye in the training yard where she'd been watching him, but no one had raised an alarm yet.

Not that she'd be safe much longer if Sandrian was so careless as to send her another message in the middle of the day where anyone might see her receive it. Gods above, what if she'd been with Cyra when the leaf had come in? The leaves were expensive, not the kind of magical object a normal person would have around, and she would've been at a loss to explain to Cyra or anyone else why someone was sending her one.

On the other hand, she'd been expecting this message for days now and was eager to see what it said. She was ready for this job to be over, so she hoped the leaf contained either orders to abort her mission or the go-ahead to kill the Lord and Lady of Hiraeth.

Talyn's hand was on the door to her bedroom when the stone on the bracelet she wore suddenly glowed green, and she swore under her breath. She thought Cyra had gone to lunch, but apparently the lady wanted a bath before eating, and Talyn – or Leeda, as Cyra knew her – was being summoned to help.

Talyn tapped the stone to indicate she was aware of the summons and was on her way, but she went into her bedroom first to stash the message.

She pulled the curtains on her window, lit the lamp near her bed, and sat down on the mattress. She quickly unfolded the message leaf and read the three-word note. She stared at the words, letting them sink in, then folded the paper and slipped it into her pillowcase on the underside of her pillow before heading out of her room and up to Cyra's quarters on the fourth floor.

Cyra was already undressed and in her robe when Talyn entered the master chamber a few minutes later. A tray of food with enough for two people sat on one of the tables, but the lord was nowhere to be seen.

Talyn groaned inwardly. Cyra was self-sufficient, and the tray for two confirmed what Talyn had suspected. The lady didn't want help with her bath. She wanted company.

"Leeda, did you have lunch yet?" Cyra asked. She gestured to the tray. "I didn't want you to go hungry while you helped me with my bath."

Talyn surveyed the tray of sandwiches, fruit, cakes, and a bottle of wine. She didn't want to encourage Cyra, but she was hungry, and she likely wouldn't get a chance to eat if Cyra kept her here, so she took a plate and added a few items.

"Thank you, my lady."

Cyra had befriended her former lady's maid, Raina, but Raina lived in Polaris now after the attempted coup a few months ago. The woman was the illegitimate child of the late Lord Ursan, and she'd begun training as the potential heir apparent for Polaris's Triumvirate seat. Quite a step up, to say the least.

Cyra clearly missed her friend, and she'd been trying to establish a relationship with Talyn ever since they'd met. Cyra still saw Raina on occasion, but the women's respective duties kept them away from each other often. Talyn, on the other hand, was always at Cyra's beck and call, always just a summons away when the lady felt lonely.

"How's your day been?" Cyra asked, and Talyn stiffened.

She tried to avoid answering questions whenever possible because Cyra had truth seeing abilities, and it was difficult to carefully word her answers so she wasn't outright lying. This question was innocent enough, but it would only lead to more.

"It's been fairly productive," Talyn said. "How has yours been, my lady? You seem to be in better spirits today."

It was no secret in the house that Cyra's father Aramis had been killed a few days ago when he'd accompanied the lord and lady on some business they had, but for once the servants were short on the details of how or why he'd been killed. Only Talyn herself knew Aramis had died confronting Sandrian and a small group of his forces in an abandoned temple on the outskirts of Rowe.

She knew this because Aramis's death was due to information she herself had passed to Sandrian.

The healer was an innocent man who hadn't deserved to die, and his death weighed heavily on Talyn, as did the grief Cyra now carried. The people Talyn killed usually deserved it to some degree, and she wasn't used to feeling guilt over someone's death.

Cyra gave Talyn a small smile. "I received some good news today. The deal to buy that vineyard outside of Solandis went through. I'm officially a vineyard owner again."

"Congratulations, my lady. That's wonderful," she said truthfully.

Despite herself, Talyn didn't mind Cyra, and she was happy the news of the vineyard had cheered the lady up.

Talyn's work didn't really allow her to make friends, something she'd resigned herself to a long time ago. Cyra didn't even know her real name, nor had she ever seen Talyn's real face – no one had – and that kind of deception wasn't conducive to friendship.

Most of the forms and faces Talyn took nowadays were female. She could only stretch herself so wide or tall, although her natural height gave her a few more options in her shifting. Other shapeshifters might be able to push themselves further, but even with Talyn's own limits, the possibilities were still endless. She could make herself taller or shorter by several inches either way. She could narrow her hips or plump her breasts if she thought the situation called for it, but she'd found that holding a shape with larger breasts – her own real ones were decently large – for too long made her back hurt for several hours after she returned to normal.

As a child she'd transformed into little boys on occasion because their body size and proportions weren't that different from little girls at that age, but she stopped doing so as she grew up and her body became that of a woman and changed in ways beyond her control. There'd been a time her body had grown so rapidly that she would shift back to her true form only to find it now looked different, her breasts a bit larger, her formerly slender, gangly legs now more shapely.

She'd been about fourteen when she changed into a male again for the first time since childhood, and the feel of the foreign appendage between her legs had taken her by surprise. She hadn't bothered to make *that* change to her body when she was a child, hadn't even known the thing was there at the time, but there it was now.

Still, the notion of what she could do with a cock didn't occur to her until she was nineteen. She'd needed to infiltrate the house of a man who liked young, effeminate men, so she'd taken the form of his favorite servant after the boy had gone to bed for the night. She'd been shocked to feel the dick between her legs start to harden after she'd killed her target, and an idea was born.

She'd gone straight to the nearest brothel when she was done with her job, intent on trying out the cock. She sat in the lounge of the place for almost half an hour, watching the prostitutes work the room. The women there weren't as skilled at seduction as the courtesans in the pleasure house where her mother worked, but she'd finally caught the gaze of one she thought was pretty, and the woman had serpentined her way across the room to ease down onto Talyn's lap.

Talyn's eyes had rolled back in her head as the woman ground her ass against her cock, and she'd nearly thrown the girl onto the floor in her haste to rise and get to one of the private rooms.

She'd been sure she was doing the prostitute a favor. She was, after all, a woman herself, so she knew what a woman felt during sex and thus what they wanted. She'd had grand visions of satisfying the prostitute so thoroughly the woman might even refuse payment for her services.

In reality, the sex had been quick and awkward. The male body Talyn wore was too unfamiliar, the movements too foreign from the man's side to be in any way satisfying for the woman who nevertheless grunted and moaned beneath Talyn in a poor imitation of pleasure.

It occurred to Talyn later that letting the prostitute be on top might've helped, but she'd been too excited by the prospect of getting the full male experience to consider it at the time.

Talyn had dropped a few coins into the woman's hand afterward, thanked her, and left hurriedly to go find a safe place to change back into a form she understood better.

She'd changed into a male a few times after that, but she'd learned her lesson and hadn't attempted sex as a man again since.

As a rule, Talyn wasn't usually aroused by women, but she could appreciate Cyra's beauty nonetheless as she helped the lady disrobe.

She'd done her best to keep Cyra at arm's length during her time here. Figuratively speaking at least. She had to touch Cyra to attend her, and the consequence – as she'd seen today in the training yard – was that Cyra had unwittingly syphoned Talyn's ability to port.

That's how Talyn assumed Cyra had taken the power anyway. The rumor among the servants was that the lady had only to touch someone to syphon their ability, and thus far Talyn had found the servants were generally correct in their information. Talyn could only hope Cyra either hadn't syphoned her masquing ability as well, or at the very least, didn't know she had it.

"My lady, you have a bruise on your back," Talyn pointed out as she helped Cyra down into the bathtub.

She used to think Cyra got the bruises from her husband, but she knew better now. She'd seen today exactly when Cyra had gotten the bruise in question.

The guard Cyra had been sparring with earlier had executed a skillful dodge of Cyra's attack, and he'd brought his sword around before Cyra could recover from her miss. Even Talyn had cringed when Cyra cried out from the hit and fell to the ground, but the guard had been at her side instantly, on his knees apologizing. Cyra had shaken him off, picked herself up, and readied to face him again.

Cyra winced now as she sat back against the tub. "I forgot about that one," she said. "I can never reach the ones on my back. I'll have to call-"

She cut herself off, and Talyn swallowed. Cyra had been about to say she needed to call Aramis, and guilt gripped Talyn all over again.

Gods above, she wasn't used to feeling guilty.

"I'll have to call a healer to take care of it," Cyra finished.

"Is your training going well?" Talyn asked, hoping to steer the conversation toward Samhail, or at least away from Cyra's father. She put some jasmine-scented soap on a sponge and began to wash the lady.

"Well enough, I suppose," Cyra said. "My magic is coming along, but as far as my combat training, I'm not exactly warrior material. I need a lot more muscle and at least another six inches of height."

Talyn couldn't stop her next words.

"Nonsense," she said. "It may help to be big and strong like that man …Samhail, is it? But speed, agility, and quick thinking can be equalizers in a fight."

Cyra turned to look at her curiously, and Talyn shrugged.

"I've seen a lot of fights," she said.

It wasn't a lie. She'd also *been in* a lot of fights, but Cyra didn't need to know that. She urged the lady to sit forward so she could wash her back gently, taking care around the bruise.

"Samhail has speed, agility, and quick thinking as well," Cyra said.

Talyn had seen enough to know that was true.

"If you're trying to become like him, it's not going to happen," Talyn said as she filled a pitcher with water and poured it over Cyra's back. "Don't compare yourself to a warrior like that. Find your own strengths and hone those. Then pay attention so you can find your opponents' weaknesses and exploit them. As great a warrior as Samhail is, he must have some weaknesses, right?"

Cyra shook her head. "If he does, I have yet to see them."

It had been worth a try.

"You seem to know a lot about fighting," Cyra observed.

Talyn tensed. "I had to fend for myself early on," she said after a pause. "Learning to fight was a necessary evil."

That was true as well, although her more lethal skills had been developed out of desire rather than need.

"Do you have any family?" Cyra asked.

Fuck. Somehow she'd let Cyra lead her right into a personal conversation. She needed to get out of it quickly before she had to either lie or reveal something she didn't want to reveal.

"I never knew my father," Talyn said as she massaged almond-scented soap into Cyra's long, dark hair. "My mother still lives in Rowe as far as I know, but I haven't seen her in a while."

"My parents were taken by the Great Flu," Cyra said, and Talyn frowned before she realized the lady was talking about the parents she'd grown up with in Fernweh.

"You don't have any siblings?" Cyra asked, and Talyn's hands stilled.

She didn't want to talk about this with Cyra. She considered lying, but Cyra had turned to look at her by then.

"Not anymore," Talyn said softly as she worked on Cyra's hair. It occurred to her a second later that simply saying 'no' would have sufficed.

"Can I ask what happened?" Cyra ventured.

"No." See? Easy enough to say.

The word was sharper than she'd intended, though, and Cyra flinched, obviously taken aback at Talyn's tone.

Talyn didn't care. This wasn't information the lady needed to know, and she had a right to keep it to herself.

"I'm sorry. I didn't mean to pry," Cyra said, recovering.

"No, I'm sorry, my lady," Talyn said quickly. "Please forgive me for snapping at you."

"It's fine," Cyra said. "I should know better."

"Close your eyes, my lady," Talyn said as she poured a pitcher of water over Cyra's head to rinse away the soap in her hair.

She had the sudden impulse to push Cyra's head under the water and hold her there as her assassin's instincts acted up, but she recalled Cyra could breathe underwater. She'd gone down to a shipwreck at the bottom of the ocean with the merman to retrieve the collar and rings Sandrian had wanted not too long ago.

Talyn shuddered to think of the prodigious power Cyra must have to accomplish that journey as a full human. There were also rumors among the servants that the lady had killed a sea monster of some kind.

"I just know so little about you," Cyra went on, and Talyn sighed inwardly. For one wonderful moment she'd thought Cyra might be done questioning her.

"There's not much to tell, my lady," Talyn said.

She moved to the side of the tub and re-soaped the sponge to wash Cyra's front. Cyra's nipple peaked as she ran over it, and Talyn paused a moment, then ran over the second breast. That nipple stiffened as well, and it suddenly occurred to Talyn how she might be able to cut this visit short. There was at least one person the lady would prefer to spend her time with rather than Talyn.

"Does Lord Bressen please you, my lady?" Talyn asked.

Cyra lifted her head off the rim of the tub. "What? Why do you ask?"

Talyn dipped the sponge lower under the pretense of washing Cyra's stomach, but her hand dipped close to the apex of the lady's thighs, and Cyra relaxed back against the tub again as her legs fell open a little more.

Cyra's baths were usually routine affairs, Talyn's touch purely functional, but today the lady seemed a bit more...stimulated than normal, and Talyn was sure she could use this to her advantage.

"I...I don't mean to overstep," Talyn said. "It's just that I don't have any female friends to talk about this with, and I hoped you might be willing to share with me."

It was exactly the right thing to say. Cyra opened her eyes, and her face lit up with a smile.

"Raina and I used to talk about everything," Cyra said. "I'm happy to talk to you as well if you need advice or-"

"I'm really more curious about you and Lord Bressen," Talyn cut in before the lady could start asking questions. "You seem very happy together, and I was just wondering what he does that pleases you?"

If she could get the woman thinking and talking about Lord Bressen, perhaps Cyra would dismiss Talyn and call him instead.

Cyra smiled. "Bressen does a lot of things that please me."

Talyn moved the sponge over Cyra's breasts again, increasing the pressure, and Cyra cocked her head.

"Leeda?"

Talyn froze. She'd been trained in seduction and had hoped to subtly arouse Cyra, but maybe she was more out of practice than she thought.

"I'm sorry, my lady," Talyn said. "I didn't mean to be so forward. I'm just trying to understand. I was confused when I found you and the lord that day…"

Cyra nodded absently as if remembering the day Talyn had burst in on her when Bressen's head was between her legs.

"It seemed like you were in pain," Talyn prompted.

Cyra gave a soft laugh. "I was for a while," she said. "Bressen kept bringing me to the brink of my release then stopping. I thought I was going to go mad. He'd finally just let me climax when you arrived."

Talyn scowled. The practice was known as edging in the pleasure houses, and some courtesans specialized in it for those patrons who liked to prolong their pleasure by being brought to the 'edge' of their release without going over. Talyn herself didn't see the appeal, but then, delayed gratification wasn't exactly in her nature.

"And you enjoyed that?" Talyn asked.

Cyra huffed another laugh. "No, not really. He was trying to make a point, and all I wanted to do was climax."

Talyn ran the sponge down one of Cyra's arms. "Have you thought about getting your revenge on him?"

"Revenge?" Cyra asked, a little alarmed. "How would I do that?"

"Nothing bad," Talyn assured her quickly. "Maybe just give him a taste of his own medicine. Let him feel what it's like to be frustrated and unable to do anything about it."

Cyra was quiet a moment. "I'm listening," she said finally.

"Lord Bressen is usually in meetings around now, isn't he?"

"I think he's meeting with Axenus and Samhail," Cyra said.

"And you can make him feel what you're feeling, can you not?"

Talyn couldn't see Cyra's face from where she crouched behind her, but she sensed the lady's brow rise.

"I can," Cyra said slowly.

"Then make him feel what he can't have right now."

"I…I'm not sure I should do that," Cyra said, but Talyn caught the tone in her voice, the tone of one willing to be talked into something.

"They discuss you in those meetings, don't they?" Talyn asked, and Cyra nodded.

"Maybe it's time you reminded your lord you're right here."

Cyra paused, then smiled. "You're right. I *should* remind Bressen it's not polite to have conversations about me when I'm not there."

"I could help you if you want," Talyn offered.

Cyra was quiet for another long moment, and Talyn could almost hear the arguments running through the woman's head, but she was optimistic. Her offer bound them together as conspirators, and Talyn knew from experience this made people more likely to do things they wouldn't normally do. They felt less culpable when they could share the blame with someone else, and Talyn was the demon on the lady's shoulder, pushing her toward temptation.

"My mother was a courtesan," Talyn said. "I learned a little about pleasure from her. About what drives a man wild. I don't want to press you into anything. I only offer what service you might find helpful."

She left out that some of her own training had been hands-on – literally – in the same pleasure house where her mother worked.

That seemed like another lifetime ago.

"What…do I need to do?" Cyra asked softly.

"Touch yourself," Talyn said softly against Cyra's ear as she guided the lady's hand into the water between her legs. "Touch yourself the way you want your lord to touch you."

"I…"

"Close your eyes, my lady," Talyn said, and she leaned around to see that Cyra had done so. "Now connect with your lord's mind and let him feel what you're feeling."

Talyn ran the sponge down Cyra's chest again. She circled each breast with it, letting her thumb flick the lady's nipples as she went. Cyra let out a deep breath as her hand moved between her legs.

"Would Lord Bressen be angry to find me touching you like this?" Talyn asked softly.

Cyra huffed a small laugh. "I doubt it. It would probably arouse him."

Talyn suspected as much, but she'd wanted Cyra to say it, to realize it.

"Then let him see my hands on you," she urged.

Talyn abandoned the sponge to knead Cyra's breasts and pinch her nipples gently between her fingers. The peaks stiffened even more, and Cyra moaned softly as her hand began to move faster.

"Is that how he touches you?" Talyn whispered, and Cyra nodded.

"With just his fingers, or does he use his tongue as well?" Talyn asked.

Cyra smiled, her eyes still closed. "I love when he uses his tongue."

Talyn felt a tightening between her own legs as she watched Cyra stroke herself. She closed her eyes and imagined what it might be like to have Samhail's large hands on her body, to feel their roughness on her skin. She'd watched him enough that she could almost imagine the hot warmth of his mouth on her breasts, his hard length inside her…

Talyn had heard plenty of stories about Samhail from the other female servants in the house, but she wasn't sure how true they were. As much as these women desired the man, Samhail had apparently never taken any of them to bed, probably out of respect for Bressen, so as not to create drama or chaos within his household.

Nevertheless, the women claimed to have heard and seen plenty.

One of the kitchen servants had heard from someone, who knew someone, who knew someone else who swore that Samhail's cock was large enough to split a woman in half. One maid was certain his cock turned to stone when he shifted into a gargoyle, and another insisted she'd seen Samhail come out of Bressen and Cyra's bedchamber half-dressed in the wee hours of the morning weeks ago at the Citadel.

Cyra whimpered, drawing Talyn's attention back to her. The lady arched her back, which pushed her breasts up, and without thinking, Talyn closed her mouth over one nipple. Cyra cried out as Talyn swirled her tongue around the bud and sucked it into her mouth.

"Does it feel good when Samhail does this?" Talyn asked before biting down gently.

Her eyes flew open a second later as she realized what she'd said. She shouldn't have let herself get caught up in the fantasy, but she couldn't help imagining what it would be like to have Samhail touch her like this. She hadn't been this attracted to a man in…ever, and thinking about him had distracted her from what she'd been saying.

But Cyra didn't seem to notice the slip.

"Mmm, yes," Cyra murmured. She began to thrust her hips up to meet her hand. "I love it when they do that."

Talyn lifted her head from Cyra's breast. Wait, had the lady just said "*they*?" No, she must've misheard.

Talyn lifted the sponge again and squeezed it so that water trickled down Cyra's neck. She leaned in close to blow on the wet skin, and gooseflesh rose on Cyra's arms. The lady let out a soft moan and drew her knees up farther in the tub as she rocked against her hand.

"Oh gods," Cyra breathed as the water churned around her.

The lady seized in pleasure a few seconds later, and Talyn felt her own body cry out for a release. She was wet and aching, but she'd have to wait until she could get back to her own bedchamber to do anything.

Talyn and Cyra both jumped as the door to the bathing chamber slammed open. Lord Bressen filled the doorway looking thunderous. His cock bulged against the front of his pants, and his power seemed to ripple off him like smoke.

A small shiver ran up Talyn's body at the sight of him, and, as if he sensed it, Lord Bressen's eyes flicked to her.

"Out, Leeda," he said. "I need to speak with my wife."

Talyn looked at Cyra, suddenly wary of leaving her alone with the lord, but only heat filled Cyra's gaze. The lady bit her lip as her eyes remained locked on her husband.

"You can go, Leeda," Cyra said without looking at her. "Lord Bressen can help me finish my bath."

In the doorway, the lord let out a low growl.

Talyn rose and wiped her wet hands on her skirt, then hurried out of the room. The lord moved out of the way to let her pass, and the door slammed shut behind her. Seconds later she heard splashing followed by Cyra's squeals.

Talyn paused, wary of leaving, but a moan came from behind the doorway as Cyra began to invoke the gods again, and Talyn decided it was safe to go.

She felt a little bad for manipulating Cyra as she made her way back to her room. In some ways she pitied the lady. Cyra was lonely. Her best friend was halfway across the country, and she usually only saw her husband at night when his work was done, although clearly there were exceptions.

Cyra would likely be busy for the foreseeable future getting her new vineyard up and running, but that might only exacerbate her loneliness if it took her away from her friends and husband even more. She might even forego her trainings with Samhail and Axenus for a while, and that would be even less time she'd spend with people who cared about her.

If Cyra's connections with those around her started to fray, Talyn could only imagine the disastrous repercussions there might be for a being of Cyra's power. She'd seen the storm the woman created on the beach several nights ago, and it had been truly terrifying on a number of levels. It made her feel at least a little more certain about what she had to do.

Talyn slipped inside her room and went straight to her pillowcase to pull out the message leaf from Sandrian. The three-word command remained as she'd read it earlier, the ink seeming overly stark against the paper as she let the words sink in.

She read them one more time before she lit the leaf on fire and watched the flames burn away the evidence of Sandrian's order:

Kill them both.

Chapter 4

Talyn

Talyn turned the daggers over in her hands as she stood outside the door to Cyra and Bressen's bedchamber later that night. It would take two ports to get where she needed to be. One to get onto the other side of the door without opening it, several steps, then another port to get to the center of the bed where the lord and lady slept curled around each other.

She'd have to go for Bressen first, so she hoped whatever position he was in gave her good access to his heart or throat. If he awoke before she was able to kill him, she wasn't sure how long it would take him to realize what was going on. She needed him dead before he opened his eyes. Once the lord was taken care of, then she'd worry about Cyra.

Cyra would be both easier and harder to kill. Easier because, even with the recent boost to the lady's powers, Talyn was sure she could kill Cyra before the lady realized what was happening. Harder because she didn't actually want to kill the woman. Talyn had never changed her mind about a job she took before, but she was reconsidering it now.

History had branded syphons as extremely dangerous perimortals that needed to be eliminated before they could amass too much power, but Talyn had a hard time picturing the woman who'd tried desperately to befriend her these last few weeks as a power-hungry despot in the making.

The lady *had* committed a crime, Talyn reminded herself, perhaps more than one, although the details varied depending on which of the servants she spoke to. One swore Cyra had melted the minds of the people in Fernweh who'd burned her family's vineyard. Another claimed she'd set a building on fire with the men inside it before the merman had doused the flames. Still another claimed Cyra had turned all the villagers to mice and set cats on them, then laughed as the felines hunted the rodents down. That last had been said with approval rather than censure.

Talyn wasn't sure which version to believe, if any, but Cyra had done *something* to the people of Fernweh in retaliation for the destruction of the vineyard. She knew that much. Cyra herself had let it slip that she was supposed to be under house arrest, although clearly no one had dared to enforce the restriction.

Talyn smiled wryly and shook her head at her own hypocrisy. It was a cruel irony that she was trying to sit in judgement of Cyra considering her own drive for vengeance had made her what she was.

She'd been only sixteen when she'd gone after the man who'd torn apart her family. It had been easy to lure him to the abandoned building on the outskirts of town that night ten years ago, letting him think she was a prostitute. He'd been confused when she suddenly shifted into someone else — that face she always wore when she killed someone now - and his confusion changed to shock when he'd felt her dagger sink into his side. She hadn't killed him, though. Not immediately. She'd spent the next several hours letting his screams be a balm to the pain of her loss.

In the end, the man's death hadn't brought Talyn any peace. If anything, it had only ignited the need to shed more blood, the desire to purge the world of people like him. Thus she'd begun her journey toward becoming the most dangerous and notorious assassin on the continent.

Talyn didn't always have the luxury of killing only those who deserved it, but if the person hiring her was worse than the person she was asked to kill, she had no problem taking her client's money, then killing them both. She considered it a service to mankind.

Now, here she was standing outside the bedroom of a couple who were — as far as she could tell — relatively decent people. The lord was an arrogant ass, but that wasn't an offense worthy of death, much as she wished it was. Likewise, she had a hard time picturing Cyra hurting anyone unless she was protecting someone she cared about.

Talyn swore under her breath. She'd already taken half of Sandrian's money for this job, and if she backed out now, her reputation would take a serious hit. She'd have to kill Sandrian to keep him from spreading the word of her failure.

For that matter, it wouldn't be hard to justify killing him anyway. He'd kidnapped and threatened Lord Aidan's consort in order to get a few pieces of jewelry. For what reason, she still didn't know, but at this point she could make the case that Sandrian deserved her dagger more than Cyra and Bressen did.

Talyn shook away the thoughts. She needed to stop weighing the morality of it. She was the last person who had any right to judge anyone, and she was being paid to do a job, so she'd do it. She still might kill Sandrian later, just because she wanted to, but she'd finish this job first.

Talyn steeled herself. If the gods were good, this would be over in a few seconds.

She ported.

Talyn blinked in confusion as she rematerialized in the same place she'd been standing in front of the door. She ported again, but once more she found herself standing in front of the same door. She frowned, but the issue hit her a second later.

The room was warded. Fuck.

Talyn's stomach twisted as she realized she'd likely just set off an alarm that told whoever created the wards that someone had just tried to breach them. She had maybe seconds before Bressen or Cyra came crashing through the door to find her standing there.

Talyn ported again, but this time she materialized in the hall outside the sitting room where she'd been. Then she ported again and again and again, as fast as she could to get back down to her own room before someone came looking for her.

She made it as far as the first floor when a wave of power rocked the house, causing her to stagger. She'd felt such a surge before and knew what it meant.

Lord Bressen was awake, and he was furious.

It was well-known among the servants that when Lord Bressen was especially angry, his power pulsed, strongly enough that anyone within a few hundred feet could feel it. This had been more than just a pulse, though. This had been a surge strong enough to shake the floor under her feet, like a small earthquake.

Talyn was about to port again when the front door of the house flew open, and several guards rushed in. Talyn shifted instead into the form of Yarris. She'd seen him leave the house to head toward the city and assumed he must have the night off. Hopefully in the chaos, no one would realize he wasn't supposed to be there.

"What happened?" one of the guards asked Talyn as he rushed up.

The man was in his late thirties and not quite as tall as some of the other guards, but he was solidly built. He had dark blonde hair and a closely trimmed beard. Sully, the Captain of the Guard at Tide's End.

"I don't know, sir," Talyn answered.

"With me," Sully ordered as he charged up the stairs, and Talyn had no choice but to follow him and the other guards who'd come in.

Just before they reached the landing to the third floor, two large figures barreled into the stairwell before them to head for the fourth floor.

Samhail and Axenus.

Talyn and the rest of the guards followed on their heels, and within seconds Talyn found herself in the last place she wanted to be, back on the fourth floor facing the Lord and Lady of Hiraeth, who were now standing in the hall outside their sitting room.

Lord Bressen wore only a pair of loose black pants that hung low on his hips and gave a tantalizing view of his toned upper body. Cyra had wrapped herself in her silky bathrobe and stood pressed against him while he wrapped an arm protectively around her shoulders.

Right here, right now, Cyra didn't look like the destructor Sandrian insisted she was, but merely like a scared young woman seeking comfort from her husband.

"What happened?" Samhail asked as their whole group stopped in front of the lord and lady.

Unlike Lord Bressen, the pair of black leather pants Samhail wore were tighter and showed off every muscle of his lower body.

Sweet gods, were those his thighs or just well-shaped tree trunks?

At least he was wearing a shirt. The gods had some mercy on her.

"Someone or something set off the wards on our bedroom," Bressen said, and Talyn was surprised to hear how shaky his voice sounded beneath its skin of ire. "Gods damn it, Cyra just put them up today. I didn't expect them to be tested so soon."

Talyn closed her eyes to curse her luck. If Sandrian had sent her that message only a day earlier, the room would have been unwarded, and her targets would now be dead.

"Could they have gone off accidentally?" Axenus asked. "Maybe it was just an animal. Did you see anything?"

"When my power pulsed, I didn't sense anyone nearby," Bressen said. "Just the two of you on the third floor and the guards and servants on the first floor. Whatever it was disappeared quickly."

Talyn's stomach turned over. She didn't realize he could sense people nearby through those pulses.

"How could they get away so quickly?" Cyra asked.

"Someone may have tried to open a portal into the room," Axenus said. "That would have set off the wards, and we know Magdalene has that power."

Talyn frowned. She'd met Magdalene when she met Sandrian, but she thought the woman was a seer.

"Someone might've tried to fly in as well," Samhail said. "We should check the grounds and the skies."

"Agreed," Bressen said. "Axenus, stay with Cyra. Samhail, with me."

Bressen turned and went back inside, presumably to head for the balcony off his bedroom. Talyn blinked as a loud whoosh sounded, and a pair of huge leathery bat-like wings topped with sharp talons sprang free from Samhail's back as he disappeared into the bedroom behind the lord.

Gods damn her, those wings…

"Spread out inside the house and do a thorough search," Sully ordered the guards. "Lord Bressen didn't sense anything, but we're going to make sure there's no one here."

Thank the gods. This was the opportunity Talyn needed.

Sully began to assign guards to specific floors, and Talyn managed to maneuver herself into the group that was assigned to the first floor. She hurried off with them, then broke off toward the servants' wing as soon as she got the chance.

She was nearly back to her room when her bracelet glowed green, telling her Cyra wanted to see her.

Fuck. She'd been so close.

She shifted back into the guise of Leeda and, for the third time in the last few minutes, trekked up the stairs to the fourth floor. At least her legs would be strong by the end of this job.

Axenus opened the door when she knocked, and he let her in.

"My lady, is everything alright?" Talyn asked. "I felt something shake the house."

She didn't have to fake her nervousness. If Cyra asked her the wrong question and she tried to lie, this could go very badly.

"I'm sorry to drag you out of bed, Leeda," Cyra said. "The shaking you felt was Bressen's power. It seems someone tried to break past the wards on our bedroom tonight."

Talyn feigned concern. "My lady, are you okay?"

"I'm fine," Cyra said. "I wanted to be sure you were alright. Is all well down in the servants' quarters? Did you see anyone you didn't know?"

Talyn shook her head. "No, my lady. I didn't see anyone."

She glanced quickly at the merman who stood with his arms crossed near the balcony looking out over the water. He wore a loose pair of pants with an untucked tunic, and his garnet-colored hair hung around his shoulders as he surveyed the scene outside. The light iridescence of his skin shimmered in the lamp lights.

"Did you need help with something, my lady?" Talyn asked. She really didn't want to be here when Bressen and Samhail returned. She needed to get back to her room to rethink her strategy.

"No, I just…"

Whatever answer Cyra had been searching for was cut off as the sound of beating wings drew their attention back to the balcony. Samhail landed a second later, and Talyn's eyes flared in awe at the sight of his giant black wings stretched out behind him. The balcony was big, but the wings nearly spanned the whole space, blocking out the night sky. He tucked them back against his body as he entered the bedroom, but they didn't disappear, and Talyn wondered exactly how the metamorphosis worked.

"Nothing?" Axenus asked him.

"Not that I saw," Samhail said, "but I didn't go very far. There's something about this whole thing that doesn't sit right with me. I had a feeling I should come back, that it was better to be here."

Samhail's eyes scanned the room as if the threat he sought was right in front of him. Indeed it was, but his gaze passed right over Talyn as if he didn't even see her, and she softly let out the breath she'd been holding.

"My lady, if you don't need anything," Talyn started to say, but she stopped when Samhail's gaze snapped back to her.

It had been a mistake to draw attention to herself, and Talyn dropped her eyes, hoping he'd go back to ignoring her.

No such luck.

"Leeda, was it?" Samhail asked, stepping toward her, and Talyn resisted the urge to retreat from him.

She knew exactly what he was thinking, knew he was remembering a few days ago when he'd caught her in the hall outside Bressen and Cyra's rooms. He was wondering if she was the one who'd set off the wards.

"Yes, sir," she said, eyes still down.

His bare feet appeared in front of her, and every muscle in Talyn's body tensed. She was certain he was going to ask her if she'd been up here again. Regardless of whether she lied or not, that she'd been here once before in the dead of night made her suspect.

Talyn lifted her head and gave him her most imploring look. She had to convince him without words not to say anything about finding her that time. She begged him with her eyes to keep her secret because if they started asking her questions, she was done for.

"Samhail?" Cyra asked. "Is something wrong?"

Samhail hadn't taken his eyes off Talyn yet, and she tried to shake her head the barest amount.

Please, she thought. *Please don't say anything.*

"I was just wondering if Leeda might have noticed anything," Samhail said finally. "She's up here often."

"Not in the dead of night," Cyra said. She looked at Talyn in question.

"My lady, I was down on the main floor when I felt the lord's power pass through the house," Talyn said. "I saw nothing there."

A more experienced truth seer might've noticed the answer that wasn't exactly an answer. The truth seers Talyn had met were used to people carefully wording their answers to avoid lying, but Cyra wasn't that experienced with her powers. She was too guileless to suspect her own lady's maid of trying to skirt the truth.

Samhail's gaze bore into Talyn for another few seconds before he stepped back, seemingly satisfied with her response.

"You can go back to bed now," Cyra told her kindly when Samhail was no longer looming over her.

"Thank you, my lady," Talyn said. She bobbed a quick curtsey and tried not to hurry from the room too fast. She didn't want to give them any reason to call her back and ask more questions.

Aside from the lord, Samhail was probably the biggest threat to her, Talyn mused as she hurried back down to the first floor, hopefully for the last time tonight. Cyra was powerful, but the lady was still too trusting and – all things considered – not ruthless enough to do what she needed to do in the face of a threat.

Talyn needed to know more about Samhail. He was close to both Cyra and Bressen, and he'd hunt her to the ends of the continent if she killed them. It was possible she might need to kill him too if she wanted to accomplish her mission and not have to look over her shoulder the rest of her life.

A memory sparked in her mind, and she recalled seeing Samhail touch Cyra's cheek tenderly today at the end of their training session. Then he'd shocked the three hells out of Talyn and hugged the lady.

His behavior had struck her as odd at the time, not quite in line with the warrior's normally gruff demeanor, but it seemed even more so now as Cyra's slip earlier in the day took on new meaning.

They. "I love it when *they* do that," Cyra had said today when Talyn had sucked on her breast.

It hadn't hit her before, but now that she thought about it, Samhail's eyes had lit on Cyra when he'd returned from searching the grounds. There'd been something in his look that made Talyn wonder if there was more to their relationship than it appeared, something that made Talyn…

Jealous.

Chapter 5

Talyn

The next morning, Cyra skipped her training sessions with both Axenus and Samhail and visited her new vineyard with Bressen instead. As an added bonus, Axenus left that day on a trip for the lord. Talyn didn't know where, but she learned he'd be gone a few days.

That left her alone in the house with Samhail. Well, alone with Samhail, the servants, and the extra guards that were now on duty after her failed attempt to get through the wards last night, but close enough.

Luckily, most of the servants and guards were stationed on the first floor. One guard was also stationed on each floor above, but otherwise, Bressen's steward Ferris was generally the only other servant on the upper floors unless the floor was scheduled for cleaning.

Talyn thus resolved to find a way to 'run into' Samhail today.

She had enough suspicions about what was going on between Samhail and Cyra that she needed to find out more. Or so she convinced herself. After all, if the gargoyle and the lady were close, she might be able to use that as leverage. If they were having an affair, perhaps she could use it to sow discord between Cyra and Bressen. If she could separate them – maybe even get Cyra to leave the house unaccompanied – she might be able to kill them easier.

Any hopes she had of killing them at night were gone now that their bedchamber was warded when they went to sleep. That would've given her ample time to escape before the bodies were discovered, but it wasn't to be. She'd have to devise a plan to kill them during the day and not be discovered doing it. She was used to killing mortals or – at best – low to mid-level perimortals, but four of the most powerful perimortals she'd ever encountered lived under this roof, and she wasn't taking any chances.

Talyn had already checked outside the house, specifically in the training yard, but Samhail wasn't there. Next, she'd cleared the first floor and had just begun looking on the second where most of the leisure rooms in the house were.

Talyn approached the door to the great room and peered around the corner to see if anyone was there. She drew back quickly at the glimpse of the huge form with white hair seated at one of the tables.

Perfect. Samhail was alone and in a common area. All she needed was an excuse to talk to him.

Then an idea struck her. It was a dangerous idea, but if she managed to pull it off, she might learn a lot.

After a quick pause to reconsider the wisdom of what she was about to do, Talyn willed her body to take the form of the Lady of Hiraeth. The body of Leeda she normally wore was taller and plumper than Cyra, so she shrunk an inch or so, and her curves pulled in. Her olive-colored skin also paled to Cyra's more porcelain complexion.

Talyn walked down the hall to where she'd seen a mirror. The reflection that looked back was an almost perfect re-creation of Cyra.

Whether it was perfect enough to fool Samhail remained to be seen.

Samhail was seated in a chair at a rectangular table where Talyn imagined the inhabitants of the house might play cards or games in their spare time. His boots were propped up on another chair, and she wondered why he didn't just sit in one of the more comfortable cushioned seats by the fireplace.

The great room had a set of double doors that normally stood open, but she quietly pulled them closed behind her as she entered. At the very least, she didn't want a passing guard to just be able to look inside. She'd seen the guard stationed on this floor return to his post after making his rounds, so she should have a little while before they were disturbed.

Samhail was facing away from the doors, but he looked up and turned to her as she approached. Whether he'd heard her soft footsteps or somehow sensed her, she wasn't sure, but she made a note of it.

"Back from the vineyard so soon?" Samhail asked as she approached.

"I forgot something and had to come back," she said, smiling at him. "I thought I'd see what you were up to since we don't have training."

"Doing a bit of research," he said, holding up the book.

Talyn swayed her hips as she closed the distance between them, and the movement didn't go unnoticed. Samhail's eyes dipped briefly before coming back up to meet hers.

She sidled up next to him and reached an arm across to half-close the book in his lap so she could see the title on the cover. It was something about a history of battle strategies, but the subject of the book was incidental. She was more concerned with making sure her breasts were in Samhail's face, and she saw in her periphery that his gaze had indeed flicked to her chest.

"It looks like a real page-turner," she said to him, straightening back up and putting a hand on his shoulder.

"It's actually been interesting so far, but I haven't found anything in it yet about how to fight a war without hurting your enemies."

Talyn blinked at him. "What?"

"Axenus reminded Bressen and I the other day that the symbionts are all human and likely unwilling victims. He wants to find a way to separate the symbionts from their human hosts, but in the meantime, that means trying to win a war without killing anyone."

Talyn sighed. "That's a noble idea, but wars are full of innocent victims. Rulers send unwilling soldiers into battle all the time. It's the nature of war."

Samhail nodded. "That's my feeling too, but if I can find a way to minimize the life lost, I'll look. I'm not sure how much of Sandrian's army will be made of symbionts from Rowe, but he's clearly been raiding Thasia's own towns and villages to fill his ranks. We'll be fighting and killing our own people."

Talyn gave him a sympathetic look and trailed her hand inward so it came to rest on his neck. He went still, and she pushed her luck further by letting her thumb run gently up and down the side of his neck. He still didn't move, but his breathing had shallowed.

Talyn bent closer as she pretended to read over his shoulder.

"You're a good man to consider such things," she said next to his ear.

He exhaled heavily.

Talyn slid one hand down the front of Samhail's chest and let it rest lightly on the hard swell of his pectoral. She felt the muscle twitch under her hand, but she couldn't yet tell if he was aroused or just uncomfortable. Perhaps it was both. She needed to go a little further, but she had to be careful not to push him too far.

Talyn straightened up, making sure to draw her hand slowly back up Samhail's chest and over his shoulder before she walked around in front of him. She looked down at him and caught his gaze. There was definitely something blazing there as he looked at her.

Be patient, she told herself.

When Talyn wanted a man, she had no problem being bold. Had she been attempting to seduce Samhail as herself, she would've just thrown her leg over him to straddle his lap, but Cyra wasn't nearly so forward. The lady was more reserved in her interactions with her husband, at least in public. Cyra didn't swing her hips when she walked or do anything openly flirtatious. Her touches were soft and discrete, although the lord himself had no problem pulling his wife into possessive embraces.

Still, she only had so much time. She couldn't be too subtle either.

Talyn held Samhail's gaze for another second before she leaned over to pull the book out of his hand.

Gods, he had such large hands. She couldn't think right now about how they might feel on her body.

Samhail let her take the book from him, but he angled his head in question. Talyn just turned around and sank down onto his lap. She leaned back against his chest and held the book up in front of her as if she meant for them both to read it while she sat there across his legs.

Samhail's entire body went rigid as he inhaled sharply, and she wondered if she'd misread something about his relationship with Cyra. Then she felt him harden beneath her backside and smiled. No, she hadn't misread anything.

"Cyra," Samhail said in a hoarse whisper. "What are you doing?"

Talyn nestled herself against him more, making sure to rub her ass against his groin. He grunted and hardened even more.

"I'm reading," she answered, as she flipped a page in the book.

"You know that's not what I'm asking," he said. His breathing had become ragged, and Talyn realized just how much he wanted her…how much this man wanted his friend's wife.

She shifted herself on his lap so she was looking into his face again. There was something there behind the obvious desire that she couldn't read. Anger perhaps?

"What's wrong?" she asked as if she really had no idea why every muscle in his body was tense. She reached a hand up to lay it on his face, but he grabbed her wrist before she could touch him.

Samhail's nostrils flared at her question. "You're sitting on my lap," he said matter-of-factly.

"And that's a problem?" Talyn asked, pulling her hand back.

It was a genuine question. She needed to get a better sense of where the boundaries lay between Samhail and the lady. That he hadn't yet thrown her off his lap suggested she wasn't completely wrong to think there was something between them. His reaction told her they weren't having an affair, but the bulge she felt in his pants and his hesitation to remove her likely meant their relationship also wasn't entirely innocent.

Samhail raised a brow at her. "You don't think it's a problem?"

Talyn resisted the urge to frown at how he'd answered her question with a question, but she threw caution to the wind and played a hunch.

"Surely you and I have done worse than this," she said, leaning toward him so her breasts brushed against his chest.

He didn't retreat, but his chin rose a notch. "Of course," he said, "but Bressen was there those times, and I had his permission to touch you."

Talyn just barely managed to keep her jaw from falling open. Her mind reeled at Samhail's admission as she played through the possibilities. The two most likely scenarios were that Samhail, Bressen, and Cyra had engaged in a threesome at some point or that the lord was a voyeur and liked to watch his wife with other men. Possibly both.

She was certainly no one to judge other people's sexual proclivities – to each their own – but the idea that the unassuming young woman whose body she currently wore had fucked both Samhail and Bressen, perhaps at the same time, shocked her more than she cared to admit.

Not that she blamed the woman. Both men were magnificent, and she would've been more than happy to welcome them to her own bed under different circumstances. Or Samhail at least. She wasn't sure she'd be able to tolerate the lord long enough to fuck him.

Talyn's jealousy flared again. She couldn't help picturing Samhail holding himself above Cyra, thrusting into the lady while she wrapped her legs around his hips, and Talyn's chest burned at the thought.

She tamped down hard on the emotion. It was ridiculous to be jealous of whatever Cyra had with Samhail, and she was angry at herself for feeling this way.

"What if *I* give you permission to touch me?" Talyn asked Samhail when she got her shock under control.

The knot in Samhail's throat bobbed, and he took his legs off the chair they'd been propped on. Talyn waited to see what he'd do, whether he meant to rise and dump her off his lap, or whether he was giving himself more leverage to touch her. For the moment, he did neither.

"I thought we agreed our last time was *the* last time," Samhail said.

Talyn took a moment to digest that information as she stared at him. If she had to name the look in his eyes, it was somewhere between annoyance and pleading, and she was now positive Samhail and the lord's wife had slept together at some point. Clearly there'd been something between Cyra and Samhail – or Cyra, Samhail, and Bressen – but she couldn't conceive of exactly what.

In any case, she had to stop staring, or he was going to get suspicious.

Samhail's face had hardened, but he didn't move to throw her off. He wanted her to get off his lap of her own accord, and she almost did.

Instead, she slipped her arms around his neck and kissed him.

Gods, she shouldn't have done it. She hadn't meant to, but Nemesis take her, she'd been overwhelmed by the urge to press her lips to his.

His smell was intoxicating, leather and something earthy that made her want to be outside. Her nipples stiffened into peaks as they pressed into his chest, and she was all too aware of the swollen length of him beneath her. His lips were surprisingly soft, and she tasted something savory on him. Or maybe that was just how he tasted.

Talyn ground her mouth harder into Samhail's, and he jolted back against his chair. He didn't push her away, though. Rather, his lips parted to allow her tongue to delve into his mouth, and his own met hers, thrust for thrust.

She realized a moment later, however, that his arms were still at his sides. He'd succumbed to the assault from her mouth, but he was resisting the urge to touch her, to wrap her in his arms.

Talyn pulled back and searched his face. Desire still raged in his eyes, but his hands hung at his sides, and she ached to have them on her body.

"You won't touch me," she said. A statement, not a question.

"I can't," he said, his voice a dry rasp. "Not without Bressen here."

"Then I guess I'll have to do the touching for us both," she said as her eyes locked with his.

What she was about to do was far bolder than Cyra would ever be, but Talyn didn't care. Something had broken loose inside her when she'd kissed him, and her own need was building. It was no longer about Cyra and Samhail and what they were to each other. Now it was about her own desires and her growing need for the man who sat there trying resolutely to resist her. His resolve was a challenge, and she wanted to break it.

She slid off his lap, and his eyes widened as she knelt in front of him.

"Cyra," he breathed, shaking his head. It was a plea.

"Yes?" she asked as she undid the fastenings of his pants.

His breath was labored as he opened his mouth to say something, but no sound came out. Talyn knew he wanted to object, but he couldn't bring himself to say the words, and until he did, she was going to do whatever she wanted to him. She finished with the fastenings of his pants and pulled the flaps apart.

Talyn held back her gasp as his cock sprung free. Samhail was a large man in general, and she'd expected his cock to be large as well, but Protector save her, this was something else entirely. As if the size of his cock wasn't enough, the hair between his legs was also stark white.

Talyn's mouth suddenly watered as she took in the appendage standing upright before her. He wasn't just big. He was hard as all hells.

She met Samhail's eyes. There was desperation in them, but whether it was desperation for her to stop or to keep going, she wasn't sure.

Talyn grasped Samhail at the base of his shaft, and his cock pulsed under her hand. He groaned, and she searched his face again. She still couldn't read his expression.

She ran her hand up his cock and grazed her thumb over the head to wipe at the precum beaded there. He wasn't just long, he was thick as well.

"Fuck, Cyra. Please," Samhail said.

"Please what?" she asked softly, still not sure if it was a plea to continue or to stop. She suspected the latter, but she'd choose to believe the former until convinced otherwise.

When he didn't answer, Talyn leaned forward slowly toward the head of his cock without taking her eyes from his. She wanted him to know exactly what she intended to do, but she'd give him every opportunity to stop it. Part of her hoped he would, given that he thought she was Cyra, but another part wanted desperately to take him into her mouth and run her tongue up and down that beautiful hard shaft.

She'd never intended it to go this far. She'd planned to tease him a bit, maybe even kiss him lightly. She'd never planned to get on her knees in front of him and take him into her mouth, and she wasn't quite sure how she'd let herself go so far off course.

Talyn opened her mouth and was about to slip her lips over him when Samhail reached forward and grabbed her upper arms. She cried out at the strength of his grip.

"Cyra!" he growled. He was breathing hard now as his chest rose and fell with the effort of restraining both himself and her.

Talyn felt an unexpected wave of relief. She was breathing hard as well, and she pulled back away from him. He released her arms to let her go, and she got unsteadily to her feet.

She looked down at his cock, still hard and standing straight up out of his pants. She wanted him. More specifically, she wanted him inside *her*, the real her. If Samhail was going to fuck her, she didn't want it to be while she was wearing the body of another woman.

It would never happen, of course, and the thought disappointed her more than she could admit.

Talyn swallowed as her eyes locked with Samhail's again. They stared at each other for several long seconds.

"You're right," she said, forcing the words past the lump in her throat. "I should…I should go now."

Her feet felt weighted down with stones as she got herself to move. There was nothing but silence behind her as she left the room without looking back. She only prayed she hadn't just made a huge mistake.

Chapter 6

Samhail

Samhail barely made it back to his quarters in time after leaving the great room. He summoned a towel from the bathing chamber, fumbled to get his pants open, and yanked them down his hips before thumping heavily into one of the armchairs in his room. It only took two strokes of his hand before he exploded into the towel, gritting his teeth to hold back the roar that threatened to erupt along with his seed.

He pleasured himself twice more before his lust subsided enough to keep him from getting hard all over again.

The first time, he let himself imagine Cyra's mouth slipping over him as she knelt there before him on the floor. He remembered all too well from their two previous times together what it felt like to have her lips wrapped around him as her tongue ran up his length. He remembered the soft moans she made as her head bobbed over his groin, and her whimpers when she tried to press him deeper into her mouth.

The next two times, he envisioned climbing between her legs and thrusting into the slick warmth of her sheath. He started out gently – he always needed to be gentle with the women he bedded – but by the last time, not even his fantasy could contain his lust, and he imagined driving wildly into Cyra as she cried out with pleasure beneath him.

He avoided Bressen and Cyra the rest of that day. He skipped lunch and didn't come down for dinner. Instead, he raided the kitchen after dark, nearly scaring the cook half to death when the man came to investigate the banging cabinets and clinking plates.

He also couldn't sleep that night. Each time he closed his eyes, he saw Cyra's face hovering above his cock, ready to take him into her mouth, and he got hard all over again.

He knew he still desired Cyra. She felt so good around his cock, and he loved the soft moans she made when he thrust into her. Both times he'd had her, he wanted her again almost immediately. But he'd known from the first time he saw her together with Bressen that there was something far stronger than lust between them, and he wouldn't come between that.

Something had been different with Cyra this time, though. It was her, but…not her, and he tried to pinpoint exactly what was off as he lay in bed staring at the ceiling.

Her scent was different for one. Cyra usually smelled of jasmine and almond, but what he'd smelled this time was citrusy, like the lemon verbena that infused the air in the summer near his childhood home, and it stirred a longing in him. He thought he'd smelled that scent somewhere else recently, but he couldn't place where. He'd have to ask Cyra, eventually, if she'd changed the soap she used to bathe.

Her scent was only the most obvious difference, though. Something had *felt* different about Cyra as well, but he couldn't put his finger on what. There was something…missing?

Then there was the way she'd touched him.

Cyra could be bold behind closed doors on occasion, but she'd never been an aggressive woman, especially out in the open. The Cyra who ran her hands down his chest, sat on his lap, then rubbed her ass against his cock simply wasn't the Cyra he was used to. Cyra wasn't a seductress, but that's exactly what she'd been doing today. Seducing him.

That was the biggest problem.

The confident, sensuous Cyra who'd approached him today in the great room had stirred his blood in a way she never had before. It was almost as if she'd been someone different, and the urge to throw her down on that table, rip off her clothes, and fuck her until she screamed his name had haunted him all day. He normally controlled his lust well enough, but it had taken all his strength to push her away when she'd dropped to her knees and pulled out his cock.

He didn't understand why she'd done it. Cyra loved Bressen with all her heart, and Samhail had a hard time believing she'd jeopardize her relationship with her husband just to suck his cock. Even if she'd changed her mind about their last time being the last, she knew they couldn't do anything without Bressen there. She was the wife of his oldest friend, and that wasn't a line he'd cross.

It made him angry the more he thought about it. It had taken him weeks to quell the desire he felt for Cyra, but he'd done it. Yet it had taken barely more than a brush of her hand against his neck to reignite that wanting. It was cruel of her to make him want her again, and he felt betrayed by her teasing.

Regardless, he'd let things go way too far. He shouldn't have kissed her back, but he loved the way she'd taken charge. She usually let him dominate her when they kissed, but she'd plunged her tongue into his mouth like she owned it, owned him, and he'd surrendered fully.

Samhail

Samhail avoided Bressen and Cyra the following day as well. Cyra went to the vineyard again in the morning, so it saved him from having to cancel their training, but he did cancel his sparring session that afternoon with Bressen. He took his meals either before Bressen and Cyra arrived in the dining room or after they were done.

On the third day, he met them leaving the dining room just as he was coming in. His eyes met Cyra's as they passed each other, but she didn't seem the least bit phased by what had happened in the great room. He expected to see her grin at him or look ashamed or at least blush, but he saw nothing in her expression to suggest she was thinking about what she'd done…about what *they'd* done.

"Samhail, I have some business to take care of this morning while Cyra is at the vineyard," Bressen said, drawing his attention, "but I need to speak with you after lunch."

Bressen looked serious, and Samhail cursed inwardly. Had Cyra finally told him what happened? Would Bressen beat the shit out of him for it? Throw him in the dungeon? Attack his mind until he was nothing but a drooling pile of flesh?

"Of course," he said and thanked the gods his voice sounded steady.

Samhail tried to eat after Cyra and Bressen left, but his gut roiled with the uncertainty of his upcoming meeting with Bressen. He couldn't avoid what had happened any longer. He needed to confront Cyra.

He should've told Bressen about what happened already, but he'd wanted to ask Cyra first why she'd done it. He needed to do that now. He needed to know what he was walking into with Bressen this afternoon.

After forcing down some breakfast, Samhail went outside, let his wings unfurl behind him, and launched into the sky toward Cyra's vineyard. He'd gone with Bressen and Cyra once to look at the place when they were still negotiating with the owner, and he remembered generally where it was. It wasn't far by flying, and twenty minutes later, he started his descent toward the rows of vines that striped the land in neat rows.

He was almost to the vineyard's manor house when something slammed into him from above and made him drop several feet in the air. Pain shot down his back and through his wings as something pulled at the joint where they connected, and he roared as he reached behind him to grab whatever it was. His hand found a head of short hair over his shoulder, and he gripped just enough to yank it forward. A pained grunt sounded above him, but the weight on his back and the pressure on his wings didn't ease.

Without being able to beat his wings, Samhail was dropping in the sky, the open wings catching just enough air to barely slow his fall. He gave a second hard yank on the hair in his hand, and something kicked off his lower back to separate itself from him.

Free of whoever or whatever had been on top of him, Samhail beat his wings furiously to slow his descent. He managed to get just enough loft at the last minute to keep from crashing into the ground, but he landed hard and stumbled forward to trip onto the grass. He was up a second later with his swords drawn, scanning the skies. He swung around just in time to see something large barrel toward him before it hit him. The blow knocked both the swords from his hands as well as the breath from his lungs.

Hands free, Samhail grabbed at the body on top of him and rolled with it, forcing it beneath him. He raised a huge fist, ready to bring it down into his attacker's face, but he pulled up short when he saw who was grinning up at him.

"What the fuck are you doing here?" Samhail asked in shock as he stared down at his younger brother, Surgeon.

The other gargoyle chuckled. "You've lost your edge, brother," Surgeon said to him. "We never would have been able to get the drop on you like this so easily years ago."

Samhail growled and sunk his fist into Surgeon's stomach instead of his face. Surgeon grunted and coughed hard, but Samhail felt better to have expended some anger. Then something clicked in his head.

"Wait, did you say 'we?'" Samhail asked, but he knew the answer even before something else slammed into him from his blindside.

The force knocked him off Surgeon and sent him tumbling over the ground. He came to rest on his back with his wings pinned under him, and he was about to rise when the blade of one of his own swords appeared at his neck.

A tall, well-muscled woman with long white hair like his own stood above him. Her eyes were the same deep brown as their father's, as opposed to the midnight blue ones he'd gotten from their mother.

"He's definitely getting old and slow," his sister Serise drawled from above him. "We could've killed you twice over by now, Samhail."

Samhail glared up at the woman standing with her great, leathery wings outstretched behind her.

"Do you want to cry mercy, brother?" Serise cooed at him.

Samhail slapped the sword aside and sent it flying out of Serise's hand.

He kicked one leg out to knock her feet from under her, and she sprawled forward with a cry of surprise. Samhail threw his arm out to summon back the sword he'd just knocked away, and it was in his hand a second later. He rolled over and pointed the blade at the back of Serise's own neck where she lay face down on the grass.

"Did no one teach you to respect your elders?" he asked her coldly.

He turned toward Surgeon who'd picked himself up off the ground and was advancing toward them. Samhail threw out his hand and a percussive forcefield hit the other gargoyle, throwing him back again onto the ground. Samhail got to his feet, still keeping the sword at Serise's neck while he summoned his second sword back to his hand.

"What in the three hells is going on out here?" came a female voice.

Samhail's head snapped to the manor house to see Cyra rushing toward them.

"Cyra, stay back!" he called to her. He wasn't sure why his siblings were here, but he didn't think he'd like the reason, and he didn't want them anywhere near her.

Cyra ignored him and came to stand right next to him. "Samhail, put your swords away please."

"You don't understand," Samhail said as he shunted her behind him. "These are-"

"Your brother and sister," Cyra cut in. "I know."

He turned and blinked at her. "What?"

Cyra smiled at him. "You just defeated my two new bodyguards."

Samhail was so stunned he almost dropped his swords. Almost.

"Your what?" he asked incredulously.

Cyra sighed. "Let Serise up and come inside. I'll explain everything."

Samhail looked down at his sister. She hadn't moved yet, and neither had Surgeon after he'd been knocked down again. Samhail grunted and pulled his wings back in before sheathing his swords. He didn't wait around to greet his siblings but followed Cyra into the manor house.

They entered a spacious area that was set up much like a tavern, with a bar, tables, and chairs where patrons could presumably come to drink wine. The furniture was all dark wood, but the walls were white, and ornate crown molding ran along the ceiling. Three huge metal chandeliers hung from a beam in the center. The floor was stone, but three intricately woven rugs covered most of it.

Samhail followed Cyra through the room, down a hallway, and into what he assumed was her office. He paused before pulling the door shut behind him. Part of him wanted to keep it open to avoid a repetition of the incident in the great room, but he also didn't want anyone to overhear their conversation, especially not with his brother and sister around.

A large desk stood in front of floor-to-ceiling windows that looked out over the vineyard, but Cyra didn't head for it. Instead, she went to a plush leather couch on the side of the room and sat down at one end. She motioned for Samhail to sit next to her, but he pulled a chair over from in front of her desk and sat across from her instead.

Cyra raised a brow at him. "To what do I owe your visit?" she asked when he didn't say anything.

"Why are my siblings here?" he asked, ignoring the question.

Cyra sighed. "That's why Bressen wanted to talk to you this afternoon. We would've mentioned them sooner, but you've been…aloof the last couple days."

She looked at him questioningly, but he remained silent.

"*Bressen* decided," she went on, emphasizing her husband's name, "that I needed additional protection. He reached out to your father the other day. As I understand it, he wanted to ask him about helping us fight Sandrian and Magdalene, but while they were talking, he asked if any of your siblings might be available to guard me. He just wanted to know if it was a possibility before he asked you what you thought, but your father went ahead and sent Surgeon and Serise. They arrived late last night. Bressen was going to tell you when you met with him later. We didn't mean for you to find out this way."

Samhail inhaled deeply and tried to get himself under control. Surgeon and Serise were twins and the youngest of his four siblings. The two of them had gone everywhere together as children, and while Samhail hadn't realized they still did, he should've at least known to look for Serise when he'd discovered Surgeon here.

He chastised himself mentally for that slip-up. He'd been so distracted by the conversation he needed to have with Cyra that he'd let his guard down, and he was ashamed the twins had taken advantage.

Surgeon and Serise were actually the siblings Samhail considered the least objectionable, although that wasn't saying much. In truth, he didn't know them well. He'd already been grown and on his own before they were born, so he hadn't seen much of them. What little he knew of them had been gleaned from those rare times his family got together. Such occasions inevitably involved contests and sparring matches, and he'd found the twins to be competent warriors, if too reliant on each other.

"Samhail?" Cyra finally prompted when he hadn't said anything for almost a minute.

"It's fine," he said curtly. "I would've preferred to know about this sooner, but I'll speak to Bressen."

"We would've told you sooner," Cyra said, "but it feels as though you've been avoiding us lately. Is anything wrong?"

Samhail looked at her incredulously.

She frowned at him. "What is it? Why are you here?"

He sat back in his chair and crossed his arms. "We need to talk about what happened in the great room a few days ago."

Cyra's brows furrowed. "The great room? Back at the house? Why? What happened there?"

"I mean what happened between you and me there," he clarified.

Her brows furrowed deeper. "I don't understand," she said finally. "What exactly do you think happened?"

Samhail sighed, not sure why she wanted to make this so difficult.

"A couple days ago when you came back from the vineyard to get something," he said, deciding he'd spell it out if she was really going to make him, "you found me in the great room reading, and you…you were rather forward."

He'd meant to be blunt, but he stopped short at the look on her face. She seemed genuinely confused, and he suddenly had an uneasy feeling.

"Samhail," she said, "I never came home from the vineyard to get something. I don't know what you're talking about."

Unease pooled in Samhail's stomach, and he stood up to pace. His heart pounded in his chest. If that hadn't been Cyra in the great room the other day, then there was only one other explanation.

Fuck. It all made sense now, why she'd smelled different, acted different, and even felt different. He hadn't been able to figure out what had caused that last, but he knew now. There'd been no divine imperative tugging at him that day. Whenever he was around Cyra, the imperative made it feel like there was a barely discernable charge of static electricity running through him, but he hadn't felt it that day. To be sure, he'd felt a few other things, but not the divine imperative.

Cyra got to her feet as well and came over to lay a hand on his arm, but Samhail flinched and pulled away from her.

"Samhail?" she said anxiously. "What's wrong? You're worrying me."

"Cyra," he said, then trailed off. He had no idea how to tell her what had happened now that he was almost certain it hadn't been her he'd seen.

Cyra reached out once more, but she stopped short of touching him, apparently afraid he might pull away again. "Please," she said. "Please tell me what's going on."

"Cyra," he tried again, "two days ago, you…or someone who looked like you, found me in the great room back at the house. She…"

He dragged a hand through his long hair. He couldn't tell her this. He'd been ashamed of his behavior when he thought it was her, but the truth was even more humiliating.

"Let me see?" Cyra suggested.

He looked at her and shook his head. "No, I…"

"Please," she said gently.

Samhail squeezed his eyes shut. When he'd decided to confront her, he'd been afraid she might be angry at him for pushing her away that day. Now he was afraid she'd be angry at him for an entirely different reason.

He opened his eyes and looked into her beautiful silvery-gray ones.

"Don't hate me for what you see," he said.

Cyra shook her head slightly, and he sat back down in his chair.

Cyra's mindreading powers were growing stronger by the day, and she could read his mind without touching him, but she still laid a soft hand on the side of his face. Samhail tensed, remembering the feel of her hands on him the other day.

No, not *her* hands. Someone else's hands.

Samhail sighed and dropped his mental shield.

A couple minutes later, Cyra pulled her hand from his temple and stepped back, her eyes wide. Samhail tried to read her expression, but he couldn't tell what she was thinking.

"That wasn't me," she said, her voice barely a whisper.

"No," he agreed, "it wasn't."

"Samhail, I…" She trailed off, and he waited for her to say something more, to yell at him, to tell him how disgusted she was. Instead, she just asked, "Who was that woman? How is she able to look like me?"

Samhail stood and began to pace again, his muscled arms crossed tightly. "She's likely a masque. As for who she is, I have no idea."

"What's a masque?" Cyra asked.

"It's a rare kind of shapeshifter," Samhail said. "The majority of shapeshifters turn into animals, either one animal if they have limited powers or, if they're more powerful like Ursan was, they can turn into just about any animal they want. Masques are a powerful type of shapeshifter, but instead of turning into animals, they can change their appearance at will. They can even mirror the appearance of another person."

"And you think that's what this woman was?" Cyra said. "That she made herself look like me? Why?"

"I don't know," Samhail said, shaking his head. "If she'd wanted to kill me, she had plenty of opportunity. She could've slit my throat while she was behind me."

Cyra inhaled sharply. "So if she wasn't there to kill you, then what? It looked like she wanted to…"

Samhail caught her eyes, and they looked at each other.

"That can't be the only reason she was here," he said finally. "If all she wanted was sex, she didn't need to come to me looking like you. There are easier ways to get me into bed."

"It didn't work, in any case," Cyra said quietly. "You stopped her."

Samhail looked away. He couldn't meet her eyes right now, but he felt her presence as she came to stand beside him. She reached out to put a hand on his arm, but she again stopped herself.

"Samhail," she said. "Do you still desire me?"

His eyes met hers. "Yes. And I probably always will, but you're Bressen's wife," he said. "As I told you before, I won't let my desires jeopardize my friendship with either you or him. I should've put a stop to what happened far sooner, and I regret letting it go as far as it did."

If Cyra was shocked by the admission, she didn't show it. Instead, she shook her head and let her hand fall on his arm this time.

"She made you think she was me," Cyra said. "She made you think it was alright, that I wanted it. You stopped it before anything went too far. Under the circumstances, your restraint was admirable."

He smiled at her wryly. "We'll see if Bressen feels the same way."

Cyra opened her mouth to say something but closed it again, and Samhail wondered if she'd been about to suggest they not tell Bressen. It was out of the question, in any case. This wasn't a secret they could keep from the Lord of Hiraeth for reasons that were both moral and practical.

"Is Bressen at the house?" Samhail asked. "This is something he should know right away."

Cyra closed her eyes for a moment, and he knew she was communicating mind-to-mind with her husband.

"He's home and expecting us," she said as she opened her eyes a few seconds later. "I only told him we had something important to tell him. I'll have Surgeon and Serise meet me back there later."

Cyra closed her eyes again, presumably to send a mental message to his siblings. When she opened them, she raised her hand to draw a circle in the air. When her hand reached the top of the arc, a portal ringed in glowing blue light opened into Bressen's study back at Tide's End. Bressen stood waiting for them on the other side as Cyra widened the portal and stepped through.

Samhail hesitated as he looked through at them. He felt the separation between himself and his two friends acutely, not just physically, but mentally as well. Part of him missed the days he and Bressen had spent together in their bachelorhood, but he also couldn't imagine his life without Cyra in it now. He only hoped the momentary madness he'd succumbed to in the great room the other day didn't permanently damage his relationship with either of them.

He sighed and stepped through the portal to face the Lord of Hiraeth.

Chapter 7

Samhail

Bressen stood in front of his desk in his study as Samhail stepped through the portal after Cyra. The lord's expression was easy and light, and for some reason, that piqued Samhail's anger. His annoyance bubbled to the surface as he recalled he had a bone to pick with his friend.

"What the fuck are Surgeon and Serise doing here?" he growled at Bressen the second Cyra closed the portal behind them.

Bressen raised a brow, but Samhail didn't care. Shame and anger had made him reckless.

Bressen looked at Cyra in question, obviously wondering if this is what she'd brought them there to talk about, but Cyra only shrugged.

"They're here to help protect Cyra," Bressen answered calmly.

"Why them?" Samhail snapped.

"The short answer is that I'm counting on the divine imperative to motivate them."

That brought Samhail up short.

"You…you didn't tell them about Cyra, did you?" he asked with quiet horror. "Do they know she's…"

"A Hand of the Gods?" Bressen finished for him. "No, I didn't give your father or the twins any details. I just assumed, or at least hoped, Surgeon and Serise would feel the same protectiveness toward Cyra that you did when you first met her, even if they didn't understand why they felt it. Given what happened with Jasper, I thought it might be good to strengthen Cyra's protection. Since gargoyles are already primed to protect her, and I happen to have a personal connection to a rather powerful gargoyle family, it seemed like the perfect solution."

Samhail was silent as he processed all that. "Why didn't you ask me to do it?" he said finally.

He suspected the answer was obvious given the other news he was about to tell Bressen. Perhaps his friend no longer trusted him to spend so much time around his wife.

"I need you for other things I can't ask Surgeon and Serise to do because they don't know everything you know," Bressen said.

"In other words," Cyra said, "we didn't want you stuck following me around on guard duty when there were other more important jobs you could be doing."

Samhail's gaze swung to hers. "There are few if any things I would consider more important than keeping you safe," he said. "In another time, I'm sure it would've been considered one of the highest honors for a gargoyle to be named the personal protector of a Hand of the Gods."

Cyra smiled warmly and blushed. "You'll always be my first and fiercest protector," she said, "and I have no doubt you'll continue to fill that role whenever you're around."

Samhail refrained from pointing out Bressen was her fiercest protector, but he assumed she meant other than her husband.

"Neither Cyra nor I expect you to stop keeping her safe," Bressen said. "That will always be part of your job, but the reality remains that there are other things I need you to do, so I had to find others to help protect Cyra. More gargoyles seemed like the obvious choice. As you've said, she would've had a cadre of gargoyles protecting her in earlier times. Well, consider the three of you to be her cadre."

"But Surgeon and Serise-," Samhail started to argue.

"Answer to you," Bressen cut in.

That brought him up short again. "What?"

"They've been told to obey any orders you give them," Bressen said.

"They were less than happy about that," Cyra added with amusement, "but they were told."

The tightness in Samhail's chest eased, not from their attempts to stroke his ego, but at the news he'd at least have some control over his siblings. It was true he couldn't watch Cyra himself all the time, so the twins were the next best choice.

That didn't mean he trusted them. They'd always had an unusual attachment to one another, an attachment he sometimes thought made their judgement suspect when they needed to consider others. In his opinion, their over-dependence on each other also hindered them in battle, but perhaps he was biased. He was used to fighting on his own.

Still, the twins were a better choice than either of his two older siblings. His eldest brother Soldier was a formidable warrior who wore his austerity like a suit of armor, but his temper was quick and extremely volatile when stirred. Likewise, his older sister Sadira had a fondness for brutality that brought her just short of sadistic. Had his father sent either Soldier or Sadira to protect Cyra, he would've made Bressen send them back. The twins were odd and had their own special streak of madness, but he had to admit they were likely to keep Cyra safe, especially if they were answerable to him as Bressen promised.

"Did they actually agree to obey me?" Samhail asked, wanting to be sure before he relaxed.

"They did," Bressen said. "Grudgingly, but they did. We made sure Cyra was in the room when I spoke with them about their duties, and I have a feeling they both felt the tug of the divine imperative. It would've been hard for them to refuse anything that helps her."

Samhail mulled this over. He wasn't thrilled to have his siblings here, but for Cyra's sake he'd deal with it. Surgeon and Serise were warriors above all else, and if the divine imperative was driving them, there was little he could complain about.

"Are you satisfied?" Bressen asked him.

Samhail nodded. "For now."

"So is that the important news you needed to discuss with me?" Bressen asked, glancing between Samhail and Cyra.

Samhail went rigid as the real reason they were here came back to him. "No," he said reluctantly. "There's something else. I suspect there may be a masque among us."

Bressen's face went serious. "Why do you think that?"

Samhail looked at Cyra, and she gave him an encouraging nod.

"I was in the great room the other day when Cyra came in, or someone I thought was Cyra," Samhail said. "She was acting…out of character. When I discussed it with Cyra today, she had no idea what I was talking about. The woman who looked like her said she'd come home from the vineyard to get something she forgot, but Cyra says she didn't come home from the vineyard earlier this week."

Bressen looked between Samhail and his wife again. "There's something you're not telling me," he said. "What did you mean when you said Cyra was acting out of character?"

"It's not important," Cyra said quickly.

Bressen looked between them. "It is if both of you are trying to avoid telling me what this woman did," he said.

Samhail exchanged a resigned look with Cyra and pushed a deep breath out through his nose. He'd known they wouldn't get away with leaving out the details.

"The woman was being very…aggressive," Samhail offered. When Bressen simply looked at him, he added, "She touched me. Intimately. She sat in my lap, and kissed me, and…" He stopped as he saw Bressen's brows shoot up, and he realized he could've stopped at the kiss. That would've been enough, but Bressen had caught the 'and.'

"And what?" Bressen asked, an edge to his voice.

"Samhail stopped the woman before anything went too far," Cyra cut in. "That's all that matters."

Bressen looked at his wife, and the two of them were silent for a long moment. Samhail knew they were having a mental argument, and it was one Cyra must've lost because Bressen's head snapped back to him.

"So let me get this straight," Bressen said. "A woman who looked like my wife tried to seduce you in the middle of the great room, and it didn't occur to you to talk to either her or me about this sooner?"

Samhail heard the anger in his friend's voice, and he didn't blame Bressen one bit. He'd handled things as best he could in the moment, but he'd still let it go further than he should've.

As for trying to avoid Bressen and Cyra for the last few days, that had been nothing short of craven, and Bressen was right. He should've come to one or both of them immediately. At the very least, he should've listened to his instincts, which had told him there was something wrong with the way Cyra was acting.

Nemesis take him, he should've known.

"Well?" Bressen asked when Samhail didn't say anything.

"Bressen," Cyra said placatingly, but Samhail wasn't going to let her fight this battle for him.

"I should've come to you sooner," Samhail said. "I have no defensible reason for why I didn't."

"No, you don't," Bressen said, his voice rising. "And because you didn't come to either of us, this masque has likely been walking around our home unchecked this whole time."

Samhail inhaled sharply. It was only sinking in now that this woman, whoever she was, had been here for days, maybe even weeks, and she was probably still among them.

"You think she's still here?" Cyra asked Bressen.

"Why wouldn't she be?" he asked, his voice still sharp as he looked at Samhail. "She was probably sent by Sandrian to spy on us. We never knew how Sandrian found out about the collar and rings we retrieved from *The Stalwart*. If he has a spy in the house, that would explain it. Fuck, the masque is probably the one who set off the wards the other night."

Guilt twisted in Samhail's gut, and he felt as though he might vomit for the first time in decades. They'd had a spy living among them for the gods-only-knew how long, and he'd failed to report information that might've led them to learn this days earlier. He swallowed down the bile that rose in his throat. If something had happened to either Bressen or Cyra because he'd been too ashamed to come clean about what he'd allowed to happen, he never would've forgiven himself.

Cyra dropped into one of the chairs in front of the desk, her face ashen, and Samhail resisted the pull to go to her. Bressen was at her side in a second, and he knelt in front of her, speaking softly as his hand brushed along her cheek.

"I'll find her," Samhail said quietly, realizing even as the words left his mouth that he couldn't even be sure it was a woman they sought. How did one look for a person who could change their face and body at will?

"And how do you plan to do that?" Bressen asked, apparently thinking the same thing.

"I don't know yet," Samhail said, "but I'll figure it out."

"My negation powers," Cyra said. "If I can get close enough to the masque to negate her shapeshifting abilities, she'll go back to her original form, won't she?"

"How close do you need to be?" Bressen asked her.

"Maybe within about fifteen feet or so?" Cyra said. "Since my power boost from the gods, I think I have a slightly greater range now."

"What if she's already in her original form?" Samhail asked. "She can change into Cyra, but she may not be wandering around in a false form all the time."

"Chances are good that she's wearing at least some kind of disguise," Bressen said, standing from where he knelt beside Cyra. "If she's here to spy, I doubt she'd want to use her actual face to do it."

"Does the house have any relatively new staff?" Samhail asked.

"Several," Bressen answered. "We hired a new stable hand, a cook, a scullery maid, Cyra's lady's maid, and at least two guards within the last couple months."

"It's likely one of the women, but with a masque you can never be sure," Samhail reasoned.

Something gnawed at the back of his mind as he ran over the list of new staff Bressen had just named, then something clicked into place as he remembered where he'd last smelled the faint scent of lemon verbena.

"Your new lady's maid, Cyra," Samhail said as he furrowed his brows. "How long has she been here?"

Cyra frowned. "Leeda? A few weeks," she said. "We hired her right before the wedding, but I…I can't believe it could be her."

"Why not?" Samhail asked. "She'd be the perfect spy. She has direct access to you, so she's far better placed to gather information than a scullery maid or a stable hand."

"Besides her position, do you have any specific reason for suspecting Leeda?" Bressen asked him.

Samhail sighed inwardly. He wasn't looking forward to admitting his next news. "I found her in the hall outside your room in the dead of night a week or so ago," he said.

Bressen's brows shot up. "And this didn't seem worth mentioning earlier?" he asked incredulously.

"Honestly, not at the time," Samhail said. "I ran into her coming down the hall from your room at almost one o'clock in the morning. I questioned her, but she said she'd lost her necklace while cleaning your sitting room that day. She said it was special to her, and she couldn't sleep until she found it. I admonished her for going into the sitting room while you were asleep, but she begged me not to tell you. It seemed harmless enough at the time, and I didn't think it would do any good to get the girl in trouble. I forgot about it by the next morning. It's only now it seems like there could've been more to it."

"And why were *you* outside our bedchamber at one in the morning?" Bressen asked Samhail. "That seems like a lot of traffic coming and going in our hall for such an early hour."

Samhail remembered that night well. He'd just learned Cyra was a Hand of the Gods and that he was divinely bound to protect her. Strangely, he'd woken from a sound sleep for some reason and had the urge to check on her. He'd tried to ignore the feeling, but his mind wouldn't rest until he'd pulled on his clothes, grabbed his swords, and walked up to Bressen and Cyra's bedchamber.

Stupid idiot. There'd been so many warning signs he'd just dismissed. He didn't deserve to call himself Cyra's protector for all the times just in the last few weeks he'd failed her.

"Something woke me, and I felt the urge to get up and be sure everything was alright," Samhail explained.

"And when you found the girl in our hallway, did you think to check on us?" Bressen asked.

"Of course I did," Samhail said, annoyed. He wasn't completely inept. "I went into the sitting room and was about to look in on you."

"But you didn't?" Cyra asked.

"I didn't need to," he said, crossing his arms. "I could hear you were both awake and…otherwise occupied. So I left."

Cyra blushed, but Bressen just nodded.

"What night was this exactly?" Bressen asked.

"The night Axenus and I found you and Cyra on the beach venting her powers," he said. "The night you told us what Phaedrus discovered."

Cyra gasped.

"What?" Bressen asked.

"That was the night-," Cyra started to say, but she stopped short and glanced at Samhail. She looked at Bressen instead and must've explained in his head because he nodded gravely.

Samhail was getting tired of them having private conversations with him in the room. "That was the night of what?" he snapped, deciding he wasn't going to let them leave him in the dark on this.

Cyra and Bressen exchanged glances before Bressen answered.

"Cyra accidentally dream walked into one of Axenus's nightmares."

Samhail's eyes widened in understanding. "You know what happened to him?" he asked Cyra, and she nodded.

"And if you tell Axenus any of this, I'll-," Bressen began, but Samhail lifted a hand to cut off the threat.

"I won't say anything," he said. "I'm not that big an asshole."

Bressen gave him a look that said he wasn't convinced.

"So it's possible the masque overheard our conversation that night," Cyra said. She seemed to be replaying it in her head because a moment later she gasped in horror. "Bressen, we were talking about…" She trailed off as the rest of her thought was likely sent to Bressen mentally.

"What?" Samhail snapped, impatient now.

"The turn our conversation took," Bressen said, "might explain why the masque tried to seduce you as Cyra."

Samhail's eyes widened. "Fuck me. Were you talking about-?"

"About fucking you, yes," Bressen said wryly. "Orgies might have come up as well."

"Bressen!" Cyra said, her face flushing hotly.

"If the two of you had an orgy and didn't invite me, I'm going to be very offended," Samhail said.

"Not yet," Bressen drawled. "We're still trying to pick a date that works for everyone."

"Enough! Both of you," Cyra admonished. "This isn't the time."

Both Samhail and Bressen turned contrite, but Samhail caught the lord's wink at him out of the corner of his eye.

"So what do we do about the masque?" Samhail asked.

"Axenus gets back tonight," Bressen said. "We don't know exactly what we're dealing with, so we'll wait for him to be on the safe side. He may know something about masques we don't."

Samhail rolled his eyes but didn't say anything. What the merman could do that he, two other gargoyles, a mind wraith, and a syphon couldn't do, he wasn't sure, but he wasn't about to argue with Bressen.

"After dinner, we'll start with the new staff and call them to my study for questioning," Bressen said. "Cyra can get just close enough to negate any power they might be using, and we'll see what happens. If it turns out none of them are masques, we'll start calling in the older staff to see if the masque is pretending to be one of them."

Samhail and Cyra nodded.

"I'll find Surgeon and Serise and let them know," Samhail said.

"No need," Bressen said. "They're outside the door waiting for Cyra."

Samhail glanced toward the door. "Then I need to speak with them to be sure we're all on the same page about Cyra's protection," he said.

Bressen cocked a brow at him. "Just make sure your idea of speaking actually involves words. My wife's bodyguards need to be able to fight."

"Words only," Samhail promised, although he left out that the words would contain plenty of threats.

"And when you're done with them," Bressen added, "I'll meet you in the training yard."

Samhail tensed but nodded to his friend. It was early for their daily sparring session, but he had a feeling the lord had some extra energy to burn and perhaps some things to get off his chest. Today's training was going to be far more intense than normal, and if he was honest with himself, he was looking forward to it in a resigned sort of way. Bressen would punish him for everything he'd done or hadn't done recently, and he was ready to receive that punishment.

"Come with me," Samhail barked at Surgeon and Serise as he exited Bressen's study ahead of the lord and lady.

The twins exchanged looks but didn't move.

"Now," he said. "I believe you were told you answer to me. I need a word, and Lady Cyra is perfectly safe with Lord Bressen at the moment."

His siblings exchanged another look, darker this time, but they fell into step behind him as he led them somewhere they could speak without being overheard. He'd make it clear to his brother and sister that their lives depended on keeping Cyra safe.

Chapter 8

Talyn knew she was in trouble as soon as she walked into the room. She'd expected to face the Lord of Hiraeth and maybe Cyra when she'd been called up to Bressen's study after dinner, but she hadn't expected to see Samhail and both of Cyra's new bodyguards as well.

Lord Bressen was standing in front of his desk, leaning casually against it while Cyra stood close by, but their easy demeanors were belied by the three other warriors in the room. Samhail was even wearing his leather armor and his two swords, while the two bodyguards each carried a shortsword and dagger at their hips. If they needed this many people with this much weaponry to question her, they were expecting trouble.

Luckily fear was a natural reaction to facing such a group, so Talyn didn't bother to hide her panic.

"My lady?" she asked from just barely inside the door.

Cyra smiled at her. "Leeda, please come in. We need to speak with you a moment."

"About what?" Talyn asked. She stepped farther into the room, and the guard in the hallway closed the door behind her. A key turned in the lock with a click that echoed in her ears.

Fuck.

Talyn scanned the room for possible exits, and that's when she noticed the sixth person in the room. The merman stood next to the door she'd just entered. He'd been behind it when she came in, and she hadn't immediately noticed him when the door shut, but his shock of red hair caught in her peripheral vision as she took in the room. A quick glance told her he was armed with a sword as well.

Talyn weighed her escape routes again. She could port to the other side of the door into the hallway if things went bad, but she wanted to have other options.

The most obvious exit was the balcony to her left, but it was also the most improbable. While the balcony doors were half open, Samhail stood sentinel next to them. If she needed to go that way, she'd have to get by him first. It wouldn't be impossible, just risky. She could port right by him if she needed to, but it would put her in closer proximity to him than she wanted to be, and then she'd need to climb down the side of the house.

Talyn was careful not to catch Samhail's eye as her gaze swept past him. A lady's maid would never be so daring as to look someone like him in the eye, and she was afraid he might see something in her face that would help him make the connection between her and his supposed encounter with Cyra a few days ago.

Talyn nearly did a double take as her gaze passed over him, though. There was a large purpling bruise on his jaw as well as a couple cuts on his face. She wondered where he'd gotten them and why he hadn't had someone heal them.

She'd noticed Samhail had kept his distance from Cyra and Bressen the last few days, but the fact they were all here now and armed to the teeth likely meant they'd figured out they had a masque in their midst.

It had clearly been a mistake to try and seduce Samhail. She hadn't expected him to confront Cyra about what happened, but he obviously had. Cyra, of course, would've denied everything. Talyn had been sloppy in testing Samhail, and now she'd have to convince these people she was who she said she was, all without lying.

"Come have a seat," Cyra said, beckoning her forward, and Talyn was instantly suspicious. She didn't like this. There was something off about the whole situation, even beyond the four heavily armed guards.

She took a deep breath and stepped further into the room. Her eyes swept the space again, but the balcony was still the only logical escape route other than the main door. All the windows were closed, and the two bodyguards stood near them anyway. There was a door to the sitting room at the far end of the study, but she guessed that was locked as well.

Her best bet was still just to port back outside the main door. That the door was locked didn't matter, and once in the hall, she could simply run for it. The guards on the other side would be too surprised to do anything in time to stop her.

Talyn felt the tendrils creep into her mind then. She had her mind shield up as always, but someone was trying to break past it. No, not just one someone, but two someones. Both the Lord and Lady of Hiraeth were working together to slip past her shield. It was a subtle enough attempt that most people wouldn't have noticed, but the nature of her work had made Talyn sensitive to such attempts at incursion.

Double fuck.

Talyn had worked hard to develop a strong mind shield so her thoughts would never give her away when she took on the appearance of another, but she wouldn't be able to hold off two mind wraiths for long. In truth, she was already in trouble for even having the shield up to start. It might have bought her a little time, but Cyra and Bressen were likely wondering not only why she had the shield up at all, but how a simple lady's maid had developed such a strong one. That fear was realized a moment later when Cyra spoke.

"Leeda, do you have a mind shield up?"

The question was asked kindly enough, but Samhail, the merman, and the two bodyguards all shifted. They'd been relatively at ease before, but all four looked ready to move if she so much as glanced at them wrong.

"Did I do something wrong, my lady?" Talyn asked, ignoring her.

Talyn's hands grabbed at the sides of her skirt in a seemingly nervous gesture, but she felt the daggers strapped to each of her thighs. Both were there and ready if needed.

"That's what we need to find out," Cyra said. "I just need to know one thing."

"Anything, my lady," Talyn said, her voice overly eager.

Cyra stepped forward, and Talyn took the opportunity to shift her own stance in case she needed to flee. She was well aware just how much power the Lady of Hiraeth had, and she wasn't going to give Cyra the opportunity to use it.

That's when Talyn felt it. Cyra was about fifteen feet from her when Talyn's power simply died out, like a torch doused in a barrel of cold water. She felt a wave of nausea as the magic that always thrummed through her body vanished, as if half the blood had suddenly stilled in her veins. She hadn't realized just how much she took the feel of that magic for granted, and she sucked in a ragged breath as she felt herself begin to change, to transform back into her true self.

Horror crept through Talyn as her fingers lengthened and her copper-blonde hair spilled down her back to her waist. Her eyes flew to Cyra's, and she saw the heartbreak in them as the lady beheld what she really looked like.

Negation powers. She hadn't seen that coming.

Movement and the sound of steel being unsheathed drew her eyes to Samhail and the two blades now in his hands. She did meet his eyes then, and a moment of understanding sparked between them. Talyn winked at him, and his face darkened in rage.

A quick glance to the other side of the room showed the two bodyguards had also drawn their weapons, and she didn't need to look behind her to know that the merman had as well.

Next to Cyra, Bressen pushed off his desk, and Talyn realized she had bigger problems than she'd first thought. Not only could she no longer shift, but she likely couldn't port either. She tried just to be sure, but her body didn't budge, and she felt the hollowness in the pit of her stomach anew. She had no way to get out into the hall, and if the balcony was now her only way out, getting past Samhail had just gotten infinitely harder.

"Who are you?" Bressen asked, speaking for the first time. His voice was deep and full of authority, a voice accustomed to being answered.

Only one set of tendrils was still probing at her mind shield now. She assumed they were his and that Cyra had dropped her attempt to break through the shield when she'd discovered the woman who'd been attending her wasn't who she thought she was.

Talyn locked eyes with the Lord of Hiraeth. She'd never looked into them before, and she realized now just how piercing they were.

She smiled sweetly at him. "I'm sorry, but you haven't earned that answer yet, my lord," she said and bolted for the balcony.

Samhail moved to block her, but she'd been expecting him to. She might not have her powers anymore, but she still had speed and agility.

Her powers had died when Cyra got close to her, and she wondered if there was a critical range under which the negation powers worked. It was a long shot, and if she was wrong, she'd end up splattered on the ground below, but it was her only option. She needed to get far enough from Cyra to regain her ability to port.

Talyn made for the side of the balcony farthest away from Samhail. She was counting on him to lunge for her, and he did. Instead, she pivoted and whirled around him the other way as his momentum carried him past her to the spot where he thought she'd be. She shouldered open the partially closed doors, then ran for the edge of the balcony. She lifted her skirt in front of her to step up onto the balcony railing and launched herself off it. She didn't have time to second-guess before she was out over open air, her legs kicking out in a full stride.

For one glorious second, she felt a spark of her power return, but it died again quickly as something vice-like closed over her wrist. Talyn cried out as her body jerked to a halt in mid-air, and she swung back toward the balcony. The force of the jolt turned her around, and she saw that Samhail had grabbed her wrist as she leapt.

She came crashing back into the side of the balcony and the breath was driven from her lungs as her body hit the stone. She coughed and inhaled deeply, then cried out again as Samhail jerked her roughly upward.

Talyn grabbed her skirt with her free hand and pulled it up to get at the dagger strapped to her thigh. As Samhail dragged her back over the banister, she unsheathed the dagger and plunged it into the top of his forearm where his leather vambrace ended. His flesh was denser than she anticipated, and the blade only penetrated a couple inches.

Samhail yelled out in pain, but he didn't release her wrist right away. Instead, he yanked his arm back while still holding her, only releasing her a second later. Talyn flew back across the balcony and hit the stone wall near the door where she crumpled to the ground. She managed to avoid hitting her head, but her shoulder felt like it might be dislocated, and the side of her back had struck the stone hard. Pain radiated up her body, and she was sure she'd felt a rib or two crack. She tried to inhale deeply, but the pain in her torso allowed her only shallow breaths.

Talyn looked up from the ground to see Cyra and Bressen in the doorway of the balcony with the two bodyguards close behind them. She was out of time. She needed to get away from Cyra and pray the distance helped return her powers. Gritting her teeth against the pain, she forced herself to her feet as quickly as she could and threw herself gracelessly over the balcony railing.

Wind rushed past Talyn as she fell, her hair whipping around as she tried to gauge the distance she'd fallen. Her back was to the ground, so she couldn't tell how far she'd gone, but the pain from her cracked ribs kept her from being able to turn herself in the air. She'd had hopes of being able to grab something on the way down, but her injuries now made that unlikely.

Above her, three huge forms with bat-like wings soared out over the balcony and dove for her, the largest form in the lead.

Talyn felt the surge of her power return, and relief flooded through her. She couldn't tell how close she was to the ground, so she didn't hesitate for a second.

She ported just as Samhail's large hands reached out for her. She didn't even know where she planned to port to until she hit the floor somewhere in the house and rolled.

Talyn groaned as her already-injured ribs and shoulder protested the additional impact. She allowed only a couple seconds to collect herself before she looked up to see where she'd landed. She was inside the ballroom on the first floor, but it was only temporary safety as she saw Samhail and the two bodyguards hovering just outside the large windows.

"Ballroom!" one of them shouted back up to the balcony just before Samhail's giant form crashed through one of the windows.

Glass shattered inward, tinkling and skittering across the marble floor, but Talyn didn't bother to avoid it as she hauled herself to her feet and ran for the door. She got only a few feet before a percussive force hit her from behind, and she pitched forward, crying out in more pain as she felt a couple more ribs crack this time.

She looked back to see Samhail stalking toward her with the two bodyguards flanking him. All three had huge leathery black wings splayed out behind them. She knew Samhail had wings, but she hadn't realized the bodyguards did as well. Were they gargoyles too? She hadn't had time to learn anything about them. The woman had long white hair like Samhail, but the man had short silvery gray hair.

Talyn didn't even try to get up this time. She'd hoped to conserve her porting power, but she had to use it now or she'd never get out of here alive. She ported into the hall outside the dining room, then used the wall to drag herself to a standing position. Every movement was agony as her cracked ribs and dislocated shoulder screamed in pain, but she knew it wouldn't take Samhail and the others long to figure out where she'd gone.

She hurried down the corridor as quickly as she could using the wall to steady herself, but it was only a couple seconds before the doors to the ballroom crashed open, one coming completely off its hinges as it fell to the floor. Fear like she'd never known surged through her at the look in Samhail's eyes as he closed the distance between them, the two other warriors close behind.

Talyn was prepared for the forcefield this time, and she flattened herself against the wall as it reverberated down the hall. She stumbled under its impact, and her broken ribs screamed in protest, but she was still standing when it passed, and she ported further down the hall.

As soon as she rematerialized, she was lifted off the ground and began to drift backward. She ported again, but she was gripped once more by the force as soon as she reappeared and was dragged backward. It must be some kind of summoning power.

She ported twice more, but each time she was dragged back as Samhail and the two bodyguards got closer and closer.

Exhaustion and pain hit her then, and Talyn stopped struggling to let herself glide down the hall toward them. Her porting ability took a lot out of her, but now she was also drained from her injuries and from fighting to escape. She had only enough energy to port a few more times, and it was senseless to waste that energy trying to get away when she'd only be summoned back. She still had one dagger strapped to her leg, so she'd have to find a way to use it.

Talyn managed to twist herself in the air so she was floating forward rather than backward, and Samhail's dark eyes bore into her as his summoning power brought her to him. Anger was etched on every inch of his face, and Talyn's neck went straight into his outstretched hand as she reached him.

Her eyes widened as he squeezed his fingers around her throat, completely cutting off her air. One of her hands clawed at his wrist as her other hand with the injured shoulder flew to her thigh to pull up the dress and grab her second dagger. She swung the dagger up to stab his arm again, but he was ready this time. He caught her wrist and twisted it so she dropped the blade. She would have cried out, but his hand was still cutting off her air, and she was starting to see stars as her vision faded. She had to port again or he was going to kill her.

Talyn ported behind the three winged beings this time and stumbled along the wall as she gasped for air. She tried to run, but she bounced off some kind of barrier instead. She looked around in panic and realized she was contained in a glowing bubble. She tried to port outside of it, but she only planted face-first into the inside wall of the bubble as it allowed her no further.

She turned to Samhail and the bodyguards and saw it was the winged woman who had her hand out this time controlling the bubble.

"It was a valiant effort," a voice drawled from Talyn's other side, and she turned to see Bressen standing in the hall, having just come out of the ballroom. Cyra and the merman were right behind him, but Talyn didn't feel her power die out this time. Not yet anyway.

"I give you points for style, and I admire your courage for jumping off a balcony without wings," Bressen continued, "but that's the best I can do. Now who are you?"

Talyn could barely breathe. Every shuddering inhale sent shooting pain through her ribs, so she just smiled and leaned against the wall before sliding down it to sit on the floor. This did nothing to help her cracked ribs, but it was all she could manage at this point. She looked up at the Lord of Hiraeth but didn't say anything as she took shallow breaths.

Bressen crouched down next to the bubble, and she met his eyes.

"We can do this the easy way or the hard way," the lord said lightly, "but you'll answer my questions either way."

Talyn smiled again weakly and used her last bit of strength to shift herself into the Lady of Hiraeth. Cyra gasped behind Bressen, and Samhail growled as he lurched forward, but the male bodyguard put an arm on his chest to hold him back. Bressen's face darkened, but he held up a hand to warn Samhail back. His gaze was cold as he looked at Talyn.

"Do your worst," Talyn said in Cyra's voice a second before her power was again cut off and she shifted back into herself.

Then those tendrils were clawing at the shield in her mind again. They were much more aggressive now, much more merciless, and Talyn cried out as she felt them tear at her mental barrier in earnest. Without her powers to bolster the shield, it didn't stand a chance.

"Bressen!" she heard Cyra say, but the pain didn't stop.

Talyn screamed as the tendrils slashed violently through her shield and laid her bare. It was as though a seam had been ripped open, and she felt the edges of her consciousness fray under the power of the lord's insistence. Somewhere far away she heard Cyra telling him to stop, but she knew he wouldn't. She could feel his resolve like iron chains as he held her mind prisoner.

Who are you? Bressen's voice sounded inside her head, compelling her to answer. She tried to resist the probing of his mind, but her response came against her will.

Talyn of Avril, she said, and the pain eased ever so slightly.

And why are you here? Bressen asked.

Talyn gritted her teeth and tried to throw up her mind shield again. The second she did, pain like she'd never known coursed through every inch of her body. She knew she was screaming, knew she must be writhing on the floor, but all of that seemed far away as nothing but the excruciating agony of her body ripping apart from the inside out ricocheted through her mind.

None of that, Bressen said coldly in her mind, *or I can make things even more unpleasant for you. Now why are you here?*

Sandrian sent me, she answered, *to spy on you. To learn whatever I could that might help him.*

Help him do what? Bressen asked.

I don't know his plans, she said. *I just do as I'm asked.*

And what have you been asked to do?

Talyn tried to resist answering, but he sent another jolt of pain through her.

It upsets my wife to see me do this, Bressen said conversationally. *She doesn't have the heart or the stomach to torture someone. Luckily, I do.*

Talyn felt the pain again, this time for longer. She'd been tortured before, but nothing like this. Those times the pain had been concentrated in one place, a broken finger, a slash on her leg, a punch to her gut. But this…this was different. This pain was everywhere, from the crown of her head to the tips of her toenails.

Let's try this one more time, Bressen said. *What were you asked to do?*

Talyn tried once more to hold the answer back, but Bressen's will pulled it to the surface of her consciousness.

Sandrian wanted to know when you'd retrieved the jewelry from the ship, Talyn answered. *I told him.*

She sensed rather than saw the lord nod, as if he'd expected as much. *What else?* he asked.

Talyn fought with everything she had left not to answer the question, but the words were pulled from her mind as if they were a fish on a line.

I was ordered to kill you both four days ago.

The pain she'd felt before was nothing to what jolted through her. If she'd thought her body was being torn apart earlier, it was being shredded now. She arched off the ground as her scream reverberated off the walls. Her ribs were probably breaking fully as her body seized up, but she couldn't tell because every fiber of her being was driven well beyond the limits of its endurance. She wasn't sure how she wasn't dead yet already, but for the first time in her life, she would've welcomed the nothingness simply to make the pain stop.

It wasn't only her body breaking, but her mind as well. Bressen's power stabbed into her like knives, burying themselves in her brain and slicing her to ribbons. It was only a matter of time before she fractured completely and her brain simply exploded into mist.

Then the pain eased, and Talyn heard someone else in her mind.

Bressen. Cyra's soft voice was a balm. *Let her go.*

Cyra, get out of here now, he answered.

Let her go, the lady repeated.

Cyra, he said, his voice angry but breaking, *just do what I ask and leave. I don't want you to see this.*

And I don't want to see it, she said, *but I almost lost you once to the darkness. I won't lose you this time either.*

She was planning to kill you, Bressen said.

But she didn't, Cyra said, *and I presume she had ample opportunities to do so. Please, Bressen. Stop.*

There was a long pause before Lord Bressen answered his wife.

No.

Talyn screamed again as her body jerked in pain. She felt as if her joints were separating, and she tried desperately to reconnect herself.

If you have nothing more useful to share with us, Bressen's voice came to her again, *then it's time for you to go.*

Bressen, no! Cyra's voice cut through Talyn's mind, and then both the pain and the presences in her head were gone.

Talyn was vaguely aware her body had eased back onto the hard, cold floor, but her head was mercifully quiet. She was relieved to feel only the pain in her ribs and shoulder now, then even that was gone.

Was she dead? Or had she somehow been healed? Cyra had healing powers, but she doubted the lady would use them on her.

Talyn felt someone in her mind again, but it wasn't the lord this time.

Sleep now, Cyra told her softly, and Talyn had neither the power nor the will to resist.

Chapter 9

Samhail

Samhail looked at the unconscious woman on the couch in Bressen's study and tried to wrap his mind around what had just happened. He ran his fingers absently over the bruise on his jaw – the one Bressen had given him today during their sparring session – then let his hand fall.

The woman looked peaceful now, as if she were just dozing while they discussed her, and it registered somewhere in his mind that she was unexpectedly beautiful. That hadn't stopped him from wanting to squeeze her throat until she passed out, though. He could easily have crushed her windpipe or snapped her neck earlier, and it had taken all his control not to do either of those things when he'd had her in his grasp.

Luckily, she'd chosen to port again and then Serise had taken over with her containment bubble. He didn't want to know what he might've done if the woman hadn't ported out of his hand, and that was enough to make his shame rise up anew. He'd never lost control like that. Even when Morland had controlled his mind all those years ago, he'd still felt more in command of himself than he had when he'd had this woman by the throat.

Now they knew where Cyra's porting ability came from, in any case.

Samhail had thought maybe the woman might have wings when she first tried to jump off the balcony, but when she hadn't manifested any the second time she'd jumped, he assumed she'd decided on death over capture. When he dove after her, he hadn't been trying to capture her, but rescue her. He'd been stunned when she disappeared in mid-air only about ten feet from the ground, so much so that he'd nearly planted face-first into the hard stone himself before he pulled up in time.

He'd been impressed despite himself when he realized she'd thrown herself off the balcony to put enough distance between her and Cyra to

"

get her powers back. That he could want to kill the woman, rescue her, and be impressed by her within the span of a minute made his head reel.

"Did you find out who she is?" Axenus asked Bressen.

Samhail and the twins had resumed the posts they'd had earlier, and Bressen leaned against the front of his desk again, which was where he usually stood when he needed to think about something. Only Cyra and Axenus sat in the chairs in front of the desk.

Bressen was currently glaring at his wife for negating his powers and forcing him out of the woman's head, but he turned away from Cyra to answer Axenus.

"Talyn of Avril," Bressen said with a shrug. His tone said the name meant nothing to him.

The name meant something to the twins, however, because both of them jolted, and their eyes shot to the woman on the couch. Samhail thought the name sounded familiar as well, like something he'd heard in passing, but he couldn't place it.

"*Talon* of Avril?" Surgeon repeated in disbelief. "Or do you mean the *Raptor* of Avril?"

"Raptor?" Bressen asked, giving Surgeon his attention. "I'm pretty sure she said Talyn, but who or what is this Raptor?"

"The Raptor is only the most deadly assassin on the continent," Serise said as if they should all know this. "At least, that's her reputation. She was given that nickname because she seemingly comes out of nowhere to take out her targets, the way an eagle or hawk drops from the sky to snatch up its prey."

"Assassin?" Samhail asked, suddenly more alert. He pushed himself off the wall where he'd been leaning. Fear flooded through him as he remembered this woman had been posing as Cyra's lady's maid for the-gods-knew how long. "Was she here to kill someone?"

"Yes," Bressen said. "Me and Cyra."

Samhail's blood went cold, and the desire to kill the woman lying on the couch rose up again.

"Sandrian hired her," Bressen went on. "Up until recently, she was only supposed to spy on us, but Sandrian gave her the go-ahead to kill me and Cyra four days ago. She was undoubtedly the one who tripped the wards around our bedchamber. Her porting explains why she was able to get away so quickly. Once she realized she tripped the wards, she ported back to her room so I couldn't sense her up here."

If Samhail's blood had run cold before, it turned to ice now. The idea that this assassin had been alone with Cyra for days if not weeks was going to give him nightmares.

"But why hasn't she tried since then?" Cyra asked.

"Perhaps she was afraid of getting caught?" Samhail offered. "Killing you in your sleep would've given her plenty of time to escape. If she tried to kill you during the day, she would've had to fight her way out. For that matter, once she killed one of you, the other would've torn her to shreds."

"Thank the gods we had you syphon warding power when you did, or we'd both be dead," Bressen said to Cyra. His tone straddled anger and relief, and Cyra shuddered in her chair.

"So what makes this woman the most deadly assassin on the continent?" Bressen asked, turning his attention to Serise. "How many has she killed?"

Serise shook her head. "No one knows for sure. It could be dozens, it could be hundreds. Anyone who's admitted to hiring her claims to have seen someone different. Until now, it was still possible The Raptor was just a myth, a story born from various accounts of assassinations stitched together to create the idea of some legendary killer, but it appears she does exist. That she's a masque makes sense. She must change her appearance every time she meets a potential client so no one can identify her."

"Unfortunately," Surgeon said, "That means no one knows for sure what her body count is. There may be people she's killed that we don't know about because the fool who hired her didn't realize who she was, or it may be that half of the people she's supposed to have killed were actually killed by others hoping to capitalize on her name and reputation."

"The only part of the lore that never seems to change," Serise said, "is that she made her first kill when she was sixteen. I don't know where that rumor came from, but it always seems to crop up when I hear The Raptor mentioned. Three hells, this is the first confirmation she's female. Many people assumed The Raptor was male, but the times I talked to someone who claimed to have met the assassin, they swore she was female."

"If this is The Raptor," Surgeon said, "we're likely the first people to ever see what she really looks like."

"I don't care what she looks like," Bressen snarled as his eyes flashed red in anger, "or even if she is this Raptor. She came into my home and inserted herself in our lives with every intention of killing my wife. She should be in Revenmyer already, if only so I'm not tempted to kill her myself with my bare hands."

Cyra stood up and went to her husband. She rested one hand on his hip and the other on his chest. She looked into his eyes, and Samhail knew she was speaking into his mind. The effect was immediate, and Bressen's body visibly relaxed under Cyra's touch.

No one could calm Bressen like Cyra. Ironically, the times the lord swung to extremes of fear and rage, it was because he perceived a threat to her. She was both the reason for his violence as well as the cure for it.

Samhail himself had felt burning anger and aggression on Cyra's behalf at times, but unlike Bressen, she couldn't – and wouldn't – touch him like that to ease his inner turmoil. Only brutality released his rage.

He recalled when Cyra and Raina, who was Cyra's lady's maid at the time, had snuck out of the Citadel and gone into the city to drink. They'd gotten into trouble on the docks when four men had attacked them, but luckily he and Bressen had been nearby at the time, and they'd arrived in time to prevent anything from happening.

Bressen had seen in the men's minds how they'd intended to take turns raping the women in every way they could. Samhail had managed to keep hold of his anger and disgust, but Bressen's rage had poured off him. Bressen had wanted to take the men apart piece by piece, but he'd decided instead to let Samhail take care of them.

Samhail had been pleased when Bressen turned the men over to him to punish. He'd wanted to hurt them, and if Bressen hadn't let him, he would've found another way to release his rage.

He'd spent all night with those men. Three of them anyway. The fourth had been pulled into the Scion River by a nixie and was granted the much quicker, easier end of drowning and being feasted on by the many carnivorous things living in the river waters.

The other three men had endured hours of agony at Samhail's hands. He'd started by breaking each of their fingers, one at a time. They'd been unable to move or scream under Bressen's mind control, but Samhail had seen the pain in their eyes, seen it in the tears that streamed down their faces as he beat them. Each shattered bone and dislocated joint had eased his fury just a little more, but it was castrating them that had finally released the last of his pent-up fury.

When Cyra had asked him later what he'd done to the men, he told her he'd left their pricks somewhat intact. That had been true. He hadn't touch their cocks, only removed their balls, and those he'd ground under the heel if his boots until they were a flattened, bloody mess.

Only then had he left the men. He'd sent Bressen a message to release his mental hold on them, and Samhail had returned to the Citadel to wash their blood off himself. He hadn't felt like being with a woman for days after that, which was odd because bloodlust usually went hand-in-hand with erotic lust for gargoyles.

Samhail looked at the woman on the couch. Under other conditions, he would've wanted to fuck her. The servant she'd been disguised as was pretty enough, but her true form was nothing short of exquisite. Her wavy hair was long and thick and a beautiful shade of reddish blonde. Her full lips were parted slightly in sleep, and long lashes covered eyes he was almost certain had been pale green. She was taller than most women, and her extra inches were divided pleasingly between her legs and torso.

It was hard to tell the exact shape of her body since the servant's dress she wore was rather shapeless and baggy, especially now that she'd shifted back into her true form.

Samhail couldn't deny the chase had aroused him. It had likely aroused Surgeon and Serise as well. Such was the nature of the gargoyle libido, where fighting often led to fucking.

Samhail glanced at his brother and sister, and indeed, both were also looking at the woman with a hungry gleam in their eyes.

"Samhail?"

Samhail shook himself mentally and searched for whoever had just called his name. His eyes locked with Bressen's.

"I'm sorry, what did you say?" Samhail asked.

"I asked if you're up for an interrogation tonight," the lord said.

"Interrogation?" Samhail repeated. The word didn't register in his mind for a moment. Then it clicked into place what Bressen wanted, and his eyes darted to the woman on the couch.

"What kind of interrogation?" Cyra asked warily. "What are you and Samhail going to do?"

"We're going to get answers out of her," Bressen answered. "And we're going to ensure she never has a chance to hurt you again."

Far from being relieved, Cyra's eyes widened in panic.

"You're going to hurt her," she said. She glanced at Samhail. "You're going to have Samhail hurt her."

Bressen didn't say anything, but his face hardened.

"You can't. You…" she trailed off, looking from Samhail to Bressen.

Bressen frowned at her. "Cyra, why are you concerned for her? She lied to you for weeks, pretended to be your lady's maid, and the whole time she was only waiting to kill you."

Bressen paused and his frown deepened. "Wait, how did she lie to you without you seeing it? Is that part of her masquing ability?"

Cyra considered this. "I don't think she ever did lie to me," Cyra said. "Not directly anyway. I thought her skin turned red briefly when we first met her and she said she was unpacking our trunks, but I don't recall seeing it any other time."

"What about when she told you her name was Leeda?" he asked. "If her name is Talyn, why didn't she glow when she gave you her name?"

Cyra thought again before a look of understanding passed over her.

"Because she didn't tell me her name was Leeda," Cyra answered. "I'm almost positive she said I could *call* her Leeda. It was a good evasion. She must know I have truth seeing powers."

"What about all the other times you spoke?" Bressen asked.

Cyra shrugged. "She avoided talking about herself. I was always trying to get her to open up, but she'd change the subject as soon as she could. The times I did get her to answer me, she was probably telling me at least a partial truth."

"We both looked into her mind when we first hired her. How did we not see who she was?" Bressen asked.

"I might have an answer to that," Axenus offered. "I remember hearing somewhere that masques can also mask their minds to a small degree. They can put up a kind of mental façade that reinforces who they claim to be if a mind wraith tries to read their thoughts. It's a bit different than a mind shield, and the façade will only stand up to a cursory examination, but I assume that's all you did? Just looked into her mind long enough to be sure her story held up?"

Bressen and Cyra looked at each other and nodded.

"Had you delved into her mind more intensely," Axenus went on, "you probably would've been able to see past the façade, but you had no reason at the time to suspect she was anyone but who she claimed to be, so you didn't."

Bressen pushed off his desk and swore under his breath. "Samhail, take her down to a holding cell, please," he said. He turned to Cyra. "Once we have her secured in the cell, you'll need to release your hold on her mind so she can answer questions."

"No," Cyra said, her voice tinged with desperation as she held onto his arm. "Please, Bressen, not tonight. You're too angry. You'll push her too hard. You'll…"

Cyra trailed off, and Bressen raised a brow at her. "I'll hurt her?" he suggested. "Yes, I plan to hurt her. At least until she tells me everything I want to know."

Cyra's face fell, and she stepped up to Bressen again to press her body into his. She laid one hand on this chest while the other trailed gently down the side of his face.

"Cyra," he said in gentle warning.

"Please, not tonight," she said more softly. "I don't want to lie in bed alone while you and Samhail are downstairs torturing this woman."

Bressen closed his eyes in frustration, but Samhail knew her plea had broken his resolve.

"You can question her when I'm at the vineyard and won't be around to hear…" Cyra trailed off, then swallowed. "She'll be here tomorrow."

Bressen sighed heavily. "Fine. The interrogation can wait a day."

He leaned in to kiss Cyra's temple before he turned to Samhail.

"Make sure she's locked in good," Bressen said to him.

Samhail nodded, strangely relieved he wouldn't have to help Bressen torture the assassin tonight. He'd never tortured a woman before, and the idea left him uneasy, which was ridiculous, especially given who this particular woman was. Still, he'd been given enough of a reprieve to get used to the idea before tomorrow.

Samhail went to the couch and lifted the unconscious woman into his arms. The scent of lemon verbena hit his nose, and he remembered the first time he'd smelled it about a week ago when he'd caught Leeda – Talyn – in the hall on the fourth floor. She'd told him she was looking for her lost necklace at the time, but that had been a lie. He'd need to remember to find out tomorrow why she'd really been there.

The interrogation would actually be easier if Cyra was there to tell them if Talyn was lying or not, but Cyra was obviously having trouble reconciling that the lady's maid she'd befriended – again – was a cold-blooded killer. Cyra might want to kill and maybe even torture Magdalene, but she wasn't ready to do that with this woman.

He couldn't decide if having Axenus there would help or hurt their cause. The merman was perceptive and might be almost as good as having Cyra there, but Samhail wasn't sure what Axenus's feelings on torture and interrogation were. He'd have to ask Bressen later.

Until then, The Raptor of Avril would spend the next few hours in a cage with her wings clipped.

Chapter 10

Talyn

Talyn knew he was there. She hadn't heard him enter, but she suddenly had the feeling of being watched before the whiff of leather told her exactly who it was. She waited almost a full minute to see if he'd say something before she spoke.

"How long do you plan to stand there staring at me before you say whatever it is you came down here to say?" she asked.

She'd been lying on the cot in the holding cell with her eyes closed, but she opened them and swung her legs off the side. It had been a couple hours at least since she'd been brought down here, and she hadn't expected any visitors, but Samhail's huge body now filled most of the doorway outside the bars of the cell.

Talyn looked him up and down. She remembered running her hand over that broad chest a few days ago. Gods above, he was so big, and so...

It was too bad he now wanted to choke the life out of her.

Talyn got off the cot and walked to the door of the cell. She made sure to stay well out of Samhail's long reach.

"Have you come to interrogate me?" she asked. "I imagine you have some questions of your own you want to ask before your lord takes another crack at me." She smiled sweetly at him, and his eyes darkened.

He reached through the bars, and Talyn took a quick step back. He smiled harshly at her jumpiness and tossed a pile of clothes on the floor at her feet. Keeping her eyes on him, Talyn reached down and picked up the pile. There was a pair of pants, a sweater, and some boots.

"What's this?" she asked.

"Cyra was afraid you'd be cold down here in that dress," Samhail said. "She thought you might be more comfortable in those."

His tone said he found the lady's concern misplaced.

Talyn sighed. She'd learned over the last couple weeks Cyra had a kind heart, but she hadn't expected anything like this given the circumstances. Then again, she hadn't expected her injuries to be healed either, but she'd woken with no pain and everything seemingly mended.

"You drew the short straw to bring them to me?" she asked.

"I volunteered."

Her eyes narrowed. "Why?"

"If I didn't, Cyra would've come, and I don't want her near you."

"No, we couldn't have that," Talyn said silkily. "We don't want her finding out what happened the other day, do we."

"She knows everything."

Talyn frowned. She'd underestimated these people at every turn, and it was starting to annoy her.

"There's something between you and the lady," she challenged.

Samhail huffed a laugh.

"You've clearly shared her bed," Talyn pressed, ignoring his huff.

"Cyra is a friend and the wife of my lord," he said. "That's all that's between us."

It was Talyn's turn to laugh.

"You don't seriously expect me to believe that," she said. "You all but admitted to me the other day you've fucked her. Remember?"

Samhail didn't answer, but his expression deepened into a scowl.

"What did you say when I suggested you'd done more than kiss her?" Talyn asked, pretending to try and recall. She put a hand on her chin and tapped her cheek in mock thought. "I believe you said something about Lord Bressen being there and you had his permission to touch her?"

Talyn watched his expression closely, but it didn't change. She shrugged and went over to her cot to toss the pants, sweater, and boots on top of it. She turned half toward the wall and pulled the dress she was wearing slowly over her head so she was naked. She'd had to discard the undergarment she was wearing earlier because it was too loose and kept slipping down. When she had her powers, her clothing adjusted with her body – a benefit of the magic – but this cell was lined with caronium.

Talyn listened for a reaction from Samhail as she stood there naked, but she didn't hear anything. There didn't seem to be an undergarment, so she just took her time as she stepped into the pants and pulled them leisurely up her legs, being sure to shimmy her hips and ass as she did so. The pants were a little tight and short, but there was enough stretch to the fabric that they were comfortable. She didn't think they could belong to Cyra. Talyn's legs were longer and her hips wider than the lady's, so Cyra's pants wouldn't have fit her this well.

Next, she pulled the sweater over her head, making sure to arch her back and thrust her breasts out before she turned back to the door. She half-expected to see Samhail had left since she hadn't heard anything while she was changing, but he was still there watching her.

"The only ways I can interpret what you said," Talyn went on as she sat on the cot to pull the boots on, "is that the lord either likes to watch you fuck his wife, or both of you fucked her together. So which was it?"

Talyn again watched Samhail closely as she spoke. She thought she saw the barest tick in his jaw, but she couldn't be sure. He'd learned to control his reactions better than the last time she'd seen him.

"You delivered your package," she said, annoyed. "Why are you still here if you have nothing to say?" She stood again and took a few steps toward the cell door.

"I wanted to see '*The Raptor*,'" he said, emphasizing the moniker with disdain. "I'm told you have quite a reputation, but I'm having trouble understanding why."

She raised a brow and crossed her arms. "Oh?" she said, her ire rising. "Would you have been more impressed if I'd actually managed to escape a syphon, a mind wraith, a merman, and three gargoyles with a few broken ribs, a dislocated shoulder, and limited access to my powers? Sorry to disappoint you, but even I have my limits. If anything, you should all be ashamed it took the six of you so long to subdue me."

He was glaring at her now. Good. She hoped she struck a nerve.

"Am I supposed to be impressed, knowing you were here to kill my friends?" he asked.

She noted he didn't correct her about the bodyguards being gargoyles.

"Not really," she said, "but while we're at it, I'm not so sure you lived up to your reputation either."

Samhail's brows flicked up. "You've heard of me?"

"Your name occasionally makes the rounds in certain circles," she said. "I have to say, I expected more. The wings are a neat trick, but your fighting skills leave something to be desired. I assume the lady healed your arm?" She made a show of looking at the spot where she'd stabbed him.

His expression became shadowed, and she noticed now the bruise on his jaw and the cuts on his face were gone.

"It was barely a scratch," he said.

"Your scream suggested otherwise."

Samhail crossed his arms. "That wasn't a scream. If you want to know what a scream sounds like, Bressen can come refresh your memory."

Talyn blanched at his words. She would've given anything not to react, not to show him how much Bressen's incursion had affected her, but the memory of the Lord of Hiraeth clawing into her mind was still too raw. Just the thought of it made her stomach roil, and she took an involuntary step back. To her surprise, Samhail's expression softened.

"I'm sorry," he said. "That was a low blow."

If his concern surprised her, his apology outright shocked her, but she waved a hand to dismiss it. "It was nothing I can't handle," she said, but her voice had gone a bit hoarse.

"I know what it feels like to have Bressen break into your mind," he said. "It's not pleasant."

'Not pleasant' was easily the understatement of the century, but that's not the part that caught her attention

"Why would he break into your mind?" she asked.

Samhail shrugged. "It's part of our training. He tries to break into my mind while we fight, and I try to keep him out. It helps me strengthen my mind shield, and it helps him work on breaking past my shield while he's also trying to keep me from breaking his jaw or his ribs."

Talyn's mouth fell open. "You let him try to break in on purpose?" she asked incredulously, and Samhail nodded.

"You're insane," she said.

He shrugged again. "So I've been told on occasion."

Talyn's mind shield had been tested once or twice over the years during her work, but she'd never thought to have a mind wraith purposely try to break through it for practice.

Most mind wraiths she'd encountered only had the rudimentary ability to read someone's mind. A few had the power to compel, but none had the level of power Lord Bressen did. He'd been about to will her to die when Cyra had stopped him. Talyn was sure of it, and she shuddered at how close she'd come to death.

"How long was I unconscious?" Talyn asked.

She'd woken up about an hour ago, and her internal clock was telling her it was still the same night, but she wanted to check.

"We moved you down here about three hours ago," he said.

"So it's around ten o'clock?" she asked.

He nodded, then frowned. "Why?"

"Just curious," she said. "What does the lord plan to do with me?"

"You'll likely go to Revenmyer after we question you tomorrow."

Talyn couldn't hide the jolt that jumped through her at his words. As if their 'questioning' wasn't bad enough, the thought of Revenmyer sent something crawling up her spine. Sandrian had spent twenty-five years in the prison, and even after being out for months, he still had a hollow look about his face. She didn't know what he'd experienced, but she didn't want to imagine whatever it was that made him look like that.

"On what charge?" she asked. "I wasn't aware changing my appearance was a crime."

"But assassination is," Samhail said, his face hardening again.

"And who have I supposedly assassinated?" she asked. "The lord and lady both seem alive and well to me."

"You *intended* to kill them," he said.

"Intentions aren't crimes," she said. "And trust me when I tell you that if I'd wanted to kill them, they'd be dead."

It was true enough. There were other times she could've killed them, just not as easily. Why she hadn't tried again, she didn't know.

"So why aren't they dead?" he asked, and she could almost feel the rage simmering below his calm exterior.

Talyn paused to consider that. "Maybe I just don't think Cyra deserves to die," she said finally. "The lady's grown on me."

He raised a brow. "And Bressen?"

"If arrogance were a crime, he'd be dead already," she said. "Don't get me wrong, I really want to stab him, but until tonight, I didn't have a good reason to kill him. I try not to kill people unless they deserve it."

"An assassin with a conscience?" Samhail scoffed.

"You're still alive, aren't you?" she said. "Surely you realize I could've slit your throat the other day while you were busy fantasizing about your lord's wife." Her tone was harsher than she'd meant, but she didn't let herself consider why.

"I wasn't fantasizing," he growled. "I was reacting to an aggressive seduction. That you looked like Cyra at the time was incidental."

Talyn's laugh echoed off the walls in the cell. "I can't tell if you actually believe that load of bullshit, or if you just expect *me* to believe it."

"I don't care what you believe."

"You wanted the lady," Talyn purred. "Just admit it."

His lips curled into a brutal smile. "And *you* wanted *me*. Just admit it."

Talyn's mouth fell open. She tried to deny his accusation, but she couldn't bring herself to say the words.

"You like to remind me of what I did that day," Samhail growled, "but as I recall, you pulled my cock out and were ready to swallow it before I stopped you. Did Sandrian pay you to do that as well, or would you have expected me to?" His eyes gleamed wickedly at her.

Talyn snapped her mouth shut and glared at him. "Sometimes you have to do unappealing things for the job," she spat back finally.

"Unappealing?" he scoffed. "You certainly looked like you were enjoying yourself. You were playing with fire, though. You don't realize how close I came to bending you over that table and shoving my cock inside you. What would you have done then? Would you have revealed yourself or stayed in Cyra's form and let me fuck you?"

His dark eyes flashed, and Talyn swallowed hard, trying to ignore the tightening between her legs. He was right. If there really was something between him and Cyra, she'd been playing with fire by teasing him.

She pushed out a long breath and came right up to the bars. If he wanted to grab her throat, let him try.

"Think what you want about why I did it," Talyn said, "but I learned some valuable information that day."

"Like what?"

"Like you're not as tough as you think you are."

"I'm not the only one."

"I guess we'll never know," she sneered. "You're too comfortable out there on the other side of these bars. Let's take *your* powers away and see what's left. I bet all that muscle just slows you down."

Her eyes locked with his. This close, she could see his pupils were midnight blue, not black as she'd first thought. Somehow she hadn't noticed that the other day.

Samhail turned and stalked off, and Talyn let out a long breath. She closed her eyes and leaned her forehead against the cool metal bars.

"Coward," she said softly to his retreating form before she pushed off the door and went to lay back down.

She'd just closed her eyes when the sound of the key turning in the lock made her shoot off the cot again. When she turned to face the door, it was open, and Samhail's form filled the entrance.

Chapter 11

Talyn

Nemesis take her. He'd actually called her bluff.

Fear and adrenaline mingled in Talyn's blood, making her lightheaded. When her wits finally returned, she began strategizing what in the three hells she was going to do now that she actually had what she'd been hoping for. She'd fought big men before, but no one like Samhail.

The caronium-lined cell would take Samhail's powers as it had hers, but one good swing of his fist would still end her. She wasn't sure now that goading him into this had been a good idea. A few minutes ago, getting him to open that door had been her main goal, and she'd even given herself a better-than-decent chance of taking him down if she got him to step in here, but her confidence disappeared along with the bars between them.

Talyn looked at the key in Samhail's hand and quickly memorized its contours. More than a decade of sneaking into places had made her good with locks, and knowing which key opened her cell was crucial. If she ever got her hands on the keyring, she wanted to be able to find the one she needed right away.

Samhail closed the cell door behind him, and Talyn flinched as it locked shut automatically. He turned back to her and held the keyring up as he walked into the cell a few steps.

"This is what you wanted, isn't it?" he asked. "To fight me without my powers? Well, here's your chance. Let's see if you can take these from me." He jingled the keys before he shoved them into the front pocket of his pants and waved his hand in a gesture that invited her to come at him.

Talyn smiled. Gods damn him. She never could resist a challenge.

"And if I do take them?" she asked. She reached behind her to start braiding her long hair quickly into a tight plait.

He shrugged. "If you can take them and get to the door in time, then I suppose you're free."

She raised a brow at him. "That simple?"

"That simple."

Talyn finished braiding her hair and looked around for something to tie it with. She remembered the dress she'd been wearing had a small ribbon tied into a bow in the front, and she picked up the garment to rip the bow off.

As she did, her foot kicked the pitcher of water she'd been given and it tipped over, soaking the hem of the dress.

"Dammit," she swore as she laid the dress on the cot and began to tie the end of her braid.

Samhail eyed her impatiently.

"You don't tie your hair back when you fight?" she asked as she finished tying the ribbon off.

"No," he said, and she was pleased to hear he sounded annoyed.

"So what are the rules?" she asked as she faced him.

He raised a brow. "You want rules?"

Talyn shrugged, then smiled. "No, I suppose not," she said as she reached for the dress again.

In a blink, she whipped the wet end of the dress at Samhail's face so it snapped toward his eyes. The water gave the fabric just enough weight that it stung more than it might otherwise have, and he grabbed at the garment as she'd hoped he would. She dove through his legs feet-first still holding the dress so he was yanked forward by his hold on it. She turned as she went under him so she was facing him, and she slammed her feet into the backs of his knees as hard as she could.

Samhail's legs buckled under him, and he fell forward, landing hard on his knees on the stone floor. Talyn was up and on him a second later.

Samhail grunted in pain as Talyn threw one of her knees into his back, then wrapped her elbow around his neck so her forearm pressed at the artery there.

It usually took Talyn about ten seconds to subdue someone like this, to make them black out, but she realized immediately that ten seconds was nine seconds more than Samhail was going to give her. She let out a strangled cry as he reached behind him to grab her arm with one hand and a handful of her sweater with the other, then yank her forward. She yelled as she went flying over his shoulder and hit the floor on her back. She coughed hard as the wind was knocked out of her, and she tried to sit up, but Samhail pushed her shoulders back down.

Anger surged through Talyn as she realized he wasn't actually trying to fight her, just subdue her. In a fight, he might've tried to hit her while she was down, but he seemed content to hold her shoulders to the floor. She should have been relieved he wasn't trying to hit her, since – at best – he would've knocked her unconscious with one blow, but his lack of effort just pissed her off.

Normally Talyn would've thrown her legs back behind her from this position to wrap them around his neck and pull him forward, but Samhail was too big for that. She'd never have enough leverage to pull him forward all the way, so instead she rolled back, planted her feet on his collarbone, and kicked out with both legs as hard as she could. It was just enough to push him off-balance and send him pitching backwards.

Talyn flung her legs forward again to spring onto her feet and into a crouch. She whirled around to face him but stayed low. Those long arms and huge hands of his were the most dangerous parts of him, so if nothing else, she needed to stay out of his reach.

Samhail picked himself up off the floor and rubbed the spot on his chest where she'd kicked him.

"Not bad," he said, "but you should've gone for my groin when you slid under me, not my knees. That would have given you more time."

She smiled at him. "Probably, but I'll admit I couldn't bring myself to risk damaging that work of art between your legs."

Samhail blinked at her in shock, and she took the opportunity to launch herself at him. She came in low and tried to kick his feet out from under him, but here again she'd underestimated his size. Her kick met his ankle, but it didn't budge his foot. She paused only a moment before she swung her elbow down toward his thigh instead.

Her elbow never connected. Samhail closed a hand around the braid at the nape of her neck, and Talyn cried out as he dragged her upward by her hair so she was looking into his eyes.

"That's why I never tie my hair back when I fight," he said as he held her against him. "It's too easy to grab when it's all tied together. I'd rather lose a few handfuls of it than give someone control of my head."

Talyn bared her teeth and growled at him. She'd never actually had to tie her hair back when she fought. She'd always been able to change her appearance before, so she usually went into a fight with short hair, and the issue had never come up. Braiding her hair back this time had seemed like the smart thing to do, but apparently not.

Fine. Lesson learned.

"Give up yet?" Samhail asked in amusement as she struggled to free herself from his grasp.

She stopped struggling and smiled at him again. "Why would I give up when I have you right where I want you?" she asked sweetly.

Talyn lifted one of her legs and stomped down as hard as she could on Samhail's foot even as she reached into his front pocket and pulled the keyring out of it. Samhail yelled out as his hand loosened on her hair. Talyn slipped the keyring onto her arm then reached up and grabbed Samhail's head with both hands. She pulled his head down as hard as she could onto her knee as she also brought it up to meet his face. A bone crunched, and she imagined his nose was now broken.

Samhail grunted as he dropped to one knee, and Talyn brought her elbow around as hard as she could into his temple. He fell forward onto the floor, and Talyn skirted around him toward the door. She didn't have more than a few seconds at most. She reached outside the cell and slipped the key into the lock. It clicked, and she started to pull the door open when Samhail's hand closed on her ankle in a vice-like grip.

She cried out and had just enough time to pull the key back out of the lock before she was yanked backward. Her feet came out from under her, and she barely managed to soften her fall before she hit the floor and was dragged back across it on her stomach.

Talyn thrashed and tried to kick out, but Samhail's second hand closed over her other ankle, and she could do nothing but let herself be hauled toward him. She tried to dig her fingers into the floor, but there was nothing for her to catch her grip on, so she tucked her arms under her body and held onto the keyring as tightly as she could. She had to do whatever she could to keep hold of it.

Talyn tried to crawl forward on her elbows when Samhail let go of her ankles, but she felt him above her, and a moment later his body came down on top of hers to pin her to the cold stone. His weight forced the air from her lungs, and she gasped as she tried to inhale. Above her, Samhail's weight eased just enough for her to take a breath, but that was as much leeway as he gave her. She realized instantly the futility of trying to struggle against him.

Talyn's body relaxed, and she eased her forehead down onto the stone as she tried to catch her breath.

"Playing possum now?" he asked.

She let out a frustrated laugh. "You use your size as a weapon. I don't have any way to fight that."

Actually, Talyn usually knew exactly how to use people's size against them in a fight, but there was apparently a threshold for that. Samhail was just too big and solid for most of her techniques to work on him.

Samhail lifted his weight briefly as he rolled her over so she was facing him, then he settled his body back down on top of her. Blood ran down his face from his nose, and she felt a surge of satisfaction that it was indeed broken. She also felt something hard against her hip, and her eyes widened. Gods above, did he have an erection?

"Would you prefer me to have used my fists?" he asked.

Talyn glared at him as she tried to ignore the evidence of his arousal pressed against her. She wasn't going to give him the satisfaction of admitting she was glad he hadn't hit her.

"We use what tools were given," he went on. "You seem to know that plenty well. You may not have an answer to my size, but I'll admit I underestimated you. It's not easy to break my bones, but you can now claim my nose."

She narrowed her eyes. He seemed almost like he was trying to console her, and that only annoyed her more.

They stared at each other for several seconds before he spoke again. "So…a work of art?" he asked, grinning down at her.

She growled and managed to get a hand up between them to push on his chest, but he didn't budge at all.

"I was trying to distract you, and it worked. Don't flatter yourself."

That was only partially the truth. It was an impressive cock that she really wouldn't mind touching again, but the Nemesis would take her before she admitted that to him.

"Yes," he said, "distraction seems to be *your* tool of choice."

Talyn met his eyes, and there was something in them that made her stomach flutter. She had to get out from under him before he decided to act on what she saw there.

"What would your lord and lady say if they came down here now to find us like this?" Talyn asked.

Samhail didn't say anything as he considered the question.

"For that matter," she went on before he could answer, "how do you plan to explain your broken nose to the lady when she heals you?"

Samhail shrugged. "Luckily she's not the only healer I know."

He reached down between them, and Talyn tensed, ready to fight, but he wasn't trying to touch her as she'd feared. His real intention was worse. She did fight then as she felt him tug at the keyring.

"No!" she yelled as he pried it from her grasp.

She bucked under him and tried to reach for the keys, but he grabbed her wrist with the same hand holding the keyring and pinned it to the floor. Talyn felt the ring press into her wrist as she continued to try and throw him off, but she finally gave up when she realized she wasn't going to move him.

"Sorry," he said, "but I have to take these back."

"You should probably get that nose looked at," she hissed at him. "It looks a bit crooked."

To her chagrin, he just chuckled, and a moment later his weight was off her as he picked himself up from the floor.

Talyn rolled to her feet, but she stayed in a crouch. She watched as he pulled the unlocked door the rest of the way open and walked out. He closed it shut behind him, and the lock clicked into place automatically. Only then did Talyn dare to stand up fully.

"Tell Cyra I said thank you for the clothes," she said as she dusted herself off. "Let's do this again sometime when I have my powers."

Samhail's eyes raked down her body and back up again, and she had a feeling he was remembering when she'd stripped naked. A quick glance at the front of his pants told her he was still aroused. If she'd known it was that easy to make him want her, she would've tried to seduce him again instead of fight him.

"I'd love to fight again, but I don't think it's going to happen," he said. "Regardless, you'll still lose. The porting is a neat trick, but it won't help you against me."

Talyn scoffed at that bit of arrogance, and her hands curled into fists at her sides. She didn't care how attractive he was. She was going to slit his throat the next time she saw him.

Samhail grinned at her as if he knew exactly what she was thinking, then he turned and walked down the hall to leave.

Talyn went to the bars to look after him and couldn't help smiling at the limp in his gait from the foot she'd stomped on. She let out a sigh of relief when he turned the corner, and his footsteps receded up the stairs.

She waited another few minutes before she dared to reach into the waistband of her pants where she'd tucked the key to her cell. She'd just barely managed to unhook the ring, slip the key off it, and re-hook it as Samhail had dragged her back along the floor. Then she'd shoved the key into her pants when he'd turned her over and prayed he wouldn't feel it there. If he'd decided to act on his arousal and touch her or undress her, he would've found it, but luckily he'd left her alone.

She only hoped no one would notice the keyring now contained one less key than it had before. At least not until tomorrow when she'd already be long gone.

Chapter 12

Samhail

Samhail swirled the amber contents of his glass before taking a sip. One of the downsides to being his size was that it took a lot of alcohol to get him drunk, so even four drinks in, he was barely feeling the effects.

He sat alone at the bar of the tavern. Men tended to drift away from him when he was in a room, and none of the women in the place had yet gotten the courage to approach him, although a busty blonde had been watching him since he came in. He'd considered making eye contact with her to let her know he was open to finding a companion for the night, but he'd talked himself out of it twice now. His cock might be in the mood, but he wasn't.

His broken nose and the bruise on his foot were healed already. A city the size of Solandis had a dozen or so healers living there, but only four – three now since Aramis's death – were perimortal.

Cyra was technically a healer as well, but she didn't work regularly as one, and there was no way in the three hells he would've gone to her to mend these particular injuries anyway. He would've had to explain how he'd been injured, and doing so was out of the question.

He deserved the broken nose and bruised foot. First, he'd been arrogant enough to let the assassin goad him into getting in the cell with her, then he'd been stupid enough to underestimate her fighting ability. Gargoyle bones didn't break easily, yet she'd managed to crack his nose.

Even worse, he'd nearly let her escape. A few more seconds, and she'd have made it out of that cell and locked him in without his powers.

He shuddered to think what Bressen would've done if the assassin had gotten out. Bressen was his oldest friend, but he didn't delude himself into thinking there wouldn't be consequences if he fucked up that royally.

He must've gone temporarily mad to have done something so reckless.

Actually, he'd been making stupid decisions for days now, all of them related to this woman. He needed to get his head on straight.

Samhail drained his glass and signaled for the barkeep to refill it. He took another sip when the glass was full again, but a moment later the tavern went unnaturally quiet, and his skin prickled.

He tensed, ready to move, but he swore under his breath when two large figures appeared next to him on either side and leaned on the bar. Neither of the twins was as big as him, but they were still imposing when they walked into a room. Patrons of the tavern were probably getting ready to flee if it looked like they were there to make trouble.

"Brother, fancy meeting you here," Serise purred to him.

"We were just out on the town looking for some fun, and here you are. How fortunate," Surgeon added.

Samhail didn't believe for a second they'd found him by chance.

"What the fuck do you want?" he asked.

"Just to catch up with our favorite older brother," Surgeon said.

"We missed you the last time the family gathered for some friendly competition," Serise said, sounding exaggeratedly dismayed.

"I was busy on a job and couldn't leave," Samhail said. "And don't let Soldier hear you call me your favorite, even if that's utter bullshit."

"If he thinks you're our favorite," Serise said with a smirk, "we're not the ones who'll need to watch our backs."

She was right. Soldier was more likely to attack Samhail himself over a remark like that than to hold the twins accountable for it. It wasn't that Soldier actually cared about being the favorite older brother. He cared about the competition. Samhail couldn't be the favorite anything if he was dead. Or at least maimed.

He didn't think Soldier would go so far as to kill him. At least he hoped not. Since the gargoyles had all but wiped themselves out centuries ago with infighting, new laws had been put into practice among their kind that levied steep penalties for killing each other unless there was a very good reason.

Grievous bodily injury was fine, but not death.

"Why are you really here?" Samhail asked them, although he suspected the point of their visit was just to annoy him.

"We were wondering how you figured out there was a masque in the house," Surgeon said. "Lady Cyra said you were the first one to suspect, but I can't see how the idea came to you, unless…"

Surgeon let the thought trail off as he contemplated the possibilities.

"Unless what?" Samhail snapped.

"Unless perhaps the assassin did something to make you suspect her presence," Serise supplied. "The look she gave you when Lady Cyra snuffed her power was rather intriguing. It seemed as though the two of you might have had occasion to…interact."

Samhail didn't respond other than to take another sip of his drink.

"You and Lady Cyra are clearly close," Surgeon said knowingly. "Is it possible the little assassin let you think you'd gotten closer to her than you really had?"

Samhail clenched his teeth, and a muscle began to tick wildly in his jaw. The twins were insane, but they weren't stupid, and they were closer to the truth than they realized. There was no way he was going to let them know it, though.

"Are you actually accusing me of trying to fuck the wife of the Nemesis Incarnate?" he said, turning to look Surgeon in the eye. "And the wife of my oldest friend at that?"

Bressen may be his friend, but the man was still a lord and a gods damned powerful perimortal. Moreover, it was no secret how Bressen felt about the woman he'd married. One would need to have a death wish to risk coming between him and Cyra.

"Then correct our misconception," Serise said. "How did you know there was a masque?"

Samhail took another sip of his drink before answering. He could tell them most of the truth.

"You're right. The assassin came to me looking like Cyra," he said. "She was fishing for information. I realized it wasn't Cyra when I remembered she was supposed to be at the vineyard that day. When you attacked me, I was coming to verify with Cyra that she hadn't been home on the day in question."

The twins were quiet as they eyed him, mulling this over.

"And the look the assassin gave you earlier tonight?" Serise asked.

"She was gloating that she tricked me into thinking she was Cyra."

The twins exchanged glances. "We don't believe you," they said together.

"I don't care what you believe," Samhail muttered, sipping his drink.

"We don't believe you," Serise went on as if he hadn't spoken, "because we feel it too."

He went still. He knew what she was talking about.

"Feel what?" he asked, playing dumb.

"That pull toward Lady Cyra," Surgeon said. "The desire to protect her, to…" He trailed off, searching for the right words. "You may not have fucked the lady, but you want to," he continued finally.

Samhail's hand was at his brother's throat in the next instant, and Surgeon's eyes bulged in his head as he tried to pry Samhail's fingers loose.

Samhail sensed Serise move, but he reached back and caught the wrist she swung toward him. He wrenched her hand back, and she cried out as she dropped the dagger she'd been aiming toward his shoulder. The twins had never been a match for him before, and nothing had changed.

"You'll mind your tongue when you talk about Cyra," Samhail said, his voice low and deadly.

The entire tavern had gone quiet again before chairs scraped on the floor as patrons decided they didn't want to see what happened next between the three giant warriors.

"Stop!" Samhail bellowed, and movement once again ceased. He looked around at the people crowded near the door who now weren't sure whether it was more dangerous to stay or to disobey him.

"Sit back down. We're leaving," Samhail told them all.

He let go of Surgeon and Serise, downed the remaining contents of his glass, and threw several gold coins onto the bar. The money was far more than was needed to cover his tab, but the rest was an apology to the tavern owner for disrupting his business tonight.

Samhail grabbed Surgeon and Serise by the collars of their shirts and dragged them through the tavern. Patrons scattered back away from the door to let them pass, and Samhail didn't stop until he'd pulled them outside into the street. He shoved them both forward and glared at them as they turned to face him.

"I don't care what you accuse me of," Samhail said, barely containing the rage in his voice, "but don't ever discuss Bressen or Cyra out in public in front of their people, especially not if you're going to spew outlandish theories. That's all they need is for someone to overhear you say something stupid and then have the gossip mills get ahold of it."

The twins had the decency to look contrite.

"You're right, of course, brother," Surgeon said hoarsely as he rubbed his throat. "It won't happen again."

"See it doesn't," Samhail snarled.

He turned to leave, but Serise's voice stopped him.

"You feel it though, don't you?" she asked, and there was a subtle plea in her tone. "The pull? You must."

Samhail was quiet for a long moment. He thought about trying to convince them they were imagining things, but it was better if they knew what they were feeling and why. He didn't need to tell them everything.

"You're feeling the divine imperative," he said finally.

They looked at him incredulously.

"What? How?" Surgeon asked.

"Cyra serves the Trinity. That's all you need to know. Bressen asked Father for your help because he knew the imperative would guide you. This isn't just another job. It's your sacred duty to protect Cyra."

The twins continued to stare at him. They might be angry no one had told them, but he knew they'd fulfill their obligation. The temples may have betrayed the gargoyles, but that didn't negate their responsibility to the Trinity, a responsibility every single gargoyle he knew took seriously, including all his siblings, despite their many faults.

"Is she a priestess?" Serise asked.

"Something like that," Samhail said.

He had no intention of explaining what Cyra really was, a Hand of the Gods, a servant to the Nemesis itself. That was information Bressen didn't want known, and his siblings didn't need to know it to do their jobs.

"But-"

"You don't need to know the details," Samhail cut in before his brother could ask anything else. "The only thing you need to know is that Cyra is very important to the Trinity, and it's your duty to make sure nothing happens to her."

Surgeon and Serise both straightened as if they now had a sense of the honor bestowed on them.

They weren't even close to the cadre Cyra deserved, but for the first time since he'd learned Bressen had taken them on, Samhail felt better. He might not fully trust Surgeon and Serise, but he knew they'd protect Cyra with their lives. They were being given the opportunity every gargoyle hoped for. The opportunity to be relevant again.

"And how does the little assassin figure into all this?" Surgeon asked.

"She works for Sandrian," Samhail said. "Beyond that, we're not entirely sure. Bressen will question her tomorrow to see what she knows."

He tamped down the prickle that walked its way up his spine at the thought of the interrogation that lay ahead. Bressen could break into Talyn's mind to find out what he wanted to know, but he risked making a person go mad when he attacked like he'd done earlier. It was a miracle he hadn't already shattered the woman's mind.

Instead, Bressen would enlist Samhail to help 'persuade' the assassin to talk, and for once Samhail wasn't looking forward to what he'd have to do. Normally he was more than happy to help Bressen deliver punishment or get people to talk, but those people were usually cowards content to prey on others who were weaker than them.

That wasn't Talyn. She was a skilled assassin who'd – incredibly – held her own against him in a fight without her powers. Granted he'd been going easy on her. He could've snapped her neck and been done with it at least half a dozen times during their fight in the cell, but she'd still given him more of a challenge than anyone in the recent past – aside from maybe Bressen and Maziren – and his gargoyle nature demanded he give her a grudging respect for that.

For fuck's sake, she'd jumped off a balcony to get away with only the hope her powers would return before she hit the ground. The woman had nerves of iron. It wouldn't be easy to torture her if she refused to talk, and he had a sinking feeling she'd refuse.

Samhail suddenly felt very tired.

"I'm going to bed," he told the twins as his wings flared out behind him, causing several people on the street to cry out in surprise and jump back away from him. "I assume you know what you need to do now?"

They nodded.

"And you know if you fail to keep Cyra safe, the wrath of the Trinity will be the least of your worries?"

They frowned at the underlying threat but nodded again.

Samhail launched himself into the air without another word and flew back toward Tide's End. The twins might not like him threatening them, but they knew he was serious about holding them accountable. Sandrian and Magdalene were still out there, most likely trying to come up with another strategy to get their hands on Cyra, and right now Surgeon and Serise were the first line of defense against them.

Samhail landed on the balcony of his rooms back at the manor a while later and undressed. He took a quick bath to get the grime off him from the – not one, but two – fights he'd had with the assassin today, then climbed into bed naked.

Now that he was in for the night, he regretted not trying to find a woman. A good fight always got his blood pumping and made him want to fuck, but that was especially true tonight after he'd fought the assassin.

Who was he kidding? He'd been semi-hard since she'd stripped in front of him. Gods above, he'd never seen legs like that on a woman, long and shapely with just enough muscle tone to give them a little extra curve in all the right places.

And her ass. He dreamed about watching his cock pump in and out between the beautiful swells of an ass like that. He hadn't gotten a good look at her breasts, but if the rest of Talyn was any indication, they were probably lush and firm.

He groaned. His cock was hard, and he'd need to take care of it, but it felt inappropriate to get himself off while thinking about the assassin who'd tried to kill his two friends. What was wrong with him?

Samhail shook some oil from a bottle on his night table into his palm and wrapped his hand around his cock. He stroked himself and tried to think about one of the women he'd seen in the tavern. In the past, he sometimes pictured Cyra when he did this, but he'd tried to get away from doing so as much as possible recently, especially after the incident in the great room. Cyra was no longer available to him, so it would only make things worse to think about her when he pleasured himself.

The memory of the blonde with large breasts he'd seen at the tavern came to him as he stroked himself in earnest. She would've been his first choice if Surgeon and Serise hadn't forced him to leave early, and he settled in to imagine himself fucking her. Within seconds, though, the blonde's hair had taken on a reddish tinge in his mind, and her blue eyes had turned pale green. Shapely legs wrapped around his hips as he thrust between them, and…

Samhail shook his head to banish the image of the assassin, but he couldn't get his mind to latch onto the face of the blonde from the tavern. Every time he tried, Talyn's face replaced hers, and it only made him harder as he pictured her lips around his cock, moving up and down his length as her beautiful green eyes looked up at him. For days now it had been Cyra in his mind as he remembered that time in the great room, but now it was Talyn he pictured there kneeling before him with her mouth wrapped around him.

"Fuck!" he gritted out as he stroked himself faster.

His hips arched off the bed of their own accord as he finally gave in to the fantasy. He could almost feel her lips and tongue on him, and he imagined bending her over the table in the great room to fuck her hard while she cried out his name.

Samhail clenched his teeth to stifle the roar of pleasure that surged up his throat as he came. Milky white jets of his seed spurted into the hand he held over the head of his cock as it pulsed against his fingers, releasing over and over again until he eased back against the bed, fully spent. He summoned a cloth to clean up, then settled in under the covers and hoped to the gods he'd be able to sleep now.

Tomorrow was going to be a long day. Talyn would undoubtedly mention during her interrogation what had happened in the cell, so there was little chance he'd get away without Bressen knowing about it.

Even worse was what he'd have to do to her. The thought of breaking her bones or cutting her smooth skin to get the answers Bressen wanted disturbed him more than he cared to admit. The screams he'd elicit tomorrow weren't the kinds of screams he wanted from her.

No, tomorrow they'd both regret that The Raptor of Avril had ever come to Tide's End.

Chapter 13

Talyn

Talyn waited until about two in the morning before she attempted her escape. She'd sharpened her internal clock over the years so she could always tell what time it was, and Samhail's confirmation that it had been around ten when he'd come to see her helped recalibrate that clock. She hadn't been sure if the incursion into her mind had knocked it off kilter, but it still seemed to be working.

A guard had come to check on her around one in the morning, and she'd pretended to be asleep, but no one had come down since. She also hadn't heard anything to indicate there was a guard on duty, but she still opened the door to her cell as quietly as possible before she crept out.

She breathed a sigh of relief when she felt her power return the moment she stepped away from the cell, and she ported a few feet just to be sure everything was fine. She looked around the corner to see if there were any guards, but there weren't.

Talyn went up the stairs quietly to the main level of the basement then ported through the locked door and made her way down the hall. She ascended the stairs to the first floor and, finding the door unlocked, opened it to peek into the house.

The door to the basement was between the kitchen and foyer, and she saw no one as she crept toward the front door. Under other circumstances she might've raided the kitchen for food or looked for weapons, but given who she'd be up against if she was caught, she couldn't take any chances. She needed to get as far from here as fast as possible, so she ported out the front door and slipped into the night.

There was no guard immediately outside the door, but Talyn knew from the time she'd been here that guards patrolled the grounds. Luckily, she knew more or less where their rounds took them.

She ported quickly from one concealed spot to another as she headed for the stables. The one thing she did need was a horse, or she'd never get far enough away by daybreak. Everything else – food, clothing, money – she could steal when she was far enough away. Her powers made her a great assassin and spy, but they also made her a competent thief as well.

A small house stood next to the barn, and she imagined that's where the hands and grooms lived, but no one was around when she slipped into the stables.

She looked in the first stall but immediately moved on. The size of the giant black warhorse in it told her exactly who it belonged to, and she had no desire to give Samhail any more reason to chase her down than he already had. A horse that size wasn't ideal anyway. She needed something small and fast.

Likewise, Talyn left the horse in the stall across from Samhail's alone as well. She knew the dappled gray mare was Cyra's, and although she was sure the horse was fast, stealing it all but guaranteed they'd come after her. Part of her was hoping they might cut their losses and assume they'd never see her again, although she knew better.

The next horse was a majestic, pure white stallion that she knew instinctively must belong to the lord. She would've put money on it that he owned a black horse like Samhail, but apparently that wasn't the case.

Talyn made her way toward the end of the stables. If she took a horse from the back, maybe it would buy her a little more time before they noticed she was missing.

She found a bay-colored gelding in one of the back stalls that looked like he might be fleet of foot. She opened the door to his stall and started to lead him out when a voice stopped her.

"Hey, who's there?"

Talyn had made it a point to get to know the stable hands, and she recognized the voice. She was standing on the other side of the horse so he couldn't see her, and she shifted quickly into one of the other hands.

"It's just me," she said, coming out from behind the horse wearing the body of a gangly young man with unruly light brown hair and a slightly crooked nose.

"Ben?" the hand asked. "What are you doing out here? Where are you going with Regent?"

"He was restless," Talyn answered. "I was going to give him some exercise to tire him out."

The hand looked at her for a long moment. Too long.

"Maybe we should ask Travis first," he said, and Talyn heard the unease in his voice.

Nemesis take the man. She'd hoped to avoid hurting anyone.

Talyn didn't give the man any further chance. She ported behind him and wrapped her arm around his neck to apply pressure to his artery.

It took the young man a second to realize where she'd gone and another second after that to figure out what she was doing. He wasted three more seconds grabbing at her arm to loosen her hold. By then, Talyn already had five of the ten seconds she needed to render him unconscious. She knew by the sixth second his vision was likely going fuzzy, and after the seventh, he'd started to sag against her. By the eighth second, he was already out, and she lowered his body to the ground.

Now she really had to move fast.

Talyn grabbed some rope, tied the man up, and dragged him into the newly vacated horse stall. She tore a piece of his shirt off and shoved it in his mouth, then secured the cloth with another piece of rope. She closed the door to the stall and led the horse, Regent apparently, over to where the tack hung on the wall. She saddled and bridled him as quickly as she could and led him out of the stable. She'd have to walk him carefully to the edge of the property and hope none of the guards saw them.

She'd learned once she could port with another person, but it took more out of her, and the larger the person, the more tiring it was. She didn't think she'd be able to port a horse without knocking herself out.

It turned out to be unnecessary anyway. Talyn made it far enough away from the house that she was out of the guards' line of sight, and she mounted up. She didn't hear an alarm raised, so she turned Regent southwest and spurred him into a gallop. She had to put as many miles between herself and Tide's End as she could by morning.

Talyn

Several hours later, Talyn knelt by a stream and cupped some of the cold, clear water into her hands to drink. Next to her, Regent lowered his head and drank as well.

The sun had crested the horizon a couple hours ago and light spilled through the trees of the forest. The stream was a peaceful enough place to stop, and it was covered overhead by the tree canopy. She'd pushed Regent hard and put a decent amount of distance between her and Tide's End, but she doubted she was far enough ahead that Samhail or one of the other gargoyles couldn't still catch up with her. She'd ridden out in the open to start, but now that the sun was up, she opted for a slower pace in the woods and hoped the tree cover would keep her hidden from anything flying above.

When she'd drunk her fill, Talyn sat down on the large boulder nearby and surveyed the forest around her. Sunlight dappled the ground and gave the place a cheery feeling. It looked like a good place to rest for a few minutes, and she dared to relax for a minute.

Until the shadow of something large passed overhead.

Talyn froze.

No, they couldn't have found her yet. She'd been moving slower than she would've in the open, but not that slow. She'd known someone would find her cell empty when they brought her breakfast, but she'd counted on at least another hour before they had any hope of catching up to her.

How fast did gargoyles fly anyway?

Talyn stood quickly and masqued her features into those of a girl she'd once seen in a tavern. She used the image any time she wanted to blend in with a crowd, since the girl had such plain features.

She tugged on Regent's reins to get him moving, but he nickered at having his drink interrupted, and her eyes flew up to scan what little sky she could see above the tree cover. She didn't move for two whole minutes as her heart thundered in her chest, but when nothing happened, Talyn again pulled the reins and started to lead the horse away.

The beat of leathery wings behind her made her whirl in time to see Samhail's huge form break through the trees and land hard a few feet from her. Her shriek was only partially for show as she backed away from him.

Of course it was Samhail who'd found her. Of course.

Somehow he looked even bigger than she remembered. He was wearing simple leather armor and had his two swords sheathed across his back. His splayed wings cast a shadow over her, and she shrank away from him as she imagined any woman alone in the woods might do. Her first instinct was to port, but that would give her away immediately. She had to at least try to pretend she was someone else.

"W-who are you? *What* are you?" Talyn cried, letting very real fear edge her words. "Please, don't hurt me!"

Samhail crossed his arms and gave her a look that said she wasn't fooling anyone.

"Stay back!" she said holding out her hands to ward him off.

"Even if a woman traveling alone in the woods this early in the morning wasn't suspicious," he said, "your horse has Bressen's crest on its saddle." He ticked his head briefly toward Regent.

Talyn glanced quickly at the saddle and saw he was right.

Gods damn it.

She thought about trying to convince him she was a servant out for a ride, but he wasn't going to buy it. She sighed and shifted back.

"I thought it would take you longer to find me," she said. "Do they serve breakfast to prisoners at dawn at the manor?"

"I'm just a fast flyer," Samhail said. "I also had a feeling you'd choose the tree cover over riding in the open."

She frowned. "And how did you know I'd do that?"

"Your powers are about subterfuge and concealment," he said. "I gambled you'd lean toward the familiar. You're not really an out-in-the-open type of person."

She narrowed her eyes at him. It was true, but she didn't think he'd meant that as a compliment.

"I assume you took the key to your cell off the ring sometime before I took it back from you?" he went on.

"If you say so," she said. She wasn't about to admit anything to him.

Samhail moved toward her, and she stepped back. He stopped.

"So is the plan to bring me back alive, or is my corpse good enough for Lord Bressen?" she asked.

"He left it up to me."

"And what's your preference?"

He shrugged. "I haven't decided yet."

"You seemed ready to kill me yesterday."

Samhail took another casual step toward her, and she took an answering step back. She pulled on Regent's reins to move the horse partially in front of her.

Samhail only stepped to the side so he had a more direct path to her. They could maneuver around each other like this all day.

Talyn sighed and stepped back to sit on the boulder near the stream once again. She crossed a leg over one knee and leaned back to eye him. She was still ready to move if he attacked, but Samhail raised a brow at her seemingly relaxed pose.

"So what do we do now?" she asked.

His brow rose higher. "What do you mean?"

"I mean," she said, "I have my powers back, and you have your powers, but as far as I can tell, we're at a stalemate here."

"How do you figure?"

She shrugged. "Well, I can try to run, but you can fly, so you'll only catch me."

He nodded.

"But when you catch me," she went on, "I'll just port out of your reach. We could end up doing that all day until one of us gets tired."

"I see your point," he said. He paused as if considering their options. "Should we fight again?" he suggested.

Talyn narrowed her eyes at the eagerness she thought she heard in his voice, but she shook her head.

"To be honest," she said, "the thought of fighting you for the third time in two days just sounds exhausting, powers or not. As you pointed out, my tendency is to attack by stealth. You're more of a…How would you put it? An out-in-the-open type of person. Our fighting styles aren't compatible."

"You didn't strike me as the type to give up so easily," he said, leaning against a tree. "I figured you'd welcome a rematch now that we're on more even footing."

"We're not exactly even," she said. "I don't have a weapon, and you have two. That's the very definition of uneven."

Talyn tensed as Samhail reached behind him and unsheathed his swords, but she was shocked when he tossed her one of the blades. She caught it deftly by the handle and looked up at him with incredulity as he pulled his wings back into his body.

"Better?" he asked.

Talyn's mouth hung open another few seconds before a slow smile curled onto her face.

"I could use another foot of height and probably two hundred pounds of muscle to really make us even," she said, "but I suppose this is a start. You actually want to fight?"

"I want you to stop whining about how you could beat me if you had your powers," he said. "You have your powers, and you have a sword. Now prove you can beat me."

Talyn scowled at him. "I don't whine. I only meant-"

She ported behind Samhail and brought the sword screaming down toward his shoulder. In an instant, Samhail was facing her, and his blade met hers in a clash of steel only inches from his body.

Talyn's eyes widened at the speed with which he'd turned and blocked her blow. Nemesis take her, he was fast. She'd seen him train before, but she still hadn't expected such speed from someone his size.

Talyn ported back a few feet to give herself room – both literally and figuratively – to reconsider her strategy.

Samhail tsked. "It's hardly sporting of you to attack me from behind."

"Not that it mattered," she pointed out. "It's really not fair you get to be both big and fast."

"Are you ever going to stop complain-"

His words were cut off as Talyn attacked again, slashing and thrusting her blade at his torso. She decided not to point out he also had the advantage of wearing armor and just tried to land a blow.

Her moves were exploratory, her hits designed not necessarily to kill, but to wound, to feel out his fighting style and abilities. They were moves that forced him to defend against her blade while also keeping her far enough out of his reach that she could retreat if necessary.

Once she had a better sense of his tendencies and weaknesses, then she'd exploit them. It was how she usually approached an opponent.

After several sequences of attacks, though, Talyn had yet to discern any obvious weaknesses in Samhail's fighting. He didn't seem to favor any one side of his body or any particular move. He also hadn't tried to attack her yet either, preferring instead to simply defend against her assaults.

His refusal to attack pissed her off, which she suspected was the point. He was trying to goad her into being reckless, and it was working.

Talyn feinted in one way, then spun the other. Samhail almost fell for it, but he'd apparently learned from his mistake on the balcony and corrected his course. Talyn still managed to spin around him, and she swung her blade up, barely missing his head.

They both stepped back to regroup, breathing a bit harder.

"Close, but you missed," Samhail said with the hint of a smile.

"Did I?" she asked, smirking at him. She held up a small lock of stark white hair a few inches long between her fingers.

Samhail's face darkened, but Talyn only winked at him and tucked the hair into the pocket of her pants. She'd shifted her own hair into a short bob to avoid a repeat of the incident in the cell, and she'd make herself bald if she needed to.

Talyn had hoped to draw Samhail into attacking by keeping his hair, but he didn't take the bait, so she ported behind him again, then immediately ported back to where she'd been and swung her sword. The move worked to the extent that Samhail did indeed turn after her first port, but he still blocked the blow she aimed for his back by thrusting his sword blindly behind him to stop her blade almost by sheer luck.

Talyn gaped for a moment, then slashed low for his ankles. He was facing her again by that time, and her blade once again sang off his. His other hand reached out to grab for her, but she did a backflip out of his reach, catching his chin with her foot as she went.

It was the only hit she'd managed to land on him so far.

Samhail grunted and brought his hand up to rub his jaw. He flexed it and eyed Talyn as she circled him.

"Not bad," he said.

"Are you planning to attack at any point or are you just going to stand there and fend off blows all day?" she asked, letting her annoyance show. He was trying to tire her out, she realized. "You were the one who wanted to fight me, so fight me."

"Are you sure that's what you want?" he asked as his mouth quirked.

"Yes!" she said, holding her sword ready.

His grin widened, and Talyn had a sinking feeling.

"Just remember," he said, "you asked for this."

Chapter 14

Talyn

Samhail's attack was lightning fast, and Talyn barely got her sword up to block the blows he rained down on her. Her hand vibrated from the ringing of his blade against hers, and for a few seconds she had the overwhelming feeling she'd made a huge mistake in challenging him as he forced her backward in the small clearing.

This is what she'd been hoping for, though. A fighter relying on defense rarely left themselves open, but when they went on the offensive, they eventually became vulnerable, and Samhail was no different.

Instead of blocking his next attack, Talyn dodged it by slipping under his swing to bring her sword up as she slid by. She felt the resistance as the tip of her blade scraped along his armor before she rolled forward and back onto her feet. She looked up quickly, not sure how far her blade had sunk in. She was both thrilled at finally getting a hit past him, but also strangely nervous to see what kind of damage she'd done.

Nemesis damn her. She wasn't going to be able to fight him if she was afraid to hurt him. Why in the three hells was she afraid to hurt him?

Samhail's eyes met hers before they both looked down at the cut that slashed his armor across the sternum. Talyn held her breath as he snaked a hand underneath it. When his hand came back, the tips of his fingers were just barely red with blood. It was a scratch, but she'd still managed to cut through the armor. Or rather, Samhail's own razor-sharp blade had.

"Nice move," Samhail said inclining his head in acknowledgement. He sounded genuinely impressed, then he twirled his sword in his hand. "My turn now."

Talyn's eyes went wide, and she whirled to the side as he attacked again, even faster than before. She just barely blocked four of his blows and had to port out of the way of his fifth and sixth swings, both of which would've drawn blood if she hadn't moved.

"How did you get the nickname 'The Raptor?'" Samhail asked with a growl of annoyance. "You're more like a gods damned hummingbird."

Talyn barked a laugh. "Hummingbirds are vicious, aggressive little birds," she said. "I'll take that as a compliment."

She ported to his side and came around swinging, but Samhail had already turned, and she abandoned her swing when she saw his hand out in front of him instead of his sword. She realized just in time what he intended to do and threw herself out of the way of the forcefield that reverberated by her. Unfortunately, she didn't have time to get out of the way of the second one, and she was thrown back several feet as it hit her, causing her teeth to jar together.

Talyn's sword came loose from her hand, and when she looked up, it lay on the ground between them. If she tried to go for it, he'd hit her with another forcefield, so she did something insane instead.

She pretended to go for her sword, but as soon as she saw him move, she ported right next to him and crouched down to grab the dagger she knew was in his boot before she ported away again.

Samhail pivoted to face her and stared at the dagger in her hand.

"How did you know I had that?" he asked.

"Lucky guess."

In truth, she'd trained herself to notice the signs of hidden weapons, but it also wasn't hard to guess a warrior like him probably had something in his boot. When she was dressed for a fight, she normally carried several small daggers in her own boots.

"Be careful with Fred," Samhail said. "I'll want him back."

Talyn blinked at him in shock. "You…named your dagger Fred?" she asked incredulously.

Samhail shrugged one shoulder. "It's a long story."

"Please tell me you didn't name your swords as well," she said. "You didn't strike me as the type to name your weaponry."

Her eyes dipped to his groin briefly. In her experience, only men who were compensating for other inadequacies named their weapons, and she knew firsthand Samhail was exceptionally…adequate.

When Samhail didn't answer, she rolled her eyes. "You did name them, didn't you."

Samhail held out a hand to summon the sword she'd left on the ground so he now had both again.

"Let's just say they only acquired their names recently and somewhat by accident," he said.

Her brows flew up. "How does one *accidentally* name their swords?"

Again he remained quiet.

"Alright," she said, "but now I need to know what their names are."

Samhail held up the blade in his right hand. "This is Righteous Hand." He raised the sword in his left. "And this is Lefteous Hand."

Talyn stared at him. "Sweet gods," she whispered. "You didn't."

Samhail cocked his head in acquiescence, and a second later he lunged for her again, both blades swinging.

Talyn ported in low and swiped for his leg. She felt the resistance of the blade as it sliced across his thigh and heard his grunt of pain, but any elation she might've felt at drawing blood was dampened by the sharp sting in her own arm as Samhail's sword drew across her bicep.

Talyn cried out and gripped her hand over the wound as blood welled up between her fingers.

Ridiculous names aside, the blades were sharper than anything she'd ever seen, and the man wielding them was nothing short of deadly.

And her only defense against him was a knife named Fred.

Talyn groaned inwardly as she clutched at her arm. She wasn't used to fights lasting this long. She usually had only to slit someone's throat and be done with it. She still considered herself to be in pretty good shape stamina-wise, but fighting Samhail was exhausting. Not to mention, this was her third fight with him in less than twenty-four hours, and she'd barely slept. She might be able to get in a few more lucky blows, but she was at the point where she could admit she was outmatched.

Not that giving up was an option either. She couldn't let Samhail bring her back to Solandis or Lord Bressen would throw her in Revenmyer, and that was a fate she'd avoid at all costs. If he didn't kill her, of course.

She'd managed to wound Samhail twice now. The only thing she could do was try to wound him again badly enough that he'd have to go back to Solandis to be healed, and then she'd just ride as fast as she could to get as far away from him as possible.

Talyn scanned Samhail's armor looking for places he was vulnerable, but he saw her do it.

"Looking for your killing blow?" he asked, his voice deceptively light.

She met his eyes, apology written on her face. "I can't let you take me back to Solandis."

She attacked then, no longer worried about hurting him. She'd never get close enough to kill him, but she had to wound him good if she was going to get away. She swiped out with the dagger before porting around him to slash again. She struck quickly each time, swinging once then porting around him so he was turning in a circle to keep up with her. If nothing else, maybe she could make him dizzy.

To his credit, Samhail still managed to block each blow she leveled at him, even if just barely. Faster and faster Talyn attacked, trying to find an opening. Her power was beginning to wane from too much porting. She needed to end this, or she wouldn't have enough left to hold him off.

She saw her opportunity on the next swing where he'd left himself open on one side, and she swung out with her dagger.

She realized it was a trap a moment too late. She tried to pull up, but her momentum carried her right into him. He dropped his swords and one of his hands wrapped around her throat while he grabbed her dagger-wielding wrist in his other and wrenched it behind her back. She cried out and dropped the dagger.

She ported once more, but she didn't go far enough, and Samhail found her wrist again to pull her back. One steely arm wrapped around her waist and crushed her against his body while the other closed partially around her throat again. His thumb tipped her chin up so she was looking into his dark eyes. Paradoxically, they shone bright with adrenaline.

Talyn opened her mouth, whether it was to concede the fight or tell him to go to hell, she wasn't sure, but she never got the chance. Samhail's mouth crashed into hers for a punishing kiss, and she jolted against him, first in surprise and then again at the heat that shot through her veins with the feel of his lips on hers.

Samhail's kiss was brutal and hungry, an extension of the battle they'd been having, and the only thing Talyn could do was sag against him as his mouth ravaged hers.

She moaned unwillingly as his tongue invaded her mouth, attacking her own. Her lips would be swollen when he was done with her, and she might even have a bruise on her neck, but she didn't care. The fight had stirred something in her, and she'd lost the will to resist.

Samhail's kiss softened when he realized she was no longer fighting him. It was still fierce but no longer as violent. It ceased to be a conquest and became a claiming as his lips roved over hers, his tongue now more exploring than demanding. His hand moved from her throat to the back of her head, and his fingers threaded through her hair as he let go of her waist. A moment later, that hand ran down her arm, raising gooseflesh.

Samhail gripped her hair even tighter, and Talyn moaned again as she pressed herself shamelessly against his solid, unyielding body.

His hand left her arm for a moment, but it was back on her wrist a couple seconds later, and something about the touch set off alarm bells in her head. Her eyes flew open as she heard a click and felt hard metal close around her wrist before her power winked out.

Talyn's hair fell down her back again as the loss of her power cut off the shift that kept it short, and she jerked her mouth from Samhail's to look down at the caronium cuff now clamped tightly on her.

"You fucking bastard!" she yelled as she pushed away from him.

"I suppose it's too much to hope you'll come quietly?" he asked.

Talyn let out a mirthless laugh before she launched herself at him. She swung at him with her fist – for all the good it would do – but he caught her hand. Then she sent her knee toward his groin.

He just barely turned in time so her knee sunk into his thigh instead, and he yanked her around to pull her against him. Arms like iron wrapped around her, pinning her back to his chest, but Talyn struggled ferociously against him long after it was apparent there was no way to escape his hold.

It was several minutes before she finally stilled against him, breathing hard. She wanted to scream at how stupid she'd been to let her guard down all because he'd kissed her. That kiss was the kind of devious, underhanded, sneaky move that…well, that she'd use.

Nemesis fucking take her.

"For what it's worth," Samhail said, leaning in so his warm breath caressed her cheek, "The kiss wasn't planned. It's rare I find such a worthy opponent and I…got caught up in the moment."

He brushed his lips against her ear, and Talyn jerked her head away.

"I hope you're a light sleeper," she said, her voice low and cold, "because one of these days you'll wake up with my blade against your throat, and I'm going to enjoy the look on your face when I slit you open."

His chest rose and fell heavily against her back as he sighed deeply. "I suppose I deserve that."

"You haven't gotten what you deserve yet," she spat, "but you will."

"At least you learned from your mistake. I notice you went for my groin this time. No more concern for the work of art between my legs?"

Talyn screamed and renewed her struggles against him. He tightened his hold on her, and she grunted as it became hard to breathe. She went still again, and his arms loosened a fraction.

"Enjoy your cock while you still have it," she growled. "I'll cut it off if I ever get the chance."

He had the nerve to chuckle, which only enraged her more. She tried to throw her head back into him, but he was so tall her skull only found his collarbone instead of his face.

"It's time to get you back to Tide's End," he said.

Talyn's stomach dropped, and she shook her head frantically as she renewed her efforts to pull away from him.

"No, please!" she said, panic in her voice. "I can't go to Revenmyer. Just…Just let me go, and I promise I'll never come near any of you again."

"Even if I trusted you to stay away, I can't do that," he said.

He eased his arms from around her but only to shift his grip to her elbow so he could pull her toward the horse. She dug in her feet, but it did nothing against his strength. She stumbled forward after him, unable to plant herself.

"What if I can give you Sandrian?" she said desperately.

Samhail stopped and turned toward her. "I'm listening."

"I know how to get to Sandrian," she said. "I can hand him to you if you let me go."

Samhail scoffed and pulled her toward the horse again. "And I'm supposed to believe you'll bring him to me if I let you go?"

"I will. I promise," she said still trying – and failing – to keep herself from being pulled along in his wake.

"Unfortunately, you're not high up on the list of people I trust right now, so I'll have to pass on that offer."

"Fine, don't let me go," she said. "Let me bring you to him."

Samhail stopped to face her again.

"Where is he?" he asked. "Bring him here."

Talyn shook her head. "He's back in Rowe, and he won't cross the border, but he expects updates from me. Come to Rowe with me, and I'll arrange for him to meet us."

"And why would you do that?" he asked. "He hired you. Why would you betray him?"

"Sandrian misrepresented himself to me," she said. "He lied to me about the Lord and Lady of Hiraeth. I only knew Lord Bressen by his reputation as the Nemesis Incarnate, and Sandrian used that to paint himself as the victim of Lord Bressen's cruelty. He led me to believe Lady

Cyra was dangerous as well, that she was just as much of a monster as her husband. It's how Sandrian convinced me to take the job."

That and the ridiculous amount of money he'd offered her.

"And you don't think they're monsters anymore?" Samhail asked.

"Don't get me wrong," she said. "Lord Bressen is an arrogant prick, and I thought for a while he was abusing his wife, but then I found out you were the one giving her all those bruises."

Samhail looked surprised for a moment before his face eased. "Ah, her training."

"The point is, yes, there was a time or two I was tempted to kill Lord Bressen," she said, "but purely for personal reasons. The more I saw of him, the more I realized he wasn't the cold, cruel monster Sandrian made him out to be, and Cyra certainly isn't evil either. Sandrian used me to get information about them, and then he kidnapped an innocent man to lure them out so he could get the items they retrieved from the ship."

Samhail's expression darkened. "You're the reason Sandrian knew about the collar and rings," he said. "We suspected as much."

Talyn sighed. "Yes."

"You're the reason my friend, my brother, almost died," he went on. "You're the reason Cyra's father is dead."

His tone made Talyn pull back despite his hold on her arm.

"I didn't know what he planned to do," she said. "I swear. You have no idea how much I regret what happened to Cyra's father."

She hadn't meant to admit the last part, and she didn't know why she'd done so now.

Samhail yanked her up against his chest. He grabbed her by her upper arms, and she winced as his fingers bit into her flesh. She'd have bruises there later.

His eyes flashed with anger, but Talyn didn't turn her gaze from his. He stared at her for a long time, and his head dipped briefly in a way that made her think he meant to kiss her again, but he didn't.

"Here's how this is going to work," he said finally. "You and I will travel together to Rowe where you'll send Sandrian a message to lure him out of hiding. Then when he shows himself, I'll rip his head off."

Talyn blinked at him. "I suppose that's one way to do it. We won't be bringing him back to Revenmyer then?"

"He lost any chance of that happening when he kidnapped Jasper and got Cyra's father killed," he said. "I'm not giving him a chance to hurt anyone else I care about."

Talyn nodded. That was something she understood.

"What will you tell Lord Bressen?" she asked.

"As little as possible," he said. "He needs deniability, so he can't know we're going into Rowe. He can't go in himself, or it would be considered a hostile action, an invasion. I may be his friend, but I'm a mercenary by trade, and I'm free to cross borders for my work as needed, especially to retrieve a fugitive. As long as Bressen doesn't know what we're doing, he can't be accused of acting on behalf of the state in anything that might stoke tensions between Thasia and Rowe."

Samhail let go of her and reached into the pocket of his pants to pull out a message leaf and a small pen. He wrote something on the paper, hesitated a moment, then held it up between his middle and forefingers before the paper vanished in a puff of smoke.

"Here are the rules," Samhail said, turning back to Talyn and shoving the pen back in his pocket. "First and foremost, you're my prisoner. You'll do what I say, when I say it. If you try to escape or attack me, not only will you regret it, but the deal is off."

"Do what you say?" she asked carefully. "What does that mean?"

Samhail narrowed his eyes before he understood her concern.

"I won't order you to fuck me if that's what you're worried about."

Talyn thought a moment. "Anything else?"

"The caronium cuff stays on at all times," he said. "I'll get my own horse in the next town we come to, since the one you stole is a bit small for me, let alone both of us."

Talyn glanced at the gelding she'd chosen specifically because he'd looked light and fast. Regent perked his head up as if he knew they were talking about him, and Talyn could've sworn there was relief in the animal's eyes.

A message leaf appeared in a puff of smoke in front of Samhail's face, and he snatched it out of the air. His brows pinched as he read it, and he was quiet for several seconds. Finally, he pulled out his pen, wrote something on the back of the leaf and sent it on its way again.

"Just remember, I can fly faster than that horse can run," Samhail said, turning his attention back to her. "The first time you make me regret giving you this chance, we head straight back to Solandis, and you can take your chances with Bressen and Revenmyer. Is that understood?"

"Understood," she said.

"Then let's get going. There should be a town about five miles from here where we can get breakfast and another horse."

Talyn swallowed as she thought about what she'd just agreed to. She let her gaze roam over Samhail's chiseled jawline, his long white hair, and the heavily muscled body built for fighting. That body was probably also incredible in bed, and under other circumstances she would've jumped at the chance to find out, but she was his prisoner now.

The feel of Samhail's mouth crashing into hers came back to her, and she absently touched her puffy lips. The effect of his kiss, brutal and punishing as it was, had been devastating to her sensibilities.

Samhail was dangerous, and not just as a fighter or as her captor. He was dangerous to her ability to think straight and make smart decisions. He was dangerous to her body, which seemed to gravitate toward him when he was close by, and she'd just agreed to spend several days alone with him traveling to Rowe.

Talyn added one more item to the list of regrets she now had about taking this job.

Tandem Read: Go to *Nemesis Rising* (Bk 4), Chapter 1

Chapter 15

Talyn

It was mid-morning when Talyn and Samhail entered the nearby village and asked the first person they saw to direct them to the local stable. Samhail wouldn't let Talyn ride the horse she'd taken. He could've flown while she rode, but he didn't trust her to be more than an arm's reach away, even if he could fly faster than she could ride.

So they'd walked.

In silence.

For miles.

Samhail didn't strike Talyn as the kind of man who chatted, so she wasn't surprised their journey had been so quiet, but she couldn't help feeling there was something else beneath his silence.

Hatred most likely. She'd put him in an extremely vulnerable position the other day and had tricked him into revealing a very personal secret. She didn't think he took too kindly to that. Not to mention the fact that she'd been at Tide's End to kill his two best friends.

In truth, she was shocked he'd agreed to her deal, and even more shocked he'd let her live long enough to make it.

"Is anyone here?" Samhail called as they approached the house next to the stables on the outskirts of town where they'd been directed.

A man came out, and his eyes widened as he saw Samhail. To his credit, he didn't run.

"Can I help you?" the man asked warily.

"I need a horse," Samhail said. "A large one."

The man opened and closed his mouth, seeming to search for something to say. "For you?" the man finally ventured. "I'm not sure I have one big enough."

"What about him?" Samhail asked, pointing out into the pasture where a giant dark gray stallion with pale gray dappling near his shoulders stood grazing.

"He…he's really more of a draft horse," the man said. "I rode him once bareback, but I'm not sure he'll take a saddle. Three hells, I'm not sure I even have one big enough for him."

Samhail fished a small bag of coins out of his pocket and dropped several gold ones into the man's hand.

"Let's find out for sure," he said as the man's eyes widened.

Two hours later, Samhail sat atop the large horse. The animal had accepted a saddle and bridle easily enough, but the biggest saddle the stable owner had didn't quite fit around the horse's thick body. They'd had to enlist a leather worker in town to craft an extension for the saddle's girth so it could be fastened.

Samhail nudged the horse with his heels, and after a moment's hesitation, the animal moved forward in a slow walk. Samhail dug his heels in more, and the stallion picked up its pace.

The horse was a docile beast that wasn't inclined to be energetic, but it obeyed Samhail's commands willingly enough, and he soon had it galloping around the yard.

"Thank you for your help," Samhail said to the man as he reined the horse up in front of him.

The man nodded his head. "Anytime," he said. "Always happy to help out Lord Bressen's man."

They'd made introductions earlier, and Samhail had told the stable owner he was on an assignment for the lord, which was only partially true.

"It's time to go," Samhail said to Talyn as he dismounted from the horse. "This took longer than I would've liked, and I want to put in some miles before it gets dark."

Talyn only glared at him as he came over to release her from where he'd tied her hands to a nearby fencepost. She'd been free most of the day as they went shopping for supplies in town, but when it came time to try out the horse – who was apparently named Guster – he didn't trust her to be alone with the stable owner, so he'd tied her to the fence.

Talyn didn't say anything to him as she headed for her horse.

"You'll ride with me the rest of the day," he said, stopping her.

She looked at him incredulously. "You can't be serious. We have two horses now, but you want me to ride with you on that monstrosity?"

"You'll ride with me until I can trust you enough to ride alone," he said. He leaned toward Guster and patted the horse. "Don't listen to her. You're perfect," he told the beast.

Talyn only blinked at him. She looked at the stable owner, but he was eyeing her wrist with the caronium cuff on it. He'd been friendly to her until Samhail had tied her to the fence.

"No," Talyn said, shaking her head. "It's ridiculous for us to share a horse when we have two."

"Get up there now, or I'll throw you over the front, and you can ride that way."

Talyn crossed her arms and glared at him again, but she uncrossed them quickly and stepped back when he started toward her.

"Fine! Fine!" she said, holding out her hands to ward him off. "I'll get on the horse."

He stepped to the side so she could pass, and she hauled herself up into the saddle. She was annoyed to find her legs didn't reach the stirrups once she was up, not that she would've been allowed to use them anyway.

Samhail tied the reins of Talyn's horse to the saddle of his own, then mounted up behind her. She ground her teeth at the feel of his hard muscles pressed up against her. The weather had turned milder this week, but it was still chilly, and she found it infuriating that her body ached to lean back into his warmth as they set off. Talyn now had a cloak, which Samhail had bought her earlier, but his body heat seemed to penetrate even that.

Talyn tried to sit forward, but it was nearly impossible to get away from him. His arms caged her in on either side, and it seemed like he only leaned further forward every time she tried to pull away from him. Finally, she gave up and let herself lean back against him, but she was too aware of his body to be able to sit still.

He might hate her, and she might find him to be an arrogant, infuriating prick, but none of that mattered to her body. She didn't have to like him to fuck him. Three hells, some of the best sex she'd ever had was with a man she'd absolutely loathed. She'd been in Bader working for a client who'd hired her to kill his business rival, and she'd eagerly taken the job when she'd learned the rival had been using children for labor, keeping them under horrendous conditions and paying them far below what an adult might be paid.

The man who'd hired her hadn't cared about the children. He'd almost considered using them himself, but he'd decided they weren't worth the trouble and that the easier solution was just to kill his rival.

Talyn couldn't stand the man who'd hired her, but he'd been unfairly attractive, and she hadn't been with anyone in some time, so she'd fucked him after the job was done. The sex had been uninhibited and raw. She'd been riding her blood lust, and her employer had been celebrating the demise of his rival. He'd let her tie him to his bed, and she'd ridden him until they'd both exploded with ecstasy. Then she'd left him tied there naked with her undergarment shoved into his mouth, and she'd told his servants on her way out he didn't want to be disturbed.

Talyn smiled at the memory as she tried to settle in for the journey.

An hour later, however, she was still fidgeting. She was all too aware of Samhail's thighs pressed to the backs of hers, and that leather and earth scent of his had wrapped itself around her brain and wouldn't let her think of anything else. Her eyes fixed on the way his hands held the reins, and the direction her thoughts took as she looked at them left her aching at her core. She was also almost certain the lump she felt against her tailbone was his erection.

Talyn shifted again and tried to decide if she felt the lump twitch.

"Stop moving," Samhail growled.

"I can't get comfortable," she said. "Just let me ride the other horse."

"No."

Talyn groaned and shifted again.

"It's not too late to throw you over the front of this saddle," he said.

"I don't know why you think that's going to help anything."

"Maybe you'll stop moving if I slap your ass every time you do."

Talyn's mouth dropped open, but she clamped it shut again. She wouldn't take the bait, but fine. If he was going to be stubborn, she'd make him regret riding like this.

She leaned back against Samhail to nestle into his chest, and she smiled to feel his body tense against hers. She ground her ass slowly into his groin, and the lump against her backside seemed to get harder.

Talyn gasped as Samhail's hand shot up and closed around her throat, not hard enough to cut off her air, but hard enough that she understood the warning in it.

"*Don't* do that," he snarled in her ear, each word clipped.

She grinned and ground into him harder, then moaned softly for good measure.

Samhail jerked on the reins to stop the horse and tightened his hold on her throat.

"What the fuck are you doing?" he asked, his voice full of fury.

"Trying to convince you I should ride my own horse," she said hoarsely against the palm of his hand.

"No, what you're doing is playing with fire," he shot back. "You're alone with a man you don't know, trying to arouse him for spite. You may be the most feared assassin in Rowe, but if I decided to throw you on the ground and fuck you, you wouldn't be able to stop me."

"On the continent," Talyn said.

"What?"

"The most feared assassin on the continent," she corrected. "Not just in Rowe."

"Fine, on the continent," he said. "Either way, you'd be at my mercy if I decided to fuck you raw."

Talyn paused, not sure why that thought aroused her rather than frightened her. She almost told him as much, but she said instead, "You won't do that." She didn't know how she knew that, but she knew.

"Wouldn't I?" he asked menacingly. "You were the one who started this a few days ago. Can you blame me for wanting to finish it?"

Talyn froze, suddenly unsure of her assessment of him. No, she couldn't blame him for wanting to finish it, but she didn't want to think he was the kind of man who'd take a woman unwillingly.

But he was bluffing. She knew he was. Wasn't he?

"You won't," she said softly.

"And how do you know that?"

His voice was labored in her ear, and she felt him trying to get control. Her eyes widened. He really did want to fuck her, she realized. Badly.

Talyn swallowed against the hand still wrapped around her throat.

"If you were the kind of man who'd take a woman against her will, you wouldn't be trying so hard to warn me about the consequences of teasing you. You'd have just fucked me already," she said. "You may be dangerous and deadly, but you're not the type of man to violate a woman."

"Like you violated *me*?" he asked.

His voice had grown quiet, and Talyn went still against him.

"You came to me looking like another woman, someone I trusted," he said. "You sat on my lap and kissed me, then pulled my cock out to take me into your mouth, all looking like her. You violated us both."

His voice grew sharper as he spoke, and Talyn tried to swallow against the hand on her throat as it tightened, nearly cutting off her air.

"You're right," she gasped out. "What I did was wrong."

In truth, she did regret what she'd done, insofar as it was an abuse of his trust. She didn't necessarily regret kissing him or touching him, but she did regret that she'd done it looking like Cyra. She could see why he felt violated, and there was a part of her that wished she hadn't done it.

Talyn had always lived her life as someone else. It was common for her to appear to others as people they knew, for her to insert herself into their lives and pretend to be their friend or loved one so she could get close to them and kill them. Gods, she'd even come to a man looking like his wife once and let him fuck her before she killed him.

She'd done a lot she wasn't especially proud of, but what she'd done to Samhail made her feel truly ashamed for the first time in a while. She didn't know why this time was different than all the others, but it was.

The pressure of his hand on her throat eased a little, and Talyn felt the breath Samhail pushed out against her cheek.

"This isn't going to work," he said finally. "I don't trust you with your own horse, and I won't last much longer with you grinding against me. I do have my limits. I have to take you back to Solandis."

Talyn's body turned to ice, and she tried to shake her head as best she could with the hold he had on her throat.

"No, please," she croaked out. "Please. I'll behave myself. I promise."

Samhail

Threatening to take Talyn back to Solandis had been only partially a bluff. Samhail was prepared to do it if he needed to, but he suspected just the threat of going back to face Bressen and Revenmyer would be enough to set her straight.

She was testing her limits. She'd been living at Tide's End long enough to observe them all and realize they weren't bad people. In particular, she'd watched him with Cyra and knew he was capable of caring for another person. She'd seen a side of him no one outside of Bressen, Cyra, and perhaps Axenus had ever seen, and it made her think she could tease him with impunity.

She was right that he'd never take a woman unwillingly, but he had to convince her there'd still be consequences if she pushed him too far.

And he was damn near at his breaking point right now. He was furious with his body for reacting to her the way it did. He'd been semi-hard since they left that last village, and his cock grew harder every time she moved.

Having her tucked against him like this was agony, and part of him regretted making her ride with him, but he was too stubborn to put her on her own horse now.

He didn't understand it. He should hate her.

Correction. He *did* hate her.

But he also wanted her. Apparently his body didn't give a fuck that she was supposed to be his enemy. He fucking wanted her. He wanted to pull her off this horse, rip her clothes to shreds, and bury his cock inside her until she lost her voice screaming his name.

But he couldn't.

She was his prisoner and a dangerous one at that. He didn't think for one second the caronium cuff on her wrist made her any less so. She was fast and resourceful, and he knew if he gave her any slack whatsoever, she'd find a way to escape or kill him.

And gods damn him if that didn't make him want her all the more.

Fucking hells. Why had he agreed to this? More importantly, what was wrong with him that he got hard thinking about how dangerous she was?

"I'm supposed to believe that? That you'll behave yourself?" he asked her. "What kind of a fool do you take me for?"

"I swear," she said. "You win. I can't go to Revenmyer."

He didn't blame her for being terrified of Revenmyer. He'd been to the prison several times over the years, and the place made his skin crawl. The only thing that got him through those visits was knowing he could leave at any time. Unlike the inmates.

"You'll sit still and stop trying to arouse me?" he pressed.

"Yes," she said, nodding as best she could.

"And you promise not to try to escape?"

She went still, and he could almost hear her mind working furiously to see if there was a way to avoid promising him that.

"Promise me that and mean it, or I'll turn this horse around and we'll head back to Solandis. Better yet, I still have a message leaf. I can tell Bressen where we are, and Cyra can portal us back right now."

She stiffened even more, but he didn't say anything else as he let her weigh the options of promising not to escape versus finding herself back in a caronium-lined holding cell within the hour.

"Fine," she said quietly. "I promise not to try to escape."

Samhail pulled his hand back from her throat, and she sucked in a deep breath. He tried not to notice the way it pushed out her breasts.

Samhail urged the horse back into a walk, and she relaxed against him.

Getting her to stop fidgeting would help, but only a little. In truth, just having her pressed up against him between his legs was driving him mad. He had to fight the urge to nuzzle his face into her hair and inhale deeply. Her scent was intoxicating, and Samhail tamped down the impulse to wrap an arm around her waist and pull her head to the side to bare her neck to him. He longed to run his teeth down that long column of her throat and feel goosebumps rise on her skin.

Samhail mentally shook himself and urged the huge draft horse into a canter. The ride was far from smooth with a horse this big, but that was the point. The jolting made things less comfortable and kept him from thinking about how much he wanted to touch the woman in front of him.

Samhail

It was nearly dark when they finally stopped for the night. The next good-sized town was still several hours away, so they'd aim to get there tomorrow around lunchtime.

They'd had time to buy supplies while the leatherman in the last village was working on the extension for the girth, so they at least had food and blankets. Samhail had also made sure to stop into the apothecary for turrow berries and a few other necessities. When the dried berries were steeped in hot water, they made an effective contraceptive for both men and women, and one he normally took regardless of whether he was fucking someone at the time or not. The berries worked best when taken regularly, and he'd need them again at some point. Not right now, of course, but…eventually.

He and Talyn had spoken little the rest of the ride, and they were both quiet now as they sat by the fire eating their dinner. They'd camped by a stream and had managed to drive a fish into a shallow part where it got trapped among the rocks. Talyn had made a fire while he prepared it.

Bressen had sent him another message leaf while he cooked, but he hadn't bothered to respond this time, only crumpled it up and tossed it into the flames. He knew Bressen was furious with him for not bringing the assassin back, but something told him he was doing the right thing, and he knew Bressen would never understand that.

Samhail kept half an eye on Talyn the entire time. He had several weapons on him, including his two swords, a few small knives, and Fred, who he'd reclaimed. Despite her promise not to escape, he didn't think her word would mean much if she got her hands on something sharp.

The situation in his pants hadn't gotten any better either. If anything, the blood pumping through his veins as he stayed alert and ready to fight only made things worse. The ever-present danger Talyn posed, his three fights with her, and his last few days of celibacy were making things extremely uncomfortable for him at the moment.

He went off into the woods to relieve himself in more ways than one after Talyn returned from her own trip into the trees. After emptying his bladder, he spit on his hand, wrapped it around his cock, and stroked himself hard and quick, not wanting to leave her unattended for too long.

He hadn't gone far into the woods, but it was far enough he didn't think Talyn could hear him, although he could still see her. He kept his eyes on her as he imagined what she would feel like beneath him while he pushed inside her, the sounds she'd make, and how she might taste if he got his tongue between her legs. After that, he'd only needed a few strokes before he shot milky ropes of his seed onto the side of a tree.

"Which side of the fire do you want?" Talyn asked as he returned.

She had one of the blankets they'd bought draped over her arm, and she surveyed the ground around the fire like she was trying to decide which patch of grass would be most comfortable.

"You choose," he said.

Talyn looked over the ground once more, then laid out her blanket and climbed under it. Samhail retrieved his own blanket and threw it down next to hers.

"What in the three hells do you think you're doing?" she asked as he lowered himself down and sidled up next to her.

"Getting ready to sleep," he answered.

"Not right here you're not," she snapped, sitting up.

"You didn't think I was letting you sleep anywhere but right next to me, did you?" he asked. "I need to be able to feel if you move, and I can't do that from across the fire."

"I promised I wouldn't escape."

"I know."

"And you don't trust my word?"

"No."

Talyn huffed and tried to get up, but he grabbed her around the waist and pulled her back down. She squeaked indignantly, but he spoke before she could utter a protest.

"You sleep right next to me, or you sleep in a cell beneath Tide's End," he said. "Your choice."

Talyn glared at him, but he kept his expression hard.

He wasn't particularly looking forward to sleeping this close to her, but he needed to be touching her while he was unconscious. He was a light sleeper by necessity, and he'd feel if she tried to move. Being this close to her after riding with her all day was going to be brutal, though.

Finally, she laid down and turned her back to him. He settled in behind her, and tried to press up close, but she elbowed him in the stomach, and he grunted.

"No touching," she said. "I need my space when I sleep."

"You're going to be cold," he argued. "We should take advantage of our combined body warmth."

"No touching," she repeated, and Samhail sighed heavily.

He turned over on his back to look up at the sky and wondered again what the fuck he'd been thinking. The woman was stubborn and infuriating, and he'd willingly agreed to spend the next few days traveling with her before they walked into a lion's den.

He sensed Talyn shiver next to him, and the hint of a smile tugged at his lips. Let's see just how stubborn she was willing to be.

He waited until she shivered again.

"Cold?" he asked.

She didn't answer, and he turned over on his side, so he was facing her back. She only pulled the blanket up tighter around her.

When she shivered a third time a few minutes later, he snaked an arm around her waist and pulled her back against him. A noise escaped her throat as if she'd been about to protest, but she cut it off. Her blanket was between them, and he'd thrown part of his own over her, so she now had two blankets plus his own heat. His body always ran warm, and he suspected that warmth had killed any objections she'd wanted to make.

Samhail felt the tension in Talyn's body, but he was reassured to have her pressed against him now, and he closed his eyes to drift off. Thankfully his dick was cooperating at the moment, so maybe he'd be able to get some sleep after all. Tomorrow would be soon enough to once again let his fantasies torment him.

Tandem Read: Go to *Nemesis Rising* (Bk 4), Chapters 2-3

Chapter 16

Talyn

Talyn woke the next morning feeling like a wagon had run her over. Or maybe a gargoyle. Her body was stiff and tired, and muscles she didn't remember she had ached. It had been a long time since she'd had to do that much fighting in such a short amount of time.

She heard the crackle of a fire and let her eyes flutter open. The first thing she saw was Samhail. He stood across from her with his shirt off, and he seemed to be washing his upper body with a wet cloth.

Protector save her. This was the first time she'd seen him with his shirt off, and what riches that shirt had been hiding. His chest was broad and rippled with muscles from one shoulder to the other while his torso narrowed into a toned waist and deep V that disappeared into his pants. And his stomach…sweet gods, she could actually see eight clearly defined abdominal muscles there. She'd never seen a man with eight before.

Samhail ran the cloth across his shoulder and down one arm, and she followed its progress over his bicep, around the tricep, and down to the corded sinews of his forearm. Dark markings she assumed were tattoos covered his skin from wrist to mid-forearm in a pattern of black bands, diamonds, and herringboned rectangles that faded away below his elbows.

"Are assassins always this lazy?"

Talyn jumped at the sound of Samhail's voice and snapped her mouth shut. It was dry from hanging open, and she kicked herself for letting him catch her staring.

She sat up and pulled the blankets close against the chilly morning air.

"What?" she asked, not yet awake enough to make sense of the words.

"It's already eight in the morning. I was going to rouse you if you didn't wake on your own soon. Do assassins normally sleep in?"

Talyn tried to blink away the drowsiness from her mind. She never slept this late, especially not recently while she'd been working for Cyra, but she'd been more exhausted than she realized. She'd expended a lot of energy the last two days trying to get away from Samhail and the others, then she hadn't slept much the night before as she'd waited for her opportunity to escape. She'd fought Samhail again yesterday morning, then they'd traveled all day. It was no wonder she'd slept so soundly she hadn't even felt Samhail get up.

Talyn threw off the blankets and fought the urge to shiver against the cold. She stood up and headed into the woods to relieve herself. When she returned, Samhail tossed her a warm, wet cloth.

"In case you want to clean up," he said as she caught it.

Talyn reached the cloth up her sweater and ran it under her arms, across her chest and around whatever parts of her torso she could reach. She was about to undo her pants and wipe between her legs when she glanced at Samhail and saw him watching her, much as she'd been watching him earlier. His mouth wasn't open, but there was no mistaking the look on his face. Desire.

His eyes met hers, and she smirked at him. She unfastened her pants slowly, and his eyes dipped down to watch. She turned away from him and plunged the cloth between her legs to wipe there. She let out an audible moan for his benefit and heard him growl behind her.

When she was done, she turned back to face Samhail and tossed the cloth to him. He caught it against his chest, and his eyes met hers again. There was fire in his gaze, but whether from anger, desire, or both, she couldn't tell anymore.

Talyn refastened her pants and stepped toward the fire. "What's for breakfast?" she asked innocently.

Nearly thirty seconds burned away as the flames snapped and popped between them. They stared at each other as Samhail held the cloth she'd washed herself with still clenched in his hand. Finally, he tossed it onto the fire. It smoked for a few seconds before catching and curling into ash.

"You will be if you don't stop testing me," he said.

Talyn didn't move, but her stomach burst into butterflies that tried madly to get out.

"Let me ride my own horse today," she said, and there was more pleading in her voice than she'd intended. She couldn't spend another day pressed up against him, and she had a feeling he knew it too.

Several more seconds went up with the smoke of the fire until he finally nodded.

"Fine," he said, "but I promise you'll regret it if you make me hunt you down again."

"I'm not going anywhere," she assured him. "Now really, what's for breakfast?"

Samhail picked up a plate he'd set on a rock nearby and handed it to her. It had a hard biscuit, some fruit, and a piece of dried meat on it.

Well, she'd lived on worse.

"There's tea in the pot," Samhail said, pointing to a small pot heating near the fire.

Talyn grabbed a cup and poured herself some. She could tell by the pink hue of the liquid that it likely contained turrow berries…which made the tea a contraceptive.

Talyn looked up at Samhail and found him watching her again. She smiled at him, raised the cup in salute, then tossed the drink back in one gulp. He was still watching her when she looked back at him, but now there was the hint of a grin on his face. He didn't say anything, but just reached for his shirt to put it back on.

Twenty minutes later, they'd packed up camp and were riding southwest again, each on their own horse, much to Talyn's relief. She had no idea what possessed her yet again to tease Samhail with that cloth. He really was going to snap one of these days.

Perhaps part of her hoped he would.

They reached the next town by lunch that day and stopped to eat at one of the taverns. Samhail hadn't spoken to her the entire ride, and she couldn't decide if she was relieved or disappointed by that.

They tied their horses outside – Samhail's huge draft horse looking odd next to the other horses – and went in. The tavern bustled with mid-day activity, but the place gradually went quiet as gazes moved their way one by one and conversation died.

"I take it this usually happens when you walk in a room?" Talyn asked.

Samhail just grunted and moved toward an empty table in the corner. He took a seat against the wall, and Talyn took one next to him rather than across, so they were both facing out into the tavern. She knew he'd spot trouble, but she couldn't bring herself to sit with her back exposed.

A young woman, barely more than a girl, approached their table nervously. She was probably the daughter of the owner, and Talyn tried to reassure her with a smile. The girl edged away from Samhail, and Talyn kicked his foot under the table to get him to drop his scowl. He took the hint, and his expression eased.

"Two ales and whatever you have for lunch," Samhail told the girl.

"Mutton pie?" she offered.

Samhail nodded once, and she hurried off.

Talyn surveyed the tavern as she normally did whenever she entered a place. Most of the patrons looked like local townsfolk, and all of them seemed to have gone back to their drinks and food after their initial shock of seeing Samhail. All but one.

"The man near the kitchen door has been staring at you since we walked in," Talyn said casually. She was careful not to look at the man directly so as not to catch his attention.

"I know," Samhail said as he took a drink from the tankard the barmaid set before him.

The man near the kitchen was big, and he wore thin plated armor over his shoulders and chest. A broadsword in a scabbard stood propped against the wall next to him. His hair was dark, but not quite black, and his neatly trimmed beard made him look older than he likely was, although if he was perimortal, that didn't mean much. A scar marred one of his cheeks from his ear to the edge of his beard, and the scowl on his face almost put Samhail's to shame.

"Do you owe him money?" Talyn asked Samhail.

"No."

"Did you kill his friend?"

"Possibly."

"Did you fuck his sister?"

He gave her a sidelong glance. "Also possible."

Talyn rolled her eyes. "Any other ideas why he's been eyeing you like he wants to eat your liver?"

"I have my suspicions."

"Care to share them?"

"No."

"Maybe you should take this cuff off and give me a sword, just in case you need help."

Samhail's dark eyes met hers with amusement. "I won't need help."

Talyn shrugged. "Suit yourself."

"I always do," he said.

Their food arrived, and they ate as the man continued to watch them from across the tavern. Samhail seemed oblivious to his stare, but Talyn observed the man closely, occasionally catching his look when his eyes strayed to her every few minutes.

When they finished their meal, Samhail stood and laid some coins on the table. "Let's go. It's time to get back on the road," he said.

Talyn stood and glanced at the man across the tavern again. His eyes followed Samhail as they left. Samhail could likely handle him easily, but the man's attention put her on edge for some reason.

Outside, they untied their horses, but they hadn't gone more than a few steps before an aggressive voice called out from behind them.

"Samhail!"

They both turned, and sure enough, the man from the tavern stood there holding his broadsword.

Talyn hadn't been able to tell how tall he was when he was sitting down, but she saw now he was easily over six feet, possibly around Lord Bressen's height. Samhail still had more than half a foot on him, but the man seemed solid enough, and he looked plenty at ease with the giant sword he held.

"Do I know you?" Samhail asked him.

"No, but I know *you*," the man said. "Or I know your reputation anyway. You're supposedly the best, but I intend to show otherwise."

Talyn loosed a breath. She saw it now, the hazard of Samhail's reputation. There was always someone looking to prove they were better than him by knocking him off the top. This man wanted to make a name for himself, and he thought to do so by defeating Samhail in a fight.

The good thing about her own line of work was no one knew who she was. She was the most feared assassin on the continent, but no one had ever challenged her because no one knew her identity. Her anonymity was a blessing in so many ways, and this was just one of them.

"I'm Kostas of Avitas," the man said, raising his voice so the gathering crowd could hear. "It's a name you'll want to remember."

Samhail sighed. "You don't want to do this, Kostas."

"I challenge you to a fight," Kostas went on, ignoring Samhail.

"Not interested," Samhail said as he turned back to his horse.

"Unfortunately, I won't take no for an answer," Kostas said. "The bounty on your head is too enticing."

Talyn's head jerked to Samhail as he frowned.

"Bounty?" Samhail asked, turning back to the man.

Kostas looked surprised. "Were you not aware King Sandrian of Rowe has promised a reward to anyone who brings you in?"

"Sandrian is no longer the king there," Samhail said.

"I don't care," Kostas bit out. "He's offering a lot of fucking coin for anyone who brings you in. There's a bonus if you're alive, but the reward to bring you in dead is enough to make it worth my while regardless."

"How much am I worth dead?" Samhail asked.

"Fifty thousand Rown sovereigns," Kostas answered.

Talyn arched a brow. That was an enormous sum, but Samhail looked unimpressed.

"And how much am I worth alive?" he asked.

"A hundred thousand."

Talyn's brow shot even higher. Three hells, for that much she'd have been tempted to go after Samhail herself.

Actually, the bounty was perfect. It would give her a reason to contact Sandrian and set up a meeting with him. She could tell him she'd captured Samhail and wanted to collect the bounty. She might have to offer Samhail as a consolation for failing to kill Bressen and Cyra, but either way, this was the in she needed.

"And where can I find Sandrian when I bring Samhail to him?" Talyn asked, intrigued.

Samhail glared at her, but she gave him half a shrug. "Just keeping my options open."

Samhail turned back to Kostas. "You should hold out for more," he told the man. "Those sums are hardly worth your life."

"I'm not a greedy man," Kostas said, grinning. "Draw your swords."

"I'm not going to fight you," Samhail said.

"Can I fight him?" Talyn asked quietly. "I bet I can take him in less than three minutes, even without my powers."

Samhail looked between her and Kostas. "It wouldn't take you more than a minute, but we don't have time for this bullshit."

Talyn arched a brow at the compliment, but Kostas spoke before she could respond.

"That hair of yours would look great woven into my horse's tail," he told Samhail. "He can use those locks of yours to flick flies off his ass."

Samhail didn't take the bait. He ignored Kostas and put his foot in the stirrup to mount his horse.

"And your woman will look great on all fours in front of me while I fuck her ass," Kostas added. He mimed grabbing Talyn's hips and thrusting into her as he gave her a leering look.

Talyn rolled her eyes and held up the wrist with the coronium cuff for Kostas to see. "I'm not his woman. I'm his prisoner," she said. "And don't kid yourself. You can't handle me any more than you can handle him."

Kostas didn't seem amused. "We'll see about that," he snarled. "Maybe you'll learn to stay quiet when my cock is down your throat and you're choking on my cum."

"Please let me kill him," Talyn begged as she turned to Samhail.

She jolted in surprise to see how dark his expression had gotten. The last time she'd seen that kind of fury on his face, his hand had been crushing her throat.

Samhail didn't answer. Instead, he went to his saddlebag, opened it, and pulled out a length of rope. Talyn frowned as he handed it to her.

"Absolutely not," she said, shoving it back at him. "If you think you're going to tie me up again while you-"

"It's not for you. It's for me," he said. "I want you to tie my right hand behind my back."

Talyn's eyebrows jerked up. "You want me to what?"

"The only way this will be fair is if I fight him with one hand tied behind my back," he said as he turned around and put his right hand behind him at his waist. "Tie my hand."

Talyn pursed her lips to hide the smile that threatened. This man was arrogance personified, but there was something she found...intriguing about him. And if he could humiliate Kostas by beating him with one hand, all the better.

Talyn wrapped the rope around Samhail's wrist and tried not to think about tying him to a bed and riding the fuck out of him. Her core ached to think about what that long, hard length of him might feel like between her legs. Gods, she'd probably feel him in the back of her throat...

Samhail glanced back at her, and Talyn realized her hands had stilled on the ropes as her imagination had taken over.

"Problem?" he asked, his tone suggesting he knew exactly where her thoughts had gone.

"Just trying to decide on the best knot to use," she lied before resuming. She looped the rope through his belt and finished securing his hand behind him.

When they turned back to Kostas, the man's face was red with fury.

"I'm going to enjoy carving out your heart and presenting it to King Sandrian," he growled to Samhail. "You'll regret this insult."

Talyn came around to stand in front of Samhail, and he looked down at her in question.

"The left side of his armor is more dented than the right," she said. "He likely leaves that side vulnerable when he swings. Also, the toe of his right boot is worn. Watch for him to drag it, and you can trip him up."

Samhail cocked his head. "I noticed the armor, but I didn't see the boot. Good catch." He paused. "It's almost as if you want me to win."

Talyn gave him a wry smile. "I'd just prefer to collect the reward myself than to let him have it."

In truth, Talyn didn't know why she'd given Samhail the advice. It would've made her life much easier to be rid of him, but she didn't want to see Kostas win. The man was a piece of shit.

"Of course," Samhail said with a knowing grin before he unsheathed Lefteous Hand and strolled toward Kostas.

People around them in the street scattered out of the way when Kostas surged forward to meet Samhail, and the clang of steel split the air as their swords hit. Kostas attacked relentlessly, and for the first few seconds, all Samhail could do was block his blows.

Admittedly, Kostas was a better fighter than Talyn had assumed, but she could tell right away he was no match for Samhail. For that matter, he wouldn't be a match for her either. If Kostas somehow got the upper hand on Samhail, she'd be able to dispatch him quickly enough.

Kostas was quick for his size, but Samhail was still faster, and he blocked every blow Kostas aimed at him. Had Samhail been using both his swords, the fight would've been over by now, but he was slightly off-balance from having the hand tied behind him. She didn't think he yet regretted tying it, but it was indeed a hindrance that kept him from attacking the way she knew he was capable of.

Samhail's sword clanged off Kostas's armor on his left. The man did indeed leave that side open when he fought, but Samhail's blow was just high and missed the vulnerable joint between the metal plates. The hit knocked Kostas off-balance, though, and his right toe dragged in the dirt as he tried to recover, just as Talyn had predicted.

Samhail took advantage and brought his sword back around quickly to catch Kostas near his neck. The blade found the seam in his armor and blood welled up where the sword slashed. The cut likely wasn't deep enough to be mortal, but Kostas's hand still flew to the wound, which exposed the area under his arm. Samhail didn't hesitate but drove his blade in under Kostas's arm until the sword punched all the way through his torso so the tip jutted out the top of his other shoulder.

Kostas's eyes went wide in the few seconds between when he realized what had happened and when his body went limp. Samhail pulled his blade out and pushed Kostas to the side.

It had all taken less than two minutes.

Samhail straightened, then reached his sword behind him and cut the rope tying his hand.

The street was barren of people, most having fled when Kostas first charged Samhail. The rest had disappeared the moment the outcome of the fight was determined.

"Are we leaving him there?" Talyn asked Samhail as he returned to his horse and pulled a cloth from his saddlebag to wipe the blade. He resheathed the sword when it was clean.

"We don't have time to deal with a body," he said. "Someone will bury him." He used the cloth to wipe as much blood from his hand as he could, then stowed it back in his saddlebag and mounted his horse.

Talyn looked back at the body on the ground. Rivulets of blood had begun to spiderweb away from the widening pool of crimson under

Kostas. The man's eyes were still open wide in surprise, but Talyn couldn't bring herself to feel sorry for him.

She mounted up next to Samhail, and they wheeled their horses around to head back out of town.

"If we were so short on time, you should've taken care of him with two swords," Talyn offered as they rode. "You wasted time having me tie you up so you could toy with him."

"Maybe I just wanted you to tie me up," Samhail said.

Talyn's mouth fell open a moment before she shut it so fast her teeth clicked together. It took her a second to recover. "I'm happy to tie you up whenever you want. I can tie you to a tree when we stop for the night."

"And you think that will give you enough of a head start?" he asked.

"I'm very good with knots."

"And I'm an excellent hunter," he countered, his voice huskier.

Talyn swallowed. Why did her stomach flutter at the idea of him stalking her as prey in the night?

"I'll make you a deal," Samhail said. "I'll let you tie me to a tree tonight if you want, and you're welcome to try and escape. But if I catch you again…then I get to tie *you* up."

Talyn's stomach somersaulted as every muscle in her lower body tightened. What was wrong with her? That shouldn't arouse her.

"Would you take the caronium cuff off?" she asked.

He was silent a moment. "No," he said finally.

"That's hardly fair then."

He shrugged. "You're my prisoner. It's not supposed to be fair."

She clenched her jaw.

"So you're not going to take me up on my offer?" he pressed.

Talyn paused. "If you did catch me and tie me up, what would you do with me?" she asked.

Gods, why was she asking him this?

She felt Samhail's gaze on her, but she refused to look at him. "I suppose you'd tie me to a tree as well and make me sleep there all night?"

she suggested.

She sensed rather than saw Samhail's grin. "No, I wouldn't tie you to a tree." He paused. "Do you really want to know what I'd do?"

Talyn opened her mouth to answer, but no words came out. She did want to know. She just didn't want to have to ask him.

"I…no," she said finally.

"No?" Samhail asked, lifting a brow. "Are you sure?"

She swore there was disappointment in his voice.

Talyn swallowed again. She couldn't handle knowing. "I…"

"There's so many different options," Samhail mused anyway. "But I suppose I'd start by tying your hands behind your back."

Talyn kept her eyes forward. She wouldn't look at him. She wouldn't.

"Then I'd put you on your knees and make you finish what you started back in the great room at Tide's End."

Talyn's head snapped around so fast she was sure she pulled something in her neck. Her gaze locked with his, and she couldn't tear her eyes away from his dark, smoldering look. It was a look that told her he wanted her, but he hadn't yet forgiven her for what she'd done when she'd pretended to be Cyra. It was a look that promised both rapture and retribution at once.

Talyn tore her eyes from his and closed them. She struggled to keep calm as her breathing quickened.

"I'd thread my hands through your hair and hold you there while I fucked your mouth with long, deep strokes," he went on, his voice a rasp. "You've seen my cock. How much of me do you think you can take?"

Talyn's eyes flared. Samhail's own eyes blazed as the ghost of a grin played along his lips. Now she wasn't sure if that's what he really wanted to do or if he was just trying to shock her.

She wouldn't object if he did any of it, and she felt the blush stain her cheeks at that realization before she looked away.

"Do you want to know what I'd do after that?" he asked her.

"No!" she said, entirely too fast. She was sure there was a wet spot on her saddle already.

Samhail chuckled. "So do you want to tie me to a tree tonight and try to run, little hummingbird?"

"Don't call me that," she said.

The nickname annoyed her enough to clear her head. It wasn't that she disliked the association. Hummingbirds were little warriors in their own right, and she'd happily accept the comparison. It was more that the nickname was too close to…to what? An endearment? It was the best she could come up with for why she didn't like it.

"You didn't answer my question," he said.

"One deal at a time," she said, willing the tremor in her voice to stop. "Ask me again when we're done with our first one."

Their horses' hooves clicked off several seconds of silence.

"Coward," Samhail said so softly she wasn't sure at first he'd said it.

Talyn didn't react. It was a challenge, pure and simple, payback for when she'd said it to him from her holding cell below Tide's End. He was daring her to take him up on his offer, but she wouldn't. She couldn't.

What she needed to do was get away from this man before he turned every one of her senses upside down. She'd promised him she wouldn't try to escape, but for her own sanity, she'd need to break that promise.

But that wasn't all she'd have to do.

He'd found her easily enough the first time. There was only one way to make sure he couldn't find her again.

Samhail had to die.

Tandem Read: Go to *Nemesis Rising* (Bk 4), Chapters 4-7

Chapter 17

Talyn

Talyn and Samhail spoke very little the rest of the day, and while this wasn't unusual when they were riding, the silence felt almost palpable. Talyn might just be imagining things, a paranoia now that she'd decided to escape and kill him, but it unnerved her in a way she'd never experienced before.

They had to camp in the woods again that night, since there wasn't a town nearby, and Talyn was beginning to think Samhail planned it that way on purpose. He seemed to be trying to keep her away from people, either so she couldn't seek help from them, or because he was afraid she might use them against him. Like she might take hostages.

Talyn could handle the hard ground and the unpredictability of sleeping outside if she had to, but she much preferred a soft bed and the option of a hot bath. Hells, even a room temperature bath would be fine at this point, but that apparently wasn't in the cards.

Talyn glanced at Samhail across the fire as he finished eating his share of the pheasant he'd brought down. He'd made her come with him while he hunted so he could keep an eye on her, and she hadn't protested. She was curious how he'd hunt without a bow and arrow, but it turned out his method was faster and easier. He'd stunned the bird with a forcefield.

Talyn tore her eyes from Samhail and looked into the fire. If she watched him too long, she'd rethink her plan, and she couldn't do that. It was either him or her.

"You've been quieter than normal."

Samhail's voice boomed through the small clearing after the protracted silence of the day, and she jumped.

"You're not exactly chatty yourself," she said defensively.

He shrugged. "No, but I've come to expect at least the occasional sarcastic comment or observation from you. What's wrong?"

"Nothing's wrong. I'm just tired," she said. "I think your ego is sucking up all the air around us."

He chuckled. "That's more like it."

"Can we please find a town to stay in tomorrow? I need a bath and an actual bed to sleep in."

"Do you ever stop complaining?"

"When I stop complaining, you accuse me of being too quiet."

He cocked his head to concede the point. "Fair enough." He wiped his hands on a cloth – he seemed to have an endless supply of them – and leaned back to look at her.

"So how did you become an assassin?" he asked.

Talyn huffed a laugh. "Is it the part of the journey where we share our origin stories?" she asked, looking up. "Shall I tell you all about my dark tragic past?"

His gaze felt like a heavy cloak on her.

"Is there one?" he asked.

"A dark tragic past?" she said. "Of course there is. Do you think I chose to become an assassin because all the seamstress jobs were taken?"

"But I don't get to hear the story?"

"Not tonight. Feel free to tell me yours, though. I suppose mercenary was your fallback after being a shepherd fell through?"

"Not shepherd. Minstrel. I love the lute, but I can't play for shit."

Talyn smiled despite herself as she pictured him with a lute slung across his back instead of his swords.

He started to speak again, but Talyn cut him off.

"I'm going to sleep," she said as she stood up and went to her horse to retrieve her blanket and the cloak she usually rolled into a pillow.

"I suppose we should get some rest," he said with a sigh.

"Stay up if you want," she said, but he ignored her and collected his own blanket.

Talyn lay down facing away from the fire, but as she suspected, Samhail laid his blanket down next to hers and climbed in behind her. He sidled up so his body wrapped around hers.

"You don't have to sleep so close," she grumbled.

She froze as his fingers grazed across her cheek before he pulled the hair back from her ear and neck. The gesture was almost sensual, and for a moment she couldn't hear over the alarm bells clanging in her head. She waited to see if he'd do something else, but after a moment, Samhail's arm only snaked around her waist and pulled her to him as before.

"Yes, I do," he said.

His leather and earth scent curled its way up Talyn's nose, and she closed her eyes. She was too aware of every place his body touched hers…including the hard length of him pressed against her backside. With anyone else, it wouldn't even be a question. She'd turn over, push him onto his back, and throw a leg over him to ride him until they both collapsed in pleasure.

But something was different with Samhail. Instinctively she knew if she crossed that line with him she'd be done for. So she wouldn't cross it. Not now, and – after tonight – not ever.

Samhail's hand inched down her stomach toward the apex of her thighs, and the muscles between her legs tightened in anticipation. The desire to part her legs and let him slip his fingers inside her was nearly overwhelming. Talyn couldn't remember ever wanting anyone this badly before. Her body actually ached with the need for him.

She could let him touch her, couldn't she? Just this once?

"No," Talyn managed to say, the word nearly lodging in her throat. It was more plea than command, but Samhail's hand stopped immediately.

He exhaled deeply and moved his hand back up, but he pulled her even tighter against him. Talyn stifled her whimper at the feel of his cock against her ass. His breath tickled her ear, and she shut her eyes firmly as she willed herself to fall asleep. She was tired enough, but her body was alive everywhere he pressed against her.

It was twenty minutes before she heard Samhail's even breathing. Only then did she let herself relax enough to try to sleep.

Easier said than done. It was another three quarters of an hour before her body finally wound down enough to let her drift off, her plan clear.

Talyn

Talyn woke again exactly an hour later the way she'd trained herself to do. It had taken years, but she'd set her internal clock to know when she'd slept for an hour, and she could make herself wake thoroughly and immediately at that time.

Her eyes opened to the darkness of the forest as she took stock of her situation. Samhail's arm was still around her waist, her back pressed firmly against his chest, and she still felt the warmth of his breath against her ear. She refused to indulge in the nagging desire to just enjoy his closeness and instead reached up carefully to pull the small piece of metal out of her mouth from where she'd tucked it between her gums and cheek. She gave a quick prayer of thanks to the Protector she hadn't swallowed the hairpin in her sleep, then brought it down to her wrist to start working at the lock on the caronium cuff.

Being able to pick a lock on shackles or caronium cuffs was a must in her line of work, but she hadn't had to do it in a while. She'd managed to steal the hairpin from one of the shopkeepers while they'd bought supplies in that first town. She hadn't planned on using it except in an emergency, but as far as she was concerned, the situation with Samhail was now just that.

Five minutes later when she still hadn't unlocked the cuff, Talyn had to admit she was out of practice. That or they'd upgraded the locking mechanism on the cuffs since the last time she'd had to do this. She was about to give up and try breaking a few bones in her hand when the cuff suddenly popped open with the loudest click she'd ever heard.

Talyn froze as she listened hard for any change in Samhail's breathing, but his chest still rose and fell steadily against her back. She waited a couple minutes more before carefully slipping the cuff off her wrist and tossing it gently aside into some tall grass. She felt her power ramp up inside her the second it was gone, and she breathed a shallow sigh of relief.

Talyn reached out next to find the rock she'd spotted earlier. She'd surveyed the area before choosing a spot to settle down for the night, and she'd chosen this area because of the large, sharp rock that lay close by.

Inch by inch, Talyn reached out her hand until her fingers closed over it. The rock was just light enough for her to pick up with one hand but also heavy enough to crack Samhail's skull with a hard enough swing.

She felt an unfamiliar pang at the thought. She rarely hesitated or had regrets once she decided someone needed to die, but she had them now. It seemed to be her new normal since meeting these people.

Samhail wasn't innocent, she reminded herself. He had plenty of blood on his hands, more than enough to justify killing him, but something kept her from swinging the rock. Instead, she lay there tucked up against him with her hand closed over the hard, jagged stone, willing herself to just do it.

The rock felt brutally rough and cold under her fingers, and she told herself her delay wasn't hesitation, but calculation. She didn't have the leverage or angle to swing the rock with any force from this position. She'd need to port out of Samhail's arms and then strike quickly.

She'd nearly decided to do it when Samhail's voice cut through the darkness, making her jump.

"Can you hurry up and decide whether or not you plan to hit me with that rock so I can go back to sleep?" he said.

Fuck.

Talyn's blood rampaged through her veins as her heart threatened to beat out of her chest. He'd caught her, so the question now was whether she should let go of the rock and hope he was willing to forget she'd just been planning to kill him or go ahead and strike.

Before she realized she'd made a decision, instinct took over, and

Talyn ported behind Samhail. She swung the rock down toward his head the second she materialized, but he moved faster than she expected, and he caught her wrist only inches from his head. An instant later she was flipped backward, and then he was on top of her, pinning her body beneath his. He slammed her hand into the ground, and Talyn cried out in pain as the rock jarred loose from her grip.

There was no time to second-guess her decision. She'd made her move, and now she had to follow through.

Talyn ported out from under Samhail and reappeared near the horses. There was only about a quarter of a moon in the sky, and she could hardly see in the dark, but she'd taken good note of her surroundings earlier. She pulled both of Samhail's swords from their sheaths and turned to face him when a strong force tried to pull the swords from her hands. She lost her grip on one of them and it flew straight into Samhail's outstretched hand, but she managed to hold onto the other one, tightening her grip on it.

Nemesis take her. She forgot he had summoning powers. She had to keep her head on straight or she was going to lose it. Literally.

Talyn could barely make out Samhail's outline in the darkness, and the fact he was wearing all black didn't help. Only his white hair was slightly visible, and she tried to focus on that.

The flash of the moon in the polished steel of his sword was the only warning she had when Samhail attacked. His blade sang through the night toward her, and she somehow blocked it with her own. She ducked low and rolled to one side, swinging out as she went. She aimed for where she thought his ankles might be, but the clang of steel on steel told her he'd blocked her again.

Talyn's eyes were adjusting to the dark more now, but she could still only see Samhail's outline against the patch of starry sky through the trees. He moved then, not toward her, but toward a denser section of forest so she could no longer make out where he was at all. If he attacked from there, she'd never see him coming, and panic bubbled up like bile. She had few options, but she had to try one more idea before she ran.

"I don't suppose we can forget I just tried to kill you and go back to sleep?" she called in the general direction of where she thought he was.

She had no intention of going back to sleep, but she hoped he might respond so she could gauge where he was.

Samhail didn't take the bait. Silence greeted her question as she scanned the forest for movement.

A twig snapped to her left, and she swung the sword out in a blind arc, hoping to catch something. Anything. Instead, something hard came down on her hand and knocked the sword from her grip. Then her arms were pinned to her sides as Samhail's iron hold closed around her. She ported instantly and ran as fast as she could through the trees.

She ran blindly, feeling her way in front of her and praying to the Protector she didn't trip over any roots or break an ankle in a hole. The branches of trees whipped across her face, scratching her skin, but she didn't dare try to run slower or more carefully. She didn't hear anything behind her, but she knew better than to think Samhail wasn't following.

In the back of her mind, Talyn realized he was hunting her, just like they'd jested about earlier. Well, not just like. The idea of being hunted had aroused her earlier, but bone-deep fear was the only thing she felt now. Samhail wouldn't fuck her if he caught her. He'd kill her.

Talyn ducked behind a large tree and ported as far as she could to her right. She did it twice more so she was nearly a hundred and eighty degrees away from where she'd been. She only hoped Samhail didn't realize she'd changed direction. She tried to run as quietly as she could now, and the only sounds she heard besides the thudding of her heart in her ears were the night noises of the woods all around her.

Too late she heard the rustle ahead, then something huge slammed into her. The force of the impact would've knocked her to the ground, but Samhail's arms again circled her like steel bands as they punched the air out of her lungs.

She was about to port again when white-hot pain lanced through her shoulder near her neck, and she screamed. Something sharp seemed to have pierced her skin, and Talyn's hand flew to the spot to feel what it was. Her fingers found Samhail's head, and it took her a moment to understand what was going on. Then it came to her.

He'd bitten her. Nemesis take him, he'd actually bitten her.

Talyn tried to port, but for some reason she couldn't. She rammed a hand into his shoulder as hard as she could while her other wrapped in his hair to pull him away, but he didn't budge.

Samhail's mouth moved against her shoulder, and numbness began to creep through her body. Her eyes widened as she tried to push on him again, but her muscles had started to seize up.

Oh gods, no.

His face, Talyn thought as panic once again set in. She needed to go for his face. She moved her hand up either to poke his eyes, or maybe scratch him, but she couldn't do either. Her limbs felt heavy as a tingling sensation spread through her, and her hand fell away from his face as she found she could no longer hold it up.

"What…are you doing to me?" she managed to ask, terror infusing every word. Her tongue felt large and awkward in her mouth, and the words came out slurred.

Talyn sagged against Samhail as her legs gave out, and his arms tightened around her to hold her up. She felt the pressure of his grasp, but her skin seemed to lose all feeling as the pain in her shoulder faded along with all other sensation in her body.

"No," she whispered. "Samhail, please…"

Whatever else she might've said was lost as her jaw locked up and words were no longer possible. Her eyelids fluttered, and the small bit of light she could still see went completely black as she succumbed to darkness.

Chapter 18

Samhail

Samhail knew the moment Talyn regained consciousness the next morning, even before her head snapped back against his chest. He thought she was trying to headbutt him, but then her head lolled to the side, and he had to catch her as she fell forward.

He'd been riding since dawn with Talyn nestled in front of him, and it was a sweet agony with her between his legs, her limp body leaning back against him. He ached to touch her, but he wouldn't do it while she was unconscious. As it was, he'd had to manhandle her to get her into the saddle as he'd climbed up with her tucked under his arm earlier.

He wasn't sure how long she'd be out after he bit her, but once she was, he'd at least been confident he could get through the night without having his head smashed in.

He'd carried her back to the camp, laid her under the blankets, and curled his body around hers again. He resisted the urge to touch her face as he had earlier. He wasn't sure what had made him do it before, but she'd stiffened against him when he had.

He held her the next morning as he waited for her to wake, but she hadn't, even when he shook her. Eventually, he'd just gotten up and prepared to leave, pulling her into the saddle with him when she remained unconscious.

They'd been on the road almost two hours when he finally felt the subtle change in her body that told him she was awake. That's when her head had snapped back against his chest.

He'd summoned the caronium cuff she tossed away, but he couldn't bring himself to put it back on her. He felt too guilty for biting her, and she'd already proven she could get out of it, so she could port now if she wanted to. He hoped they could come to an agreement, though.

"I can't move," Talyn said, her voice slurred. "Why can't I move?"

"The toxin is still wearing off," he said. "It may be a little while before you have full use of your body again."

It surprised him she was still feeling the toxin's effects, but this gave him more time to figure out how to make this work with her.

"Toxin?" she asked as if trying to wrap her mind around the word.

"From when I bit you," he said. "Gargoyle fangs can release a mild toxin if needed. It has sedative and paralytic properties. I've never actually bitten anyone before, so I'm not sure how long it lasts."

"And you'd thought you'd experiment on me?" she asked, her voice sounding more like her own with the return of her indignation.

"You didn't give me much choice."

A pause. "You could have just let me go," she suggested quietly.

He sighed. "No, I couldn't."

That was true in at least two senses. He couldn't return to Solandis and tell the Lord of Hiraeth he'd simply let the woman who'd been sent to kill Cyra go. Bressen was his friend, his brother in every sense other than blood, but he was certain Bressen's understanding wouldn't extend that far. Letting Talyn go now would have far-reaching consequences for his relationships with both Bressen and Cyra.

In another sense, and one he was loath to admit to himself, he couldn't let Talyn go because…well, because he didn't want to. She'd tried to maim or kill him at least three times now, and for some reason he had yet to wrap his head around, that had only stirred his blood…and his cock.

He wanted her. He'd given up denying that by now. He supposed it was his gargoyle nature that appreciated her strength and fighting ability, and the more Talyn fought him, the more he wanted her.

Samhail, please…

Her words when she'd felt the toxin take hold had almost broken him. It was the first time she'd used his name, and there was something about the sound of it on her lips that drove him mad with longing.

He'd bitten her because it was the only way he could think to stop her, but he'd regretted it almost at once. He'd felt the exact moment the fight had left her and wished instantly he could take it back. Her body had gone limp in his arms, and the fear he'd heard in her voice tore at him.

He'd expected to see such fear when he stepped into the holding cell with her the other day. He'd waited for her to show regret about goading him, but instead her eyes had flared, and she'd begun strategizing.

Last night, though, it had bothered him deeply to see her subdued and helpless. More than he'd ever admit to himself. Likewise, he'd begun to panic when his attempts to wake her failed. It was a new feeling for him because he didn't panic. Ever.

He'd only ever bitten his siblings when they were children and first learning to use their powers, but gargoyles were immune to their own toxin, so he hadn't known what to expect using it on a full human.

In truth, he'd kept his teeth sunken in Talyn's soft flesh longer than intended, not because he was unsure of how the toxin worked, but because he'd been shocked by how much he enjoyed the taste of her blood. Gargoyles didn't feed on blood the way some creatures did, but a couple of his siblings enjoyed the taste of it. His sister Sadira claimed the people she took to bed, men and women alike, let her drink from them as part of their pleasure.

It was possible for gargoyles to bite someone without releasing the toxin, but Samhail had never tried it either way, so he hadn't been prepared for what he experienced when he first bit Talyn. He'd let himself enjoy the taste of her too long, so she'd likely received more toxin than necessary. It was just one more thing he could feel guilty about.

"How long have we been riding?" Talyn asked as her head rested against his shoulder. "I imagine we're halfway back to Solandis by now?"

"We're still on our way to Rowe," he corrected.

"What?" she asked, her head lolling toward him. "Why?"

"Did you want me to take you back to Solandis?" he asked.

"No, of course not, but I don't understand. I tried to kill you last night.

Why would you want to keep going?"

Because he was an idiot who hadn't learned anything from the first three times she'd tried to kill him? Because he didn't know what Bressen would do to her if he brought her back to Solandis, and for some reason, he didn't want to see her hurt? Or because this way he got to have her all to himself for just a little longer? All of the above?

Idiot, idiot, idiot. He'd deserve it if she succeeded in killing him.

"I expected you to try to kill me or escape at least once more before you gave up and accepted the situation," he said. "I'm hoping you finally got it out of your system, and we can proceed as planned. Have you?"

Talyn was silent for a long moment before answering. "I suppose we'll find out."

Samhail smiled. He'd expected nothing less from her, and he almost looked forward to the next time she attacked him, because there *would* be a next time. He was sure of it.

"I can always bite you again if not," he suggested, and her intake of breath made him instantly regret the words.

Gods damn it. He didn't do regret.

There was another long pause before Talyn spoke again. "You mentioned fangs."

"I have them in my gargoyle form, and I can call forth parts of that form at will."

"Like your wings?" she asked.

"Like my wings."

She seemed to take this in. "What does your gargoyle form look like?"

"I've never looked in a mirror after I shift," he said wryly.

"Of course not, but surely you have some idea," she pressed him.

"I do," he said, "and maybe the next time you decide to try and kill me, you'll find out."

It was said lightly, but he let the hint of a threat creep into his voice on the chance it gave her any pause whatsoever about attacking him again.

He doubted it would.

"Tell me about gargoyles," she said. "I've seen the carved ones on the roofs of temples, but I've never met a real one until now."

"You've met three so far," he said, although she seemed to know that already, if her taunt to him back in the jail cell was any indication.

"Surgeon and Serise are gargoyles as well."

"Yes."

"Did you know them before they came to work for Lord Bressen?"

"Unfortunately, yes."

"How?"

Samhail sighed. "They're my younger siblings. Twins."

She paused. "You don't seem particularly close to them."

"I'm not," he said, and he could almost feel her eyebrows rise.

"Okay, we'll come back to that later," she said, "but what about the gargoyles on the temples? Are they some kind of tribute to your kind?"

Samhail snorted in disgust.

"Not tributes then," she said. "So what are they?"

"You're full of questions today," he observed.

"My mouth is the only part of my body I can move at the moment," she said sardonically.

He wished she hadn't said that because thinking of her mouth made him think of the other things she could do with it.

Samhail cleared his mind before those thoughts could take hold. Talyn wasn't in any state to do any of the things he wanted to do with her.

Plus she'd just tried to kill him a few hours earlier. Why did he have to keep reminding himself of that?

"The temple gargoyles?" Talyn prompted when he didn't answer.

"Gargoyles are an ancient race," Samhail said finally. "For as long as the gods have existed, gargoyles have been the guardians of their temples. Thousands of years ago, each temple would've had one or more true gargoyles in residence to protect the temple and its priests and priestesses. When the gods went to war, the gargoyles were their army. We defended the Trinity when false gods rose up to challenge them."

"I've been in my share of temples," Talyn said. "I've never seen one with its own real gargoyle."

"Should I even ask why you had occasion to visit so many temples?"

"You'd be surprised how many people want a priest or priestess dead, and maybe even more surprised how often they deserve it."

His brows rose. "How many have you killed?"

"Five priests and one priestess," she answered without hesitation.

"And what did they do to deserve the wrath of The Raptor?"

"Two of the priests were rapists," she said. "The third liked to touch children, and the fourth had a habit of killing young women. I was hired to kill the fifth because he was the High Priest of the temple, and the next priest in line wanted his position. It's not a job I'd normally take, but I discovered in my observation of the High Priest that he was skimming from the temple coffers to support his habit of hiring prostitutes."

"So you killed him, and the priest who hired you ascended to High Priest?" Samhail asked.

"No, the priest who hired me was the one who liked to touch children. I took his money, killed the High Priest, then killed him too."

He gave a short laugh. "I'm almost afraid to ask about the priestess."

"She was having an affair with a married nobleman," Talyn said. "When the man tried to break it off with her, she killed him. The man's wife hired me to take care of the priestess."

"So you only kill those who you think deserve death?" he asked.

"Mostly. Early on I took whatever jobs I could get, but as I developed a reputation, I could be more selective about who I worked for. I now have a certain…code I live by when deciding if I'll take a job."

"Do you meet your own code?" he couldn't help asking.

"You mean, if I was hired to kill myself, would I decide I deserved to die?" she asked.

"Yes."

"Yes, I would," she said without hesitation.

Samhail mulled that over. "Given that you tried to kill me last night, I assume I meet your code."

"Yes," she said, again without pause. "But we've gotten off topic. You were telling me about gargoyles."

"I find discussing you far more interesting," he said.

"I don't. Now, I believe you were about to tell me why most temples no longer have a resident gargoyle."

Samhail exhaled heavily. "Most haven't had a gargoyle for hundreds if not thousands of years," he said. "Much of the gargoyle population was decimated in a series of religious wars several thousand years ago, and the rest were the victims of infighting. Gargoyles tend to have quick tempers, and like most perimortal beings, we don't have many offspring, so we don't replenish our population very fast."

"Are Surgeon and Serise your only siblings?" she asked.

"My family seems to be the exception to the rule of procreation," Samhail said. "I'm one of five. Surgeon and Serise are the youngest, and then I have an older sister, Sadira, and an older brother, Soldier."

"Hmm. You're a middle child. That explains a lot."

Samhail ignored the comment.

"So then most temples don't have a gargoyle because there aren't enough to go around?" she asked.

"Yes and no," he said. "It's true there aren't many of us, but the temples also decided they didn't need us anymore. At the end of the holy wars when there weren't enough gargoyles to guard all the temples, many High Priests and Priestesses made alternate plans. Some had stone gargoyles carved on the outsides and insides of temples, and they asked the Trinity to bless the statues to act as wards against evil. When the temples remained safe, they assumed the substitute gargoyles were doing their jobs, and they decided having the statues carved was far less expensive than hiring the real thing. Most of my kind now work as mercenaries, although I know a few who work as the personal guards for various monarchs and heads of state as well."

"And you," she said, "you're somewhere in between? As near as I can tell, you work both as a mercenary and as some kind of personal…I'm not sure what, for Lord Bressen."

"I work mainly as a mercenary, but Bressen is like a brother, so I make myself available whenever he needs me," Samhail said.

Talyn seemed to consider this. "So you're not there just to give Lady Cyra fighting lessons?" she asked.

"Cyra asked me to train her months ago," he said. "She was drugged one night by Lord Jerram, and I think she wanted to do something to feel more in control. Learning the basics has been good for her."

Talyn was quiet a moment. "It's kind of you to do that."

Was it just him, or did she sound…jealous?

He shrugged. "It's been more difficult for me to train her lately than I anticipated. She's much smaller and weaker than me, so I've had to be careful not to hurt her. She'd probably benefit more from working with someone like you."

Talyn's head jerked. "Are you actually suggesting I help train the Lady of Hiraeth to fight?" she asked. "As if her husband will ever let me near her again?"

"I'm just making an observation."

She was right. Bressen would never let Talyn within ten miles of Cyra, especially not with a sword. Whatever had made him imagine having her in Solandis, living there, working with him, was nothing but a fantasy.

"The merman, Axenus," Talyn said. "He trains Cyra in magic?"

"Yes."

"And has he slept with her as well?" she asked. "Do the three of you just take turns fucking her, or do you fuck her all at once?"

Samhail pulled hard on the reins of his horse, and Talyn pitched forward. He caught her around the shoulders and hauled her back against his chest before wrapping his hand around her throat. It seemed to end up there at least once a day now.

"That's enough," he growled against her ear. "It's none of your concern who Cyra takes to her bed, although I can assure you, she's not nearly as promiscuous as you seem to want to believe. Understand?"

Talyn let out a soft noise. "I understand," she said. "I was just curious. You can tell a lot about a person by their sexual appetites."

"Is that so?" he asked, letting his breath caress her ear. "And what are *your* sexual appetites?"

He shouldn't ask, but now that she'd brought it up, he had to know.

He lifted her chin so he could brush his lips down her cheek. He thought he felt her tremble, and he had to stop himself from trailing his lips lower to her neck. Gods, her scent was driving him mad. He hadn't had this much lack of control around a woman since he was in his teens and just discovering the joys of having a dick.

"How badly do you want to know?" Talyn asked huskily.

Samhail groaned and moved his hand from her throat to slide it down to her waist. He pulled her back against him so his cock pressed against her backside.

"Do you feel that?" he rasped in her ear.

"I assume you have an erection?" she said. "Unfortunately, I still can't feel most of my body, so if you do, then it's lost on me."

Samhail frowned. "The toxin hasn't worn off yet?" he asked, straightening in the saddle again. "You still can't move your body?"

"I believe that's what I just said."

"Fuck."

Samhail tightened his arm on Talyn's waist and dismounted, pulling her down with him. He lifted her into his arms and looked around. He spotted a large bolder off to the side and carried her over to prop her up on top of it. She swayed, and he put his hands around her waist to steady her as he knelt before her.

"Are you sure the toxin will wear off?" she asked, concern in her voice. "What if I'm like this permanently?"

Samhail shook his head. "The toxin shouldn't be permanent. You likely just got too much and it's taking a while. I may have…bitten you too long."

"Bitten me too long?" she repeated indignantly.

"We can head to the next town to find a healer," he said, concern shading his voice. "If we can find a perimortal healer, they should be able to draw the rest of the toxin out."

Samhail looked over her body, as if he could somehow see whatever was preventing her from moving. His gaze snagged on her foot as he thought he saw one of her toes flex inside her boot.

Relief flooded him. Toe movement had to be a good sign.

"Did you feel your toe move?" he asked as he bent lower to look.

He caught movement above him, and something clenched in his chest as he knew instantly he'd made a fatal mistake. He heard his swords being drawn from their scabbards a second before Talyn's body disappeared from the rock and the sharp steel of his own blades crossed against the front of his throat. A knee pressed hard into his back, trapping him between it and the blades.

Possum. She'd been playing fucking possum, and now she had him right where she wanted him, on his knees with his own swords poised to slit his throat. He swallowed against the blades and felt the sharp sting of the edge nick his throat.

Well, he'd told himself he'd deserve it if she succeeded in killing him, and he did indeed deserve it. He'd been doing monumentally stupid things since the woman first crossed his path.

Take that fight with Kostas, for one. He wasn't the kind of man to grandstand, yet he'd had her tie his hand behind his back. It hadn't been about impressing her but about punishing Kostas. He hadn't just wanted to beat the man, he'd wanted to humiliate him after he'd threatened Talyn.

Samhail held himself unnaturally still so he didn't accidentally slit his own throat before Talyn had a chance to do it herself. His blades were as sharp as steel could be, and any wrong move might open his neck.

Samhail almost laughed to think of all the warriors nearly twice Talyn's size that had tried to kill him over the decades and died for their efforts. It was fitting his death would finally come at the hands of a beautiful woman with legs he'd never get a chance to feel wrapped around him.

He'd let his guilt over biting her distract him, make him lax, and she'd taken full advantage. Part of him had to admire her for that.

"Just make it quick and clean," he said softly. "That's all I ask."

"I will," she whispered behind him.

He wouldn't close his eyes. He'd die with them open. He promised himself that much.

Samhail smiled then. He was strangely at peace as he stared straight ahead and waited to feel the searing slice of the blades across his throat, the gush of warm blood down his chest, and the chill of dark oblivion.

Chapter 19

Talyn

Talyn could barely hear over the din in her head as blood thundered through her veins. She was breathing hard, but not from exertion.

She stared at the back of Samhail's head where he knelt before her, the swords she'd stolen from him pressed against the front of his throat, and she willed herself to just pull them across and slice his neck open. She finally had the upper hand. She could end this now and be free of him.

She'd been trying to keep her body as limp as possible for the last several minutes so Samhail didn't realize the feeling was coming back into her limbs. Part of her couldn't believe the ploy had worked, but she'd seen her advantage when he admitted he'd never bitten anyone before and didn't know how long his toxin worked.

She'd almost given herself away when he'd pulled her against him. The first time, her body had nearly reacted instinctively to his hand on her throat. It had taken every ounce of her self-control not to fight back or port. Then she'd felt his breath in her ear and his lips against her cheek, and she was almost certain he'd felt her tremble.

She was sure he must've suspected something when he pulled her back against his cock, and she'd felt that hard length of him. She managed to stay perfectly still, although her traitorous body had instantly gone wet between her legs. She was afraid he might be able to smell her arousal, but apparently not.

One of Talyn's hands twitched now, and Samhail flinched as the blade bit into his skin.

Nemesis take her. There was no going back now. If she didn't kill him, he'd most definitely kill her. She had to do this.

Talyn felt the tremor in her hands start to work its way up her arms.

She'd promised him a quick, clean death, but if she didn't stop shaking, the swords would tear his skin to shreds before she managed to end him. There'd be nothing quick or clean about it.

The tremor reached her chest, and Talyn tried again to make herself pull the blades across his throat, but her arms refused to obey the command. All it would take was two easy strokes, and she'd be free.

Not even two, just one. If she could manage to move just one of the blades, she'd never have to look over her shoulder again.

Well, that wasn't completely true. If she killed Samhail, the Lord and Lady of Hiraeth would hunt her to the ends of the world, but that wasn't something she'd worry about now. Her more immediate concern was taking care of Samhail and getting back to Rowe.

Talyn's hands twitched again, and Samhail took in a sharp breath.

She needed to do this now. It was kinder to do it quicker rather than nick his throat with a thousand tiny cuts.

Talyn closed her eyes, and the muscles in her arms clenched tightly as she promised herself she'd do it. She held her breath and…

"Fuck!" she screamed and pulled the swords from his throat.

She staggered backward away from him as her breath came in ragged gasps. Her arms shook violently, and she could barely hold the blades, which now felt like lead in her hands.

She couldn't do it. She couldn't fucking kill him, and it was likely to be the last mistake she ever made. It was a simple action she'd done hundreds of times before, yet she was powerless to do it this time. What was wrong with her?

Movement drew her eyes, and Talyn looked up to see Samhail standing before her. Two thin red lines on his neck trickled blood.

Talyn huffed a wry laugh and turned the swords over to hand them to him, handles first. She'd signed her own death warrant.

"I just hope you're better at making it quick and clean than I was," she said, smiling sadly. "I won't kneel, so just do it. There are rewards for proof of my death around the continent if you care to claim them."

Samhail reached forward slowly and took the swords from her. She was still breathing hard, and there was a vibration in her chest she couldn't quell. She closed her eyes and lowered her head, instinctively shielding her neck as she waited for the blow. She wished she had the courage to bare her throat to him and let him do it, but her last few threads of self-preservation won out.

She felt the tip of the cold steel under her chin, and she tensed as she waited for Samhail to push the blade through her neck. She sucked in a breath as the sword pressed upward instead, tipping her head back so she had to look up at him.

Nemesis take the man. He was savoring this, wasn't he. He was going to draw out her death, lord his victory over her.

To hells with that.

Talyn opened her eyes, intent on staring him down and letting him see every ounce of her defiance. She expected to see a cruel grin on his face as he reveled in her defeat, but she started in surprise at what she saw. The intensity in his eyes stole her breath, and she shuddered at the seriousness of his expression.

Her legs almost gave out as dread trickled through every limb. He wasn't going to kill her. He was going to do something much worse. Torture her? Take her to Revenmyer?

Despite her determination not to flinch, Talyn jerked back when Samhail pulled the blade away from her throat and thrust the two swords into the ground. He surged toward her, and her eyes widened in alarm as she stepped back, bracing for whatever he meant to do.

She waited to feel his fists slam into her. With his strength, he could break her bones into pieces with little effort. Or perhaps she'd feel the unyielding pressure of his hands on her throat again, cutting off her breath until her life faded away.

Talyn made a strangled sound of surprise as Samhail's lips instead collided with hers, and his tongue pressed into her mouth for a searing kiss. He snaked an arm around her waist and dragged her against him while his other hand threaded through her hair to hold her in place. His mouth was ravenous as it moved over hers, and she could do nothing but stand there in shock as she struggled to think beyond the relief and sensual heat that now pulsed through her.

Samhail kissed like he fought. Relentlessly. Unmercifully. Passionately. Her lips would be swollen again like last time when he was done with her, but she found she didn't give a fucking damn.

Talyn's body finally unfroze enough to respond in kind. She grabbed for his chest, but her fingers scraped against his leather armor, and she had to settle for gripping the heavy fabric of his sleeves. Her tongue met his stroke for stroke as she let her body pour its tension out in the kiss. Samhail drank her in, and a moan escaped her as a new kind of tremor shuddered through her. He answered with a groan of his own as he pulled her closer.

Talyn could barely wrap her mind around what was happening. She'd gone from nervousness, to elation, to panic, to fear, to…whatever this was, all in the span of about a minute, and her senses had yet to catch up.

She remembered wanting to feel Samhail's arms around her when she'd come to him as Cyra, but she hadn't realized just how much she'd needed to feel his embrace. That she looked like herself now seemed all the sweeter, and she tried to absorb his touch so she could remember what it felt like later.

This was why she couldn't kill him. She wanted him.

He still made her want to scream sometimes with his arrogance and high-handedness, but if anything, it only made her want him more. She'd never met a man who could dominate her body the way he could, not just with his strength, but with his sensuousness and ardor. She'd never wanted to give in to a man the way Samhail made her want to give in to him. Every part of her had surrendered to him completely the moment his lips touched hers.

Talyn let out a cry as the world suddenly went sideways, and she found herself on the ground under Samhail. His mouth was on hers again a second later, and her mind wavered somewhere between panic and rapture. Samhail's body was massive and powerful, and the assassin in her balked at being trapped beneath him like this. The way he caged her body in set off warning bells in her head.

Paradoxically, another part of her enjoyed the feel of having him on top of her, a part of her that saw his body not as a cage, but as a shield. Her head was too muddled right now to decide which was more likely, or perhaps they were both equally likely. She only knew this was dangerous.

There was always danger in Talyn's life, but it never seemed more present than right now with Samhail's mouth on hers and his body pressing her to the ground. This was a different kind of danger altogether, the kind where she'd let him do absolutely anything he wanted to her.

As if sensing her thoughts, Samhail began to tug up her sweater, and with an effort of will, she pulled her mouth away from his.

"What are you doing?" she gasped, trying to press firmly against his chest, but not quite succeeding as much as she'd hoped.

Samhail pulled back to look at her. "Kissing you," he said before his mouth dipped back down to tease a path along her neck.

Talyn closed her eyes again and suppressed a moan as every nerve he hit ignited another one somewhere else in her body.

"What are you doing with your hands?" she clarified.

His hand found the hem of her sweater and slipped up it, but she laid her own over his to hold it still. Samhail raised his head again.

"I thought that was pretty self-explanatory," he said, "but if you need me to spell it out, I'm trying to get to your breasts. I desperately need to have one of them in my mouth so I can run my tongue over your nipples and then suck-"

"I understand what you're trying to do," she cut in before he could finish the thought. "What I don't understand is what's happening here."

He cocked his head in confusion. "Again, I thought my intentions were fairly transparent." His voice grew husky. "After I explore every inch of your body with my tongue, I plan on plunging my cock into that tight little sheath between your legs and fucking you so hard you won't be able to ride a horse for days."

Talyn's mouth fell open. Gods above. She'd heard plenty of men say things like that before, and she usually just rolled her eyes, but when Samhail said it, the tension between her legs only coiled tighter.

Samhail started to lower his head to hers once again, but he snapped it up a moment later to look down at her in alarm. "You're not a virgin, are you?" he asked.

Talyn couldn't help the bark of laughter that erupted from her throat. She clamped her hand over her mouth to stifle any further outbursts, and it was a few seconds before she could pull it away and shake her head.

"No," she said, still trying to suppress a smile. "I'm not a virgin."

"Thank the gods," Samhail said, real relief in his voice. "I'm not the kind of man a woman should have for her first time."

Talyn had to agree. She'd seen the size of his cock, and she wouldn't wish that on anyone for their first time. It was bigger than anything she'd ever had inside her, and while she found the prospect of pushing herself down onto that huge, glorious length of him exciting, she couldn't imagine an untouched virgin trying to take him inside her. She still remembered the pain of her own first time, and the man – barely more than a boy – had been averaged sized.

Samhail frowned down at her. "So if you're not a virgin, then why are you stopping me?"

That was a damn good question. She'd been fantasizing about him since she'd met him, and her body was screaming at her to take everything he was offering right now. It was her mind that held back, and she wasn't entirely sure why.

"I just tried to kill you," she said, deflecting the question.

"I know. It was making my cock hard as fuck," he said.

He brought his mouth down on hers again, and Talyn went limp as she gave in. His kiss was still insistent, but his lips moved over hers slower now, so it was more an exploration than a conquest. His tongue delved in to play with hers, and Talyn struggled to focus on anything but the desire making her lightheaded.

Samhail's hand closed over her breast through her sweater, and the jolt of pleasure oddly cleared her mind. She pushed on him again, and he pulled away reluctantly.

"I thought you were going to kill me. Why didn't you?" she asked.

"I could ask you the same question," he said as his hand slid down to rest on her hip. "I have sword marks on my neck right now that say I should be dead. Why am I not dead?"

She shook her head slowly. "In all honesty, I don't know. I really tried to kill you, but I couldn't."

He brushed her hip lightly with his thumb, and Talyn's world narrowed to that one gods damned finger. She tried to ignore the flutter that stirred in her stomach at the touch.

"So why haven't you killed me yet?" she asked. Then her eyes widened again. "Wait, are you planning to fuck me and then kill me?"

She started to move out from under him, but Samhail's hold tightened on her. "Easy," he said, his voice calming. "I'm not planning to kill you."

"Why not?"

He chuckled. "You seem disappointed. Did you want me to?"

"No, of course not, but I don't understand why you don't want to. Aren't you afraid I'll attack you in your sleep again?"

"No," he said without hesitation. "If you couldn't kill me when you had me on my knees with two swords to my throat, then I'm not worried you're going to crush my head in with a rock while I sleep. Now answer my question."

Talyn furrowed her brows. "What was your question again?"

"If you're not a virgin, why do you keep stopping me?"

Talyn raised a brow. "It's awfully presumptuous of you to think that because I'm not a virgin I want to fuck you. Maybe I just don't want you."

It was Samhail's turn to raise a brow. "Your body is clearly saying otherwise," he said. He slid his hand off her hip and over her stomach where he slowly undid the first fastening on her pants. "I'm fairly certain if I put my hand between your legs, it will come back dripping wet. Should we see if I'm right?"

His voice had gone husky again, and Talyn bit her lip. She knew she should stop him, but all she could think of was how much she wanted him to push his hand into her pants. She thought about him brushing his thumb over the sensitive spot at her apex, and her hips lifted unconsciously. She imagined him slipping a finger into her and her riding his hand until she felt the release she so desperately needed right now.

Samhail's eyes flashed when her hips pressed up against his hand, and he popped two more fastenings on her pants.

Talyn's mind screamed at her to stop him, but she said nothing, did nothing, as his hand slipped into her pants and found the knot of nerves between her thighs. She jerked as his fingers stroked over her clit on their way to her soaking wet folds, but he didn't even pause as he pushed two long fingers inside her.

Talyn made a noise that was part whimper, part moan as Samhail began to stroke between her legs. She forgot they were enemies, forgot to be annoyed at him, and forgot she'd promised herself she wouldn't give him the satisfaction of seeing how much she wanted him. She forgot it all as Samhail pumped his fingers slowly in and out of her.

"This isn't…a good idea," she managed to say between pants.

"I disagree. This is the best idea I've had in days," Samhail said as he lowered his head again to press his lips against her neck. His teeth scraped lightly over her skin, and Talyn couldn't help the shiver of bliss that traveled down her body all the way to her toes. She pushed her hips up as she gave in to the urge to ride his fingers as she'd imagined.

Talyn struggled to bring her mind back from the brink. She didn't think she'd ever wanted a man as much as she wanted Samhail right now, yet something was holding her back, almost like when she'd tried to kill him. The desire was there, but the ability to act wasn't.

Talyn let out a strangled sound of frustration and pushed against

Samhail's chest again. "No, I can't! Let me up."

Samhail lifted his head from her neck reluctantly. Talyn saw the momentary indecision in his eyes, but then he slowly took his hand out of her pants. He didn't let her up, though. Instead, he brought the fingers that had been inside her to his mouth and sucked on them.

"Mmm. You taste so fucking good," he rasped. "I can't wait to get my tongue between your legs."

Talyn swallowed hard. Her voice would break if she tried to speak, so she only pushed on his chest again, and he shifted his weight to let her pull herself out from under him. Talyn got to her feet unsteadily, and Samhail followed a moment later. Her eyes dipped to his groin where the evidence of his arousal was very, very apparent.

"I'm sorry," she said as she refastened her pants. He was likely to feel some discomfort for a while. She was feeling a rather acute discomfort herself that she tried to ignore. "But this is a business arrangement, and I try not to mix business with pleasure."

Liar. She mixed them all the time.

He cocked his head. "Business? I wasn't aware you were being paid to take me to Sandrian."

"Even exchange," she said. "I take you to Sandrian, and you don't let Lord Bressen throw me in Revenmyer."

"And after I have Sandrian and our business arrangement is over?"

"Then maybe we can revisit our boundaries."

"*Our* boundaries?"

"Fine. *My* boundaries."

Samhail stepped closer to her, and Talyn clenched her teeth as she craned her neck up to look him in the eyes. She was taller than most women, and she wasn't used to having to look up so far at someone. It was…disconcerting.

"We should get moving if you're not going to kill me," she said.

"I might be rethinking that decision," he grumbled, but there was the curl of a smile on his lips.

"Well, we should put some miles in while you make up your mind," she said as she turned to head for the horses.

She untied her horse's reins from Samhail's saddle, but when she turned around, he was right there.

"You've used up your second chances," he said. "Behave yourself from now on, or I won't have a choice. You're on your honor not to use your powers against me."

Talyn looked down at her bare wrist. She'd almost forgotten about the caronium cuff. Apparently he hadn't been able to find the one she'd tossed away.

Talyn flinched as Samhail raised his hand. He paused at her flinch, but then he lifted the hand to her shoulder and pushed her hair away from her neck. She didn't understand what he was doing at first until his finger brushed the wound where he'd sunk his fangs into her. She couldn't tell if her tremble was from the memory of her body going numb or from the unexpected gentleness of his touch. Yet there was an implicit threat in the touch as well, a reminder that he had a way to subdue her if needed.

"Do we have an understanding?" he asked softly.

"Yes," Talyn said, meeting his gaze. "I'll behave, and you'll keep your hands to yourself."

His brows pinched into a deep frown. She knew he didn't want to agree to that, but he nodded finally.

"Fine. I won't touch you until you ask me to," he said. His lips curled into a grin. "Because you *will* ask me, hummingbird. I've tasted your nectar, and it's only a matter of time before you give me more."

Chapter 20

Talyn snapped to attention a couple hours later when her horse knickered, and she surveyed the area for signs of trouble. She was annoyed to realize she'd been lost in thought about Samhail kissing her, and she hadn't been paying attention to her surroundings as they rode. It was wholly unlike her, and she chastised herself for such carelessness.

She needed to get her head on straight and stop daydreaming like some kind of foolish, lovestruck maiden. For fuck's sake, it was like she'd never been kissed before.

Well, not like *that* she hadn't anyway.

Talyn eyed her horse. Animals were great at sensing danger, and she often counted on them to provide advanced warning. She listened closely now for the faintest sound, the scrape of a sword leaving its sheath, the winding of a crossbow, or the snap of a twig under a heavy boot.

There was nothing.

Not ready to relax yet, she scanned the trees for movement or a pop of color that might be out of place among the shades of green and brown that dominated the landscape. Again nothing. Her horse's knicker was apparently just that. Only a knicker.

What finally convinced her there was no imminent threat was the ease with which Samhail rode just ahead of her. All his muscles were relaxed – or as relaxed as she'd ever seen them get with him – and he rode with the barest arch to his back that bespoke a lack of tension in his spine. It was the want of urgency in his body that calmed her own nerves. If Samhail wasn't worried, she didn't need to be either.

Samhail's posture could be deceptive, though. Even if she'd let her own guard down, she suspected every one of Samhail's senses was alive and alert for danger, despite what his seeming relaxation might say.

She was shocked he'd let her ride her own horse. Not that it really mattered anymore. Without the caronium cuff, he couldn't keep her from porting. He had to trust she wasn't going to run or try to kill him again.

Strangely, she had no desire to do either anymore. She still didn't know what they'd do when they met Sandrian, but she at least accepted they were going to see him, and she might as well make the most of this time with Samhail. The gods knew he was nice to look at, even if she couldn't touch him.

They hadn't spoken again since getting back on their horses. Talyn wasn't much more of a conversationalist than Samhail was, but the silence was starting to grate on her.

For the gods' sakes, she'd almost slit his throat earlier, but instead of killing her as he should have, he'd taken her to the ground, kissed her soundly, slid a couple fingers inside her, then licked her wetness off them.

Surely they had some things to talk about.

"Why don't you get along with Surgeon and Serise?" she asked suddenly, and her voice cut the quiet like a knife.

She wasn't sure where the question came from, but she'd needed to say something, just to break the silence.

Samhail gave her a half-glance over his shoulder before turning forward again. He didn't answer, and Talyn pursed her lips at the dismissal before nudging her horse forward to pull up next to his.

"People who ignore me usually find it doesn't end well," she said.

He snorted. "And what are you going to do if I ignore you? Scratch up the front of my neck some more?"

Talyn scowled at him. "I'm already regretting not following through on that," she said. "But why not just answer me and make this journey less monotonous on both of us?"

He sighed. "I don't get along with any of my siblings," he said with a shrug. "Gargoyles aren't really brought up to value family bonds, and truth be told, my siblings aren't the kind of people I like to associate with.

Surgeon and Serise aren't as bad as Sadira and Soldier, but the twins have always had their own special relationship with each other, so there wasn't much room for anyone else with them. Then, of course, there's the fact that they're both batshit insane."

Talyn raised a brow. "And Lord Bressen still hired them to protect Lady Cyra? That seems risky."

"They won't hurt Cyra."

"How can you be so sure?"

He paused. "Just trust me. They won't."

"Because you'd make them regret it?"

A smile cracked his lips. "I would, but that's not the only reason."

"And you're not going to tell me the other reason?"

"No."

She frowned. "What exactly is between you, Cyra, and Bressen?" she asked. She didn't really expect him to answer, but she had to ask. Her curiosity was killing her.

Yes…curiosity. That's all it was.

"That's, as you said, between us," he answered.

"You just put your hands down my pants and tried to fuck me with your fingers," she countered. "I'd like to know if I'm getting into the middle of something between you and two of the most powerful perimortals on the continent. I want to be sure Cyra isn't going to burn me alive or turn me into a pig the next time I see her."

He chuckled. "She won't."

"And I'm supposed to take your word for that?"

"Yes."

Talyn growled her frustration and jerked the reins to guide her horse off the path toward a stream.

"What are you doing?" Samhail asked, following her.

"I need a break, and my horse needs water," she snapped as she slid off her saddle.

Samhail dismounted and led his horse to the stream to drink as well.

"Why are you so intent on knowing what's between me, Bressen, and Cyra?" he asked. Then he added, "*If* there was something."

"When I was sitting on your lap as Cyra," she said carefully, aware she was treading on dangerous ground, "you said you couldn't do anything because you didn't have Lord Bressen's permission to touch me…uh, her. Tell me that wouldn't make you curious."

"What's your theory?" he asked.

"I told you before, either the lord likes to watch his wife with other men, or the two of you fucked her together."

"Jealous?" he asked with a half smirk.

"Jealous that you got to fuck Cyra?" she said, turning to him with a sly smile. "A bit. The lady is beautiful, and she moans rather prettily."

His mouth actually fell open at that.

"And just in case you're wondering," she said, doubling down, "I've fucked a woman before when I shifted into a man, so if you want to compare cocks sometime…"

She let the thought hang in the air. He'd probably never considered she could take the form of a man – most people didn't – and she wondered suddenly how he felt about that. To her surprise, his expression changed from one of shock to intrigue.

"Gods damn me," he said, and his eyes went unfocused as if he were imagining it. "I'd pay a fortune to watch you and Cyra in bed together."

Talyn rolled her eyes. She was pretty sure he was still picturing her as a woman in bed with Cyra, but she'd let him have this.

"So am I right?" she asked.

"Right about what?"

"Does Lord Bressen just like watching you with his wife, or did the two of you fuck her together?"

He looked at her a moment. "Tell me how many people you've assassinated, and I'll answer your question."

Her eyebrows went up. That's all he wanted to know?

"Two hundred and seventy-two," she said.

He looked surprised. Whether it was surprise that it was so many or surprise she knew the exact number so readily, she wasn't sure.

"How old are you?" he asked.

"Answer my question first."

He was quiet a long time, and she thought he wasn't going to answer.

"Bressen and I shared Cyra on the last Harmilan," he said finally.

Talyn fought back the twisting in her stomach. She'd been dying to know what had happened – was certain he'd fucked Cyra – but now that she knew the answer, she felt anything but triumphant. She felt…queasy.

"I'm twenty-six," she said past the knot in her throat.

"Fuck," Samhail said, shaking his head.

That wasn't quite the reaction she'd been expecting, but she didn't question him.

"And you made your first kill at sixteen?" he asked. "Is that true?"

Talyn stiffened but nodded. "I didn't kill again for another year or so after that, but yes. I was sixteen the first time I killed someone."

He eyed her as if seeing the girl she'd once been, and she turned away from him.

"Who did you kill?" he asked.

"A very bad man."

"Bad how?"

He stepped closer to her, and her skin prickled at his nearness. If he touched her right now, she might just give in to him.

He didn't touch her, though.

"He was a murderer and a rapist," she said. "He'd killed several women I knew of by the time I found him."

"What did you do to him?"

"I…did more or less what he did to his victims. Tortured him. Violated him. Killed him. I spent five hours letting him die slowly."

"Why him?"

She huffed a laugh. "Why not him?"

"There must've been a reason you chose him specifically. Something that brought him to your attention?"

She smiled sadly. "There was."

Several seconds blew away on the wind before his hand closed on her arm, and he turned her toward him. She had to crane her neck up.

"It sounds like revenge," he said.

She shook her head. "Not revenge. Punishment."

She flinched for a second time as he lifted his hand to brush the back of his finger down her cheek. Her body was too used to reacting defensively when someone raised a hand to her, but his gesture was achingly tender, and she struggled to keep her face passive. When he reached her chin, he held it lightly while his thumb brushed over her bottom lip, and she fought the urge to port away from him.

His touch was too familiar. Too gentle. Too... risky.

Samhail began to lower his head, and her eyes flared. Gods above, he was going to kiss her again.

A hundred thoughts tumbled over each other in Talyn's mind as she tried to decide whether to pull away or let him kiss her. She was shocked by how much she wanted to feel his lips on hers again, but there was a voice in her mind screaming at her to turn away. She smothered it and parted her lips in invitation.

So much for his promise not to touch her again.

Samhail tipped her head up further, and she almost moaned when his mouth brushed hers. She managed to swallow back the sound, but the next press of his mouth was more insistent, and his tongue slipped in to tease hers as she closed her eyes, letting herself enjoy the kiss.

She'd nearly let herself go completely when she felt the muscles in his body tense. His head snapped up, and a second later, the horses knickered.

Samhail stepped back from her just as the thwack of a crossbow split the air, and he grunted loudly as the bolt found its mark.

Samhail

Samhail's shoulder kicked back as the shaft of a bolt suddenly appeared there, stuck in his hard leather armor. The armor had stopped most of the bolt, but the tip broke through, and he felt the pinch of its sharp point scratch his skin. If he hadn't been so distracted by the woman in front of him, he'd have realized sooner they weren't alone in the woods.

"Get behind me!" Samhail yelled as he pulled the bolt from his armor and shoved Talyn behind him.

He reached up to unsheathe his swords, but that's when the second and third thwacks sounded. Sharp pain stabbed his stomach and his side under his arm where the armor didn't cover his body, and he jerked forward, instinctively curling inward to protect his torso from further harm. He'd exposed the area when he reached up for the swords, and the enemy had taken advantage of his momentary vulnerability. He staggered back against the nearest tree to brace against it.

"No!" Talyn cried, and then she was at his side, her hand on his chest.

Samhail had sustained plenty of wounds in battle, and ones like these normally wouldn't have made the list of his top twenty worst injuries, but he felt instantly something was wrong. The bolt stuck in his side was especially agonizing, having likely broken a rib on the way in, but more than that, he'd felt his power drain after they'd hit.

Caronium-tipped weapons were common in state-funded militaries, but it was odd for anyone else to have access to them given how regulated caronium was.

Samhail grabbed the shaft of the bolt under his arm to pull it out, but a voice halted him.

"Leave it, or the next bolt is to your head," a man said as he emerged from the woods with a crossbow aimed straight at Samhail's face.

Samhail froze as another fifteen or so men emerged from the trees now as well, two more with crossbows aimed at him.

"Who are you and what do you want?" Talyn asked the man. She stepped in front of Samhail, and he growled as he tried to pull her away, but she shook him off.

The man who'd spoken leered at her as his gaze raked down her body, and Samhail had the urge to pluck the eyes out of his head.

"We'll deal with you after we get some answers out of your man here, sweetheart," he said huskily.

"He's not my man," Talyn said coolly. "He tried to strangle me to death a couple days ago, and I almost slit his throat earlier today."

The man blinked, and Samhail flinched inwardly at her words.

"Well then, it looks like we're rescuing you," the man said, "and I'm sure you'll find some way to show your appreciation for that."

Talyn chuckled. "Oh, don't worry. I'll be more than happy to show you how I feel, but first tell me what kind of answers you're looking for. Maybe I can help."

The man considered her before answering.

"He looks like someone we were told to find. Do you know his name? We're looking for someone called Samhail."

Samhail looked at the man more closely. They were looking for him specifically? Why?

"I'm afraid this isn't who you're looking for then," Talyn said, feigning regret. "His name is Percy."

Talyn was turned away from him, so she couldn't see the glare he shot her, but the man with the crossbow did.

"You're lying," the man said. "We were told to find a huge man with long white hair, and this brute here fits that description perfectly. I don't think there are many men on the continent that look like that."

"And if he were this Samhail you're looking for," Talyn asked, "what would you want with him?"

"King Sandrian has offered a rich reward for his capture. Or his head," the man said. "Even split between us all, we'd be wealthy beyond our wildest dreams." He indicated his companions.

The bounty. Gods damn Sandrian.

The man smiled at Talyn, the leer still in his eyes, and Samhail once again had to stop himself from attempting to break the man's spine.

The caronium in the bolts was making him too weak. He had to get them out soon before he couldn't stand anymore. Wearing a caronium cuff was one thing, but having the metal lodged in his gut and ribs was quite another. If Talyn kept the man talking, he might find an opening.

"If you were to help us bring in Samhail," the man said to Talyn, "we could split the reward one more way. Are you sure that's not him?"

"Sandrian is no longer king of Rowe," Talyn pointed out, ignoring the question. "How do you know he'll make good on the reward?"

"He may not be king yet, but he will be soon," the man said. "When that happens, he'll reward all those who helped him regain power, like us."

"So you're doing all this on a gamble Sandrian will eventually retake Rowe?" Talyn asked incredulously. "What if he doesn't? Then you've done all this for nothing, made yourselves outlaws for nothing."

Some of the other men shifted, but the man with the crossbow said confidently, "Sandrian will retake Rowe. We have faith in that, and then those of us who've been loyal to him will be rewarded."

"Where are you supposed to take Samhail when you capture him?" she asked.

The man's expression faltered slightly, as if he realized she might be using him to get information.

"Come with us and find out," he said. "You can stay with me. I won't let the rest of the boys touch you."

There was a murmur of grumbling behind the man, but he held up a hand and the others went quiet again.

"I see," Talyn said. "Well, I think I know everything I need to know."

She turned to Samhail, and he tried to read her expression. She couldn't really be considering the man's offer…could she?

Of course she could. She'd been hired by Sandrian, and something curdled in his stomach that had nothing to do with the nausea he felt from his wound. When would he learn not to give her any more chances?

"You can't trust them," he gritted out between the pain.

Talyn smiled at him. "I need to borrow Fred."

Faster than Samhail could've expected, Talyn bent and pulled the dagger out of his boot. Then she was gone.

She reappeared a second later behind the man with the crossbow and jabbed the dagger into his neck. Her other hand pushed the crossbow down in case his finger squeezed the trigger by reflex, and it turned out to be a good move. The crossbow fired harmlessly into the ground as blood poured down the man's neck, soaking his clothing. He made a guttural noise as the blood dripped into his throat, and he slumped to the ground.

The other men were momentarily stunned as they looked at their fallen companion, but Talyn didn't wait for them to regain their heads. She disappeared again to port right behind a second man with a crossbow. She slit his throat as well before swiveling around to plunge the now-bloody dagger into the heart of the man standing right behind her. Then she was gone once more, appearing behind the third man with a crossbow.

By this time, the men realized what was happening.

Having seen two of his other companions fall already, the third crossbowman turned the second he saw Talyn disappear, so she appeared in front of him instead of behind him. He fired, but Talyn realized the danger just in time to throw herself out of the way of the bolt that would've lodged itself right in her stomach. Instead, it lodged in the leg of one of the other outlaws, who screamed in pain and fell to the ground.

The flurry of sudden activity finally spurred Samhail to move. He yanked the crossbow bolt out of his side and felt hot blood spill down his hip. His vision blurred momentarily with the pain, then he pulled the bolt from his stomach as well. He waited to feel his strength and power return, but he was as weak as ever, and now he was bleeding profusely.

Samhail tried to stagger forward. Talyn was fast and had her powers, but she was taking on at least twelve men right now. He had to help her.

Samhail reached up and drew his swords, the movement sending gut-twisting pain shooting up and down his torso. He allowed himself only one grunt before he launched himself at the nearest man. Luckily, the man's attention was focused on Talyn, so Samhail took him completely unaware as his sword cleaved the man in half.

Before the body even hit the ground, Samhail was moving again, slashing out at the next outlaw while spearing a third in the gut. The spike of adrenaline made his vision go fuzzy for a moment as he stumbled forward to engage another outlaw, and the momentary loss of sight gave the man an opening to slash him across the thigh with his own blade. The cut wasn't overly deep, but the leather of Samhail's pants became instantly wet with blood.

Samhail slashed out with both swords, and deep gashes in the shape of an X opened across the man's chest. The man's scream rent the air before he pitched forward to land face-down on the ground.

Samhail wheeled to face the next attacker, but he came up short when he realized there were none left. All fifteen of the men now lay on the ground in puddles of blood, and Talyn was nowhere to be seen.

He swore violently, but he jolted a second later as Talyn appeared at his side. He just barely managed to keep from swinging out instinctively at her sudden appearance.

"Nemesis take you!" she yelled at him. "Why did you pull the bolts out? You're bleeding all over the place."

"The tips were caronium," Samhail gritted out.

His weakness had returned now that the adrenaline spike was subsiding, and he sank to his knees.

"We need to get you to a healer," she said kneeling down beside him. "We passed that town a ways back. We need to get back there."

Talyn stood up and hurried over to the nearest body. She used Fred to cut the leg of the man's pants off and then pulled the belt from around his waist. She folded the pant leg into a tight square and pressed it to Samhail's side over the wound to staunch the blood.

"Hold that there," she ordered, and Samhail obeyed.

Talyn looped the belt around Samhail and fastened it over the wound to hold the cloth in place. Luckily the man she'd taken the belt from was on the heftier side because the leather just barely managed to close over the thick muscles of Samhail's torso. He grunted as Talyn pulled the belt tight and secured it. She repeated the process for his stomach wound.

"My power isn't returning," Samhail said. "It should've come back when I pulled the bolts out. Maybe there was something else on them."

Talyn went over to examine one of the bolts he'd pulled out.

"The tip is missing," Talyn said. "It must still be in the wound. We'll have to get it out before you can be healed." She paused and narrowed her eyes as she examined the bolt more closely. "It almost looks as if the point was meant to come off so it would lodge in its target."

Samhail heaved himself to his feet with a groan, and Talyn dropped the bolt to hurry back to him. She positioned herself under his arm and wrapped a hand around his waist as if she might actually be able to hold him up. He didn't bother trying to lean on her. His weight would've buckled her knees, but he let her lead him back toward his horse. He managed to mount with some difficulty, and Talyn mounted her own horse to lead the way to the town they'd seen a few miles back.

Samhail used the rest of his strength to stay upright in the saddle, but through his haze of pain, one thought shone through.

Talyn hadn't betrayed him or left him to die. She'd saved his life.

Chapter 21

Talyn

Talyn urged her horse into a quick walk. She was afraid a swifter gait might only aggravate Samhail's wounds.

It took them half an hour to get back to the town, and it was nearly dark by then. Samhail looked pale and barely conscious. He'd managed to stay upright in his saddle, but she had to get him to a healer soon or he wouldn't make it with all the blood he'd lost. His own fast perimortal healing might've helped him if it hadn't been for the damned piece of the crossbow tip that was apparently still lodged in him. Getting that out would be a priority.

Talyn stopped the first person she saw and asked where to find the healer. The woman pointed her toward the healer's house but said the man was out delivering a baby on a farm a couple miles away. Talyn swore and asked the woman to direct her to the nearest inn instead.

A couple minutes later, Talyn and Samhail stopped their horses in front of the inn the woman directed her to, and Talyn went inside. Thankfully the innkeeper was inclined to be helpful, especially when she explained who she had outside. The man didn't recognize Samhail's name, but he certainly knew Lord Bressen, and he sprang into action when Talyn explained that Samhail was one of the lord's most trusted generals. She wasn't entirely sure that's what Samhail was, but it seemed accurate enough for her purposes.

The innkeeper sent one of his staff to ride for the healer and then came outside to help Talyn get Samhail off his horse. The innkeeper's eyes widened to see the warrior, but whether he was more concerned by Samhail's size or how awful he looked, she wasn't sure.

Between the two of them, they got Samhail off his horse and down the hall of the inn to a room. Talyn sent a silent prayer of thanks that the room was on the first floor, since they never would've been able to get Samhail up the stairs if they'd had to.

She chastised herself mentally for taking so much time to question the outlaw. She hadn't realized the head of the bolt had been made of caronium or that its point was designed to break off and remain in its victim. She would've acted sooner if she'd realized what the bolt had been doing to Samhail, but she'd seen an opportunity to get some information and hadn't wanted to let it pass.

Talyn and the innkeeper laid Samhail down on the bed, and Talyn sent the man to get her some water, alcohol, clean cloths, and a pair of tweezers, although she didn't hold out much hope he'd find the last. She was surprised when he returned a few minutes later with all four items, explaining that his wife had a pair of tweezers she used to pluck her eyebrows. Talyn had blinked at that, but she thanked the man and got to work on Samhail.

She wasn't sure how quickly the healer would be able to get here, even if he knew how urgently he was needed, so she'd just have to do what she could in the meantime. She didn't like how much paler Samhail had gotten just in the last few minutes.

"What are you doing?" Samhail asked as he watched her clean the tweezers in the alcohol.

"I'm going to get the tip of that bolt out of your wound," she said. "The healer is on his way, but I'm not waiting."

"Have you ever done something like this before?" he asked.

"No," she admitted, "but how hard can it be?"

She almost laughed at the grimace that crossed his face.

"Do you know which wound that bolt came out of?" she asked.

"My side, I think. But it's possible there are tips in both wounds if that was how they were designed."

"Turn over," she said.

He rolled over so she could more easily reach the wound on his side, and Talyn unbuckled the belt from around his ribs. He lifted himself slightly so she could tug it out from under him.

"Something tells me I'm going to need this," he said as he took the belt from her and folded it a couple times before clamping his teeth down on the leather.

"If I'd known you were going to be a big baby about it, I would've knocked you out and been done with it already," she grumbled.

Samhail glared up at her, but Talyn just smiled.

"Relax," she said, "I have a very steady hand. If they could still speak, all the people I've killed would tell you so."

Samhail pulled the belt out of his mouth. "The cuts on my neck say otherwise."

Talyn shrugged. Fair enough. She'd been chattering on mostly to calm her own nerves, but she knew it couldn't be helping him much. She lifted the cloth off the wound and winced at how jagged and red it looked. Him ripping the bolt out certainly hadn't helped.

Talyn took a deep breath and slowly pressed the tweezers into the wound. Samhail's entire body tensed in pain, but she kept pressing, moving the tweezers in as slowly as possible so she might feel when they hit the tip of the bolt. The tweezers were almost two inches into the wound when she felt them butt up against something hard.

"I think I found it," she said, more to herself than him. "I'm going to try and grab it."

Samhail didn't say anything, but she felt his breathing get shallower, as if he was trying to hold as still as possible.

She'd been pressing the tweezers into the wound in their closed position, but she carefully let them open now and tried to push them down further. Samhail's muscles clenched even more. He grunted but didn't move otherwise. When she'd gone in a little farther, Talyn pressed the tweezers together again and felt them close on something solid. Praying she had a good enough hold on the tip of the bolt, she started to draw them back out. Blood welled up from the wound anew and she pressed a clean cloth carefully around the hole to keep it clear. Samhail closed his eyes and grunted again, but he remained unmoving.

Slowly, ever so slowly, Talyn pulled the tip of the crossbow bolt out of the wound. She lost her grip on it once and had to re-grab it with the tweezers, but a few moments later she saw the piece of metal crest the surface. She pulled it the rest of the way, then dropped it onto the bedside table. Her shoulders relaxed, and she exhaled deeply as Samhail's body eased next to her as well.

"Does that feel any better?" she asked, pressing another clean cloth to the still-open wound. "Are your powers returning?"

"Somewhat," Samhail said as he removed the belt from his mouth. "I can feel them again, but they're not at full strength."

"There must be another tip in your stomach," she said. "Give me the belt back so I can bind this again, and then I'll see about the other wound."

Samhail handed her the belt, and she slipped it back around him. He was quiet as he watched her pull the leather tight and buckle it.

"You could've handed me over to those men," he said.

"They were looking for glory and reward," Talyn said, "and they would've shared me among them if given half a chance, willing or not. I never would've handed you over to men like that."

"And if they'd been a different kind of men?" he pressed.

"Do yourself a favor and don't overthink this. Suffice it to say, I'm not sure Sandrian himself is the type of person I want to work for anymore, so I'm inclined to see where this little adventure takes us."

Samhail rolled onto his back again as she finished buckling the belt, and their eyes met. She knew they were midnight blue, but they looked black in the dim light of the room.

"You're an efficient killer," Samhail said. "I'll give you that."

He was looking at her shirt, which had a relatively small amount of blood on it given the number of men she'd just killed. Talyn stiffened, but Samhail shook his head.

"I meant that as a compliment," he said. "We'd have been in big trouble if you hadn't dispatched those men as quickly as you did."

She cocked her head at him. "You seem surprised at my efficiency," she said as she cleaned the tweezers in preparation to go after the second tip. "You're aware of my reputation as an assassin, are you not?"

"Reputations aren't always earned," he said. "Most of the people who supposedly hired you never saw the same person, so it's impossible to know if they were actually hiring you or someone they thought was you."

Talyn smiled. "True. I always use a different face when I meet with potential clients. It's hard for the authorities to track you if they don't know what you look like."

"I suppose your victims never see the same face either," he said.

She went serious. "The opposite. Everyone I kill sees the same face."

Samhail furrowed his brows, and she knew he was about to ask her to explain when she noticed the streak of red further down his body.

"Your leg is bleeding," she said in surprise. "When did that happen?"

"One of the men slashed me. It's just a scratch."

Talyn pressed near the wound, and blood welled up under her fingers.

"It's not a scratch," she said grabbing for more of the clean cloths the innkeeper had brought. She pressed them down onto his leg. "Hold that there. And where the hell is that damned healer?"

Talyn unbuckled the belt from around his stomach and handed it to him to put in his mouth.

"I wasn't trying to kill you the other day," he offered, "just…keep you from escaping."

Talyn was confused before understanding dawned on her.

"Your hand crushing my throat said otherwise," she said with a little more bite than she intended. She wasn't sure why he wanted to bring this up now.

He nodded in acknowledgement. "I might've lost control a bit. I was extremely angry at the time."

Talyn went still again before she sighed and looked away. "I might've overstepped with you that day in the great room," she admitted. "At the time it seemed like a good way to get information, but I can see how what I did was…"

She stopped, uncertain how to describe what had happened. She'd put Samhail in a vulnerable and exposed position – both literally and figuratively – and in hindsight she didn't blame him for being furious at her. She could only imagine how she might've felt if things were reversed and a masque had come to her as someone she trusted. She shuddered now to think about it.

"It was a violation," she said finally, "and for what it's worth, I'm sorry. I shouldn't have done it."

"How far were you planning to take it?" he asked.

Talyn's eyes flicked back to his. She could see the blue in them again, and that eased her mind.

"I don't know," she said, shaking her head. "I hadn't planned to do half of what I did. It…it was good you stopped me because your guess is as good as mine how much further I would've taken it."

"Why?" he asked, his brows knitting together again. "You say you didn't plan to do half of it, so why did you do any of it?"

Talyn opened her mouth to explain, but she had no idea what to say. She was spared from trying to come up with an answer when a knock sounded at the door, making both her and Samhail jump.

Talyn got up and opened the door, Fred hidden behind her back. A man in his thirties with dark brown skin and a neatly trimmed black beard stood in the hallway.

"I'm Caleb," the man said. "I was told you needed a healer?"

"Yes, come in," Talyn said. She opened the door for him and put the dagger back onto the dresser.

Caleb entered and took in Samhail lying on the bed. Like the innkeeper, his eyes widened slightly at the sight of the warrior, but he recovered quickly and went over to examine Samhail.

"What happened?" he asked.

"We were attacked by outlaws," Talyn said. "He was hit with

crossbow bolts. The heads were made of caronium, and it looks like the tips were meant to break off and embed in the wound. I managed to get one tip out with some tweezers, but he hasn't fully recovered his powers. Either I missed a piece of the bolt or there's a second one in his stomach. Is there any chance you're perimortal?"

Caleb looked between them, seeming uncertain. Then he nodded.

"Only a few people in town know I'm perimortal," he said, "but yes. I have a little power. Just keep that to yourself please. Some people in these small towns still fear our kind."

Talyn stepped back as Caleb extended his hands out to hover over Samhail, his power searching the battle-hardened body for injuries. She breathed a sigh of relief that he was a perimortal healer and not a mortal one. She would've taken either at this point, but it was far better for Samhail to have a perimortal given their situation.

Caleb placed his hand lightly over the wound on Samhail's side.

"You weren't hurt?" he asked her over his shoulder as he worked.

"No, I'm fine," Talyn said.

Caleb hesitated a moment before asking, "And the outlaws?"

"Beyond your abilities to help," she answered.

Caleb stilled, then nodded. He was quiet for several minutes before he lifted his hand to reveal that the wound in Samhail's side was now gone, except for a lightly pink scar.

Talyn pushed out a long breath in relief.

Caleb hovered his hand over the stomach wound next and frowned.

"What is it?" Talyn asked.

"I feel the caronium," he said. "You were right. There's still a piece."

"Can you get it out?" she asked.

"I should be able to," Caleb said.

He turned his attention to Samhail. "You're… a gargoyle?" he asked tentatively, glancing at Talyn.

"Yes," Samhail said, his voice hard. "Is that an issue?"

"Not at all," Caleb assured him quickly. "It just helps to know all the details before I heal someone. There can be subtle but important differences between fully human perimortals and demi-human ones.”

Caleb held his hand over Samhail’s wound, and when he pulled it back, a small piece of caronium hovered just above his palm. He dropped the tip on the nightstand where Talyn had put the other. He placed his hand back on top of the wound, and when he pulled it away again minutes later, the hole was completely closed up.

Lastly, Caleb turned his attention to the slash on Samhail’s leg, and about a minute later he sat back to examine the newly healed wound.

“I couldn’t fully prevent the scars,” Caleb said to Samhail, indicating the slightly raised pink skin where the wound on his stomach had been, “but I did my best to make them minimal. I’m not a terribly powerful perimortal, so my abilities have their limitations.”

“They’re not my first scars, and they won’t be my last,” Samhail said. “I probably needed a few more anyway. Thank you.”

Caleb nodded and stood up. “Is there anything else I can do for you? Was anyone else hurt?”

“No,” Talyn said. “Thank you for your help.”

Caleb nodded. “Very well. I’m heading home. Let me know if you need anything else before you leave town. I suggest you stay here tonight and rest before moving on.” He looked at Samhail. “You lost a lot of blood, and that’s something your body will have to replace on its own.”

Samhail fished in his pocket and pulled out a gold coin. He tossed it to Caleb, who caught it and nodded his thanks.

Talyn walked Caleb to the door and saw him out.

When she turned back, Samhail was standing up. She looked down at the blood streaked across the blanket and moved toward the bed to start pulling it off.

“I’ll get you some new bedding from the innkeeper,” she said as she balled up the stained sheets and blanket and moved to leave.

“Get *us* some new bedding,” he corrected.

Talyn paused at the door. “The inn isn’t full,” she said. “There’s no reason for us to share a room.”

“Nevertheless, we will.”

Talyn huffed a laugh. “You still don’t trust me not to run, even after I saved your life?”

“I’m grateful to you for helping me, but I need you to stay where I can keep an eye on you. I’m already operating outside the bounds of what Bressen would condone. If he found out I let you have your own room…”

Samhail trailed off, and Talyn’s face hardened.

“Of course,” she said bitterly. “We wouldn’t want you to get in trouble with Lord Bressen. Can I go get new bedding now, or do you need to accompany me to do that as well?”

Samhail frowned but nodded his head toward the door to indicate she could go. Talyn turned without another word and stalked off.

She found the innkeeper easily enough, and he insisted on accompanying her back to the room to help make the bed himself. He brought up some dinner with him as well. Samhail was standing where she’d left him, and the innkeeper set to work as she and Samhail ate. When the bed was remade and the innkeeper left, the room was silent again as Talyn and Samhail looked at each other.

“Your bed is ready,” she said as she sat down in one of the chairs. She threw one leg over the other and crossed her arms.

“Our bed,” he corrected her again.

“Oh no,” Talyn said. “You can make me sleep in the same room as you, but you can’t make me sleep in the same bed.”

“Actually, I can,” he said and started toward her.

“What are you doing?” Talyn asked as she sat up in the chair. She uncrossed her legs and arms, ready to move. “Lie down. You’re supposed to be resting.”

Samhail didn’t answer but just reached down as if he planned to pick her up in his arms. She instantly ported across the room.

He didn’t seem surprised. Instead, he simply changed course to pursue her on the other side.

"What are you doing?" she repeated as she backed away from him. He kept coming, and she ported again to the opposite side of the room when he got close.

"I can do this all night," she said, as he turned once again to face her.

"Can you?" he asked. "Because I seemed to recall the night we chased you through Bressen's house that your porting power was starting to wane by the end. I suspect there's a limit to the number of times you can do it before you need to rest."

Talyn stiffened, and she knew he could see the truth of his theory in her posture.

"The question is," he said, "whether you really want to wear yourself down making me chase you all over this room in my weakened state for the next half hour, or whether you just want to save us both some trouble and get into bed."

Talyn glared at him, then eyed the bed. It wouldn't be so bad to sleep with him. They'd done it in the woods. This wasn't any different…

"You can transform into Cyra before you come to bed if it makes you feel any better," Samhail said, his tone sardonic.

Talyn jerked her head back to him. There hadn't been any real venom in his voice, but there was something about the look in his eyes that suggested he hadn't fully forgiven her yet.

Or maybe he wanted her to come to bed looking like Cyra?

"I apologized for that," she said.

"But you never answered my question about why you did it."

She wasn't sure why the question made her angry, but it did. He had every right to ask it, but she still felt her temper rise as he looked at her.

"I don't know why I did it," she snapped. "Maybe I was just trying to break you. You seemed so resistant to touching me – her – and I wanted to see what it would take to make you give in."

Talyn glared at him across the room, something she seemed destined to do several times a day now. She couldn't read his expression, but when he stepped toward her, there was something different than anger in his eyes, something feral. He crossed the distance between them slowly, and Talyn planted her feet, promising she wouldn't retreat this time.

Samhail stopped directly in front of her, and she raised her eyes defiantly to him. She always forgot how gods damned big he was.

"I think I know why you did it," he said huskily.

She crossed her arms. "Oh? Do tell."

She inhaled sharply and grabbed his biceps as his hand slipped around her waist to splay across the small of her back. She felt every one of his long fingers as he pulled her against his body, and she tried not to think about the wall of muscle now pressed against her.

She turned her face away from his, but his other hand came up to turn her head back. He tilted her face up and then ran his thumb along her jawline before tracing it back lightly over her lips. Prickles of anticipation skittered across her skin as she waited to see what he'd do next.

Samhail lowered his head toward hers. Something in her mind screamed for her to port away from him, but something more insistent kept her in place. His lips just barely brushed hers, and her mouth instinctively lifted to meet his, chasing the promised kiss.

Samhail lifted his head and smiled down at her, and she realized she'd done exactly what he expected her to. He'd been testing her reaction to see if she'd pull away from his lips or lean toward them, and damn her if her traitorous body hadn't just told him everything he needed to know about why she'd done what she'd done the other day.

Talyn was about to step back when Samhail pulled her more firmly against him, and his mouth descended to claim hers. His fingers threaded through her hair, holding her prisoner to his onslaught. Not that she had any intention whatsoever of pulling away. Heat shot through her body, and she reached up to grip the steely bands of his biceps again, her fingers digging into his arms. Her legs turned liquid, and she was grateful now for the hand anchored at her back keeping her upright.

Their mouths parted an inch or two, just enough to take in several ragged breaths, and then they were crushed against each other again, each second only building the hunger between them rather than sating it. When they parted again, Talyn realized her feet were dangling off the ground while Samhail held her up against his body. She hadn't even felt him lift her, and the abandon with which she'd given in to him caused a wave of panic to surge. There was a growing ache between her legs, but she wasn't ready to admit yet that he was the only one who could ease it.

Talyn ported without thinking and then stumbled as she fell against the wall on the opposite side of the room with Samhail no longer supporting her body. She heard a frustrated growl behind her and turned to face him. He stood where she'd left him, breathing heavily.

"You made your point," Talyn said, still trying to catch her breath. "I admit it. I enjoyed teasing you before, but it won't happen again."

"It was more than that," he said.

"No," she said, shaking her head, "it wasn't, and it can't ever be more. Especially not when you're in love with another woman."

He blinked. "You think I'm in love with Cyra?"

"I know you are."

"No, I'm not," he said emphatically. "First of all, gargoyles don't really fall in love. It's not in our nature. Second, wanting someone and being in love with them are very different things."

Talyn paused at that first bit of information. "But you admit you want her?" she went on, and her stomach knotted, as it seemed to do every time she thought of Cyra and Samhail together.

"*Wanted* her," he said, emphasizing the past tense. "I won't deny Cyra is a beautiful woman, and I desired her in the past, but all that's over now."

"What exactly is over?" she asked. "Your desire for her, or just your ability to have her?"

His back went rigid before he answered. "Both."

Talyn closed her eyes. Somehow it was and wasn't the answer she'd wanted to hear.

"Talyn," he said, and she opened her eyes again.

He took a step toward her, and she pressed against the wall, holding out an arm to ward him off. "Don't come any closer."

He stopped dead. "Talyn," he said again, his tone firmer.

She wasn't sure if she'd ever heard him use her name before now, but she didn't appreciate the sternness in his voice, as if he was trying to reason with a child.

She steeled her expression, and his jaw tightened. Finally, he nodded and moved to put out all the lamps in the room but the one by the bed.

Her sigh was one of both resignation and relief, but it was short-lived as he peeled off his clothes and got into bed naked.

"Nemesis take you," she said as her breath hitched at the sight of his well-muscled thighs and that impressive manhood between his legs. "What the hell are you doing?"

Samhail pulled the covers up over himself and shrugged his broad shoulders. He threaded his hands behind his head on the pillow. "My clothes are covered in blood, and my spare pants and shirt are in my saddle bags. I'll get them tomorrow."

"You can't sleep like that."

"Actually, I can. I rather enjoy sleeping naked."

"You know what I mean. You're not allowed to sleep like that if I'm going to share a bed with you."

Samhail quirked a brow at her. "I'm not *allowed?*"

"Please put some clothes on," she tried. "I'll get them from your saddlebags for you."

"I'm too comfortable to get up and put them on now."

Talyn growled. "You're an infuriating man."

He shrugged again. "You don't have to come to bed," he said, "but I'm turning out that last lamp. If you don't want to stumble around in the dark, I suggest you find where you're going to sleep."

Talyn glowered at him and stalked over to the bed, but she realized as she got closer to the light that her own clothing was still covered in blood. It wasn't nearly as bad as his had been, but it still wasn't something she wanted to sleep in. She'd have to take both her shirt and her pants off and sleep in her undergarments.

She looked up to find Samhail eyeing her with a smile tugging at the corners of his mouth. He'd realized the same thing and was waiting for her to undress. Well, if he thought he was going to see anything, he'd be waiting a while. She turned off the last lamp so the room went dark, then hurriedly pulled off her shirt and pants so she wore only her lower undergarment and a wrap of cloth she'd wound around her chest to bind her breasts. She felt her way to the bed and carefully climbed in under the covers as far from Samhail as she could.

Talyn sighed inwardly. A few days ago, she'd been ready to practically impale herself on him. Now she was afraid to be in the same bed with him to do nothing but sleep.

What did his relationship to Cyra matter after all? If Talyn was being honest with herself, she still wanted him. It wouldn't be the first or likely the last time she'd take a lover just for a night or two of pleasure. It would certainly make the rest of the journey more tolerable if she was able to enjoy his body along the way.

Something wouldn't let her take that step, though.

Talyn listened to hear if Samhail's breathing was regular with sleep yet, but she couldn't tell. She closed her eyes. She was reasonably certain he wouldn't touch her now, and the day's events were starting to catch up with her. Soon her own breathing slowed, and she fell asleep with the warmth of Samhail's body drifting across the bed under the covers.

Tandem Read: Go to *Nemesis Rising* (Bk 4), Chapters 11-12

Chapter 22

Talyn

Talyn woke to the smell of leather and earth in her nostrils the next morning. She was also pressed up against something very large and solid.

With a sinking feeling, she forced her eyes to flutter open and confirm her worst fear. Sometime during the night, she had indeed rolled over to Samhail's side of the bed and nestled up against him. Her hand now rested on his chest as it rose and fell with his deep breaths. Her head also lay on his shoulder and…fuck. Yes, that was her knee on his thigh.

He was also still naked, she remembered belatedly.

Nemesis take her. She needed to move back to her side of the bed without waking him, but the chances of being able to do that seemed remote. She'd just decided to chance it when Samhail's deep voice rumbled against her ear.

"Still trying to figure out how to get back to your side of the bed without waking me?" he asked.

Talyn pinched her eyes shut and exhaled deeply. "Yes. Any ideas?"

"Well, I wouldn't advise moving your knee any higher. That's not going to help anything."

Talyn groaned. "I assumed that for myself. Anything else?"

"Let me think," Samhail said as his free hand came up to brush along the arm she'd slung across his chest. Gooseflesh rose there as he tickled the skin with his feathery touch. Sensing this would only lead to a place she didn't want to go, Talyn started to pull her limbs back from him, but he caught her hand before she could retreat.

"Just give me a minute," he said. "We'll figure this out."

She grunted and pulled her hand free so she could roll back to her side of the bed. She threw off the covers and slipped out, then dipped to pick her clothes up off the floor. She quickly donned her blood-spattered shirt before she turned around to find him on his side watching her.

"What?" she asked. "Why are you watching me get dressed?"

He gave a shrug of one shoulder. "I'd prefer to watch you get *un*dressed, but I'll take what I can get for now."

She rolled her eyes. "Two days ago you were ready to kill me. Now you want to fuck me. Are all gargoyles like this, or did I just get lucky?"

He shrugged again. "All gargoyles are lusty by nature. We have a lot of sex, but I'll admit I want you more than I want most women I've met."

She willed the flutter in her stomach to settle down at that admission. "And why is that?" she asked, trying to keep her voice steady.

His eyes ran up and down her body as she pulled her pants on, and she felt her face heat. A blush? Seriously? She never blushed.

"I have my reasons," he said. He wasn't smiling, but the quirk of his lips held the potential for one.

"You only want me because you can't have me," she said.

He arched an eyebrow. "That sounds like a challenge."

Talyn huffed a laugh. "Save your energy. I'm unseducible."

"That definitely sounds like a challenge."

"It's not. It's a statement of fact. Now, if you'll excuse me, I need to go get a change of clothes out of my saddle bags and see if there's a possibility of getting a bath here."

"Can I trust you not to ride off without me?"

She looked at him like he'd said something ridiculous. "I had a several-hour head start last time, and you still caught up to me. I'd be stupid to think I might get far enough this time before you found me again, and then we'd be heading back to Solandis."

"Smart woman," he said.

Talyn shot him an annoyed look and slipped out the door.

Samhail

Samhail took a deep breath as the door clicked shut, and he tried to will the throbbing in his cock to stop. He didn't have time to pleasure himself before Talyn returned, so the only other option was to calm himself enough that he didn't explode. He'd thought briefly this morning about trying to coax her into letting him between her legs when he'd found her pressed up against him, but he thought better of it.

He knew Talyn wanted him as much as he wanted her, but pushing her before she was ready to admit her desire would be counterproductive. He wasn't sure why she was denying the attraction now after she'd been ready to swallow him whole and probably more just a few days ago, but he was willing to give her more time to figure things out, even if it made things very – very – uncomfortable for him until then.

It had been a pleasant surprise to find her curled up against him when he woke, but it was a frustrating one as well. He'd hardened almost instantly when he realized half her body was thrown over his, and he'd laid there as still as stone for at least fifteen minutes savoring the feel of her until he felt her eyelashes flutter open against his shoulder. Her body stiffened when she realized what she'd done, and he gave her another couple minutes to decide how to escape before he dashed her hopes of getting away without him noticing.

He'd been surprised she hadn't pulled away immediately when he spoke to her, but she'd let him tease her another few seconds before she finally retreated. Then he'd hardened more when she got out of bed.

He'd seen her fully naked before when she boldly changed in front of him in that jail cell, but he'd still been too angry with her at the time to appreciate how stunning her body was. When she'd gotten out of bed, though, his mouth had practically watered, even half-clothed as she was.

Talyn was tall and leanly muscled, yet the flare of her hips and the promise of the breasts beneath her chest wrap gave her body curves that made him grit his teeth with longing. He imagined his hands gripping those hips, his mouth on her breasts, and her legs…Gods above, the Creator had achieved perfection with those long shapely legs that he ached to have wrapped around him.

Samhail mentally kicked himself for thinking about her like that. It only brought on a fresh wave of desire, and he needed to start calming himself all over again.

The door swung open, and Talyn re-entered. She tossed Samhail's spare pants and shirt next to him on the bed, her own change of clothes in her hand.

"The innkeeper is filling the tub down the hall for a bath if you want one," she said.

"A bath sounds wonderful."

"Take yours first if you want."

"No, you go first."

He wasn't sure he'd be able to walk if he tried to get out of bed now, and having her bathe first might give him enough time to take care of his situation. Picturing her in the bath might even help.

Talyn shrugged and started for the door, but she stopped with her hand on the knob and looked at him.

"Why are you still in bed?" she asked. "You're not the type to lie around."

"I'm just resting. My strength is still drained from yesterday."

Talyn narrowed her eyes, and her gaze dipped to his groin. He was turned on his side so his cock didn't tent the bedding, but she seemed to sense what was under the sheets. A wicked grin split across her face, and warning bells went off in his head at the look in her eyes.

"Do you have a little problem?" she cooed, crossing her arms.

"As you've seen, it's really more of a big problem," he said wryly.

Talyn rolled her eyes. "Should I call the healer back?"

Samhail rolled onto his back so his erection was indeed tenting the bedding now, and Talyn bit her lip as her eyes focused there. He enjoyed the flush of pink that rose in her cheeks.

"I don't think it's something the healer can take care of," he said.

There was a long pause, then, to his immense surprise, Talyn tossed her clothes on a chair and walked slowly around the bed. She sat down and pushed herself into the middle toward him. Samhail's breath caught as she took the top of the bedding that covered his waist and slowly pulled it back, exposing his body to the knees. His breathing turned more ragged as her eyes fixed on his erection.

"That looks…uncomfortable," she said softly.

He grunted. "You have no idea."

Before he realized what she intended, Talyn wrapped her fingers firmly around the base of his cock and ran her hand up to the head. Heat shot out of every pore of his body as her touch sent his blood screaming through him. He thought he'd been hard before, but it was nothing compared to what he was now with her hand wrapped around him.

"Fuck!" Samhail ground out as his hips arched off the bed.

Talyn ran her hand firmly down his length then back up again. Her finger ran over the drop of precum that beaded at his head before she put the finger to her mouth and licked the moisture from it. Samhail's breath hitched as her hand returned to his cock, and he tried to keep from spending himself like some inexperienced youth being touched by a woman for the first time.

"Talyn," he rasped, and this time her name was a benediction on his lips. "What are you doing?"

"Taking care of your problem," she said as she moved her hand up and down him more urgently.

Samhail pressed his head back against the pillow and groaned. "You don't…" He tried to speak, but he couldn't seem to get his mouth to form words. "You shouldn't…"

Talyn's hand slowed, and he opened his eyes to look at her. Nemesis take him, if she stopped now, he wasn't sure he'd ever walk again.

Talyn's eyes locked with his, and something stirred in his stomach at the gleam there. He only had time to inhale before she slipped her lips around his cock, and he came undone.

Samhail reached back to grab the bedpost, and the wood groaned ominously as a growl of pleasure ripped from his throat. He tried desperately not to buck his hips under her, but he couldn't keep them from twitching as her lips and tongue began to work his cock while her hand stroked him at the base.

He looked down and saw her hair had fallen across her face. He wanted to see her soft mouth wrapped around him, so he reached forward to brush her hair back, and the sight of her full lips moving up and down him almost made him come right then. His release was building fast, and he tried to hold it back. He didn't want this to be over so soon.

Talyn's tongue circled around his crown before she took a long lick up the underside of his shaft. She plunged her mouth back down on top of him, and he groaned loudly. Gods, she was fucking good at that, and fire burned in his chest as he thought about her doing this to other men.

Samhail gripped the bedpost harder as she pressed her mouth down onto him hard. He felt his cock hit the back of her throat, and the muscles there contracted around him as she swallowed.

"Fuck! Talyn!" he swore again, and he threaded his hand through her hair as she moved her mouth and hand faster.

He kept his hand lightly on her head, being careful not to push down. If she felt like she was choking, he didn't doubt she'd bite him, and somehow that knowledge pushed him over the edge. His balls tightened as the eruption built inside him.

"Talyn, I'm going to-," he tried to warn her. He pushed back gently on her shoulder, but she only plunged her mouth down so that she was taking nearly all of him.

Samhail roared as his pleasure exploded and his seed spilled down her throat. He felt her swallow, the muscles squeezing around him, and he let out a loud groan as his cock throbbed again and again so that he pumped even more of himself into her. His torso jerked forward so he was half-sitting up as he tightened his fingers in her hair.

She drove her mouth over him a few more times as he shuddered beneath her. Finally, she pulled back, letting her lips slide one final time over his length, and Samhail collapsed back onto the bed, breathing harder than he could ever remember breathing before.

"Nemesis take me," he whispered.

His eyes sought hers, and she looked up at him with a satisfied grin on her face. "I figured I owed you that one," she said.

She started to get off the bed, but Samhail moved quickly, and a second later she was on her back beneath him. He was afraid she might port out from under him, but she just stared up at him.

"Let me return the favor," he said, his voice still hoarse from his climax. "Let me make you scream with pleasure."

She smiled up at him. "You seem so confident you can."

The grin he gave her was beyond wicked. "I know I can," he said and started to lower himself down her body.

Talyn stopped him with a light press of her hands to his chest. "Not now. We need to get going soon."

Samhail looked down at her. He wanted so badly to bury his face between her legs and feast on her, and he didn't know why she was stopping him. For that matter, he didn't know how she'd gone from refusing to let him see her undress last night to swallowing his cock. He didn't understand this woman.

Samhail wasn't ready to let her go just yet, though. He lowered his lips to hers for a hungry kiss, and she moaned as his tongue invaded her mouth, the mouth that had just brought him such exquisite bliss.

His body started to stir again, and he pulled back reluctantly. If he kissed her any longer, he'd need another release.

"You'll let me pay you back later," he said.

A statement, not a question.

"Maybe," she said.

"I don't like leaving my debts unpaid, and now I owe you two."

She looked at him questioningly.

"Saving me yesterday, and helping me now," he explained.

She shook her head. "I don't do things like that expecting repayment. You don't owe me on either count."

"And if I want to owe you?"

She shrugged against the mattress. "We'll see if the opportunity presents itself for you to repay me."

Talyn pressed again on his chest, and he leaned back, letting her slip out from under him and off the bed. She picked up her clothes from the chair and left the room to head down the hall for her bath.

Samhail stretched out on his back. His cock was hard again already, so he'd have to pleasure himself once more before she got back, but her ministrations had at least taken the sharp edge off his desire. He might almost be able to sit on his horse once he'd gotten himself off again.

One thing was for sure. He was most definitely going to make sure the opportunity did present itself for him to pay her back.

With interest.

Chapter 23

Talyn

They had breakfast after they bathed, and then they were on their way again. Samhail was even more laconic than normal as they rode, seeming to be lost in his own thoughts, but she caught him glancing at her every now and then.

If she'd known sucking his cock would throw him this off-balance, she'd have done it a lot sooner. Three hells, he'd even let her buy a set of daggers to wear at her hips when they replenished their supplies before they left town.

Talyn still wasn't sure why she'd done what she had. She'd promised herself she'd keep Samhail at arm's length, especially after he'd bragged about being able to seduce her, but then she'd seen the evidence of his desire under the sheets, and he'd started to tell her she *shouldn't* do it…

That's what had made her do it. The challenge. When he'd tried to put her off, she'd suddenly wanted to see him fall apart under her touch. She'd wanted him at her utter mercy, and damned if he hadn't surrendered. Feeling him unravel under her lips had been a heady, powerful feeling.

Now he knew which one of them was really in control.

Or so she hoped. He'd never know how close she came to letting him put his head between her legs, how much willpower it had taken to refuse his offer to make her scream with pleasure, but she was proud of herself for refusing. Had he dared to put a finger between her thighs, he would've seen just how soaking wet she was. She'd need to insist on a room of her own tonight so she could give herself a release.

They rode most of the day with only a few stops for the sake of the horses. They passed one small town after lunch, but Samhail insisted there was a larger town further on they could make before nightfall if they hurried, so they hadn't stopped.

They were tired and hungry when they reached the town around dusk that evening and headed first to find an inn. Unfortunately, Samhail had nixed any chance of her getting her own room, and she'd been too tired by then to argue with him.

Now they sat in the dining area of the inn eating what had blessedly turned out to be a delicious stew of goat meat flavored with rosemary and ale and loaded with potatoes, carrots, and a few other vegetables Talyn couldn't name.

They'd spoken very little that day, and definitely not about this morning, but Talyn wondered what would happen later tonight when they were both in bed together again.

"Can I get you anything else, love?" the barmaid asked as she took their empty bowls.

The woman's gaze lingered on Samhail, and Talyn resisted the urge to roll her eyes. Yes, Samhail was attractive to a degree that bordered on sacrilege, but did every woman they encountered in these towns have to let him know? It was a wonder his ego fit in the same room as him.

Even worse, the women they met didn't seem at all concerned Talyn was there as well. She never gave any hint that she and Samhail might be together, but it still seemed bold of these women to flirt with him the way they did with her sitting right there. The barmaid in that last town where they'd healed him had gone so far as to plop down into Samhail's lap at breakfast and whisper in his ear. Talyn had kept her eyes on the hand Samhail rested on the woman's hip the whole time, only glancing away when he moved the woman gently off his lap looking disappointed.

Not that she was jealous. It just annoyed her the way women threw themselves at him.

"I'll have an ale," Samhail told the woman. He looked at Talyn.

"Nothing else for me," she said, but it was moot considering the barmaid had already turned to head toward the counter.

"I'll wait in the room if you need some time with her," Talyn offered.

She managed to keep most of the irritation out of her voice, but she took a sip of her water to wash the rest of it down.

Samhail raised a brow. "You think I want her?"

"I don't care if you do," Talyn said. "I just don't want you to think you have to watch me every moment. If you need to go take care of gargoyle things," she waved a hand in the air, "then feel free."

Samhail's brow remained raised. "Gargoyle things?"

"Weren't you the one who told me gargoyles have a healthy libido?"

"Ah. Those gargoyle things."

"Yes, those."

Samhail shrugged. "Do you think I just jump into bed with every woman who wants me? I still need to find them attractive."

Talyn ignored the ego in that statement and looked at the barmaid. She seemed pretty enough. Her long dark hair was straight and fell to her waist, which was pinched in tightly with a corset that also pushed her ample breasts up so they nearly spilled over the top. Her face had a doll-like quality to it, and her caramel-colored skin looked soft enough that even Talyn was tempted to touch it.

"And you don't find her attractive?" Talyn asked dubiously. "Gods, even I'd fuck her if I had a dick."

Something thumped against the table, and Samhail's wince told Talyn he'd likely knocked his knee into the underside.

He let out a deep breath. "Under other circumstances I might."

Talyn frowned. "What other circumstances?"

He grinned. "Let's just say recent events have reset my standards."

Talyn did roll her eyes this time.

The barmaid returned with Samhail's ale and set it down before him.

"Will you be in town a while?" she asked him, still ignoring Talyn. "You have to at least stay for the Verdaiya festival tomorrow."

"Verdaiya?" he asked.

"It's a local term," the barmaid said with a giggle that made Talyn want to stab her. "It's just our term for the first day of Spring."

The glass of water Talyn had been sipping from hit the table with a clunk loud enough that both Samhail and the barmaid looked at her.

"Tomorrow is the first day of Spring?" Talyn asked. Her mouth had suddenly gone dry.

The barmaid nodded. "Yes. Why?"

Talyn shook her head and picked her glass up to take a drink. Samhail and the barmaid were still looking at her.

"On second thought," Talyn said, setting the water down, "give me a glass of fyrebyne."

Samhail cocked his head at her in question, but the barmaid turned and headed toward the bar again looking annoyed.

"Fyrebyne is strong," Samhail observed. "Are you sure you wouldn't rather have an ale?"

She glared at him. "I'm going to need something strong if I have to sit here all evening and watch her try to get into your pants."

He smiled. "Jealous?"

"Absolutely not," she said. "I told you, I could care less who you stick your cock in, as long as it's not me. I just don't want to have to watch it."

Samhail leaned back in his seat and grinned at her. "I bet Cyra can see you glowing red with that lie all the way from Solandis."

Her glare sharpened, but she was spared from having to answer by the arrival of her fyrebyne. She tossed the bright red liquid back and chased it with the last of her water as the strong spirit burned its way down inside her chest. Then she stood.

"I'm going back to the room," she told Samhail. "I assume you'll settle our tab as usual."

She didn't give him a chance to answer. Instead, she bumped her hip into the lingering barmaid as she left so the woman fell onto Samhail. The woman's cry of indignation turned to one of delight as she landed across his lap, and Talyn smiled to herself. That should keep him busy for a while.

Talyn hurried back up to their room as her mind reeled. How had she not realized what day it was?

Once inside, she shut the door, then leaned against it, breathing hard. She was always so composed, so strong…

Every day but this day.

Talyn closed her eyes and tried to inhale deeply. She swallowed the fyrebyne down again as it threatened to come back up.

That day ten years ago was as clear in her mind as if it had been today. There'd been so much blood. She could still feel how sticky it was on her hands, how it had made her shirt cling to her body.

That was the day the girl she'd been had died. The next day – the first day of Spring – she'd been reborn as The Raptor.

Talyn pushed herself off the door and stood in front of the mirror that sat on top of the dresser. She watched as her face shifted, as it grew rounder, as the red in her hair deepened, and her eyes turned more hazel than green.

The face that stared back at her was familiar, but she had the sudden fear she might not have gotten it right. After all, it had been twelve years since she'd seen her sister. Was the chin right? Had Julia's lips been fuller? She couldn't remember now, and a lead weight settled in her stomach at the realization that her memory of her sister's face was fading.

Talyn fingered the locket at her neck. Julia had indeed given it to her – she hadn't lied to Samhail about that – but Talyn had meant to have a miniature portrait painted of her sister to put inside. She'd never had the chance before Julia was killed, though, so the locket had sat empty at her throat, no picture to help her remember her older sister's face.

The locket wasn't actually empty anymore, but what she kept there now wouldn't help her remember Julia.

Talyn let the rest of her body shift to what she thought her sister's had looked like. Her clothes shifted as well so she now wore a dress, something simple like Julia had always preferred.

She grabbed her cloak from where she'd thrown it over a chair and slung it over her shoulders. She probably only had seconds before Samhail came looking for her. If she was going to leave, she needed to go now.

She pulled open the door to their room and looked down the hallway. It was clear, so she slipped out and hurried toward the back staircase. She went down the stairs as quickly as she could and emerged onto the side street next to the building. She peeked around the corner, and when she didn't see Samhail, she stepped onto the street and started walking.

She'd counted about ten taverns alone just on that one main street when they rode in. Only two general stores and one apothecary, but ten taverns. Clearly the people in this town had their priorities.

She passed at least four of the taverns before she found one that had the atmosphere she was looking for. The first had been too refined, if the finely-dressed patrons inside were any indication. The second had been too dark and dismal, the kind of place people went to drink alone in the shadows. By contrast, the third and fourth had been too busy and too…cheerful, as evinced by the upbeat music drifting through the open door of one of them. The fifth tavern was the right balance, busy but not so busy people were packed into it.

Talyn took off her cloak and hung it on a hook by the door before heading to the bar. She felt a few pairs of eyes on her as she took a seat next to a man who didn't even try to hide the way his eyes roved over her.

Her sister had always been pretty. She wouldn't have made as much as their mother had as a courtesan, but she would've had a regular group of clients. Of course, it was better that their mother's madame hadn't wanted Julia. Her sister had been too innocent, too delicate for the business of sex work.

Although now that she considered it, maybe it would've been better for her sister if she'd been hardened a little. Maybe her last days would've been easier…

Talyn shivered and ordered an ale from the barkeep.

"Are you cold?" the man who sat next to her asked.

Talyn looked up at him. "If you're going to offer to keep me warm, save your breath," she said, although not unkindly.

The man chuckled. "Oh, you won't need me after a glass or two of ale here. This place makes theirs with ginger. It gives you a nice warm feeling after a while."

As if on cue, the barkeep set her drink down in front of her.

"Put that on my bill, Henry," the man told the barkeep.

Talyn thought about arguing with him, but then decided better of it. "Thank you," she said instead.

"I'm Terrick," the man said.

"Julia," Talyn said before taking a sip of the ale. It did indeed have a bite of ginger that smoothed into a warming sensation on her tongue.

"Aren't you going to introduce us to your friend, Terrick?"

Talyn turned to see two more men standing around her.

"Wasn't planning on it," Terrick said to the man who'd spoken, but his tone was friendly.

"How rude," the man said, but he was smiling. He looked at Talyn. "I'm Selvin, and this is Drue."

He gestured to the third man, who wore an expression that was as close to a scowl as one could get without actually scowling. Drue nodded to her and grunted in greeting.

"Hello. I'm Julia," she said, already halfway to forgetting their names.

It was fine. She hadn't necessarily wanted to drink alone, so if they wanted to keep her company, she'd let them. She was sure she could handle them if they tried anything.

"I've never seen you in town," the man sitting next to her said.

Gods, what was his name again? Terrick?

"I'm just passing through," she said as she took a long swig of her ale.

It was warm going down her throat, and she willed it to start numbing her mind. Maybe she should've gone for another glass of fyrebyne. Selvin looked uncomfortably like a young man she'd known once. Someone she'd cared for.

Talyn took another long drink of her ale.

"Do you like the ale?" Terrick asked her.

She shrugged. "It's not bad."

Twenty minutes later, Talyn was ready for her third glass of the ginger-infused drink. The three men had all pressed in around her and were taking every opportunity to touch her when they could. A brush of her shoulder here, a hand on her leg there. One of them – Drue she thought – had even trailed his hand down the length of her neck after pushing a lock of hair behind her ear.

Between the alcohol, the ginger, and the press of bodies around her, Talyn was feeling pleasantly warm. She'd even forgotten for a while about what's-his-face and the barmaid he was probably fucking in their bed at the inn. Actually, they'd likely use the woman's bed instead. He probably hadn't even noticed Talyn was missing yet.

Cool air rushed in as the door to the tavern opened, and Talyn savored the feel of it on her flushed skin. The chill that stole over her next had nothing to do with the night air, though, and everything to do with the fact the tavern had gone unnaturally quiet.

"Nemesis damn me," Selvin whispered, and Talyn sighed.

She didn't need to look to know exactly who'd just walked in. She glanced quickly anyway, only because it would've seemed odd for her not to look when the entire place was suddenly so transfixed by the man who now stood in the doorway.

Her glance confirmed Samhail had finally found her, but she only took another sip of her drink, refusing to acknowledge his presence. She'd seen the expression on his face, and she knew enough about him by now to read his mood.

He wasn't angry. No, the slight narrowing of his eyes, the stern set of his jaw, and his barely pursed lips told her he was, in fact, quite furious.

Chapter 24

Samhail

Samhail knew it was her the moment he entered the tavern. There was a passing resemblance between Talyn and the woman sitting at the bar – an almost too obvious one – but that wasn't what convinced him it was her. It was the fact that she looked away from him a full thirty seconds before everyone else in the tavern did that confirmed it.

Samhail was used to being the center of attention when he walked into a room. Indeed, the entire tavern had gone quiet as he entered, all eyes fixed on him. The woman looked at him as well, but only for a few seconds before she turned away. By contrast, the eyes of every other person there followed him all the way to the bar where he took a stool two seats away from her. The stool groaned under the weight of his solidly muscled frame, and the people in the tavern slowly went back to their conversations as they decided he wasn't there for trouble.

He glanced at the woman again. Her hair had more of a rusty hue than the hints of copper in Talyn's strawberry blonde waves, but there were similarities in their faces. This woman had Talyn's pert nose and high cheekbones, but that wasn't what he found most familiar about her.

It was the way she held herself, the gracefulness with which she crossed one leg over the other on her stool. It was in the way her head tilted and turned on her long neck so regally it would make a swan envious. And there at the base of her throat was the locket she'd once told him she'd lost in Cyra and Bressen's sitting room.

The faint scent of lemon verbena that drifted to Samhail down the bar stirred something in his chest, and he inhaled deeply without thinking. Yes, he knew without a doubt it was Talyn.

She'd known what she was doing when she bumped the barmaid into his lap. It had taken him nearly five minutes to get the woman off him and pay their tab, but by then Talyn had already been gone when he reached the room.

He didn't think she'd run. Her things were still there, and her horse was still in the inn's stable. She'd clearly been upset when she left, and the fyrebyne had suggested to him she might be looking for more alcohol, so he'd started searching taverns.

He'd been sure it would be pointless to look for her. She could shift her appearance, so there was no way for him to know what she looked like. He'd just hoped she might do or say something to give herself away. As it turned out, it had been easier to find her than he'd expected, as this was only his third stop. She wasn't trying very hard to hide.

Samhail ordered an ale from the barkeep as he opened an ear to eavesdrop on her conversation with the three men who currently had her attention. One man sat between her and Samhail while two stood next to her. Their chatter was banal, idle conversation mixed with the men's not-so-subtle attempts to keep Talyn's attention on them over the others. They were all mortals as far as he could tell.

Talyn finished her drink and called for another, and Samhail wondered how many she'd had already. There was an urgency in the way she took a deep gulp from the new glass the barkeep set before her.

The two men standing next to her both rushed to pay for her drink, and Talyn raised her glass to them before taking another long swig.

Samhail recognized the hunger in the eyes of the men around her. The man seated next to Talyn reached out to put his hand on her knee, and Samhail's arm twitched as he watched from the corner of his eye. Talyn didn't seem to notice the hand, and he tamped down the urge to spin the man around on his barstool and plant a fist into his face.

In answer to their companion's boldness, the two other men pressed in closer to Talyn, and Samhail gritted his teeth.

He was guilty of doing the same thing when he was interested in a woman, of finding excuses to step in closer to her or brush her arm with his hand, but seeing these men do it now made him want to rip the legs off his barstool and beat them bloody. That Talyn didn't discourage them flared not only his anger, but some kind of dread deep within him he couldn't explain.

He had no claim on her. She could do whatever she wanted with whomever she wanted, and he had no right to say anything, but knowing that and being able to accept it were two different things.

Feelings of jealousy were new to him, and although he'd never felt them before, he knew that's exactly what this was. He and Bressen had shared women a few times, but there'd never been any jealousy between them, even with Cyra. Perhaps it was because Bressen was more like a brother to him than his own siblings, but jealousy also wasn't a common emotion among gargoyles. Lust and promiscuous sex were common and accepted among his kind, so jealousy simply had no place in their world.

Samhail almost shook his head. He had no idea now how Bressen had ever shared Cyra with him. Samhail hadn't even fucked Talyn yet, and he already knew there was no way he'd share her with anyone, even Bressen.

Talyn was his.

Or she would be soon, and he wanted to pull her onto his lap right now so these men knew it. He ached to claim her mouth and run his hands over her body until every inch of her smelled like him as a warning to anyone else who might be foolish enough to think they could have her. If he didn't know she'd strenuously object, he'd pull out his cock right here, haul her down on top of it, and make her ride him in front of the entire gods damned tavern.

A soft cracking sound brought Samhail back from the spiral he'd been heading down, and he lifted his hand off his glass of ale to see there was a small fracture snaking up the side of it.

The glass didn't appear to be leaking, so he glanced back at Talyn and the three men. One of the men standing near her now had his hand on her hip, and Samhail pulled his own hand away from his glass so he didn't accidentally crush it into shards. He couldn't sit here and watch this all night. At some point, especially if he kept drinking, he'd get the urge to throw one of these men across the room.

He didn't know why Talyn was here, or why she looked the way she did, but he'd leave her to it. Now that he knew where she was, he could go back to the room and wait for her to stumble in later…

No, he should stay. He didn't want to leave her here alone with three men when she was drunk. She could easily take on all three of them when she was sober, but what if they somehow knocked her out?

Samhail's hand clenched into a fist just thinking about it, and he was about to drag her back to their room, consequences be damned, when he tuned in to their conversation again.

"If I win, I get a kiss," one of the men next to Talyn said.

"That's reasonable," she said, slurring her words a bit.

"Then let's do it," the man said as he rose and strode toward a large dart board on a wall across the room. Instead of darts, the board had two sets of throwing knives stuck in it.

The man plucked the six knives out of the board and handed three to Talyn as she came up next to him and set her drink on an empty table. The two other men followed, and at the bar, Samhail turned around on his stool to watch. Talyn and the man had the attention of several other patrons in the bar as well.

Samhail had never actually seen Talyn throw knives before, but given what he knew about her, he'd bet everything he had on her to win.

The man stepped up and sent his first knife cartwheeling through the air. It lodged itself in one of the outer rings of the board, and he frowned.

"I must be a bit rusty," he said. "Your turn, sweetheart."

Talyn stepped up to the throwing line and aimed at the board. She pulled her arm back and let the knife fly. Samhail expected it to hit the bullseye, but instead the knife bounced off the wall next to the board before clattering loudly to the floor, and a couple of patrons snickered.

Samhail narrowed his eyes. Talyn was either drunker than she seemed, or she was missing on purpose. There was no way in the three hells The

Raptor of Avril, assassin extraordinaire, was bad at throwing knives.

"I must be rusty too," Talyn purred, flashing the man a smile.

She swayed but caught her balance on the back of a chair, even as three sets of male hands grabbed for her waist to steady her. The men's hands lingered before releasing her, and Samhail began contemplating which of their bones he wanted to break first.

Fingers were always a good start. He'd work his way up to their necks.

Talyn's opponent grinned at her and stepped back up to the line. His next knife was closer to the middle of the board but still not near the center. He stepped aside so Talyn could take her turn.

Her next throw also hit the wall, but at least it stuck there this time.

Samhail ground his teeth. He was sure she could beat this man easily, even drunk. She was losing on purpose, and he wasn't sure why. If they'd been betting money, he might've suspected she was drawing the man in to make him put more money on the table, but if he'd heard right, they were playing for a kiss. Did she want to kiss him or…?

Was she doing this on purpose to drive him crazy? Make him jealous?

The man's third knife stuck in the outer ring of the bullseye, and his two companions cheered.

"I don't think you can win now, sweetheart," the man said to Talyn.

She sighed. "No, but I'd like to at least hit the board one time."

"Let me show you," the man said.

He stepped in behind her and closed his hand over hers. His other arm crept around her, and he laid a hand against her stomach as he whispered into her ear, apparently giving her instructions as he moved her arm to demonstrate the proper throwing motion.

At the bar, Samhail drained his ale and fought the urge to rip the man's hand clean off his body.

"Like this?" Talyn asked as the man finally stepped away from her.

She let her third knife fly. It stuck in one of the mid-range rings, and the three men cheered as Talyn pretended to be surprised at her improvement.

"It's time to pay up," the man said to her.

Talyn smiled and stepped toward him. The man didn't waste any time pulling her against him and closing his mouth over hers. One of his hands slithered up her side while the other threaded through her hair. His tongue dove between her lips, and after a few seconds, Talyn laid a hand on his chest to gently push him away.

Samhail's vision went red as something he'd never felt before roiled inside him. The beast in him normally only stirred when there was real fighting to be done – bloody fighting – but it stirred now, and for several seconds he wasn't entirely sure he could stop it from coming out. He turned and gripped the edge of the bar as he saw the dark slate of his gargoyle skin creep up his arms from out of the markings on his forearms.

Fucking hells, he couldn't change here. Not over this.

Samhail closed his eyes and willed his gargoyle form back into dormancy. His skin prickled, and he felt his blood raging through his veins as he fought the shift. It took every ounce of his strength to hold it back, to keep his wings and horns from springing out or his fangs from emerging. He felt his body trying to grow, felt the beast trying to burst out of him. It roared in his chest, and when he opened his eyes, he saw the blue glow of them reflected against the surface of the bar.

Not here, not now, he repeated to himself. *Not here, not now. Please…*

Samhail finally felt the beast withdraw as he breathed deeply. When he looked up again, mercifully, Talyn was no longer in the man's arms.

A low growl rumbled from his throat as he realized she was now playing against the second man in the group.

Hearing Samhail's growl, an older man who'd been sitting at the bar next to him downed his drink and left the tavern quickly.

Over at the dart board, the second man had landed two of his knives relatively close to the center. One of Talyn's knives was again stuck in the wall, but her second shot had made it into one of the outer circles. The man threw his last knife, but it was far in the outer rings like Talyn's second shot. Talyn threw her last knife and then jumped in triumph as the knife landed a few inches from the bullseye.

"Did you see that?" she asked, throwing her arms around the neck of the second man. "I got it near the center!"

"That deserves a reward!" he said as he wrapped his arms around her and claimed her mouth.

Samhail gripped the bar again as the man's hand slid down to cup Talyn's ass, and she squealed as he dragged her against him.

He'd kill the man.

He'd kill all three of them. He'd rip their spines out one by one, then throw Talyn down and fuck her in the puddle of their blood for making him do it.

Samhail blinked and shook his head, unsure where such a dark thought had come from. This woman pulled at something inside him that he hadn't even known was there. She seemed to call to his beast, and Nemesis damn him, the beast was answering.

"My turn," the last man said as he went to retrieve the knives out of the board.

He handed Talyn her three knives and stepped up to the throwing line. Instead of just taking his first shot, though, the man fired all three knives at the board, one after another. They stuck just off the center making a triangle around the bullseye, and he turned back to Talyn with a self-satisfied smirk.

"Just pay up now, honey," he said as he stepped toward her.

The man's hand came up to brush the hair back from her neck, and Samhail's eyes flicked to the spot at the crook of her shoulder where he'd bitten her. The mark was still there, and he frowned. Either the mark was unaffected by her shift into another form, or she'd chosen to keep it there when she shifted, and now he desperately wanted to know which it was.

The man's hand skimmed across the fang marks without noticing them, but Samhail thought he saw Talyn shiver.

Samhail dug his fingernails deeper into the bar. He wasn't sure he could watch her kiss a third man without tearing the top off it.

The man leaned in to claim his victory kiss from Talyn, but she held a hand up to his chest to stop him. Samhail saw the hard glint in her eyes even from across the room, and hope swelled in his chest. She'd been willing to play her part as long as the challenge hadn't been serious, but this man had thrown down a gauntlet, and Samhail knew she'd pick it up.

"Still," Talyn said, pressing the man back, her voice less slurred, "I'd like to take my three shots."

The man shrugged and moved out of the way. Talyn drained the ale from her glass and stepped up to the line.

In quick succession, she threw the knives at the board, each hitting the bullseye dead-on so the blades formed a tight cluster in the middle. A murmur went up from those in the tavern who'd been watching, and one of the men with Talyn swore under his breath.

Talyn shrugged at the third man who was now gaping at her.

"Sorry," she said. "It looks like I win after all."

The man's face darkened. "Bitch! You were playing us."

"I was playing along," she corrected, "and I would've continued to do so if you hadn't been a jackass about it."

"Fuck you!" he said as he grabbed for her. His hand closed around her wrist, and he jerked her toward him. "I'm taking my kiss."

Chapter 25

Samhail

Samhail's barstool hit the floor as he launched himself off it to get to Talyn. He fully intended to rip the man's arm off, but he pulled up short when he saw the blade she had pressed to the man's groin. He didn't know where she'd pulled it from, but the man stopped dead as his most sensitive part was now threatened.

For the first time since he'd arrived, Talyn looked directly at Samhail.

"Here to rescue me?" she drawled, and he could hear she was drunker than her knife-wielding skills might suggest.

"Here to rescue *him*," Samhail said, nodding to the man with the dagger between his legs.

"Are you planning to fight me then? What round is this now? Four? Five? I've lost count," she said.

She took her dagger from the man's groin and faced Samhail.

"Maybe when you're sober," he said.

Her chin went up. "I don't need to be sober to beat you," she said, but she had to catch herself from swaying again.

The three men looked at her as though she was raving mad for talking to him that way, but Samhail just inclined his head toward the door. "You should leave before she starts throwing knives again," he told them.

The men didn't need to be told twice and hurried out of the tavern.

Samhail turned to Talyn. "It's time to go."

She reshed the dagger at her thigh under her dress and sunk onto one of the chairs at the empty table. "I just need a minute," she said as her head lolled on her neck. Her inebriation was likely returning now that her adrenaline surge was gone.

"I can carry you," Samhail said.

"I can walk," she snapped. "Just wait."

Samhail looked around the room and heads everywhere swiveled back to their drinks as the hum of conversation rose again around the tavern.

"So who is this you're wearing tonight?" he asked, gesturing to the unfamiliar form.

Talyn looked up at him in confusion. She lifted a hand and felt along her cheek, as if she'd forgotten she was wearing another woman's face. She cocked her head at him and rose from the chair.

"Why?" she asked, grinning sensually. "Do you like her?"

Talyn pressed herself against Samhail and ran her hands up his chest to curl them around his neck. His muscles clenched where she touched, and he grabbed her wrists to return them to her sides.

"Change back into yourself," he said quietly.

"I can't do it here," she said. "It would cause a stir."

"Then let's go. You'll need time to sleep this off."

He took her elbow and steered her toward the door.

"You're no fun," she said petulantly.

Talyn shook off Samhail's grip as they emerged into the cool night. He'd grabbed her cloak from the rack by the door, and he laid it over her shoulders as they turned back toward the inn.

"You could've just told me you wanted to go for a drink," he said as they walked.

"Maybe I wanted to be alone," she said.

"It didn't look like you wanted to be alone."

She turned to grin up at him. "Jealous?"

"Were you trying to make me jealous?" he countered.

She scoffed. "Why would I want to do that?"

"You tell me."

Talyn stopped walking, and he turned to face her.

"If I was trying to make you jealous, it worked," she said. "You looked ready to pull those men off me from the moment you walked in."

Samhail raised a brow. "I didn't realize you knew I was there."

"Everyone else was giving you plenty of attention," she said poking a clumsy finger into his chest. "You didn't need any more from me."

Samhail caught her hand gently in his own, and she seemed momentarily stunned as she looked up at him.

"Whose face is this?" he asked again.

"No one's," she said, looking away. "Just a random woman."

He took her chin between his thumb and forefinger and turned her face back to him.

"There's a resemblance," he said. "Is she related to you?"

Talyn smiled. "Do you think she's pretty?" she asked, her voice turning sultry again.

He ignored her question. "Change back."

She pouted. "You don't think my sister is pretty?"

Samhail stiffened and his face went serious. "This is your sister?"

"Was," Talyn corrected him. "This *was* my sister."

Her face had gone serious as well, and Samhail searched her eyes in the light of a street lantern.

"What happened to her?" he asked.

Talyn's features slid back into her own.

He'd seen her shift a few times now, and it still unnerved him to watch, but this time there wasn't much she had to change to shift back to herself. She looked more like her sister than he originally realized.

"She was murdered," Talyn said, "by a man who killed numerous other women. Tonight is the anniversary of…" She trailed off.

"The anniversary of her death?"

She shook her head. "We couldn't tell how long she'd been dead when they found her body," Talyn said. "Maybe a week? The cuts and bruises were…extensive. Today is the anniversary of the day I killed the man who murdered her."

Samhail sucked in a breath, and he realized he was still holding onto her hand. "Your first kill was the man who murdered your sister," he said, letting the knowledge sink in.

The look in Talyn's eyes was far away as she stared through him, but she met his gaze suddenly, and Samhail saw something in her expression he couldn't discern at first. She rested her free hand on his chest and slid it up over his shoulder around his neck. She pulled him down, and Samhail yielded to the pressure until she'd brought his lips to hers.

She slipped her tongue into his mouth, and Samhail groaned as he pulled her against him, giving in to the urge he'd had all night to kiss her. He could taste the gingered ale on her lips as his tongue met hers, and his cock hardened.

He knew she was drunk, knew he'd have to let go of her soon, but he could have this one moment. It wouldn't be so wrong to let himself enjoy the feel of her against him for just one minute. Just one gods damned minute, and then he'd let go and bring her back to the inn to sleep it off.

Talyn broke the kiss first. "The alley," she breathed.

He furrowed his brows in confusion. "What about the alley?" he asked. He looked down the nearest street to scan the shadows for threats.

"We can go down the alley," she said. "Fuck me against the wall."

His eyes narrowed even more. "What?"

Talyn took his hand and tried to pull him toward the narrow street between two buildings, but Samhail didn't budge. He could easily imagine her legs wrapped around him while he thrust into her against a wall, but that wall was not down a dirty side street. She was out of her fucking mind if she thought he'd rut her in a back alley.

He'd fuck her anywhere she wanted after they crossed that initial bridge, but not this time. Not their first time, and not when she was drunk.

"No," he said firmly. "No alley. We need to get back to the room."

She paused, then nodded and started to lead him back toward the inn again. He followed, hoping she'd forget about any thoughts of sex tonight by the time they got back. He had no intention of taking her tonight, regardless of where they were. She was upset and drunk, and he wasn't such a cad that he'd take advantage of her in this state. He needed to get her back to the room and into bed to go to sleep. It was likely going to be a long night for him, but if that was the case, then so be it.

He managed to get her back to the inn without further delays. Talyn's last drink seemed to catch up with her because she grew more unsteady with each step, and by the time he got her to their room, he'd had to sling an arm around her waist to hold her up.

Samhail unlocked their door and swung Talyn up into his arms to carry her in. He'd left a lamp on, so dim light filled the space, and he carried her to the bed to lay her down on it.

"Why is the room spinning?" she asked.

"Because you're drunk," he said as he pulled off her boots. He poured a glass of water from the pitcher by the bed and sat her up. "Drink this."

She obeyed, and he laid her back down when she finished. Next, he lifted her legs and tucked them under the covers before pulling the blankets up over her shoulders. "Try to get some sleep. You'll feel better in the morning," he told her.

He turned and strode across the room to where he'd left his saddle bags. He pulled his shirt off and folded it before laying it down on top of the bags. He stared at the blank wall as he debated the pros and cons of sleeping on the floor instead of in the bed with Talyn. He was used to sleeping in uncomfortable places, but he hated to do so when there was a perfectly good bed with plenty of room right there. He just needed to stay far away from the infuriating…tempting woman in it. The hardness in his cock had started to ease, but getting into bed with Talyn might be an issue.

The gentle touch of two hands on his bare back jarred Samhail out of his contemplation, and he swung around, instinctively ready to fight. The tension left him when he saw Talyn behind him. He hadn't heard her get out of bed, and he wondered if she'd ported to him. Then his eyes went lower, and he swore violently.

Nemesis damn him. She was fucking naked.

Samhail shut his eyes tightly and decided the gods must hate him. Why else would this woman he wanted so badly be standing here completely naked in front of him when he couldn't have her? If they didn't hate him, then they were at least testing him, although he had no idea to what end.

Samhail opened his eyes again when he felt Talyn start to work at the fastenings of his pants. He caught her hands, but not before his cock went rock hard again.

"Get back into bed," he said through gritted teeth.

"Come with me," she purred, trying to press closer to him.

"I'll come to bed in a minute," he said, "but we're not going to do anything but sleep."

She pouted. "I thought you wanted me."

"I do want you," he said softly, "but not like this."

Talyn's face shifted, and Samhail pushed her away abruptly as Cyra's image looked up at him.

"How about like this?" Talyn asked. "Would you rather fuck me if I looked like this?"

"Change back," Samhail growled at her, taking another step back, "and don't ever wear that face again." His voice was low and menacing.

Talyn took a step back as well, seemingly surprised at the ferocity of his reaction, but she didn't shift.

"Are you still in love with her?" she asked.

"I told you before," he said, "gargoyles don't fall in love, and even if they did, I was never in love with Cyra. I desired her once, but no longer."

"You don't want her anymore?"

"No," he said in frustration. "I want *you*, Talyn."

She blinked at him, and her features slid back into her own.

Samhail relaxed. He didn't realize how much he meant all that until now. There was a time he'd wanted Cyra. She was one of the few people he cared about deeply, but he'd been fine with not taking her to bed again until the day Talyn had come to him as Cyra and tried to seduce him. He realized now, though, that it hadn't been Cyra he really wanted. It was Talyn all along. She may have looked like Cyra, but the way she'd touched him that day had most definitely not been like Cyra.

Cyra had never aroused his lust this much. She was steady and even-tempered and alluring in her own way, but Talyn was fiery and forward and dangerous. He'd enjoyed Cyra's innocence, the way she brought out protective instincts in him he didn't even know he possessed, but there was something about Talyn that stirred his blood and drove him mad. His gargoyle nature appreciated her strength and her ability to fight, and he couldn't help imagining what it would be like to have her writhing beneath him as he drove into her, taking her to greater and greater heights of ecstasy. He wanted her legs wrapped around him as he buried himself inside her, wanted to watch those lush breasts bounce as he thrust into her and made her cry out with pleasure.

"You want me?" Talyn asked, taking a step closer to him.

"Yes," he said, "but not tonight. When you're sober. I want you when you'll be able to remember and enjoy everything I plan to do to you."

"And what if I want that now?" she asked.

He shook his head. "It's not going to happen now."

He recognized the gleam of challenge in her eyes too late. One moment she was there, and then she was gone. Samhail didn't have time to react before she kicked the backs of his knees like she'd done in the jail cell, and he fell forward onto them.

He had to stop letting her do that.

Then she was in front of him again, and he was at eye-level with her beautiful breasts. They were full, with pert pink nipples that he ached to suck into his mouth. His hand twitched, eager to palm one of them, but he held himself in check.

Drinking and porting didn't mix well, though, because Talyn swayed and stumbled backward. Samhail grabbed for her, and his hands wrapped around her hips to pull her toward him. Still unsteady, she fell forward, and he found himself with his forehead resting between her breasts.

He pulled back from her, but not very far. He couldn't take his eyes from the two creamy globes so close to his face. Gods, how he wanted to knead that soft flesh, to take her nipples into his mouth and run his tongue around them, to gently bite them and hear her moan.

He settled for planting a few soft kisses between her breasts before trailing his lips lower to kiss her stomach. Then he forced himself to stop as he began to get ideas he shouldn't. Now was not the time to lay her on the bed and lick her until she begged him to take her.

With some effort of will, Samhail pushed her carefully away from him.

The gods really did hate him. He needed to find a temple somewhere between here and Rowe and make a sacrifice or two. Or twenty.

"Samhail," Talyn whispered. "I want you."

He closed his eyes and shook his head. "All that ale you drank wants me," he said, opening his eyes again. "When you can say you want me without the alcohol giving you courage, then I'll be more than happy to fuck you until you forget how to walk. Until then, you need to go to bed."

Talyn searched his face for something as he knelt there quietly, letting her look at him. Her eyes were starting to get heavy.

"Let me put you to sleep," he said softly.

He still gripped the enticing swells of her hips, and he fought the urge to run his hands all over her body. She was finally starting to calm.

Talyn nodded, and Samhail released a breath of relief. He stood up and turned her around to guide her back to the bed. He pulled down the covers, and she dutifully climbed in. He thought briefly about making her put her clothes back on, but she was being cooperative, and he didn't want to risk sidetracking her. Naked would have to do for now.

Talyn's eyes fluttered shut as he pulled the covers back up over her body, and sleep finally seemed to wash over her.

Thank the gods. Any longer and his resolve about not taking her would've shattered into a million pieces. His cock strained against his pants. He'd have to pleasure himself before he could fall asleep.

He wondered if he'd be able to do it in bed next to her, but he decided that would be tempting fate, so he grabbed one of the cloths he usually carried in his bags and sat down in the armchair across the room.

He nearly ripped the fastenings of his pants trying to free his cock, but the first stroke of his hand down his shaft was such a relief that he groaned. He gripped it tighter and thrust his hips as he ran his hand faster and faster over his length. He closed his eyes and recalled the feel of Talyn's mouth on him. His cock throbbed in his hand, and thoughts of what he'd do with her the next time he had the chance were all he needed to bring himself to a release so strong he saw stars.

Chapter 26

Samhail

The next morning, Samhail was immediately aware that he was no longer on his own side of the bed. He'd been careful to lay down as far from Talyn as he could after he'd pleasured himself, but sometime during the night, he and Talyn had rolled toward each other, and she was now tucked up against him, his front to her back. He'd curled an arm around her body to pull her in close, and her head was nestled into his shoulder as his fully-awake dick pressed tightly against the small of her back.

He caught that citrusy, lemon verbena scent of hers when he inhaled, and it made him strangely happy. He could lie like this all day.

"Still trying to figure out how to get back to your side of the bed without waking me?" Talyn asked quietly.

Samhail chuckled and nuzzled his face into her hair. "Not at all," he said as he pulled her tighter against him. "I was trying to decide how much longer to let you sleep before I woke you up and slid my cock between those beautiful thighs of yours," he said.

A soft moan escaped her, and his cock twitched. Gods, how did she make his body react so easily?

"How are you feeling?" he asked, willing himself not to think about her soft body pressed up against him.

"Like someone is driving a stake into my brain," she said.

"That's to be expected given how much you drank."

"It wasn't *that* much," she argued without conviction.

"How much do you remember about last night?" he asked.

She was quiet a moment. "Enough that I probably owe you an apology," she said finally.

He lifted his head. "An apology? For what?"

Another pause. "For throwing myself at you."

Samhail pulled away enough to roll Talyn onto her back so she was facing him and his body was half on top of hers. That was a mistake because it only reminded him how very, very naked she was.

Samhail took a deep breath and tried to calm the blood that was coursing faster through his body now, especially to one part in particular.

"Never apologize for telling me you want me," Samhail said. "Next time, just say it when you're sober."

Talyn opened her mouth as if to speak but then closed it again, and he wondered if she'd been about to say it. She didn't, and the wall she erected whenever she came too close to admitting her desire for him was back up again.

Talyn nodded lightly. "I understand."

Samhail kept his face impassive as he tamped down the flicker of hope that had bloomed in his chest when she'd opened her mouth. It was fine. She was still feeling the aftereffects of her night of drinking, so this wouldn't be ideal for their first time together anyway. That didn't necessarily mean they couldn't do anything, though.

Samhail lowered his head slowly to hers, giving her every opportunity to push him away. When she didn't move, he kissed her, gently at first, then with more insistence as he parted her lips with his tongue. She returned the kiss, angling her head up to his and meeting his tongue in a kind of sensual dance.

Samhail lifted his head. "Maybe I can pay one of my debts now."

Talyn opened her mouth again, but the words seemed to die as he peeled the covers back from her body. She was breathing harder, and when she didn't say anything to stop him, Samhail dipped his head to her breast and closed his mouth over it. Talyn gasped and arched off the bed as his tongue licked around her nipple while his hand closed over her other breast to knead it gently.

"Samhail!" she rasped.

Her hands threaded through his hair as her chest heaved beneath him.

His hand on her breast trailed lower until it reached the apex of her legs, and he gripped one of her thighs to pull it open. His fingers grazed her clit before sliding further until he slipped two long fingers inside her.

"Gods above!" she gasped. "I-"

Whatever she'd been about to say was cut off by a loud knock at their door, and Talyn put a hand on his forearm to stay him.

Samhail growled and swore violently under his breath. "Go away!" he yelled toward the door as he continued to push his fingers leisurely in and out of Talyn despite her hand on his arm.

"I'm sorry to disturb you, sir," came the terrified voice from the man outside, "but there are two, um…winged persons here to see you."

Samhail's head jerked up from where it still hovered over Talyn's breast. It couldn't be. The gods could not hate him *this* much.

"Tell them I'm not here," he said.

"I wish I could, sir," the man said, "but they already know you are."

"Fuck," Samhail said, pulling his fingers from Talyn and rolling away from her to sit up in bed. He was going to kill Surgeon and Serise, or at least beat them both to bloody pulps.

"Fine. Tell them I'll be down in a few minutes," Samhail said.

"Um…" There was a pause on the other side of the door.

"What?" Samhail snapped.

"They want to see both you and the woman," the man answered in a quavering voice.

"Then they're out of luck," he growled. "They'll get me or no one."

"But, sir, I…I…," the man said, falling into a terrified stutter.

"We'll both be down shortly," Talyn called out from beside Samhail.

"Thank you, miss!" the man said, and they heard the quick retreat of his footsteps down the hall before she could take back what she'd said.

"Forget it," Samhail said to her. "You need to stay here."

"They'll just come up to look for me if I don't come down."

"They'll have to get past me, and that's not going to happen."

"I assume it's your brother and sister," Talyn said. "What makes you think you can take them both?"

Samhail quirked a brow to let her know he was offended by the very idea she'd question that. "Because I've done it before," he said anyway.

He didn't bother to note that Surgeon and Serise had actually gotten the drop on him a few days ago when they'd first arrived. His siblings had the element of surprise then, but in a straight fight, they'd never beaten him, either together or separately.

Talyn looked at him in disbelief. "You've fought them before?"

Samhail shrugged. "The last time my family got together," he said. "Gargoyle gatherings tend to involve a lot of fights and competitions. Just let me deal with them."

Samhail threw the covers off and got out of bed. He'd slept in his pants just to be sure he wasn't tempted to do anything.

"You can do the talking," she said, "but I'm coming with you. I can't sit up here wondering if one of them is going to burst through the door because they got past you. I'd rather face them head on."

"I told you they won't get past me," he said as he grabbed his shirt from where he'd left it last night.

"If you say so," she said, "but I'm still coming. If there's going to be a gargoyle battle royale, I don't plan on missing it."

Samhail sighed. He didn't think it would actually come to the battle she seemed to hope for, but he understood she didn't want to sit up here and wonder what was happening. More to the point, he had no way to make her stay in the room, so she might as well come down where he could keep an eye on her.

"Fine," he said. "Get dressed, unless you're willing to be a diversion."

She gave him a look that said she wasn't willing to go that far and slipped out of bed with the sheet wrapped around her. He almost laughed at her modesty now, given that she'd undressed last night and strolled naked across the room to seduce him. He never knew what to expect from her, and it was intriguing. Alluring. Maddening.

Gods damn him. He wanted her so much.

Talyn

Talyn wasn't sure what made her pull the sheet off the bed and wrap herself in it while she looked for the clothes she'd stripped off last night. She'd already paraded around naked in front of Samhail twice now. It wasn't like she could hide anything he hadn't seen before. Her need for the sheet must be overcompensation for her behavior last night, a way to convince either herself or him she wasn't quite the harlot she must've come across as. Gods above, she'd actually tried to get him to take her against a wall in an alley. Thank the Protector he'd had enough sense to refuse her flat on that suggestion, although the wall might still be a possibility under different circumstances…

Talyn didn't remember much from last night, but her proposal of the alley was one of a few stronger impressions in her mind. She also recalled with a decent amount of clarity the dagger-throwing games with those three men and the moment Samhail had first walked into the tavern.

Granted she'd been more sober earlier in the night, but the fact that the noisy tavern had gone almost dead quiet when he walked in made the memory stick with her. Samhail had a presence wherever he went, and she'd felt both thrill and dread when she'd turned to see him standing there. Somewhere in the back of her mind she'd known he'd find her. Perhaps she'd even hoped he would, but he hadn't acknowledged her when he sat down, so she'd been happy to keep the game going.

She knew he'd watched her the entire night. She could feel his eyes as she flirted with the three men at the bar, and he'd even gone so far as to turn around on his stool to watch the knife game. She thought he might rip the top off the bar when she'd purposely lost the first game and kissed that man. She'd felt the anger radiating off him, although whether it was directed at her, the man, or both of them, she wasn't sure. Regardless, she'd loved knowing she was driving him crazy.

Somewhere over the course of the night, however, she'd completely lost her own self-restraint, and Samhail had found his. She was grateful she couldn't remember too much more after they returned to the room because she was sure she'd made a fool of herself.

The only other thing she could remember perfectly was Samhail's reaction when she'd shifted into Cyra. She wasn't sure what reaction she'd been hoping for when she did it, whether turning into the lady would've convinced him to fuck her, or whether she had wanted him to reject her in that form. As it turned out, he'd done the latter, and she'd been relieved.

More importantly, his fierce response to her shift had been genuine. He'd shoved her away so fast and so resolutely that there was no doubt in her mind about his feelings, or lack thereof. If he still wanted Cyra, there might've been some hesitation on his part, but there was none.

That had been her last doubt about Samhail. If she was going to give in to this desire she felt for him, she wanted to be sure it was completely mutual, and he wasn't simply interested in her because she could become some other woman he really wanted more. She still didn't know why it mattered to her, but it did.

Yet she'd hesitated again this morning. Samhail had given her the opportunity to tell him she wanted him, but she'd let it pass. She'd come so close. It had been on the tip of her tongue to ask him to take her, but she hadn't said it in time, which, in hindsight, was for the best since they couldn't have acted on it anyway. She also wasn't feeling well after all that drinking, so having to wait was fine.

Talyn watched Samhail out of the corner of her eye as she got dressed. Part of her couldn't believe he hadn't taken advantage of her drunken advances last night. Any one of those three men she'd met at the tavern would've fucked her in a heartbeat, no matter how drunk she was, yet Samhail had refused her.

She wanted to thank him for that. She'd almost said it this morning when she was enveloped in his arms, but then his mouth was on hers and on her breast, and the ability to form words had left her altogether.

Talyn shielded her eyes as she and Samhail walked out the front door of the inn. By some miracle, the day was cloudy, but even the muted light was still too much for her to handle. She squinted at the two large figures standing several feet from the door. Surgeon and Serise hadn't bothered to stow their wings, and they were garnering quite a bit of attention from people passing by on the street.

"Ah, he lives after all," Serise cooed to Samhail as they stopped in front of the twins.

"We thought the masque had slit your throat and left you for dead somewhere, brother," Surgeon added cocking his head toward Talyn.

Samhail crossed his arms. "Well, now that you've seen I'm alive, you can go home. I thought you were supposed to be guarding Lady Cyra."

"We're on a special assignment for his lordship," Serise said.

"Find the wayward gargoyle and bring him back," Surgeon said, "along with the assassin. Dead or alive is fine for the latter."

"Which reminds me," Serise said, waving a hand at Talyn.

If she hadn't been hung over, Talyn might've seen it coming, but she'd been too preoccupied by the pounding in her head to realize what was happening. In the next second, she found herself inside one of Serise's containment forcefields, and her eyes flew to Samhail in panic.

"Let her go, Serise," Samhail growled at his sister. He uncrossed his arms and stepped toward her, but Serise didn't back down.

"I can't do that, brother," she said with mock regret. "We have our orders straight from Lord Bressen."

"Bressen doesn't understand what's going on," Samhail said.

"Then perhaps you should've explained it to him better in that pitifully short message you sent him a few days ago," Surgeon said.

"Better yet, explain it to us now," Serise added.

"Let Talyn go first," Samhail said.

"Talyn?" Serise arched a brow. "It seems you've gotten rather familiar with the little assassin in your time on the run, brother."

"It's easier than addressing her as 'assassin' the whole time," Samhail said dryly. "And we're not on the run. We're traveling to Rowe."

"So you're heading to Rowe with the assassin who was hired by the former king of Rowe to kill Lady Cyra?" Surgeon said incredulously.

"Can you perhaps see why Lord Bressen is worried about your judgement?" Serise asked.

"I don't want to discuss this out in the open," Samhail said nodding to the people passing by on the street who weren't trying to hide their interest in the scene playing out. "Let Talyn out of the forcefield and let's go inside. I'll explain everything."

"You think to hamper us by bringing us indoors where we can't use our wings," Surgeon said.

"Put your wings away," Samhail said. "You don't need them. Also, I don't need to bring you inside to have an advantage. You know I can take you both out easily enough right here."

The twins looked at each other with disdain, but that look was their undoing. With their eyes off him, Samhail lunged forward at the two gargoyles. They were standing only slightly close together, but it didn't matter. With his impressive arm span, he grabbed Serise's head in one hand and Surgeon's head in his other and brought their skulls together with a sickening crack that made Talyn wince. The twins dropped like stones onto their knees in the street as they pressed their hands to their heads in pain, and the forcefield fell off Talyn. Samhail simply stood over his siblings with his arms crossed again.

"Now, are you going to come inside and listen to me?" he asked. "Or should I finish you off here on the street?"

"Lead the way, brother," Surgeon grunted, still on the ground.

Samhail did just that, turning on his heel to head back into the inn. Talyn waited for the twins to pick themselves up unsteadily off the ground and retract their wings, intending to bring up the rear, but they clearly had no intention of letting her get behind them.

Serise smiled and gestured for Talyn to go first. "After you, assassin."

Talyn shrugged and followed Samhail inside. If he wasn't worried about giving the twins his back, she wouldn't be either.

A few minutes later, they were seated at a table in the inn's restaurant.

The innkeeper set down plates of breakfast in front of Talyn and Samhail while Surgeon and Serise fingered the mirror lumps on their foreheads.

"So, brother," Surgeon said. "Would you care to explain the note you sent to Lord Bressen several days ago?"

"I thought the note was fairly self-explanatory," Samhail said before he took a bite of his eggs.

Surgeon raised a brow and fished into his pocket where he pulled out a small, folded piece of paper. He opened the message leaf and read aloud. *"Found the assassin. I have a plan. Trust me. - Samhail."*

Samhail gave Surgeon a look as if to ask what was unclear about that.

"Lord Bressen bid us tell you that, while he is in fact a mind reader, he's going to need to know a little more," Serise said.

"So if you'd care to fill in the blanks?" Surgeon suggested.

Samhail shrugged. "The Raptor has seen the error of her ways, and she offered to turn Sandrian over to us."

Talyn narrowed her eyes at him regarding the first part.

"And how will she do that?" Serise asked.

"Sandrian has a bounty on me," he said. "She'll turn me in to him."

Surgeon and Serise both sat up straighter. They exchanged looks, and Talyn wondered if they were considering just how much of a reward they might get for turning in their own brother. Serise's next question didn't ease her mind on that count.

"Alive or dead?" she asked.

"Either," Samhail answered. He held his fork up with a piece of steak on it. "I assume he wants to torture me to death himself, but he'll take me dead if that's the only way."

Talyn frowned at his blasé tone as he popped the steak into his mouth, but more than that, she was surprised by the surge of alarm she felt at the thought of Samhail being hurt.

"He's not the only one," Serise muttered under her breath, and Talyn threw her a look that promised violence if Serise dared to try anything.

"Is there anything else we should know?" Surgeon asked.

"Yes. We encountered outlaws who had crossbow bolts tipped with caronium," Samhail said, and the twins' eyes widened. "The points were designed to break off inside the wound."

"How do you know that?" Serise asked.

Samhail lifted his shirt to reveal the two scars where the bolts had hit him, and the twins exchanged glances again.

"Were you able to remove the points?" Surgeon asked, and Talyn had the suspicion he asked not out of concern for Samhail's welfare, but because he was searching for a weakness in his brother.

"Talyn removed one of the points. A healer took care of the rest," Samhail answered.

Two sets of eyes swung to Talyn in unison, and her chin went up.

"It seems the little assassin has been handy to have around," Surgeon said sardonically.

Talyn wasn't used to being called little, but she supposed she seemed small to the gargoyles. Surgeon and Serise weren't quite as big as Samhail, but they still towered over her.

"She saved my life," Samhail said to Surgeon.

"Well, no one's perfect," Serise purred. "We can forgive her for that."

Talyn gave the woman another sharp look that made Serise's lips curl, and she shoved a piece of biscuit into her mouth before she could threaten Samhail's sister.

"She also seems rather protective of you, brother," Serise said, still grinning harshly at Talyn. "It's a good thing her looks aren't as lethal as she is, or I'd be dead twice over by now." She looked back at Samhail. "Can we assume you've discovered other reasons to keep her around?"

Samhail's face darkened, and Talyn felt his body coil next to her.

"The nights have been rather cold," Surgeon said, his eyes running over Talyn's chest. "Does she warm your bed for you too, brother?"

"Mind your tongue about her," Samhail said with venom, "or you'll find yourself without it... *brother.*"

Surgeon and Serise exchanged smirking glances, and Talyn knew they'd just confirmed what they took to be a weakness in Samhail. Her.

"She is a rather enticing little piece. Will you share her?" Serise said, letting her eyes roam over Talyn. "I bet she holds a dagger to your throat when she rides your cock. Or do you hold one to hers? Please tell us."

"Normally I wouldn't be inclined to fuck your leftovers, brother," Surgeon added, "but in this case-"

Talyn and Samhail moved at the same time. Samhail shot out of his seat, and his hands slammed down on the table, nearly collapsing it.

Talyn was far less subtle. Both Surgeon and Serise screamed as Talyn ported in between them and drove a dagger into each of their hands. The daggers pierced all the way through and stuck in the wood so both twins had a hand pinned to the table.

Samhail still had murder in his eyes when they met Talyn's, but her look said she had this under control, so he cracked his neck and sat down.

"Now then," Talyn said to the two gargoyles as they groaned in pain, "this was a friendly reminder to keep your hands to yourself around me. Understood?"

The twins nodded.

"Wonderful," she said. "If you don't mind, we really do need to be on our way. If you have any extra message leaves, though, we'll take those so we can keep Lord Bressen updated."

Surgeon reached into his pocket with his unpinned hand and pulled out several blank message leaves to lay on the table. Samhail swiped them up and put them in his own pocket.

"Are there any other questions you have for Samhail?" Talyn asked, and both gargoyles shook their heads.

Talyn pulled the daggers out of the table at the same time, and the twins clutched their wounded hands to their chests.

"You should probably get back to Solandis and have Lady Cyra look at those," Talyn said. "I tried to avoid any major bones or tendons, but as you said, Serise, no one's perfect."

Talyn smiled sweetly at the other woman, and she was surprised to find the gargoyle grinning back at her.

"I like her, brother," Serise said to Samhail. "You should invite her to the next family gathering. She and Sadira would get along well."

Talyn couldn't tell if the comment held the undercurrent of a threat, but Samhail's growl suggested it did. She ignored it and sat down again to finish her breakfast. She felt a little bad about the two bloody palm prints on the table the innkeeper would have to clean up now.

"What should we tell Lord Bressen?" Surgeon asked as he wrapped a cloth napkin around his hand.

"Tell him we're working on a plan to lure Sandrian into the open, and as soon as we have something definite, we'll contact him," Samhail said.

Surgeon nodded and glanced at Talyn's wrist. "No caronium cuff?" he asked Samhail.

"She got out of the one I put on her," he said.

The twins raised simultaneous brows.

"Do you need a new cuff?" Serise asked. "We have one."

Talyn gave Samhail a look that said he better not dare. He ignored it.

"No, I still have the one she escaped from," Samhail said. "There's no point putting it on her if she can get out of it."

Talyn looked at him in shock. He still had the cuff but hadn't tried to put it on her again?

"Besides," he went on, "she promised to behave herself, and if she doesn't..." He let the thought hang for a moment as he glanced at her with the hint of a smile. "...I know how to get her under control."

Talyn let out a sharp laugh. "Just because I let you think you're in control doesn't mean you are," she purred to him.

The gaze he returned was so full of heat she went instantly wet between her thighs. That hadn't been the effect she was going for.

"Oh, they've definitely fucked," Surgeon said as he watched them.

"No, they haven't," Serise said as a knowing grin lit her face. "But they want to, and they will. Soon."

Talyn and Samhail both glared at the gargoyle woman.

Samhail popped a last piece of steak into his mouth before he stood. "Tell Bressen we'll be in touch soon," he said.

"Give me back a message leaf so we can have Cyra call us a portal to Solandis," Surgeon said.

He reached out to Samhail, but Samhail only laid his hand at the small of Talyn's back to steer her toward the stairs to their room.

"If you leave now, you might make Callanus by lunchtime," Samhail said over his shoulder. "Stop at the Priory and ask for Phaedrus. He can draw you a portal back to Tide's End."

"You can't be serious," Serise said to him.

He turned to face her. "I am. That should give Talyn and I enough of a head start so you can't call Bressen before we're ready for him."

Surgeon tsked at him. "Trouble between you and the lord?" he asked. "I thought you were Lord Bressen's dutiful little lapdog. Since when don't you come when he calls?"

Samhail paused. "Since Bressen lost his objectivity about this," he said as he caught Talyn's eye. "He's too angry about the threat to Cyra to see Talyn's usefulness where Sandrian is concerned."

Both twins raised a brow. The same brow, in fact.

Talyn couldn't help the twinge of disappointment at Samhail's claim that he was only doing this because she was 'useful' to them, but she shook herself mentally. What had she expected? That Samhail was trying to shield her from Bressen because…because he cared for her?

"And you believe you're being objective?" Serise asked dubiously.

Samhail didn't answer but just urged Talyn toward the door.

"Best get between her legs soon, brother," Serise called after them as they began to ascend the stairs. "The lord will catch up to you soon, and I doubt there will be much left of her when he's done!"

Tandem Read: Go to *Nemesis Rising* (Bk 4), Chapters 13-16

Chapter 27

Talyn

Talyn and Samhail passed into the Derridan territory later that morning as the exchange with Samhail's siblings continued to ricochet around in her head.

Samhail wanted her. He'd made that clear enough, but he'd also made it clear that the only reason she wasn't in Revenmyer right now was their deal. She also knew that, as Serise had said, there might not be enough of her left to lock away once Lord Bressen eventually caught up with them.

Talyn shuddered as she remembered having the lord in her head. She'd felt just how easy it would've been for him to rip her mind apart, to leave her as a shell of herself who'd waste away until she succumbed to death. By comparison, willing her to die – which he also could've done – would've been a mercy.

Talyn's horse tossed its head and knickered, and she quickly surveyed the area for signs of trouble, but nothing stood out.

She kicked herself mentally. Gods damn her, she'd let her mind wander again. When in the hells had she gotten so complacent?

She felt safe around Samhail, she realized. She'd let her guard down because she trusted him to have her back, and she *never* trusted anyone to have her back. She shouldn't now either.

Talyn was used to living her life on the edge, used to never trusting anyone and looking for danger around every corner, but she'd been daydreaming about Samhail. She'd dared to wonder what it might be like if he actually wanted more from her than Sandrian and a quick fuck.

She sighed at her own stupidity. She did want to ride his cock one of these nights, but she wasn't looking for a relationship. Her life was just easier when she didn't have someone else to worry about.

She ignored the voice that kept trying to remind her how happy Cyra was to have Bressen, how the lady's eyes lit up when he entered a room, and how she smiled unconsciously when she spoke of him. No, the ache in her stomach was *not* jealousy or loneliness or a toxic mix of the two.

Serise was right. Once this was over and Samhail had his fill of her, once they'd found Sandrian and captured or killed him, Talyn would be on her way to Revenmyer, and Samhail wouldn't be able to stop it.

Assuming he'd even want to. He might welcome the convenient way to get rid of her after he was done with her.

Talyn shook her head. She was doing it again. Fucking hells.

They continued to ride in silence, but they didn't reach a town before dark, so they made camp in the woods. It was a bad time not to have shelter because there was a cold snap, and they spent the night huddled together under blankets for warmth. On one hand, Talyn enjoyed the feel of Samhail's large body wrapped around hers as they tried to fall asleep. His body always ran hot, and having him curled around her with his warm breath on her neck and his arm tucking her tightly against him was…nice. On the other hand, the cold weather kept them from picking up where they left off the previous morning after being interrupted.

They didn't dally under the blankets the next morning either, but rose, ate, and got underway as quickly as possible. Thankfully the chill was broken by the early Spring sunshine around mid-morning. Talyn actually removed her cloak and laid it across the back of her saddle.

Her desire to talk also returned with the Spring warmth, so she spurred her horse up next to Samhail's a few hours into their ride.

"I misspoke yesterday when I said you don't seem close to Surgeon and Serise," Talyn said, and Samhail's body jerked to attention as if he'd let his mind wander as well.

"What?" he asked.

"I said I was mistaken when I observed that you aren't close to your siblings. The three of you are downright hostile to each other."

"Gargoyle families aren't close," he said. "Parents aren't especially nurturing, and – like most perimortals – families often only have one child, so sibling bonds are rare. My family is an anomaly. Five children is nearly unheard of among perimortals, let alone gargoyles."

"Yet having so many siblings didn't bring you closer," she said.

"Having five children gave my family a degree of prestige among our kind, but no, it didn't broker any love between the five of us. If anything, it stoked rivalry because we had to fight for our parents' attention, unlike others who didn't have siblings to compete with."

"Do you love your brothers and sisters?" she asked.

Samhail actually turned in his saddle to look at her. "Do I love them?" he asked incredulously. "I don't even like them."

"Yes, but you can love someone without liking them."

He raised a brow. "Can you?"

"I think so. I mean, they're still your blood. Would you mourn any of them if they died?"

Samhail was silent as he considered this.

"I suppose I might mourn my parents," he said finally. "They weren't especially loving, but they cared about my upbringing. My older siblings, Soldier and Sadira would be just as happy to kill me as look at me, so no, I wouldn't mourn either of them. I'd probably be happy to be rid of them. As for Surgeon and Serise…"

He paused to consider again.

"I'm not sure I'd mourn them per se," he said. "I can at least stomach being in the same room with them. I suppose I'd recognize their deaths as a loss in some way, but I wouldn't mourn them. Not in the way Cyra mourns her father, in any case."

"Do *you* mourn Aramis?" she asked. She wasn't sure why she wanted to know all this, but for some reason she seemed compelled to…get to know Samhail? To learn who and what he cared about?

She didn't need to ask about Cyra and Bressen. She knew he cared for them deeply and that he'd mourn their passing.

She didn't really expect him to mourn Aramis, but to her surprise,

Samhail didn't answer right away. He opened and closed his mouth, as if he thought to answer, but then reconsidered.

"Do you?" she prompted, surprised.

"I…Aramis was a good man from what little I knew of him," Samhail said finally. "I don't mourn him as a loved one would, but I deeply regret my part in his death."

She blinked. "Your part in his death? What are you talking about?"

"I should've protected him. He risked himself to save us, to heal me when I was wounded, and then I left him alone to go fight. I should've gotten him to safety first. I failed him, and I failed Cyra."

She was taken aback by the depth of emotion in his voice, and his own guilt sent a prickle up her spine, reminding her that she too had played a part in the healer's death.

Talyn hung her head, and a few seconds of silence were trampled under their horse's hooves before Samhail spoke again.

"I…take it you were close to your sister?"

His tone sounded like he felt compelled to reciprocate her curiosity, but she didn't call him on it.

"My sister practically raised me," she said. "Our mother is a highly sought-after courtesan, so she wasn't around much."

She sensed his head whip toward her, but he didn't question her on that little admission, so she went on.

"I got my masquing power from my mother. As you might imagine, her ability to change her features to become anyone her customers want makes her very in-demand. She was rarely home when I was growing up, so my sister took care of me. Julia was nearly twice my age, but her father was likely mortal because her masquing power was limited. She worked in a printing house."

Talyn paused, but when Samhail didn't speak, she went on.

"My masquing power, on the other hand, is as strong as my mother's. The madame of her pleasure house had already begun to train me to follow in my mother's path. Had my sister lived, I'd likely be a courtesan myself right now, but it seems the gods had other plans for me."

Samhail

Samhail realized his mouth was hanging open, and he clamped it shut. Fucking hells. He couldn't wrap his mind around the idea that the woman riding next to him had been groomed to become a courtesan.

To start, she was such an effective fighter that the warrior in him balked at the idea she might never have become who she was, that her potential in that area might have gone unrealized.

More than that, he bristled inwardly to think of other men touching her, of them grunting above her as they fucked her. It made him want to tear something, or someone, in half.

Talyn claimed it was the ability to become anyone a potential lover wanted that made her and her mother so valuable, but the irony was that – in this form, her true form – she was already the most beautiful woman he'd ever seen. He couldn't imagine anyone else he might find more desirable, including Cyra. Cyra was beautiful, but he had to admit she'd lost some of her luster next to Talyn.

He marveled at the bright green of Talyn's eyes, and he ached to thread his fingers through the soft strands of her coppery hair. The times he'd seen it up close, he'd noticed some strands were mostly blonde while others were of varying hues of coppery red, and they blended together to give her hair its unique color.

Her body was perfect as well. Her breasts were large, but not overly so. Her waist was narrow, and she had a flat stomach that showed off just a little definition of her abdominal muscles. Her hips flared out in a way that would give him plenty to hold onto when he was pounding into her from behind, and her legs were long, with an enticing amount of muscle tone that drove him crazy. He'd never considered himself to be someone who appreciated a woman's legs until he'd seen Talyn's, then that's all he could look at. Gods, how he wanted those legs wrapped around him.

Talyn was taller than most women, and he hadn't realized what a difference that made until he'd kissed her. He still towered over her by just over a foot, but it was much easier to kiss her when he didn't have to stoop as far to reach her lips. It was…comfortable.

No, there wasn't a gods damned thing he'd change about Talyn.

Samhail shook away the thoughts as his pants became painfully tight.

"Your father was perimortal?" he asked, trying to steer the conversation toward topics that wouldn't arouse him.

"I assume so," Talyn said. "Both my sister and I were unplanned pregnancies from my mother's work. She takes at least two kinds of contraception, but as you probably know, it's more effective when both partners take it, and many of her clients don't bother." She paused. "On the other hand, I suspect the madame may have tampered with my mother's contraception occasionally. I think she wanted my mother to get pregnant so she'd have children with masquing abilities that could grow up to work in the pleasure house."

Samhail looked at her aghast, but she only shrugged.

"My porting ability may come from the man who sired me," Talyn went on, "or it might be a power buried deep in my mother's line that decided to manifest."

Samhail nodded absently. He couldn't get the idea of Talyn working as a courtesan out of his mind. He hadn't visited a pleasure house in quite some time because he was usually able to find a willing partner that he didn't need to pay, but he couldn't help wondering what he would've done if he'd walked into one and found Talyn working there. He'd probably become a regular.

Or would he? There was no doubt she was beautiful, but a significant amount of her appeal for him was wrapped up in how dangerous she was, how lethal and strong and stubborn she was. She didn't back down from a fight with him, even when most men did. Would her beauty have been enough to make him want her as badly as he did now, or would Talyn as a courtesan have been merely a passing fancy for him?

He felt a hollowness in his stomach at the idea that, if her life had gone differently, he might've been content to fuck her once and move on, never having a clue of the potential fire that smoldered inside her.

"Do you smell smoke?" Talyn asked.

Samhail jolted and his eyes widened at her words. She couldn't possibly know what he'd been thinking.

Then he smelled it too.

Samhail reined up his horse and sniffed the air. The acrid smell of something burning was faint, but it was there, and he looked around for the source.

"There," he said, pointing to plumes of smoke billowing over a hill in the distance.

Talyn turned to where he pointed. "Should we-"

"Yes," he said and reeled his horse around to spur it toward the smoke. He didn't wait to see if she'd follow, but the pounding of a second set of hooves behind him told him she had.

It took them twenty minutes to reach the source of the smoke, and they reined up just outside a small village.

Samhail tied his horse to a tree and pulled his swords from his back. Talyn had just finished tying her horse, and she unsheathed the daggers from her belt. Together they walked carefully into the town, looking for an enemy that no longer appeared to be there.

Samhail surveyed the area. Several buildings burned around them, and a film of smoke hung in the air. It was a familiar sight to ones he'd seen before. He'd accompanied Bressen to several towns recently where there'd been attacks. In all cases, they'd arrived too late to help. They'd found buildings on fire, several people injured or dead, and – more recently – some of the villagers had been taken, mostly men.

Now, as Samhail looked around, he noticed two things. The first was that there seemed to be fewer bodies on the ground than normal. It was possible there would be more as they got further into the town, but for now the casualties seemed minimal. On the other hand, he didn't see many men. Several women ran for cover with children, and a few elderly villagers huddled where they could, but he didn't see any men of fighting age just yet. They might find differently as they made their way further into the town, though.

"It seems fairly deserted," Talyn observed.

"That's my impression as well," he said.

They walked on further, but the few people they saw fled from them.

"We need to get someone to talk to us, to tell us what happened," Samhail said. He looked expectantly at Talyn, and she raised a brow.

"You think they'll talk to me?" she asked.

"They're more likely to talk to you than me," he said. "In case you haven't noticed, people don't normally gravitate toward me."

She looked as though she might argue with him, but she bit back whatever she'd planned to say.

"Fine. Stay here then," she said. "No one will come near me with you hovering around."

Samhail stopped walking and forced back a smile. He had to admit he liked the idea of no one coming near her when he was around. Not that it had worked that other night at the tavern with those three men. It still made him see red to think about them kissing her, but they hadn't known she was with him at the time. Next time he'd be sure they knew.

Talyn broke away from him and headed toward where they'd seen two women and a child disappear into a building. He followed at a distance, unwilling to let her completely out of his sight.

Before Talyn stepped inside the building, though, a woman darted out from behind a wagon, seemingly to find a better hiding place.

"Wait!" Talyn called to her.

The woman didn't stop, but Talyn ported in front of her. The fleeing woman screamed, but Talyn quickly sheathed her daggers and grabbed her by the shoulders.

"I'm not going to hurt you," Talyn assured her. "We're here to help."

"We?" the woman asked, then screamed again as she saw Samhail.

Talyn put her hand on the woman's face and turned her head away from him.

"We're here to help," she repeated. "Can you tell us what happened?"

The woman didn't speak right away as she tried to calm herself. Finally she found her voice. "Soldiers. They came up over the hill and attacked."

"Soldiers?" Talyn asked. "You're sure?"

"I didn't recognize where they were from, but they all wore dark blue uniforms," the woman said. "At least, some of them wore uniforms. The others were…"

"Were what?" Talyn prompted when the woman didn't go on.

"They weren't human. They were…some kind of blue monster. They had glowing eyes and long claws. There were maybe fifteen of them."

"What happened then?" Talyn asked.

"They attacked," the woman said, "but they seemed to be trying to round up the men." The woman's look turned pleading. "They took my husband. Please, can you get him back?"

"Which way did they go?" Talyn asked.

The woman pointed west. "That way. They had large wagons with cages that they herded the men into. The men they didn't turn, that is."

"Turn?" Talyn asked. "What do you mean by 'turn'?"

"Those monsters," the woman said, "when they clawed some of the men, the blue seeped off them into their wounds and…It turned them into whatever those things were."

The woman shuddered, and Samhail didn't blame her. He'd seen the things up close, and everything about them was disturbing, even for him.

"How long ago did the wagons leave?" Samhail called out, and both Talyn and the woman looked at him.

"Maybe fifteen minutes ago?" the woman said.

Talyn locked eyes with him again, and he knew they were thinking the same thing. The wagons weren't that far ahead and would be moving slowly. They could catch them before they got far with the townspeople.

"Let's go," Samhail said to her, and she nodded.

"Wait!" the woman said. "I thought you were going to help us."

"We are," Talyn said. "We're going to find your men."

The woman paused, then nodded in understanding.

Talyn let go of her and jogged back to where they'd left the horses as Samhail fell into stride next to her. Talyn untied her horse and mounted up, but Samhail fished in his saddlebag for a message leaf and pen.

"What are you doing?" she asked.

"I'm sending a message to Aidan to let him know the town was attacked so he can send help," Samhail said. "I'm not signing it, so he won't know who sent it, but he should be told what happened."

Talyn nodded and waited for him to send the message. As soon as it vanished, she kicked her horse forward, and Samhail swung himself up onto Guster to follow her.

They soon found that the soldiers – or whoever they were – had left a fairly obvious trail to follow. Samhail and Talyn rode fast, although not as fast as they had to get to the village.

"There," Talyn said when they crested a hill several minutes later.

Off in the distance, they could see a procession with several wagons moving slowly ahead of them.

Samhail pulled his horse up next to hers.

"What should we do?" she asked. "There's not as many as I expected, but I'm still not sure we want to take them on with just the two of us."

Samhail thought for a moment. He could easily take them all on in his gargoyle form if he shifted, but he wanted to see where they were going. This was the first time they'd been lucky enough to catch up with an actual band of attackers, and it was an opportunity to learn about them.

"Let's follow at a distance for now," he said. "They're likely traveling back to a base camp. I want to see where they go. We'll figure out what to do once they stop."

Talyn nodded and they urged their horses into a walk, going just fast enough to keep the caravan in sight without overtaking them.

"The blue monsters the woman was talking about," Samhail said as they rode. "We call them symbionts. They-"

"I know what they are," Talyn said. "Or, at least, I've encountered them. I even fought them before."

He frowned at her. "When did you fight them?"

"I was at the gambling den in Solandis when they attacked Cyra and Raina," she said.

"What?" Samhail said, his head snapping to her.

"I…think I'm the reason they attacked the den in the first place," she went on. "Sandrian had me reporting Bressen and Cyra's movements to him, so I sent him a message that night telling him Cyra and her friend had gone into town for the evening. Raina tried to misdirect me by suggesting they were going to a different tavern, but I managed to hide in the room, and when they left, I ported through Cyra's portal before she closed it." She paused. "From there I let Sandrian know where they were."

Samhail couldn't help the growl that rumbled up his throat.

"I'm sorry," she said. "I wish I hadn't done it given what happened, but Sandrian wanted to know if Cyra ever left the manor without Bressen. I think he was looking for an opportunity to take her. He must've sent the symbionts that night to do it."

"You said you fought them," he said.

"Yes, I didn't realize until later Sandrian had sent them," she explained. "They attacked everyone, including me, so I defended myself."

He frowned. "I don't remember seeing you. I assume you'd shifted?"

"I was the young man with the dagger," she said. "You pulled one of them off me and shoved your sword through his chest. You probably saved my life."

Samhail stared at her. He vaguely remembered a young man there who'd been trying to fight the symbionts. One of the creatures had cornered the boy and was about to slash open his stomach when Samhail had grabbed the thing by its neck and yanked it backwards. He'd thrown it against a wall and driven his sword through it. He'd waited until the blue shell dripped away from it, but when he turned back, the boy was gone.

"So you know how hard their exterior is and that they can heal quickly if you don't kill them fully," he said.

"Yes, and I know they can infect others who are wounded."

"Then you know enough to stay away from them," he said. "When the caravan stops, I'll take care of whatever attackers we find while you free the prisoners."

She looked at him incredulously. "Bullshit! You can't possibly think I'll let you take on those things by yourself."

"I do, and you will, because I can take them on without any danger that they'll infect me."

She looked like she was about to argue back when understanding crossed her features.

"Your gargoyle form," she said. "You intend to shift."

"Yes. They can't wound me in that form, so I'll fight them while you release the townspeople."

She let out a long breath, but he was relieved she didn't argue.

He had a feeling it wasn't something that would happen often, so he enjoyed the momentary victory as they rode on.

Chapter 28

Talyn

It was about half an hour before the caravan stopped in the middle of a field. Tents had been erected in the space and even a larger pavilion in the center. A few men had been left behind to watch the camp and tend the fires, and they let out a cheer as the caravan rejoined them.

Tree cover had allowed Talyn and Samhail to catch up to the group, and they tied their horses far enough away from the encampment that the animals wouldn't be seen or heard. They grabbed their weapons and crept closer, all the way to the edge of the tree line where they hunkered down behind a large stand of rocks.

"Rather bold of them to camp out in the open like this," Talyn said.

"Even bolder of them to fly that flag," Samhail answered.

Talyn found the banner flying from a post above the main tent and gasped. She wanted to believe she wasn't seeing things correctly, but the sword with an eye in its pommel that was wrapped in thorny vines on a burgundy background was a sigil she knew well.

"Rowe?" Talyn said in disbelief. "What's a unit of Rown soldiers doing this far into Thasia?"

"That's what I intend to find out," Samhail said as he looked up over the rocks. "Looks like about seventy of them, no?"

Talyn nodded. "About that many. Why?"

Samhail was silent for a long time, and Talyn was about to prompt him again when he began to take his armor off.

"What are you doing?" she asked as he removed his double scabbard and handed it to her.

"I'm going out to fight them," he said.

"And you don't need your swords?"

"No."

"You're going to shift?"

"Yes."

Talyn paused. "If what that woman back in the village said is true, some of those men are villagers that were turned into symbionts. Are you going to kill them?"

Samhail stopped and sighed deeply. "I'll do my best to injure rather than kill, but my strength in my gargoyle form is difficult to control. I may not be able to hold myself back. I'll try to leave one or two conscious for questioning."

Talyn nodded. She wanted to bring as many of these men back to their families as possible, but she didn't want Samhail to put himself at risk by going easy on them either. She wasn't sure what his gargoyle form entailed, but fighting seventy men on his own still seemed mad.

"Take my swords and go release the villagers out of the cages," he said as he pulled his shirt over his head and laid it on the ground. "Only fight the men you have to. Do not, under any circumstances, try to come help me."

Talyn's indignant response died in her throat as he began to undo his pants. Her original comment was replaced by a hissed, "What in the name of the Trinity are you doing?"

Samhail's mouth quirked up in half a smile. "Getting ready for battle."

"It looks like you're getting naked," she said, trying to hush her voice.

"I have to," he said. "I don't have another pair of pants with me."

Talyn just stared at him as he toed off his boots. A second later he pushed his pants down his legs and tossed them on top of his shirt.

Protector save her. Her eyes dipped immediately to his groin and the thick length of him that was just as damned impressive when it was slack.

Stop looking at his cock…Stop looking at his cock…

Talyn tore her eyes away from his manhood and tried to forget what it felt like between her lips the other day.

No such luck. All she could think about was how silky smooth the skin had been as she'd licked up his length. The bead of liquid on his tip had been pleasantly salty, and…

Her eyes locked with Samhail's, and he was smirking at her. She was biting her lip, and she released it.

"Be careful. Don't die," she said. She tried to make her voice strong, but the words slipped out in a whisper.

He raised a brow. "Are you actually concerned for me? A couple days ago you were ready to slit my throat."

She shrugged. "You've grown on me."

He smiled and shifted position so he was in front of her where she crouched on the ground.

Talyn inhaled sharply as he took her hand and wrapped it around his cock. She felt him start to harden.

"A stroke for luck?" he rasped.

"You're insane," she said, not taking her gaze from his.

He only smiled and thrust once into her hand. He groaned and made to pulled back from her, but she tightened her fingers around his shaft, and he groaned even louder.

"Protector keep you safe," she said and gave his cock another hard stroke before releasing him.

Samhail had closed his eyes, but he opened them and leaned forward. He hooked his hand around Talyn's neck to draw her to him, and his mouth covered hers. She instinctively leaned into him, parting her lips, and he kissed her thoroughly, his tongue delving in deep to taste her. She was breathless when he finally pulled back.

Then he stood and strode naked toward the encampment.

Talyn could only stare after him as his already large body began to grow. His wings unfurled from his back, but they weren't soft and leathery the way she'd seen them before. Rather, they seemed to be made of stone. Indeed, a dark, slate-gray coating was creeping over all of Samhail's skin, and a long, powerful tail now swept back and forth at the base of his spine. His legs elongated and changed shape to those of a lion or wolf, or some other beast with clawed toes. Sharp, lethal-looking claws tipped his fingers as well. She hadn't seen what happened to his long hair, but it was suddenly gone, replaced by huge, curved horns that curled around the sides of his stone-gray head.

Nemesis fucking damn her. He was incredible.

A cry went up from the encampment as soldiers spotted Samhail stalking toward them, and within seconds the camp was a flurry of activity as men ran for their weapons.

Talyn didn't move yet. She watched as Samhail and the soldiers drew closer to each other. She saw the symbiont shells grow over several of the men and hoped to the gods Samhail was as invincible as he seemed to think he was.

He was.

The soldiers hit Samhail as a wave, swords and spears flashing in the sunlight that peeked through the clouds as they attacked, but the blades just glanced off him. He swept one long stone-like arm out in front of him, and a row of soldiers went flying backward. All of them cried out in pain, and only a few stirred after they hit the ground.

Without thinking, Talyn breathed a sigh of relief.

She shook herself and unsheathed Samhail's swords, then ran toward the encampment. There was no longer any question Samhail could take care of himself.

No one noticed Talyn as she headed toward the wagons. All eyes were trained on the massive gargoyle now slashing and battering his way toward the camp, and Talyn reached the prisoners without issue.

Four soldiers had been left to guard the wagons, but none appeared to be symbionts. Still, Talyn wouldn't take any chances as she strode toward them, one of Samhail's razor-sharp blades in each hand. The swords were long — almost too long for her to wield — but they were surprisingly lightweight for their size.

The guard who noticed her signaled his compatriots, and they all turned to face her. They looked more curious than anything.

It hit Talyn all of a sudden how strange it was to face these men as herself. Under other circumstances she would've shifted into a guard and snuck into the camp, but the thought hadn't even occurred to her this time. After a decade of always being someone else out in the open, it had only taken her a few days to get used to being in her own body.

It had nothing to do with the way Samhail looked at her, she assured herself. Nothing to do with the way he always reacted so strongly whenever she took on another visage, or how his face eased when she shifted back. Not at all. It was just…Well, in this case, she didn't need to shift. She was rescuing people, not assassinating them. There was no reason to hide her identity.

Talyn ignored the four guards for the moment and addressed the men in the wagons behind the soldiers.

"Gentlemen," she said, "I'm here to rescue you."

The guards chuckled, but the men in the cages only looked between each other with horror or concern on their faces.

Talyn rather enjoyed such looks of incredulity. It made it all the sweeter when people realized just what she could do.

"Are any of these guards men from your town?" Talyn asked the prisoners, indicating the four soldiers with one of her swords.

The men only looked at her in confusion, the soldiers included.

"Is it alright if I kill these four guards?" she pressed the prisoners.

They began to murmur among themselves, but all four of the guards laughed outright this time.

"Planning to stick your sword in me, honey?" one of the guards sneered at her. "Better not miss, or I get to stick *my* sword in *you*." He grabbed his groin as he said it, and his companions all laughed.

"What are you doing? Run!" one of the prisoners shouted to Talyn.

All laughter died as Talyn ported in front of the soldier who'd spoken and plunged one blade into his chest, then the other into the chest of the man right next to him. The swords slid in like their bodies were made of pudding, quickly pushing through their torsos and coming out the other side. Talyn was surprised to find the blades buried to their hilts, and the men looked equally surprised.

Talyn jerked both swords down, and the blades tore through flesh and bone to leave twin foot-long gashes in the men's bodies. They both tried to scream before the noises were lost in the gurgle of blood that rose up their throats and spilled over their lips.

"I don't miss," Talyn couldn't help saying to the man who'd spoken, but his eyes were already glassy and vacant.

The third guard recovered from his shock and drew his weapon, but Talyn pulled back her blades and sliced at him. His head went flying into the air before hitting the ground with a thud. She felt his warm blood spray her face and splatter her shirt, but she ignored it as she looked down at the two blades in her hands.

Gods above. She had no idea how Samhail kept his swords this sharp, but she wasn't planning to give them back to him now. She'd barely felt any resistance when the sword had sliced through the man's neck like it was nothing more than a column of water.

The men in the cages suddenly all yelled at once, and movement in Talyn's periphery caught her attention. She whirled to see a dark blue hand sweep through the air toward her, and she threw herself sideways out of the way just in time to avoid serious injury. One sharp claw grazed her upper arm, though, leaving a thin cut that soaked her sleeve in blood.

Talyn wheeled to face the last guard and cursed her luck that he'd turned out to be one of the symbionts. It figured she'd left him for last so he'd had time to turn.

And now she had an open wound. She'd have to be careful. If she remembered correctly, that's how the symbionts entered someone's body, through a bleeding cut.

The symbiont slashed at her again, and she swung one blade to deflect the blow. The sword cut through the creature's arm to leave a deep gash, and it screamed in pain, a terrible high-pitched sound that hurt her ears. Had the thing been human, its arm would've gone flying, but with the hard blue shell on its body, the sword – while it had done more damage than a normal blade – hadn't fully severed the limb.

An otherworldly roar like nothing she'd ever heard before sounded from somewhere behind Talyn, and she turned to see several men fly into the air as if they'd been thrown. Samhail towered above the tents as he swept his massive stone-like arms at the soldiers who tried to attack him. Occasionally he picked a man up and threw him across the field.

Talyn turned back to the symbiont in time to dodge another swipe of its claws, but she didn't have time to deal with it anymore. It looked like Samhail had things in hand on his end, but she wouldn't take any chances.

The villagers in the cages were screaming and rattling the bars, seemingly trying to break free to help her, but she wished they'd just be quiet. She wasn't used to fighting with so much noise.

She ported behind the symbiont and slashed one blade across its back before driving the other with all her might into its torso where its heart should be.

The creature let out another ear-piercing cry, then the dark blue symbiotic shell began to drip from its body, mixing and swirling with the crimson streams of its human blood.

Talyn didn't wait to watch the body fall. She yanked her sword from its torso and ran for the cages. The men inside were all shouting, and she caught snippets of incredulity mixed with delighted cries of praise.

Talyn spotted the keys on the belt of one of the dead soldiers and grabbed them to unlock the first cage.

"Get back to your village," Talyn ordered the men as they piled out of the first wagon. She noticed now that there were even a few women among the group.

She ran to the other three wagons and opened them as well, then turned to head toward Samhail.

She was stopped by a hand on her arm. She nearly struck out at the person who'd grabbed her, but she held her swing just in time. It was one of the women she'd just released.

"Come with us," the woman said.

Talyn shook her head. "I have to help my…"

She stopped, not quite sure what to call Samhail. Her friend? Her companion? Technically he was still her captor, but that didn't seem like the right way to describe him anymore.

"Just go," Talyn said to the woman. "Get back to your family. We'll take care of things here."

The woman hesitated, then turned and followed the group of villagers hurrying away.

Talyn broke into a run, heading toward where Samhail's head moved above the camp. She sprinted between the tents, stopping only when stray soldiers or symbionts crossed her path. They all inevitably fell under her blades, some quicker than others.

By the time she reached him, Samhail had fought his way to the edge of the camp, and he was surrounded by at least thirty soldiers and five symbionts all still trying – and failing – to take him down. In his gargoyle form he was about nine or ten feet tall, and the soldiers hacked and slashed at whatever parts of him they could reach. Their blades only glanced off him, sparking on the stone of his body. A few men with crossbows tried to shoot him, but the bolts bounced off and fell harmlessly away.

There was an ever-growing pile of bodies that littered the ground near him as their blood soaked into the dirt to create a thick, reddish mud. Puddles of blue from now-dead symbionts also spattered the area. Whether Samhail had given up any semblance of trying to spare the soldiers or whether he simply hadn't been successful, she didn't know.

For a moment, Talyn just stared at Samhail as he swiped his arms across a group of men, bowling them over and likely breaking half their bones in the process. She was mesmerized by the beast in front of her, all fury and wrath. He was beautiful in the way raw, unchecked power can sometimes be beautiful, the way a storm of ferocious wind and rain and lightning can be both glorious and terrifying. His eyes glowed with an eerie blue light, and they held her attention as she watched, so enthralled that she didn't see the attack coming in behind her.

Thankfully Samhail did.

His bellow of warning made the symbiont who'd been rushing toward Talyn draw up short. The pause gave her just long enough to whirl and realize it was there, although not long enough for her to dodge when it swung. Its claws caught her across the abdomen, and she fell backward as her own blood seeped into the already-splattered front of her shirt.

Burning pain seared across her stomach as Talyn clutched at it and looked up at the creature. Its attention wasn't on her, though, but on the giant form she now sensed behind her. Talyn tilted her head back to see Samhail looming over her, his wings splayed menacingly, and his maw open wide to bare sharp fangs.

The roar that Samhail let loose vibrated in her chest and sent an icy chill trickling down her spine. The symbiont tried to launch itself at Samhail, but the gargoyle caught it around the waist and lifted it into the air. Without pausing, he ripped the creature's head off, and Talyn gasped as the body hit the ground with a thud next to her. The head rolled away to rest up against a tent, and the blue shell seeped away from it to reveal the wide-eyed expression of horror on the man's face beneath.

The sound of steel striking stone rang out behind her, and Talyn turned on the ground to see the few remaining soldiers and symbionts still hacking or clawing at Samhail. A sweep of his tail crunched bones and sent the last of them flying into the air where they landed in heaps of their own limbs and didn't rise again.

Then all was quiet.

Talyn looked around as she held a hand over her stomach, but none of the soldiers stirred. All appeared to be either dead or knocked unconscious. She had a feeling that any who were still alive would wish they were dead when they came to.

Samhail's snarl drew her attention, and Talyn lurched backward as he took a step toward her. His body began to shrink, and the gray stone-like skin slid back down his arms as if it were being sucked into the tattoo-like markings around his wrists. White hair sprouted from his head and spilled down his back and chest even as the blood-covered claws at his hands and feet pulled back in. The pale blue glow flickered out of his eyes and the huge spiral horns on either side of his head curled back up behind his ears. Between his legs, what had once been a stone codpiece-like bulge swung free into his cock, and Talyn might have laughed at the sight of it if she didn't think her stomach would hurt.

Then Samhail was kneeling beside her, fully back in his human form. His beautiful, blood-covered, *naked* human form.

Chapter 29

Talyn

"How bad is it?" Samhail asked her, his voice surprisingly hoarse.

Talyn scanned his body quickly but didn't see any wounds. The blood coating his hands, arms, and chest didn't appear to be his own.

"It's only a scratch," she said as her wince belied the statement. It wasn't too bad considering, but it was more than a scratch.

Samhail lifted Talyn's hand off her stomach. There were three jagged rips across her shirt, and beneath them Talyn felt the burn of torn flesh.

"Not all of that blood is mine," she assured him. "Really, it's not bad."

Samhail ignored her and scooped her up into his arms as easily as if she were a doll. He turned and headed toward the heart of the camp.

"Where are you taking me?" she asked.

"The pavilion in the center," he said. "I'm hoping they have medical supplies there."

"I told you, it's just a scratch," she said.

"I'll be the judge of that," he said, his voice angry. "And the next time I tell you to stay out of the way, stay out of the way."

"I wasn't in the way," she snapped back.

"You weren't paying attention, and that thing almost slashed you open. If you're going to stand there and fantasize about me, make sure you do it where it's safe."

Talyn let out an indignant cry. "I wasn't fantasizing about you!"

"If you say so. Either way, you were somewhere you didn't need to be. I told you I could handle this."

"I may not have taken out as many soldiers as you did," she said with irritation, "but I took out my fair share of them."

"I can see that," he said as they passed some of the bodies that bore the evidence of her blades. Samhail's tone suggested he was impressed.

They reached the large tent in the center of camp, and Samhail slipped inside with Talyn in his arms. The air was warm, and Talyn let herself relax against his body. He looked around to be sure no one was there, then strode for a large table in the center of the room. He perched Talyn on the edge of it, then swept the maps and other papers off it before pushing her further onto it. Without a word, he grabbed the hem of her shirt and pulled the garment over her head.

"Hey!" she yelled. "A little warning please before you start pulling my clothes off."

Talyn tried to swat him away, but Samhail ignored her and pressed her down onto the table with a hand to her shoulder before once again pulling away the arm she'd crossed over her stomach.

"Let me see the wound," he said, and he leaned down to examine it closely. He let out a breath. "It's not as bad as I was afraid."

"I told you," she grumbled.

"It still needs to be cleaned and dressed," he said as he looked around the tent again.

Apparently finding what he was looking for, Samhail stalked off toward one corner, and Talyn bit her lip as she watched the muscular swells of his backside flex while he walked. Nemesis take her, she'd never seen an ass like that before.

Samhail grabbed a box of medical supplies off a pile of other boxes, then Talyn was treated to the front view of him coming back. His thigh muscles flexed with every step, and his cock hung long and thick, even without being erect.

She bit her lip. How had she ever resisted him this long?

Samhail seemed oblivious to Talyn's blatant staring as he set the medical box down next to her on the table and opened it up to look inside.

"Do you see water around anywhere?" he asked, looking up again.

They both scanned the tent.

"There," Talyn said, pointing to a large canteen sitting on a table.

Samhail strode across the room to retrieve it, also grabbing a cloth, possibly a shirt, that lay over a chair. He opened the canteen and poured some water over his hands and arms as he walked, then wiped his hands on the shirt. He repeated this again until his hands were as clean as they could be without a bath.

When he got back to her, Samhail poured some of the water over her stomach to rinse away the blood, then wiped the wound with a clean part of the shirt. Talyn winced as the water stung the wounds but didn't say anything. Samhail pulled some clean cloths and wraps out of the medical box, as well as a bottle of alcohol.

"This will probably hurt," he said and poured some of the alcohol across the slashes on her stomach without warning.

This time Talyn cried out and sat up as she tried to clutch her hand across her stomach again, but Samhail caught her wrist before she could.

"You need to keep your hands away from the wound or I'm going to tie you down," he said.

Heat flashed in Talyn's eyes. "Promises, promises," she said with a wicked grin. "Now who's fantasizing?"

Samhail met her eyes with an answering flare that sent desire scorching through her body. They just stared at each other for a long moment before Samhail let out a slow breath. He put his hands on either side of the table around her and leaned in close so his lips were near her ear. Talyn shivered as his breath tickled the wisps of hair at her temple, but she refused to pull back from him. He wasn't touching her, but it felt like he was. Her skin prickled with his nearness, and she struggled to keep her breathing even.

"Are you sure it's just my fantasy and not yours as well?" he asked huskily. "Are you sure you wouldn't secretly love it if I tied you to this table, spread your thighs wide, and made you come over and over again on my tongue until you begged me to stop?"

Talyn clamped her mouth shut as quivers of excitement danced through her. His words struck her like lightning, and she decided it was better not to answer him. She looked away, and he chuckled softly as he ran his nose up the side of her cheek and puffed a hot breath against her ear. Talyn couldn't hold back the full-body shiver that rolled over her, and Samhail hummed approvingly as he pressed a clean cloth to her wound.

"Hold this," he said softly.

Talyn obeyed, pressing her hand over the cloth to hold it in place, and Samhail pulled back to wind a roll of gauze around her mid-section. He stopped as he caught sight of her arm.

"Why didn't you tell me your arm was hurt as well?" he asked.

"Because it's even less of a wound than this is," she said. "You've probably cut yourself worse shaving."

Samhail growled low in his throat and finished winding the gauze around her waist before he picked up the alcohol again to address her arm. His touch was surprisingly gentle, soft enough that the brush of the callouses on his hands gave her gooseflesh.

Samhail stopped as the bumps rose on her skin. He didn't move for several seconds as he looked at her arm. He ran a thumb lightly over the bumps, and they peaked even more over her skin.

"Are you cold?" he asked softly.

"No," she said, and several more seconds slipped by while they looked at each other.

"If either of these get infected," Samhail said as he went back to attending her arm, "scratches or not, they'll become a much bigger problem. I'd have thought you of all people would understand that."

Talyn saw his eyes dart over her upper body, lingering here and there on the various scars that adorned her arms and torso. She remembered being surprised he had so few scars on his own body, but she understood why now. He likely did much of his fighting in his gargoyle form, which seemed impervious.

Her eyes fell to the new scars on his side and stomach from the crossbow bolts. She saw only a couple other scars besides those, and she made a mental note to ask him about them at some point.

His scars weren't the only thing that drew her eyes, though. The wide expanse of his smooth, golden chest held her gaze as she watched his muscles ripple while he worked on her.

Nemesis take her. She couldn't *not* touch him.

Talyn raised her hand and placed it on the pectoral muscle over his heart. His body went rigid, and he stopped wrapping gauze around her arm. Both of them seemed to realize at the same time he was standing between her legs where they hung off the table.

"Is something wrong?" he asked as he finished tying off the gauze. His voice was strained.

Talyn didn't answer but trailed her hand down his chest, making sure to let her finger flick over his nipple. Samhail's entire body jerked at the touch, and he let out a low groan. Her hand continued lower, savoring every bump and dip of the taunt muscles of his stomach as they clenched tightly under her fingers.

"I just realized why you have so few scars," she said. "Your gargoyle form, it's…" She searched for the right word.

"Disturbing?" he supplied.

She raised her face to his in surprise and shook her head. "No. It's magnificent," she breathed, and Samhail sucked in a breath.

Talyn's hand continued lower, and his eyes widened as she reached his groin. Her hand closed around the base of his cock, and he grunted loudly, closing his eyes. She felt him harden beneath her touch, and he leaned forward to brace his arms on the sides of the table as she stroked her hand slowly up his length. The skin there was like silk over stone, and a pleasing pressure built between Talyn's legs as she remembered the feel and taste of him in her mouth.

She heard the sound of cracking wood and glanced down to see Samhail's hands nearly splintering the sides of the table. She leaned forward so her face was right next to his. She heard the raggedness of his breathing and felt the warmth of it on her shoulder. It brought on a fresh wave of gooseflesh.

She'd wanted him for so long, yet she'd felt like she needed to deny herself the pleasure of touching him. All of a sudden it made no sense, and her hand instinctively closed more tightly around his cock.

"Talyn," Samhail groaned, his voice a desperate, hoarse whisper. He thrust his hips involuntarily against the table "Gods above, I can't-"

"I want you, Samhail," she whispered into his ear, her own voice husky with need. "Right here, right now. Prove to me what a fool I've been to deny you."

His eyes flew open as he lifted his head, and Talyn gasped at the primal, predatory need in them. His eyes flashed blue, like the light she'd seen in them before, and he looked like he might devour her whole.

"We're in the middle of an enemy camp," Samhail reminded her as her hand made another lazy stroke between his legs, causing both him and the wood beneath his hands to groan again. "We're both covered in blood and surrounded by bodies."

"So then an orgy and voyeurism are off the table," she said, "and since I'm not partial to necrophilia-"

Samhail silenced the thought as his mouth crashed down on hers. He dragged her to the edge of the table so his hips were nestled between her thighs and his naked erection pressed up against her core, her pants the only barrier between them.

Then she was kissing him back with equal fervor, her need to have him inside her so strong she thought she might go mad without him. Her hands wanted to be everywhere at once, threading through his hair, running up his arms and over his shoulders, grabbing his hips. His own arms were anchored around her shoulder and waist to hold her against him, as if someone might try to pull her away.

Samhail pulled back from her and reached down to yank off her boots. Talyn unwrapped the cloth that bound her breasts and started to work at the fastenings of her pants, but her fingers trembled with anticipation.

When Samhail had discarded her boots, he pressed her back onto the table so he could get to her pants. He managed to work the fastenings free, although she was certain he'd been seconds away from just ripping them open. He grabbed the waist of both her pants and undergarment and yanked them down her legs before tossing them aside. He took a moment just to look at her body laid out for him before he started to kneel in front of her. Talyn sat up and grabbed for his shoulders.

"No!" she cried. "Inside me. Now."

Samhail didn't hesitate. He stood, and his hands closed over her hips as he positioned himself between her legs. He braced his arms on either side of her, and she felt the head of his cock probe at her opening. She let out a desperate whimper at the mere thought of him entering her, but he didn't move.

"Please tell me this is what you want," Samhail rasped out, his self-restraint seeming to hold on by a thread.

"Yes! Fuck me now!" she cried, and he was pressing inside her before the words were fully out of her mouth.

He entered her slowly, although it seemed to pain him to do so, and Talyn moaned as she savored the feel of each inch of him sliding into her. She grimaced at the slight burn between her legs as his cock stretched her wider than she'd ever been stretched, but she was soaking wet for him, and her body – used to shifting – adapted quickly to his hard, thick length.

He stopped to let her adjust for a few seconds then pushed in further. Talyn's eyes flared as she realized he'd only been halfway in. Gods above, she already felt like he was rearranging her organs.

With a final small thrust, Samhail buried himself as deep as he could go, and Talyn gasped at the feeling. There was a slight sting of pain, but overall her body throbbed in welcome to have him finally inside her.

Samhail stopped again to let her get used to him, but he was breathing heavily, and Talyn knew it was from the effort of holding back.

She swallowed at the feeling of him filling her, stretching her, and she grasped his forearms. "You need to fuck me now."

"Thank the Nemesis," he breathed as he began to move.

He still went slowly at first, but he drove faster as her slickness coated his erection, smoothing his strokes. She cried out at his first hard thrust, and he stopped, but Talyn wrapped a leg around him and pulled him toward her, urging him to keep going.

"Both," Samhail ground out. "Wrap both of your legs around me."

She did as he asked, and he groaned deeply as he began to move in earnest. He took long, fierce strokes that Talyn swore she could feel all the way in the back of her throat, but her body sang to finally be joined with his. She silently chastised herself for denying this pleasure for so long, but she still needed more of him. She wanted to wrap herself around him, but the table was hard, and it made positioning herself awkward. She looked to see if there was grass on the ground in the tent, but she saw something even better off to the side.

"Samhail," she gasped, and he slowed enough to look down at her. "The bedroll."

He looked where she pointed. Indeed, the captain of this regiment must use the tent as both a bedroom and a war room because there were blankets and a pillow laid out on the ground off to the side.

"Hold onto me," Samhail said as he wrapped his arms around her and swept her off the table, his cock still buried within her.

Talyn tightened her legs around his waist as her arms encircled his neck, and he swore softly. She pressed her mouth to his, and her tongue delved in to battle his own as he walked them to the bedding. He lowered her down carefully on top of the blankets as his body covered hers, and Talyn moaned as the new position pushed him into her deeper.

"Nemesis take me," she breathed at the feel of his solid weight on top of her. He began to thrust again, and Talyn's eyes nearly rolled into the back of her head at how good it felt.

"I have occasionally been mistaken for a god in bed," Samhail drawled, "but I promise, I'm the one taking you, not the Nemesis."

Talyn started to retort, but his mouth silenced her, and then she was screaming into him as he thrust powerfully inside her, pushing her closer and closer to the release that had been building slowly for the last week.

She wasn't sure how she hadn't shattered already. It wasn't possible for that sweet tension between her legs to coil any tighter, but just when she was sure she'd break, Samhail brought her even higher. She writhed beneath him, unable to keep still as her need for release became more urgent. If she didn't come soon, she'd go mad.

"You feel so fucking good," Samhail rasped as he sunk into her again.

She bucked underneath him, meeting his thrust and driving him inside her to the hilt. He grunted and rocked his hips on his next stroke to hit a spot she never knew existed. Her head kicked back against the bedding as he pushed her right to the brink, then his second rocking thrust sent her diving over it.

A crackle of energy shot through her core and skittered across her skin as Talyn's head snapped back again. She screamed, and her fingernails raked violently across the back of Samhail's shoulder as wave after wave of bliss crashed over her. Her inner muscles clenched around him, and a roar ripped from his own throat, not wholly unlike the one she'd heard him make in his gargoyle form. His hot seed spilled into her as he continued to thrust, and Talyn gripped his hair as she pulled his mouth down to hers to drink in his rapture.

It was the most intense feeling of pleasure she'd ever experienced in her life. Her limbs became liquid as any sense of time and place momentarily left her. She was no longer in a tent on a killing field in the middle of Derridan. She was somewhere between worlds where there was only her and Samhail and the ecstasy of their own bodies finally joined together. It was as if she was whole now, having never realized she might once have been in pieces.

Samhail drove into her twice more before his body shuddered, and he eased down on top of her, his face buried in her hair.

This time, Talyn welcomed his weight. She knew he was still holding himself up because she remembered him crushing her into the floor back in the jail cell, and she knew she wouldn't be able to breathe if she was taking his full weight. She couldn't breathe anyway, but that was for an entirely different reason.

They lay there panting for several long minutes before Samhail propped himself up on his elbows to look down at her. He hadn't withdrawn yet, not that he could have if he'd wanted to. Talyn's legs were still wrapped firmly around his waist, and she had no intention of freeing him just yet. It didn't seem like he had any thoughts of making her either.

"You're so gods damned beautiful," he said to her, and a knot lodged in Talyn's throat.

Men had told her she was beautiful before, but always when she'd been wearing another face. No one ever saw her as she really was. She hadn't worn her true form for this long in more than a decade.

Samhail saw her – the real her – and the thought almost made her eyes tear up, but she blinked back the moisture.

"I've been imagining what it would be like to be inside you for days," Samhail said. "To have your legs wrapped around me just like this. I was afraid I'd built it up too much in my mind and the reality could never live up to my imagination."

"And now?" she asked. The words were almost a croak.

"It was better than I could've dreamed," he said. "I don't think I've ever come that hard in my life. I want to live inside you like this."

She laughed softly, and he brushed a strand of her sweat-matted hair back from her forehead.

"Are you alright?" he asked. "Did I hurt you?"

She shook her head. "I'm fine."

"How was it for you?" he asked, and she almost laughed at the genuine concern in his voice.

"I can't tell you," she said.

He frowned. "Why not?"

"You already think you're a god in bed. If I have to admit it's true, you'll be impossible to deal with."

His deep chuckle sent shivers over her skin. "I was under the impression you already thought I was impossible to deal with," he said.

"You are, so imagine how much worse it'll be if I admit you're incredible to fuck."

"Fine. I see your point. I won't make you admit to my godhood, but I still want some idea how you found my performance."

"It was adequate," she said.

"Adequate!" he choked, leaning back.

"I don't want you resting on your laurels if we do this again," Talyn said. "You need a goal to work toward."

"*If* we do this again?" Samhail said. "The word you're looking for is *when*, because I plan to fuck you every morning, mid-day, and night from now on."

"That's ambitious of you."

"Ambitious would be never letting you leave this bed."

Liquid heat pooled between Talyn's legs at his words, but she said, "At some point those bodies outside may make staying here unpleasant."

Samhail's face went serious, and he sighed. "I supposed we do need to do something about them."

"Like what?"

Samhail started to withdraw, and Talyn reluctantly loosened her legs so he could pull out. He was no longer hard, but he was still big, and she felt the void inside her as he left her body. He rolled off to sit next to her on the bedroll, and she sat up as well.

"I need to bring Bressen in at this point," he said. "A regiment of Rown soldiers camped out in Derridan is something he and Aidan should be aware of."

Talyn's stomach twisted at the thought of seeing Lord Bressen again, and she felt the phantom pain in her head from when he'd broken into her mind. He'd wanted to kill her, and only Cyra's mercy had saved her. She wasn't eager to come face to face with him again.

"You'll send him a message? Tell him where we are?" she asked.

Samhail nodded. "I have to."

Talyn looked away, but he gripped her chin and turned her face back.

"He won't hurt you again," he said. "I won't let him."

"I wish I could say that was comforting," she said dryly.

"Bressen isn't a cruel man," he said, letting go of her chin, "but he's fiercely protective of Cyra. If we can convince him you're not a threat to her, you'll be fine."

"Do you believe I'm not a threat to her?" she asked.

Samhail regarded her for a few seconds before answering. "If everything you've said to me is true, then no, I don't think you're a threat to her, but I also don't have Cyra's truth seeing abilities. I have to take everything you've said on faith."

"And do you have faith I'm telling the truth?" she pressed.

He didn't hesitate this time. "Yes."

She nodded. "For what it's worth, I have no intention of harming Cyra, or anyone else you care for. I told you I'd help, and I will."

"Good," he said, "because I would really like to do this with you again, and that will be very difficult if I have to kill you."

She quirked a brow at him, but he just smiled and captured her mouth for a lingering kiss before he got to his feet and extended his hands down to her. She took them so he could pull her up, and she practically flew onto her feet at his effortless tug.

"You're bleeding through the bandages," he said, frowning down at her stomach.

Talyn looked down to see the bandage Samhail had wrapped around her was already soaked through with blood. She'd forgotten all about the wound when he'd been inside her. Her whole torso was also smeared with blood, but that had been transferred from Samhail's own body. They'd been too caught up in their arousal to clean themselves first, and she felt a bit queasy now at the feel of the sticky blood drying all over her body.

She glanced back at the bedroll and cringed. The covers were smeared crimson as well, like some kind of macabre painting.

"We need to get rid of those blankets," she said.

Samhail looked at the bedroll and grimaced before turning toward the table to get more dressings for the wound. He whirled again at Talyn's cry of alarm.

"What is it?" he asked, scanning the tent for threats.

"Your back!" Talyn gasped. "Gods above, it looks like you've been mauled by a wild animal."

Talyn looked down at her hands. The fingertips of one hand were crusted with dried blood, and she felt his skin under her nails now.

"What did I do to you?" she asked, rushing over to examine him.

Four long, gouging scratches ran down one side of his back, starting at his shoulder and extending more than a foot. The marks were red and angry, and several small trickles of blood meandered down his back.

"I scratched you," she whispered. "Badly."

"Believe me, I'm aware," Samhail said, half turning to grin at her. "I think it's what sent me over the edge."

Talyn's brows shot up. "You enjoyed it?"

He shrugged. "There's often an overlap between pleasure and pain."

"There's something wrong with you," she said shaking her head. "You should have a healer look at that. I'm not sure how gargoyles heal, but those scratches are deep enough to scar. I assume Cyra can-"

Talyn stopped herself. If Cyra came with Bressen, Samhail would enlist the lady to heal them, but it would be all too obvious how he'd gotten those scratches. Talyn's face heated at the look she imagined she might get from the Lord and Lady of Hiraeth if they saw what she'd done. Aside from her humiliation, it might be harder to convince Bressen she meant them no harm when he saw what she'd done to his friend's back.

Samhail turned around and took Talyn's hands in his, examining her fingertips. Finding the offending hand, he brought it to his lips and kissed the pads of her fingers, still crusted with his blood.

"If the marks are deep enough to scar," he said, "I have every intention of letting them do so."

Her eyes widened. "Why?"

"I don't have as many scars as someone else in my line of work might.

I welcome a few more. Scars are reminders of the battles we've fought, and these will always serve as evidence of my greatest victory."

He smirked at her, and Talyn's mouth fell open with an indignant squeak. Samhail pulled her against him and kissed her hard, and any protest she might've made died unvoiced.

"You can't just kiss me every time you want to silence me," Talyn said when he finally lifted his mouth from hers.

"I can," he said, kissing her again, "but what I think you meant to say is that I shouldn't."

"What I meant to say is you're an infuriating and frustrating man."

"You're not the first to tell me so," he said, "but scold me later. I need to send a message to Bressen. Stay here while I go get my clothes."

Talyn nodded and bent to pick up her own clothes as Samhail strode out of the tent. She found a bucket of water in the corner and washed herself as best she could to get the blood off her body, then she pulled her undergarment and pants on before rewrapping her breasts. Before putting her shirt back on, she removed the newly blood-soaked bandages from her stomach and pressed fresh cloths onto the wounds before winding more gauze around her to hold them in place. Only then did she slip her bloody shirt back over her head.

The tent flap opened and Samhail strode back in, fully dressed again. It looked as though he'd found a way to clean up as well, and he'd also retrieved his two swords. He went straight to the table again, set the swords down on top of it, and proceeded to write a note on a message leaf. When he was done, he held the paper up between his middle and forefingers and the note disappeared in a puff of smoke.

Talyn swallowed. Lord Bressen would soon know where they were.

She crouched down and gathered up the papers and maps that Samhail had swept off the table when he laid her there.

"We should take a look at these," she said. "There might be something that will tell us more about what they're up to."

"Agreed," Samhail said coming over to stand behind her as she dumped the papers back on the table.

Talyn felt him at her back, not touching her, but close enough that the heat from his body warmed her own skin. A few seconds later, he slid his arm around her and pulled her against him. She bit her lip as one of his hands clamped onto her hip to hold her in place as he ground his groin into her backside.

"This is not productive," she said softly.

His hand moved higher so he could run his thumb over her nipple through the wrap, and she sucked in a breath as her head fell back against his chest.

"I disagree," he said.

Talyn grinned and leaned forward over the table. She arched her back so her ass pressed into Samhail's groin, then undulated her backside against him. Samhail groaned and gripped her hips with both hands to pull her back so she could feel his new erection pressing into her.

"Gods damn me," Samhail growled. "I should have fucked you a few more times before I sent that message to Bressen."

Talyn laughed softly and ground her ass into him harder.

He growled. "Fuck it. I'm sure there's time for one more."

Talyn cried out as his fingers looped over the waist of her pants to pull them down, but the blue light of a portal flared next to them, and they jumped apart.

Samhail swore violently under his breath, and Talyn straightened quickly to make sure her pants were back in place. The portal widened, and through it they saw Cyra standing in Bressen's study back in Solandis. Talyn felt a momentary sense of relief at seeing the lady there instead of the lord, but it was short-lived as a dark form moved in front of Cyra.

Then the Lord of Hiraeth stepped through the portal into the tent, and his piercing turquoise eyes went straight to Talyn. The air was suddenly thick with his power, and Talyn had the feeling that everything she'd done up to this point had been a huge mistake.

Chapter 30

Samhail considered Bressen more of a brother to him than any of his blood siblings, but the look on the Lord of Hiraeth's face when he stepped through the portal was anything but brotherly. Bressen's eyes immediately lit on Talyn, and his face darkened.

Samhail had the instinctive urge to step in front of her, but two things stopped him. One was the certainty she wouldn't appreciate the blatant attempt to try and protect her. The other was the raging erection currently pressing at the front of his pants. The evidence of his arousal wasn't likely to help their case where Bressen was concerned, so he needed to get himself under control first.

"Samhail," Bressen drawled, and Samhail wondered if that had been a flash of red in his friend's eyes. "I was starting to think you forgot about us. It was a pleasant surprise to get your message."

Samhail was about to speak when Surgeon and Serise stepped through the portal, and he clenched his jaw shut. Fucking hells.

Cyra closed the portal behind them and came up to stand next to her husband as the twins took up positions behind her. Samhail tried to read in her face how she felt about this reunion, but her expression was impassive. He suspected she wasn't as angry as Bressen, though.

Samhail glanced at Talyn. Her body was tense, as if she was ready to run – or port – if needed.

"I know you don't agree with how I've handled things," Samhail said to Bressen, "but I had my reasons for doing things this way."

"I suspect I know your reasons," Bressen said, his gaze shifting between Talyn and Samhail, "but what makes you think I don't agree?"

Samhail bristled at the obvious implication he was thinking with his cock, but he ignored the comment for now.

"You sent *them* after us," Samhail said, giving Surgeon and Serise each a glare. They grinned back at him.

Bressen smiled as well and nodded behind him. "And you sent them back with holes in their hands. Or rather, the assassin did."

"They deserved it," Talyn and Samhail said at the same time.

Surgeon and Serise stopped smiling.

Bressen chuckled. "At least the verdict is unanimous."

His head ticked toward Cyra the barest amount, and Samhail knew she must've said something into his head. When several seconds went by and neither said anything else, he was sure the two of them were having a silent conversation in their minds.

"What I think Bressen means to say," Cyra said finally, "is that we were worried about you, Samhail."

"I understand," he said, "and I apologize for worrying you, but I needed to do it this way to give you deniability." He looked at Bressen again. "As you're aware, I can get away with things you can't in your role as a Lord of the Triumvirate."

"So you were protecting me?" Bressen said, raising a brow.

"In a way," Samhail said.

"Or were you protecting someone else?" the lord asked as he looked pointedly at Talyn.

"That's not what I was doing," Samhail said, looking instinctively at Cyra for confirmation. He wasn't sure if it was the truth or not, but Cyra didn't react, and neither did Bressen.

"Regardless of your motivations," Bressen went on, "now would be a good time to tell us what in the hells is going on."

"I need a favor first," Samhail said.

Bressen's brows rose again. "Oh?"

"Talyn was injured in the fight against the soldiers," Samhail said. He turned to Cyra. "Can you heal her?"

Cyra opened her mouth to speak but stopped short, and Samhail knew

Bressen must again be speaking into her mind because she shook her head slightly before saying, "I'm happy to do what I can. I just need to have Lord Aidan join us first."

Cyra turned and opened another portal behind her. This time they saw Aidan on the other side, along with Maziren, his captain of the guard. The two stepped through to join them in the tent.

Samhail had developed a relatively good relationship with the new Lord of Derridan during the trials the man had undergone to win his position, but Aidan's expression as he stepped through the portal was as hard as stone. Samhail thought he even saw a glint of hatred in the man's eyes. Aidan's demeanor toward him had changed recently, but he was having trouble pinpointing exactly when or why it had.

Maziren's eyes lingered on Talyn, and the captain's hand went to rest on the pommel of the sword at her hip. Her eyes flicked to Samhail next, and he gave her a look that warned her not to do anything rash.

"Someone needs to start explaining now," Aidan said as Cyra closed the portal behind him. "What's going on? Why are you all in Derridan?"

"I'll explain in a minute," Samhail said. "First, Cyra needs to-"

"Why don't you go talk to Bressen and Aidan outside," Cyra suggested, cutting him off. "I'll stay here and take care of Talyn."

"No!" Samhail and Bressen both said together, then looked at each other in surprise.

Cyra arched a brow at them. "Talyn and I will be perfectly fine here on our own. Won't we?" She turned to Talyn. "I assume you're not planning to assassinate anyone?"

Talyn frowned but nodded. "No assassinations today, my lady. I don't mean you any harm."

"She speaks the truth," Cyra told Bressen, and his mouth thinned into a hard line.

Samhail looked to Aidan, and he thought he saw surprise on the lord's face at the mention of Talyn's name. Perhaps Aidan had heard of her.

Aidan's expression shifted then, but Samhail didn't understand what he saw. Experience told him it was lust in the lord's eyes, but that didn't make sense. Aidan didn't take women to his bed as far as he knew. More importantly, Aidan was happily married to a man he loved deeply. Samhail must've mistaken whatever it was he thought he saw.

"Fine," Samhail said as he turned back to Bressen. "This way."

He led the way out of the tent while Bressen, Aidan, and Maziren followed. He didn't think Talyn and Cyra were in any danger from each other, but he was wary of what they might end up talking about, especially in front of Surgeon and Serise.

It was eerily quiet outside. The only sounds were the snapping of the Rown banners in the wind and the occasional crackle of the fires.

"What is this?" Aidan asked as he looked up at the banners. "I thought we were in Derridan."

"We are," Samhail said.

"Then why are we in the middle of what is obviously a camp of soldiers from Rowe?" Aidan asked.

"Because these soldiers invaded Derridan," Samhail said. "They attacked a town a few miles east of here. I was the one who sent you that message of the attack, Lord Aidan."

Aidan frowned but nodded.

"The camp looks deserted," Bressen said. "Where are the soldiers?"

"This way," Samhail said as he headed toward the spot on the outskirts where he'd engaged most of the soldiers.

They soon encountered the occasional body on the ground lying in its own blood. One was headless, and Samhail felt a new appreciation for Talyn's skills as a fighter. He'd fought with women warriors before and had a healthy respect for them, but none had the grace and speed he'd seen Talyn fight with. Her ability to port helped her a lot and kept her out of harm's way, but that didn't diminish her fighting ability in his eyes.

"Your handiwork, I take it?" Aidan said to Samhail as he stepped over a man whose entrails had spilled out onto the ground.

"No. Talyn's," Samhail said.

He glanced at Bressen, but far from being impressed, the lord's face only hardened more at the revelation. It occurred to Samhail belatedly that showing Bressen just how deadly Talyn could be after they'd just left her alone with Cyra might not have been the best idea.

The metallic smell of blood became thicker in the air as they arrived at the place where Samhail had taken on most of the regiment. It mingled with the occasional whiff of shit or urine, since soldiers often soiled themselves when they saw him in his gargoyle form.

Samhail's foot sank into the ground where it had been softened into mud by the blood that soaked in. Bodies littered the landscape in crumpled heaps, evincing far more blunt-force damage than those Talyn had left. Broken bones that pierced the skin abounded, as did limbs that were twisted at odd angles. Bodies had buckled in ways that made one hope they'd been long dead before they reached that state.

In truth, Samhail often found it difficult to see the aftermath of what his gargoyle form wrought in battle. He much preferred the quick, almost elegant deaths his blades allowed, as opposed to the mangled messes that were left behind when he shifted. As he'd anticipated, he'd been unable to control himself enough to keep anyone alive – or at least conscious – for questioning, and he felt a stab of guilt that at least some of the villagers would never return to their families.

Their return had been doubtful anyway once they'd been turned to symbionts, but now it was certain they'd never go home.

Even worse was that there was a small part of him that always thrilled when he shifted into the beast, when its bloodlust filled his head, and he could give himself over to the mindless destruction that came so easy in that form. He could rampage through dozens or even hundreds of men at a time, confident they couldn't harm him. That feeling of invincibility and the almost primal urge to annihilate that he felt when he was in his beast form were heady, and there were times the need to give in to those feelings burned through his blood like wildfire.

It was why he tried to limit the time he spent in that form. Not because it felt bad, but because it felt so good. Too good.

Bloodlust inevitably gave way to simple lust when he finally shifted back to his human form, and it wasn't unusual for him to spend the next few days after a battle fucking one or more women until the insistence of that lust finally subsided.

It was why he'd been hesitant to shift this time, why he'd considered the consequences of doing so for far longer than he might normally have considered them. Talyn was with him, and he'd been afraid of what he might do to her when he shifted back. He'd been having enough trouble controlling himself around her as it was, and he'd been genuinely afraid his battle lust might make him try to take Talyn against her will, or that it might at least make him push her into doing something she wasn't yet ready to do.

He'd eventually reasoned that because there were relatively few soldiers to take care of this time – nowhere near the hundreds or thousands he might kill in a major battle during wartime – he'd be able to control the lust.

He'd only just barely been right.

Samhail had been both terrified and enraged when he'd turned to find Talyn standing in the camp watching him tear men apart. For one, he hadn't wanted her to see him that way, grotesque in his gargoyle form and half-crazed with battle fury. For another, her presence had instantly stirred his carnal lust so that it mingled dangerously with the bloodlust raging through his system, so he wasn't sure where one ended and the other began. Thankfully, his gargoyle form prevented him from acting on his lust since his cock was drawn back against his body, protected by what amounted to a stone codpiece.

That hadn't stopped him from wanting Talyn when he saw her, but it had at least allowed him to refocus when he'd seen the creature running to attack her. She'd had her back turned and was oblivious to the assault, so he could only roar a warning. Luckily Talyn had moved just in time, and the precious few seconds had allowed him to get there and tear the thing's head off before it could attack again. She'd been injured, and his only thought had been to kill the symbiont before it could seep inside the wound and turn her.

He'd been afraid to look at her face to learn what she thought of his brutality, but seeing a moment ago just how many men she'd cut down herself made him realize she was used to such carnage.

Talyn's wound had been a strange kind of blessing. Taking care of her injury had distracted Samhail from wanting her, although the need had still been pumping there below the surface. It had taken a monumental effort to focus on Talyn's wound as he knelt over her on the ground, but it had taken his mind off sex for at least a little while.

Then he'd taken her into the tent, and she'd touched him.

She'd put her hand on his chest, and the beast had roared somewhere deep inside him. The need to push her back onto the table and bury his cock deep inside her had been so strong he'd almost blacked out, but he'd used every remaining ounce of his willpower to keep himself in check. He'd never hurt a woman before, never forced himself on anyone, and the Nemesis would take him before he'd do it now.

How he'd managed to stay still when she'd trailed her hand down his stomach and then lower, he had no idea. He was sure the bottom of the table bore the marks of where he dug his fingernails into the wood when she'd wrapped her hand around his cock. Still he'd managed not to move, even with his blood pumping through his veins like molten steel and the beast roaring in his head to take her, fuck her, claim her.

Then she'd said those four words that had been his salvation. *I want you, Samhail.*

He'd almost sagged to his knees in relief. He'd even tried to get down at one point, intent on making what he was about to do as good for her as possible, but she'd stopped him, and here again his relief had been overwhelming. He still wanted to taste her, still owed her that, but he'd been more than happy to defer it to a later time.

He'd made himself ask her one more time if she was sure it was what she wanted. If she'd said no at that point, his heart would've stopped beating. She'd said yes, though, and finally pushing inside her had been the single most intense feeling of his life.

He'd forced himself to go slow so he didn't hurt her. He was a large man in general, and he had a cock to match, so he'd eased inside her rather than plunging in as his body wanted to do.

He barely remembered the rest. They'd moved to the bedroll off to the side of the tent at some point, but his mind had been such a haze of rapture and need that he'd been unaware of anything but the feel of being inside her, of how fucking amazing she'd felt writhing beneath him with her body closed tightly around him. That he'd been able to hold out long enough for her to take her own pleasure was nothing short of a miracle. He'd felt the sting of her fingernails rake down his shoulder when she'd climaxed, but it had only made him come harder.

Bressen's voice jolted Samhail back from his musings.

"I see that blue substance," Bressen said. "Were they symbionts?"

"Some of them were," Samhail answered. "Not all. They turned some of the people while they were still at the village, then they brought a few wagons of people with them here. I assume they were planning to turn them eventually. Talyn freed the prisoners."

His eyes met Bressen's, and they seemed to have a momentary standoff about how genuine Talyn's help was.

"Still think Derridan can stay out of this war?" Bressen asked Aidan.

Samhail could see the fury in Aidan's face as he clenched his jaw, and Samhail blinked in surprise. Aidan wanted to stay out of the war? Clearly he'd missed a few things while he was away.

"I suppose not," Aidan finally said through gritted teeth.

"I've seen enough," Bressen said. "Let's get back to the tent."

Samhail was just as eager to get back, so he turned to follow the two lords. Women talked to each other when given enough time, often about things they had no business talking to each other about, and it was that, more than anything, that quickened his steps as they headed back toward the center of camp.

"Was she worth it?"

Samhail's mind snapped back from imagining the highly damning conversation he was sure Talyn and Cyra were having, and he looked down at the tiny woman walking beside him as they followed the lords. Maziren had spoken just loud enough for him to hear, and she had the hint of a knowing grin on her face.

"Was who worth what?" he asked in a low voice, playing dumb.

She shot him a look that said he knew exactly what she was talking about, but she spelled it out anyway. "Was fucking the assassin worth pissing off Lord Bressen?"

He opened his mouth to speak, but she cut him off.

"And don't deny you fucked her. I saw the blankets on the side."

Samhail felt his face drain of color. Fuck. They'd forgotten to get rid of the bloody blankets.

"How was she?" Maziren asked as she gave him a side-eyed smile. "She has incredible legs, and you know I like the tall ones."

Samhail clenched his teeth. Yes, Maziren did seem to like her bedmates tall. Including him.

It had happened – or almost happened – about a week after they'd started sparring together when he'd been in Derridan for the trials. He was always a bit aroused after a good workout, but he hadn't thought Maziren would be interested. She was usually reserved around him, and he'd also seen her slip off one night with one of the castle maids, yet she'd invited him out to a tavern with her one evening.

He'd been shocked as all hells when she'd straddled his lap after a few drinks and kissed him. He'd kissed her back, and they'd left shortly after. They'd made it back to her room, shed their clothing, and fallen into bed.

Unfortunately, that's as far as they'd been able to go. Maziren was a comically tiny woman compared to him – under five feet tall – and she'd clearly been in pain when he tried to push inside her. For his own part, he'd felt like he was splitting her in two. They'd tried a few different positions but eventually gave up. He'd put his head between her legs instead and let his tongue work its magic until she'd clamped both hands over her mouth to hold in her screams. He'd been about to get up and get dressed when she'd urged him onto his back and taken his cock in her hands to stroke him until he'd roared his pleasure and spilled himself all over his chest and stomach.

They'd gone back to being nothing more than sparring partners the next day and hadn't spoken of it since.

Samhail suspected she'd only wanted to bed him because of his reputation. Even if they didn't know who he was, women recognized he was an elite warrior and often took him to their beds for the prestige of being able to say they'd had him. Not that he'd ever complain about it.

"Yes, she was worth it," Samhail said to Maziren finally.

She raised an intrigued eyebrow. "Do tell."

"No."

She shrugged. "Fine. Do I have a shot with her?"

He ground his teeth again. Honestly, he didn't know. Talyn had admitted to fucking a woman. For all he knew, she might be interested in Maziren, but he didn't want her to be. He wanted her all to himself.

"You'd have to ask her," he said.

"But you'd rather I didn't," Maziren said knowingly.

He didn't answer, partially because they'd reached the tent again and partially because he wouldn't admit he didn't want her to have Talyn.

Surgeon and Serise stood guard outside, and Samhail was grateful they hadn't been privy to whatever was going on inside.

He held his breath when they re-entered and saw the two women standing together. Talyn and Cyra both clammed up as if they had indeed been deep in conversation.

He glanced toward the place near the side of the tent where he'd fucked Talyn, but the bedroll was gone. He felt a measure of relief at the thought that maybe Talyn had been able to get rid of it before anyone else besides Maziren saw it.

"Everything alright?" Bressen asked the two women, taking the words out of Samhail's mouth.

"Perfectly fine," Cyra said, giving her husband a pointed look. "Talyn and I were just catching up while I took care of her wounds. Neither were anything serious."

"That's good," Samhail said, still eyeing the two women as he tried to gauge what they might've been speaking about right before they entered.

He caught Talyn's eyes, but her expression gave nothing away as he stood next to her again. His positioning didn't go unnoticed by Cyra.

"And what about you?" Cyra asked Samhail, her eyes roving over his body looking for injuries.

"What about me?" he asked.

"Were you injured?" Cyra asked. "Any wounds I can heal?"

Samhail stiffened, unsure if she was asking because she knew about the scratches on his back or if she suspected something and was fishing for information. "I'm fine," he said. "No injuries."

Cyra started to nod, then paused and narrowed her eyes at him. Her gaze darted around his body again as if looking for wounds he wasn't telling her about.

"Are you sure?" Cyra asked, her tone suspicious.

Nemesis damn him. He really was fine, but strictly speaking, he was injured if you counted the scratch marks still stinging across his shoulder.

"I wasn't injured in the battle," he said carefully. "I let the beast out to play for a while, and you know he doesn't bruise easily."

Cyra looked at him for another few seconds as if she thought he might still be lying, but she nodded finally.

"Is there anyone else that needs to be treated?" she asked, turning to Bressen and Aidan. "Dare I even ask what it looks like out there?"

"It's probably best you don't," Bressen said, and Cyra flinched. "I haven't checked to see if anyone is still alive, but I'll do that now."

"I meant to leave one or two for questioning," Samhail said, "but things didn't go as planned."

Bressen paused, and Samhail knew he was using his mind powers to sense any living consciousnesses besides their own. Samhail didn't expect Bressen to find any, so he was surprised when both Bressen and Cyra looked in unison toward a cabinet in a corner of the tent.

"We're in luck," Bressen said. "One person survived the slaughter, and he's been here in the tent with us the whole time."

Tandem Read: Go to *Nemesis Rising* (Bk 4), Chapter 17

Chapter 31

Samhail

Samhail went rigid, and Talyn gasped softly at Bressen's words.

"Show yourself," Bressen ordered.

The door of the cabinet opened, and a man in a blue uniform marched out, likely compelled by the power of the lord's mind. He was young-looking, perhaps in his late twenties or early thirties, with reddish brown hair and a beard that could probably have used a trim. He looked terrified as he surveyed the six people surrounding him.

Talyn clutched at Samhail's wrist, her fingernails digging into his skin, and something cold and heavy pooled in Samhail's stomach as the man approached them.

It was disconcerting enough to think this man had been in the room watching him fuck Talyn, but it was more disturbing to think how vulnerable they'd been. Samhail had been distracted long before he carried Talyn into the tent, and when she'd finally touched him, he'd completely lost any sense of what was going on around him. He'd been so focused on the feel of finally being inside her that the man could easily have walked up behind him and slit his throat.

He'd left Talyn alone with the man when he'd gone to get his clothes, then they'd all left Cyra and Talyn in the tent with this soldier, who'd had ample opportunities to do them harm. That he hadn't taken any of them was either due to dumb luck or the man's own cowardice.

Realistically Samhail knew both Talyn and Cyra could take care of themselves, but that didn't staunch the surge of dread at the idea of what might've happened if the man had decided to act instead of staying hidden. From the expression of barely-contained fury on Bressen's face, his friend was thinking the same thing.

Cyra looked pale, but Talyn's jaw was clenched shut, and she was staring daggers at the man. Her ire was likely about what the man had seen them do and her desperate wish for him not to disclose it to anyone else.

The question of whether or not the man had seen anything was answered easily enough by the nervous looks he sent back and forth between Talyn and Samhail. The man hadn't just seen something. He'd seen everything, and Samhail added his own death stare to Talyn's.

"We can do this one of two ways," Bressen said to the man as he stopped in front of the lord. "You can answer my questions honestly, or I can dig the answers out of your mind in the most painful way I can think of. What will it be?"

"I…I'll answer your questions," the man said tremulously.

"Good choice," Bressen said. "Let's start with your name."

"Reginald of Dorhaven," he said.

"And are you a soldier or an officer?" Bressen asked.

"I'm just a soldier," Reginald said.

"Lie," Cyra cut in.

Bressen's face darkened. "Did I forget to mention my wife is a truth seer?" he said to the man. "You have one more chance before we do this the hard way. Care to try again?"

A look of panic crossed the man's face.

"I…I'm the captain of this regiment," Reginald said finally.

Cyra nodded to confirm he spoke true.

"And why was the captain of this regiment hiding in a cupboard while his men were out fighting and dying?" Aidan asked, his voice dripping with disgust and rage.

"I was surviving," Reginald said desperately. "When I looked out of the tent, there was a huge monster out there. I could see even from here we didn't have a chance, so I hid. Someone needed to be alive at the end to report back what happened. I don't even know where the beast went. For all I know, it could still be stalking around outside somewhere."

He looked pleadingly at everyone in the tent.

"I'm fairly certain the beast has gone back to sleep now," Bressen said shooting Samhail a quick smile. "Who were you going to report back to? Whose army is this?"

"We fight for Rowe. For the king," Reginald said, straightening.

Bressen cocked his head. "You were sent by King Alessi?" he asked.

Reginald swallowed and glanced at Cyra.

"Answer me or Samhail starts breaking bones," Bressen told him. He gestured to Samhail, who took a step forward as Talyn let go of his wrist.

Samhail was inclined to break some bones anyway, just for what the man had witnessed. The captain had seen Talyn naked, so at the very least Samhail might need to gouge his eyes out.

Reginald's face drained of color. "We fight for King Sandrian," he said quickly. "The rightful King of Rowe."

Bressen exhaled deeply. "And what exactly is the rightful King of Rowe up to? Why is he sending forces into Derridan?"

"We should take him back to Seatherny," Aidan cut in. "This is hardly a place to interrogate someone."

Samhail frowned at Aidan. The lord seemed almost…nervous.

"We'll question him now," Bressen said, his tone brooking no argument. It was a tone Samhail hadn't heard him use in months – the tone of the Nemesis Incarnate – and even Aidan clamped his mouth shut.

Bressen shook his head. "This is taking too long. I'll read his mind."

"Wait," Cyra said, frowning. "You and I both sensed his presence. He's not one of the symbionts. Why isn't he one of them?"

All eyes turned to Reginald.

"I…," the man said looking around wildly as if for an escape.

Enough was enough. Samhail stepped forward and grabbed Reginald by the front of his uniform. He lifted him into the air with one arm and slammed him down on the table. *That* table.

He grabbed the man's arm and started to bend it back the wrong way. Reginald screamed, and Samhail eased the pressure a little.

"Start talking, or we'll see how far back your arm bends before your elbow breaks," Samhail snarled.

Anger swelled inside him. He didn't want to deal with this craven. He wanted to get Talyn alone again so he could spend the next several hours doing everything he'd thought about doing with her the last few days.

"I'm immune!" Reginald yelled as Samhail reapplied pressure again. "They tried to turn me, but the creature wouldn't take to me. It's rare, but sometimes the interaction just doesn't work."

Bressen held up a hand, and Samhail eased up again.

"And is that why you're here?" Bressen said. "Sandrian is trying to build an army of those things by turning our own people?"

Reginald nodded. "Yes."

"It doesn't make sense," Talyn said stepping forward. "They only turned some of the villagers. They took the rest with them. Why not turn them all at once?"

Samhail bent Reginald's arm, urging him to answer, and he cried out.

"We can only turn so many at a time," the man said, explaining quickly before Samhail could twist his arm again. "Once one of the creatures turns someone, it needs a day or two to recover before it can split again. Likewise, once someone is turned, the creature needs about three days to fully bond its host and build its strength before it can split. We turn a few people when we attack, then we take any men and women who look strong enough to act as hosts and turn them later."

There was silence in the room as they all looked at each other aghast.

"I'm not sure whether to be relieved or horrified by that," Cyra said finally. "It could be worse, but…sweet gods."

"We need to get to Sandrian immediately," Bressen said. "It's time to find out everything this man knows."

Reginald's body seized, and he began to scream as Bressen attacked his mind. Samhail let go of the man and looked at Talyn. She'd gone a bit pale, and she'd drawn her daggers, although she didn't seem to realize she'd done so. He put a bracing hand at the small of her back. She jumped but didn't move away.

"Bressen, stop!" Aidan shouted as he stepped forward and pushed on Bressen's shoulder. On the table, Reginald stopped screaming as Bressen turned to the other lord.

"What are you doing?" Bressen asked Aidan sharply.

"What are *you* doing?" Aidan countered. "I'm the lord of this territory. You don't have any authority to question this man, let alone torture him."

Both of Bressen's brows shot up. "I don't have the authority?" he said incredulously. "This man is an invader. He brought a unit of soldiers into your territory to attack your people, and you want to get into a pissing contest with me over who gets to interrogate him?"

"Is everything alright in here?"

Everyone turned to see Surgeon and Serise in the threshold of the tent, their swords drawn.

"Everything is fine," Aidan snapped at them. "I was just reminding Lord Bressen that he's out of his jurisdiction, and that – Nemesis Incarnate or no – he's not the only lord here."

Samhail glanced at Maziren, and she met his eyes. She seemed just as concerned as him that Aidan would fight Bressen on this. It was true Bressen was out of his jurisdiction, but given the circumstances, an exception seemed in order.

Then several things happened very quickly.

"Stop the assassin!" Aidan yelled as he surged toward Talyn.

Samhail's head snapped to Talyn. She still had her daggers out, but she didn't look about to attack. Indeed, she looked shocked to have Aidan suddenly lunge at her. Talyn braced herself for Aidan's attack as Maziren drew her sword.

Dread gripped Samhail as Aidan caught Talyn's wrists in his hands. If Maziren thought Talyn was a threat to Aidan, she'd attack. On instinct, Samhail grabbed the back of Aidan's jacket and yanked him backward. Talyn jerked forward as well with Aidan's hold on her, but she ported out of his grip a second later and reappeared ten feet back from their group, only one of her daggers still in her hand.

Aidan himself somehow careened into Reginald, who'd gotten up off the table in the chaos, and the two of them toppled to the ground.

"Samhail!" Bressen shouted, and Samhail reached down to pluck Aidan up off Reginald.

"Lord Aidan!" Maziren shouted as she lifted her blade, her eyes wide with fear. "Are you hurt?"

Samhail noted the wild look in her eyes as she took in the blood on the lord's hands and down the front of his shirt. Samhail looked for injuries on Aidan, but Cyra's cry a second later told him instantly what had happened.

They all looked down to see one of Talyn's daggers – apparently pulled from her hand by Aidan – lodged in Reginald's chest. The man's eyes were wide, and they darted around as he coughed up blood.

"Fuck! Cyra!" Bressen said as he dropped to his knees next to the man. "Can you heal him?"

Bressen pulled the dagger from Reginald's chest and made room for Cyra to kneel next to him. She put her hands over Reginald's wound and began to heal him, but she lifted them a couple seconds later.

"It's too late," she said, sighing heavily. "He's gone."

Samhail stood stunned, the back of Aidan's jacket still curled in his fist. He looked down at the lord and thought he saw…satisfaction?

What in the fucking hells had just happened?

Bressen stood slowly, his eyes on Aidan.

"Aidan, what did you do?" he asked softly.

Aidan's chin went up a notch. "He tried to grab for the dagger in my hand. I defended myself."

Bressen didn't move, but Samhail felt his friend's power pulse over them. The metal poles of the tent and the furniture inside all rattled as Bressen's eyes flashed red with anger.

"We needed that man to find Sandrian," Bressen said, his seemingly calm voice belying the rage Samhail knew was churning inside him. "You killed the only person who might've been able to help us find him before it was too late."

"I was defending my life," Aidan insisted. "No thanks to this monstrosity and his assassin." He waved his hand in disgust at Samhail and Talyn. "She had her daggers out and was going to kill the man herself. You do remember she works for Sandrian, right? She wanted to kill him before he could spill his secrets."

"No! I wasn't going to kill him!" Talyn cried. She still stood back away from the group, her one remaining dagger clutched in her hand. She looked down at it as if remembering it was there and shoved it back into its sheath. She looked pleadingly at Cyra.

"You're mistaken, Aidan," Cyra said. "She's telling the truth."

Aidan huffed in annoyance and turned away. Samhail looked at Maziren to see what she thought of this, but she seemed as uncertain as ever as she slowly resheathed her blade.

"It seems we need to do things the hard way now," Bressen said. "Samhail, you and the assassin had a plan to draw Sandrian out?"

Samhail jolted as reality came crashing back to him, and he met Bressen's gaze.

"Sandrian has a bounty on my head," he said. "Talyn was going to send him a message to say she captured me and get him to meet us."

"Fine, we'll do that then," Bressen said.

Samhail dug in his pocket to pull out a message leaf. He put it on the table, and Bressen shifted his attention to Talyn. The lord held his hand out, inviting her forward to take the leaf.

Talyn looked like she'd prefer to bolt, and Samhail prayed she didn't. Finally she stepped forward, took the pen Bressen held out to her, and began to write on the leaf. She finished a few seconds later and held it up to show Bressen. He read it and nodded, and she held it between her middle and pointer fingers until it disappeared in a puff of smoke.

"And exactly what are we supposed to do when, or if, Sandrian answers?" Aidan asked.

"We arrange to meet, then set a trap for him," Bressen said.

Aidan didn't look impressed. "You're going to get us all killed."

Bressen raised a brow. "And what would your plan be?"

Aidan shrugged and shook his head. "I don't know. Continue raising our armies as you wanted and meet Sandrian on the battlefield."

"So he can strike our forces down with his lightning?" Samhail asked.

He was starting to get annoyed with Aidan. This wasn't the same cunning, deliberate lord he'd met back in Derridan months ago, the one who liked to outthink his enemies as much as fight them. What had happened to that man? He needed to ask Bressen if Aidan seemed off.

The minutes marched by while they waited for a reply.

"What's taking so long?" Cyra asked finally.

"Perhaps Sandrian doesn't trust his assassin anymore," Bressen said as his eyes fell on Talyn, and her chin ticked up a notch.

Just then, a message leaf poofed into existence before Talyn, and she plucked it out of the air. She read it briefly and handed it to Bressen.

"Sandrian wants to meet tomorrow morning on the Rown border," Bressen said after reading the leaf. "He sent coordinates."

"Why tomorrow?" Cyra asked. "Why not now?"

"I'm not sure," Bressen said. "He's likely wary of a trap and wants to plan, which is fine, because we need to plan too." He turned to Aidan. "Do we have your permission to enter Derridan tomorrow to meet with Sandrian?" he asked sardonically.

Aidan's brows furrowed. "So long as you know I'll be there as well to oversee things."

Bressen cocked his head in amusement. "By all means, Lord Aidan. Oversee away."

"Now, if you don't mind," Aidan said, "I need to get my men over here to clean up this mess."

"Of course," Bressen said with a nod. "We'll leave you to it."

Cyra was already tracing a circle in the air for a portal. She opened it wide and led the way as Samhail, Talyn, Bressen, and the twins followed.

As soon as it closed behind them back at Tide's End, Bressen rounded on Samhail.

"We need to speak. Now," he said to him.

Samhail nodded. He'd known this was coming.

"I'll get Talyn settled in a room," Cyra said.

"I already have a room here, my lady," Talyn pointed out.

"In the servants' quarters," Cyra said. "It's not really appropriate to have you stay down there anymore."

Talyn hesitated. "And where would be more…appropriate?"

Cyra smiled. "Don't worry. You won't be back in a holding cell."

Talyn relaxed, and she followed Cyra as the lady led her toward the guest floor, Surgeon and Serise falling in behind them.

Unease stirred in Samhail as he watched Talyn go. He didn't like having her out of his sight, but he turned back to Bressen.

"Are we going to talk in your study?" he asked the lord. "Or will we be 'talking' out in the training yard like last time?"

Bressen considered the question. "Let's start in my study," he said, "and I'll decide if we need to move our discussion to the training yard."

Samhail nodded. "Lead the way. Just know that if we end up in the training yard again, I won't let you win this time."

Bressen raised a brow. "*Let* me win?"

"I took the hits last time because I felt guilty about what happened. This time I don't have anything to be sorry for."

Bressen's brow rose higher, then he shrugged. "Very well. Let's hear all about your adventures with the assassin. You have five minutes to convince me you don't deserve a cell in Revenmyer next to hers."

Tandem Read: Go to *Nemesis Rising* (Bk 4), Chapter 18

Chapter 32

Talyn

Talyn debated not answering her door when a knock sounded several hours later, since there was only one person it was likely to be. She was surprised he hadn't just broken the door down, though, so it was that courtesy alone that made her open it.

"Yes? What can-," Talyn started to say, but the words caught in her throat as she took in the giant figure filling the threshold.

Nemesis take him, the man wasn't fighting fair.

Samhail leaned against the doorframe with his chest bare and the top two buttons of his pants undone, giving her a tantalizing peek into what lay below. His skin looked smooth, and she ached to run her fingers over the ridges of muscle that created a rolling landscape over his torso. It took every ounce of her willpower not to reach for that broad chest and run her hands down his stomach to explore what those open buttons at his waist promised.

"Is there a problem?" Samhail drawled when she didn't finish.

"You're half naked," was all she could say.

"And that's a problem?" he asked, a smile quirking his lips.

Talyn sighed and dragged her eyes back up to his face. "I see you escaped your meeting with Lord Bressen unscathed. Is there something I can help you with?"

Surprisingly enough, she'd escaped her own meeting with Lord Bressen unharmed. He'd called her in to see him after he was done with Samhail, and their conversation hadn't gone at all as she'd expected. For one, he hadn't invaded her mind.

Samhail shrugged and pushed past her into the room. "Bressen is mostly bluster. As for what you can help me with, you can help me understand what made you think we wouldn't be sharing a room tonight."

Talyn begged to differ about Lord Bressen, but she didn't say so. Instead, she bit her lip as she caught sight of the nail marks that still streaked red and jagged down Samhail's back from the top of one shoulder. She must've been frenzied with lust to have made such marks.

She still didn't understand his decision to let the marks scar over. If he didn't want Cyra to see them, he could find another healer before it was too late. If they scarred, he'd forever have to explain the marks to anyone who saw him shirtless, including future lovers. She wasn't sure the next woman who saw them would find them quite so intriguing.

Talyn herself was torn about the marks. On one hand, they were evidence of how fully and completely she'd allowed herself to let go with him, and part of her was ashamed to have left such blatant evidence of her lack of control on his skin. Another darker part of her was proud of them and wickedly delighted that any woman who had him after her would see she'd marked him. She'd learned he was more than a hundred years old, and he'd likely taken dozens – hundreds? – of women to bed during that time, yet she alone had marked him. Or at least, she was the only one whose mark he allowed to remain etched on his skin.

What that said about who they were to each other wasn't something she was willing to consider at this time.

"I was thinking we both needed a good night's sleep for tomorrow," Talyn said, meeting his eyes when he turned around. "And you snore."

"I don't snore," he said firmly, "and I have hundreds of witnesses who will swear to that."

Jealousy welled in Talyn as her mind went straight to thoughts of his bed partners, but then she remembered he'd been a soldier and had probably slept near hundreds or even thousands of other men at some point. At least, that's who she hoped he was talking about.

"Well, of course. No one else is going to have the balls to tell someone like you that you snore," she said, crossing her arms.

He quirked a brow in amusement. "But you do?"

"I can grow a pair if you like."

She was rewarded with the look of shock on his face as he remembered she could do exactly that.

"Snoring or no," she went on, "you should sleep in your own room."

"I can do that if you insist," he said, and she was both surprised and annoyingly disappointed at his easy acceptance.

Until his next words.

"Right after I fuck you in all the ways I've been imagining since this afternoon."

Talyn swallowed. "I never agreed to anything after the tent," she said.

She'd given in to her desire for him then, and she didn't regret it, but now that she'd had a little time and space to think about it, the idea of doing more with him seemed unwise. She could see how it would be all-too-easy to get attached to him, and that could have dire consequences.

"Maybe not, but you still want me," he said. "I can see it in your eyes. I knew it the minute you opened the door."

Talyn's chin went up. "It's perfectly rational to be rendered speechless when a half-naked man knocks on your door. It doesn't mean I want you."

"Fair point, but you do want me. That much I know."

"Do you?" Her hackles rose at his arrogance.

"I do, and I'm happy to prove it to you."

"And how exactly do you plan to do that?"

"Let me kiss you," he said, "and if you can still tell me you don't want me, I'll go back to my room and won't bother you again."

"And if I can't?" she felt compelled to ask.

"If you can't, then I'm going to throw you down on that bed and fuck you until you scream my name so loud the guards break down the door," he said, his voice wicked with promise.

Talyn pressed her thighs together at the liquid heat that pooled in her core. She shouldn't have asked. She definitely shouldn't have asked.

She reached out to grab something and steady herself, but there was nothing near her, and the gesture didn't go unnoticed by Samhail.

"Do we have a deal?" he asked, smirking.

She could refuse and just make him leave, but her pride wouldn't let her. Refusing his challenge was as much as admitting he was right, that she did want him. She'd accept it and simply resist him enough to say the words. At least that way she'd get to kiss him one more time.

"Fine," she said. "If you're going to make me prove it to you, then go ahead and kiss me."

She turned her face up to his in stubborn challenge, and his expression said he was beyond amused.

Samhail stepped forward, and every muscle in Talyn's body tensed. For once, it wasn't because she expected him to attack, but because she was already coiled with a different kind of anticipation. She refused to move, though. She'd stand there, let him kiss her, and then she'd lie through her teeth about wanting him and show him the door.

His smile as he approached was downright predatory, and Talyn had the sinking feeling she'd made a huge mistake in agreeing to his terms.

Samhail's hands curled around her upper arms as he pushed her backwards, and Talyn gripped his biceps.

"What are you-," she asked in alarm, but her question was cut off when her back hit the door. His lips came down on hers a heartbeat later, and Talyn let out an involuntary whimper as his mouth claimed hers. His tongue delved in deeply, and her whimper was followed by a muffled squeal of surprise when he pressed one of his legs between hers and pulled her onto it so she was straddling his thigh.

"What are you-," she tried to ask again, more desperately this time, but his mouth once again cut off the question.

Talyn couldn't move as Samhail's muscled body pinned her in place against the door, his mouth ravishing hers. He slipped one hand around her back, and his other hand gripped her hip to rock her back and forth along his thigh so the sensitive bud between her legs began to twist with exquisite sensation.

She managed to wrench her mouth away from his long enough to gasp out, "That's not fair." Then his lips were on hers again, and she couldn't summon the will to do anything more than dig her fingers into his biceps even harder. Not that it did any good. The muscles didn't give at all under her grip. His body was so remarkably solid and unyielding.

As the pressure between Talyn's legs built, her hips started to undulate of their own accord so she was riding Samhail's leg all on her own.

Somewhere she found the will to turn her head from his again and stop her hips, although she couldn't do more than catch her breath.

"Say it," Samhail breathed into her ear as Talyn panted against him. "Tell me *truthfully* you don't want me, and I'll leave."

Talyn swallowed hard. "I...I...don't want..."

Samhail pulled her harder against his thigh, and Talyn gasped as she now sat on his hip.

"You don't want what?" Samhail asked as his lips and tongue traced a path down her neck.

"I don't want...," Talyn said again, trying to force the words to come out. "I don't want...to want you," she finished finally.

It was the best she could do, and Samhail pulled back to look at her.

"That wasn't what I was expecting," he said.

"You wanted the truth. It's the truth."

"I don't doubt it, but it's not what you needed to say to get me to leave. If anything, it's an admission you do in fact want me."

"Nemesis take you. You knew that already," she said, frustration at both him and herself infusing her words.

"Then why are you trying to deny it?"

"It...It's too complicated to want you," she said, shaking her head.

His eyebrows shot up. "You'll need to explain that to me later, but right now I'm way too aroused to make sense of it. I just need to know one thing. Do you want me to fuck you, or do you want me to leave?"

Talyn closed her eyes. Letting herself give in to him again was going to make it that much harder later on to let him go – and she did need to let him go – but in this moment, she couldn't bring herself to tell him anything but the truth.

"I want…I want you to fuck me."

"Thank the gods," Samhail growled as he pulled her away from the door and carried her to the bed, one arm anchoring her against his hip.

He set her down on her feet and made quick work of her clothing as he pulled it off and threw it across the room. When he was done, he pushed her down onto the mattress and climbed on after her. Talyn began to reach for him, but he put his hands on her knees and pressed them open before lowering his head between her legs.

"Samhail!" she cried out, but he only wrapped his arms around her thighs to hold her in place.

"I have a debt to pay," he said, and then his mouth was on her.

Talyn arched off the bed as Samhail began to lick and suck and tease between her legs. His tongue flicked over her core before his lips closed firmly over her clit to suck on it, and Talyn couldn't stop the scream of pleasure that tore from her. She reached down to thread both her hands through the silky, white strands of his hair and tried to remember how to breathe. Gods above, the man's hair had no business being that soft, and his tongue definitely had no business being that skilled. She wasn't sure what he was doing down there, but it was like nothing she'd ever felt before. She struggled to keep her eyes from rolling back in her head as he drove her to heights she didn't know were possible.

Talyn's release built quickly, and she cried out again as her climax tore through her. Her entire body shuddered with pleasure before she eased back down into the bed. She tried to catch her breath, but Samhail gave her only a few seconds of reprieve before his tongue began to work again, swirling around her clit, then spearing inside her.

To her shock, she felt her release build again quickly. Too quickly. She'd shatter if she let him keep going, and as much as she craved the second release he was pulling her toward, she wasn't ready for it.

"Samhail! Please!" she cried out, trying to pull at his shoulders.

Samhail lifted his head, and the sight of him looking up at her from between her legs almost sent her over the edge.

"You have no idea what hearing my name on your lips does to me," he growled, his expression almost feral. "Tell me what you want."

"I want…," she managed between gasps. "I want you inside me."

"I'm not done feasting on you yet."

She shook her head. "Please. I need you inside me."

Samhail eased himself up off the bed, never taking his eyes from her. She forgot he still had pants on, and she bit her lip as she watched him unfasten them the rest of the way and pull them off. His cock was already erect, and her eyes widened to remember how big he was.

Samhail knelt back on the bed, and Talyn sat up to pull him toward her, but she yelped in surprise as he pushed her back down and flipped her on her stomach. He came down on top of her, covering her body with his, and one of his knees nudged her thigh open so he could press his cock between her legs from behind.

"This is how I want you," he whispered against her ear.

He paused, and she understood he was giving her a chance to object.

Talyn's heart hammered in her chest. She'd never let anyone take her from behind. It was the first rule of being an assassin: never let anyone get behind you where you couldn't reach them. Never be vulnerable.

The thought of denying Samhail was there and gone in an instant, though. Inexplicably, she trusted him to let him take her this way.

"Yes," she whispered.

He groaned as he pushed inside her slowly, sheathing himself into her as far as he could go. She gasped and tipped her head back against his shoulder.

"Are you alright?" he asked, not moving.

"Stop asking me that and just fuck me," she growled as she arched her ass up against him.

Samhail chuckled softly and began to thrust, slowly at first, then with increasing insistence. Talyn fisted her hands in the sheets as she felt every inch of him slide in and out of her, felt herself stretch around him again as he filled her more than she'd ever been filled. His hands came down on top of hers, and his fingers threaded into her own as the rocking of his hips sent shockwaves of pleasure through her.

He began to drive harder, and Talyn arched up to meet him so their bodies crashed into each other. She couldn't tell if the pulsing between her legs was him, her, or both of them, but she needed more.

"Samhail," she gasped, and his name was a plea of need on her lips.

"Gods damn you, Talyn," he gritted out. "You have no business feeling this fucking good. I'll never get enough of this."

She pushed back against him again, and he growled before suddenly pulling out of her.

Talyn cried out at the feeling of emptiness. "What are you-," she started to ask, but she yelped in surprise as he pulled her up onto her elbows and knees before he plunged back into her.

Talyn cried out and fisted her hands into the covers so tightly she thought she might shred them as he drove into her hard and fast, each thrust bringing her closer to splintering into a million tiny pieces. She pressed her face down into the bedding, letting it smother her cries, but Samhail turned her shoulder to pull her away from it.

"Let me hear you," he rasped. "I want to hear every noise you make when I'm fucking you."

His hands clamped tightly around her hips as he pulled her back to meet his thrusts, and the erotic slap of body against body only seemed to increase the frenzy for both of them. He pounded into her relentlessly, and Talyn obliged him with every moan and gasp and scream he elicited until she shattered with pleasure seconds later.

She cried out as her climax coursed through her, and her inner walls clenched around him. That seemed to send him over the edge as well, and he roared as he released inside her with a few final thrusts, each bringing aftershocks of languid bliss that spread out from her limbs before she collapsed onto the bed.

Samhail eased himself down with her, and they lay there panting against each other, his thick length still inside her. Neither of them seemed inclined to move, and it was several minutes before he broke the silence.

"I have a confession," he said, his voice graveled with spent arousal.

"Now?" Talyn asked drowsily. Her body refused to move.

"Yes."

"And what is this urgent confession?"

Samhail brushed Talyn's long hair away from her shoulder to bare her neck and back. He traced a finger over the place near her neck where she knew his half-healed bite marks dotted her skin.

"I want to taste you again," he said, kissing her shoulder.

Talyn blinked as her pleasure-addled mind struggled to wrap itself around his words. "You just tasted me."

"Not that way. Well, not *just* that way," he said softly against her ear before brushing another kiss against her shoulder and pressing his mouth into the crook of her neck. "I want to bite you again."

Talyn's eyes went wide, and she jerked against him as fear shot through her. Samhail wrapped his arm around her waist to pull her against him and keep her from bolting off the bed.

"I won't," he assured her quickly. "Don't port. I promise I won't bite you unless you let me."

Talyn's heart hammered again, although for a different reason than before, but she stayed still. Samhail didn't loosen his grip on her waist, not that it would've helped if she decided to port. She wasn't sure why she hadn't done so already.

"And why would I let you do that?" she asked.

"Because I can bite you without using the toxin, and because I'm told some people actually enjoy the feel of being bitten during sex."

To emphasize his point, he ran his unfanged teeth gently across her neck as he moved his hips. His cock was still inside her, and although it was no longer rigid, something nevertheless stirred between her legs.

She inhaled deeply as arousal threatened to grip her again. Her fear ebbed with his promise that he wouldn't bite her unless she said he could, and she had to admit to herself – and only to herself – that there was something oddly stimulating in the feel of his teeth grazing along her skin.

"Not today," Samhail said. "When you trust me more."

"Not today," she agreed, ignoring his comment about trust. She already trusted him far more than she should, and that terrified her.

Samhail's grip around her waist loosened.

"We should get some sleep," he said. "Do you still want me to go back to my room?"

Talyn hesitated, then shook her head. "You can stay as long as you behave yourself."

"Define 'behaving myself.'"

"No biting."

"Is that all?"

She hesitated again. "For now."

She sensed his smile.

"Then I accept your terms."

He finally pulled out of her, and Talyn got up to turn out the lamps. When she returned, he was already under the covers, and he held the blankets up for her to slip under as well. He pulled her against him, and Talyn was surprised she didn't feel the urge to tell him she needed some space. She was getting too used to having his body pressed up against hers, of having him between her legs. This wouldn't end well.

But that was a problem for another day.

First Talyn needed to worry about tomorrow and their meeting with Sandrian before she could figure out what to do about Samhail. She let her head sink deeper into the pillow, and Samhail buried his face against her neck as he tightened his hold on her. His thumb stroked back and forth slowly just under her breast, and for several seconds, that thumb was all she could feel.

With anyone else, the possessiveness in the touch would've annoyed her, but it didn't with Samhail. Rather, it made her feel…cherished.

It was a stupid thing to feel. It made it seem like there was more than lust between them, and there wasn't. There was a physical attraction that was oddly fueled by the frequency with which they fought, but to read more into it was asking for trouble.

Talyn didn't need to be with anyone. Being with someone was too messy given her line of work. It was too messy in general.

She closed her eyes and tried to clear her mind. She needed to get some sleep and stop thinking about the huge man nestled up next to her. The man whose warmth radiated off him. The man whose large hands were capable of great violence to his enemies, but whose hands could also touch her with such gentleness…

Talyn didn't remember finally falling asleep, but she awoke the next morning enveloped in Samhail's scent and the feel of his body still wrapped around hers. She wasn't surprised to see his chest inches from her face when her eyes fluttered open.

She rarely spent the night when she fucked someone, and the times she did, she always insisted on leaving a comfortable gap in bed between herself and them. That she gravitated toward Samhail during sleep was wholly unlike her. It must be his warmth.

Talyn sighed. Regardless of the reason, she had to admit she enjoyed waking up with him like this. It was one of the peculiarities that made this thing between them all the more confusing. And concerning.

"Still trying to figure out how to get back to your side of the bed without waking me?" Samhail asked.

Talyn smiled. "No, just wishing we could stay like this the rest of the day, forget about Sandrian and Rowe, and just…" She trailed off, not sure exactly what else she wanted other than to remain in Samhail's arms like this until thirst, hunger, or something else forced her from them.

"If you enjoy this so much, why don't you…want to want me, as you put it?" Samhail asked. "You said wanting me complicates things. What did you mean?"

"Do we have to talk about this now?" she asked as she rested her head against his chest.

"Yes."

She sighed again. "Fine. I don't want to want you because the more we do this, the harder it's going to be to give you up later when we go our separate ways. Assuming Lord Bressen lets me leave at all. I do want you, but I can't keep you, so it's better if we don't get used to this."

Samhail was still, and Talyn could almost sense his raised eyebrows.

"There are two flaws in your reasoning," he said finally.

"Oh? And they are?"

"First, you're assuming we have to go our separate ways. We don't."

"We don't?"

"No. You travel for work. I travel for work. There's no reason we can't travel together. I can help you with your jobs, and you can help me with mine."

She lifted her head. "Are you suggesting we become partners?"

Samhail shrugged. "Is there a reason we shouldn't?"

There was. Talyn had kept her anonymity because no one knew what she looked like or where she'd strike next. She could slip in and out of cities and towns without being noticed, but Samhail drew attention wherever he went. He was always noticed. If someone figured out that The Raptor always struck when he was in town, he'd either be blamed for her kills, or the local authorities would start taking a closer look at who he traveled with. Either way, working together put both of them in danger.

It was on the tip of Talyn's tongue to tell him all this, but he'd only argue with her, so she kept silent. There'd be time enough later to poke holes in his plan and convince him it wouldn't work.

"And the second flaw in my reasoning?" she asked.

"You said you can't keep me, that you'll eventually need to let me go. You're assuming that *I* plan to let *you* go. You may not be planning to keep me, but I'm definitely planning to keep you."

A kaleidoscope of butterflies took flight in Talyn's stomach, and she tried to tamp down the inexplicable happiness his words elicited.

"It's not possible," she forced herself to say.

"Why not?"

"It...just isn't. Think about what you're suggesting."

"I have, and I very much like the idea of keeping you."

She sat up and met his eyes. "For how long? Do you just envision us going around killing people and fighting monsters during the day and then fucking each other silly at night until one or both of us gets tired of the other and we go our separate ways?"

"I wouldn't have put it that way, but I suppose that was more or less my thinking," Samhail said. "If it helps, I have no plans to ever get tired of you. And I also plan to fuck you during the day," he added.

She huffed a laugh. "As comforting as that is, you must see how ridiculous it sounds."

He shrugged. "Maybe, but it sounds less ridiculous than simply letting you walk away from me when all this is over. Not when I can barely think of anything else besides kissing you, or tasting you, or being inside you."

Talyn's breath caught in her throat.

"I don't know what will happen between us a month from now or a year from now," he went on. "I just know I'm not ready to give you up yet, so I won't. I don't usually make long-term plans, and I don't intend to start now. If the time comes for us to part ways, then that's something we'll deal with when we need to."

"You're absolutely mad," she said, her eyes searching his for any signs he was kidding. There were none.

He shrugged again. "I've been accused of worse."

Samhail reached up and brushed a strand of Talyn's hair away from her face, then trailed his fingers down her cheek. The unexpected tenderness of the gesture caught her off-guard and cut short any other response she'd thought to make.

"We should probably get up and get ready," she said instead.

Samhail grimaced. "There's just one problem with that."

She suspected she knew what the problem was, but she asked anyway. "And what's the problem?"

He took her hand and brought it down under the covers between his legs to rest it on the hard, swollen length of his cock. "That."

"Hmmm," she said wrapping her hand around his shaft, making him groan. "That's a big problem indeed."

She stroked her hand up over his crown, and Samhail closed his eyes, exhaling deeply. "Fuck," he murmured under his breath as she did it again.

"So what can I do to help with this big problem of yours?" she asked.

Samhail opened his eyes to look at her from under lids heavy with desire. His lips turned up in a wicked grin, and his hand moved between her legs to press against her thighs.

"Just let me between your legs," he said. "I'll take care of the rest."

Talyn did open her legs, and he settled between them as if he belonged there and nowhere else. She gasped as he sheathed himself into her to the hilt, and much to her delight, he took care of the rest.

Chapter 33

Talyn

A couple hours later, Talyn flexed her grip on the handles of Samhail's swords as they waited for Sandrian at the border of Rowe and Thasia. Something didn't feel right, but she couldn't put her finger on what.

Next to her in the clearing, Samhail knelt on the grass, his hands tied behind him with a slip knot. An unlocked caronium cuff was wrapped around his wrist, giving the illusion he was subdued.

"I seem to end up on my knees in front of you a lot," Samhail said quietly. "I'm starting to think you like me this way."

Talyn closed her eyes and vowed not to let him drag her into a conversation that would only distract them both. They needed to keep their wits about them until this was over.

"Hush," she said, opening her eyes. "You're supposed to be drugged."

"Give me something good to put in my mouth, and I'll be quiet," he countered. "Although I can't promise you will be."

Talyn glared down at him, but he only licked his lips at her. She swore under her breath and turned away.

Gods damn him. The man was incorrigible.

Blue light flared in front of them, and Samhail dropped his head.

Talyn watched the portal open before them and looked through it to where the former King of Rowe stood on the other side. He didn't move, though, and Talyn's unease grew. She finally called to him when it looked like he had no intention of stepping through.

"I hear there's a reward for this one," Talyn said.

Sandrian frowned at her. "And who are you?"

Talyn blinked in surprise until the issue hit her. She shifted into the black-haired woman in her forties she'd been wearing when she first met him. She'd worn her own form for so long lately that she forgot no one else knew what she looked like.

"Better?" she said, and recognition hit him.

"Ah, a masque. Of course," he said, smiling at her. "I'd despaired of ever hearing from you again, my dear assassin. I gave you an order, then you seemed to disappear. Did you accomplish your task?"

"No," Talyn admitted as she shifted back into her own form. "I failed, and they discovered me. I had to run."

All true. Talyn didn't see Magdalene through the portal yet, but Cyra had warned her the woman might have truth seeing powers, so she needed to be as honest as possible. She'd had a bit of practice in this.

"They sent the gargoyle after me," Talyn went on, "but luckily he's easily distracted by anything with breasts and a firm ass."

She just barely heard Samhail's murmur of agreement next to her.

Still Sandrian didn't step through, and Talyn's mind raced. She needed to get him onto this side of the portal.

"How did you subdue him?" Sandrian asked. He eyed Samhail, and the gargoyle swayed slightly as if drunk.

"A little essence of horkaine root makes anyone who drinks it lethargic and docile for hours," Talyn offered.

It was true. She just left out that she hadn't actually given Samhail any.

Sandrian nodded. "He's tied up?"

Talyn nearly smiled at the nervous edge to the man's voice. He could wield lightning, but the idea of even an incapacitated Samhail worried him.

"And he's wearing a caronium cuff," she assured him.

"This doesn't make up for your failure," Sandrian said to her, still not moving, "but the gargoyle is a good consolation prize. Bring him here."

Talyn hesitated. Did he suspect something, or was he just being overly cautious?

"I'll need help," she said. "He's not easy to move."

She hoped there was enough truth in her words to avoid suspicion.

Sandrian raised a brow. "How did you get him out here?"

"He was more cooperative earlier," she said.

Samhail took that moment to fall forward onto the ground. The thud he made was loud enough that Talyn wondered for half a second if something had really happened to him. The man deserved a gods damned award for that performance.

"Nemesis take me," she swore as she crossed her arms over her chest. "Estimating the dosage for a man his size is harder than it seems."

Sandrian paused again, then grinned and finally stepped through the portal. Magdalene was behind him, and the woman stepped through as well. Talyn saw the cruel gleam in Sandrian's eyes as he looked at Samhail's prone form, and she stepped in front of his body.

"About the reward," she said.

"You've already been paid for a job you didn't do," Sandrian said. "I'll consider him compensation for that."

Talyn was about to argue that she'd only been paid half of what she was owed, but the ground suddenly began to shake, and she had to catch herself as she stumbled forward. Behind Sandrian and Magdalene, the earth split open as a wide chasm formed between them and the portal they'd come through. At the same time, vines broke through the ground where they stood and wrapped around them so they were held in place.

"Magdalene, you and I have unfinished business," Cyra snarled at the woman as she stepped forward, her obfuscation glamour lifting. She carried a shortsword in a sheath on her hip.

Samhail tugged at the slip knot of his bindings to release them and got to his feet as he dropped the caronium cuff on the ground. The rest of their group – Bressen, Aidan, Maziren, and the twins – emerged from the woods as Bressen's obfuscation glamour lifted from them all. Bressen, Maziren, and the gargoyles were armed with longswords while Aidan bore a shortsword and a crossbow that he aimed toward Sandrian.

Magdalene only smiled as the vines holding her and Sandrian loosened and fell away. "Did you get that power from your auntie?" she scoffed to Cyra. "I've had that one for a while. You'll have to do better than that."

One of Serise's containment fields appeared around Sandrian and Magdalene next, but Magdalene only sent her power into the ground and a shriek rent the air behind Talyn as the containment field disappeared.

Talyn turned to see Maziren pull Serise back up from a hole that had opened beneath the gargoyle woman.

Sandrian began to laugh. "You traitorous bitch," he said to Talyn. "I knew I couldn't trust you. I knew they'd get to you. Luckily I planned for just such an eventuality."

Talyn was instantly on guard as she scanned the area around them. Then she saw it.

"Samhail, the grass next to them," she said urgently.

Samhail was silent a moment as he looked where she indicated, then he swore violently. "Bressen!" he yelled. "There's something behind them on the grass."

Sure enough, the grass there was matted, as if dozens of invisible people, or more likely symbionts, were standing on it.

"You're not the only one who can cast obfuscation glamours, Lord Bressen," Magdalene purred to him.

"And you may have taken one of ours, but we've taken one of yours," Sandrian said as his grin widened.

Movement in her periphery caught Talyn's attention, and she saw Aidan pivot so his crossbow was aimed straight at Bressen. He pulled the trigger, but Serise was right behind him. As if she'd known what Aidan had planned, she slammed her arm down on the crossbow just in time so it loosed its bolt into the ground at the lord's feet instead of into his head where it had been aimed. Her other hand came around, and she punched Aidan, sending him sprawling to the ground.

Talyn's mouth fell open. Samhail had hinted earlier they couldn't trust Aidan, that the lord 'wasn't himself,' but was he actually a traitor?

Talyn glanced at Maziren, Aidan's personal guard. The woman looked as if she wanted to attack Serise, but she held back.

Another crossbow thwack sounded from somewhere across the field, and Bressen's shoulder kicked back as a bolt lodged in it. Cyra shouted just as Bressen swore, and a moment later, several crossbows came flying toward them from across the field to land at Surgeon's feet, the gargoyle likely having summoned them out of the enemies' hands.

The sound of feet pounding toward them caught Talyn's ear, and she looked to see the matted grass closing in on them.

"They're coming!" she shouted.

"Get behind me!" Samhail yelled to her as he grabbed his swords back.

Talyn cursed him under her breath and drew her daggers instead.

Samhail swiped blindly in front of him with the blades as the unseen horde reached them. The swords met with the resistance of bodies, but a second later, three slash marks appeared across Samhail's chest, and he yelled in pain. Another set of slashes appeared across his side, and he spun to try and knock away his invisible attackers.

Fear shot through Talyn at the sight of Samhail's open wounds, and she jumped forward to stab her daggers where she assumed his attackers would be. The blades hit something, but they glanced off it, and she swung again, desperate to keep the symbionts away so they couldn't turn him.

Gods above, how were they supposed to fight what they couldn't see?

As if in answer, a thick fog suddenly engulfed the clearing. Talyn couldn't see more than ten feet in front of her, but what she *could* see was the outline of bodies where they displaced the fog. There were three of them on Samhail, and she surged forward to drive her dagger down into the base of one's neck. The thing screeched a high-pitched wail, then became visible as the dark blue substance dripped off it, leaving only its host's body on the ground.

Next to her, Samhail's body jerked as more slashes appeared across his torso. Gods, if one of the symbionts managed to turn him…

"You have to shift!" she yelled to him.

Samhail growled in anger as he swiped his blades in front of him to push any attackers back, but Talyn was relieved to see him begin to shift. He drove his swords into the ground as his wings flared from his back and his body grew. The layer of stone skin creeping over him covered the half dozen or so sets of slashes he'd taken so far as his claws and horns emerged, and he let out a roar that reverberated through the misty air.

The shift complete, Samhail grabbed at the nearest void in the mist, and his hands closed around the creature. He tore its head from its body and tossed both aside.

Talyn realized she needed to get away from him. He wouldn't hurt her on purpose, but visibility was limited, and she didn't want to be mistaken for an enemy if he ripped before looking.

She resheathed her daggers, grabbed the swords he'd discarded, and looked around for something to fight. She jolted as one of the twins in gargoyle form emerged briefly from the fog to barrel past her before being swallowed by it once again.

Three voids shot toward Talyn, swirling the mist in their wake, and she slashed at one of them. She was rewarded with a shriek, but the thing only swung around again as Talyn tried to stab for the other two voids. She thrust forward with Samhail's blades, and the two creatures impaled themselves on the swords as they tried to get to her. She shoved the blades forward to be sure they were in and then jerked them upward. Strangled cries came from the invisible forms, and she withdrew the swords so the forms fell around her.

Talyn turned back and slashed the third creature across the neck, and it fell next to the other two, leaving three human bodies on the ground in puddles of blood and blue symbiont sludge. She didn't pause to look at them. It wasn't a courtesy she'd allow herself. Their deaths would be marked only as another number in her body count. Between the outlaws and the soldiers she'd killed recently, that count had swelled quickly in the last few days.

Two hundred ninety-eight. Two hundred ninety-nine. Three hundred. A milestone.

A long, wailing scream rent the air and echoed around the clearing, as if each misty droplet of water sent it bouncing, and the roar of three gargoyles answered from somewhere in the fog.

"Cyra!" Bressen's panicked shout also answered his wife's scream.

The scream seemed to come from Talyn's right, but it was hard to tell in the chaos.

She slashed her sword toward another void that barreled toward her. It stuck in something solid, and she followed up with her second blade as she aimed toward where she assumed the creature's head would be. The symbiont fell to the ground, its headless body again visible as the parasite leaked from it.

Talyn turned and ran toward where she thought she'd heard Cyra. The lady had saved her life, and Talyn was partially responsible for the death of the woman's father. She owed it to Cyra to come to her aid.

Talyn cried out as claws raked across her back. She felt the cool air through the torn flaps of her shirt as blood trickled down her back, but she kept going. She charged across the clearing, not daring to port since she could barely see anything. She knocked bodies out of the way as she went by, throwing her shoulder into them when she saw voids.

"Cyra! Answer me!" Bressen's voice called again.

Two forms emerged just ahead of Talyn. Cyra was on her knees while Magdalene stood over her, reaching toward her. Cyra seemed to struggle as what looked like ice or frost seeped over her chest.

Talyn ported immediately. She appeared next to Magdalene and slammed into the woman, sending them both toppling to the ground. Talyn tried to raise a sword to strike, but Magdalene put a hand to her chest, and Talyn grunted as a huge forcefield sent her flying backward.

Talyn landed hard and dropped the swords as her head kicked back against the ground. Her vision went momentarily black before stars flared again behind her eyes. She had the sensation of falling as her eyes fluttered open, and it took her a second to realize she was indeed falling.

She tried to clear the cobwebs from her mind, then a scream tore from her throat as she realized what had happened. She'd been near the chasm Cyra had opened to cut off Sandrian's retreat, and Magdalene's forcefield had pushed her over.

Talyn ported upward immediately. Once, twice, then a third time. Her third port brought her to the lip of the chasm, and she grabbed for the edge, but there was nothing to hold onto. She fell back as her fingers came away with only grass and dirt.

She was about to port again when she felt her body being pulled upward by the familiar feel of someone's summoning power. A brutally strong hand, rough as stone, closed around her wrist, and Talyn looked up to see two glowing blue eyes. She blinked as Samhail's stone face came into focus, his arm outstretched before him, and she followed it to where his huge stone hand held onto her.

She yelped as he tugged her up, and she was momentarily weightless before he dropped her back on her feet. He let go, and she stumbled forward, catching her balance. They looked at each other for half a second before they both turned toward Cyra and Magdalene.

Power flowed between the two women as they seemed locked in some sort of magical battle. Talyn could feel the strength of the energy pulsing between them as it reverberated through her chest.

"I'll help her," Talyn promised Samhail.

He hesitated, but four symbionts broke through the fog then, and he turned to engage them with a roar. He pushed them back into the mist where the outlines of other symbionts still writhed in the disturbing parody of a ghostly dance, and Talyn wondered how Bressen and Maziren were faring against the creatures.

Talyn didn't see Samhail's swords, so she drew her daggers and took a step toward Cyra. A voice stopped her, though.

"I finally realized why you look so familiar."

She whirled to see Aidan standing a few feet away with his crossbow trained on her, the dark head of a caronium-tipped bolt aimed at her chest. She was about to port behind him and drive her dagger into his neck when he spoke again.

"You look just like your sister. At least, I assume she was your sister."

Talyn's entire body locked up as her eyes met his.

"I couldn't pinpoint the resemblance right away," he went on, smiling at her, "but now it's all I can see." He shook his head and looked at her as if in awe. "You did have a sister, did you not?"

Did.

He used the past tense, as if he knew her sister was dead, and something closed around Talyn's throat.

"How did you know Julia?" she asked, willing her voice not to shake.

"Julia? Was that her name?"

"How did you know her?" Talyn asked again, anger moving in.

He smiled. "Let's just say she and I shared an intimate week together."

Talyn closed her eyes and tried to quell the tremble in her chest that was starting to work its way into every part of her body. She wasn't sure if her legs would be able to hold her up in a few seconds.

"What does that mean?" she asked.

She was afraid she knew, but…it couldn't be what she suspected.

Aidan shrugged. "It means I spent a lot of time with your sister before she died."

No. She'd killed the man who murdered Julia. There were any number of other explanations for Aidan's words. He'd mistaken her for someone else. Or he'd somehow found out about her past and was just trying to get in her head.

But now that the doubt was there, she couldn't ignore it. It dug its claws into her brain, into her heart, and wouldn't let go. Her chest tightened at the possibility that, not only was the man who'd murdered her sister still alive, but she'd killed the wrong person for it.

The man she'd killed was guilty of at least two other crimes she knew of, but was it possible he wasn't guilty of the one crime that mattered? He'd told her as much at the time, had begged her for his life, but she'd been deaf to his pleas.

Gods, the things she'd done to him. She'd never again killed anyone as cruelly and violently as she had that day.

Aidan looked up as the sky grew dark and the temperature dropped, but Talyn barely noticed the change as she tried to wrap her head around what the lord had just said.

He'd spent several nights with her sister, but he hadn't known her name. There was only one reason she could think of that explained why.

"You killed my sister," Talyn said. It was as much a question as a statement, and her voice shook with both fury and shame.

Aidan didn't answer, but the cruel look in his eye told her everything she needed to know.

Gods above. It wasn't possible. He was a gods damned Lord of the Triumvirate.

Talyn launched herself at Aidan as her daggers flashed through the air. He pulled the trigger on his crossbow, but she ported a fraction of a second before the bolt would've hit her. She appeared behind him and thrust her dagger down toward his neck with a fierce shriek she was sure she'd never be able to make again.

A pulse of power shuddered over the field, causing her to stumble sideways, and somehow Aidan turned in time to deflect her blow. He grabbed the blade, and the dagger turned instantly to sand that fell to the ground in a pile.

Fuck. She'd forgotten his transfiguration powers.

She was surprised enough by the sand that she didn't see Aidan's fist coming until it had just about struck her. Her reflexive attempt to dodge probably saved her from being knocked unconscious, but Aidan's punch still connected partially with her temple and knocked her to the ground. Stars burst before her eyes, and her vision faded first to bright white, then to black before she blinked her surroundings into focus again.

It had grown almost as dark as night around them, and Talyn felt an inexplicable dread that had nothing to do with Julia as she shivered. It seemed to have dropped at least ten degrees since they first got here, and there was a strange noise building in her ears that she tried to dispel by popping them. It didn't help.

"Get back through the portal!" a frightened voice shouted from somewhere to her left. Magdalene.

The mist started to clear, and bodies littered the ground in pools of dark blue and crimson as Talyn picked herself up. Three hulking forms – the gargoyles – were scattered around the clearing, still fighting with the last of the creatures.

A tall figure in black clothes – Lord Bressen – was also picking himself up off the ground as Sandrian ran from him toward a portal. The one on the other side of the chasm was closed, and Magdalene had created a new one on this side to aid their retreat.

Aidan stood in front of her, and her eyes met his. He seemed to debate a moment, then he turned and ran for the portal as well.

Alarm jolted through Talyn as Magdalene and Sandrian reached the portal and stepped through. Aidan ran toward it, only yards from escaping, and fire burned in Talyn's blood. She had to stop him. She had to kill him.

No, not yet. Aidan hadn't actually admitted to killing Julia. She was almost certain he had, but she'd been wrong once before. She needed to be absolutely certain she had the right man this time. She needed incontrovertible proof. She needed…to be able to read his mind.

Nausea churned in Talyn's stomach at what she had to do, and she only had seconds to do it. She spared one more second to consider her decision before she ported to where she'd been standing earlier with Samhail. The caronium cuff he'd discarded still lay on the ground, and she grabbed it. Her power blinked out when she touched it, but she shoved it in her pocket, and the power returned when she no longer had direct contact with the metal.

Talyn ported in two quick jumps to Lord Bressen and pulled the cuff from her pocket before snapping it on his wrist.

"What the-," he started to say, but she sunk her fist into his stomach.

He grunted, but he didn't go down as she'd hoped. Still, she'd surprised him enough that she was able to pull the sword from his hand.

She looked toward the portal. Aidan was just stepping through. It was now or never, and she was already damned.

"I'm so sorry, Lord Bressen," she said before she grabbed his arm and ported with him.

One jump had her within feet of the portal, and one more took her and Bressen through it just as it closed behind them, cutting off Cyra's scream and Samhail's roar of fury.

Tandem Read: Go to *Nemesis Rising* (Bk 4), Chapters 19-20

Chapter 34

Talyn

Talyn kicked the backs of Lord Bressen's knees to send him crashing to the floor in front of her, then pressed the sword she'd taken from him to his throat.

Before her, Magdalene, Sandrian, and Aidan all stood staring at her in shock. Aidan drew his sword, but no one moved to attack her.

Talyn took a moment to gauge where she was. They were in the great hall of a stone castle or fortress, but one that didn't look like it had been used in a while. The tapestries on the walls were dusty and moth-eaten, and a few hung askew, no one having bothered to set them aright.

Windows lined both long walls, providing ample daylight for now, but torches in sconces stood ready to be lit later in the evening. There was no furniture in the room, save for a large chair that was set up on what appeared to be a small makeshift dais made of several large stone blocks pushed together.

A 'throne' of sorts.

Sandrian was the first to recover and address Talyn. "Raptor?" he said. He furrowed his brow as he looked from her to Bressen, who'd gone very still the moment her blade touched his neck. "I wasn't expecting you to return with us," he said, sounding cautiously intrigued, "nor was I expecting you to…bring a guest?"

"A prisoner," she clarified. "As a show of good faith to prove this is where I want to be."

She spoke carefully, still assuming Magdalene had truth seer powers.

Sandrian raised a brow at her declaration. "I was under the impression you'd abandoned your contract with me and switched sides."

"So were they," Talyn said coolly, "but believe me when I tell you they'll kill me on sight if I try to go back now."

Something clenched in Talyn's gut. *Samhail* would kill her if she tried to go back. She'd destroyed anything there might've been between them by taking his friend.

Sandrian's eyes fell to Bressen at her feet and the caronium cuff he now wore. "Indeed," he said. "But why should we believe you? How do I know you're not still helping him, and this is all some elaborate ruse?"

"This man tried to kill me," Talyn bit out, reangling her sword at Bressen's neck. She didn't have to feign the bitterness in her voice. "When he found out who I was, he peeled my mind open like an orange and almost willed me to die. Cyra is the only reason I'm alive."

Talyn remembered the pain of having the lord in her head. She needed to draw on that memory to sell her story.

Bressen still hadn't moved, but she felt the rage and hatred radiating off him. Getting him to help her now would be nearly impossible. What had she been thinking?

"Look at him," Talyn said, indicating Bressen at her feet. "He wants to tear me apart."

Bressen's all-too-real growl of fury was oddly welcome.

Talyn looked at Magdalene. "Tell me, lady, is anything I said untrue?"

Magdalene cocked her head to consider Talyn. Then she shook it. "No, everything you've said so far is the truth."

"You forget that I saw you with them," Aidan sneered. "You and Samhail seemed rather close."

Talyn forced herself not to port right to him and slit his throat. She had to be sure it was him this time. She couldn't live with the doubt.

She shrugged. "The gargoyle was a decent enough fuck. I didn't mind using him while I had him, but there's nothing between us."

Magdalene chuckled, drawing Talyn's gaze back.

"That's the closest thing you've said to a lie so far," the lady said with a knowing grin.

Talyn huffed a mirthless laugh. "Fine. He was a fantastic fuck."

At her feet, Bressen growled again.

Magdalene laughed. "Now you're being honest," she said. "But why did you work with our enemies to begin with?"

"I didn't have a choice," Talyn said. "They put me in a holding cell, and I escaped, but Samhail caught up to me hours later. I tried to fight him, but you can guess how that went. He put a caronium cuff on me, and he was going to bring me back. After they tortured me for information, they would've thrown me in Revenmyer, so I did what I had to do. I made a deal."

She looked at Magdalene who weighed her words, then nodded once.

Sandrian had been looking to the woman for confirmation, and Talyn saw his shoulders relax at her nod.

"So you betrayed us to save yourself," Aidan sneered.

"I did what I had to do to save myself," Talyn said. "I have no loyalty to you and your cause, and I don't delude myself into thinking you would've come rescue me if they'd thrown me in Revenmyer."

She looked pointedly at Sandrian, and he gave a brief nod to concede her assumption.

"I work for you because I'm being paid to," Talyn went on. "If you want loyalty, get a dog. Otherwise, the only thing you can expect from me is my best effort to do what I can to fulfill my end of the contract. I may have failed to kill Lord Bressen and Lady Cyra as you asked, but I bring you Lord Bressen now."

Magdalene's head snapped to Sandrian. "What? You ordered her to kill Cyra?"

Sandrian looked surprised at the anger in her tone. "Yes. About a week ago," he confirmed, disgruntled.

"You idiot!" Magdalene thundered as Sandrian frowned. "I told you I need Cyra alive. How dare you try to have her killed?"

Sandrian's expression changed from one of confusion to anger. "The woman is too powerful to keep alive," he argued. He gestured to Bressen. "They both are. The Raptor was in a position to eliminate our most dangerous enemies, and I made a decision." He glared at Talyn. "For all the good it did me."

"That wasn't your decision to make!" Magdalene spat at him. "You're using my money to pay this assassin, so you both answer to me!"

Talyn blinked in surprise. She'd always wondered where Sandrian got the money to pay her, considering he'd just left Revenmyer after twenty-five years. But what was Magdalene's stake in all this?

Sandrian opened his mouth to snap back at Magdalene, but he gasped and clutched at his chest as frost suddenly radiated out over the front of his shirt. He managed to lift a hand, and a small bolt of lightning shot from his palm to hit Magdalene. She cried out and staggered backward, but then she threw out her hand, and her forcefield sent Sandrian sliding back across the floor.

Talyn felt Bressen twitch, as if he might try to fight his way out of this in the chaos, but she pressed the sword tighter to his throat.

"Don't do anything stupid," she hissed at him, "and I'll make sure you get out of this alive."

He huffed in disbelief but remained still.

In front of them, Aidan stepped toward Magdalene, who'd subdued Sandrian with her ice again where he lay on the floor writhing in pain.

"You bitch!" Aidan roared at her as he raised his sword to strike.

Talyn's body was coiled and ready to move, but a small flicker of hope lit in her chest that maybe the three of them would destroy each other without her having to do anything.

That hope died a second later when Aidan clutched his throat and began to gasp as if his breath was cut off.

"Enough!" Magdalene thundered at the two men, and they went still. "You both need to remember who's in charge here, and if I have to remind you again, that reminder will leave much more permanent marks."

Sandrian groaned on the floor where he lay, and Aidan looked at Magdalene with loathing as he gasped for air. Finally, he took in a deep breath as Magdalene released him.

"I'll only say this once more," Magdalene said. "No one is to harm Cyra. I need her alive. Kill anyone else you want, but leave her to me. From now on, you'll obey me or face the consequences."

"You forget yourself, Lady Magdalene," Sandrian said, trying to rise. "I'm the king here."

"You're nothing at the moment," she snapped back at him. "You're a man without a country hiding in an abandoned castle. If you regain your throne, it will be because I put you there. Now shut up and let me do what I can to make that happen."

Sandrian got to his feet. He glared at Magdalene but didn't speak.

"If we can kill everyone else, then I'm starting with him," Aidan snarled, and he took a step toward Bressen.

"No!" Talyn shouted. She moved her sword from Bressen's neck to hold it out toward Aidan.

Aidan raised a brow. "Protecting your new lord?" he asked with a cruel smirk. "I thought you didn't care about Bressen. If you don't care about him, prove it. Slit his throat."

Talyn looked calmly at Magdalene. "Are they always this stupid?"

Magdalene quirked a brow, but her look said, 'You have no idea.'

"Aidan would have me kill your only leverage," Talyn said to her. "If you want Cyra, you just need to dangle Lord Bressen as bait. She'll come to you to get him back."

Magdalene looked at her appreciatively and nodded. "Under other circumstances, I'd hold your botched attempt to kill the lord and lady against you," she said to Talyn, "but your failure was fortunate, given that I need Cyra alive. And since you seem to have more sense than these two put together, I'm inclined to give you a second chance."

Talyn relaxed until the woman spoke again.

"After you let me read your mind."

Talyn went rigid. Her masquing ability could usually hide her true intentions from a normal mind wraith, but Magdalene was a syphon. Bressen had already proved that a powerful enough mind reader could see through her, and she wasn't sure she could keep her plans for Aidan a secret from the woman.

Magdalene stepped forward, and Talyn swallowed, but the lady turned her attention to Bressen instead. She put a hand on his head, and he grunted in pain as she seemed to explore his mind. His grunt soon intensified into a loud, drawn-out scream as whatever she did to him turned excruciating, and Talyn couldn't help feel a little satisfaction that he was getting a taste of his own medicine.

Her body twitched as Bressen's scream went on, though. She needed the lord, and she'd told him she'd protect him, but she didn't want to seem too eager to stop his pain.

"My lady, what are you doing?" Talyn asked. "We need him."

Magdalene lifted her hand from Bressen's head, and his scream tapered off. The lord collapsed onto the floor at their feet, and Talyn had to stop herself from bending to see if he was okay.

Bressen lay there panting, and Talyn heard him whisper something, but she didn't catch what it was. At least he was still alive.

"The lord has true hatred for you," Magdalene said.

Talyn nodded. She'd assumed as much, but it still sent a pang of regret through her. She'd seen enough of him to know he wasn't the monster the rumors claimed he was, and under different circumstances, she might have liked him, despite his arrogance.

Different circumstances that included a future with Samhail? a cruel little voice in her head asked, but she pushed it down. That had been a long shot before. Now it was impossible.

"Your turn," Magdalene said to Talyn.

Talyn took a deep breath and stepped forward. She'd touched Magdalene during the fight, so the woman had likely syphoned her powers already. That wasn't what worried her.

Aidan knew why she'd followed them through the portal. She was sure of it. Why he hadn't said anything thus far she didn't know, but it was likely a moot point. Magdalene would know very shortly why she was really here unless her masquing power – by some miracle – kept the woman from finding out.

Magdalene laid a hand on Talyn's head, and Talyn jolted as a feeling of vertigo overtook her. She closed her eyes tightly and fought the feeling of nausea that threatened as her equilibrium shifted. The feeling wasn't painful per se, not as it had been when Bressen had torn his way into her mind, but she'd been fighting to keep him out then. She wasn't actively fighting Magdalene, so maybe that was the difference.

Magdalene lifted her hand from Talyn's head, and the ground finally stopped shifting. Talyn opened her eyes and found the lady looking at her. There was no anger on Magdalene's face, but her expression was… knowing? Had she seen why she was really there?

Perhaps she had and just didn't care. There was some obvious tension between Magdalene and Aidan. Maybe the lady wouldn't be all that bothered to lose him.

"Well?" Sandrian asked as Talyn and Magdalene continued to look at each other.

"I believe The Raptor can be valuable," Magdalene said after another moment. "And she's burned whatever bridges she might've had before by bringing Lord Bressen to us. We'll let her stay and assume she's smart enough to recognize that helping us is a good opportunity."

Magdalene hadn't shifted her eyes from Talyn's, and Talyn had the distinct feeling the woman was giving her a warning. She had one chance to prove herself.

"Thank you," Talyn said. She nodded and pulled her gaze away to look at Sandrian. "Show me the way to the dungeon, and I'll escort Lord Bressen down."

"Don't trouble yourself," Sandrian said. He motioned with a wave of his hand, and four guards stepped forward. "Find Lord Bressen a comfortable cell," he said to them.

Talyn stiffened. She'd hoped to have a word with Bressen, but she'd have to find another way to get down to visit him.

"Let's make one thing clear," Talyn said as the guards pulled Bressen to his feet. "I brought him here, so he's *my* prisoner. Nothing happens to him without my say-so."

Magdalene's brows twitched up the slightest bit, but then she nodded. "Fair enough."

Talyn watched the guards haul Bressen toward the doors, and unease settled in her stomach again. She didn't like leaving him out of her sight, but there wasn't much she could do without making Sandrian or Magdalene suspicious.

She looked at Aidan. He was watching her with what she took to be a mixture of loathing and lust, and she tamped down the impulse to gouge out his eyes.

"Come with me," Magdalene said to her. "I'll show you to a room."

Talyn glanced once more at Aidan as she followed Magdalene out. He watched her go, and she knew without a doubt he'd try something soon. She'd need to sleep this afternoon so she could stay awake later.

Talyn's feet felt heavy as she walked a step behind Magdalene through the corridors of wherever they were. An abandoned castle. That's what Magdalene had said. But where exactly?

"You want to kill Aidan," Magdalene said suddenly, and Talyn's blood iced in her veins. "Or Morland, as I know him."

Talyn frowned. An alias maybe? She swallowed but said, "I get the feeling I'm not the only one who wants to kill him."

Magdalene chuckled softly. "No, you're not. The man has a very limited view of what women are good for, and he doesn't like the influence I have over Sandrian. In truth, he's turned out to be more of a pain in my ass than I anticipated when I agreed to help Sandrian find him. I'm sure he'd kill me himself if he could, but he knows they need me to put Sandrian back on the throne."

"And what do you get out of it if Sandrian retakes Rowe?" Talyn asked. "Why help him? You clearly have your own agenda."

Magdalene gave a shrug. "Sandrian's aspirations are small compared to mine, but it costs me little to help him right now," she said. "If anything, his attempts to retake Rowe and attack Thasia provide a useful distraction while I enact my own plans."

"And what are those?" Talyn dared to ask.

Magdalene gave a small smile. "Maybe I'll tell you one of these days if you stay around. I could use someone like you once you've finished your business with Morland."

Something flipped in Talyn's gut. The woman did know, but apparently she wasn't too worried about it. As suspected, she probably wanted Talyn to take out Aidan…uh, Morland. Without him competing for Sandrian's attention, it would be easier for her to control the latter.

They stopped in front of a door, and Magdalene pushed it open to reveal a room no one had likely used for decades.

"It could use a bit of cleaning," Magdalene said, "but you'll have to see to that yourself. I don't have the staff to spare at the moment."

"Thank you," Talyn said.

Magdalene met her eyes. "I'm sure I don't need to warn you that you should get to Morland before he gets to you?"

"I'll be ready for him," Talyn assured her.

"Good. I meant it when I said I could make good use of you. You'd have a high-ranking position in my court if you chose to stay."

"Not Sandrian's court?"

Magdalene smiled. "Sandrian will have his own court, but let's just say you'd rather be in mine. And if you really want the gargoyle, I can make sure you have him."

Talyn stiffened. "What? How?"

"I have ways to hold men like him in line," she said. "You can keep him like a pet if you want. He can sleep at the foot of your bed to guard you, then you can ride his cock or his tongue whenever you want."

Talyn stared at the woman. She wore a kind smile, as if she'd just offered Talyn a precious gift. Sweet gods, this woman was mad.

"Think about it," Magdalene said, and Talyn nodded.

Magdalene turned and headed back the way she came, leaving Talyn to stare after her.

A lump rose in Talyn's throat as Magdalene disappeared around the corner. The lady had suggested she could keep Samhail at the foot of her bed like a pet, but that wasn't what she wanted. No, she wanted him back in her bed with his arms wrapped around her as if…as if he cared for her.

If Magdalene could somehow manage that after today, Talyn would give the woman anything she wanted.

Chapter 35

Samhail

Samhail felt at least two of his fingers break as he smashed his hand clean through the wall in the great room at Tide's End. Had he still been in his gargoyle form, the whole thing would've collapsed, but he and the twins had shifted back earlier before they'd returned.

Luckily, all three of them had still been in their stone forms when Magdalene's portal closed behind Talyn and Bressen. Samhail's roar and Cyra's scream had rung out simultaneously, and then the entire area began to shake as Cyra released her rage in a wave of power.

Samhail had been instantly wary of a repeat of the temple, and he'd acted without thinking. He'd seen Maziren close by and lunged for her. She'd cried out in shock as he grabbed her and shot into the sky, but he'd been just in time.

Flames had engulfed the clearing just as he got into the air, the fire so hot that everything within two hundred yards was charred to a crisp. The trees, grass, and bodies were nothing but embers and ash when Cyra's scream finally faded off, along with the flames she'd conjured. Only Surgeon and Serise, safe in their stone forms, had survived the inferno.

Samhail had landed in time to see Cyra collapse, and all three gargoyles rushed for her. Serise reached her first, and they'd all shifted back to their human forms as Serise checked Cyra. The lady was just unconscious, thank the gods, and Samhail envied her that blissful oblivion. His own mind and body roiled with a rage the likes of which he'd never felt before.

It had taken him several seconds to grasp what was going on back in the clearing when he'd seen Talyn port. The first time she'd jumped, he thought she was trying to get to a weapon, but she'd picked up the caronium cuff he'd discarded. He was confused when her next port took her to Bressen, and she'd slapped the cuff on his wrist. His mind started to catch up when both of them had disappeared, but full understanding only hit him when her next two ports took both her and Bressen through Magdalene's just-closing portal.

She hadn't looked back as the portal closed behind her, and he'd roared his fury, even as something deep in his core refused to believe she'd betrayed them. Betrayed *him*. He'd worked hard the last few days to get her to trust him, only to have her turn around and prove his own trust was sorely misplaced.

And Bressen would now pay the price for his stupidity.

"Samhail." Surgeon's voice held a warning as Samhail pulled his hand back through the wall and debated putting it through again.

"What should we do with the lady?" Serise asked. She still held Cyra's unconscious form cradled in her arms.

Samhail looked at his siblings. Both were still naked, having just shifted back, but it didn't phase him. Gargoyles learned early on to ignore casual nudity because they always lost their clothes when shifting. In truth, Samhail probably would've been fine walking around naked all the time, but he already drew too much attention wherever he went.

"I'd suggest putting her to bed, and I'll get a healer from the Priory," another voice answered.

Samhail's eyes swung to Phaedrus. He'd almost forgotten the priest was there. With Cyra unconscious, they'd needed to find another way to get home. Luckily Surgeon had found a crumpled message leaf in the pocket of his pants, and they'd sent a message to Phaedrus at the Priory. After sending Maziren back to Seatherny to report to Jasper, Phaedrus had portaled the rest of them back to Solandis.

Samhail nodded. "Do it."

Phaedrus immediately turned and opened a portal. A woman looked up from where she sat at a table reading a book on the other side.

"Emelyn, I thought you might be here. The Lady of Hiraeth needs your assistance," Phaedrus called through to her.

The woman took in the scene through the portal and immediately shut her book. She rose and stepped through.

"What in the name of the Trinity happened?" Another alarmed voice rang out through the room as Phaedrus closed his portal.

Everyone turned to see Axenus standing in the doorway staring at them. The merman's eyes dipped briefly as he took in the three naked gargoyles, but his gaze snapped back up a second later.

The room was silent as everyone looked to Samhail to answer, and he realized that without Bressen or Cyra there, he was in charge.

"Go," Samhail said to Phaedrus and Serise. "Take care of Cyra. I'll fill Axenus in."

"Sir, your hand…," the priestess, Emelyn, said hesitantly as Phaedrus opened a portal to Cyra's bedroom.

Samhail looked down and saw his hand was dripping blood onto the floor. "Later," he told her. "Take care of the lady first."

Emelyn nodded and hurried through the portal after Serise and Phaedrus before the priest closed it behind them.

Samhail flexed his hand, and pain shot through it. He'd definitely broken something, but he was too angry to feel much at the moment.

"Samhail, what the fuck happened?" Axenus asked again, striding into the room.

Samhail was momentarily thrown by the merman's language. Axenus rarely swore, but he'd apparently made an exception for this situation.

Samhail launched into the short version of finding the Rown regiment in Derridan, of calling Bressen, and of the plan they'd hatched to lure Sandrian out of hiding. He explained how Aidan had turned on them, and how Sandrian and Magdalene had snuck dozens of symbionts through the portal under an obfuscation glamour. Finally, he gave a brief summary of the battle as he'd seen it, with Surgeon interjecting his own observations.

"Where's Bressen?" Axenus asked warily when Samhail paused at the part he'd been dreading.

"Sandrian and Magdalene have him," Samhail admitted. His hands shook with fury at his sides.

"What? How?" Axenus asked, his voice rising in panic.

Samhail glanced at Surgeon, but his brother – for once – didn't seem inclined to interrupt with his own version of events. He was probably enjoying the thought of Samhail having to admit Talyn betrayed them.

"The assassin," Samhail said, the words like acid on his tongue. "As Sandrian and the rest were escaping, she took the caronium cuff I'd been wearing and put it on Bressen. She ported with him through Magdalene's portal just as it closed." He paused. "Cyra went mad, set the entire clearing on fire, then collapsed. We just got back."

The room was dead silent as Axenus stared at him in horror. Finally, after what seemed like minutes, Samhail couldn't stand it any longer.

"Go ahead and say it," he snapped at Axenus as his eyes met the merman's. "Gloat that I let her fool me. I know you want to."

Axenus closed his mouth, which had been hanging open in disbelief, and his face went serious. He shook his head. "That's the last thing I want to do," he said. "Despite what you may think, I've always trusted your instincts because most of the time they're right. That you were wrong this one time doesn't make you worthy of ridicule. It makes you human…or demi-human, in any case."

Samhail closed his eyes. It was the worst thing Axenus could've said because he knew somewhere deep down, he wouldn't have been so forgiving if Axenus had made the same mistake. He would've laid into the merman for being an idiot, for letting his dick do all the thinking. Now he'd have to admit Axenus was the bigger man, figuratively speaking, and that only made him angrier.

Axenus must have sensed the direction of his thoughts because he added, "If it helps, I've always known you weren't perfect."

The attempt at easing the tension snapped something in Samhail. He grabbed a glass decanter someone had left out and hurled it at the wall with his good hand. The vessel shattered and left a dent in the wall before it crashed to the floor and broke into more pieces.

"Samhail," Axenus said, stepping forward.

"Don't!" Samhail said, holding up a hand to ward him off. "Don't forgive me so easily. I don't deserve it. You don't understand."

Axenus cocked his head in question. "What don't I understand?"

Samhail looked at Surgeon, but his brother seemed only curious.

"It's my fault Talyn took Bressen," he said. "She went over the chasm Cyra created, and I saved her. If I hadn't saved her, she wouldn't have been able to take him. Worse yet…" He glanced again at Surgeon. "I defied the divine imperative to do it."

Surgeon's brows furrowed. "What are you talking about?"

"Talyn attacked Magdalene to help Cyra, and Magdalene hit her with a forcefield," Samhail explained. "The forcefield pushed Talyn over the chasm, then Magdalene turned back to attack Cyra again. I had to make a split-second choice to either save Talyn from falling or help Cyra against Magdalene." He let out a deep breath. "I chose to save Talyn."

He remembered that moment with crystal clarity. It had all happened in the span of seconds, but in his mind, it had felt like minutes. He'd seen Talyn get knocked toward the chasm and knew she'd fall over it before she knew it herself. On his other side, Cyra had been on the ground with Magdalene looming over her, and he'd had to decide. Did he heed the divine imperative and his own concern for Cyra…Or give in to the surge of raw panic he'd felt when Talyn rolled over that edge.

He'd done the latter and saved Talyn. He'd listened to the voice in his head that told him he'd go mad if something happened to her. He'd ignored the force in his very core that tried to drag him toward Cyra, the ancient, divinely-imbued force that insisted she was his responsibility. He'd fought back the pain in his head that tried to punish him for his failure to aid Cyra, and he'd launched himself desperately toward the chasm, prepared to dive into it after Talyn if he had to.

Talyn had tried to port, but she'd lost her hold on the chasm edge. He didn't get to her in time to grab her, but his summoning power latched onto her almost automatically, and then his hand had closed around her wrist, and he'd hauled her to safety. Something unspoken had passed between them as they'd looked at each other in shared relief, and Talyn had promised to help Cyra.

Then she'd betrayed them and taken Bressen.

One of the glasses on the table followed the decanter into the wall as Samhail released more of his rage. The high-pitched crash it made as it hit wasn't nearly satisfying enough, and Samhail ached to pick up the whole damned table and smash it against the wall. He needed to destroy things.

"You couldn't have known," Axenus said softly, but Samhail only growled at him.

"Stop trying to coddle me!" he snapped. "This is just one of the many ways I've fucked up recently."

Axenus tried to interject, but Samhail didn't give him the chance.

"Aramis is dead because of me," he cut in. "I should've protected him after he healed me, but I was too eager to get into the battle back at the temple. I should've gotten him to safety first."

"That's not your-," Axenus tried.

"The assassin escaped because of me in the first place," Samhail went on. "She goaded me into getting in that cell with her, and that allowed her to get the key away from me. It was beyond foolish."

Samhail looked at Surgeon, waiting to see the gloating smile, but his brother's face was strangely stoic.

"Then, when I caught up to her, instead of bringing her right back here as I should've, I let her talk me into making a deal. I let her worm her way under my skin and onto my cock, and now our enemies have Bressen. The gods only know if he's still alive."

The last glass hit the wall, and Samhail's chest heaved as he tried to bring his breathing back under control. There was a knot in his throat that threatened to choke him. How could he be so stupid?

Samhail surveyed the pile of glass shards below the wall. He should get something to clean up the mess. Or maybe he should walk over the shards barefoot to let the pain drive home how badly he'd fucked up.

Axenus frowned. "You said Talyn attacked Magdalene to help Cyra and that Magdalene sent Talyn over the edge of the chasm."

Samhail looked up at him. "So?"

"So why would Talyn attack Magdalene if they were working together, and why would Magdalene nearly kill Talyn?"

Samhail blinked at him. "I...don't know. To keep her cover?"

"Why bother? If they wanted to win the battle, it would've been a perfect time for Talyn to turn."

"What are you trying to say?" Samhail asked.

"He's suggesting something made the assassin turn on us toward the end of the battle," Surgeon said, breaking his silence. He looked at Axenus for confirmation.

Axenus gave a quick nod of acknowledgement. "It's possible."

Hope surged in Samhail's chest, but it died a second later. No, he'd already given Talyn too many chances. It was time to stop letting her make a fool of him.

"It doesn't matter," he said, hardening his heart. "The fact is that she turned, and if we get her and Bressen back...I'll kill her for it."

Tandem Read: Go to *Nemesis Rising* (Bk 4), Chapters 21-23

Chapter 36

Talyn

Talyn shifted into the form of Magdalene before she walked around the corner of the dungeon. The syphon was small, and Talyn could only shrink herself so far, but she was counting on the guard not being familiar enough with Magdalene to tell that she was maybe an inch or two taller than the woman should be.

She'd debated shifting into Sandrian himself. The man was averaged-sized, and she probably could've gotten close to imitating him, but the guards would likely know him better than Magdalene, so this was safer.

"I need to see the prisoner," she told the guard on duty.

He eyed her up and down, and Talyn's chin went up a notch.

"I was told no one was supposed to see him," the guard said.

"No one but King Sandrian or myself," she corrected. She made sure to use Sandrian's title to lend gravitas to the statement.

The guard gave her a hard look, and she stared right back at him, daring him to challenge her. She'd knock him out if she had to, but that would be difficult to explain later.

"This way," the guard said finally, and Talyn tried not to show relief as she followed him down the hallway to the cells.

The guard stopped in front of one, and Talyn saw the Lord of Hiraeth laying on a cot inside.

"Give me the key and leave us," Talyn told him.

The guard looked at her incredulously. "I can't do that, my lady."

She gave him a steely look. "You can and you will."

"My lady, I-"

"Do you want to know what it feels like to have your heart freeze in your chest?" she asked, and the guard went still. "However unpleasant you imagine it might be, I promise it's worse."

Talyn held out her hand for the keys, and the guard hesitated only a moment more before handing them over.

"Now leave," she said.

The guard opened his mouth to argue, but Talyn raised a hand toward his heart as if she meant to do some sort of magic. He gave her a quick bow and retreated.

Talyn waited until he'd climbed the stairs and closed the door behind him before she called out softly.

"Lord Bressen. I need to speak with you."

The lord lay on his back but didn't move.

"Lord Bressen," she called a little louder. Still he didn't move.

Talyn sighed heavily. She suspected he could hear her and was just ignoring her, but she couldn't raise her voice any further to be sure.

Talyn unlocked the cell and stepped in. He was probably hoping she'd do just that, but she was ready for him if he moved.

She felt her magic leave her as she stepped inside, and her body shifted back into her true form. She prayed the guard stayed away until she could get out of the cell and shift back into Magdalene. She tucked the key down the wrap that bound her breasts and stepped forward, but still the lord didn't move from his cot.

"Lord Bressen, we don't have time for you to play possum," she said. "I only have a few minutes, and I need to speak with you. It's in your best interest to hear me out."

The lord's head twitched slightly at her voice, and she wondered if he recognized the change from Magdalene's voice to her own.

He turned his head slowly to look at her, and Talyn gasped. His face was covered in bruises. Both of his eyes were blackened, and one was nearly swollen shut. His lips were cracked and bleeding in several places, and dried blood crusted below both of his nostrils. She strongly suspected his nose was broken and that he'd reset it himself.

"Fuck!" she swore. "Who did this to you?"

His less swollen eye narrowed. He sat up slowly and gingerly, as if every movement pained him, and Talyn vowed she'd slit the throat of everyone who'd touched him. She had no love for the lord himself, but he meant something to Samhail. Moreover, she'd told Sandrian and Magdalene that Bressen was her prisoner and wasn't to be touched, yet they'd clearly ignored her. She didn't appreciate being ignored.

"Who beat you?" she asked again when he didn't answer.

Bressen's brows rose, and he huffed a laugh. His shoulders slumped as he hung his head, and Talyn took an unconscious step toward him.

It was a mistake.

Bressen moved faster than she could've expected, especially injured. One second he was on the cot, and the next he had her pinned against the wall as his hands closed over her throat.

Talyn cursed herself for not seeing the ruse for what it was. Nemesis take her, she'd used the same ploy on Samhail only a little while ago.

Talyn clawed at Bressen's hands, but his grip was like iron. The lord might not have his powers, and he might be injured, but he was still a warrior and damn strong. She began to see stars and knew she had only seconds before she passed out or he crushed her neck.

Talyn raised her arms over her head and turned her body to the side. The movement loosened the lord's grip on her neck just enough that she could bring her elbow down hard onto his forearm. She dislodged one of his hands from around her throat, and he was pulled forward from the blow. She immediately thrust a knee up into his stomach, and he cried out in pain before letting go of her.

Talyn tried to pull him forward to crack his head into the stone wall, but he recovered too fast. He grabbed her arms and threw her across the room as if she were no more than a rag doll. She fell to the floor and yelled out as she landed on her tailbone. Her teeth cracked together, and she flexed her jaw quickly before she was on her feet again and reaching for the daggers at her thighs.

Bressen had already started toward her again, but she launched herself forward and met him halfway. Surprise bloomed on his face, more so when she used his own momentum to vault herself up and hook a knee around his neck. As she fell back down, her weight pulled him forward, and she used that to flip him onto the floor.

The lord grunted loudly as the air punched out of his lungs, and Talyn gave silent thanks to the Protector that Bressen wasn't as big as Samhail. If she tried that on Samhail, her knee would probably still be hanging around his neck while he wore her as a necklace.

Talyn didn't wait to congratulate herself. She straddled Bressen's torso and pressed one dagger to his neck while the other dug into the inside of his thigh, and he went still.

"My daggers are currently pressed against two major arteries in your body," she warned him quietly. "You can listen to what I have to say, or you can bleed out on this floor. You don't want to test my reflexes."

Bressen's open eye narrowed again. "What do you want?" he asked.

Talyn pulled back the dagger from his leg, but she continued to hold the other to his throat until she got to her feet. Finally, she pulled that one up as well and backed quickly away from him.

Bressen got to his feet again. "I should've killed you when I had the chance," he said. "Pray to the Protector I never get my powers back."

"Actually," she said, twirling one of the daggers in her hand. "I was hoping to ask you a favor, one that you'll need your powers for."

His half-swollen eye flew open wide this time. "What?"

"I'm sorry I dragged you here, Lord Bressen," Talyn said. "It was never my intention to harm you, but I didn't know what else to do. You're the only person aside from Lady Cyra who can help me, and it was easier to get you here than her because of the caronium cuff."

Bressen tried to cross his arms over his chest, but he winced and lowered them again. As bad as his face looked, Talyn couldn't imagine the bruises that must lay beneath his shirt. He'd pulled the crossbow bolt from his shoulder at some point during the battle, but she doubted the wound had been treated. For that matter, she'd need to find out if the tip of the bolt was still in him, as it had been with Samhail. She'd need to get it out for him to use his power.

"Your decision to take me instead of Cyra may be the only thing that keeps you alive if I ever get out of here," Bressen said.

Talyn gave a mirthless laugh. "If you don't kill me, Samhail will. I'm on borrowed time, and I knew that the second I chose to bring you here."

"Then why did you do it?" he asked.

"I think I might've made a huge mistake years ago, and I need your help to fix it."

He frowned. "And why would I do that?"

"Because if I'm right in what I suspect, it will ultimately benefit you."

He looked unimpressed.

"And because I tried to help Cyra against Magdalene," she offered.

Bressen stiffened, but he considered this before he finally nodded and eased himself back down onto the cot. "I'm listening," he said.

Talyn leaned back against the wall, but she kept her daggers ready.

"Twelve years ago," she said, "my older sister was kidnapped by a man who held her for a week before he strangled her to death. During that time, he raped her repeatedly, beat her, and cut her dozens of times before he dumped her into the river. She was pulled out by some fishermen when her body snagged one of their lines."

Talyn couldn't tell what the look on Bressen's face was under all the bruising, but she at least had his attention, so she went on.

"I was thirteen at the time, and I snuck in to see my sister's bloated, ruined corpse. My childhood ended that day, and I vowed to find the man responsible for her murder and kill him. It took me almost two years to track him down, but when I found him, I did to him everything he'd done to my sister and more. He screamed for mercy, but I had none. He pleaded with me, swore to me he wasn't the one who killed her, but I didn't believe him."

"I'm very sorry to hear about your sister," Bressen said, "but what does this have to do with me?"

"Before I killed him, I shifted into my sister. It's something I do now before I assassinate someone. Her face is always the last thing my victims see, but when I put on my sister's face just before I disemboweled him…"

She paused as she remembered the blank look on the man's face. There'd been momentary surprise at her transformation, but there hadn't been an ounce of recognition.

She'd convinced herself there was, though. She'd been absolutely certain of it for the last ten years, but not anymore. The look on Aidan's face when he'd seen her, *that* had been recognition, and she hadn't even been wearing her sister's face at the time. He'd simply recognized the similarities between her and Julia.

"The man I killed didn't recognize me," Talyn finished. "You'd think he'd recognize a woman he tortured and murdered, but he didn't. There was only confusion in his eyes. I convinced myself I was mistaken and killed him anyway, but today, I saw that recognition in Aidan's face. The fucking bastard went so far as to tell me I looked like my sister."

She looked at the lord. He sat silently on the cot without moving, waiting for her to go on.

"I know you don't owe me anything, Lord Bressen, that you'd happily kill me if given half a chance, and I fully expect you will someday," she said, "but I'm almost certain Aidan killed my sister and at least half a dozen other women very brutally. If that's the case, then I plan to kill him, also rather brutally. But I was wrong once before. I can't be wrong again. I need you to look into his mind and see if he's really the one who murdered my sister. That's why I brought you here. I needed some way to convince Sandrian I was still loyal to him, and I needed to get someone with mind powers close to Aidan to confirm he's the man I seek. Once I kill him, I'll get you out of here, and you can do with me whatever you feel is necessary. Send me to Revenmyer, kill me if you must, but let me avenge my sister first, once and for all."

The lord still didn't move, and Talyn felt the need to fill the silence.

"I didn't mean for you to be hurt. I knew you likely would be, but I was counting on being able to keep you as safe as possible. I failed you in that, and, for what it's worth, I'm sorry. I shouldn't have dragged you into my personal vendetta, but I didn't know what else to do. I've failed my sister for the last ten years." She swallowed. "And I gave up Samhail to make things right."

Bressen's back straightened at her words, and she went on, hoping that maybe if she laid herself bare, showed him all her vulnerabilities, he might agree to help. She had nothing left to lose.

"Whatever you may think of me, Lord Bressen," she said, "I care for Samhail, and knowing I betrayed his trust for this will be the single greatest regret of my life."

She swallowed hard as the enormity of her loss backhanded her like an iron gauntlet.

"If you won't do it for me," she said, fighting back the tears that threatened in her eyes, "do it for my sister. She was innocent of any wrongdoing, and I've seen enough of you and Cyra to know you're not people who condone evil."

She stopped talking then and looked at him. She'd said everything she possibly could to get him to help her. If he refused now, there was nothing else she could do.

Well, maybe there was one more thing.

Talyn reached into the pocket of her pants and pulled out a small metal hair pin. She stepped toward Bressen, getting closer than she should've, and held it out to him. He took it and looked at her in confusion.

"Regardless of whether you agree to help me or not," she said, "you can use that to open your caronium cuff. Stick the prongs into the keyhole, twist them counterclockwise, then jerk them to the left. That will open most cuffs. I suggest you practice on the one you're wearing so you can get out of it if they take you out of your cell."

She stepped back and looked at him. He just stared at her, and she realized he wasn't going to answer her one way or another right now.

"I'll be back to treat your crossbow wound as well," she added. "We have to be sure the tip didn't break off inside, or the caronium cuff will be moot."

Talyn turned to head for the door as she pulled the key to the cell from its hiding place in her cleavage.

"I can read his mind for you," Bressen said, stopping her in her tracks, "but I can't let you kill Aidan."

Talyn jerked back around to look at him. "What? Why not?"

Bressen stood and took a couple steps toward her. "That isn't Aidan. An old enemy of ours, Morland, has taken over Aidan's body, but I sensed Aidan's consciousness still inside. Cyra did too. Morland has pushed Aidan deep down and locked him out of his own mind, but he's still there. We have to find a way to pull Morland out of Aidan's body and put him somewhere else before you can kill him. Once we do that and help restore Aidan, you can do whatever you want to Morland."

She let her mind wrap around that as she recalled what Magdalene had told her. So Morland wasn't an alias. He was an entirely different person who'd somehow…?

Talyn shook her head. "And what if you can't? What if there's no way to remove this Morland from Aidan's body?" she asked, panicked now.

Bressen was quiet for a long moment. "There has to be a way."

Talyn shook her head again. "I can't let him live," she said, her voice half a sob. "I thought I killed him a decade ago. I just…can't."

"I'll make a deal with you," he said. "I'll read Morland's mind as soon as I can and tell you for sure if he's the one who murdered your sister. If he is, then give me a month to try and figure out how to restore Aidan. If it looks like there's absolutely no way to do it, then I'll let you kill Morland. Just a month. That's all I'll ask, for Aidan's sake."

Talyn considered the offer. It was reasonable enough. She'd waited ten years for justice already. What was another month?

The question was how she'd spend that month. If Bressen had his way, she'd probably spend it in Revenmyer. If she even lived long enough for him to put her there.

"I might not have a month to wait," she said. "Samhail will kill me if he ever sees me again."

He considered this. "I'll handle Samhail," he said finally. "For one month, you'll have immunity from me and any of my people, and you have my word that we'll all do our best to get Morland out of Aidan's body. It's something we'd do anyway."

She nodded. Yes, now that she understood the situation, she knew they'd do whatever they could to free Aidan's mind from its imprisonment. Moreover, the immunity offer was more than generous, considering what she'd done and how bad Bressen now looked.

It was only the fact Samhail wanted to kill her at all that made her gut clench. She'd almost gotten to the point where she'd been ready to consider his offer that they travel together, but that was impossible now.

"Very well, Lord Bressen. I accept your terms, if only because I don't have any other choice." She smiled sadly. "And I look forward to seeing you try to stop Samhail from killing me."

Bressen held out his hand to shake hers and seal their deal. Talyn hesitated but then took it, and they shook. She tried to pull her hand back but winced when he squeezed it tighter and pulled her closer.

"It's not Samhail you need to worry about," he said as a faint smile curled his swollen, cut lips. "It's Cyra. But I won't let her kill you either."

He let go of her hand, and she pulled back. She wouldn't let him see her flex it in pain, but his words had their desired effect. She'd forgotten Cyra would be enraged as well. She'd kidnapped the woman's husband, and if she did manage to get Bressen out of here, she'd be returning him to his wife in less-than-perfect condition.

Talyn steeled her expression. "You're too kind, Lord Bressen," she said. "Be careful or people will think you've gone soft."

He actually chuckled as he started to lay back down on his cot, but he stopped. "One other thing," he said. "Expect a visit from Morland tonight. It sounded like he had some unpleasant plans for you when he was down here earlier."

Talyn arched a brow. The lord was warning her?

"Thank you," she said. "I was expecting to see him tonight, so it's good to have confirmation."

He nodded to her and laid down.

Talyn left the cell and secured the door behind her. She breathed a relieved sigh as her power returned and she shifted again into Magdalene.

She shuddered as she remembered Samhail's bellow of rage when she'd disappeared through the portal with his friend, his brother.

Cyra was a syphon, an impressively powerful perimortal, and she'd seen firsthand how the lady's self-control slipped when it came to those who harmed the people she loved, but it was still Samhail's wrath she feared more. Or perhaps it was just the thought of the hatred he must now feel toward her that ripped her apart. Samhail would try to kill her if he ever saw her again, of that she was sure.

And she didn't think even Bressen would be able to hold him back.

Talyn

It was just after one in the morning when the handle of the door to Talyn's room turned to sand and fell to the floor in a pile. The door eased open slowly so the dim light from the torches in the hallway seeped inside the room and fell across the bed where the covers mounded over a form.

Morland stepped over the pile of sand in the doorway, his eyes fixed on the bed, but he froze when Talyn's sword appeared under his jaw and pressed to his neck.

"If you even breathe too hard, I'll slit your throat before you have time to transfigure anything," Talyn said from where she'd been waiting just on the other side of the door. "Drop the blade."

The dagger Morland had been carrying clanged loudly on the floor in the silence of the room.

She tsked. "Going to kill me in my sleep? That's not very fair of you."

The hint of a smile touched Morland's lips, but he didn't answer.

Talyn's eyes narrowed. "Show me your other hand."

Morland's smile faded, and he held up a caronium cuff, a length of rope, and a piece of cloth.

Talyn clenched her teeth so hard her jaw popped.

"Planning to rape me first like you did my sister?" she snarled.

Morland's brows lifted innocently. "I don't know what you're talking about. Your sister and I were friends. Lovers."

Rage boiled up in Talyn. "Liar!" she snapped. "You raped, tortured, and killed her! Admit it!"

Morland remained silent, and Talyn held in the string of curses that begged to be set free. He knew she was waiting for him to confess, so he wouldn't give her that satisfaction.

She couldn't kill him yet anyway, Talyn reminded herself. She'd promised Bressen she wouldn't do it as long as he was in Aidan's body. She'd agreed to give Bressen a month, so even if she got Morland to confess right now, it wouldn't matter.

"Get out of my room now," Talyn said, "or I'll cut your dick off and feed it to you, as I did to the man I killed in your stead."

Morland's smug expression faltered.

Talyn lowered the sword from his neck and stepped back. Gods, she ached to cut him at least, to make him bleed, but she needed to remember this was another man's body. An innocent man's. If they did manage to get Morland out of it, Lord Aidan wouldn't appreciate her cutting him up.

Morland stepped back into the hallway without turning around, and Talyn watched him go. He cleared the doorway, gave her a mocking half-bow, then turned and strode back down the hall without another word.

Talyn sighed and closed the door. It didn't latch without its handle, but she pulled a chair over and set it in front. It wouldn't keep anyone out, but she'd at least hear it scrape the floor if someone tried to enter.

She didn't get into the bed but curled up on the couch at the side of the room to sleep. She just needed one hour of sleep, then she'd wake and go down to see Lord Bressen again. She suspected the caronium tip of the crossbow bolt was still in his shoulder, and she'd need to get it out so he could read Morland's mind. It needed to come out in general if they were going to escape.

It was too dangerous for either of them to stay much longer. It was only a matter of time before Morland tried to hurt her or the lord again. Now that she knew – or highly suspected – what a sadistic bastard he was, getting out had taken on new urgency. Bressen had agreed to help her, and she was counting on his own sense of honor that he'd follow through.

She just hoped she could trust him to keep his word more than he'd been able to trust her to keep hers.

Tandem Read: Nemesis Rising (Bk 4), Chapters 24-29

Chapter 37

Talyn

Talyn went down to the dungeon the next morning right after breakfast. She'd had to scrounge her own food from the kitchen since there weren't formal mealtimes. Sandrian, Magdalene, and now Morland apparently all took their meals alone in their rooms, so she hadn't seen any of them yet this morning, which was for the best.

She'd made it down to see Lord Bressen again last night and had been able to get the caronium tip out of his shoulder. At least she hoped she had. She didn't trust him enough to take him out of the cell and see if he got his power back, but she was reasonably certain she'd gotten all the tip.

She'd also thought last night about ways to get her, him, and Morland out of the castle, and she'd come up with an idea just before exhaustion finally overtook her. She planned to run it by Bressen now to see what he thought, and if it worked, they might actually be gone by dinner.

She shifted again to look like Magdalene and strode straight past the guard on duty, a different one than yesterday.

"My lady, wait!" the guard said as she pushed past him.

"I'm here to see the lord," she said without stopping. "Stay here and don't disturb us."

"But, my lady, he's not in his cell," the guard said as he hurried along in her wake.

Talyn jerked to a halt and rounded on the guard. "Not in his cell? Why not? Where is he?"

"They took him upstairs a little while ago," he said.

"Who took him upstairs?" she asked, trying to hold her rising panic in check. "And where exactly did they bring him?"

"The king's man, Morland, came down with some guards. I don't know where they took him."

Fuck, fuck, fuck!

Talyn turned and sprinted back up the stairs. She'd told Morland to keep his hands off the lord, but she knew by now he didn't like to take orders from women. Why in the three hells hadn't she thought to take better precautions to keep Bressen safe? He'd agreed to help her despite everything. She owed him that much.

Talyn raced through the fortress, straight toward the throne room. She had a feeling Morland liked a spectacle, so she was sure he'd take Bressen somewhere public if he was planning to do something. She only prayed she got to him in time before Morland did anything irreparable.

The sound of jeering met her ears when she was within sight of the doors to the throne room, and Talyn knew she'd guessed right. She ported the rest of the way as fast as she could and appeared on her last leap in the middle of the room. What she saw made her stomach lurch.

Bressen knelt in the center of the room secured to the floor by a set of chains that held prisoners before the judgement of whatever lord sat in power. His hands were shackled behind his back, and she saw not one, but two caronium cuffs on his wrists.

He was naked. His clothes lay shredded on the floor where they'd been cut from his body, and dozens of dripping cuts crisscrossed every part of him. His arms, back, chest, legs, and even the bottoms of his feet bore red slashes that bled onto the floor. His face and torso, not yet healed from his last beating, showed evidence that someone – likely Morland – had taken their fists to him again.

Around the room, a dozen or so guards laughed and taunted Bressen as he struggled to hold himself upright, even now refusing to show weakness to his enemies. Sandrian sat in his throne on the dais looking amused while Morland, in Aidan's body, stood before Bressen with a large dagger. It seemed to steam or smoke as if he'd just pulled it from the fire that burned in the hearth.

"What do you think, men?" Morland said gleefully to the guards gathered around. He loomed over Bressen with the dagger. "Will his wife still want him if I remove her favorite part? I'll send it to her after I cut it off. She can have it stuffed. Maybe it will still be usable for a while until she finds someone else to fuck her."

Talyn's eyes flared wide, and Bressen struggled against his chains as they both realized what Morland intended to do.

"What do you think, Bressen?" Morland sneered at him. "Will Cyra moan for me if I fuck her with your cock?"

Bressen rattled his chains again as the guards in the room erupted in laughter and jeers.

Morland bent toward Bressen with his dagger, but Talyn didn't waste time trying to call out to him. She ported to Morland immediately, reared back her fist, and punched him across the jaw in a blow that sent him staggering backwards.

"You fucking bitch!" he spat at her as he looked up, but she grabbed his head and brought it down onto her knee. She heard his nose crunch, and he screamed as she pushed him back so he fell to the floor.

Talyn was beyond words. Aidan's body or not, her sister's murderer or not, she was going to kill him, right here, right now.

Talyn drew her daggers and dropped to her knees next to Morland, intent on plunging both blades straight into his heart.

"Talyn, no!" Bressen yelled, and the plea in his voice made her falter just enough for Morland to act.

Morland slapped his hand onto the floor next to Talyn. She cried out as the stone turned to water, and her body plunged down into it. She went under but managed to grab the edge of the floor that was still solid and pull herself to the surface, just as Morland turned the water back to stone. Only her head, shoulders, and one hand now sat above the floor as the rest of her body was trapped within the stone.

"It's time for you to learn your place, whore!" Morland seethed as he lunged toward Talyn's head with his dagger.

She ported just in time so the dagger struck stone and the tip scraped across the floor. She was on Morland a second later. She ported onto his back and wrapped an arm around his throat. She dropped the dagger still in her hand and pulled one of the smaller ones she kept in her boot.

Morland screamed as she drove the dagger into his side, not a killing blow, but one that would slow him down long enough for her to figure out what the fuck to do next.

She didn't get the chance to act further as lightning jolted through her and every muscle seized up. Her vision went white, and then she was on the ground blinking up at the ceiling. She wasn't sure how long she'd been out as the room rematerialized in front of her, but it didn't seem like long.

"Talyn." Bressen's urgent whisper filtered past the ringing in her ears. "Talyn, are you alright?"

She blinked, willing the fog in her mind to lift. There almost seemed to be concern in the lord's voice.

Well yes, he would be concerned. She was his only ally here, and he needed her to be okay to help him escape. That was now more urgent after what Morland had just tried. The time had come for them to leave.

Talyn tried to lift herself off the ground, but her body felt heavy. Her eyes flared as she spotted the hairpin she'd given Bressen lying partially hidden under a scrap of his clothes on the floor. If she could get it to him and distract Sandrian, maybe he could free himself. He had two cuffs to remove instead of one, but it was their only chance.

"The hairpin," Talyn whispered back to Bressen.

She let out a loud groan for Sandrian's benefit as she pretended to collapse back to the floor. She reached out for the hairpin, and her fingers closed around it as she struggled to push herself up again. The struggle was real enough.

"What's the meaning of this, Raptor?" Sandrian thundered as he stomped down from the dais. "I should kill you now!"

"I told you Lord Bressen is *my* prisoner!" Talyn shot back at him.

She struggled to her knees and crawled toward Bressen as she retrieved her two daggers. Next to her, Morland yelped as he pulled the smaller dagger from his side.

"I'll kill you, you filthy little whore!" Morland raged as he tried to pull himself up as well. He turned to Sandrian. "I told you we shouldn't trust her! She's with them!"

"I'm not!" Talyn snapped back. Perhaps she might've been once, but not anymore. Even if she wanted to be.

"You lie!" Morland snarled, holding the dagger out toward her. "You let that gargoyle fuck that rotten cunt of yours. You reek of him, but I'll help you get his stench off you."

He lunged for her, but she dodged and shoved him to the side. She sliced her dagger across his forearm, and Morland cried out as the small blade fell from his hand and clattered on the stone.

"Enough!" Sandrian shouted.

He stepped toward her, but Talyn sprung toward Bressen, positioning herself behind him. She dropped one dagger to grab his hair at the back of his head while she put the other dagger to his throat. He gasped as a trickle of blood ran down his neck, and Sandrian stopped moving.

"I told you no one was to touch the lord without my say-so," she said. "I told you I owed him for what he did to me, and you promised I could have him, yet you let this cretin torture him without me. If that's what your word is worth, I'll just kill him now, and we'll see how much leverage you have with Cyra when she comes to claim his body."

As she spoke, she let go of Bressen's hair and let her fingers trail down his back until they reached his hands. She placed the hairpin in his palm and felt his fingers close over it. She considered trying to pick the caronium cuffs herself – she had much more practice at it – but if someone saw her, things would go from bad to worse even quicker. She needed to provide the distraction while Bressen worked at freeing himself.

She prayed he could.

Sandrian held up his hands placatingly. "I never promised you anything," he said. "Magdalene did. But surely you understand that Morland and I have a far longer history with Bressen than you do. The urge to play with him was too hard to resist."

Talyn didn't know the details, but she knew the former king had spent the last twenty-five or so years in Revenmyer. Indeed, his otherwise handsome face still bore a hauntedness she assumed was a consequence of his time there. If she could get Sandrian to talk about it, perhaps it would buy Bressen enough time.

"He held you in Revenmyer," Talyn prompted. "For twenty years?"

"Twenty-five," Sandrian corrected.

She knew he'd feel the need to set the record straight if she purposely got some of the details wrong.

"He threatened to send me there as well," she said. "What was it like?"

Sandrian's eyes narrowed on her a moment before his gaze became distant as a memory seemed to overtake him.

The room grew quiet as everyone waited for him to go on, and Talyn heard the faint click of one of the caronium cuffs pop free.

"King Sandrian?" she prompted quickly to camouflage the sound.

She hoped the use of his supposed title would further distract from the click that had seemed to echo throughout the chamber. She remained crouched behind Bressen, her dagger held loosely at his throat.

Sandrian's eyes met hers, and for one heart-stopping moment she thought he'd seen through her subterfuge. Then he spoke.

"Be grateful you've never seen the inside of that place," Sandrian said. "There are no demons in the three hells because they're all in Revenmyer."

"Demons?" Talyn asked. She'd heard stories of the monstrous little creatures that inhabited the prison, but she didn't know much about them.

"Nightmare demoni," Sandrian said. "When you're awake, the walls writhe with them. You hear them moving around, see their red eyes blinking in and out in the darkness, feel their claws scraping against your skin. The only time you're free of them is when you're asleep, and then a whole new nightmare begins."

Talyn shuddered involuntarily, and Bressen went still in front of her. He was likely wondering if Sandrian's story was making her rethink her plans to help him. Did he still plan on sending her to the prison if they got out of this?

Samhail might've been able to talk the lord out of sending her, but that was before she'd betrayed him. What if she helped Bressen escape only for him to throw her into Revenmyer? She'd made her peace that when the Nemesis took her, she'd spend the rest of eternity in one of the three hells, but she'd at least hoped to avoid any torture in this life.

Talyn shook herself mentally. It didn't matter anymore what it cost her. She'd made a mistake bringing Bressen here, throwing him to his enemies, and it was time she accepted the consequences for that.

"What kind of nightmare?" she asked, and she felt the urgency in Bressen's body as his hands moved behind him again. He didn't want Sandrian to give her any reason to change her mind.

There was no humor whatsoever in Sandrian's smile.

"Every fear, every regret you've ever had comes to life in your dreams," Sandrian said. "Everything you've ever done that hurt someone else becomes magnified and replayed over and over again in your head, and this time you feel the pain right along with them."

Talyn swallowed. She'd killed a lot of people, and while she couldn't think of any deaths she truly regretted, that might change if she had to feel the pain of what she'd done to them every night when she tried to sleep. She'd given most of her victims a quick death, but there were a few exceptions. The man she'd thought had killed her sister, for one. His death hadn't been quick by any means, and it definitely hadn't been painless.

"You invaded Thasia," Talyn argued. "You started a war where thousands died. Didn't you deserve punishment?"

Sandrian's eyes narrowed, and Talyn knew she shouldn't have said that. Bressen knew it too, and she felt him go rigid again.

"I've killed a lot of people," she went on before Sandrian could say anything. "I deserve to be punished, and if it doesn't happen in this world, I know it will happen in the next. Perhaps it's a blessing you've served part of your sentence here already."

Sandrian stared at her for a moment before he burst out laughing. The sound was harsh and grating in the otherwise silent room, completely devoid of actual mirth. Even Morland's wheezing had stopped where he still lay on the floor close by.

"My dear," Sandrian said, "I didn't take you for the kind of fool who actually believes the gods are fair and just."

Talyn blinked at the disgust in his tone, and even Bressen paused to look up at him.

"The gods are as petty and vengeful as any human," Sandrian went on. "As for our dear Lord Bressen, have you asked him how many people he's killed over the years? How many women did he and that pile of stones you seem to favor fuck and then abandon before he took one of the most powerful beings on the continent as his wife?"

Bressen's body jerked, but Sandrian wasn't done.

"Bressen didn't avoid Revenmyer because he's a good man," Sandrian said, his voice full of scorn. "He avoided my fate because his side won the war, because he's powerful both in magic and title, and there's no one to tell him he can't do what he wants. If I'd won, you can be sure the great *Nemesis Incarnate*," he sneered the name, "would've had my cell in Revenmyer instead. And I can guarantee you he'd still be there, because I wouldn't have been careless enough to let him escape. Just as I won't be careless enough to let the two of you escape now."

Talyn's blood seemed to stop in her veins before surging forward double-time as she recognized the knowing look in Sandrian's eyes, the look that said he was no longer buying her act.

"Do you think I don't know what you're doing?" Sandrian asked coldly. "Trying to distract me?"

Talyn's head snapped to the side as movement caught her eye, and Morland lurched to his feet. The man limped to the side wall where two giant axes hung crisscrossed over each other. Still holding his hand over the wound she'd given him, Morland pulled one of the axes down and stalked back toward her and Bressen.

Talyn pulled herself up and held her daggers out, ready to fight.

"Talyn, get out of the way!" Bressen yelled.

"No!" she shot back. "I got you into this. I won't let them kill you!"

Morland let go of his wound so he could grip the axe with two hands. He swung the heavy weapon back over his head as he prepared to bring it down, and Talyn got ready to port. She had to strike in a way that would push the man off balance and keep him from bringing the giant blade down on top of Bressen.

Just as she was about to port, a force seized Talyn's mind. She'd only had a rudimentary shield up, and someone had just crashed through it, sending a sharp pain stabbing through her head.

Talyn's body threw itself out of the way of Morland's blade unwillingly, and she cried out in horror as the axe descended toward the Lord of Hiraeth. She tried to port, but her body wouldn't obey.

The wet sound of hard steel meeting soft flesh that she expected to hear never came, though. Instead, the deafening clang of metal meeting metal echoed around the room.

A scream lodged in Talyn's throat as she tried to make sense of what she'd just witnessed. At the last second, Bressen had moved out of the way of the axe's blade so it came down onto the chain holding him in place rather than onto his head.

Talyn's eyes widened as Morland raised the axe and brought it down again in the same spot, and the already-damaged chain broke fully apart.

Then Bressen was on his feet – just barely – and he yanked the chain through the rings that linked the shackles to the floor. The shackles were still on his wrists, but without the chain to bind them, he had the use of his hands again. His two caronium cuffs lay on the ground, and Talyn's heart leapt into her throat to realize he'd managed to free himself and apparently take over Morland.

The force holding her mind – Bressen's magic – released her, and she sprung to her feet ready to fight. Even as Sandrian screamed in fury, the guards around the room began to change, the dark blue shells of their symbionts creeping over their skin.

Talyn saw Sandrian's arm shoot out toward Bressen, and she reacted without thinking. She ported to him immediately, then ported again the second she touched him. They both disappeared an instant before Sandrian's lightning crackled through the space where they'd been.

Sandrian screamed and clutched his head, and Talyn knew Bressen must be clawing through the man's mind shield. She shivered involuntarily as she remembered the pain of that experience, but there was no time to dwell on it. The dozen or so guards in the room had fully shifted into their symbiont forms and were heading toward them with claws out.

Talyn shot forward to meet them, just as Sandrian sent a bolt of lightning at Bressen that made the lord jerk and fall to his knees.

"What in the name of the gods is going on?" Magdalene's voice cut through the room, and Talyn's heart dropped. They'd been lucky the syphon hadn't been here before, but their luck had just run out. They needed to get out of here. Now.

Talyn turned away from the symbionts and ported back to Bressen. She threw one of his arms over her shoulder and pulled him to his feet.

"It's time to go!" she told him.

She'd just gotten him to a standing position when the entire building began to shake, and both she and Bressen staggered sideways as the ground shifted beneath them.

"Earthquake!" Sandrian shouted as he grabbed his throne for balance.

"No," Bressen said as a slightly maniacal grin turned up his lips. "That would be my wife."

Talyn's stomach flipped. Under other circumstances she might've been relieved to learn Cyra had arrived, but she didn't think the Lady of Hiraeth would be as happy to see her.

First things first. They had to get out of this chamber before Sandrian or Magdalene did something drastic.

Talyn grabbed hold of Bressen, then ported to where Morland stood looking dazed. She hoped Bressen still had control of his mind as she grabbed Morland's arm as well.

It took her three ports to get them out into the hallway, more than usual. She couldn't port as far when bringing others with her, and she'd never tried it with two people before. She managed to port four more times down the corridor before she collapsed onto the floor.

Talyn blinked as her vision blurred. Her porting had always been the weaker of her two powers, the one that waned the quickest, and trying to take two people with her had all but drained her. Terror surged through her as she realized she couldn't move.

"There's no time for a nap just yet," Bressen said as he slid his arms under her knees and around her back to pick her up.

Talyn's head lolled onto his bare shoulder, and he started to run unsteadily. He was still naked and barefoot, and the building continued to shake around them as Cyra tried to get to her husband. Talyn was vaguely aware of Morland keeping pace next to them, his eyes vacant under Bressen's mind power.

The sight the three of them must be.

What seemed like minutes later, Talyn's vision brightened, and she realized they'd made it outside.

"Bressen!"

Cyra's relieved voice carried across the courtyard followed by a bone-chilling roar. Cyra and Axenus hurried toward them as three stone gargoyles rampaged nearby, sending symbiont guards flying.

Talyn's stomach somersaulted to see Samhail, but only a small part of it was joy. Most of it was pure dread. He was going to kill her, and she was too weak to fight him off or even run.

Talyn looked over Bressen's shoulder to see Magdalene had opened a portal to the courtyard and was just stepping through it.

"Magdalene!" Cyra growled.

"Not now!" Bressen shouted. "Open a portal and get us out of here!"

Cyra's face flashed with a moment of indecision before she turned and traced a circle in the air. A portal flared to life, and the lady threw it open wide for Bressen to barrel through with Talyn in his arms and Morland following dutifully behind. Talyn saw over Bressen's shoulder that Axenus and the gargoyles were holding off Magdalene, Sandrian, and the symbionts as they made their escape.

"Retreat now!" Cyra yelled to them, and they all turned to follow her back through the portal. She closed it behind them just in time to cut off the bolt of Sandrian's lightning that came streaking toward them.

Talyn couldn't manage to be relieved as her gaze sought Samhail. He was still in his gargoyle form, and his glowing blue eyes fixed on her. She felt the hatred radiating off him, and regret squeezed her heart.

Bressen set Talyn down on a hard stone floor and propped her against a pillar. She didn't recognize the room, but the three large chairs on the dais at one end suggested they might be in the Citadel at Callanus.

"Sweet gods! What happened?" Cyra cried as she knelt next to her bloody and bruised husband. "Bressen." She laid a hand on his cheek.

He covered it with his own as they looked at each other.

"I'm alright," he assured her.

Cyra's head jerked toward Talyn. "You!"

Talyn jolted to see the flash of red in the lady's eyes.

"Time for you to die!" Cyra said. Her voice cracked with emotion as she reached a hand toward Talyn, but Bressen grabbed her wrist.

"Cyra, wait-," he started to say, but his words were cut off by a roar that shook the room and made even the lord jump.

Samhail shifted back to his human form, and Talyn gasped as he charged her. She tried to port, but she was still too weak. All she could do was press herself against the pillar and hope her death was quick.

"Samhail, no!" Bressen yelled as he put himself between her and the charging gargoyle. He grunted as Samhail's forcefield pushed him aside.

Talyn tried once more to port, but nothing happened.

Then Samhail's hand was around her throat and both her breath and her scream were cut off.

Chapter 38

Talyn's vision blurred then began to fade as Samhail cut off her air. She clawed at his hand with what little energy she had left, but his grip was iron around her throat.

"Samhail, let go of her!"

Bressen's voice seemed far away as Talyn tried and failed to gasp in a breath. She winced as Samhail's thumb dug into the side of her neck, but she was vaguely aware he could've crushed her windpipe in a second if he'd wanted to. She couldn't fathom why he hadn't yet.

Talyn's eyes fluttered wildly as blackness overtook her. She thought she heard a roar of pain, but she knew it couldn't be hers.

Then all of a sudden, the pressure on her throat was gone, and she sucked in a great lungful of air. She forced her eyes open but jolted to see Samhail crouched before her, his face strangely placid.

He snapped awake a second later and looked around. His gaze met Bressen's and narrowed.

"What did you do to me?" Samhail asked, rising quickly.

Bressen stood as well. Both men now wore pants, likely one of Bressen's glamours, and Talyn flushed to think they were actually naked.

"I stopped you from making a big mistake," Bressen said. "Talyn is the only reason I got out of there alive and with my body parts intact."

"She was also the reason you were there to begin with," Cyra growled. "Give me one good reason I shouldn't kill her now or let Samhail do it."

Bressen looked pointedly at his wife. "Because rage and grief make people do desperate, ill-advised things, and they deserve the chance to make up for their mistakes," he said.

Cyra blanched visibly and stepped back. It was clear Bressen expected her to know what he meant, but he still seemed surprised at her reaction.

"You broke into my mind," Samhail cut in, drawing Bressen's attention back to him. His tone was somewhere between anger and awe. "How did you break in so fast? You've never broken through that fast."

Bressen exhaled a deep breath and looked apologetically at Samhail.

"I've always been able to break into your mind," the lord admitted. "I have yet to encounter a mind shield that can keep me out for very long."

Samhail stared at him.

"But…our training sessions," Samhail said, still bewildered. His face grew dark with anger. "Have you been humoring me this whole time? You've been able to break past my shield whenever you want, but you've let me think I kept you out?"

"This is a conversation for another time," Bressen told him. "We have more important concerns right now."

He turned to where Morland still stood quietly next to them.

"Is he…do you have control of his mind?" Cyra asked Bressen.

"Yes," Bressen said. "Aidan actually helped me get past Morland's mind shield. He attacked it from the inside and weakened it."

"Wait. Back up," Axenus said. "What exactly happened? Why did Talyn take you? How did you escape?"

Bressen's eyes swung to Talyn, seemingly asking for her permission to tell them, and she nodded as she rubbed her throat.

"Talyn needed my help," he said. "She realized something about Morland, and she needed me to read his mind, but he was escaping with Sandrian and Magdalene, so she made a quick decision."

He paused to give Talyn a meaningful look.

"In hindsight," he went on, "we probably have her to thank for getting Aidan back so quickly. Who knows how long it would've taken us to track Sandrian and Magdalene down otherwise."

Cyra and Samhail didn't look ready to concede that point just yet, but at least neither of them looked on the verge of killing her anymore.

Then something clicked in Talyn's head, and she pushed herself up along the pillar to stand.

"Lord Bressen, you're in Morland's mind right now?" she asked.

He nodded.

"Is he…can you…?" She couldn't get the words out. Now that she was so close to the truth, she was almost afraid to know.

"Yes," Bressen said gently. "Morland killed your sister."

Cyra inhaled sharply, and Talyn closed her eyes as her legs turned to jelly again beneath her. She reopened them and grabbed for the pillar to steady herself even as Samhail reached out to catch her. Their gazes met as he stopped himself before he touched her, and she saw the emotions warring behind his eyes.

"Morland killed Talyn's sister?" Axenus asked.

"He killed several women," Talyn said. "He liked to kidnap young women and hold them for days while he raped and tortured them. I don't know how many he took before my sister, but I learned of at least four others after her. I began tracking him, and I thought I'd found him, but somehow I got the wrong man…and I killed him."

The entire room had gone silent, and Talyn looked at Bressen to confirm her understanding of events matched what he'd seen in Morland's mind.

He nodded. "Morland laid a false trail," he said. "He led you to the other man to get you off his scent, then he left town after you killed the man. He didn't know who you were, only that someone was onto him."

Talyn closed her eyes to let it sink in how easily Morland had duped her into killing someone else. She shook her head and opened her eyes before she went on. "I only learned yesterday I might've killed the wrong man," she explained to the group. "I look a lot like my sister, and Morland recognized me. He told me I looked like her, and…there was something about the look in his eye. I just knew."

Her eyes met Cyra's and then drifted to Samhail's. She didn't delude herself into thinking she saw forgiveness or even understanding in them, but she at least dared to think the desire to kill her was gone.

"I didn't know what to do when Morland retreated with Sandrian and Magdalene," Talyn said, a hint of desperation in her voice. "I couldn't let him get away. Not once I realized my mistake. But I was wrong once before, and I had to be sure. Taking Lord Bressen wasn't planned. I just knew if anyone could see the truth in Morland, he could. I brought him to Sandrian to get me close enough to Morland to find out. It was a stupid, foolhardy plan for so many reasons, but it was all I had in the three seconds I had to decide what to do before Morland disappeared through Magdalene's portal. For what it's worth, I'm sorry."

She looked at both Samhail and Cyra, then her eyes met Bressen's. He was the one to whom she owed the biggest apology. It was a miracle she hadn't gotten him killed.

"I'm sorry, my lord," she said sincerely. Her eyes drifted over the cuts and bruises that still marred his face and upper body. "I put you in grave danger, and after you give me the month you promised, I'll submit to whatever punishment you deem appropriate."

"Month? Month for what?" Cyra asked Bressen.

Bressen didn't take his eyes from Talyn as he answered his wife.

"Talyn would like to kill Morland, but I told her I wouldn't allow it as long as Morland is still in Aidan's body," he said. "I've asked her to give us a month to find a way to get him out and restore Aidan."

More silence.

"Even if we could pull Morland's mind out of Aidan's body, what would we do with it?" Axenus asked. "In order for her to kill him, he needs some kind of corporeal form. We can't just put him into a random body and let her kill it. That would be…" He paused to consider the right word. "Problematic," he finished.

"What about putting Morland's mind into a magical object, like Praya did with the warriors in the collar?" Samhail suggested.

"It might be an option, but we don't have a magical object like that," Cyra said, "and as far as I know, we don't have the means to create one."

"Actually," Bressen said, suddenly thoughtful, "we might. There was one more unintended benefit to my kidnapping."

Everyone looked at him questioningly, including Talyn.

Bressen stepped closer to Cyra and put his hand to the side of her head. She looked at him in confusion for a moment before she gave a huge gasp and clutched his arm.

"Sweet gods above!" she said as her eyes locked with Bressen's. "Is that…Is that real?"

"Yes," he said. "A memory alteration, buried so deep even I couldn't find it. Magdalene snapped it loose when she invaded my mind."

"Did Magdalene see it?" Cyra asked. "Does she know…?"

"I don't know. I don't think so," he answered. He moved to Axenus and laid a hand on the side of the merman's head.

Axenus frowned, then his eyes widened in understanding.

"The island!" Axenus exclaimed, but Bressen held up a hand to stop him from saying more.

"You think that might be the way to get Morland out of Aidan's body?" Axenus asked Bressen.

"It's the only option I can think of right now," the lord answered.

Bressen looked at Samhail, and a few seconds of silence passed between the two before Samhail nodded, the lord having undoubtedly filled Samhail in mentally.

Talyn noticed then that Surgeon and Serise still stood behind them, both also wearing glamoured clothes. They looked annoyed that everyone else got to know what Bressen had discovered except them. Or perhaps they were just annoyed Samhail got to know.

"So what do we do with the assassin for a month?" Samhail asked.

He nodded his head toward Talyn, and something twinged in her chest. He was back to calling her "the assassin" rather than by her name.

Everyone turned to Talyn, and she met each of their eyes in turn, her gaze lingering on Samhail's.

Axenus was the only one with a neutral expression. Bressen looked torn while both Cyra and Samhail wore their distrust openly. The twins looked like they'd be happy to keep an eye on her.

"You're free for the next month," Bressen said finally. "Go where you want. Do what you need to. I trust you'll return here when the month is up. Until then, you can set your affairs in order."

Talyn's stomach dropped. Allowing her to 'set her affairs in order' meant he intended to send her to Revenmyer. She wasn't surprised by his decision, but part of her had still hoped to avoid the prison.

"What are you going to do with him?" she asked, inclining her head to where Morland still stood silently, oblivious to everything around him.

"We'll keep him in the dungeon here at the Citadel for now," Bressen said. "I need to speak to Jasper about how to handle things in Derridan until we can free Aidan, but that's none of your concern."

"I'm not leaving him," Talyn said. "I spent too long thinking I'd killed my sister's murderer only to have the rug ripped out from under me. I need to be close by."

Bressen shook his head. "I can't allow you to walk free in the Citadel. You've proven too willing to switch sides when you see an opportunity, and you spent several weeks in my household spying and plotting to kill us. I think you can see how, all things considered, I can't have you close."

Talyn did see, and she didn't blame him, but he didn't seem to realize the flaw in his thinking.

"You realize I can just turn myself into one of your staff and hide out for the next month?" she pointed out.

She should've just done it without warning them, but some part of her wanted their trust...wanted Samhail's trust back.

Bressen started to speak, but she cut him off.

"What if I let you put me in the dungeon with him?" Talyn offered.

Bressen's eyes flared, then narrowed half a second later.

"You're volunteering to be imprisoned for a month?" he asked.

"You won't let me stay here freely, and I can't let Morland out of my sight, so yes."

They all looked at her incredulously.

"Do we have a deal?" she asked when no one spoke again.

Bressen and Cyra looked at each other, and Talyn was almost certain they were having a mental conversation about it.

Bressen finally turned back to her. "If that's what you really want, then yes. You can keep Morland company in the dungeon for the next month."

Tandem Read: Go to Nemesis Rising (Bk 4), Chapter 30

Chapter 39

Talyn

Talyn lay on her back looking up at the ceiling in her cell. By now she was getting used to the feeling of the caronium suppressing her power.

So this is what it felt like to be mortal.

She'd been in the dungeon for five days, and Morland had barely moved, still under Bressen's mind control as he was. The man ate when given food, used the toilet when the urge arose, and slept when the guards put out the lights, but otherwise he either sat on his cot or paced the cell for a few minutes. Talyn assumed the last was just to give him some exercise so his muscles didn't atrophy.

She herself didn't do much more than Morland. She exercised to the extent that she could by doing pushups, sit-ups, and leg workouts, but otherwise she just read. To her surprise, Cyra had brought her some books the first day, perhaps out of a lingering sense of friendship from her time as the lady's handmaid, but Talyn hadn't seen her since.

Jasper came once a day to visit Aidan, or at least Aidan's body, but the lord consort didn't do anything besides stand at the bars and watch his husband. He never spoke to Talyn, and she never said anything to him out of respect for his need to grieve silently for the partner who was there, but not really there.

Talyn herself never had any visitors. Not during the day at least.

It was well after midnight that first night when Samhail came to see her. She was a light sleeper, but no particular sound had woken her. She'd just popped awake all of a sudden and felt him.

She was on her side facing the wall, and she didn't move as he stood outside the bars watching her. Perhaps it had been that faint scent of leather and earth that alerted her to his presence, or perhaps it was just the way her skin seemed to prickle when he was near, as if it knew something she didn't. She didn't move, and she kept her breathing as steady and even as she could, so as not to let him know she was awake.

She wasn't completely sure when he'd left because she heard nothing at all, but her body eventually relaxed, a sign he was no longer watching. Only then did she dare to turn over and verify the hallway outside her cell was empty.

He came every night that week, always in the deepest darkness. He never made a sound, never spoke to her, and always left as silently as he came, but she knew without a doubt every time he was there.

She looked forward to his visits. There was something strangely soothing about having him there, even if he never said anything, and she never acknowledged him. If he'd left her completely alone, that would've been far worse. This, at least, suggested he might still care for her.

She wasn't sure why that mattered. They had no future together. Three hells, she had no future either with or without him. She'd agreed to turn herself over to Lord Bressen in a month, regardless of what happened with Morland, and then she'd be in Revenmyer.

She didn't want to think about what it would be like in the prison, about the horrors she'd see in her nightmares. She didn't regret the life she'd chosen for herself – or perhaps the one fate had chosen for her – but if what Sandrian said was true, that wouldn't matter. She'd feel her victims' pain over and over again regardless.

Especially that first man.

The man hadn't been innocent. Morland had chosen him for a reason. He'd been stalking a woman – her – when she'd taken him, so she knew he was at least a predator, but he wasn't the man who'd killed her sister.

"Fucking three hells!"

Talyn jumped at the voice coming from the cell across the hall and bolted off her cot to see what was going on.

Morland stood in the middle of his cell looking around. He seemed lucid, his eyes no longer vacant. He strode to the bars and pulled at the door to see if it would open, but it didn't budge.

Talyn didn't move. Had he broken through Bressen's hold on him?

Morland's gaze swung up to her, and she went rigid as he looked her up and down. A malicious grin curled the corners of his lips.

"Well, well. What do we have here?" he sneered. "It looks like I'm not the only one in a cage. Is this how Lord Bressen rewards his savior?"

Talyn didn't say anything. If Morland wanted to make assumptions about why she was there, she'd let him. Maybe she could get more information out of him.

"How did you break out of Lord Bressen's hold on your mind?" she asked instead.

Morland considered the question, then shrugged. "I didn't. It seems he released me."

Talyn's body went cold, and she shook her head. "He wouldn't do that," she said.

"But it appears he has," Morland said. "Maybe he thought you were lonely and needed someone to talk to."

Talyn closed her eyes. Nemesis take her. It had been so nice and quiet down here, but she could see it now. Morland wasn't going to shut up now that he was out from under Bressen's control. Why on earth had the lord released him?

"It's a pity they didn't put us in the same cell," Morland mused. "I could've shown you exactly what I did to your sister."

Talyn's eyes flew open, and her head snapped up. The look of cruel amusement on Morland's face sent fire scorching through her veins, and she grabbed the bars of her cell to rattle them.

"You're lucky they didn't put me in there with you, or you'd learn early what the third level of hell feels like," she snarled.

Morland tsked. "Such aggression. Your sister was so much more docile, so innocent." He paused, and his smirk widened. "Did you know she was a virgin? Before me, that is."

Bile rose in Talyn's throat, and rage made her ears ring as she rattled the bars again.

"What was your sister's name again? Julia?" he asked.

"Keep her name off your filthy lips, or I'll-"

"She was still unconscious the first time I fucked her."

Talyn froze. Her chest heaved as she tried to rein in her breathing and slow her heart. It was pounding against the inside of her rib cage like it wanted to get out, but she realized her mistake now. Morland enjoyed tormenting her, and she had no way to make him stop talking. The more she showed him how it affected her, the more he was going to do it.

"It's a pity really," Morland said. "If I'd known she was a virgin, I'd have waited until she was awake to fuck her so I could hear her scream when I tore through her maidenhead. I like hearing them scream and cry. But who knew the daughter of a courtesan would be a virgin at that age."

Talyn clenched her teeth together and tried not to react, but it was too late. She'd shown him too much.

"I just couldn't help myself," Morland went on, his eyes fixed on her face. "When I pulled her clothes off, all that creamy skin called to me. I just spread her pretty legs and shoved my cock inside."

Talyn let out a jagged breath. She had to find a way to shut him up. She couldn't listen to this. Not when she didn't have any way to get to him, to make him pay for everything he'd done.

"There's nothing tighter than virgin cunt," Morland said, "and, gods, she felt so good."

"Shut up!" Talyn screamed.

"She bled all over my cock. Such a mess. I made her lick it all off when she woke up. Her mouth and throat were almost as tight as-"

Talyn shook the bars with all her might, "Shut up, or I'll-"

"You'll do what?" he cut her off. "You're over there, and I'm over here, and there are two sets of bars between us. Exactly how do you plan to make me stop telling you every little detail of my seven, long days and nights with your sister?"

Morland's smile was feral now as he reached down to undo the fastenings of his pants and pull out Lord Aidan's cock. It was erect, and she knew that remembering what he'd done to Julia was arousing him.

Talyn looked away. "I'm going to kill you," she whispered, and she saw Morland stroke himself out of the corner of her eye.

"I'll say one thing for that mortal body I had previously," Morland went on, not acknowledging her threat. "Its cock was long and thick. Lord Aidan is decently endowed, but that last cock I had made women scream so beautifully, especially when I fucked them in the ass. It really tore your sister up."

Talyn clamped her hands over her ears and stumbled to the corner of her cell farthest from Morland. She tried to hum to block out the sound of his voice, but he only shouted louder, and she could still just barely hear what he was saying despite her best efforts. Tears ran down her face as he described in gruesome, callous detail the things he'd done to Julia. When she dared to peek open an eye, she saw him stroking himself faster, and she pinched her eyes shut as tight as she could.

Protector save her. There was no way to make him stop, and she knew in that moment exactly what nightmare would haunt her dreams when she went to Revenmyer.

Talyn

Talyn had no idea how long Morland talked before he finally went to sleep. She'd looked up at one point to see the guards had left her dinner, but she didn't dare uncover her ears long enough to go eat. She couldn't stomach food anyway. She'd already vomited once during a particularly graphic part of Morland's account that she'd been unable to block out, and she was shaking too badly to eat.

The thought of what Julia had gone through – the pain, the fear, the humiliation – it had nearly driven her mad, and Morland had never slowed in his story. He'd relished telling her, had taken pride in what he'd done.

At some point, Talyn had gotten too tired to continue holding her hands over her ears. Her arms shook with the effort, and she knew her muscles would be stiff in the morning.

The dungeon had been quiet for hours now, but Talyn hadn't moved from the corner where she crouched, still trembling. Maybe if she exhausted herself enough, she'd be able to pass out tomorrow when Morland started taunting her again. Maybe she'd be able to sleep through it without him noticing.

"Talyn?"

The voice in the darkness made her jolt. It wasn't loud, but it was still jarring after so much blessed silence.

Talyn lifted her head and saw the outline of Samhail's huge form filling the doorway of the cell. There were only a couple torches burning in the dungeon at this time of night, so she couldn't see much of him, but she'd know his silhouette anywhere. She'd forgotten he usually came.

"Why are you crouched in a corner on the floor?" he asked. Concern fought with wariness in his voice. "Are...you alright?"

Talyn swallowed. Her throat was raw from trying to hum all day so she couldn't hear Morland, and her voice came out harsh and raspy.

"Morland is no longer under Lord Bressen's mind control," she said. "I don't know how he broke the hold, but-"

Samhail swore, cutting her off.

"Bressen and Cyra are away," he explained. "They left a couple days ago. Bressen's mind powers only extend so far. I'm sure he forgot Morland would be released when he got out of range."

Talyn let out a puff of air that was almost a laugh. It was somewhat comforting to think Lord Bressen hadn't released Morland on purpose to torture her, but that didn't erase the horrors she'd heard today.

"What happened? Did he threaten you?" Samhail asked.

She couldn't hold back the whimper that escaped.

"Talyn," Samhail said firmly. "What did he do? Tell me."

She swallowed again and took a deep breath before answering.

"I got to hear in exquisite detail today everything he did to my sister in the seven days he kept her," Talyn said quietly. "There was nothing I could do to make him stop talking."

There was silence as Samhail stood there looking at her. Then he turned and walked away.

Talyn's heart sank into her stomach. He didn't care. He thought she was weak for not being able to endure a day of hearing Morland talk. He…

Samhail's form moved back into view, this time in front of Morland's cell. The lock clicked open, and the door clanged loudly as Samhail shoved it open forcefully before stepping inside.

Talyn shot to her feet and hurried on unsteady legs to the bars of her own cell just as Morland's sleepy voice sounded.

"What…What's happen-?"

The words were cut off by his shriek of surprise. Talyn heard scuffling in the cell, but it was too dark inside to see what was happening.

"Samhail, to what do I owe-?"

Morland's words were cut off again, this time by a strangled noise, and Talyn imagined that Samhail now had him by the throat against a wall.

"I should break your neck right now, Morland," Samhail spat out, "or maybe pull out your tongue. You can't tell stories without a tongue."

Morland only choked out a laugh. "But you can't do either of those things," he wheezed against Samhail's hold, "because you'd be doing them to Aidan too."

Samhail's answering snarl was so bestial and vicious that Talyn wondered if he'd shifted into his gargoyle form.

There was another scuffling noise, then Morland screamed.

"That dislocated shoulder won't cause any permanent damage," Samhail said calmly, "but it'll hurt like fuck until I send the healer over in the morning."

"You can't leave me like this!" Morland yelled, but Samhail had already stepped out of the cell and pulled the door shut again.

He turned to Talyn's cell and took the ring of keys out of his pocket. Talyn's eyes flared and she backed away as he found the right key and turned it in the lock.

She looked around frantically for something to use as a weapon. Gods above, her limbs were still shaking from the strain of trying to block out Morland this afternoon. There was no way she could fight him now.

But he didn't step into the cell.

"Come here," was all he said.

"W-why?" she asked.

"You're not staying down here as long as Morland has his mind back. There's nothing I can do to keep him quiet, so I need to move you."

"But-"

"Come here," Samhail repeated. "Or I'll come in and throw you over my shoulder."

Talyn was about to tell him exactly what she thought of that, but she snapped her mouth shut. She was too tired and weak to fight him on this, so she stepped forward until she was in front of him.

Samhail took her wrist and reached into his pocket to pull out a caronium cuff that he snapped onto it.

Again, Talyn didn't feel like fighting him, so she let him do it.

"I still know how to pick the locks on these," she felt the need to point out, and she saw him smile in the dimness.

"We've made some improvements to the locking mechanism since then," he said. "Now let's go."

Talyn let Samhail lead her out of the dungeons, up to the first floor, back toward the main part of the building, then up several other flights of stairs. Finally they exited into a hallway, and she frowned as she followed him down it. She assumed he was bringing her to some other place in the Citadel where they might have backup holding cells, but this area looked like a residential part of the fortress.

Talyn stopped walking.

"Where are we going?" she asked, suddenly wary.

"Just follow me," he said without stopping.

Talyn didn't move. She crossed her arms and waited for him to realize she wasn't following him. Finally, he stopped and turned to face her.

"Talyn, let's go," he said.

"I'm not a dog," she said. "I'm not just going to come when you call."

Even in the dark she could see his grin.

"That's fine. I have other ways of making you come," he said.

Talyn forced herself not to react, but her body readied to move as he walked back toward her.

"Tell me where you're taking me," she said.

He sighed. "My room."

"The three hells you are!"

She tried to step back, but he caught her arm.

"There's nowhere else to put you," Samhail said. "I'm not leaving you in the dungeon so Morland can taunt you, and there are no other holding cells within the Citadel. I could lock you in one of the guest rooms, but I don't trust you by yourself, so that leaves us with my room, where I can keep an eye on you."

Talyn started to respond, but she jumped in surprise as the door in the hall next to her opened, and a bleary-eyed Axenus stepped out.

"What's going on out here?" the merman asked, yawning.

He rubbed the sleep from his eyes but started when he saw Talyn.

"What is she doing out of her cell?" he asked Samhail.

"Bressen's mind control over Morland wore off. He must be too far away to keep it up," Samhail said. "Morland spent the day torturing Talyn with the details of her sister's torture and murder."

Axenus's eyes snapped to hers, seeking confirmation. She didn't say anything, but she was sure he read the truth in her face.

"Gods above," Axenus said. "So where are you taking her then?"

His tone suggested he already knew the answer.

"My-"

"I can stay with Axenus," Talyn cut in before Samhail could answer.

Both men looked at her incredulously.

"You said you needed to put me somewhere you could keep an eye on me," she said to Samhail. "I'm sure Axenus can do that."

Samhail's eyes narrowed menacingly, but Talyn looked at Axenus, waiting for a reply.

The merman just stared blankly at her for a moment before he chuckled. Talyn frowned at him.

"If you think I'm going to challenge *him* and insist you stay in my room, you're even more insane than I first thought," Axenus said to her as he cocked his head toward Samhail. "Or you must think I'm more insane than I actually am. Either way, I'm not sure who'd end up slitting my throat sooner, you or him."

Talyn's frown deepened. "You aren't really afraid of him, are you? I'd bet on you in a fight over him any day."

Next to her, Samhail growled, but Axenus just chuckled again.

"Try to keep the moaning to a minimum," the merman said as he turned to head back into his room. "Some of us need our rest."

Talyn's mouth fell open as Axenus closed the door behind him, and she turned to find Samhail smirking at her.

"Nice try," he said. "Now let's go."

Talyn clamped her mouth shut again and followed Samhail as he rounded a corner into another hallway. He stopped in front of a heavy wooden door and pushed it open to let her in.

The room she stepped into was relatively sparse compared to the grandeur she'd seen at Tide's End. To be sure, the furniture was clearly expensive, but there wasn't much of it besides the bed, a couch, a few chairs, and a table. The space lacked the statues, vases, and other ornamentations that most rooms in a fortress or palace like this might boast, and she had a feeling the room's occupant preferred it that way.

Talyn's eyes drifted back to the bed. It was large and sturdy, easily able to fit Samhail and probably several companions for the night. It was also unslept-in at the moment, its covers still pulled neatly over it. Despite the late hour, Samhail hadn't gone to bed yet.

She'd always assumed he woke up to come down and check on her, but the state of his bed suggested he stayed out late, then came down to the dungeon on his way home. It made her wonder where he spent his nights…or with whom.

"Get in bed," Samhail said from behind her.

Talyn turned to see he'd already removed his shirt, but thankfully his pants were still on. She'd almost forgotten how beautiful he was. The swells of his chest muscles, the way she could count every one of the ripples on his stomach, and the sharp V of muscles that traced a path straight down to his groin all did things to her insides.

"I assume you'll be sleeping on the couch," she ventured.

"That has as much chance of happening as you sleeping in Axenus's room," he said.

She sighed. She'd figured as much, and she was too exhausted to argue, so she just climbed into the bed and tried to get comfortable.

Talyn felt the bed dip heavily under Samhail's weight as he slid in behind her, and she yelped a second later as his arm snaked around her waist to pull her back against his body.

"Samhail!" she squeaked as he settled up against her.

"Just a precaution to make sure you don't end up somewhere you're not supposed to be," he said. "Now go to sleep."

His breath brushed over the side of her face, and she smelled the slight tang of alcohol on it.

Talyn stayed awake until she felt Samhail's breathing even out and become steady. Until recently, she hadn't been able to sleep with someone else's body wrapped around hers, but – as with everything else – Samhail seemed to be the exception to the rule. Perhaps she was just so exhausted from dealing with Morland that her body no longer cared about the mass of hard muscle cocooning her in. It was oddly comfortable being nestled up next to him, and once she stopped fighting the sleep and let her eyes flutter shut, Talyn slept sounder than she ever had before.

Chapter 40

Samhail

Samhail woke to the scent of lemon verbena in his nose, the feel of a soft body tucked into him, and the ache of a raging erection pressing against his pants.

He'd let Talyn go to bed last night with all her clothes on and had kept his own pants on in the hopes the layers of fabric between them might keep his lust in check, but no such luck. Everything about this woman aroused him, and he wanted so badly to free his cock, tug down her own pants, and slip into her from behind to make her moan for him.

Nemesis take him. The woman had kidnapped Bressen and nearly gotten him killed, yet Samhail had only managed to stay angry with her for a few hours after she'd returned. He'd wanted to choke the life out of her at first, and the gods knew he'd tried. He could've crushed her throat with one squeeze, but he hadn't been able to do it. He was secretly relieved when Bressen broke past his mind shield and forced him to let her go.

He promised himself the first night that he'd just go to bed and not think about her, but he'd gone to a tavern in Callanus instead, and several drinks later, he'd found himself in the dungeon watching her.

Talyn hadn't moved on her cot, but he'd had the strangest feeling she was awake that night, and every night since, when he came to check on her. He didn't know how he knew, but he did.

Then he'd found her last night crouched in the corner looking exhausted and shaken, and any lingering anger he'd felt had dissipated. She'd told him about Morland, and his rage had returned tenfold, but this time on her behalf.

The urge to kill Morland had been overwhelming. He'd wanted to pull the man apart slowly, piece by piece, starting with his fingers and toes and working up to his head, but he couldn't do that. Not yet.

Maybe if Bressen and Cyra's mission was successful…

Samhail itched to brush the hair back from Talyn's face as she lay there sleeping. It was like a mind wraith had put some kind of compulsion on him. He wanted to touch her all the time. She'd wake instantly if he tried, though, and he wanted her to sleep. She needed it.

On the other hand, he really needed to get up and relieve himself in more ways than one, so it was inevitable she'd wake.

Samhail brushed his lips over the back of Talyn's head ever so gently, and she stirred. Reluctantly, he peeled his body away from hers.

Talyn jolted at the movement and tried to sit up in bed, but he urged her back down with a hand on her shoulder.

"Stay in bed and rest," he said. "I'm going to bathe and get ready, but there's no reason you need to get up yet."

Talyn looked at him warily but settled back down into the mattress.

"Are you locking me in here all day?" she asked.

"No. You'll need to come with me on my rounds. Until Bressen and Cyra return, you and I will be attached at the hip."

She raised a brow, and Samhail grimaced at his inadvertent phrasing.

"I mean, I won't be letting you out of my sight," he clarified.

"You don't really expect me to sleep here until Lord Bressen gets back, do you?" she asked as Samhail swung his legs out of bed.

"Planning to ask Axenus to take you in again?" he teased over his shoulder as he strode toward the bathing chamber.

She scoffed. "What's the point? Clearly he's afraid of you for some unwarranted reason."

Samhail chuckled. "Despite what I tell him, Axenus is a smart man. He's not going to put himself in the middle of…whatever this is."

Samhail stepped into the bathing chamber and was about to close the door when she asked, "And what do you think this is?"

He paused with his hand on the doorknob and looked back at the woman still curled in his bed, her beautiful hair flowing over his pillow.

He shrugged finally. "It's a battle. A battle of wills."

Samhail turned, but her voice stopped him again.

"Who's winning?" she asked.

He expected to see her grin when he looked, but her face was serious. He closed the door to the bathing chamber without answering, and, once inside, he let out a heavy breath.

She was. Talyn was definitely winning.

Samhail strode to the toilet and barely managed to get his dick to point down long enough to relieve his bladder. He was going to have to jerk himself off. He couldn't walk around the fortress with a huge bulge in the front of his pants all day, both for the sake of propriety and because it would be pure agony. Having Talyn with him all day was going to be challenging to say the least.

Samhail turned to the huge bathtub and saw the Citadel's magic had already filled it with steaming hot water. He'd get his release there. The water would help, since he'd left the oil he usually used in his bedstand.

Samhail stripped off his pants and eased himself down into the tub to let the hot water relieve the tension in his body. This woman was going to be the death of him. He wasn't sure if Bressen really did intend to send her to Revenmyer when all this was over, but he already knew he wouldn't let his friend do that. He still had slim hopes that he and Talyn might be able to travel and work together one day.

Samhail wrapped a hand around his cock and gave his length a long, firm stroke. This wouldn't take long.

He closed his eyes and let his mind drift to the woman in his bed. He imagined himself standing at the foot of it with her splayed out naked before him. She ran her hands over her body as he watched, and one drifted between her legs to pleasure herself. In his mind, she swirled her fingers over her clit, then plunge two of them inside herself. He heard her cry his name as she rode her own hand…*Samhail! Oh gods, Samhail!*

"Samhail."

His head snapped up as he realized that last one hadn't been in his head. Talyn stood in the doorway.

Fuck.

"What are you doing?" he asked, pulling his hands quickly out of the water. "I'm taking a bath."

She gave him a knowing smile. "Is that what you were doing?" she asked. "It sounded like you were in pain."

Samhail tensed as Talyn strolled into the room, but he laid his arms out across the edge of the tub and tried to pretend her presence didn't make his heart thud in his chest like a war drum.

"It used to be my job to help Cyra with her baths," Talyn said casually.

He shut his eyes and willed himself not to picture that. No such luck.

"One time she was teasing Bressen through her mind, but it was arousing her as well," she went on, "so I helped her out."

Samhail opened his eyes when he felt her fingers on his hand. She ran them up his arm and over the muscles of his shoulder as she walked around him. Her fingers brushed across his hair before finding his other shoulder and continuing their trail down his other arm.

Samhail couldn't hold down the gooseflesh that rose on his skin. Gods above. He never, ever got gooseflesh.

Talyn crouched down behind him so her lips were close to his ear. She rested a hand on his shoulder before moving it over his chest.

"I ran my hands over her breasts," she purred as she moved her hand across his pectoral muscle so her thumb brushed his nipple. "And Cyra put her hands between her legs and-"

Samhail grabbed Talyn's wrist just as her hand hit the waterline.

This woman was a demon in disguise meant to tempt him to one of the three hells. And, gods damn him, he was ready and willing to go.

"You're on dangerous ground, hummingbird," he said quietly.

"Oh? How so?"

Samhail let go of her wrist and rose from the water as she stepped back a pace.

"An animal will only take so much teasing before it bites," he said.

"And make no mistake, I'm just as much beast as I am man."

Talyn

Samhail stepped out of the tub, and Talyn bit her lip as she took in every inch of his nearly seven-foot frame. Every dripping-wet, naked inch.

Water slid down him like delicate silk sheets before trickling into rivulets that rolled over the swells and ridges of his body. It clung to him like a second skin and made each ripple of his already impressive muscles seem all the more pronounced. A droplet clung to one of his nipples, and Talyn had to stop herself from flicking it with her tongue.

Who knew it was possible to be jealous of water?

The place that drew her eye next was the hard, straight length of his cock that stood up erect from the small patch of stark-white curls at his groin. She wondered how she had ever fit the thing inside her, even as a stubborn, reckless part of her wanted to try again.

She took a step toward Samhail.

"Talyn," he warned. He held up a hand to ward her off, but she took another step toward him.

His eyes flared as she advanced on him. To her surprise, he backed away like she was a mouse trying to skitter up his leg. She half-expected him to jump up on a chair. So much for being as much beast as man.

"Stay back," he warned, and Talyn's brows shot up.

His back finally hit one of the walls, and she pounced. She pressed her hands to the wall on either side of his hips and looked up at him.

She didn't understand this dynamic they had. When she pursued, he retreated, but then they'd reverse roles, and she'd flee while he hunted her down. One of them was always running, the other always chasing.

Well, right now, she'd caught him, and she smiled triumphantly.

"Talyn," Samhail warned. "What are you doing?"

The smile faded from her face as she became serious.

"Thanking you for rescuing me last night," she said softly.

Talyn dropped to her knees in front of Samhail, wrapped her hand around his cock, and licked up the underside of it from root to crown.

"Fuck!" he swore as his body jerked. "Talyn!"

She didn't listen as she pushed her mouth over his head. He jerked again, but Talyn pushed his hips back before she plunged her head forward, intending to take him as deep as she could.

That wasn't very far, and she tried to suppress her gag reflex as she eyed just how many more inches of him she'd need to fit.

It wasn't physically possible.

Talyn pulled back and pushed her mouth forward again as her hand stroked his base. Her eyes watered as she felt him hit the back of her throat, but she forced herself to swallow, and Samhail let out a string of curses that would've made a sailor blush as he grabbed the hair at the nape of her neck.

"Talyn, you're still a prisoner," he ground out. "I can't…It's not ri-"

She cut off his attempt to explain the ethics of their situation by tightening her lips and driving herself forward onto his cock. The effort earned her a loud, almost-pained grunt, and Samhail's hips bucked forward, pushing him deeper down her throat. Tears sprung to her eyes as she choked, but she managed to swallow around his cock again as her throat loosened up.

She pulled her mouth off him for a moment. "You know, if you removed the caronium cuff, I could use my masquing power to take you deeper," she purred.

He let out a pained groan. "That might fucking kill me," he said.

Talyn laughed softly, and Samhail swore as she plunged her mouth over him again, then pulled back to let her tongue press against every bump and ridge of his cock.

"You need to stop," he gasped. He seemed to be begging her.

Talyn ignored him and pressed her mouth over him again, and this time he slid down her throat more easily. She moved her tongue against him, and Samhail's hips jerked forward. She looked up and saw his gaze fixed on her face.

"Watching you take my cock like this really is killing me," he said, his voice graveled. He took a deep breath. "But Nemesis take me, I've never been more willing to embrace death than now, watching you on your knees with your lips wrapped around me."

Talyn pulled her mouth back all the way so she could swirl her tongue over his head, and he groaned. She took him deep again, and his hand on her head urged her forward. She obliged as they began to set an ever-more insistent pace. He didn't thrust hard, but the push of his hips sent him deeper down Talyn's throat each time. Her eyes still watered as he pushed into her, but the look of utter pleasure on his face filled her with pride.

Samhail could dominate her in most things, but in this she had him at her mercy. She might be on her knees, but she'd never felt so powerful as she did now, watching him fall apart under her mouth.

Talyn dug her nails into Samhail's hips as their pace quickened, and she held him to her as she drove him relentlessly toward his release.

"Fuck, Talyn! I'm going to…Fuck!" Samhail yelled as his head kicked back against the wall.

Talyn pushed forward again as he spilled himself down her throat, and she drank him down. She pressed her tongue to the underside of his cock to feel him pulse in her mouth, and only when his body relaxed against the wall did she slip her mouth all the way off him and look up.

His chest heaved with ragged breaths as he tried to bring himself back under control. The satiated haze left his eyes as he looked down at her, only to be replaced by an intensity she might almost have called anger.

Talyn gasped as Samhail grabbed her arms and pulled her up. Then the world flipped upside down as he tossed her over his shoulder and began walking.

"Samhail! What are you doing?" she squeaked.

He didn't answer, but a few seconds later, the world turned right side up again, and Talyn found herself lying on the bed.

"Take off your clothes," he growled.

"What?"

"You either take them off now, or I cut them off."

Talyn blinked again, but she did as he ordered and started to pull her shirt and breast wrap off. She tossed them onto the floor and unfastened her pants. Samhail only watched as she slid the pants and her undergarment down her legs. Those items joined the others on the floor.

She sat on the bed naked and looked up into Samhail's eyes. They'd gone so dark they were almost black, and the look on his face was nothing short of feral.

Samhail put a knee on the bed and climbed toward her. She didn't move as he prowled forward until his body loomed over hers.

A pause the length of three heartbeats ticked off between them before Samhail grabbed the back of her neck and crushed his mouth down onto hers. Then he was on top of her, his solid body pinning her to the bed. Talyn let out a strangled moan as his tongue invaded her mouth, and she sucked in a deep breath through her nose to replace the one he'd stolen.

Samhail was always in control the times he'd fucked her. He was careful, almost gentle sometimes, and she knew it must be his way of compensating for his size. He could likely hurt his partner if he was too rough, so he seemed to hold back when he was driving inside her.

Not so with his kissing. Samhail kissed like it was a war and his tongue was a weapon to wield. He wielded it well. His kiss was meant to conquer, and Talyn was more than happy to wave a white flag.

Talyn threaded her hands through his hair to encourage him. Her lips would be swollen later from his onslaught, as they always were, but it was a small price for what he made her feel. She had a whole new heartbeat pulsing between her thighs.

Samhail pulled his lips from hers and moved down her body. He sucked one nipple deep into his mouth, and Talyn cried out as he bit down gently on it. He paid homage to her breast for what seemed like minutes before he moved to the second one and did the same.

"Protector save me, these breasts are perfect," he whispered, circling his tongue around the nipple of one.

Talyn couldn't hold herself still as she squirmed beneath him. She was a whimpering, writhing mess as he finally finished with her breasts and kissed lower down her stomach.

His fingers dug into her thighs as he spread her wide, then pulled her knees up over his shoulders. His mouth descended between her legs and Talyn screamed as he began to devour her. His tongue seemed to be everywhere as he teased the bud of nerves at her apex before thrusting it up inside her. He hummed against her center, and the vibrations had Talyn cursing and grabbing for the bedcovers with white knuckles.

"You're so wet, hummingbird," he murmured. "Is this all for me?"

"No," she gasped. "I'm thinking about Ax-"

The name choked off in her throat as Samhail nipped at her clit.

"Say his name," he warned, "and I'll make sure you don't come for the next two hours."

Talyn moaned. "I'm sorry. Please," she begged. "Please, I'm so close."

Without another word, Samhail lowered his mouth again, and within seconds Talyn clamped her thighs around his head as her climax rolled over her like a storm. She cried out as her inner muscles pulsed around his tongue, over and over again, and she heard his satisfied purr as the torrent of her release finally ebbed.

Samhail pushed her thighs open gently and got off the bed to go to his nightstand. Talyn's body came down to earth and sunk into the bed as she watched him.

"What are you doing now?" she asked as he came back around and tossed a small bottle next to her on the covers.

He didn't answer, but his hands clamped around her hips, and he flipped her onto her stomach before pulling her onto all fours.

"Samhail!" she cried as he positioned himself behind her and reached for the bottle. "What is that? What are you doing?"

She twisted to look behind her. He'd unstoppered the bottle and was splashing its contents on his hand. She jolted as his fingers rub some of the liquid over her second entrance.

Oh sweet gods.

"Samhail, no!" she cried. She tried to sit up, but he pushed her shoulders back down.

"Easy now," he said. "I'm not going to fuck your ass. Yet."

"Yet? What does that mean?"

"It means I want to start preparing you. Have you ever taken someone here?" he asked, rubbing an oiled finger over the puckered hole.

She shook her head. "No. I…I've never even let someone take me from behind. Until you."

He went still behind her.

"What? Why not?" he asked.

"Never let someone behind you. It leaves you vulnerable," she said.

There was a long pause as seconds bounced by on the bed.

"Why did you let me?" he asked finally.

"I…I don't know."

He ran a hand slowly down her back, and Talyn's skin pimpled with gooseflesh at the feel of his rough hands, calloused from a century of wielding weapons.

"Do you feel vulnerable now?" he asked.

A pause. "Yes," she admitted.

"But you'd still let me take you like this."

She nodded.

He circled a finger around her other hole. "Would you let me take you here? Not today, but soon?"

Talyn swallowed. "I…I…Maybe. Yes."

"I've never taken a woman there," he admitted. "I'm usually too big, but I have a feeling you can take me. That you can…adjust."

"Yes…If I had my powers."

"I want to fuck your ass eventually," he said, his voice deeper than normal. "I want to have you every way it's possible to have you. Will you let me start to prepare you?"

Talyn's breath hitched in her throat. She wasn't sure how far into the future he envisioned this happening, but she was curious enough to let him start 'preparing' her, as he called it.

She nodded.

"I need to hear you say it," he said, running what she thought was his thumb around the hole.

"Yes," she said. "Your finger only."

He hummed approvingly, and Talyn felt something press inside her. She pushed out a deep breath, letting her body adjust to the feel of having something foreign there.

"Are you alright?" he asked.

"Yes."

Samhail moved his finger slowly in and out of her, and she moaned softly. It was an odd sensation, but it felt better than she'd expected.

"I'm going to add a second finger," he said.

He withdrew the first, and when he pushed back in, she felt fuller, like she was being stretched more. There was a small sting of discomfort, but it eased eventually as he continued to move his fingers slowly.

"Relax your muscles," he said. "You're gripping me like a vice."

Talyn tried to loosen her muscles, and he moved his fingers faster.

"Oh gods," she said, dropping her head.

"That's it," he said, a note of praise in his tone, but her mind was focused entirely on the feel of his fingers pumping into her.

She felt the head of his cock press at her other entrance.

"Now let me fuck you, and we'll see how well you take it," he said.

"Gods, yes," Talyn whispered, and she gasped as he pushed into her.

She felt every inch of him sink slowly in, even as he continued to move his fingers in her ass. It was strange to feel something there, but she had to admit that it somehow enhanced the sensations elsewhere.

"Fuck, Talyn," he gritted out through his teeth. "I'm not going to last if you keep squeezing me like that."

Her only answer was to push back against him, driving him into her further. They both groaned and he moved faster. He pushed his fingers down so she felt them press with each thrust along his cock through the thin wall that separated them inside her.

Talyn squeezed her muscles around him, and Samhail swore again as he used his knees to push her legs wider. His free hand gripped her hip to help guide her as Talyn rocked herself back and forth. She ground her ass into him, marveling at how full she felt with both his cock and his fingers filling her. There was something about the feel of how they worked in tandem to create friction that drove her wild, and she was nearly ready to tip over the edge.

"Talyn, I'm going to-" Samhail started to say, but his words were cut off by her scream of pleasure as she drove herself back into him.

Her body convulsed around Samhail as the muscles of both holes pulsed frantically under one of the most intense releases she'd ever experienced. She let loose a long cry as she rode out her climax with several more short thrusts back against him.

Samhail pulled his fingers out of her as she relaxed, and he grabbed her hips with both hands to pound into her, chasing his own release. His rough grunts started to arouse her again, but he pulled out of her suddenly.

A long, deep groan rumbled up his throat before it turned into a roar of satisfaction, and Talyn felt something warm and wet splash across her lower back. He'd pulled out to spill his seed onto her instead of inside her.

Talyn didn't move as Samhail's grip on one side of her hips relaxed and his body eased behind her. She felt the hard ridge of his cock slide along her tailbone, and he let out a long sigh.

"Don't move," he said, and she looked behind her to see he held his hand out in the direction of the bathing chamber. A moment later, a towel flew into it, and he used it to wipe the milky substance off her back.

"You usually finish inside me," she said when he was done, and she rolled over to sit on the bed.

"You've been in the dungeon the last few days," he said. "I didn't think they were giving you turrow berry tea. I take mine every day, but it's more effective when both partners take it, and I didn't want…"

He trailed off, and something twisted in Talyn's heart at the idea he'd been concerned about getting her pregnant. She swallowed, but she couldn't think of anything to say, so she just nodded.

"If you want to bathe, you should do it now," he said. "I have a lot to do today, and you'll need to come with me."

Talyn got off the bed and headed toward the bathing chamber. They'd given her a bucket of cool water and a rag to wash herself with each day in the dungeon, but an actual bath with hot water sounded wonderful.

"I'll see about getting you a change of clothes," he said.

Talyn looked back at him. He was still standing naked next to the bed, and their eyes met before he turned to head into his closet.

"Thank you," she said to his back.

She continued into the bathing chamber, not sure where the huge knot in her throat had suddenly come from.

Chapter 41

Samhail

There was only one thing worse than Samhail's monumental failure in self-control this morning, and that was the knowing grin on Axenus's face when he and Talyn walked into the dining room for breakfast thirty minutes later.

"Wipe that smirk off your face, Axe, or I'll do it for you," Samhail growled as he went directly to the sideboard and piled food haphazardly onto his plate.

"You're awfully grouchy this morning," Axenus observed. "Was I wrong in thinking the two of you relieved some tension last night?"

Samhail didn't dare look at Talyn as he finished filling his plate and brought it to the table to let it clatter down loudly.

"As is often the case, you *are* wrong," Samhail said as he dropped into his seat across from Axenus. "We didn't do anything but sleep last night."

Axenus quirked a dubious brow, but Samhail ignored him and dug in.

"It's true," Talyn said as she sat down next to Samhail. "He didn't shove his cock down my throat until this morning."

Samhail shut his eyes as Axenus choked on his toast. Why had he thought for even a second she'd let him get away with the half-truth?

He considered pointing out that she'd been the one doing the shoving, but she'd only mention what made her come into the bathing chamber in the first place, and that was more than Axenus needed to know.

He glared at Talyn. Her cup of tea – like his – had the rosy hue of turrow berries, and she winked at him as she took a sip.

"I'm making my usual trips to Seatherny and Solandis today," Samhail said, changing the subject. "What's your plan for the day, Axe?"

"I have to go to Gendris," Axenus answered. "Kern countered our offer, and I need to discuss their proposal with the High Council."

"Does Bressen know this?" Samhail asked.

"Not about the counteroffer," Axenus said, "but he gave me authority to act on his behalf if I saw fit. If the council decides to accept Kern's terms, I can accept them on Bressen's behalf as well. The issue is that Aidan will also need to accept them, and that's obviously an issue."

Samhail exhaled deeply. "I'll let Jasper know the situation when I speak with him today."

Axenus took a sip of whatever he was drinking. Gods, the liquid in his cup looked green.

"You're bringing her with you?" the merman asked, nodding at Talyn.

"I don't have much choice," Samhail said. "I can't put her back in the dungeon with Morland, and I can't leave her unattended."

"You can, but you won't," Talyn corrected.

"Do…you want me to take her with me?" Axenus offered hesitantly.

"He won't do that either," Talyn said before Samhail could answer. "He's afraid I'd eat you alive, and he'd be right."

Axenus raised a brow at her but then looked back at Samhail. "Is that true?" he asked. "You don't trust me to keep an eye on her?"

"It's more like I don't trust her not to be a pain in your ass," Samhail said, glaring at Talyn. "Or maybe I just want to bring her with me so I can shove my cock down her throat again. At least it would keep her quiet."

Something flashed in her eyes, but he couldn't tell if it was surprise, anger, or…desire. Maybe all three.

Axenus sighed. "Forget I suggested anything," he said, shaking his head. "I'm not touching whatever this is."

Samhail

After breakfast, they all headed to the Priory. With Cyra gone, they needed to rely on Phaedrus for portaling. Samhail hated to impose on the priest, who – as Bressen recently reminded him – had other duties that kept him busy, but it couldn't be helped. Phaedrus was the only one in Callanus they knew of who could draw portals, and the alternative was to spend days traveling back and forth to where they needed to be.

The priest had managed to keep his portaling ability a secret until a few months ago. Portaling was incredibly useful, and the priest would've been called upon incessantly to move people from place to place if others knew of his power. As it was, Bressen was the only one who'd known about it for quite some time, and only because he'd read it in the priest's mind at some point decades ago. Now that Phaedrus's secret was out, Bressen had decreed only the Lords of the Triumvirate and the Priory's high priest could call upon Phaedrus to portal them, or in Axenus and Samhail's case, only those designated by the Triumvirate.

Phaedrus sent Axenus through to Gendris before he closed the portal and turned to Samhail.

"Seatherny first?" the priest asked.

"Yes," Samhail said. "Aidan's new portal master can send us to Solandis when we're done."

Phaedrus nodded and drew open a portal. Jasper and Maziren stood on the other side waiting, and Samhail ushered Talyn through into the palace at Seatherny, Derridan's capital.

Talyn

A look of shock crossed Jasper's face as Talyn stepped through the portal while Maziren's hand went to her sword.

Talyn smiled at Aidan's Captain of the Guard. She'd heard the woman was a formidable warrior, one that had supposedly given Samhail a challenge months ago, but she was confident she could hold her own against the tiny woman. She hoped to test that out some day.

"I thought she was supposed to be in the dungeon with Morland," Jasper said to Samhail, gesturing to Talyn.

"Bressen is out of range, so Morland is free from his mind control," Samhail said. "It wasn't safe to leave her down there with him. She has a caronium cuff, though, and I won't let her do anything to you."

Jasper cocked his head. "I'm not worried she'll hurt me," he said. He looked at Talyn. "I'm just surprised you were willing to let Morland out of your sight. Bressen told me…" He paused. "Never mind."

Talyn looked at the lord consort with interest. "You're not afraid of me," she observed. "Why not?"

Jasper returned her look. "I was told you helped Lord Bressen escape. He said you used a lot of power to ensure both he and Aidan…uh, Morland got away."

"True," Talyn said, "but didn't he tell you I was the one who put him in danger in the first place?"

Jasper shrugged. "He did, but he also said why, and I suppose I can't fault you. Believe me, if I could kill Morland right now, I would."

Talyn locked eyes with the lord consort, and a shared understanding passed between them before Jasper looked away again. Morland had been pretending to be Jasper's husband these last couple weeks, and she knew enough about Morland to suspect it hadn't been a pleasant experience for Jasper or anyone else in the palace.

"That reminds me," Samhail said to Jasper, "I suggest you forego your visits to the dungeon until Bressen is back. You'll only be subjecting yourself to Morland's viciousness. It's why I had to pull Talyn out."

Jasper was quiet a moment before he sighed heavily and nodded. "I understand." He gestured to the meeting table. "Shall we get on with business then?"

The three of them sat down while Maziren took up a place behind Jasper, and Talyn eyed her surroundings as she always did in a new place.

The ceiling of the room was high, and the inner wall was made of some kind of white stone, quartz perhaps. The opposite wall was made almost entirely of large glass windows that looked out over the city. It gave the room an open, airy look that was emphasized by the simple décor. The only things in it were the long table in the center, the fourteen chairs around it, and a few large potted plants that gave the bright room a pop of color. It was simple but stately.

"There's been some news from Kern," Samhail told Jasper. "I'm not sure of the details, but Axenus is in Gendris today speaking with the High Council. If they agree to Kern's terms, it sounds like Axenus will accept them on Bressen's behalf as well. Unfortunately, because something like this has the potential to affect the Triumvirate, we'll need Aidan's approval as well. The real Aidan, that is, and as you know, that's not possible right now. I'm not sure where that leaves us. Bressen appointed Axenus as a regent while he's away, so I suppose we could argue Aidan would've appointed you as regent in a case like this, but if you have any other ideas, we're happy to entertain them."

Jasper thought for a moment. "It depends on what the timeline is to respond to Kern," he said. "I'd want to wait as long as possible to see if we can restore Aidan before I make any moves on his behalf."

Samhail nodded. "Understood."

Jasper opened his mouth to speak but closed it again.

"What is it?" Samhail asked.

Jasper hesitated another moment before answering. "Has Lady Raina been included in any of these negotiations with Kern?" he asked.

Talyn saw the muscles in Samhail's jaw tighten.

"I don't know for sure, but from what I know of the High Council, I doubt it," Samhail said finally.

Jasper nodded slowly. "And does Lady Cyra know about them?"

Samhail's jaw flexed again. "I haven't asked, but I hope for Bressen's sake she does."

Jasper sighed. "Well, keep me posted."

Samhail nodded. "Have there been any issues since I was last here?"

"Nothing we haven't been able to handle," Jasper said, "but the palace staff are getting suspicious. We told them Aidan doesn't feel well, but we've had to make excuses when the healers ask to see him, so there are rumors he's gone. Short of showing them Aidan, there isn't much we can do. When Lord Bressen returns, perhaps he can bring Aidan and have him walk around the palace so everyone can see him."

Talyn cleared her throat. "I can help with your problem," she said, and all eyes swung to her. She held up the caronium cuff. "If you were willing to remove this."

"No." Samhail's response was immediate and unequivocal.

She blinked. She knew he wouldn't like the idea, but she hadn't expected quite so vehement a rejection.

"Let's not be hasty," Jasper said, holding up a hand. "I understand your reticence, but she has a point. Her power may be just what we need."

"Absolutely not," Samhail said. "You have no idea how dangerous she is without that thing. Three hells, she's dangerous even with it on."

Talyn felt a swell of pride to hear him say so, and she smiled at him. "Thank you," she said, and he glared at her.

"I agree with Samhail, Lord Consort," Maziren said from behind Jasper. "We can't let a shapeshifting assassin loose in the palace."

Talyn gave the captain of the guard a look of challenge. "Afraid you won't be able to handle me?"

Samhail flashed her a look of warning, but Maziren only straightened and returned Talyn's stare.

"Any time you want to try me, girl," the captain said.

"Ladies," Jasper said placatingly.

"Lord Consort," Talyn said, turning back to him, "I'm no more dangerous than letting rumors spread around the palace, and eventually the city, that Lord Aidan is missing. I understand I've done little to earn your trust thus far, but I think I've at least proven I won't just kill you all for the fun of it. If you don't take me up on my offer now, it may be too late by the time you realize you should've trusted me."

"No," Samhail said again, but there was less certainty in his voice now.

"Half an hour," Talyn said. "Remove the cuff for half an hour and let me walk around the palace as Aidan so as many servants and guards can see me as possible, then I'll let you put the cuff back on. I promise."

She gave Samhail a serious look that she hoped conveyed her sincerity.

"Lord Consort, no," Maziren said urgently from behind Jasper. "You can't really be considering letting this woman loose in Seatherny."

Talyn met Jasper's gaze. She wasn't sure what she saw in his face, but she wouldn't try to convince him any further. He seemed like a smart and fair man, and he'd make his own judgement. Trying to sell him on the idea too strongly would only backfire.

Several seconds rebounded off the walls in the silence of the room.

"I think we should try it," Jasper said finally. He addressed Talyn. "You think you can shift into Aidan well enough to fool his own people?"

"The one issue is Aidan's size," she said. "I can only stretch my body so far. I might have to shave an inch or two off his height, maybe make him a little leaner, but that might work to our advantage. You've told everyone he's sick, so if he looks smaller and thinner, it only sells your story. Your people will see a sicker, weaker version of Aidan, but they'll at least see him."

Jasper considered this.

"Jasper, I…" Samhail said, but he trailed off as he looked at Talyn.

She looked right back at him, daring him to say he didn't trust her. She knew she didn't deserve his trust, but she still wanted it, and it would be a stab to her gut to hear him say what she knew he wanted to.

Samhail let out a deep sigh through his nose. "Fine," he said to Jasper. "If you want me to take the cuff off her I will. We can try it."

Jasper nodded. "Is there a way to get her into our bedroom without the guards noticing? They'll need to see her come out of the bedroom to make it believable."

"Do you have a balcony, and is it unlocked?" Samhail asked.

"Yes. It should be," Jasper said. "It's on the east side of the palace. I can show you where."

Samhail turned to Maziren. "If you can distract any guards in that area or get them away somehow, I can fly Talyn up to the balcony."

A muscle ticked in Maziren's jaw, but she nodded. "If I can't talk you out of this, then yes. I can do that."

They all rose and followed Jasper out of the room toward the east courtyard. Once there, Maziren rounded up everyone in the area and made them follow her. What she planned to tell them, Talyn had no idea, but she didn't have time to consider it.

"Meet us up in the room," Samhail told Jasper as his giant leathery wings unfurled behind him.

Jasper nodded and hurried off as Samhail wrapped an arm around Talyn's waist and pulled her against him.

"Hold on," he told her only a second before his wings gave several mighty beats, and they shot upward toward the balcony.

Talyn barely held in her shriek of surprise as she threw her arms around his neck. By the time she registered what happened, her feet had already touched down on the balcony, and Samhail hurried them inside.

"Sweet gods above," she said as she steadied herself. "A little warning next time please." She tried to step away from him, but he grabbed her arm and pulled her against him again.

"Don't give me a reason to regret this," he said. "Bressen isn't around to stop me from crushing your neck this time."

He wrapped one hand gently around her throat, but somehow the way his thumb caressed the column of her neck was more sensual than threatening, and she bit her lip.

"Don't worry," she said huskily. "I won't do anything naughty before you've had a chance to fuck my ass." She ran a hand over his groin, and she felt him harden as he grunted loudly. Gods, it was almost too easy.

Samhail swore as he took his hand off her throat so he could pull hers away from his groin. He stepped back, mumbling something about the gods hating him.

The door at the other end of the room opened, and Jasper slipped in.

"Is everything ready?" he asked as he strode to Talyn and Samhail.

Samhail fished in his pocket and pulled out a small key. Talyn held the caronium cuff out to him. He took her wrist, and after a deep breath, removed the cuff.

Talyn considered porting into the closet to hide, just to see if he'd explode, but she resisted the urge. Instead, she shifted into Aidan, albeit a thinner, slightly shorter version of him.

She turned to Jasper to let him inspect her. The look in his eyes was pained, but he nodded.

"It's a good enough likeness that it'll fool anyone but me and Maziren," he said. "This may actually work."

"Are we just going to walk around the palace?" Samhail asked.

"You should probably stay here and let me and Talyn walk alone," Jasper suggested.

"Not a chance," Samhail said. "Wherever she goes, I go. I'll hang back, but I'm going with you."

"Then you'll need to meet us," Jasper said. "You can't leave the bedroom with us. Around the corner is Aidan's study. Fly over to that balcony and come out that way."

Samhail looked uncertain about leaving Talyn alone for even the minute or so it would take to do as Jasper asked, but he finally turned and strode back out on the balcony. After a look around to be sure no one was watching, he beat his wings and flew toward the side of the building Jasper had indicated.

"Are you ready?" Jasper asked her.

"Is there anything I should know before we go?" she asked.

"The guards at the door are Marsh and Elrid," Jasper said as they walked over. "Aidan knows all the guards' names and likes to greet them. I'll try to feed you names as we go. Otherwise, just keep it simple and say hello. We'll tell everyone you were feeling well enough to try walking around. We'll make a quick circuit of the main floor and then say you're tired and need to come back to rest."

Talyn nodded. "After you, Lord Consort."

Jasper reached to open the door, but he stopped and looked at Talyn.

"Is something wrong?" she asked.

"No, I…" He paused. "I just wanted to thank you for not killing

Aidan, for letting Bressen try to find a way to get Morland out of him."

Talyn went still at the look on Jasper's face. She knew it wasn't fair to kill Aidan in order to get rid of Morland, but she'd also forgotten Aidan had a husband who'd mourn him if she killed him.

Gods. How was she going to do this if Bressen and Cyra couldn't find a way to draw Morland out of Aidan's body?

Talyn swallowed down the knot in her throat. "I hope we find the solution to both our problems," she said with a weak smile.

Jasper smiled back, and they opened the door to find Marsh and Elrid facing down a tense and thunderous-looking Samhail who was trying to get them to open the door.

"Ah, Samhail," Jasper said genially. "My apologies for the delay. Aidan is still weak from his illness, and it took us a bit longer to get ready than anticipated. He's ready to see you now, though. Please follow us."

Chapter 42

Samhail

They had lunch in Seatherny, and then Jasper's portal master sent them straight to the army training camp in Hiraeth so Samhail could check on the progress of their troops.

The clang of steel instantly met Samhail's ears as they stepped through to the camp outside Solandis, and his body automatically tensed, then relaxed as he confirmed the sound was training and not real battle. Once he was sure of that, he actually found the noise rather soothing.

He glanced at Talyn and saw she was almost smiling. He furrowed his brow as something occurred to him.

"Where did you learn to fight?" he asked her as they walked toward the training field. "I don't imagine that's something they taught you at the house of pleasure."

She gave a small laugh. "You might be surprised how useful wrestling moves could be there," she said, then laughed again as Samhail stopped walking to stare at her. "I'm kidding. Mostly. But no, I learned to fight the same way these men are learning, by training in a war camp."

He frowned at her as they started walking again. "I didn't realize Rowe's war camps accepted women," he said. "We only just started a few years ago here in Thasia."

"Strictly speaking, they don't accept women," she said, "but then strictly speaking, I wasn't a woman when I trained in one."

"You signed up as a boy," he concluded.

"I learned some of my stealthier skills on the streets, but to get started, I spent a year training in the camp after my sister died. The grounds were on the outskirts of the city, but we had a horse, so I rode out one day to watch the men and boys train. That's how I met Rob."

"Rob?" he asked. He didn't like the turn her story had taken.

"Rob was about a year older than me at the time. I'd just turned fifteen, and he was sixteen. That was the age Rowe expected young men to begin their training, and he'd just started at the camp. He noticed me watching that first day and approached me later. I thought he might hurt me, but he gave me some food he'd saved from his lunch instead. He thought I was some homeless urchin who'd walked all the way out there."

The tension in Samhail's spine eased a bit to hear the boy had been kind. He liked to think he would've done the same if he'd been in that situation, but, in truth, he probably wouldn't have noticed a young girl watching him train.

He'd been much older than sixteen when he'd entered the training camp Bressen's father oversaw, and he'd been entirely too full of himself to pay attention to things like that. Bressen had been the one to take him down a peg or two. Samhail had underestimated the lord's son, thinking him to be a pampered brat, but Bressen's combat preparation had started early, and he'd come to the camp already well-trained.

Samhail had the size advantage in their first sparring match, but underestimating Bressen had cost him early on in the fight, as the small scar just under his jawline attested. He'd made the healer leave it there as a reminder not to take himself too seriously, although it had still taken him several decades for the message to really sink in.

"This Rob taught you to fight?" Samhail asked.

"Sometimes," she said. "At first, we became friends. I watched him train, then when he was done for the day, we'd spend time together. He'd walk me through what he learned. Eventually it wasn't enough. I'd shown him my powers by then, and I told him I wanted to join the army. He tried to talk me out of it, but I showed up the next day as a boy and signed up. Rowe has been unstable since Sandrian lost the war against Thasia, and at the time they needed all the fighters they could get, so they didn't look very hard at the forged documents I presented. Hells, I probably could've just walked onto the training field that day without any paperwork at all, and they would've taken me."

"And your mother had no idea you were doing this?" he asked as they stopped at the edge of the training field to watch the men practice.

She shook her head. "My mother was grieving Julia. She spent more and more time working at the pleasure house. I only saw her in the evenings when I went there for my own lessons."

Samhail's body went rigid. "Your lessons?"

"They were mostly lessons in etiquette and seduction, like how to move my body to entice someone." She shrugged. "Ultimately they came in handy when I became an assassin."

"So you didn't have to...," he started to ask, but trailed off.

"I was made to watch the other courtesans," she said, "although thankfully not my mother. I only started more 'hands on' training just before I became The Raptor."

"Hands on?" he prompted, unable to stop himself. He had to know.

"How to pleasure someone with my hands and mouth," she clarified.

He closed his eyes. "You were only fifteen?"

"I'd just turned sixteen by then. The madame was planning to auction off my virginity to the highest bidder in a few weeks. As it turned out, I gave it to Rob the day before he was sent out with the army to quell a rebellion in the Murthland province."

Samhail loosed a deep breath. At the start of her story, he'd been dreading the idea she might've given her virginity to this boy, yet now it was a relief to know she had. It was infinitely preferable to having some rich lord two or three times her age take it from her.

"How was it?" he asked.

She gave a short laugh. "About as good as it can be between two teenage virgins trying to figure out what fits where. I'd seen a lot of people have sex by then, but that didn't mean I knew what I was doing."

He chuckled. "That sounds about right."

She looked at him. "Was your first time that awkward?"

"It was awkward in an entirely different way," he said. "My two older siblings, Soldier and Sadira, took me to a pleasure house and paid a courtesan to introduce me to the joys of sex. I was fourteen."

He looked over at her when he was met with silence and found she was staring at him with her mouth open.

"Fourteen?" she said, aghast. "The courtesan actually agreed to deflower a fourteen-year old?"

Samhail gave a half shrug. "I doubt she knew how young I was. I was a very large fourteen-year old, and it's common for gargoyles to start having sex fairly young. It's cultural."

She stared at him for several more seconds. "So how was it?" she finally asked.

He shrugged again. "I suppose I should be grateful they paid for a courtesan rather than a regular prostitute. The woman knew what she was doing. I'm pretty sure I blacked out at least once or twice while she was…uh, servicing me."

Talyn's brows shot up, and he gave her a half smile.

"What happened with you and Rob when he returned?" he asked.

Her face fell, and he knew immediately what the answer was.

"He didn't make it back," she said quietly. "From what I heard when his unit returned, he fell the first day of fighting. It was quick at least. A sword through his neck."

"I'm sorry."

She shook her head. "I didn't have time to dwell on it. I'd been tracking a man I thought might've killed Julia by then, so I mourned for Rob later." She sighed. "As it turns out, I killed the wrong person."

He didn't know what to say to that, so they stood watching the training in silence.

"You have them training with spears instead of swords," she said.

He hesitated, not sure he should tell her about what they suspected was coming, but he couldn't see the harm.

"Cyra saw a vision of an army of symbionts. The men do train with shortswords as well, but we felt it was important for them to learn to fight with spears since it will give them a longer reach. They need to be able to stay away from the symbionts' claws as long as possible."

Samhail looked at her and found she was staring at him again.

"An army of symbionts?" she asked in horror, and he nodded.

Talyn shook her head in disbelief and looked back at the men.

"They're not nearly ready to face an army of those things," she said.

"Maybe you can help me train them until Bressen returns," Samhail suggested. "I'm sure they'd benefit from working with you."

"You keep trying to turn me into a trainer," she said with a smile. "In my experience, though, men aren't typically receptive to letting a woman tell them how to fight."

"These men will be when I get done with them," he said.

She side-eyed him. "You think threats will make a difference?"

Samhail paused, then grinned. "No, they need to see you in action."

She raised a brow, but Samhail put his fingers to his lips and made a loud, high-pitched whistle that echoed around the yard. Instantly all the fighting stopped as the men gave him their attention.

"What are you doing?" Talyn asked under her breath.

"Good work, men," Samhail said, stepping forward. "You've all been training hard, and I'd like to see what you've learned by putting you up against one of the best fighters I've ever had the misfortune to face."

He gestured to Talyn, and her eyes went wide.

It didn't surprise Samhail to hear soft laughter ripple over the field from the men, but it did annoy him. This is exactly why he had to do this.

"This is Talyn of Avril," he went on. "She's nearly killed me at least twice, and she's agreed to work with you for the next few weeks."

Talyn made a noise of protest, but it was lost as half the men laughed harder while the other half looked between each other, no longer sure if Samhail was joking or not. In their defense, had Talyn been a man, they still might not have believed she'd almost killed him.

Samhail put a hand on Talyn's back and pressed her forward so she was in front of him. Then he stepped away.

"A gold piece to the first man who can land a hit on her," he said.

A murmur went up from the men as Talyn snapped around to look at him incredulously.

"What?" she cried.

Samhail only addressed the men again.

"You might want to press your advantage before she can get to the weapons rack and arm herself," he said as he winked at her.

Talyn's head whipped around again to look at the long rack of weapons that stood mostly empty about a hundred feet across the yard. Almost fifty men stood between her and the rack.

She turned back to him and held up her wrist with the caronium cuff on it in question.

He crossed his arms and shook his head.

"I'm going to slit your throat in your sleep tonight," she said as she glared at him.

He only chuckled.

"And forget about ever getting between my legs again," she added.

That made him scowl.

"I suggest you stop talking and get moving," he said. "It's a long way to that weapons rack, and there are a lot of men you need to get through."

Talyn scoffed. "I don't need to get to the weapons rack," she said. "I just need to get to *him*."

She gestured to a man close by who was swinging his spear with great flourishes and who looked all too eager to engage her.

Talyn turned and shot straight for him. The man looked shocked to have her bearing down on him, but then he smiled and raised his spear high, ready to bring it swinging down on her.

Samhail sighed. Clearly the man had learned nothing in his time here. Raising his weapon like that left his entire midsection open to attack, a move that would get him killed or taken over by the symbionts.

Samhail expected Talyn to punch the man in the gut, but she dropped down to slide feet-first on the grass toward him. The man's eyes widened as her slide took out one of his ankles, and with his body unbalanced from holding the spear aloft, he went crashing forward onto the ground. The spear was jarred loose from his grip, and a moment later Talyn had snatched it up and was on her feet again. She knocked him across the back of his head with the butt of it.

It had all taken seconds, and there was dead silence in the yard as the men took in what she'd just done. Then a roar went up as half the men surged toward her. Talyn sprang into action and began to fend them off, the blade of her stolen spear flashing in the sunlight.

Samhail stood on the side and took note of which men backed away, recognizing they were outmatched, and which men barreled at her with only male bravado driving them. Only a small few stood to watch her fight, taking in her moves, and waiting for their opening.

He hadn't sent the soldiers after Talyn with any particular purpose in mind, but it was a useful exercise nonetheless. It gave him an idea which soldiers were overly cautious, which ones were reckless, and which ones might actually have some good battle sense.

It also told him who might have an issue with women on the battlefield, which was important, given that he expected a cohort of female volunteers next week. After a period of separation, he'd been hoping to mix them in with the men for training, but he'd have to keep an eye out for potential troublemakers.

Samhail knew Talyn would put on a good show for the men, but even he was surprised at how handily she took care of his troops. He hadn't appreciated just how fast she was, even without her ability to port, and she seemed to have a sixth sense about when a weapon was swinging toward her. He watched in amazement as she blocked blow after blow, even diving out of the way once just in time so the two attackers charging her from opposite directions nearly ended up running each other through with the blunted spears.

The only other fighter he'd seen come close to her skill was Maziren. Bressen and Axenus were both good warriors, fast and skilled, but

Maziren was better than them both, and based on what he saw now, Talyn might be even better than Maziren. The captain of the guard had strength on her side, which had been an equalizer against Samhail himself when they'd sparred in Derridan during the lord trials, but Talyn made up for her limited strength with raw skill. He'd assumed at first her stealth was what made her dangerous and that she had little beyond her porting ability, but he was learning more and more just how wrong he'd been.

Thinking of Maziren reminded him he needed to talk to Talyn at some point. Given how much she dwelled on his involvement with Cyra, it was probably better to tell her now rather than later that he and Maziren had been together – in a way – as well.

He knew Maziren would never say a word, but he didn't want there to be secrets between him and Talyn. He'd have to find a way to tell her that didn't make her want to kill him or Maziren. In fact, he should probably warn Maziren before he said anything to Talyn, just in case.

Samhail was pulled back from his reverie when he realized the sound of clanging weapons had stopped. He'd missed the last few minutes of the fight, and Talyn now stood alone in the center of the field, the bodies of groaning men strewn about her feet.

Damn it. He'd wanted to see if any of the men who'd watched Talyn first before engaging her had given her a challenge. He'd have to ask her if she thought any of them were particularly skilled.

Samhail stepped forward, motioning his training captains in.

"That was incredible," one of them said to him. "Please tell me she's on our side."

Samhail wasn't sure how to answer that. Instead, he gestured to the men standing around the edges, the ones who'd been too nervous – or perhaps too smart – to engage Talyn.

"Anyone still standing runs five miles," Samhail told the captains. "And starting tomorrow, they'll all work in the same group until we get them over their hesitancy to act."

The captains all nodded and two broke off to round up the men who'd be running.

"Get the rest of these men up, and see if there are any major injuries," Samhail went on to the remaining captains. "Anyone you think gave her a good fight runs a mile. Everyone else runs the gauntlet."

The captains hurried off to enact his orders.

Samhail turned to see Talyn still standing in the middle of the field, the spear she'd taken from the first man hanging by her side. He walked toward her, stepping over a few men who still lay on the ground, and stopped in front of her.

"That was impressive," he said. "I really thought one of them would eventually land a hit."

"I'm going to kill you in your sleep tonight," she said again.

Her voice shook, and at first he thought she really was angry at him, but then he noticed her legs trembling.

"You're tired," he said as it hit him that she'd just taken on about thirty men. And won.

Her answer was to collapse onto the ground to sit there with the spear across her lap.

He smiled. "Is the assassin not used to fighting for long periods of time?" he teased.

"I *will* kill you," she said again, just barely above a whisper.

Samhail chuckled, and his giant leathery wings sprang out behind him. There were gasps and murmurs from the men around them, but Samhail only pulled the spear from Talyn's hand to drop it on the ground next to her. Then he scooped her up and launched into the air with her to head to Tide's End.

Tandem Read: Go to *Nemesis Rising* (Bk 4), Chapters 31-35

Chapter 43

Several Days After the Training Camp

Samhail

Samhail let his thumb graze along Talyn's stomach as he lay in bed with her at the Citadel, more content than he could remember being in a long time. Her back was tucked up against him while she slept, and he'd curled his giant body around her to hold her close as morning sunlight streamed into the room. Despite what she'd told him once about liking her space, this was how they slept at night now, and he loved it. It was new to him as well, but he'd adapted surprisingly fast.

He brushed his thumb higher so it skimmed the underside of her naked breast. She didn't move, and he smiled. A week ago, any touch would've woken her instantly, ready to fight. That she didn't stir now told him she was comfortable enough to relax her guard around him, that she trusted him to watch over her while she slept.

He didn't let himself think too deeply about why this made him happy. If anything, it just meant she might consider staying with him once all this was over. That, in turn, meant he could continue to fuck her whenever he wanted, which was his new favorite thing to do.

He'd taken her straight to Tide's End from the training camp that first day, rather than messaging Phaedrus for a portal back to Callanus. He'd just wanted to be alone with her, and he'd pushed her against the wall as soon as he'd gotten back to his room at the manor. He'd been rock-hard already and needed a minute to collect himself after flying back with her in his arms.

"What's wrong?" she'd asked, her body tense.

"What's wrong," he'd said breathlessly, "is that watching you take out half a unit of my soldiers today made me want to fuck you so hard you'll feel my cock inside you long after I've pulled out."

Her eyes had flared, and he'd kissed her soundly before he picked her up, laid her on the bed, stripped her naked, and buried his face between her thighs. He'd made her come until her legs were shaking.

He'd given her a few minutes to recover after that as he undressed, then he'd reached into his nightstand to pull out his bottle of oil. He'd pulled the key to the caronium cuff from his pocket and removed the cuff, then flipped her on her stomach. To his relief, she didn't port.

"I'm going to take your ass now," he'd told her as he pulled her to her knees and pressed her shoulders down to open her fully to him.

"I thought you were going to take some time to prepare me?" she'd said over her shoulder.

"You have your powers back. What more do you need to prepare?"

She'd whimpered softly but didn't object.

Despite his eagerness, though, he had in fact taken the time to prepare her slowly, using his fingers to stretch her open while he massaged her clit. When she was moaning beneath him and pushing back against his fingers, only then did he slather his cock liberally with the oil and notch himself at her ass.

He wouldn't have considered trying it with any other woman, but he'd been counting on her body's malleability to accommodate him, and it did. Talyn had let out a long moan as he'd pushed past the first ring of muscle, and Samhail's eyes had rolled back in his head to feel her close around him. Even with her body's ability to shift, she was so tight.

He'd continued to go slow, entering, waiting, withdrawing, then pushing in a bit further each time until his hips were pressed tightly to her body. She let out a low groan of pleasure when he was finally all the way in, and his cock had twitched at the sound.

"Are you alright?" he'd asked, willing himself not to move.

Her breath had stuttered, and her "Yes" was nearly a whisper. He'd been about to question her again to be sure when she started to move on her own, to rock herself against him so his cock slid in and out of her.

"Fuuck." He drew out the word as the fact she was letting him claim her in everyway possible made him harder than he'd ever been.

He'd tried to go slow, but the feel of her squeezing around him had made him erupt inside her after only a couple minutes. It was the quickest he'd come in decades, but he'd been unable to hold back his climax at the feel of her and the thought of what she was letting him do. He'd always wanted to try this, but he'd resigned himself to never being able to.

He'd fucked Talyn every night since then, but only one other time in her ass. Now that he'd done it, he didn't feel the need as strongly anymore. It was enough for him to know he was the first and only one to ever claim all of her entrances, although he took care not to show her how much that pleased him.

Talyn still made a show of trying to resist him every night when they went to bed, but the one time he'd called her bluff and turned over to pretend to sleep, he'd felt her fingers trace down his back a few minutes later. She'd insisted she was just fascinated by his muscles, but she hadn't protested when he'd spread her legs, settled between them, and drove into her until she'd come three times on his cock.

Actually, for someone who once claimed to be unseducible, she spent an inordinate amount of time with him inside her now.

For one, she enjoyed being woken by sex. She'd told him once, semi-jokingly, that he could go ahead and fuck her in the morning as long as he didn't wake her, and he'd taken her up on it the next day. He'd dipped his head below the covers, parted her thighs, and licked her until she'd popped awake with a cry of pleasure.

Sometimes he hooked a hand under her knee to pull her leg open, then pushed into her from behind as she slept. He'd fuck her slowly until she woke, then he'd drive into her until she found her release. He liked to see how long it took before she became conscious and began moaning into her pillow. Once, he'd been able to slide carefully in and out of her for two whole minutes before she jolted awake and gasped with pleasure. Then he'd fucked her in earnest.

Outside the bedchamber, they'd fallen into a routine this week.

Once they got up, they bathed, dressed, and met Axenus for breakfast, where the merman would greet them with the beleaguered sigh of a man who wished the walls and doors of the fortress were thicker.

They'd gone to Seatherny once more to talk to Jasper, and Talyn had made another appearance as Aidan. The other days they trained together in the mornings. A couple times they'd gone for a run around the grounds, but usually they fought with blades to keep their skills sharp, although Samhail didn't fight as hard as he could, and he suspected neither did she.

Still, they didn't go easy on each other either, and it wasn't unusual for them to both be bloody and bruised when they were done. That inevitably led Samhail to push her into the storage room or some other secluded place and fuck her some more. Those times she begged him to take her harder, and more than once he'd had to clamp his hand over her mouth to stifle her scream so the house guards didn't come running.

Their afternoons were spent at the army training camp, and Samhail was pleased to see the men now showed Talyn a deference that bordered on awe. Even those from other units who hadn't seen her fight treated her as if she were a general, saluting her and calling her ma'am, much to her amusement. Even more amazingly, they paid close attention when she instructed them, and they seemed to try harder when she was around.

Samhail still saw a resentful look here or there, and he took note of who made them so he could tell Talyn who to keep an eye on. He had the urge to let those men see his gargoyle side, but he didn't think Talyn wanted him to fight her battles for her, so he let her handle things her own way. Usually.

Talyn's own way had included nearly breaking the finger of one man who'd dared to slap her ass one day. Within seconds she'd grabbed him and forced him to his knees where he whimpered in pain as she bent his finger back at a harsh angle.

Samhail hadn't heard what she'd said to the man when she whispered in his ear, but the man had gone pale and apologized profusely.

He should've left it at that, but Samhail hadn't been able to help himself. He'd strode over to the man on his knees after Talyn walked away, offered his hand, and pulled the man up. Then he'd grabbed the man around the back of his neck and said under his breath, "Touch something that belongs to me again, and I'll rip your hand off."

The man had gone even paler and hurried away.

It was the wrong thing to do. The next day, word had spread about Samhail's threat, and the men were too afraid to even look at Talyn. She'd been livid when she pried the story out of one of the soldiers.

Samhail had seen her stalking toward him and frowned at the murderous look in her eyes. Before he could ready himself, she'd rammed her knee into his stomach, and he'd doubled over. She'd then somehow swung her legs up around his neck and used her body weight to pull him the rest of the way so he flipped and landed hard on his back.

It had just barely worked, but his breath punched out of him when he hit the ground, and he'd had enough sense to stay down as Talyn rose and brushed herself off.

"First of all," she told the men, who were now gaping at her, "I don't belong to him. If any of you touch me inappropriately, it's me you should worry about, not him."

A murmur of ascent went up among those watching.

"You should keep your hands to yourself because I deserve your respect," she went on, "and that respect shouldn't depend on what I may or may not be to him."

There was another murmur of ascent, softer this time, and a number of men cast their eyes to the ground. Samhail hadn't bothered to move from where he lay flat on his back.

"Back to it!" Talyn yelled, and the men hurried to resume training.

She stood over Samhail then and angled her head in question. "Are you planning to lay on the ground all day?" she asked.

"Am I allowed to get up?" he countered.

"If you promise to never, ever do that again."

He got to his feet. "I apologize," he said. "You had it handled yesterday. I shouldn't have stepped in."

She only looked at him, seeming to expect more. "And?"

He frowned. Then it came to him. "And you don't belong to me."

"No, I don't," she said and walked away.

Yet, he added in his mind as he watched her go. *But you will.*

He'd given up any gentlemanly thoughts about Talyn, about how she didn't belong to him and other such chivalrous bullshit. She was his, and one of these days she'd realize it, because he didn't plan on letting her go or letting anyone else have her. He'd allowed his inner beast to take over where she was concerned, and the beast had staked his claim.

That incident had been two days ago, and it was the one time she'd actually denied him sex later that night. His balls had been as blue as sapphires by the next morning when she'd finally had mercy on him. He'd plunged into her in one deep thrust when she'd finally given him permission to touch her, and the rest was a blur of ecstasy.

Samhail groaned now as he remembered the relief of being inside her, and he tried to decide whether to spread her thighs or let her sleep.

The decision was taken out of his hands when a loud knock sounded at his door, and Talyn jolted awake.

"What was that?" she asked. She started to sit up quickly, but Samhail eased her back down.

"It's just someone at the door. Likely Axenus," he said. "I'll get rid of him, and then I'm coming back to climb between your legs."

She turned over and pulled the covers up. "It's a wonder I can still walk with how often you end up there," she grumbled.

Samhail chuckled and swung his legs out of bed. She might complain now, but in a few minutes, she'd have her legs wrapped around him, refusing to let him withdraw.

The knock sounded again, louder this time.

"I'm coming, Axe," Samhail yelled across the room. "Give a man a minute to find his pants."

He found the loose pair of sleeping pants he used to wear to bed before Talyn had become a fixture there and pulled them on, then strode across the room to yank the door open.

"I thought you knew better by now than to-" he started to say, but the words cut off in his throat as he saw who stood in the doorway.

"You thought I knew better than to what?" the Lord of Hiraeth asked silkily as he stood there with a brow raised.

"Bressen," Samhail said in surprise. "When did you get back?"

Bressen stepped forward, and Samhail instinctively moved out of the way to let him pass.

"We returned last night, but we went straight to bed," he said. His eyes lit on Talyn. "Ah, and there's my missing prisoner. I suspected I might find her here."

Talyn bolted up to a sitting position and pulled the covers over her naked body. Bressen's gaze seemed to fix on her bare wrists, and he raised a brow at Samhail.

"I was afraid we'd lost her again," Bressen said, "but I suppose you felt the best way to avoid that was to keep her close." His turquoise eyes flashed as he smiled at Samhail. "Your dedication is truly appreciated."

Samhail rolled his eyes at the sarcasm. "I didn't plan to take her out of the dungeon, but your mind control over Morland lapsed when you got too far away, and he spent the day telling her the details of how he tortured her sister."

Bressen's face went stormy, and Samhail saw the brief flash of red in the lord's eyes that marked his anger.

"The bastard left that part out when I checked on him this morning," Bressen growled. Then his face eased. "I don't blame you for taking her out then. And naturally, the safest place to keep her was in your bed."

Samhail knew his friend wasn't actually angry about finding Talyn here, but Bressen also wasn't going to let the chance to tease him slip past.

"Axe offered to keep her in his room," Samhail said, crossing his arms, "but she said it was drier in here. So did you find what you were looking for, or did you just come in here to hold my balls over the fire?"

Bressen's face went serious. "We did find what we were looking for," he said, "and we have a possible plan to extract Morland from Aidan's body. We have no idea if it will work, but we at least have an option."

"How?" Talyn asked from across the room.

She leaned forward eagerly at Bressen's words, and Samhail gave her a look that warned her to stay put. As expected, she ignored him and tugged the sheet loose so she could wrap it around herself and come over. He was actually surprised she bothered to do that much. He wouldn't have put it past her to walk across the room naked.

Samhail glowered at Bressen as the lord's eyes followed Talyn all the way across the room while she dragged the giant sheet behind her like the train of a fancy gown. She stopped next to Samhail, apparently unconcerned by her state of undress. One hand held the sheet against her chest while her other held it closed at her side.

"How?" Talyn repeated when she was in front of them.

Bressen cocked his head, amused by her demand for answers. She remembered who she was talking to a moment later and tacked a "my lord" onto the end of her question.

Samhail took a small step closer to her and let his hand rest at the small of her back. The gesture didn't go unnoticed by Bressen, who gave him a pointed look. He glared back, silently conveying that he'd protect Talyn if it came down to it.

Not that he'd actually be able to do anything. If Bressen attacked, it would be with his mind, and there was little, short of knocking Bressen out, that he could do to stop him.

Samhail didn't want to think about whether he was prepared to go that far to keep Talyn safe. The choice should've been obvious, given that it was between his oldest friend and a woman he'd met weeks ago. A woman who'd tried to kill him more than once.

Yet somehow the choice wasn't obvious at all, and he prayed Bressen wouldn't do anything to hurt Talyn.

"We found a way to resurrect Morland's body," Bressen said finally as he looked between the two of them. "Or so we think."

"Resurrect him?" Samhail asked. "How do you plan to do that?"

"It's complicated and a bit of a long story that I'm not at liberty to tell right now," Bressen said, "but the crux of it is that we recovered one of Morland's bones from the battlefield where he died…uh, where his body died, and we have a way to – hopefully – restore his body using that bone. From there, Cyra will transfer his consciousness out of Aidan and back into his original body using the rings. Then…"

Bressen trailed off as his eyes landed on Talyn.

"Then I kill him," she said.

Bressen nodded once.

"So we're resurrecting him just to kill him?" Samhail asked. "That seems a bit…backwards, doesn't it? There's no way to just extract him from Aidan and send him straight to the three hells?"

"Not that we're aware of," Bressen said. "And trust me when I tell you we've considered every other possible option here. Morland's mind needs to die, but in order for his mind to die, it needs to be connected to a body that dies. He was able to survive the last two times because his mind somehow clung onto a living body. We can't put him into a body that's already occupied, and he can't be put into a dead body, so our only option is to re-create an unoccupied living body to put him in."

"And Cyra can do that?" Samhail asked.

Bressen hesitated. "Creating the body is the tricky part," he said finally, and Samhail had a feeling there was something he was leaving out.

"As for transferring Morland's mind," Bressen went on with a shrug, "Cyra did it once by accident. Now we'll just have to see if she can do it again on purpose."

Tandem Read: Go to *Nemesis Rising* (Bk 4), Chapter 36

Chapter 44

Talyn

Talyn didn't realize she was clenching her teeth until her jaw started to ache. She released the tension as she stared at the man who killed her sister where he stood in the training yard of the Citadel.

Well, she stared at the body that man was currently occupying, much like an invading force might occupy a conquered city. If by some miracle this worked and they were able to pull Morland's mind out of Aidan's body, she wasn't sure she'd ever be able to look at the Lord of Derridan again without seeing a monster.

Aidan's voice still echoed in her mind as she recalled Morland telling her in vivid detail everything he'd done to Julia. It hadn't been the voice her sister had heard, but it was the one Talyn would hear from now on whenever she thought of Julia's killer. It was all the more reason she needed to leave as soon as this was over. Even if this did work, she was afraid she'd be too tempted to kill Aidan, innocent though he was.

Talyn glanced to her side where Samhail stood. His jaw was clenched tightly as well, and she remembered that he had almost as much reason to hate Morland as she did. He'd told her how Morland had taken over his mind during the war and almost made him kill Bressen, and she tried to imagine what it would've been like if Morland had taken over her mind and forced her to kill Julia. It made her shudder.

Across from them, Jasper and Maziren stood waiting. Maziren's body was coiled, ready to strike, but Jasper looked as if he might collapse at any moment. His normally regal posture was gone as his body seemed to sag under its own weight, and anxiety was written over every inch of his face. He was paler than she'd ever seen him, and she looked away quickly when he caught her eye.

She turned back to Morland. He looked strangely at peace standing in the middle of the training yard as he waited patiently for her to kill him. Bressen had put him back under his mind control as soon as he'd returned from wherever he and Cyra had been.

Movement caught Talyn's eye, and she saw the Lord of Hiraeth and his wife heading toward them with Cyra's two shadows, the twins, following close behind. Bressen and Cyra had left to see to some 'last-minute preparations,' but they were back.

Talyn frowned. Cyra's eyes were red and puffy as if she'd been crying.

"Cyra? Are you alright?" Samhail asked, apparently noticing the same.

Cyra lifted her chin and tried to work a smile onto her face. "I'm fine," she said. "Let's get started."

The lady stepped forward and placed a bone on the ground in front of Morland. It was an ulna, or maybe a radius. Talyn could never keep the two forearm bones straight.

She had the sudden urge to stomp on the bone, but she reminded herself that – even if they managed to resurrect Morland – this wasn't the body that had abused her sister. That body was already dead and rotting.

Talyn closed her eyes and tried not to think too closely about it. It would give her a headache if she dwelled on the details. Regardless of what body he was wearing, it was Morland's…mind? His soul?…that had hurt Julia.

She didn't know what made Morland who he was, what compelled him, in whatever form he took, to hurt people. Not just hurt them, but take joy in hurting them. Delight in their pain and suffering. Whatever that thing was, Talyn was going to kill it, once and for all.

Perhaps it was hypocritical of her. She was an assassin after all, but aside from her first kill, when she'd admittedly relished the man's pain, she'd always tried to make her victims' deaths as quick and painless as possible. More than half the time, they'd never seen her coming.

Whether that made her a good person or not, whether she deserved a place in the three hells or not, was between her and the Nemesis.

Cyra stepped back from the bone she'd placed on the ground and held her hands out toward it. For several seconds, nothing happened. Then the bone began to vibrate.

Talyn gasped as the bone suddenly lurched upright to stand on end, and some kind of substance crept over it.

Flesh, she realized with a start. Flesh was regrowing over the bone.

She looked at Samhail, but he was transfixed by the scene before him. She may never have seen the real Morland, but Samhail had, and he was watching a man he'd thought he'd killed reform himself.

"Would you like to kill him instead?" Talyn asked him quietly.

She'd been so consumed with the idea of killing Morland herself that she'd never stopped to consider Samhail might want the honor.

For a moment it didn't seem he'd even heard her, then he dragged his gaze from the regrowing body and looked at her.

"Do you want to kill him? Instead of me?" she repeated.

He looked back at the bone for a long moment, then shook his head.

"I don't care who kills him as long as it's for good this time," he said. His eyes met hers again. "Make sure you finish him."

She nodded as she gripped the hilts of the daggers in her thigh sheaths. She'd been able to take her time with the man she'd thought had killed Julia. This time she'd need to kill as quickly and thoroughly as possible. Morland's mind had already proven it could hop bodies the way bees hopped flowers, and she didn't want to give it any chance to get out again once they had it where they wanted it.

One dagger to Morland's heart, the other to his neck should do it. Or maybe straight into his brain through his ear.

An arm, a shoulder, and part of a torso now stood on the ground as, little by little, flesh and more bone knit together in front of their eyes.

Nemesis take her. This was easily the most insane thing she'd ever witnessed, and Talyn had seen her share of unbelievable things.

Minutes passed as the body slowly filled in. Another arm, the stomach and back, hips, and soon legs were all there as the naked body of Morland appeared, crouching on the ground before them.

The head was the last thing to form, and the sharp features of a surprisingly young-looking man emerged. His hair was a light golden brown, and Talyn saw his eyes were ocean blue. Morland wasn't especially handsome – not like Bressen or Samhail – but he also wasn't the hideous beast Talyn had assumed him to be.

But then that was the danger of some monsters, their ability to look just like everyone else.

Whatever force or power had been regrowing Morland seemed to finish, and the body stood up from where it had been crouched, although its eyes remained vacant.

Talyn's hands closed tighter on the hilts of her daggers.

Cyra exhaled as she looked at the body that stood before them, and Talyn remembered the lady had never seen the real Morland either.

Bressen had, though, and every muscle in his body was strung taut, even those in his face. Something ticked wildly in his jaw, and she could almost hear his teeth grinding.

Cyra stepped forward and put one hand on Aidan's forehead and the other on the forehead of Morland's newly reformed body. She wore plain gold bands on each of her middle fingers, which Talyn had learned held the power to transfer things between them. Supposedly the rings had made it possible for Cyra to accidentally move Morland's mind out of his last body and into Aidan's in the first place.

Talyn drew her daggers and stepped forward as well. The moment they had confirmation Morland was out of Aidan, she'd kill him.

"I need to let his mind go now," Bressen told Cyra, and she nodded.

They'd discussed this earlier. They didn't want to leave Bressen's mind connected to Morland's and risk creating yet another opportunity for the man to jump bodies. Cyra would have to take over holding his mind as she simultaneously tried to transfer his consciousness.

Lord Aidan's body jerked but then stood still again, and Talyn assumed Bressen had ceded control to Cyra.

"Do you have him?" Bressen asked, and Talyn heard the nervous strain in his voice.

Cyra closed her eyes and looked to be concentrating. Her brow pinched further, and she shut her eyes tighter. "Yes, but he's fighting me," she said, her own voice strained.

"Hold onto him," Bressen urged. "You're stronger than him."

"I've got him, but I'm having trouble moving him," Cyra said.

The lady's body was nearly trembling with her efforts, and Talyn's own body started to shake as well. She wished she could transfer some of her strength to Cyra or that she could help hold Morland in some way, but there was nothing she could do.

"I'm going to try something," Cyra said through clenched teeth.

"Cyra…" Bressen's tone was cautionary, but a moment later, the crackle of electricity ignited the air, and the bright blue-white webs of Cyra's lightning skittered over both Aidan and Morland. The bodies jolted and fell to the ground. Cyra cried out and collapsed as well to crumple between the two men.

Bressen yelled and rushed forward, but Talyn got to Cyra first and pressed her fingers to the lady's neck.

"She's alive. Just unconscious," Talyn assured him. "Check Morland. We need to know if-"

Talyn didn't get to finish the thought as both her mind and body were seized at the same time. Morland's body – his real body – had lurched toward her to grab the dagger she'd resheathed when she'd checked on Cyra, and she felt the tip dig into the soft skin under her jaw. At the same time, pain blinded her as Morland crashed through her mind shield to hold her so she couldn't move. He'd been a mind wraith originally, and it appeared he still was, now that he was back in his original form.

"No!" Samhail bellowed from somewhere close by, but Talyn couldn't see him and couldn't turn her head to look.

"Stay back and stay out of my head, or I'll shove this dagger up into her brain," Morland said, and Talyn almost wanted to laugh at the slightly nasal tone of his real voice.

"Bressen, don't!" Samhail's voice was pleading.

Talyn knew she was nothing to Bressen, and she didn't doubt he'd sacrifice her to take Morland out, but Samhail, it seemed, wasn't willing to do the same.

There was a short pause before Bressen spoke. "Let her go, Morland. There's no way out of this for you."

Talyn couldn't see Bressen from the way her head was angled, but she imagined a look must've passed between Bressen and Samhail.

Whatever response Morland might've made was drowned out by Bressen's voice in her mind.

Can you fight his hold on you? the lord asked her. *I can try to help. He doesn't know I'm in your mind yet, but I'm not sure how long I can stay hidden before he feels me here and tries to kill you.*

I…don't…know, Talyn thought back. The pain wasn't as bad as when Bressen himself had taken over her mind, but it was still enough that she was having trouble focusing.

Try, Bressen said, and there was resignation in his voice. *We can't let Morland go, so if you can't get control of your mind back from him…*

Bressen let the thought hang in the air, but Talyn understood. If she couldn't save herself, he'd sacrifice her, regardless of Samhail's plea.

She began to fight.

Morland's hold was like a snake slowly constricting around her mind. The first thing she did was try to slip mental fingers between herself and him so she could pull him away. She felt Bressen's mind ease the way for her by subtly loosening the coils, and she forced her way through. The coils of Morland's mind squeezed harder in answer, and Talyn's mind blurred, but she had a hold now, and she pushed against his pressure.

I can give you five more seconds, Bressen warned. *Five…*

Talyn struggled to bring the world back into focus. She heard Samhail's voice faintly, as if he were somewhere off in the distance, but she couldn't hear what he was saying.

Four…

The coils of Morland's mind slipped a bit as she felt Bressen's power help her fight. She had the sense he was disguising his presence to make it seem as though only Talyn herself was fighting back.

Three…

Talyn yanked at the coils of Morland's power, but for every bit of room she gained, he took a little back.

Two…

There was still a chance Bressen could break through Morland's mind before Morland could kill her, but she wasn't willing to take that chance. She needed to free herself, needed to throw off Morland's control…Needed to kill him.

One.

Talyn broke free of Morland's mind control only half a second before Bressen himself crashed through Morland's own mind shield. She ported just as Morland tried to drive the dagger up into her jaw, and the blade met with empty air.

Her other dagger, however, did not.

Talyn appeared behind Morland and drove her dagger down as hard as she could into his spine at the base of his neck. She felt bone crunch, and Morland's scream of pain was drowned in the gurgle of blood as it filled his throat.

She didn't stop there, though. Talyn pulled the dagger from his spine – yanking it hard to dislodge it from bone – and stabbed it into Morland's brain through his ear as she'd planned. Adrenaline surged through her, and she pulled the blade free again only to slash it quickly across his neck for a third and final stroke, just to be sure.

Talyn felt the blood fleck her face with each attack, but – far from being warm – it was cold on her skin, like a chilly Autumn rain.

She pushed Morland's corpse forward into the ground and fell backward away from it, breathing heavily.

Hard muscled arms wrapped around her shoulders and waist from behind, and she instinctively jerked her dagger toward whoever was trying to grab her. A large hand clamped down on her wrist, staying the dagger, and she was about to port when the now-familiar sent of leather and earth hit her nose.

"Are you hurt?" Samhail asked against her ear, and the whisper of his breath across her skin instantly quelled her panic.

When had his presence begun to soothe her?

"I'm…fine," Talyn said, still trying to catch her breath.

She let herself relax against Samhail as she tried to slow her heart, which beat a rapid pace in her chest.

"Is he…?" Talyn asked as she looked at Morland's body, its blood seeping into the earth.

"He's very dead," Bressen said, also looking at the body. "At least his body is."

Bressen and Samhail looked at each other, and they both seemed to have the same thought. Samhail moved faster. He let go of Talyn and surged forward so suddenly that she fell backward, and then his large hand was wrapped around Bressen's neck.

"What was the first thing I said to you when we met at the training camp?" Samhail asked Bressen, his voice a snarl.

The lord's eyes bulged as his air was cut off, but then he choked out a laugh.

"You mean after our standoff the first time we sparred?" Bressen croaked out. "You told me I was almost too pretty to hit, then you punched me."

Samhail let go of Bressen's neck, but a second later he growled in pain and grabbed his head with both hands.

Talyn didn't hear Bressen say anything, but the lord must've asked Samhail a question into his mind, because Bressen chuckled a second later and said, "I did do that, didn't I."

Then they both looked at Talyn.

"He's not in me!" she hurried to assure them as she held up a hand to ward them both off. "And if you attack me," she said to Samhail, "I'll tell everyone exactly what happened that first night I goaded you into getting into that jail cell with me."

Samhail paused, and Bressen looked at him.

"It's her," Samhail told the lord, who nodded and moved quickly to check on Cyra.

Samhail and Talyn looked to Aidan, who was just beginning to stir as Jasper cradled the man in his arms.

"Bressen, check them," Samhail said quickly.

Aidan, Jasper, Maziren, and the twins all winced as Bressen seized their minds at the same time, but their faces eased as he released them a moment later.

"Welcome back, Aidan," Bressen said. "It's good to see you in control of yourself again."

"It's good to *be* in control again," the lord said as he sat up, and Jasper buried his head in his husband's shoulder. "That's a living nightmare I hope to never again experience."

Aidan looked at Talyn, and she tried to remind herself there was no longer a monster inside him.

"Thank you for not killing me," he said to her. "I'm sorry for anything I did or said to you while under Morland's control."

Talyn swallowed, but she couldn't bring herself to answer. She only nodded. It was definitely going to take some time to disassociate Morland from the real Lord Aidan.

Cyra finally stirred then, and Bressen clutched her to his chest.

"Thank the gods," he said.

Cyra moaned softly, and Bressen gave Samhail a quick nod, presumably confirmation that Morland hadn't taken over Cyra either.

"Is he really gone?" Jasper asked, lifting his head from Aidan.

"It looks that way," Bressen said. He slipped one arm under Cyra's legs and one around her back to pick her up. The lord and lady looked at each other, and Talyn assumed unspoken words passed between them.

Everyone turned to Talyn as one then, and she felt the weight of their stares as she considered what she must look like splattered in Morland's blood. She looked down at the dripping dagger she still held in her hand and fought down a wave of nausea.

"Did it help?" Bressen asked her, his tone gentler than she'd come to expect from him.

She considered for a moment. Like Samhail, the man she'd thought she'd killed had resurfaced years later to haunt her. The same man, in fact. She suspected Samhail would always have the lingering fear in the back of his mind that Morland could still return one day, and she was sure she'd always have it as well, but for now, a small weight had lifted.

"A bit," she said.

Knowing Julia's murderer was finally dead would help, but only a little. Julia was still dead, and unlike Morland, she wasn't coming back.

Bressen nodded. "I'm taking Cyra up to rest," he said to the group at large as he turned to carry her back into the building. The twins followed them, then so did Jasper, Aidan, and Maziren, leaving Talyn and Samhail alone in the training yard.

Talyn felt Samhail's gaze burn into her, and she finally turned to look at him when they were alone.

He took a step toward her, but she took an answering step back and held up a hand. She knew he was feeling something similar to what she was, but she couldn't worry about him right now.

"I need to be alone for a while," she said. "I'm going to ask Lord Bressen if he can spare another room for me tonight."

She couldn't tell what emotion crossed his face in the split-second before he mastered himself, but he nodded.

"Follow me," he said. "I can show you to your own room."

He turned and strode toward the house. Talyn's stomach twisted at the stiff set of his back, but she was as grateful he hadn't tried to fight her on this as she was surprised by it.

She exhaled heavily as she followed him. It was time to start extricating him from her life. She'd grown too comfortable around him, too accustomed to letting him watch her back. She was too used to having him to talk to, to train with, to make her smile.

She was too consumed by his kisses and the feel of his body above her as he satiated a hunger she'd never felt until him.

…Too willing to surrender herself to his touch, to give in to his desires, to make those desires her own.

…Too dependent on his strong arms around her as he pulled her close at night and whispered how she was his when he thought she was asleep.

She had to leave. She'd stay in her own room and rest another day before she was on her way. If Bressen let her go, of course.

Yes, she'd stay away from Samhail tonight and maybe – *just maybe* – by tomorrow the idea of leaving him might not feel so much like she was ripping herself in two.

Chapter 45

Talyn

Talyn didn't sleep much that night. The bed felt strangely cold and empty. In the past she might've relished having her space back, but now she only felt exposed. She found herself jumping at every little creak and bump she heard in the room, and she cursed herself for becoming so reliant on Samhail. She'd have to completely retrain herself to be vigilant.

She was sure she looked like shit when she went down to breakfast the next morning, and she wasn't sure how to feel about the fact Samhail didn't look much better. He seemed just as exhausted as she was, and part of her wanted to believe he hadn't slept any better.

She planned to ask Bressen if she was free to go, then leave after breakfast, but she found herself saying yes when Samhail asked if she wanted to train as usual in the morning.

Their sparring was more intense than normal and devoid of the playful taunting they usually engaged in. Samhail looked as though he wanted to speak to her half a dozen times both during and after their session, but he didn't broach whatever was on his mind, and they went back to their separate rooms afterward.

Talyn found Bressen a little later, and he gave her his blessing to leave if she wanted. To her surprise, he actually urged her to stay. He'd talked to her before the whole kidnapping incident about possibly working for him, and he extended an official job offer now, but she thanked him and declined. He shared some information with her that almost made her rethink that decision, but in the end, she knew leaving was for the best.

She went back to her room and gathered her few belongings, prepared to go, but every time she tried to leave, she talked herself out of it.

She was too tired, she decided. Yesterday had been an exhausting and emotional day, then she hadn't gotten much sleep. She'd stay at the Citadel one more day to rest up, and then she'd leave tomorrow.

Or tonight. It would be better to leave in the dark hours when no one was awake and there could be no goodbyes.

Talyn

When the knock sounded at her door later that evening, Talyn wasn't at all surprised this time when she opened it to find Samhail leaning in the frame with his shirt off and the first button of his pants undone. Her lack of surprise did nothing to stave off the heat that flushed her body or to ease the tightening she felt in her core, but she kept her expression bland and her eyes locked with his.

Self-control, Talyn reminded herself. She had enough self-control to keep her eyes from straying to the gorgeous expanse of hard muscles that flexed under the smooth skin of his chest. She was not – *not* – going to look down.

"How many times do you think that's going to work?" Talyn asked as she gestured to Samhail's bare chest. She kept her eyes locked with his.

He shrugged. "I was hoping to get at least two, maybe three… hundred more uses out of it?"

Talyn rolled her eyes. "And I'm just supposed to look at you with your shirt off and that button undone…," she said, her eyes dipping to the flaps of his pants, "and…and…"

Nemesis take her, why had she looked down? She could see that shock of curly white hair peeking out from the flap of his pants, and she pressed her legs together tighter before tearing her eyes back up to his face.

"And what?" she said finally. "I'm just supposed to get on my back and open my legs for you?"

Samhail shrugged. "Actually, that's exactly what I was hoping for." He narrowed his eyes teasingly. "Is that not what you're planning to do?"

Talyn huffed a laugh. "Do you need something?"

He smiled wickedly. "Yes. I need you on your back with your thighs spread wide for me."

Talyn again kept her expression neutral as her stomach did a backflip. She started to swing the door shut, but he caught it and pushed it open.

Talyn turned into her room again, knowing he'd follow, but it was a mistake to turn her back on him. As soon as the door clicked shut behind her, she found herself yanked backward and thrown against it. Samhail pressed his body against hers, and his lips came down to cut off her cry of surprise.

She tried not to sag against the door as his tongue plundered her mouth, but her hands curled around his biceps to help keep her upright as she succumbed to his domination. Gods above, the man kissed like he was going into battle, and she lost this fight against him every gods damned time.

Talyn considered herself fairly aggressive during sex. If she saw someone she wanted, she wasn't shy about going after them, and once in bed, she usually ended up on top.

With Samhail it was different. He'd overwhelmed her from almost their first moments together, and something about submitting to his dominance just felt right. Not that she'd ever make it easy on him. Talyn enjoyed fighting him, and she suspected he enjoyed their fights as well, that he enjoyed her resistance. She'd never stop challenging him, but she had to admit that when their fights were over and he inevitably succeeded in gaining her submission, it felt so good to be beneath him, to feel his immovable weight on top of her and his long, thick cock inside her.

Disappointment stabbed through Talyn at the thought that she'd never see him again after today. Sex with him was beyond anything she'd ever experienced, and it was going to take her a while to forget how much she enjoyed it. But she *would* forget eventually. She hoped.

"Why are you here?" Talyn asked again when he finally let her draw in a breath.

"I can't stay away from you," Samhail rasped against her lips as he pressed her against the door. One of his hands clasped her just under her chin to hold her head in place while the other splayed across her lower back to pull her against him.

Talyn could have ported away, and they both knew it, but she wouldn't. Not yet.

"Why didn't you tell me what Cyra is?" she asked.

He pulled back in surprise. "She told you?" he asked.

"Lord Bressen did. I had a conversation with him a little while ago, and he filled me in."

His eyes narrowed even more in suspicion. "He told you she's…," he trailed off, apparently not trusting that she actually knew.

"A Hand of the Gods," Talyn filled in. "A servant of the Nemesis."

Samhail's brow eased, and he nodded slowly.

"I couldn't tell you," he said. "Bressen swore us to secrecy, and I wasn't going to give him a reason to make my brain leak out of my head."

She arched a brow at him.

"Why does it matter anyway?" he asked.

Talyn frowned. "It matters because you fucked her, and apparently you're divinely obligated to protect her."

In truth, she no longer cared that Samhail had fucked the lady. She liked Cyra despite herself, and Cyra was only one of many women Samhail had slept with over the years. Talyn had her share of past partners as well. They both had their own histories, and it did no good to dwell on those. No, the only reason she brought it up now was because she needed to drive a wedge between them, or she'd never bring herself to leave tonight.

Samhail's face darkened. "Yes, I'm obligated to protect Cyra – I'd protect her anyway because she's my friend – but when I had the choice to help her or you, I chose you. Instead of helping Cyra against Magdalene, I pulled you back up over that chasm."

Talyn froze. What had he just said?

She shook herself mentally. It didn't mean anything that he'd saved her over Cyra. It didn't.

"You chose me that time. What about the next?" she asked. Not that there'd be a next time.

She wasn't being fair, and she knew it, but she didn't care. She had to find a way to push him away, both physically and emotionally.

To her surprise, Samhail only smiled down at her.

"Are you jealous?" he asked.

Talyn scoffed. "I'm most certainly not jealous."

"It seems like you are."

She made a disgusted noise. "You're welcome to fuck whoever you want," she said before she ported behind him.

Samhail didn't move, even though he was now leaning against the door alone. She crossed her arms as he sighed heavily and turned to her.

"And what if you're the only one I want?" he asked.

"My apologies. I misspoke," she said, "You're welcome to fuck whoever you want, except me."

Samhail crossed his arms as well, and they stood facing each other for several seconds.

"We both know how this ends," he said finally, breaking the silence. "You resist me because for some reason you feel you need to. We'll fight. There will probably be blood. There will definitely be lots of heavy breathing, both during the fight and after, but ultimately you'll end up beneath me on that bed screaming my name. Can't we just skip to the end this time?"

Talyn's chin went up at the audacity of his statement, but she couldn't suppress the flutter that went through her stomach. Why in the three hells did it excite her so much to hear him say things like that? She could already imagine him driving inside her with that thick cock of his. She just prayed he couldn't tell how much he affected her.

"Your arrogance is truly staggering," she said as levelly as she could.

"It's not arrogance. It's inductive reasoning. I'm drawing a conclusion based on a pattern," he argued.

Talyn huffed a laugh. "Fine. Maybe it's a pattern with us, but don't pretend you don't want me to resist. The only reason you're here right now is because you like it when I fight you. If I ever just started letting you have me, you'd be tired of me before the end of the day."

There was the hint of a smile on Samhail's lips. "So you fight me to keep me interested?"

She growled in frustration. "That's not what I'm saying. What I mean is…" She shook her head. "There's something seriously wrong with you."

Samhail considered this. "I'm fine with that. Now can we just get on with this? I'm starting to get hard already just arguing with you."

Talyn's mouth fell open, and she couldn't help glancing at his groin, which only made Samhail smile.

"Get on with what exactly?" she asked, dragging her gaze back up.

"Fighting," he said. He held his arm out to the side, and one of the spare daggers she'd left on the side desk flew into his hand.

Why did she always forget he could do that?

She still had a dagger strapped to each of her thighs, but she didn't move, even as Samhail stepped toward her.

"We're not fighting," she said. "Or at least, I'm not fighting you. If you think I fight to keep you interested, then I'll have to stop doing it."

Samhail stepped forward, forcing her to look up, and he grazed the dagger lightly down her cheek. "That strategy probably isn't going to end well for you," he said huskily.

Talyn swallowed and tried not to think about why the feel of him running a dagger down her cheek excited her. There was clearly something wrong with *her* as well.

"You won't hurt me," she said. "You may be an arrogant prick, but I know that much about you."

He raised a brow and grinned. "Oh?"

Samhail struck fast, and the dagger sliced across her arm to draw a cry from her. Luckily, Talyn's body acted on reflex before she knew what she was doing, and she ported back from him, pulling her own daggers as soon as she materialized. She looked down to see a thin scratch about three inches long that was beading a tiny bit of blood along her forearm.

"Nemesis take you!" she yelled, looking up at Samhail. "What in the three hells are you doing?"

"You're right that I won't hurt you…badly," he said, "but I can give you enough of those scratches that it will feel like your skin is on fire. Fortunately, they'll heal quickly."

She narrowed her eyes at him. "You wouldn't."

His answer was to slash at her again, but this time she was ready, and she crossed her daggers in front of her to catch his own blade in the crook where they met.

"You're insane," she said, meeting his eyes. They were so dark she couldn't tell where his irises ended and his pupils began, but there was nevertheless an eager shine to them.

"No, I'm aroused," he said, his voice rough with need.

She understood then. He needed to fight her right now. She'd gotten to kill Morland. She'd gotten a sense of closure, but he'd had to wait and watch and do nothing. He needed a release, but not a sexual one. Or not *just* a sexual one. He needed blood.

Talyn shoved his blade back with her own and spun away from him to regroup. She leaned forward, ready to move as she held her daggers out, and they circled each other.

"You're right about one thing, hummingbird," he said, his eyes wicked with amusement.

"And what's that?" she asked, forgetting to care about the nickname.

He slashed again and Talyn whirled out of the way, but he was on her before she could attack. He grabbed her wrists and spun her so her arms were crossed in front of her and her back was pressed to his chest.

"I do love it when you fight me," he growled into her ear. "It makes me so hard I can barely walk." He pressed his cock into her back, and Talyn tried not to moan as she thought about what that rock-solid length of him could do to her. As it was, she let herself savor his arms around her half a second too long, and she felt the sting of his dagger again as he sliced her leg through her pants. She ported away from him again with a cry of outrage, and Samhail snarled at finding his arms suddenly empty.

Talyn slashed out with her daggers, and Samhail blocked both blows before swiping toward her stomach. Talyn lurched back just in time to miss the blade, and she countered with a swing of her own as Samhail's arm was still across his body on his follow-through. Her blade cut the top of his arm near his shoulder, barely scratching him as he'd done to her. He pulled his arm back, but before he could recover, she slashed her other dagger at his chest, and another red scratch appeared across one thick pectoral muscle.

Samhail grunted and stepped back. He looked down at his chest where a thin trickle of blood was making its way over the ripples of muscle toward his stomach. Then he eyed the cut beading blood on his arm. He inclined his head to Talyn. "Nicely done."

"Is this really what you want to do all night?" Talyn asked, trying to catch her breath. "Slash each other until we're each a bloody mess?"

"Of course not," he said. "I want to throw you down on that bed and fuck you. You're the one making it more complicated than it needs to be."

"You were the one who picked up a dagger first and slashed me!"

"I'm trying to get us through this dance you insist on as quickly as possible. As I said, you're resisting me because you feel you need to. So far we've covered the fighting, the bleeding, and part of the heavy breathing. The only thing left for me to do is fuck you until you scream my name, so do you want to cooperate and get on the bed now, or are you going to make me throw you down onto it?"

Gods damn him. He needed to stop saying things like that. Or she needed to find a way to keep her stomach from flipflopping when he did. Thankfully, his comment about cooperating pissed her off enough that she wasn't ready to give in to him just yet.

"What's your hurry?" she asked, grinning wickedly. "I don't think you've bled enough yet."

She attacked, feinting one way before shifting back the other to swing out with both blades. Samhail was ready for her, though, and he defended the attempts by first deflecting one of her daggers to the side, then swinging his own dagger around to knock her other blow down toward the floor. Talyn barely managed to hold onto both of her daggers, but the force of his deflections sent reverberations up her arms. She saw his muscles tense to lunge at her again, and she did a backflip out of the way, her foot missing Samhail's chin as he jerked back just in time.

"The only thing you're doing by fighting me is making my cock harder," he said as he shifted his weight back to a resting position.

Talyn didn't take the bait, either to look at his groin or to attack him while he was seemingly relaxed.

"There is definitely something wrong with you," she said.

He grinned. "And you love it. Do you think I don't know how wet you are for me right now?"

Talyn let out an indignant noise but realized instantly she'd fallen into his trap as he moved toward her so fast she barely had time to react. His dagger was in his right hand, so she ported next to him on his left, and instinct had her driving one of her blades toward his side to find a kidney. Reason took over at the last minute as she remembered she was aiming to scratch him, not to kill or incapacitate, and she managed to check her blow just enough that the dagger only penetrated his side half an inch.

Samhail grunted as the blade pierced his skin, and Talyn pushed out a breath as she saw how close she'd come to almost doing real damage to him. That her blade would've struck true if she hadn't pulled back was both exciting and terrifying. She looked up to meet Samhail's eyes, her own still wide with horror at what she'd almost done. His answering gaze told her he knew how close he'd come to a serious wound.

Neither of them moved for several seconds, but Samhail recovered first, and Talyn shrieked as he tossed her over his shoulder. She barely had time to register what he was doing before he whipped her back over onto the bed. Her breath hitched as she hit the mattress hard enough to bounce on it, and then Samhail was on top of her, his hands pinning hers above her head, daggers still in her grasp.

"Do not port off this bed, or you'll regret it," he growled.

Talyn only grinned at him and then ported on top of him so she was straddling his waist as he lay on his stomach beneath her. She brought one dagger to his neck to press the tip lightly at his artery while her other hand pressed into the back of his shoulder.

"I'm still on the bed," she purred at him. "Do you yield?"

There was silence for a moment before Samhail bucked her off him. Talyn cried out and pulled her dagger back from his throat, afraid of accidentally cutting him, but the moment of concern cost her, and she found herself under him again with one of his muscled legs shoved between her thighs. One of his hands held both of hers above her head as he pulled the two daggers from her grasp and tossed them aside.

"Let me rephrase," he growled against her ear, "Don't port at all, or I'll find a caronium cuff, and then I'll tie you to this bed and fuck you until you forget how to walk."

The punch of breath that left her this time came out as part moan. Did he actually think threats like that were a deterrent?

Samhail's lips crashed down on hers as his tongue pushed its way into her mouth, easily parting her lips to open the way for him to deepen the kiss. His ardor was almost brutal in its intensity, but she didn't care. She arched under him, not to throw him off, but because she was done denying that she wanted this, that she wanted *him*. She returned his kiss with equal fervor, their teeth scraping against each other as they ravaged each other's mouths.

Samhail groaned, and he let go of her wrists to find the hem of her shirt and yank it up. He broke the kiss only long enough to get the garment up over her head, and then his lips were on hers again, hard and punishing. He growled and pulled back a second later, though, as his hand found the cloth band she wrapped around her breasts.

"Nemesis fucking take me," he swore and reached out a hand to summon back one of the daggers he'd tossed aside.

"What are you doing?" Talyn asked in alarm as Samhail held the dagger near her sternum.

"Stay still," he said as he carefully slipped the dagger under the wrap between her breasts. Once it was through, he pulled up and the blade cut through the cloth easily to let her breasts spring free.

"I'll get you a new one," Samhail said as Talyn opened her mouth to admonish him. Then his mouth closed over her breast and whatever she'd been about to say died on her lips as she cried out in ecstasy.

Samhail's mouth was hot and wet, and he sucked at her breast with an intensity that was just short of painful. Talyn's hands threaded through his hair to hold him there, not that she needed to. He seemed to have no intention of letting up except for the brief second he took to move his mouth to her other breast.

Talyn couldn't see straight as the teasing flicks of Samhail's tongue on her nipple sent jolts of pleasure skittering down her limbs. She was feverish with desire when Samhail lifted his head again, and there was a wild gleam in his eye that made her breath catch in her throat.

"Why are you looking at me like that?" she asked warily.

Samhail's only answer was to open his mouth just wide enough to let her see the sharp, gleaming fangs that peeked out from behind his lips.

All the breath left Talyn's lungs as the urge to port stampeded through her. Bone-deep fear warred with exhilaration as she realized he didn't just want to fuck her. He wanted to devour her.

Chapter 46

Talyn's eyes flared wide at the realization of what he wanted to do. It was on the tip of her tongue to refuse, but she couldn't force the words past her lips.

Ever so slowly, Samhail lowered his mouth back down to her breast, his eyes never leaving hers. Talyn's chest heaved in anticipation, and she tried once more to voice the words to stop him, but they again failed her.

Samhail's mouth hovered just above her breast for a moment as her breathing became more and more ragged. She flinched and gave a small scream as his tongue circled her nipple, and he chuckled. She relaxed when she realized it wasn't his teeth, and that's when he struck.

Samhail's bite wasn't hard or violent as it had been the first time, but she cried out at the sharp stab of pain as his fangs pierced the flesh of her breast just above and below her nipple.

Talyn's hands flew to his shoulders as every instinct told her to push him away. Instead, her nails bit into his skin, and she pulled him closer.

He began to suck, and starbursts flared in her vision. The feeling danced somewhere between pleasure and pain as his mouth pulled at her breast. His tongue swirled around her nipple as he tasted the blood that seeped from the wounds his teeth had made. His body was between her legs, and her thighs clamped around him as she couldn't stop herself from writhing beneath him.

Talyn's eyes rolled back in her head as he drank deeply from her. His tongue continued to tease her nipple as each hard pull of his mouth on her breast sent need pulsing straight to her clit, where it was wedged against his body.

Samhail withdrew his teeth finally, and Talyn's breathing eased. His tongue laved the wounds he'd made, and Talyn let a deep moan ripple up from inside her.

Samhail lifted his head, and she watched as his tongue licked over his lips, cleaning the last of her blood from them. She wasn't sure if the jolt that shot through her was terror or rapture.

"You taste so gods damned good," he breathed. "I can't decide what's sweeter, your blood or that nectar between your legs."

Talyn's mouth worked on a response, but nothing came out.

He pulled back enough to yank her boots, pants, and undergarment off before he pushed her knees open.

"I'll have to compare," he said as his mouth descended on her sex.

"No teeth!" she managed to gasp out as his tongue delved in and began its exploration of her.

His chuckle vibrated against her center, and she moaned again.

Samhail circled her clit before his mouth closed over it, and he sucked greedily at her. Talyn cried out and grasped his forearms where they held her hips down. His tongue plunged inside her, and she threw back her head as her fingers threaded through his hair. His name came out in a sound that was half scream, half mewl, and she spared a thought to realize he'd been right in predicting that as well.

She didn't care. Gods above, she fought him every time on this, and every time they got to this point – which they inevitably did – she wondered why in the three hells she'd been fighting him in the first place. No one had ever made her feel like this. No one had ever brought her to the brink of insanity so she thought she might go mad from pleasure. The man had a gods damned magical tongue.

Talyn felt her release build, and she moved her hands to fist in the covers so she didn't end up pulling on Samhail's hair. She'd shred the bedding to ribbons if that tautness between her legs twisted any further.

Samhail licked all the way up her center before his tongue did the-gods-only-knew what to her aching clit, and Talyn screamed as the dam of pleasure broke, sending sweet fulfillment sweeping away everything in its path. Her breath came in ragged gasps, and her hands trembled as they continued to fist in the covers.

When her vision cleared again, Talyn was vaguely aware Samhail hadn't yet moved, and she lifted her head just enough to see him gaze up at her from between her legs with heavy-lidded eyes. He looked every bit like a predator ready to pounce.

Gods, that look.

Samhail lifted himself and prowled over her. She bit her lip as she watched him, never taking her eyes from his. When he was above her again, he reached down and began to work at the fastenings of his pants. Talyn's breath caught as he pulled the pants off to free his cock. It seemed more swollen than she'd ever seen it.

"My turn," he said as he notched himself at her entrance.

Samhail drove himself into her to the hilt with one deep, hard thrust as his mouth closed over hers to smother her scream. Her sounds turned quickly to muffled moans and whimpers as he plunged into her again and again and again, and she held onto his shoulders for dear life. The marks from the scratches she'd given him their first time had healed, and there was no longer any trace of them on his skin, but with the way he was fucking her now, she was likely to make them again. Indeed, there was something different this time about the way he moved.

Samhail's kisses were rough and deep and usually left her lips swollen, but he was more careful when he fucked her. She always felt him hold back at least a little, but not so now. The way he drove into her now was just short of painful, but she knew he needed this, needed to let go of the anger and pain and frustration of Morland…and also of her betrayal.

"Give me everything," Talyn managed to whisper brokenly into his ear as he pounded into her.

He slowed and raised himself to look down at her. "What?" he asked.

"Give me everything," she repeated. "Let yourself go, and give me all of you. I can take it."

Realization seemed to dawn on him, and he shook his head slowly.

"Talyn, no, I…"

She grab the dagger he'd used to cut her breast wrap off and slashed a thin cut across his bicep before she pressed the blade to his throat.

"Fuck me as hard as you can right now," she ordered. "No holding back. I want you to fuck me like you hate me. Fuck me like you don't care if you hurt me, or so help me gods, I'll finish what I started when I had you on your knees with your swords to your throat."

He grunted as she slashed him again across his chest and then returned the blade to his throat.

His eyes flashed as he glared down at her, and Talyn saw his restraint break. He ripped the blade from her hand and tossed it across the room. Then he pinned her hands over her head with one of his own.

"I hope you don't regret this," he said, his voice strained, "because you just opened a door I can't re-shut right now."

And then he let loose.

Talyn's eyes went wide as his first thrust made her teeth clack together, and she didn't have time to catch her breath before his next plunge made her cry out. Then he was fucking her harder and faster than he ever had before, and all she could do was try to absorb his pounding drives.

Despite his words, she knew instinctively he'd find a way to stop himself if he truly hurt her, but she didn't plan on making him stop or even slow down. For this, their last time, she wanted all of him.

Talyn gasped as a flash of blue lit Samhail's eyes, and then his wings flared out from his back. They stretched out wide, and she saw the veins in them where the light shone through the membrane. The wings seemed to almost beat lightly as he fucked her, and she got a good look at the lethal-looking talons that topped the wing joint. Samhail's eyes began to glow blue steadily, and for the first time, Talyn felt a pang of fear.

Could he shift into a gargoyle while he was fucking her? She didn't think so. He didn't have a cock in that form. At least she hoped he didn't, and the thought of suddenly having a giant stone cock inside her sent panic racing down her spine.

"Don't shift!" she cried out.

He actually smiled. "I won't," he assured her without slowing.

Tears formed at the corners of Talyn's eyes as Samhail pounded into her, but she couldn't say they were from pain. Or perhaps they weren't only from pain. In truth, she was right on the border, and in a way, the pain *was* pleasure. She needed this release as much as he did. She needed to feel this to let her forgive herself for everything she'd done to him, and for what she was going to do to him tonight when she left.

Talyn cried out in protest as Samhail pulled out of her suddenly, but he only turned her over onto her stomach. He pulled her onto her knees and quickly sheathed himself back into her.

"Oh, gods! Samhail!" she screamed as he drove into her again.

He clamped one large hand onto her shoulder while the other wrapped around her waist to hold her in place. The new position pushed him even deeper, and his grunts filled the room as Talyn curled her hands tightly into the covers.

Samhail dragged her body back against his chest as he continued to thrust into her. Her knees were splayed wide on the bed as he pumped harder. One of his arms anchored across her chest as his hand teased the nipple of her breast while his other hand dipped between her legs to massage her clit.

"Fuck! Samhail!" she swore as her body jerked against his, but he held her fast so she couldn't move.

"Come for me," he growled against her ear. "I want you dripping down my cock while your tight little sheath squeezes every last drop of my seed out of it."

Talyn moaned loudly as he punctuated the order with several hard thrusts and a twist to her nipple.

She screamed again, and her inner walls clamped around his cock in release. He grunted as she convulsed around him, but he didn't slow, and Talyn wasn't sure her body could take much more if he didn't come soon. She was so sensitive it was almost unbearable, and she dug her fingernails into his thighs hard enough to draw blood.

Samhail let out a roar and pushed her forward again as he pressed her shoulders into the mattress. He drove into her with three more pounding thrusts before he stopped, fully buried inside her. He let out a savage noise she'd never heard before, and then she felt him pulse as he spilled himself into her. He gave one last half thrust before he eased, and Talyn's own body sagged in relief.

Samhail pulled out of her, and she felt his seed drip from between her legs as they both collapsed, panting.

Several minutes later they still lay tangled around each other. Samhail had stowed his wings, and he now lay on his back with her sprawled across him. Talyn lifted her head from his chest and reached up to let her fingers trail down the side of his cheek. Unlike the ever-present dark stubble Lord Bressen wore, Samhail's face was perfectly smooth, and she wondered absently if he could even grow a beard.

She knew nothing about gargoyles and their bodies. Was it actually possible for him to get her pregnant, for instance? She wasn't worried he would, but the question made her curious nonetheless.

"How do you do that?" she asked.

"Do what?" he asked, leaning his face into her touch. The gesture seemed unconscious, and she wondered if he knew he'd done it.

She started to speak but stopped, not willing to admit the way her body craved his. It wasn't just the physical pleasure he gave her, but the way her skin tingled when he was near. She'd never felt anything like it.

"Never mind," she said.

Samhail reached up and brushed a lock of hair back from her face before pressing a kiss to her temple. Her heart ached at that for some reason, and she swallowed down the lump that rose in her throat. Nemesis take him. What was he trying to do to her?

Talyn pushed herself up from Samhail's chest and sat back. "Actually, I do have a question, and you need to tell me the truth."

"Of course. What is it?"

"Do you have some sort of magical spell on your tongue? I've never felt anything like it before."

He looked surprised for a second but then chuckled. "I do have a kind of secret weapon when it comes to my tongue," he said hesitantly.

She narrowed her eyes. "Tell me."

Samhail looked up at her for several seconds as if weighing the pros and cons of sharing his secret, and she quirked a brow.

"You might be disturbed if I tell you," he said.

She frowned. "Now you *have* to tell me so I don't have nightmares about what you've been doing between my legs."

Samhail sighed heavily and sat up to face her. He pulled her onto his lap so she was straddling his thighs, then he wrapped his arms around her waist. She had the distinct feeling he was trying to hold her in place, something they both knew was futile if she wanted to get off him.

"Just try to remember how much you enjoy what my tongue does to you when I show you this," he said, and Talyn frowned even more.

Then she gasped as Samhail opened his mouth to reveal a forked tongue, longer and thinner than his normal human tongue. Her body jerked in shock, and Samhail's arms tightened around her.

"Don't port," he said, and for the first time ever she thought she heard fear in his voice.

She shook her head. "I won't," she said softly as she raised a hand toward his mouth. "That's your gargoyle tongue?"

Talyn's fingers touched his lips, and his tongue snaked out so its forks wrapped around her forefinger, squeezing it gently.

Nemesis take her. That explained a lot.

Talyn bit her lip as his tongue drew her finger into his mouth for him to suck on. "Fuck me," she whispered. "First the wings and the teeth, now the tongue. I suppose I should be grateful you don't have a giant stone cock. You don't, right?"

Samhail chuckled again and nipped her finger gently before he let her pull it from his mouth.

"My gargoyle form is made for fighting, not for fucking," he said. "A giant stone cock is a liability in battle."

Talyn narrowed her eyes again as something occurred to her. "Do you use that tongue with other women?" she asked.

Samhail's face fell, but he nodded. "I have. In the past."

"With Cyra?" she asked, already knowing the answer, but needing to hear him say it. "Have you used that tongue between her legs as well?"

The deep exhale that pushed past Samhail's lips also carried a growl.

"I've been using my gargoyle tongue with women for more than a century now," he said. "So yes, I've used it on Cyra. I can't take back the fact that I've had her, but I'm hoping you can find a way to get past that."

Talyn just looked at him.

"Tell me what I can do to make this easier for you," he said, his voice tinged with worry. "Do you want to fuck Bressen to make us even?"

Talyn couldn't help the bark of laughter that escaped her.

"The Lord of Hiraeth and I would kill each other long before we made it anywhere near a bed," she said, "and I'm not sure Cyra would appreciate you volunteering her husband to fuck me in any case."

Samhail shrugged. "Maybe if the three of you-"

"Not going to happen," Talyn said, cutting him off.

"Fine, but if you're going to insist on destroying that fantasy for me, then tell me what you do want."

She didn't know. She thought she was past his involvement with Cyra, but learning about his tongue had dredged up lingering doubts.

Not that it mattered, she had to keep reminding herself. She was leaving and would probably never see him again. It didn't matter anymore what he'd done with Cyra.

"If it helps, you're the only person who knows about my tongue," he said. "I've never told anyone else – including Cyra – about it. I figured it was better for women to just enjoy the feel without having to think about it." He paused before adding, "Not even Bressen knows, and he knows everything about me. You're the only person in the world I've told, and

I'd appreciate it if you didn't tell anyone else."

"Your secret is safe with me."

Samhail brought his hand up to brush her cheek again with his thumb. "How do you feel about it?" he asked. "Does it disturb you to know?"

She thought a moment. It had been shocking to see it and realize that's what had been between her legs, but she couldn't deny that his use of it was…euphoric. He'd been afraid she'd find his gargoyle form disturbing when he first shifted in Derridan, but the truth was that she found him fascinating, and part of her felt the same way about his tongue now. He wasn't fully human, so it was unfair to compare him to those who were.

For that matter, there was really no comparison. Samhail surpassed any man she knew by just about every measure she could think of. She wasn't sure what she'd feel the next time his tongue was between her legs, knowing what it was, but for now at least, it didn't bother her.

She shook herself mentally. No, there wouldn't be a next time.

"I won't use it if you don't want me to," he said.

"It's fine," she said, forcing a smile. "It doesn't bother me."

"You should also move back into my rooms when we return to Tide's End," he said. "I need to stay around for a little longer while we deal with Sandrian and Magdalene, and it doesn't make sense for you to have separate quarters. I'll talk to Bressen. He won't send you to Revenmyer."

Samhail leaned in and pulled her toward him to kiss her. She let him, but her blood had stilled in her veins. He was making plans for a future that didn't exist between them, and the regret nauseated her.

"I assume there's nowhere pressing you need to be?" he asked. "I know you and Bressen have had your rough patches, but he's smart enough to recognize that your abilities can be very useful. I'm sure he can find a role for you if you're willing to work with us."

Nemesis damn her. She had to tell him. "Samhail-"

"Just tell me what you need me to do about Cyra," he said. His hand threaded into her hair as he pulled her to him so his forehead rested against hers. "You're the only woman I want in my bed, Talyn. Tell me what I need to do to prove that to you, and I'll-"

"Stop!" she said, pressing back against his chest. Her hands shook as she tried to push away from him, but his arm only curled around her, preventing her escape.

"Talyn, please," he said, and the panic on his face crushed something inside her. "I'll do whatever-"

"Stop," she said, unable to keep the quaver out of her voice. "Stop making plans."

He was silent a moment. "Why?" he asked finally, and she heard him readying for an argument.

Talyn closed her eyes. She really hadn't wanted to tell him this. It would've been so much easier just to leave in the middle of the night, but now that she thought about it, it was probably better to do it this way. Samhail would only come after her if she just disappeared on him. She owed it to him to at least explain.

"I'm leaving," she said softly. "Tonight. Alone. I already spoke to Lord Bressen, and he's not sending me to Revenmyer."

His face showed only confusion.

"What do you mean you're leaving alone?" he asked.

"I mean that…" Talyn tried to swallow down the lump in her throat, but it felt like she had a huge bite of unchewed apple wedged there. "I mean that I need to go back to my life now that things are over, and I need to go back to being by myself. I can't stay here, and I won't be traveling with you later. I need to leave."

Samhail's brows drew together as his face darkened. "I don't understand. Why don't you want to travel together?"

"Because my work relies on stealth and anonymity," she said, "and you're entirely too noticeable. It was good – great – while it lasted, but whatever this is between us can't go on anymore. Aside from the fact that we'd eventually kill each other, it's just not feasible."

Her voice broke by the end, and she locked her jaw to keep her chin from quivering. She fought back the tears that threatened and looked away from him. This was so much harder than she'd thought it would be.

Samhail was silent a long time before he shook his head. "No," he said firmly. "No, I said I didn't intend to let you go, and I meant it."

"That's not your choice," she said, trying to sound angry rather than like her insides were being torn to ribbons.

Samhail's hand tightened in her hair, forcing her gaze back to his, and she saw he was looking for some sign she was only kidding. She willed her expression to remain neutral. She couldn't let him see how much it was killing her to do this.

"No," Samhail said, shaking his head again. "I won't let you go."

"You can't stop me," she whispered. "It's not your choice."

Samhail opened his mouth to speak but rethought what he was going to say and closed it. He appeared to be waging some kind of internal battle behind his dark eyes.

"No, I won't let you go," he said again finally, as if he'd come to a decision. He inhaled deeply, then spoke again, as if making some kind of proclamation. "Talyn of Avril, I…I claim you by Right of Primacy."

Talyn's brows shot together. She had no idea what that meant, but the words eased something in Samhail's face, as if he'd somehow made peace with what he'd just spoken.

"What do you mean you claim me?" Talyn asked as his words sunk in. "What's the Right of Primacy?"

Samhail lifted his chin. His hands still threaded through her hair keeping her head trapped. She tried to lift herself off his lap, but his muscles tensed around her, holding her fast in his embrace.

"Samhail, what's the Right of Primacy?" she asked again, growing angry. She shook her head to dislodge his hands, and he let go of her hair.

His face hardened as if steeling himself for a battle.

"It's a gargoyle custom," he said, his tone more assured now. "In the human world, the nearest equivalent would be…marriage. For all intents and purposes, we're now mated, and you're my wife."

Chapter 47

Samhail

He had no idea what made him do it. It was easily the stupidest, most ill-conceived thing he'd ever done, and he and Bressen had done some truly stupid things in their younger days.

But he hadn't been able to help it. When Talyn said she was leaving, every fiber of his being had screamed at him to do something, to find some way to keep her from going, but he knew he'd made a huge mistake as he watched Talyn's eyes widen impossibly large at the news she was now his wife.

Fuck. This was not going to end well.

To his shock, though, Talyn only laughed.

"I'm sorry," she said. "Can you repeat that? I can't have heard you right. I thought you just said that we're now married and I'm your wife."

He put as much apology into his expression as he could.

"Samhail?" she said, her tone growing more serious. "Tell me I didn't hear you right."

"You heard me right," he said softly. "I've claimed you by Right of Primacy. By gargoyle custom, you now belong to me. It's not a marriage per se, but it's as close as gargoyles get."

Talyn tried to lift herself from his lap, but he tightened his arms, trying to hold her in place. He wasn't surprised when she ported away from him. She appeared next to the bed looking thunderous, and he dropped his arms now that they held empty air.

"I belong to you?" she said incredulously. "No. Absolutely not. Unclaim me now."

"I can't," he said as he rose from the bed to face her. The chances were good she'd try to kill him again, so he should probably be ready. "The Right of Primacy doesn't work like that. You can either accept the claim, or you can reject it and-"

"I reject it then," Talyn cut in angrily. "I reject your claim."

Samhail let out a long breath. "It's not that simple. In order to fully reject the claim, you need to defeat me in battle."

She blinked at him.

"In gargoyle society, we more or less live by the notion that if you're powerful enough to do something, you can do it," he said, hoping he might be able to explain before she snapped and attacked him. "There are a few notable exceptions, but in general, if you want something, you claim it, including a mate. If that mate doesn't want the bond, they can reject it, but they need to prove their superiority by defeating the one making the claim in battle. Only that can nullify the claim."

"I'd have to kill you?" she asked, and her tone suggested she might be more than happy to do that right about now.

"Not kill," he said. "Just defeat. You'd need to incapacitate me to the point I couldn't continue. Essentially, you'd need to get me in a position where you *could* clearly kill me if you wanted to, and I wouldn't be able to stop you."

"Fine," she said, glaring at him.

He was ready for it when she swiped her dagger off the floor and came at him. He dodged her swing and grabbed her wrist, then twisted her arm until she cried out and dropped the blade.

"There are rules," he said with a sharp look. "And we need witnesses."

Talyn narrowed her eyes at him, and she tried to wrench her hand free from his grasp. She ported a few feet away when he didn't release her.

"How dare you!" she stormed, and he saw actual tears glisten in her eyes. "How dare you claim me like I'm some kind of object to possess?"

"I'm sorry," he said quietly. "I didn't know what else to do when you said you were leaving. It was a mistake."

"Well, it was all for nothing. Claiming me won't get me to stay," she said, and the bitterness in her voice crushed something in his chest.

"You have to defeat me before you go, or things may end up being difficult for you," he said.

"What the fuck is that supposed to mean?"

"Look at your finger," he said.

She raised her hands to look at them and gasped when she saw the faint markings on the middle finger of her right hand, markings that were a perfect miniature replica of those on Samhail's wrists and forearms.

"What in the three hells is that?" she yelled, trying futilely to rub the gray markings off.

"It's my mark," he said, hating every word. "It will become darker if you accept my claim. It will only disappear if you defeat me and the claim is officially rejected. As long as you have that mark, any gargoyle you meet will be obligated to bring you back to me so the claim can either be finalized or broken."

Talyn's face was a mask of fury as she looked between him and her hand. A moment later the markings disappeared as she used her powers to mask them, and she held up her hand in triumph.

"Looks like I'll just have to keep them covered," she sneered at him.

"No one may be able to see it, but if a gargoyle comes near you, they'll be able to sense it," he said.

He didn't think it was possible, but her face darkened even more.

"You bastard!" she yelled, launching herself at him.

Any other woman would likely have beat against his chest, but Talyn came in swinging for his face. Her punch knocked his head to the side and sent pain shooting through his jaw. Her next fist landed in his stomach, and he grunted as his breath whooshed out of him.

Samhail let her punch, kick, and elbow him for several seconds without trying to defend himself until she pulled her knee back, presumably intending to send it into his groin. Then he grabbed her and swung her around to pin her back against his chest. He expected her to port, but she only fought his hold as he held his arms over hers, trapping her still-naked body against his.

"How could you?" she asked when she finally stilled. Her voice was soft, but he heard every bit of hurt and anger in it.

"I'm sorry," he said, just as quietly. "If I could take it back, I…Well, I shouldn't have done it in the first place. But now that I have, you have a decision to make."

She huffed an angry laugh and pulled away from him. He let her go so she could turn to face him.

"Some decision," she said. "Accept your claim or fight you?"

He sighed heavily. "In theory, you could accept the claim and leave anyway. I wouldn't stop you."

Letting her go with his mark on her would be like having his entrails ripped out and thrown on the floor, but he'd do it.

"We'd be bonded, but you'd never have to see me again," he said.

"So I'd just have to walk around with your brand on me for the rest of my life, reminding me that you own me?" she said, and he flinched at the venom in her voice.

Talyn looked down at her finger, the markings once again faintly visible. Samhail looked at them as well, and something feral rose up in him at the sight, something that roared in his mind that she was his and that he'd die before he let her go. He tamped the feeling down, knowing it would only make her angrier if she sensed the direction of his thoughts.

"What are the rules if I challenge your claim and we fight?" she asked, and something cracked open inside him.

"We need witnesses. Surgeon and Serise can do it," he said. "But you need to understand I can't just let you win. I have to try my best to defend the claim. Invoking the Right of Primacy is a serious matter in gargoyle society. One doesn't claim it lightly. A gargoyle will generally only do it if they're absolutely certain their potential mate wants to enter into the bond, and then sometimes not even then. My parents lived together and raised five children without ever bonding through the right."

She raised a brow at him. "And you thought claiming me after all the times I've tried to kill you was a good idea? What part of holding your swords to your throat suggested I wanted to be bonded to you forever?"

"My mistake," he said. "I clearly misunderstood you letting me live."

He didn't realize it was possible for her to glare any harder, but she did. He wasn't going to beg her forgiveness, though. Claiming her had been a decidedly bad idea, but he couldn't bring himself to regret it. He wanted her. Letting her go was no more an option than cutting off his own hand at this point.

The irony was that, by claiming her, he'd all-but assured he'd lose her.

"So you have to try your best to defeat me," she said. "I understand."

"Do you? Because you've never fought me at my best, Talyn," he warned her. "I've always held back at least a little, but Surgeon and Serise know what I'm capable of. They'll know if I'm holding back this time, and if they judge that I'm throwing the fight, my life is forfeit. Any gargoyle, including them, can kill me for tarnishing the right."

He watched the range of emotions cross her face, from surprise to anger to fear. That last one lingered, and he dared to hope maybe she didn't really want him dead after all.

Talyn nodded. "Fine. I understand," she said, her tone clipped but resigned. "When can we do this?"

"Tomorrow if you want. I just have to ask Surgeon and Serise to stand witness. They'll determine the winner."

She frowned. "Do you trust them?"

"Gargoyles have few laws, but those surrounding the Right of Primacy are among the most sacred. They'll be fair because their own lives are on the line if they aren't."

Talyn blew out a long breath. "Is there anything else I should know?"

"If I win, the bond will automatically take hold," he said. "Those markings on your finger will darken and become permanent."

He saw her jaw clench, but she didn't say anything. He knew it was time for him to leave, but he had one more thing to say to her.

He stepped toward Talyn, and her eyes dipped to his groin, the evidence of his need for her growing there again. Her body tensed as she prepared to either fight him or port, but she didn't move. When he was right in front of her, he raised a hand to brush her cheek, but she pulled away from him and turned her head.

"Don't," was all she said, and he thought he heard her voice break.

"Talyn, please look at me."

She didn't turn her head, and he grabbed her chin to force her face around. He needed her to look at him when he said this.

"You're unlike any woman I've ever met," he said. "I may care for Cyra, but that's nothing compared to what I feel for you."

Her eyes flared at Cyra's name, but she held his gaze.

"I've never met an opponent I feared to face in battle. I've never met someone I wasn't absolutely certain I could defeat," he said. "Until you."

Something flickered in her eyes, but she kept her jaw clenched tight, refusing to speak.

"I'm never prepared for you," he said. "I've never felt closer to defeat than when I face you."

She swallowed.

"And I'm not just talking about your fighting ability," he went on. "I claimed the Right of Primacy because I was facing defeat with you, and I had no other options. I've never wanted anyone the way I want you, and you were slipping through my fingers."

He saw the clench in her jaw ease, even as her body went still.

"Make no mistake," he said, his voice hardening. "I don't regret claiming you, because I want you more than I've ever wanted anyone or anything in my life, and I think that's been true since I met you. But the right is brutal by nature, and I'll have to hurt you tomorrow to enforce my claim. I don't want to hurt you, but I'll do what's necessary to keep you, even if it means you hate me."

He released her face, grabbed his pants off the floor, and strode out of her room naked. He only prayed no one was in the hallway because he wasn't going to stop long enough to get dressed.

Thankfully he didn't encounter anyone on his way back to his room, and he slammed the door behind him as he stalked in. He tossed his pants onto the back of a chair, then leaned over it as he tried to calm himself.

He looked down at his hard cock, standing at attention. Fuck. The woman drove him mad. She fought him every gods damned step of the way, but that only inflamed him more.

Samhail detoured to the bathing chamber to grab a small towel before laying down on the bed. He had to relieve this need, or he'd be tempted to go back to Talyn's chamber and beg her to let him fuck her. There was no chance whatsoever she'd agree after all that, so this would have to do.

Samhail splashed some oil from a bottle near the bed on his hand and began to run his hand roughly up and down his cock.

Gods, what this woman did to him.

He groaned as he pictured her breasts bouncing while he thrust into her. He loved to feel her beneath him, to hold her down while he fucked into her, but there was something so gods damned erotic about knowing he could only hold her there as long as she allowed it. It brought an urgency to their fucking, a kind of razor's edge he ran along because he knew she could be gone at any moment.

Samhail squeezed his cock tighter, and he came with a growl that rumbled around the room as he pumped milky white jets of his seed into the towel. He collapsed back on the bed when his muscles finally eased.

He needed to get up and find Surgeon and Serise to let them know they'd be needed tomorrow.

That was a conversation he dreaded. He wasn't looking forward to admitting he'd dared to claim the Right of Primacy only to have Talyn reject it. The twins would laugh themselves hoarse.

Then he needed to find Bressen and explain what he'd done. Cyra would have to be on hand tomorrow in case they needed a healer, although he was afraid her presence might only make things worse.

Something Talyn said hit him all of a sudden. She'd already spoken to Bressen, and he'd not only told her he wouldn't be sending her to

Revenmyer, he'd told her what Cyra really was. Bressen never would've told her the latter unless he'd invited Talyn to stay.

Hope rose in his chest at the thought Bressen might've already offered Talyn a position in his war cabinet. She'd clearly turned it down, but at least one hurdle was out of the way. If he could somehow survive tomorrow and not lose Talyn in the process, there was at least a place for her here in Thasia.

A place for her with him.

Tandem Read: Go to *Nemesis Rising* (Bk 4), Chapter 37

Chapter 48

Samhail

Samhail stared across the Citadel's training yard the next day at the woman who'd twisted him in knots these last few weeks. She was still so beautiful despite, or perhaps because of, the murderous glint in her eyes.

The area around the yard had been cleared of guards and servants so no one would be able to see the fight. Only Talyn, Cyra, Bressen, and the twins stood there at the moment. Aidan, Jasper, and Maziren had gone back to Seatherny yesterday, and Axenus was – mercifully – away on another diplomatic mission for Bressen. If Samhail had had to deal with Axenus's sardonic looks on top of everything else, he would've snapped.

Bressen stepped in front of Samhail suddenly. The lord wasn't tall enough to fully block his view of Talyn, but Bressen's turquoise stare could be magnetic, and Samhail reluctantly tore his eyes from her.

"Should I ask what the fuck you were thinking?" Bressen asked.

Samhail huffed a laugh. "I have no idea what I was thinking."

"Why didn't you tell me about this claiming thing before anyway? Why is this the first I've heard of it?"

"When did you want me to bring it up? When we were cutting down soldiers on the battlefield, or afterwards when we were fucking women?"

Bressen inclined his head to concede the point. "Is there really no way to stop this now?" he asked.

"The only way is if Talyn changes her mind and accepts my claim, and she won't do that. It's part of the reason I…"

The words tapered off. He wasn't sure he could confess what he felt for Talyn. Bressen knew him well enough, though.

"You actually love her, don't you," he said, surprised.

"Yes," Samhail said without hesitation. He'd stopped trying to deny he loved Talyn days ago, stopped trying to convince himself that gargoyles couldn't fall in love, because there was no denying he was hopelessly, irrevocably in love with her.

When she'd told him last night she was leaving and had refused to consider any plan that might allow them to stay together, he'd racked his brain to think of something to keep her here. The only two options he'd come up with were locking her back in a cell under Tide's End or claiming the right. It had been a toss-up which would piss her off more, but he'd chosen the option he'd hoped against hope she might accept.

It hadn't surprised him she'd immediately rejected the claim. Ironically, part of him would've questioned his decision if she'd simply accepted it and hadn't chosen to fight him on it. He liked her fight, which only accorded with his belief that anything worth having was worth fighting for, even if it meant fighting the woman he wanted herself.

Bressen was quiet a moment. "You know if you win this fight, you'll really lose her, right?"

Samhail growled in frustration. "I'm aware."

"So what are you going to do?"

Samhail shrugged wearily. "Pray to the gods she beats me." His eyes drifted back to where Talyn was speaking with Cyra now.

"I thought you couldn't lose on purpose?" Bressen asked.

"I can't. That's why Surgeon and Serise are here. They have to certify the results, and if they think I'm losing on purpose, they can declare me in violation of the right."

"And that's bad?"

"I'd essentially be a pariah and a target among gargoyles."

Bressen flinched. "So how are you going to ensure she wins without throwing the fight?"

Samhail's eyes dropped to meet Bressen's again. "You don't think she can beat me," he said, as if he just realized his brother felt this way.

Bressen raised a brow. "Can she?"

"That woman broke my nose and escaped Tide's End without having her powers. She's had me on my knees at least twice, and the last time she had both my own swords at my neck. There was nothing I could do but wait for her to kill me. I'm only here because she decided to let me live."

Bressen's expression was one of utter shock. "She almost killed you?"

Samhail lifted his chin and pointed to the faint scar lines on the middle of his throat where his own swords had cut him as Talyn tried to steady her shaking hands that day.

"Fuck me," Bressen whispered, leaning in to look.

"She's an excellent fighter, and her porting makes her hard to track."

"Alright," Bressen said, leaning back again. "So she has a chance. But just so I'm clear, the only thing you need to do is ensure she injures you grievously enough to declare her the winner without purposely allowing her to wound you?"

"Sounds about right."

Bressen gave him a dubious look. "What the fuck were you thinking?"

Samhail smiled. "The issue is that I wasn't thinking."

"Or you were letting the wrong head make decisions?"

"That too," Samhail said, shaking his head. "No offense to Cyra, but I've never been between a sweeter pair of legs than Talyn's. I can't even think straight when I'm fucking her."

"Welcome to being in love, brother," Bressen chuckled. "I can't remember half of the first month with Cyra because I spent so much of it in a rapturous haze. Every time I was inside her I swear I forgot my own fucking name. I still do sometimes."

Samhail chuckled as well. "I remember that haze, and I swore I'd never make the same mistake." He sighed heavily. "At least you're enjoying your madness. Let's hope I live to enjoy my own."

Talyn

Talyn was trying to read Samhail's lips as he spoke to Bressen when Cyra appeared in front of her, capturing her attention.

"Are you sure you want to do this?" Cyra asked, her tone clearly indicating what she thought of the idea.

Talyn glowered at her. "No, of course I don't want to do this, but I don't have a choice."

Cyra paused. "You could always just accept-"

"Accept his claim?" Talyn cut in.

Cyra nodded. "Why not?"

Talyn frowned. "Do you understand what you're asking me to do? The man claimed me like I was a plot of land."

Cyra shrugged. "He's a gargoyle. I've learned to accept they have their own way of doing things."

That brought Talyn up short, and she just stared at Cyra.

"Let me ask you," Cyra said, "are you actually opposed to being with Samhail, or are you just opposed to the way he tried to make it happen?"

Talyn clenched her jaw. "I can't be with a man who places so little value on letting me make my own decisions," she said.

"As I understand it, you were planning to leave," Cyra said. "It seems like he was trying to tell you he was willing to fight to keep you here."

"He wasn't fighting. He was claiming," Talyn repeated.

Cyra gave her a frustrated look. "If you'll forgive me for saying so, I know Samhail well enough to know he doesn't want to own you. He likes you because you're strong and because you challenge him. I'm willing to bet he expected you to reject the claim and fight him."

Talyn went still as she considered that idea for the first time. Nemesis take her, Cyra was right. That was just the kind of backwards thing Samhail would do. He enjoyed fighting her, for the gods' sakes. Leave it to him to find another way to get her to engage him in combat.

She wasn't sure if that made her more or less angry at him.

"You never answered my question," Cyra said, jolting Talyn out of her thoughts.

"What was your question?" Talyn asked, trying to remember.

"Are you actually opposed to being with Samhail?"

Talyn blinked. She hadn't let herself consider that. She'd always known she *couldn't* be with him for a multitude of reasons that now seemed unimportant. Whether or not she *wanted* to be with him didn't feel like a question she had the luxury of asking herself.

Talyn opened her mouth to answer the lady – to say what, she had no idea – but Surgeon and Serise stepped forward then, cutting her off.

"Combatants, step forward!" Serise called out.

Talyn turned away from Cyra and walked over to meet Samhail in front of the twins.

"Samhail of Bragden, you've claimed the Right of Primacy over Talyn of Avril," Surgeon said. "Talyn has rejected your claim and chosen to exercise her right of refusal by combat."

Talyn scowled at the barely contained smile on Surgeon's lips. He seemed to find it amusing Talyn had rejected his brother's claim. It almost made her want to accept it just to wipe that look off the gargoyle's face.

"Have you agreed on the terms of the battle?" Serise asked.

Talyn's scowl deepened as she looked at Samhail. He hadn't mentioned any terms to her beyond what he'd told her yesterday.

"We haven't discussed them yet," Samhail said, "but I propose that both weapons and powers be allowed."

Talyn's eyes widened. She didn't realize the rules allowed opponents to determine things like whether weapons or powers could be used, but she did realize Samhail could've proposed they not be allowed to use their powers. Her ability to port was the thing that gave her any chance against him, and he wasn't trying to take it away from her.

It would mean Samhail could use his powers as well, so she'd have to watch out for that, but it was a huge boon to be able to port.

The weapons were also a blessing, albeit a lesser one. Without a weapon, she'd be left to fight a man twice her size in hand-to-hand combat. Back in her jail cell, she'd had the element of surprise against him, and the smaller quarters had played to her advantage against someone that big, but out here there was little she could do against him without a blade.

Something twisted in Talyn's chest to realize he was giving her every possible chance to beat him.

"And what about-," Serise began to ask, but Samhail cut her off.

"Talyn isn't a gargoyle, so I won't use my gargoyle form in any way," he said. "Including my wings."

Talyn's mouth fell open to learn that after all this, he could still have opted to use his giant stone gargoyle form to fight her. Gods above. The fight would've been over before it started if he'd insisted on that.

Indeed, Surgeon frowned at Samhail.

"Brother, are you sure you-"

"I won't use my gargoyle form," Samhail insisted, cutting Surgeon off. "If I'm going to prove I deserve my claim, I'll do it in a fair fight."

Talyn's eyes met Samhail's for the first time then, and she had to steady herself at the look of longing she saw in them. She almost never cried, but she blinked back the tears that threatened to gather.

Nemesis fucking damn him. She wanted to hate him for what he'd done, for what he was forcing her into, but instead she found herself wishing she hadn't rejected his claim.

Talyn looked away. There was still time for her to call this off and accept the claim, but she couldn't bring herself to do it. Pride wouldn't let her. Neither would that last thread inside her that insisted she couldn't be with him, couldn't put her trust and hopes for happiness in him. She was an assassin. That kind of life just wasn't in the cards for her.

"May the better fighter win," she said, glancing back at him.

She'd meant to sound confident and proud, but her voice broke over the words, and something shifted in Samhail's face as he looked at her.

"I'd like to speak to Talyn alone for a minute," Samhail said without looking at his brother and sister.

The twins turned and retreated to the side to give them some privacy.

"I won't accept the claim, so save your breath," Talyn said when they were out of earshot.

The corners of Samhail's mouth turned up the barest amount. "I didn't think you would."

"Then what exactly did you want to talk-"

Her words were cut off as Samhail's hand shot out and wrapped around the back of her neck. His lips stifled her cry of protest as they came down on hers, and his tongue delved into her mouth as he held her hostage to his kiss.

Her cry of protest turned to a whimper as she tried halfheartedly to push on his chest, but his other hand came up to cover hers, and then she couldn't fight it anymore. This might be their last kiss, and Talyn let herself enjoy it as she tried to memorize the taste of him and the feel of him against her. She wanted desperately to wrap her arms around his neck and lean into his body, but she couldn't do it with Cyra, Bressen, and the two gargoyles looking on.

Samhail lifted his lips and turned his head to whisper in her ear.

"Whatever happens today, I need you to know I'm in love with you, Talyn of Avril," he whispered.

Talyn let out a choked cry and tried to jerk back from him, but his hand tightened against the nape of her neck, keeping her from pulling away. The side of his forehead rested against hers as he went on.

"You need to know I'll be fighting as hard as I can to win, not because the Right of Primacy demands it, but because I don't want to lose. I can't lose," he said, speaking faster, more urgently now. "I can't lose *you*. I don't regret claiming you. I know I don't own you. No one could ever possibly own a woman like you, but whether you accept my claim or not, we both know the truth. You. Are. *Mine*."

He punctuated each of the last three words, and something backflipped in Talyn's stomach, even as the traitorous muscles between her legs clenched in anticipation.

"You're mine," he repeated. "I think you know that, and one of these days you'll admit it. But for now, if you need to fight me, then go ahead and fight me. You were right. It only makes me want you more. If you wanted to get away from me, then you picked the wrong way to do it."

His voice had turned to a growl, and Talyn swallowed as she fought to keep herself from whimpering at his words. Protector save her, he had no business saying such things to her.

Samhail released her head and pulled back suddenly. She nearly stumbled forward but caught herself in time. She tried to speak, but Samhail turned abruptly and strode back to where Bressen waited for him, the lord's own mouth wide-open in surprise.

She forced herself to turn and walk back to where Cyra stood. Her legs felt unstable beneath her, but she managed to make it back with her head held high, her anger growing with each step.

How dare he do and say those things to her right before their fight? He was trying to put her off-balance, and it was fucking working.

By the time she stopped in front of Cyra, she didn't even believe what he'd said anymore. He'd used a kiss to distract her once before, and he was doing it again to ensure he didn't have to suffer the indignity of losing to her. She'd seen the way Surgeon smiled at her rejection of him.

Worse than that, Samhail had told her before that gargoyles didn't fall in love. He must think her an idiot to believe it now.

"What did he say to you?" Cyra asked cautiously as Talyn examined the weapons on a nearby rack.

"Nothing of importance," Talyn snapped. She was in no mood to have this kind of conversation with one of Samhail's former lovers.

"That was quite a lie you just told me," Cyra said, sounding awed. "I've never seen anyone glow that red before."

Talyn glared at Cyra before going back to checking the weaponry.

"Whatever he said obviously upset you," Cyra went on. "You can't fight him like this. You need to have your head straight if you have any chance of beating him."

Talyn smiled wryly. "Anxious for me to beat him so you can be rid of me?" she asked without looking up. "Don't worry. I'll be gone soon, and you'll have him all to yourself again."

Cyra grabbed Talyn's arm, and Talyn met the lady's eyes just in time to see a quick flash of red in them.

"Let's get a few things perfectly clear here," Cyra said, annoyance evident in her voice. "The only thing I want with regard to Samhail is his happiness, and for reasons I'm still not entirely clear on, you seem to make him happy. My involvement with Samhail is over. It's you he wants. Any fool can see that in the way he looks at you."

Talyn huffed a laugh and shook her head.

"He told you he loved you just now, didn't he," Cyra said knowingly.

"He lied to me," Talyn said.

"No, he didn't. Whatever he said to you was the absolute truth or I would've seen him glow red."

Talyn paused, then shook her head. "It doesn't matter. I can't stay."

"Why not?" Cyra asked, her voice growing desperate.

Talyn didn't get the chance to answer as Surgeon and Serise called for them to get ready to begin. She took one last look at the weapons and chose a shortsword to go with her dagger. She wasn't as good at fighting two-handed as Samhail was, but the sword was more of a decoy weapon anyway. If she was going to beat Samhail, she'd do it with her dagger.

Talyn looked at Samhail and was relieved to see he had his two usual swords. He had long arms and long swords, but she didn't intend to be out in the path of them. She planned to stay as close to him as possible.

Samhail was too fast and too good with his swords for her to have any hope of fighting him in the usual way, but if she stayed within a foot or two of him, he wouldn't have room to swing the razor-sharp blades at her. The swords, coupled with his reach, normally afforded him a cushion to keep attackers at bay, but she could port inside his reach and attack with her dagger where he wouldn't be able to block her with his swords. It was her only chance. She'd have to be sure to stay away from his elbows and fists, but at least she'd be safe from his swords.

Just then, she also noticed he wasn't wearing his leather armor, except for his vambraces. She herself was wearing vambraces and a soft leather vest over her shirt that would afford a small degree of protection to her torso from mild swipes, but she'd refused any other type of armor. She wasn't used to fighting in it, and she needed as much mobility as possible.

She wasn't sure what to think of Samhail's lack of armor. A former version of her would've been offended, would've assumed he was trying to show her he wasn't afraid she'd hit him, like when he'd had her tie his hand behind his back to fight Kostas. The newer version of her, the one that wouldn't let her admit how much she cared for him, wanted to believe he was trying to make the fight as even as possible. If she wasn't wearing armor, he wouldn't either.

Talyn and Samhail both stepped forward to the center of the training yard and stopped about ten feet from each other. Even from this distance she had to look up at him, and she tried not to notice every rippling muscle on his body, from his lightly flexing biceps to his corded legs and everything in between.

How did she always forget how big he was?

Surgeon and Serise again came up to stand to the side between them.

"Are you both ready?" Serise asked.

"Yes," they said together.

"Serise and I will bear witness to this fight and determine a winner," Surgeon said. "We'll also decide if there are any infractions that violate the Right of Primacy." He glanced at Samhail, who glared at him.

"Will you accept the results as we determine them?" Serise asked.

"Yes," they said again.

"Very well then," Surgeon said as he and Serise stepped back. "You may begin when this dagger hits the ground."

Surgeon held up an ornate ceremonial dagger with a bejeweled silver handle. He raised it, paused, then threw it down so it stuck in the ground.

Talyn only saw the dagger hit the ground out of the corner of her eye. She didn't need to see it. She only needed to see Samhail. Her eyes were locked with his midnight blue ones, and she saw everything she needed to know in the way his pupils flared.

The fight for her freedom – or perhaps for her love – was on.

Chapter 49

Talyn ported as soon as the dagger hit earth, not directly behind Samhail, but just off to his left side. In all the times she'd seen him fight, she'd never been able to tell if he was weaker with one arm over the other, but porting to his left put her right hand, the one with her dagger, toward his back. She slashed out with the dagger, but Samhail had moved as soon as the ceremonial dagger hit as well. He was already swinging around, anticipating her port, and she had to abandon her attack to duck and roll out of the way of the fist and sword hilt that came swinging toward her.

She was on her feet again in a second, and she ported in front of him to thrust the dagger forward, aiming for the middle of his stomach. He swung his arm up between them and knocked her blow out of the way, though. Talyn nearly lost her blade when his arm hit hers, but she managed to hold onto it.

Samhail's other hand swung down as he tried to hit her with the pommel of his sword, the blade too long to slash her from this angle, but she brought her own shortsword up to deflect the blow. Her sword scraped along his leather vambrace and shifted his hand just far enough so the pommel came down on her shoulder instead of her head. Talyn cried out and ported immediately. She reappeared a few feet away and tried to roll her shoulder to ease the throbbing there.

Samhail didn't give her a second to recover. He lunged toward her with swords raised, and Talyn ported again, but not far. She appeared at his side, and his own momentum carried him across the tip of her dagger so the blade slashed a shallow cut along his side. The cut would have been deeper, but Samhail must've tried to change course as soon as he saw her port, so the dagger only grazed him instead of cutting him open.

Talyn heard Cyra's cry of fear when Samhail looked down at the red staining his shirt, but neither of them looked to the lady. Instead, they both attacked again.

It was all Talyn could do to stay one step ahead of Samhail. He moved like lightning, his swords flashing like bolts in the bright sunlight as she tried her best to stay inside his reach as much as possible. She wished there was a cloud cover because she kept having to blink from the flare of steel.

Staying inside his reach kept her safe from his blades, but as she'd feared, Samhail's heavily muscled arms and large hands kept her from being able to land anything more than minor blows. Her entire body would be black and blue from the fists and elbows she'd taken from him. She had to do something soon, or she'd be in too much pain to move.

So far she'd been lucky enough that most of Samhail's blows had been glancing, but her luck ran out on his next swing. She ported to his side and was about to stab her dagger at him when Samhail swiveled, and one of his swords caught the sun just right so it flared in her eyes. She squeezed them shut on instinct, but when she opened them again, the first and only thing she saw was the back of Samhail's fist flying toward her head.

Stars erupted in Talyn's vision as pain spiked through her temple, and everything went black for a moment. She heard someone shout her name, possibly Samhail, but she was too stunned to tell.

When she opened her eyes, she was on the ground and seeing double. She blinked to clear her vision and was relieved when she saw only one of everything again.

A large shape loomed a few feet away, and she lifted her head to see Samhail standing there, swords hanging at his sides as though he meant to drop down next to her and be sure she was alright. He took a step toward her, then stopped and glanced to his side where the twins stood watching him closely.

He seemed to realize at the same moment Talyn did that he couldn't check on her, couldn't show her mercy, and he raised his swords to attack again as he lunged toward her while she struggled to her feet.

Talyn managed to get herself into a crouch before she ported behind him. She shoved her shoulder into the back of his knee, and he swore as he fell backward. She ported out from under him, and by the time his body hit the ground, she'd reappeared on top of him, straddling his torso. Her dagger plunged toward his chest, but Samhail dropped his swords and grabbed her hands. He twisted one hand so she cried out in pain and dropped her shortsword. His other hand ripped the dagger from her and tossed it away.

Talyn shrieked in surprise as he flipped them both so he was on top of her as he pinned her hands to the ground.

"I need to stop letting you knock my knees out from under me," he said in annoyance.

"Do you give up yet?" Talyn asked as he held her down.

Samhail arched an eyebrow then smiled. "You should know by now I'll never give up where you're concerned."

Talyn ignored the shiver of pleasure that shot through her at his words and ported instead. She appeared on his back and wrapped an arm around his neck. As she did, she shifted into a man, the largest man she could get her powers to stretch her body into, and she wrapped her legs around his waist to keep him from pulling her off as she squeezed her arm against his throat. She yelled as he grabbed her shirt and dragged her over his shoulder anyway so she landed hard on her back and the breath punched out of her. Her eyes widened as his fist came flying toward her face, and she shifted into a doe-eyed girl who let out a frightened scream.

"Fuck!" Samhail swore as he diverted his fist just in time to smash it into the ground instead.

Talyn ported over to where he'd thrown her dagger and picked it up, then shifted back into her own form.

"That was playing dirty," Samhail said as he picked himself up.

They were both breathing heavily now.

"No, playing dirty would have been turning into Cyra," she retorted, and he growled.

Samhail was weaponless, and Talyn had the impulse to port back to him, but she needed half a second to rest. She couldn't do this for much longer. She could already feel her porting power start to wane.

"Aren't you going to pick up your swords?" she asked him, nodding to the two blades still on the ground.

A smile curled his lips.

"No, because I know what you're trying to do," he said. "It was a solid plan, but it's time to end this."

Samhail held his hand out, and the ceremonial dagger Surgeon had thrown to the ground flew into it.

Talyn swallowed. Fuck. There went her advantage.

Her eyes widened a second later when he held his hand out toward her, and Talyn tried to throw herself out of the way of the forcefield that erupted from his palm. It was too big, and she cried out as she was thrown back hard on the ground, her chest vibrating from the blow.

Talyn coughed and tried to inhale as she picked herself up on her elbows. Fear spiked her adrenaline as Samhail strode toward her, and she tried to rise, but another forcefield slammed into her, and she went rolling back on the ground. Thankfully she'd at least managed to hold onto her dagger. She needed to end this. Between her exhaustion, her injuries, and her waning power, she was quickly losing any advantage she'd had.

Talyn rallied her power and ported right in front of Samhail. He'd started to turn, anticipating she'd appear behind him, but he corrected himself just in time. Talyn barely dodged his swinging arm as it grazed her temple, and she stumbled a little before porting.

She ported again and again as she had that time in the woods, hoping to make him dizzy or at least keep him off-balance, but he kept up with her just enough to deflect any attacks she made.

Finally, she ported once more but reappeared back in the same space she'd left, thrusting her dagger out blindly, hoping to hit something. Samhail had started to move and was bringing his dagger around as well, but he stopped with a grunt as they found themselves face to face. Talyn's dagger met with the resistance of flesh even as pain stabbed through her own stomach.

Time ground to a halt as their eyes met. Samhail's eyes went wide with fear and pain, and nausea churned in Talyn's gut as all of her limbs went numb. She could only see the hilt of her dagger because the blade was now stuck fully inside Samhail's chest.

Panic made her lightheaded. Gods above, had she hit his heart, or was she just wide of it? She sent a desperate prayer up to the Protector that she was wide.

Talyn tried to pull the blade from Samhail's chest so Cyra could heal him, but her fingers had gone slack, and she couldn't seem to grip it. Her hand loosened on the handle and dropped to her side.

And then she was falling.

Both Cyra and Bressen screamed as Talyn hit the ground. She heard the thud next to her as Samhail fell a second after she did, and she tried to turn toward him, but pain shot through her midsection. That's when she saw the handle of the ceremonial dagger sticking out of her own stomach, its jewels glittering in the sun. It was several seconds before her pain-addled brain realized they'd stabbed each other at the same time.

Talyn reached a shaking hand toward the blade stuck just above her navel. Her hand was covered in blood, and she felt something wet and warm dribble over her lips as she coughed.

She turned her head and found Samhail lying on the ground close to her. Cyra was already kneeling next to him, terror and panic in the lady's eyes, her voice frantic. Behind her, Lord Bressen's face was ashen as he yelled to Samhail.

Talyn saw Cyra reach for the dagger in Samhail's chest to pull it out, but he caught her wrist.

"Heal Talyn first," he rasped.

"I'll get to her," Cyra said, her voice laced with terror. "Your wound is worse."

"Talyn first," Samhail insisted, not letting go of Cyra's wrist. "Please."

"Samhail, I-"

Samhail didn't let her finish. He grabbed her shirt and pulled her down close to his mouth. Talyn could hear the soft rasp of his voice as he whispered in her ear, but she couldn't make out what he was saying.

Jealousy made her go cold as she imagined him saying his goodbyes to the woman, telling her he loved her as he'd said to Talyn only moments ago, and tears welled in her eyes. One trickled out of the corner toward her hairline, but she couldn't move.

"Gods damn it!" Cyra shouted as Samhail released her shirt and she pulled away from him. She turned to the twins. "One of you hold a cloth over Samhail's wound to staunch the blood until I can get to him. And the Protector save you if you let him die because there is nowhere in the world you'll be able to hide from me."

Cyra got up and moved over to Talyn as the two other gargoyles moved in around their brother to attend to his wound.

Talyn shook her head as the lady knelt next to her. "No, Samhail..."

"He'll only let me touch him if I heal you first," Cyra said, anger roiling in her voice. "Gods fucking dammit! Aramis should be here to do this!"

Tears rolled down Cyra's face, and Talyn searched her memory for who Aramis was. It came to her a second later. The lady's father and a healer, but he was dead now.

"Please, help Samhail first," Talyn said, pushing back Cyra's hands.

"Bressen, help me!" Cyra called to her husband.

Talyn's sluggish brain realized too late what Cyra was asking. In her weakened state, Bressen took over her mind easily, and her body went limp. His power was an anesthetic, numbing the pain in her stomach and paralyzing her limbs. She could do nothing but watch as Cyra pulled the jeweled dagger from her stomach and laid her hands over the wound to repair the damage.

Talyn's eyes shifted to where Samhail lay on the ground. His skin, normally so tan, looked pale, and it shined with a fine sheen of sweat. His breathing seemed entirely too shallow.

Talyn's mouth moved, but she couldn't speak, and she felt another tear trickle down the side of her face as he looked back at her.

Don't die, she mouthed to him, but he gave no indication he understood her.

Talyn didn't know how much time passed as she lay there with her eyes locked on Samhail's, but she gradually realized the pain in her abdomen had lessened.

"Give me a clean cloth," Cyra ordered, and someone, either Surgeon or Serise handed her one. "Bressen, let her go."

A second later, the feeling returned to her limbs, and she tried to sit up. Cyra pressed the cloth to Talyn's stomach.

"Hold this here," Cyra told her. "It's not completely healed yet, but I have to help Samhail first."

Talyn grabbed the cloth and held it to the still-bleeding hole in her stomach. Healers healed from the inside out, so Cyra had repaired the worst of the internal damage first. She'd come back later and take care of the flesh wound after Samhail was out of danger.

Talyn rolled onto her side and pulled herself along the ground to him.

Cyra was already kneeling next to him, and she reached for him, but Samhail again grabbed her wrist.

"Samhail! Let go!" Cyra cried. "I healed most of her injury. She's fine!"

Samhail ignored the lady and turned his head to Talyn. "You win. Accept the victory."

Talyn blinked. "What?"

"Samhail! Let me heal you!" Cyra screamed. "Bressen, help me!"

"I can't!" Bressen said. "His shield is up. I'd have to break past it."

"Accept the victory," Samhail repeated, his voice weak and graveled.

Talyn's breath hitched as she realized what he'd done. By insisting Cyra heal her first, he'd made sure Talyn was well enough to fight while he wasn't. He was allowing her to claim the victory in the challenge.

"Oh gods," Talyn whispered.

"Talyn!" Cyra screamed, bringing Talyn back to her senses. "Accept the gods damned victory before he dies!"

Talyn opened her mouth, but the words caught in her throat. It was dawning on her that accepting the victory meant she was no longer his, and fucking hells, she wanted to be. He was right. She was his and had been for a long time.

Talyn's mind went blank. Accepting the victory would break the bond with him, but not accepting it would likely kill him. Either way, she'd lose him, and she let out a strangled cry.

"Talyn!" Cyra screamed as Samhail continued to clutch her wrist.

The lady's voice jarred her back to the present as she realized what she needed to do.

"I accept it! I accept the victory!" Talyn yelled.

She looked up at Surgeon and Serise, who were standing over Samhail, and for once she saw concern in their eyes.

Surgeon nodded. "The victory is legitimate," he said. "Talyn of Avril has won her challenge against Samhail of Bragden's claim on her."

"It's done! Let Cyra heal you!" Talyn told him, her own panic rising now as she watched the color slowly drain even more from his skin.

Samhail released Cyra's wrist, and his hand fell to the ground.

Cyra cried out and laid her hands over his wound as she sent her power into him.

Talyn looked at her own hand and saw Samhail's claiming mark was gone. Far from relief, the sight of the empty finger made her feel hollow, and her stomach ached in a way that had nothing to do with the still-bleeding wound there.

She looked back to Samhail. His eyes were glassy, and Talyn screamed as she inched closer to him.

"Samhail! Don't you gods damn die on me!" she yelled at him. She put her hand on his cheek. "Samhail! Look at me!"

He blinked slowly, and she knew she was losing him.

"Samhail, listen to me! Are you listening?"

His eyes focused for a moment, and he nodded weakly.

Talyn pushed some locks of white hair back behind his ears as if to be sure nothing would interfere with what she had to say.

"Samhail, I claim you by Right of Primacy. Do you hear me? I claim you by right as mine!"

He blinked.

Talyn looked up at Surgeon and Serise, who looked stunned.

"Can I do that? Can I claim him?" Talyn asked.

The twins glanced at each other before turning back to her.

"I…don't think it's ever happened before," Serise said, "but I don't know of any rules against a non-gargoyle claiming a gargoyle."

Talyn looked down at her right hand. There was nothing on her finger, but she saw something peeking out from under her vambrace on the back of her hand. She tore the vambrace off and saw the faint, ornate lines of a design that looked something like a feather. It started at the base of her hand, then curled around her wrist and halfway up her forearm.

Talyn grabbed Samhail's hand and saw that the middle finger on his right hand bore the gray feather-like marking as well.

"Fuck me," Surgeon said in awe.

Talyn held up Samhail's hand so he could see it. "Look. You're mine now. Do you accept my claim?"

Samhail's eyes shifted to the faint markings on his finger before he looked back at Talyn. He opened his mouth, and she leaned in to hear.

"Can I think about it for a while?" he asked weakly.

Talyn's mouth fell open and then clamped shut again. A feeble grin curled the corners of Samhail's lips, and she had the urge to hit him.

"No," she said. "And you're still weak enough I can beat you if you challenge my claim, so I'd advise against that as well."

"You're not giving me much choice," he said.

"No, I'm not," she said. "Now are you going to accept my claim, or do I need to stab you again?"

Cyra made a disgruntled noise as she continued to work on healing Samhail's wound, but he only chuckled, then groaned in pain.

"Stay still," Cyra scolded him. "Nemesis damn me, I should've let you both bleed to death."

The words were harsh, but her lighter tone told Talyn that Samhail was out of danger. She met his eyes again. The shine was back in their midnight blue depths, and her breath caught at his look.

"Yes," Samhail said. His voice sounded stronger now as the smile shimmered on his face. "I accept your claim, Talyn of Avril. I'm yours."

She smiled back as tears streaked down her face. "You're mine, and I'm yours until the Nemesis takes us."

He shook his head. "Not even then. The Nemesis may take me, but I'll still belong to you. I love you now and always, hummingbird."

Talyn broke into sobs and laid her head on his shoulder.

"I love you too," she said as she cried against him, "but stop calling me that, or I really will stab you again."

Tandem Read: Go to *Nemesis Rising* (Bk 4), Chapters 38-39

Chapter 50

Samhail

There were only three people that Samhail imagined might be knocking on his door right now, and it turned out to be the last of the three he expected.

Words died on his tongue as he took in Talyn standing there, her hand resting on the doorframe, her hips arched to one side to accentuate the already stunning curves of her body.

She wore only two items of clothing. The first was a white shirt fully unbuttoned to reveal a trail of bare skin down the center of her body where it gave a teasing view of the perfect globes of her full breasts beneath the fabric. His eyes dipped to the second item of clothing, an undergarment – a tiny scrap of black fabric – that peeked between the flaps of the shirt at her hips.

Samhail's cock hardened instantly, and he forced a deep breath out through his nose. He'd gone looking for Talyn earlier in her room after he'd cleaned up, but she hadn't been there, and he'd had the sick feeling she'd left without saying goodbye after all.

Relief and lust flooded his veins to see her here now.

"We need to talk," Talyn said casually, drawing his gaze back to hers.

Samhail blinked as he tried to get his brain to recognize the sounds coming from her lips as words. Words with meanings. What the fuck had she just said again?

His mind snapped back as comprehension dawned.

"You want to talk?" he said, and she nodded.

Samhail stepped out of the way to let her inside, and she pushed off the door frame to enter. She was barefoot as well, and damn him, she even had beautiful feet.

As soon as she was through the door, he slammed it behind her and grabbed her arm. She gasped as he yanked her back and pushed her against the door to press his body into hers.

"You didn't really think you could show up to my door dressed like this and think we'd just talk, did you?" he growled at her.

He slid his hand into her shirt to close over her breast, and she moaned. Her nipple was already a stiff peak against his palm, and she gasped as he kneaded the breast then flicked the nipple with his thumb.

"Samhail…," she breathed, but he cut her off.

"You just walked into the den of a predator dressed like dinner," he went on. "Don't expect to leave here without being eaten."

He dropped to his knees and hooked his fingers on the waist of her undergarment. Talyn sucked in a breath as he yanked at the garment and tore it free from her body. He pulled one of her legs up over his shoulder so she was almost sitting on it, and she yelped as he buried his face at her apex to feast on her.

"Fucking hells!" Talyn cried as Samhail shifted to his gargoyle tongue and let it wrap around her clit to squeeze gently.

He smiled as she began to pant. He licked up and down her center, spearing his tongue into her on each pass.

She grabbed his head with both hands as she undulated her hips to grind against his face, and Samhail pressed his mouth in deeper, licking and sucking at her as if she'd be his last meal. She was so wet, and he savored the taste of her on his tongue as she dripped against his mouth.

His tongue flicked quickly against her clit, and Talyn threw her head back against the door with a loud thud. He tried to look up to see if she was alright, but her fingers tightened in his hair to hold him in place.

"Gods above, don't you dare stop," she said, and he redoubled his efforts with a small chuckle that made her moan.

She yelled out a moment later, and he felt her muscles pulse around his tongue as he thrust it in and out of her. He tightened his hold on her leg and waist as she continued to rock her hips against his mouth, chasing the last throes of her climax.

When she finally stopped shuddering in his hold, Samhail turned his head to the side and sunk his fangs into the inside of her thigh.

Talyn let out a sharp scream, but she just kept her grip on his hair as he drank from her, letting her sweet blood coat his tongue. He lifted his head a minute later and licked her blood from his lips where it mixed with the slickness of her arousal.

"I think your blood is even sweeter just after you come," he said.

She was panting where she leaned against the door, and he put her leg down before rising to his feet. He pulled her shirt off, and she squeaked as he tossed her over his bare shoulder.

"Gods damn it, Samhail!" she yelled, but he ignored her as he carried her to the bed and dropped her onto it.

She turned and scurried toward the head of it as he unfastened his pants and pulled them off. By the time he'd discarded them, she had his dagger in her hand.

He chuckled, not surprised she knew or guessed he always kept a blade under his pillow. He held out a hand and tried to summon the blade from her, but she held it firm.

Triumph crossed her face at having held onto the dagger, but it was short-lived as he moved his hand lower and latched his summoning power onto her ankle instead. She gave another sharp cry as his power yanked her down the bed toward him and his hand closed around her ankle.

Talyn sat up and swung the dagger at him, but he tugged her ankle forward even more, and she fell back against the mattress. He crawled over her and caught her wrists to pin them above her head. She growled in frustration but didn't port.

He grinned. She wanted to fight, but she didn't really want to escape.

Samhail lowered himself on top of her and nestled his hips between her thighs as he used his knee to push her legs apart farther.

Talyn let out a soft whimper he knew was one of need, not defeat, as he notched his cock at her entrance. She pushed her hips forward, urging him on, but he held himself still.

"This is your last chance," he said.

His muscles strained with the effort of not slamming into her. The only time the urge to fuck for gargoyles was stronger than after a battle was after a Primacy bond was confirmed. He'd been in no shape earlier to claim his new mate, but he'd rested and couldn't hold back any longer.

He'd nearly mauled her just now when she'd appeared at his door half-dressed with the evidence of her desire already wetting that damned black scrap of cloth. He'd managed to hold back long enough to make her come on his tongue, but his restraint was about to snap like a frayed string holding on by its last fiber. Had he been a man with less self-control, he'd have taken her to the floor right there in the doorway and fucked her raw.

"Last chance for what?" Talyn asked, her brow creasing.

"Your last chance to stop this," he said, his voice strained with need.

She frowned deeper. "I thought the bond was already permanent. Are you saying I can still break it?"

"No," he said as his body started to shake from holding back. "The bond is permanent. You are and will always be my wife. There's no changing that now."

"Then what are you talking about?"

"If I take you now," he said, "if we consummate this mating, then I'm never letting you go again. If you want your freedom, port now and run as far from here as fast as you can. I won't stop you."

He didn't have the capacity at the moment to decipher the emotions that crossed her face at his words. He only knew she was still beneath him.

"But if I take you now," he went on, "if I let myself slip into you and feel you close around me, if I feel your body pulse and clench around my cock and hear you moan my name, then there's nowhere in this world you'll be able to run from me hereafter. There's nowhere you'll be able to hide that I won't find you and drag you back."

She inhaled sharply, and he willed himself not to move.

"So tell me what you want me to do, Talyn," he said.

He held his breath as she looked at him.

"What I want," Talyn said, her expression like stone, "is for you to stop talking and fuck me like I'm your wife and this is our wedding night."

It took a moment for her words to sink in, then a feral grin crossed his face. He found a small reserve of self-restraint, just enough to ask her, "And how do you want me to take you? Like this? From behind?"

She thought a moment. "Neither actually. I'm taking *you* this time."

She wrapped her arms around him and threw her hips to the side, apparently intending to flip them so he was on his back with her on top.

Samhail didn't so much as budge at the attempt.

He quirked a brow at her, and Talyn sighed heavily as she relaxed her hold on him.

"Fucking gargoyles," she muttered. "I'm going to need a little cooperation from you on this."

He smiled in amusement. "You were just off-balance. Try it again."

She gave him a wry look but tried to flip him again. This time they turned so fast that only his hands on her waist kept her from flying off the bed, and he now lay on his back with Talyn straddling his hips.

He groaned as her core settled over his cock, and she slid herself over him, coating his steely length with her wetness. He closed his eyes as his hands tightened on her waist, and she ran her hands down his torso.

"Hmm, what should I do with you now that I have you at my mercy?" she purred, rocking her hips so she slid along the length of his cock again.

"I think you promised to fuck me," he said, need rasping his words.

"Did I?" she asked innocently.

She leaned over and let her hair fall across his chest. His nostrils flared, but he didn't move. She leaned over him further to kiss and nip a trail down the center of his chest that made him groan, all the while rocking herself gently over his swollen cock. His hands slid lower to her hips where they urged her to move faster. She moved her mouth back up and fastened it over one of his nipples, biting gently.

"Don't test my control, hummingbird," he warned. "I can have you on your back again in a heartbeat, and I know how to tease as well."

"That sounds like a threat."

"It's a promise. Don't make me beg."

Having mercy on him, she lifted herself and reached down to guide him to her entrance. She started to ease onto him, letting his head part her slowly, but she was so wet her body swallowed him quickly, and they both groaned as she bottomed out on his cock.

"Fuuck," Samhail said, drawing out the word. His fingers moved to her thighs, biting into the flesh. She'd likely have bruises there tomorrow, but he couldn't help it.

She slid up his length to his head before slamming herself back down.

"Nemesis take me," he growled as he watched her breasts bounce with the movement. "Why haven't we done it this way before?"

"Because you're a domineering male who insists on being on top?" she offered.

"Not anymore," he said as she plunged herself down on him again. "From now on you'll ride me like this at least once a day."

"Still making demands?" she said.

He snaked his hands up her back, but she grabbed his wrists and pinned them next to his head.

"No touching," she breathed into his ear as she rode him harder, and his body practically shook beneath her.

She let go of his hands and leaned back as she ground her hips into him. He tried to move his hands, but she pushed them back down and tsked at him.

"Your hands stay there, or I'll stop," she said. She stopped for just a second to emphasize the point, and the snarl that left him was savage.

Her laugh was mischievous as she slid down his length then ground herself into him, and Samhail threw his head back against the mattress.

"Fuck!" he swore again. His hands started to lift off the bed again, but he remembered her threat in time and let them fall back down.

"Good boy," she purred as she continued to ride him.

Talyn slid one of her hands up his chest, then up the column of his neck before she curled her fingers around his throat and squeezed.

Samhail's eyes flared, and his growl rumbled against her palm.

She ran her second hand up to wrap around his throat as well.

"What are you doing?" he choked out against her hold.

"Reminding you who you belong to," she said as she pushed down onto his cock with fierce thrusts, and Samhail swore he went even harder.

She plunged herself down again and again, crying out softly with each thrust as she pushed them closer to an abyss that would swallow them both whole. Starbursts flared behind Samhail's eyes, but whether they were from pleasure, lack of air, or both, he wasn't sure. He didn't care.

"Talyn," he ground out. "Please, I need to touch you." His hands nearly vibrated from the effort of holding them next to his head.

"Yes. Touch me," she breathed as she moved her hands to his chest.

His hands were on her in an instant, trailing up her back to anchor around her shoulders. He pulled her down onto him, driving him impossibly deeper before he drew her forward for a punishing kiss. Talyn screamed into his mouth as he thrust his hips up into her, and her eyes rolled back into her head as their bodies pounded together frantically, both chasing a release that always seemed just a pace ahead.

Talyn pulled back from him and undulated her hips against his before she began to ride him faster, her hands pressed against his chest for balance as his own latched around her thighs.

Samhail watched her breasts bounce heavily against her chest and knew he wouldn't last much longer. She was so gods damned perfect.

Talyn broke first, and she cried out as her body clenched around his cock. Samhail followed only a second later, roaring as he slammed up into her with brutal force, arching his body off the bed while he spilled himself into her. His hands splayed across her back as they slowly rocked to a halt, panting against each other.

Talyn collapsed against his chest and went limp. "I'm not sure I can move," she whispered against him.

"I'll tie you to my body if you try," he promised, and she laughed.

They lay there unmoving for several minutes before Samhail spoke.

"What did you want to talk about?" he asked as he traced patterns on her back with his finger.

Talyn lifted her head. "What?"

"When you came in, you said we needed to talk," he reminded her. "What did you want to talk about? Or was that just an excuse to get into my pants?"

She huffed indignantly and started to move, but he pulled her back down to kiss the marks his teeth had made on her shoulder. There were four little scars where his fangs had pierced her skin, and he loved seeing them. She didn't bear his gargoyle mark, since it had disappeared when she'd won her challenge to his claim, but his fang marks were still there, and that was almost as good. She had marks on her breast from his bite as well, and he planned to remake those every now and again to ensure they didn't go away.

The marks of Talyn's fingernails down his back had healed so he could no longer see them, but he intended to do what he could to get her to remake them. If he succeeded, he'd get them to scar-over permanently because he wanted as many of her marks on his body as he could have.

He had something even better than scars, though: her claiming mark.

Samhail looked at the feather-like design on his hand that ran down his middle finger and across his hand to the base of his thumb. Surgeon and Serise had teased him about bearing Talyn's mark rather than the other way around, but he loved the mark and would display it proudly.

"So talking?" he asked again when she didn't answer.

"I thought we should discuss how this will work now that we're bonded, at least as far as gargoyles are concerned," she said, sitting up.

Samhail sat up as well so she was straddling his lap. He wrapped his arms around her hips to pull her close.

"That's easy," he said. "The way it's going to work is that you'll stay with me at Tide's End, at least until we've finished this conflict with

Sandrian and Magdalene, then we'll decide together where to go. In the meantime, you'll move into my rooms permanently, and I'll fuck you whenever I get the chance, which – trust me – is going to be a lot."

She laughed softly. "Given this some thought, have you?" she teased.

"That's just off the top of my head," he said. "We'll have to talk to Bressen to see if there's something for you to do. I'm sure he'll agree to let you continue helping me train our troops for one."

"Actually, that's what I wanted to talk to you about," she said. "I already spoke with Bressen yesterday, and he offered me a job. I turned it down at the time, but I met with him a little while ago and accepted it."

"That's perfect!" he said. He drew her in and kissed her soundly. "What does he want you to do?"

Her face fell, and Samhail's stomach sank.

"What is it?" he asked.

"Well, it's clear my powers make me a good spy," she said, "so Lord Bressen offered me a position as his spymaster."

Samhail's first reaction was again elation until the implications hit him.

"He's sending you away," he said. Anger twisted in his chest.

"Not for long periods," Talyn assured him, "but yes. I may be gone for a few days, or even weeks, at a time, and you won't be able to come with me. You're too noticeable."

"No!" Samhail thundered. He lifted her off him and launched himself out of bed to grab up the clothing he'd tossed on the floor.

"Where are you going?" she asked, following him off the bed.

She strode over to him naked and grabbed his arm when he didn't answer. "Samhail!"

"I'm going to set Bressen straight about this," he said as he jerked one leg into his pants.

"No, you're not," she said, her hand still closed on his arm. "Lord Bressen gave me a choice. He's not making me do this. I accepted the position because my powers are perfect for this, and I can help out."

Samhail got his other leg into the pants and yanked them up.

"I don't care," he said. "He's not taking my mate away from me already. If the roles were reversed, and I was trying to send Cyra away, he'd fight me tooth and nail on it, so that's what I intend to do."

Samhail turned to stalk toward the door, but Talyn ported in front of him and put both hands on his chest. He had to pull up short to keep from running her over, and he growled his displeasure at her.

"Samhail, stop!" She tried to push him back, but he didn't budge.

He glared down at her. "He's not taking you," he said firmly.

Her face softened. "No, he's not. I'm volunteering to go, but I'm coming back. I promise. I'm not leaving you."

The breath rushed out of Samhail in a long, deep exhale, and he knew she'd hit on the real reason this sent panic surging through him. It wasn't that she was going. It was that he was afraid she wouldn't be coming back.

"I need you," he said, the words more choked than he wanted.

She smiled and put a hand to his cheek. "I need you too, and I fought too hard to get you to just give you up."

Talyn took his hand that bore her mark and held it up for him to see.

"This means you belong to me," she said. "Trust me when I tell you I'll be back whenever I can to claim what's mine."

The smile that spread across Samhail's face was smug, and she gave him a look that warned him not to be an ass. He reached up and ran his fingers gently over the bite marks on her shoulder.

"At least you have something to remember me by when you're gone," he said huskily.

She smiled. "Oh, I have more than those marks." She reached up and opened the locket that always hung at her neck to pull something out.

Samhail frowned, not understanding at first what the object was. Then recognition hit him. It was the lock of his hair she'd cut off with his own sword when he'd first caught up with her after her escape. She'd braided the strands into a small plait, rolled it into a coil, and put it in the locket.

"You kept my hair?" he asked incredulously.

She shrugged, blushing. "At first it was a trophy. Evidence I'd fought the great Samhail and lived to tell the tale."

He raised an eyebrow as she wound the braided locks absently around her finger. She had no idea how appropriate the gesture really was.

She met his eyes. "After a while, keeping it meant something different. I tried to get rid of it when I thought I was leaving, but I couldn't bring myself to do it." She hesitated. "I needed a piece of you to take with me."

A lump formed in his throat. Gods above. What this woman did to him. He reached out, pulled her close, and kissed her, more tenderly than he'd ever kissed her before. It was a kiss of love, not lust.

Samhail let out a deep breath as he pulled back from her. "I suppose that's acceptable," he said, "but there's still one more thing. Who's going to protect me while you're gone?"

She blinked. "Protect you? What are you talking about?" she asked as she put the hair back in her locket.

"I accepted your Right of Primacy claim. That means you're responsible for my protection. Had you accepted *my* claim, it would've been my job to always keep you safe, but since you rejected mine and forced me to accept yours, it's now *your* job to keep *me* safe."

"Forced you?" she sputtered.

He crossed his arms. "As I recall, you'd stabbed me in the heart and were looming over me while I bled out when you claimed the Right of Primacy. I was hardly in a position to resist. You even threatened me if I didn't accept your claim." He shrugged. "I was afraid for my life. What else could I do?"

Talyn rolled her eyes. "I changed my mind about coming back."

She tried to walk past him, but he spun her back around and pulled her close to kiss her.

"So about that protection," he prompted as he lifted his lips.

"I'll leave Axenus in charge of that while I'm gone," she said.

"Oh, fuck no," he said, and she laughed.

"I'm not letting Bressen take you away just yet, in any case," he said. "I need at least a little time to enjoy my victory."

Talyn raised a brow. "Your victory? You lost the challenge."

He smirked. "Did I?"

She started to answer then paused. "Son of a bitch," she said finally.

Samhail chuckled and swept her up to toss her back on the bed. She squeaked in protest at his manhandling, but his huge body came down to cover hers, and she arched into him.

"It took longer than expected, but I knew I could crack that stone heart of yours," he said as he laid a hand against her heart. He slid it lower to begin kneading her breast, and she moaned. His mouth replaced his hand, but he looked up when she swore.

"What's wrong?" he asked.

"I just realized Surgeon and Serise are now my in-laws," she said.

Samhail growled. "First of all, don't mention my siblings in this bed," he said. "Second, the only thing you should be thinking about right now are the benefits of being mated to a gargoyle."

"There are benefits?" she asked.

He grinned. "Oh yes." He moved further down her body and slid his hands between her thighs to push her legs open. "For one, we have incredible stamina."

She cocked her head in interest. "Oh?"

He snaked his gargoyle tongue out to lick his lips. "Then, of course, there's my tongue, and-"

Talyn put a finger to his lips to silence him. "You can stop there. The tongue alone is worth it."

He chuckled as he lowered his head between her thighs. "I belong to you, Talyn of Avril, and I intend to spend the rest of my life showing you exactly what that means."

She opened her mouth to speak, but she gasped instead as his tongue went to work, and he spent the next few hours treating her to all the benefits of having a gargoyle of her own.

Epilogue

Praya looked out over the water as she stood on the beach near Tide's End and tried to assure herself they'd done the right thing. Ariel stood next to her, both of them hidden under an obfuscation glamour, visible only to each other and the other two people on the sand with them.

Well, the only two *live* people.

Praya watched Lord Bressen carry the shrouded body of the man once called Morland to the edge of the water and lay it down. He stepped back and put a hand at the small of Cyra's back as she stepped forward.

Cyra held her hand over the body, and a moment later it became a pile of sand. Then the lord and lady stepped back as the surf surged.

Swells gathered on the water and crashed onto the beach to wash over the pile of sand formerly known as Morland. It took only a minute or so for the waves to pull it out to sea, the water dragging each grain into its depths, just as Praya was sure Morland's soul was now being dragged to one of the three hells. Probably the lowest hell if even half of what she'd heard of the man was true.

"You still don't think we should've come back," Ariel said softly.

It was a statement rather than a question. Her wife always knew what she was thinking. Whether Ariel had minor mind powers of her own, or whether Praya just gave off such strong signals that Ariel couldn't fail to pick up on them, her wife could always read her like a book.

Usually a very dirty book. But not today.

Praya shook her head. "No, the last few hours have convinced me we needed to return." Although maybe not for the reasons they first thought.

She would've said more, but the lord and lady now trudged back up the sand to where she and Ariel stood by the dunes.

Praya tried to meet Cyra's eyes, but her attention was drawn to the small dark creature that sat on the woman's shoulder. Less than a foot tall, the thing looked like a cross between the ugliest puppy she'd ever seen and something out of a nightmare. Whenever the thing blinked, one glowing red eye always blinked half a second later than the first, and Praya couldn't decide if the quirk was amusing or unnerving.

She looked away from the nightmare demoni. She'd seen some of them centuries ago from a distance when she'd first lived on the continent, but this was the first time she'd seen one up close. Demoni usually came in a horde – a wrath, to properly name the group – and it wasn't wise to get too close to them.

This one seemed to be a kind of pet. It rode on Cyra's shoulder, surrounded by a faint cloud of black smoke that wafted off its body. Lord Bressen didn't like the thing, if the occasional scowls he threw its way were any indication.

"Thank you for your help," Cyra said, and Praya pulled her attention back to the lady, her fellow Hand of the Gods.

Praya nodded. Cyra seemed stable at the moment, but Praya sensed the woman's mental equilibrium shifting, as if it stood on sand and the tide was winnowing it away, just as the tide had taken Morland's body.

Death. That's what Praya sensed around Cyra, even more than she had the first time she'd met the woman. Cyra had used her powers to kill very recently, and not just her syphoned powers. She'd used those special powers given to her by the Nemesis itself.

The first time they'd met on the island, the lady had been relatively weak and unpracticed, but something had changed since then. Cyra now radiated power, just as her husband did, and that power worried Praya. She'd been nervous to come back and face Magdalene, but she now wondered if Cyra might turn out to be the greater threat.

"I helped fix a flaw in the natural order," Praya said.

Bressen slipped his arm around Cyra's waist and pulled her close as he kissed her temple. She leaned into him, but the demoni shifted on her other shoulder.

"Now that Morland is dealt with, we need to figure out what to do about Magdalene," Bressen said. "If what Talyn told us is true, Sandrian is just a pawn in whatever game she's playing."

Cyra met Praya's eyes, and Praya felt Ariel take a careful step closer to her. On Cyra's shoulder, the little demoni blinked its staggered blink and resituated itself. It wrapped a clawed hand around some of Cyra's hair near her neck and held on, as if it expected her to start moving.

"I feel the gods stirring," Praya, said. "Something is changing with the Trinity, and it's because of Magdalene."

"She wants to restore the continental Triumvirate," Cyra said.

Praya shook her head. "Not exactly. She wants to return to a time when syphons ruled the continent, but I don't think she intends to share that power with us, no matter what she told you."

"She wants to take your power for herself," Bressen said.

"We've been taught to view the Trinity almost as one entity in three beings, but they're more fractured than one might think," Praya said. "The gods don't get along perfectly, and there are times when one will grow more powerful until the others do something to restore the balance."

Bressen looked at his wife. "The Protector must be working through Magdalene to gather power."

Praya clamped her teeth together, and she was glad the lord had phrased that as an assumption rather than a question. She wouldn't have wanted to respond.

As the oldest of the current syphons, Praya had gradually become more and more attuned to the gods and the shifts in their power, even out on the island, but it wasn't the Protector she sensed gathering power now.

It was the Nemesis rising.

Tandem Read: Go to *Nemesis Rising* (Bk 4), Chapter 40-Epilogue II

Did you like this book?
Indie authors very much appreciate your help spreading the word about their books. Please consider rating or reviewing the book on Amazon, Goodreads, or the platform of your choice. You can also share the book on social media or recommend it to others.

Thank you so much for reading!

Acknowledgements

As always, many, many thanks to my alpha reader Karen Pasquale. I really made her work for this book and the next one, since the tandem read was a slog to map out. She's excellent at helping me fill in the story gaps, and she doesn't let me off the hook when I try to gloss over parts of the story that need to be told.

Thanks to my husband Pat for his absolute and unwavering support of my writing and his continued acceptance of my dalliances with Bressen and Samhail. Sorry, Honey. Still no dragons, though.

Thanks to my beta readers – Joshua Hamel, Liza Boritz, Mindy Petruck, Emily Rice, Heather Lee, Erin Estabrook, Lana Zadrosny, and Denise Philbrick – for their keen eyes and great feedback. Everyone notices something different, and these books are so much better for each of you and your unique perspectives. I love hearing your thoughts on the books, and I thank you from the bottom of my heart.

And a special thanks to Josh for creating such an awesome character in Samhail (aka Sammhael) and then letting me turn him into a Romantasy hero. Don't tell Bressen and Cyra, but Samhail is my favorite, and I'm forever grateful to you for letting me use him.

Thanks to my cover designer Mick Estabrook for his endless patience and understanding, even when he disagrees with me about the design. Mick, thanks for not saying, "I told you so," whenever I come around to your way of thinking several days later and make you change things.

A huge thanks to all my friends and family for reading the books and then yelling at me to get my ass in gear and write the next one so they can read it. Other writers I know complain that the people in their lives say they'll read the books, then never do, but I'm extremely fortunate to have people around me who have actually read and genuinely enjoyed the books. Your support means the world to me.